PB-1

X

Cancer Ward

ALEXANDER

CANCER

Translated from the Russian by
NICHOLAS BETHELL and DAVID BURG

SOLZHENITSYN

WARD

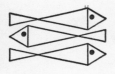

FARRAR, STRAUS AND GIROUX

New York

Contents

Letter to the Fourth Congress of Soviet Writers

May 16, 1967

To the Presidium and the delegates to the Congress, to members of the Union of Soviet Writers, and to the editors of literary newspapers and magazines:

Not having access to the podium at this Congress, I ask that the Congress discuss:

I. The no longer tolerable oppression, in the form of censorship, that our literature has endured for decades, and that the Union of Writers can no longer accept.

Under the obfuscating label of Glavlit, this censorship—which is not provided for in the Constitution and is therefore illegal, and which is nowhere publicly labeled as such—imposes a yoke on our literature and gives people unversed in literature arbitrary control over writers. A survival of the Middle Ages, this censorship has managed, Methuselah-like, to drag out its existence almost to the twenty-first century. Of fleeting significance, it attempts to appropriate to itself the role of unfleeting time—that of separating good books from bad.

Our writers are not supposed to have the right, are not endowed with the right, to express their considered judgments about the moral life of man and society, or to explain in their own way the social problems and historical experience that have been so deeply felt in our country. Works that might express the mature thinking of the people, that might have a timely and salutary influence in the realm of the human spirit or on the development of a social conscience, are proscribed or distorted by censorship on the basis of considerations that are petty, egotistical, and—from the national point of view—shortsighted. Outstanding manuscripts by young authors, as yet entirely unknown, are nowadays rejected by editors solely on the ground that they "will not pass" with the public. Many members of the Writers' Union, and even many of the delegates at this Congress, know how they themselves have bowed to the pressures of the censorship and made concessions in the structure and concept of their books—changing chapters, pages, paragraphs, or sentences, giving them innocuous titles—just for the sake of seeing them finally in print, even if it meant distorting them irremediably. It is an understood quality of literature that gifted works suffer most disastrously from all these distortions, while untalented works are not affected by them. Indeed, it is the best of our literature that is published in mutilated form.

Meanwhile, the most censorious labels—"ideologically harmful," "depraved," and so forth—are proving short-lived and fluid, in fact are changing before our very eyes. Even Dostoevsky, the pride of world literature, was at one time not published in the Soviet Union (even today his works are not published in full); he was excluded from the school curriculum, made unavailable for reading, and reviled. For how many years was Yesenin considered "counter-revolutionary"?—he was even subjected to a prison term because of his books. Wasn't Mayakovsky called "an anarchistic political hooligan"? For decades the immortal poetry of Akhmatova was considered anti-Soviet. The first timid printing of the dazzling Tsvetaeva ten years ago was declared a "gross political error." Only after a delay of twenty to thirty years were Bunin, Bulgakov, and Platonov returned to us. Inevitably, Mandelshtam, Voloshin, Gumilev, and Kliuev will follow in that line—not to mention the recognition, at some time or other, of even Zamyatin and Remisov.

A decisive moment in this process comes with the death of a troublesome writer. Sooner or later after that, he is returned to us with an "explanation of his errors." For a long time the name Pasternak could not be pronounced out loud; but then he died, and since then his books have appeared and his verse is even quoted at official ceremonies.

Pushkin's words are really coming true: "They are capable of loving only the dead."

But the belated publication of books and rehabilitation of names does not make up for either the social or the artistic losses suffered by our people as a consequence of these monstrous delays and the suppression of artistic conscience. (In fact, there were writers in the 1920s—Pilnyak, Platonov, Mandelshtam—who called attention at a very early stage to the beginnings of the cult of personality and the peculiar traits of Stalin's character; but these writers were silenced and destroyed instead of being listened to.) Literature cannot develop in between the categories of "permitted" and "not permitted," "about this you may write" and "about this you may not." Literature that is not the breath of contemporary society, that dares not transmit the pains and fears of that society, that does not warn in time against threatening moral and social dangers—such literature does not deserve the name of literature; it is only a façade. Such literature loses the confidence of its own people, and its published works are used as wastepaper instead of being read.

Our literature has lost the leading role it played at the end of the last century and the beginning of this one, and it has lost the brilliance of experimentation that distinguished it in the 1920s. To the entire world the literary life of our country now appears immeasurably more colorless, trivial, and inferior than it actually is or than it would have been if it were not confined and hemmed in. The losers are both our country—in world public opinion—and world literature itself. If the world had access to all the uninhibited fruits of our literature, if it were enriched by our own spiritual experience, the whole artistic evolution of the world would move along in a different way, acquiring a new stability and attaining even a new artistic threshold.

I propose that the Congress of Soviet Writers adopt a resolution which would demand and ensure the abolition of all censorship, open or hidden, of all fictional writing, and which would release publishing houses from the obligation to obtain authorization for the publication of every printed page.

II.   The duties of the Union toward its members.

These duties are not clearly formulated in the statutes of the Union of Soviet Writers (under "Protection of copyrights" and "Measures for the protection of other rights of writers"), and it is sad to learn that for a third of a century the Union has not defended either the "other" rights or even the copyrights of persecuted writers.

Many writers have been subjected during their lifetime to abuse and slander in the press and from the rostrums of congresses and conferences, without being afforded the physical possibility of replying. More than that, they have been exposed to suppression and personal persecution (Bulgakov, Akhmatova, Tsvetaeva, Pasternak, Zoshchenko, Platonov, Alexander Grin, Vassily Grossman). The

Union of Writers not only did not make its own periodicals available to these writers for purposes of reply and justification, not only did not come out in their defense, but through its leadership was always first among the persecutors. Names that adorned our poetry of the twentieth century found themselves on the list of those expelled from the Union or not even admitted to it in the first place. The leadership of the Union cravenly abandoned to their distress those for whom persecution ended in exile, labor camps, and death (Pavel Vasilev, Mandelshtam, Artem Vesely, Pilnyak, Babel, Tabidze, Zabolotsky, and others). The list must be cut off at "and others." We learned after the 20th Party Congress that there were more than six hundred writers whom the Union had obediently handed over to their fate in prisons and camps. However, the roll is even longer, and its curled-up end cannot and never will be read by our eyes. It contains the names of young writers and poets whom we may have known accidentally through personal encounters, whose talents were crushed in the camps before being able to blossom, whose writings never got further than the offices of the state security service in the days of Yagoda, Yezhov, Beria, and Abakumov.

There is no historical necessity for the newly elected leadership of the Union to share with its predecessors the responsibility for the past.

I propose that all guarantees for the defense of Union members subjected to slander and unjust persecution be clearly formulated in Paragraph 22 of the Union statutes, so that past violations of legality will not be repeated.

If the Congress does not remain indifferent to what I have said, I also ask that it consider the interdictions and persecutions to which I myself have been subjected.

1) It will soon be two years since the state security authorities took away from me the manuscript of my novel, *The First Circle,* thus preventing it from being submitted to publishers. Instead, in my own lifetime, against my will and even without my knowledge, this novel has been "published" in an unnatural "restricted" edition for reading by an unidentified select circle. My novel has thus become available to literary officials but is being concealed from most writers. I have been unable to obtain open discussion of the novel within writers' associations or to prevent misuse and plagiarism.

2) Together with this novel, my literary papers dating back fifteen to twenty years, things that were not intended for publication, were taken away from me by state police. Now, tendentious excerpts from these papers have also been covertly "published" and are being circulated within the same circles. The play, *Feast of the Conquerors,* which I wrote in verse from memory in camp, where I went by a three-digit number—and where, condemned to die of starvation, we were forgotten by society, no one outside the camps coming out against such repression—this play, the work of the remote past, is being ascribed to me as my very latest work.*

3) For three years now, an irresponsible campaign of slander has been conducted against me, a man who fought all through the war as a battery commander and received military decorations. It is being said that I served time as a criminal, or surrendered to the enemy (I was never a prisoner-of-war), that I "betrayed" my country and "served the Germans." This is the interpretation now being put on the eleven years I spent in camps and in exile for having criticized Stalin. This slander is being spread in secret instructions and meetings by people holding official positions. I vainly tried to stop the slander by appealing to the Board of the Writers' Union of the RSFSR and to the press. The Board did not even react, and not a single newspaper printed my replies to the slanderers. On the contrary, slander against me from rostrums has intensified and become more vicious within the last year, making use of distorted material from my confiscated papers, and I have no way of replying.

4) My novel, *Cancer Ward,* the first part of which was approved for publication by the prose department of the Moscow writers' organization, cannot be published either by chapters—rejected by five magazines—or in its entirety—rejected by *Novy mir, Zvezda,* and *Prostor.*

5) The play, *The Reindeer and the Little Hut,* accepted in 1962 by the Sovremennik Theater, has thus far not been approved for performance.

6) The screen play, *The Tanks Know the Truth;* the stage play, *The Light That Is in You;* a group of short stories entitled *The Right Hand;* the series, *Small Bite*—all these cannot find either a producer or a publisher.

*See page 544.

7) My stories published in *Novy mir* have never been printed in book form, having been rejected everywhere—by the Soviet Writer Publishers, the State Literature Publishing House, and the Ogoniok Library. They thus remain inaccessible to the general reading public.*

8) I have also been prevented from having any other contacts with readers either through public readings of my works (in November 1966, nine out of eleven scheduled meetings were cancelled at the last moment) or through readings over the radio. Even the simple act of giving a manuscript away for "reading and copying" has now become a criminal act (ancient Russian scribes were permitted to do this five centuries ago).

Thus my work has finally been smothered, gagged, and slandered.

In view of such flagrant infringements of my copyright and "other" rights, will the Fourth Congress defend me? Yes, or no? It seems to me that the choice is not without importance for the literary future of several of the delegates.

I am of course confident that I will fulfill my duty as a writer under all circumstances—even more successfully and more unchallenged from the grave than in my lifetime. No one can bar the road to truth, and to advance its cause I am prepared to accept even death. But may it come about that repeated examples will finally teach us not to stop the writer's pen during his lifetime.

At no time has this ennobled our history.

ALEXANDER SOLZHENITSYN

One Day in the Life of Ivan Denisovich was the only work of Solzhenitsyn published in book form in Russia.

Letter to the Writers' Union

September 12, 1967

To the Secretariat of the Board of the Union of Writers of the U.S.S.R.—All secretaries:

Even though supported by more than a hundred writers, my letter to the Fourth Congress of the Union of Writers has been neither published nor answered. The only thing that has happened is that rumors are being spread in order to assuage the alarmed public. These rumors—highly uniform and evidently coming from one source—aver that *Cancer Ward* and a book of my stories are being printed. As you know, this is a lie.

In a conversation with me on June 12, 1967, some of the secretaries of the Board of the Union of Writers of the U.S.S.R.—G. Markov, K. Voronkov, S. Sartakov, and L. Sobolev—declared that the Board deemed it a duty to refute publicly the base slander that has been spread about me and my military record. However, not only has this refutation failed to materialize, but the slanders continue: at instructional meetings, at activist meetings, and at seminars, a new batch of fantastic nonsense is being disseminated about me—e.g., that I have run off to the Republic of Arabia or to England (I would like to assure the slanderers that it is rather they who will run off). Prominent persons persistently express their regret that I did not die in the camp, that I was liberated. (Incidentally, immediately following *Ivan Denisovich,* the same regret was voiced. This book is now being secretly withdrawn from circulation in public libraries.)

These same secretaries of the Board promised at least to "examine the question" of approving publication of my latest novel, *Cancer Ward.* But in the space of three months—one fourth of a year—no progress has been made in this direction. During these three months, forty-two secretaries of the Board have been unable to make an evaluation of the novel or to make a recommendation as to whether it should be published. The novel has been in this strange and equivocal state—no direct prohibition, no direct permission—for over a year, since the summer of 1966. While the journal *Novy mir* would now like to publish the novel, it lacks the permission to do so.

Does the Secretariat believe that my novel will silently disappear as a result of these endless delays, that I will cease to exist, and that therefore the Secretariat will not have to decide whether to include it or exclude it from Soviet literature? While this is going on, the book is being read avidly everywhere. At the behest of the readers, it has already appeared in hundreds of typewritten copies. At the June 12 meeting I appraised the Secretariat that we should make haste to publish the novel if we wish to see it appear first in Russian, that under the circumstances we cannot prevent its unauthorized appearance in the West.

After the senseless delay of many months, the time has come to state that if the latter does happen, it will clearly be the fault (or perhaps the wish?) of the Secretariat of the Board of the Union of Writers of the U.S.S.R.

I insist that my work be published without delay.

ALEXANDER SOLZHENITSYN

PART ONE

1. No Cancer Whatsoever

On top of everything, the cancer wing was Number 13. Pavel Nikolayevich Rusanov had never been and could never be a superstitious person, but his heart sank when they wrote "Wing 13" on his admission card. They should have had the ingenuity to assign number 13 to some kind of prosthetic or intestinal department.

But this clinic was the only place where they could help him in the whole republic.

"It isn't, it isn't cancer, is it, Doctor? I haven't got cancer?" Pavel Nikolayevich asked hopefully, lightly touching the malevolent tumor on the right side of his neck. It seemed to grow almost daily, yet the tight skin on the outside was as white and inoffensive as ever.

"Good heavens, no. Of course not." Dr. Dontsova soothed him, for the tenth time, as she filled in the pages of his case history in her bold handwriting. Whenever she wrote, she put on her glasses with rectangular frames rounded at the edges, and she would whisk them off as soon as she had finished. She was no longer a young woman; her face looked pale and utterly tired.

It had happened at the outpatients' reception a few days ago. Patients assigned to a cancer department, even as outpatients, found they could not sleep the next night. And Dontsova had ordered Pavel Nikolayevich to bed *immediately*.

Unforeseen and unprepared for, the disease had come upon him, a happy man with few cares, like a gale in the space of two weeks. But Pavel Nikolayevich was tormented, no less than by the disease itself, by having to enter the clinic as an ordinary patient, just like

1

anyone else. He could hardly remember when he had been in a public hospital last, it was so long ago. Telephone calls had been made, to Evgeny Semenovich, Shendyapin, and Ulmasbaev, and they rang other people to find out if there were not any VIP wards in the clinic, or whether some small room could not be converted, just for a short time, into a special ward. But the clinic was so cramped for space that nothing could be done.

The only success he had managed to achieve through the head doctor was to bypass the waiting room, the public bath and a change of clothing.

Yuri drove his mother and father in their little blue Moskvich right up to the steps of Ward 13.

In spite of the slight frost, two women in heavily laundered cotton dressing gowns were standing outside on the open stone porch. The cold made them shudder, but they stood their ground.

Beginning with these slovenly dressing gowns, Pavel Nikolayevich found everything in the place unpleasant: the path worn by countless pairs of feet on the cement floor of the porch; the dull doorknobs, all messed about by the patients' hands; the waiting room, paint peeling off its floor, its high olive-colored walls (olive seemed somehow such a dirty color), and its large slatted wooden benches with not enough room for all the patients. Many of them had come long distances and had to sit on the floor. There were Uzbeks in quilted, wadded coats, old Uzbek women in long white shawls and young women in lilac, red and green ones, and all wore high boots with rubbers. One Russian youth, thin as a rail but with a great bloated stomach, lay there in an unbuttoned coat which dangled to the floor, taking up a whole bench to himself. He screamed incessantly with pain. His screams deafened Pavel Nikolayevich and hurt him so much that it seemed the boy was screaming not with his own pain but with Rusanov's.

Pavel Nikolayevich went white around the mouth, stopped dead and whispered to his wife, "Kapa, I'll die here. I mustn't stay. Let's go back."

Kapitolina Matveyevna took him firmly by the arm and said, "Pashenka! Where could we go? And what would we do then?"

"Well, perhaps we might be able to arrange something in Moscow."

Kapitolina Matveyevna turned to her husband. Her broad head was made even broader by its frame of thick, clipped coppery curls.

"Pashenka! If we went to Moscow we might have to wait another two weeks. Or we might not get there at all. How *can* we wait? It is bigger every morning!"

His wife squeezed his hand in an effort to transmit her courage to him. In his civic and official duties Pavel Nikolayevich was unshakable, and therefore it was simpler and all the more agreeable for him to be able to rely on his wife in family matters. She made all important decisions quickly and correctly.

The boy on the bench was still tearing himself apart with his screams.

"Perhaps the doctors would come to our house? We'd pay them," Pavel Nikolayevich argued, unsure of himself.

"Pasik!" his wife chided him, suffering as much as her husband. "You know I'd be the first to agree. Send for someone and pay the fee. But we've been into this before: these doctors don't treat at home, and they won't take money. And there's their equipment, too. It's impossible."

Pavel Nikolayevich knew perfectly well it was impossible. He had only mentioned it because he felt he just had to say something.

According to the arrangement with the head doctor of the oncology clinic, the head nurse was supposed to wait for them at two o'clock in the afternoon, there at the foot of the stairs, which a patient on crutches was carefully descending. But the head nurse was nowhere to be seen, of course, and her little room under the stairs had a padlock on the door.

"They're all so unreliable!" fumed Kapitolina Matveyevna. "What do they get paid for?"

Just as she was, two silver-fox furs hugging her shoulders, she set off down the corridor past a notice which read: "No entry to persons in outdoor clothes."

Pavel Nikolayevich remained standing in the waiting room. Timidly he tilted his head slightly to the right and felt the tumor that jutted out between his collarbone and his jaw. He had the impression that in the half hour since he had last looked at it in the mirror as he wrapped it up in a muffler, in that one half hour it seemed to have grown even bigger. Pavel Nikolayevich felt weak and wanted to sit down. But the benches looked dirty, and besides, he would have to ask some peasant woman in a scarf with a greasy sack between her feet to move. Somehow the foul stench of that sack seemed to reach him even from a distance.

When will our people learn to travel with clean, tidy suitcases! (Still, now that he had this tumor it didn't matter any longer.)

Suffering miserably from the young man's cries and from everything that met his eyes and entered his nostrils, Rusanov stood, half leaning on a projection in the wall. A peasant came in carrying in front of him a half-liter jar with a label on it, almost full of yellow liquid. He made no attempt to conceal the jar but held it aloft triumphantly, as if it were a mug of beer he had spent some time lining up for. He stopped in front of Pavel Nikolayevich, almost handing him the jar, made as if to ask him something, but looked at his sealskin hat and turned away. He looked around and addressed himself to a patient on crutches: "Who do I give this to, brother?"

The legless man pointed to the door of the laboratory.

Pavel Nikolayevich felt quite sick.

Again the outer door opened and the matron came in, dressed only in a white coat. Her face was too long and she was not at all pretty. She spotted Pavel Nikolayevich immediately, guessed who he was and went up to him.

"I'm sorry," she said breathlessly. In her haste her cheeks had flushed the color of her lipstick. "Please forgive me. Have you been waiting long? They were bringing some medicine, I had to go sign for it."

Pavel Nikolayevich felt like making an acid reply, but he restrained himself. He was glad the wait was over. Yuri came forward, in just his suit, with no coat or hat, with the same clothes he had worn for driving, carrying the suitcase and a bag of provisions. A blond forelock was dancing about on his forehead. He was very calm.

"Come with me," said the matron, leading the way to her little storeroom-like office under the stairs. "Nizamutdin Bahramovich said you'd bring your own underwear and pajamas. They haven't been worn, have they?"

"Straight from the store."

"That's absolutely obligatory, otherwise they'd have to be disinfected, you understand? Here, you can change in there."

She opened the plywood door and put on the light. In the little office with its sloping ceiling there was no window, only a number of colored-pencil diagrams hanging from the walls.

Yuri brought in the suitcase silently, then left the room. Pavel

Nikolayevich went in to get changed. The matron had meanwhile gone off somewhere, but Kapitolina Matveyevna caught up with her.

"Nurse!" she said. "I see you're in a hurry."

"Yes, I am rather."

"What's your name?"

"Mita."

"That's a strange name. You're not Russian, are you?"

"No. German. . . ."

"You kept us waiting."

"Yes, I'm sorry. I had to sign for those . . ."

"Now listen to me, Mita. I want you to know something. My husband is an important man who does extremely valuable work. His name is Pavel Nikolayevich."

"I see. Pavel Nikolayevich, I'll remember that."

"He's used to being well looked after, you see, and now he's seriously ill. Couldn't he have a nurse on duty with him permanently?"

Mita's troubled face grew even more worried. She shook her head. "Apart from the theater nurses, we have three day nurses to deal with sixty patients. And two night nurses."

"You see! A man could be screaming his head off and dying and no one would come!"

"Why do you think that? Everyone gets proper attention."

("Everyone"—what is there to say to her if she talks about "everyone"?)

"Do the nurses work in shifts?"

"That's right. They change every twelve hours."

"This impersonal treatment, it's terrible. My daughter and I would be delighted to take turns sitting up with him. Or I'd be ready to pay for a permanent nurse out of my own pocket. But they tell me that's not allowed either."

"I'm afraid not. It's never been done before. Anyway, there's nowhere in the ward to put a chair."

"God, I can imagine what this ward's like! I'd like to have a good look at it! How many beds are there?"

"Nine. Your husband's lucky to go right into a ward. Some new patients have to lie in the corridors or on the stairs!"

"I'm still going to ask you to arrange with a nurse or an orderly for Pavel Nikolayevich to have *private* attention. You know the people here; it would be easier for you to arrange it." She had already clicked open her big black bag and taken out three fifty-rouble notes.

Her son, who was standing nearby, turned his head away in silence.

Mita put both hands behind her back. "No, no! I have no right. . . ."

"I'm not giving them to you!" Kapitolina Matveyevna held the fan of notes into the front of the matron's uniform. "But if it can't be done legally and above board. . . . All I'm doing is paying for services rendered! I'm asking you to be kind enough to pass the money on to the right person!"

"No, no." The matron felt cold all over. "We don't do that sort of thing here."

The door creaked and Pavel Nikolayevich came out of the matron's den in his new green and brown pajamas and warm, fur-trimmed bedroom slippers. On his almost hairless head he wore a new raspberry-colored Uzbek skullcap. Now that he had removed his winter overcoat, collar and muffler, the tumor on the side of his neck, the size of a clenched fist, looked strikingly ominous. He could not even hold his head straight any longer, he had to tilt it slightly to one side.

His son went in to collect the discarded clothing and put it away in the suitcase. Kapitolina Matveyevna had returned the money to her purse. She looked anxiously at her husband.

"Won't you freeze like that? You should have brought a nice warm dressing gown with you. I'll bring one when I come. Look, here's a scarf." She took a scarf out of her pocket. "Wrap it round your throat, so you won't catch cold." In her silver foxes and her fur coat, she looked three times as strong as her husband. "Now go into the ward and get yourself settled. Unpack your food and think what else you need. I'll sit here and wait. Come down and tell me what you want and I'll bring everything this evening."

She never lost her head, she always knew what to do next. In their life together she had been her husband's true comrade. Pavel Niko-layevich looked at her with a mixture of gratitude and suffering and then glanced at his son.

"Well, are you off then, Yuri?"

"I'll take the evening train, Father." He came toward them. He always behaved respectfully in his father's presence. He was not by nature an emotional man, and his goodbye to his father now was as unemotional as ever. His reactions to life all ran at low voltage.

"That's right, son. Well, this is your first important official trip. Be sure to set the right tone from the start. And don't be too soft, mind. Your softness could be your downfall. Always remember you're not Yuri Rusanov, you're not a private individual. You're a representative of the law, do you understand?"

Whether or not Yuri understood, it would have been hard at that moment for Pavel Nikolayevich to find more appropriate words. Mita was fussing about and anxious to be going.

"I'll wait here with Mother," said Yuri, with a smile. "Don't say goodbye, Dad, just go."

"Will you be all right on your own?" Mita asked.

"Can't you see the man can hardly stand up? Can't you at least take him to his bed, and carry his bag for him?"

Orphan-like, Pavel Nikolayevich looked back at his family, refused the supporting arm Mita offered and, grasping the banister firmly, started to walk upstairs. His heart was beating violently, not at all, so far, because of the climb. He went up the stairs as people mount—what do they call it?—a sort of platform where men have their heads cut off.

The matron ran on upstairs in front of him carrying his bag, shouted something from the top to someone called Maria, and before Pavel Nikolayevich had finished the first flight was already running past him down the other side of the staircase and out of the building, thereby showing Kapitolina Matveyevna what sort of solicitude her husband could expect in this place.

Pavel Nikolayevich slowly climbed up onto the landing—a long, wide one such as is only found in old buildings. On this middle landing, but not obstructing the traffic, were two beds occupied by patients, with two night tables beside them. One of the patients was in a bad way; he was physically wasted and sucking an oxygen balloon.

Trying not to look at the man's hopeless face, Rusanov turned and went on, looking upward as he climbed. But there was no encouragement for him at the end of the second flight either. A nurse—Maria—was standing there, her dark, icon-like face lit by neither smile nor greeting. Tall, thin and flat-chested, she waited for him there like a sentry, and immediately set off across the upstairs hallway to show him where to go. Leading off the hall were several doors, just left clear by more beds with patients in them. In a little windowless alcove, underneath a constantly lit table lamp, stood the nurse's writing table and treatment table, and nearby hung a frosted glass wall closet with a red cross painted on it. They went past the little tables, past a bed too, and then Maria pointed her long, thin hand and said, "Second from the window."

And already she was rushing off. An unpleasant feature of all public hospitals is that nobody stops for a moment to exchange a few words.

The doors into the ward were always kept wide open, but still as he crossed the threshold Pavel Nikolayevich was conscious of a close, moist, partly medicinal odor. For someone as sensitive to smells as he, it was sheer torment.

The beds stood in serried ranks, with their heads to the wall and narrow spaces between them no wider than a bedside table, while the passageway down the middle of the ward was just wide enough for two people to pass.

In this passageway stood a thickset, broad-shouldered patient in pink-striped pajamas. His neck was completely wrapped in thick, tight bandages which reached almost to the lobes of his ears. The white constricting ring prevented free movement of his heavy block of a head, overgrown with a fox-brown thatch.

He was talking hoarsely to his fellow patients, and they were listening from their beds. On Rusanov's entry he swung his whole body toward him, the head welded to it. He looked at him without sympathy and said, "Well, what have we here? Another nice little cancer!"

Pavel Nikolayevich saw no need to reply to such familiarity. He sensed that the whole room was staring at him, but he had no wish to examine these people whom chance had thrown in his path or even to exchange greetings with them. He merely waved his hand at the fox-haired patient to make him get out of his way. The other allowed Pavel Nikolayevich to pass, and again turned his whole body, head riveted on top, to look after him.

"Hey, friend, what have you got cancer of?" he asked in his throaty voice.

Pavel Nikolayevich had already reached his bed. He felt as if the question had scraped his skin. He raised his eyes toward the impudent lout and tried not to lose his temper. All the same his shoulders twitched as he said with dignity, "I have cancer of nothing. I have no cancer whatsoever."

The fox-haired patient snorted. Then he passed judgment so that the whole ward could hear:

"Stupid fool! If it's not cancer, what the hell d'you think they put you in here for?"

2. Education
Doesn't Make You Smarter

Within a few hours, that first evening in the ward, Pavel Nikolayevich became haunted with fear.

The hard lump of his tumor—unexpected, meaningless and quite without use—had dragged him in like a fish on a hook and flung him onto this iron bed—a narrow, mean bed, with creaking springs and an apology for a mattress. Having once undressed under the stairs, said goodbye to the family and come up to the ward, you felt the door to all your past life had been slammed behind you, and the life here was so vile that it frightened you more than the actual tumor. He could no longer choose something pleasant or soothing to look at; he had to look at the eight abject beings who were now his "equals," eight sick men in faded, worn, pink and white pajamas, patched and torn here and there and almost all the wrong size. And he could not even choose what to listen to; he had to listen to these uncultured creatures and their wearisome conversations which had nothing to do with him and were of no interest to him. He would have loved to command them all to be quiet, especially the tiresome fox-haired one with the bandage grip round his neck and the constricted head. Everyone called him simply "Yefrem," even though he was not a young man.*

It was impossible to restrain Yefrem. He refused to lie down and never went outside the ward, just paced restlessly up and down the

*This is a mark of disrespect in Russian. An older man would normally be addressed by his first name and his patronymic, as in Pavel Nikolaievich, meaning Pavel, son of Nikolai. (Translators' note)

10

central aisle. From time to time he would screw up his face as if he was being injected and clutch his head. Then he would start walking up and down again. After these walks he always stopped at the foot of Rusanov's bed, leaned the rigid top half of his body toward Rusanov over the rails, thrust his broad, pock-marked, sullen face forward and lectured him:

"You've had it, Professor. You'll never go home again, see?"

It was very warm in the ward. Pavel Nikolayevich was lying on top of the blanket in his pajamas and skullcap. He adjusted his gilt-rimmed spectacles, glared severely at Yefrem, as he knew so well how to do, and replied, "I am at a loss, comrade, to know what you require of me, and why you are trying to intimidate me. I don't ask questions, do I?"

Yefrem just snorted maliciously.

"Who cares about your questions, you still won't be going back home. You may as well give back your glasses. And your new pajamas."

After this crude outburst, he straightened his clumsy body and started pacing up and down the aisle again, like a man possessed.

Of course, Pavel Nikolayevich could have cut him short and put him in his place, but somehow he could not summon his usual will power. It was already low, and it had sunk even lower at the words of this bandaged devil. He needed support, but instead he was being pushed down into a pit. In a matter of hours he had as good as lost all his personal status, reputation and plans for the future—and had turned into one hundred and fifty-four pounds of hot, white flesh that did not know what tomorrow would bring.

His face probably revealed his melancholy state, for on one of his subsequent walks Yefrem stopped opposite him and said quite peaceably, "Even if they *do* let you go home, you'll be back here pretty quick. The Crab loves people. Once he's grabbed you with his pincers, he won't let go till you croak."

Pavel Nikolayevich did not have the strength to protest, and Yefrem set off again. In fact, there was no one in the room to rein him in. All the others there seemed either apathetic wrecks or non-Russians. Along the other wall there were only four beds because the stove jutted out. The one directly opposite Rusanov's, foot to foot with his across the aisle, was Yefrem's. The other three were occupied by youngsters: a simple, rather swarthy boy next to the stove, a young Uzbek with a crutch, and by the window, thin as a tapeworm and doubled up on his bed, a youth whose skin had turned quite yellow and who lay groaning continuously. In Pavel Nikolayevich's row there were two Asians on his left, then a young Russian lad by the door, tall with short-cropped hair. He was sitting reading. Next to Pavel Nikolayevich in the last bed by the window lay, it seemed, another Russian, but being this man's neighbor was hardly a matter for rejoicing. He had a villainous cutthroat's mug. It was probably the scar that made him look that way: it started by the corner of his mouth and ran along the bottom of his left cheek almost to his neck. Or perhaps it was his black, uncombed hair standing up on end in all directions, or else his coarse, tough expression. The cutthroat had pretensions to culture, however. He was reading a book, and had almost finished it.

The lights were switched on, two bright lamps hanging from the ceiling. It was already dark outside. They were waiting for supper.

"There's an old guy here." Yefrem would not let up. "He's lying downstairs, he's being operated on tomorrow. Back in '42 they cut a tiny cancer out of him and said, 'Fine! It's nothing! Off you go!' See?" Yefrem seemed to be rattling on but his voice sounded as though he was the one being cut open. "Thirteen years went by and he forgot about that clinic, drank vodka, screwed women—he's a bit of a lad, wait till you meet him. And he's got a cancer *that* big in him now." He smacked his lips with pleasure. "I guess it'll be straight from the operating table onto the mortuary slab."

"Now then, I've had quite enough of your gloomy predictions!" Pavel Nikolayevich brushed him aside and turned away. He hardly recognized his own voice; it sounded so plaintive, so lacking in authority.

No one uttered a sound. The emaciated young man by the window in the other row was also being a nuisance. He kept twisting and turning. He tried sitting up; that was no good. He tried lying down; that was no good either. He doubled up, hugging his knees to his chest. Unable to find anything more comfortable, he laid his head not on the pillow but on the frame of the bed. He was moaning very softly, the grimaces and spasms on his face showing his pain.

Pavel Nikolayevich turned away from him too, lowered his feet into his bedroom slippers and began idly inspecting his bedside table, opening and shutting first the little door of the closet where his food was tightly packed, and then the little top drawer which contained his toilet requisites and his electric razor.

Yefrem still kept pacing up and down, arms folded tightly across his chest. Sometimes he winced with stabbing internal pains, and droned a refrain like a funeral dirge:

"Ye . . . es, it's a ter'ble situation we're in, a ter'ble situation."

Pavel Nikolayevich heard a smacking sound behind his back. He turned round carefully—even the slightest movement of his neck was painful—and saw it was his neighbor, the cutthroat, who had snapped shut the book he had now finished and was turning it over and over in his large rough hands. Diagonally across the dark-blue binding and also down the spine, stamped in gold and already dulled, was the signature of the author. Pavel Nikolayevich could not make out whose signature it was, but he didn't care to address a question to a type like that. He had thought up a nickname for his neighbor—"Bone-chewer." It suited him very well.

Bone-chewer gazed at the book with big sullen eyes and addressed the whole room in a shamelessly loud voice:

"If Dyomka hadn't picked this book out of the cupboard, I would have sworn it was specially sent our way."

"What about Dyomka? What book?" responded the lad by the door, looking up from his own.

"You wouldn't find one like it, not if you turned the whole town upside down." Bone-crusher looked at the broad, flat back of Yefrem's head. His hair had not been cut for months—it would have been too uncomfortable—so it stuck out of the top of his bandage. Then he looked at Yefrem's strained face. "Yefrem! That's enough of your whining! Here, read this book!"

Yefrem stopped dead like a thwarted bull and looked at him dazedly.

"Read? Why should I read? We'll all kick the bucket soon."

Bone-chewer's scar twitched. "That's the point! If you don't hurry you'll have kicked the bucket before you've read it. Here you are, quick!"

He held out the book, but Yefrem did not move.

"There's too much reading here. I don't want to read."

"Are you illiterate or something?" said Bone-chewer, trying halfheartedly to talk him into it.

"What do you mean? I'm very literate. When I've got to be, I'm very literate."

Bone-chewer fumbled for his pencil on the window sill, opened the book at the back, looked through it and made some marks here and there.

"Don't be afraid," he murmured, "they're nice, short little stories. Here, just these few here—try them. I'm fed up with your whining, do you hear? Read a book."

"I'm not afraid of nothing!" Yefrem took the book and tossed it on the bed.

Ahmadjan, the young Uzbek, came limping through the door on one crutch. He was the only cheerful one in the room. "Spoons at the ready!" he shouted.

The swarthy boy by the stove came to life.

"They're bringing the grub, boys!"

In came the food orderly in a white coat, carrying a tray above her shoulder. She shifted it in front of her and started going round the beds. Except for the tortured young man by the window they all stirred themselves and took the plates off the tray. Everyone in the ward had a bedside table. Only Dyomka, the young lad, did not have his own but shared one with the big-boned Kazakh, whose upper lip was swollen with a hideous uncovered, reddish-brown scab.

Quite apart from the fact that Pavel Nikolayevich did not feel like eating at all, even the sort of food he had brought from home, one glance at the supper—a rectangular, rubbery suet pudding with yellow jelly on the top—and that filthy gray aluminum spoon with a double twist in the handle, served as another bitter reminder of where he had landed, and of what a mistake he had probably made in agreeing to come to the clinic.

Except for the moaning lad, they set about their food like one man. Pavel Nikolayevich did not take the plate in his hands, but tapped the edge of it with his nail, looking round to see who he could pass it on to. Some of them were sitting sideways to him, others had their backs to him. The young man by the door was the only one facing him.

"What is your name?" asked Pavel Nikolayevich, without raising his voice. It was the young fellow's job to hear what he said.

There was a clatter of spoons, but the boy understood it was himself being addressed and answered readily enough, "Proshka . . . er . . . er . . . I mean, Prokofiy Semyonich."

"Take it."

"Yeah, all right . . ." Proshka came over, took the plate and nodded gratefully.

Pavel Nikolayevich felt the hard lump under his jaw and suddenly realized he was not one of the milder cases here. Only one out of the nine of them was bandaged up—Yefrem—just in the place where they might cut Pavel Nikolayevich open too. And only one of them was in great pain. And only that healthy-looking Kazakh in the next bed but one had that deep-red scab. And as for the young Uzbek's crutch, he hardly leaned on it at all. And there was no sign of any tumor or deformity on any of the others. They all looked like healthy people. Especially Proshka. His face glowed all over, as if he were on vacation, not in a hospital; he had a fine appetite, judging by the way he was licking that plate clean.

There was a gray tinge about Bone-chewer's face, it was true, but he moved freely, talked without restraint, and was attacking his dessert with such relish that the idea flashed through Pavel Nikolayevich's mind that he might be a malingerer who had attached himself to a state feeding place, because in our country the sick are fed free of charge.

But Pavel Nikolayevich was different. The lump of his tumor was pressing his head to one side, made it difficult for him to turn over, and was increasing in size every hour. Only here the doctors did not count the hours. All the time from lunch to supper no one had examined Rusanov and he had had no treatment. And it was with this very bait that Dr. Dontsova had lured him here—immediate treatment. Well, in that case she must be a thoroughly irresponsible and criminally negligent woman. Rusanov had trusted her, and had lost valuable time in this cramped, musty, dirty ward when he might have been telephoning and flying to Moscow.

Resentment at the delay and the realization of having made a mistake, on top of the misery of his tumor, so stabbed at Pavel Nikolayevich's heart that he could not bear *anything,* from the noise of dishes scraped by spoons, to the iron bedsteads, the rough blankets, the walls, the lights, the people. He felt that he was in a trap, and that until the next morning any decisive step was impossible.

Deeply miserable, he lay there covering his eyes from the light and from the whole scene with the towel he had brought from home. To take his mind off things he began thinking about his home and his family, and what they would be doing now. Yuri would already be on the train. It was his first practical inspection. It was very important he should look well. But Yuri was not assertive and he was a bungler; he might make a fool of himself. Aviette was spending her vacation in Moscow. She would be amusing herself a bit going to theaters. But her main aim was business, finding out the lay of the land, perhaps making a few contacts. After all, it was her last year at university; she had to take her bearings on life. Aviette would make a clever journalist. She was very businesslike, and of course she would have to move to Moscow. Out here wouldn't be big enough for her. She was so intelligent and talented; there was no one else in the family to touch her. Pavel Nikolayevich was unresentfully glad that his daughter had grown up far more educated than himself. She hadn't had much experience yet, but she was so quick to catch on! Lavrik was something of a dropout, indifferent to his studies, but his talent lay in sports. He'd already been to a sports tournament in Riga where he'd stayed in a hotel like a grownup. And he was already racing their car about. He was taking driving lessons with the Cadet Force and hoped to get his license. In his second semester he'd failed in two subjects; he'd have to work a lot harder. Then there was Maika—she was most likely already at home playing the piano (she was the first one in the family to play). And Julebarse would be lying on the mat in the corridor. Last year Pavel Nikolayevich himself had taken him for his morning walk, since he felt it was good for his own health. Now Lavrik would take him instead. He liked to let the dog chase passers-by a little and then say, "It's all right, don't be frightened, I've got him."

But the harmonious, exemplary Rusanov family, their well-adjusted way of life and their immaculate apartment—in the space of a few days all this had been cut off from him. It was now on the *other* side of his tumor. They were alive and would go on living, whatever happened to their father. However much they might worry, fuss or weep, the tumor was growing like a wall behind him, and on his side of it he was alone.

Thinking about home did not help him, so Pavel Nikolayevich tried to distract himself with affairs of state. A session of the U.S.S.R. Supreme Soviet was due to open on Saturday. Nothing important was expected to happen; the budget would be approved. There had been shooting in the Taiwan Strait. . . . When he left home for the hospital that morning, the radio had just begun broadcasting a long report on heavy industry. But here in the ward there wasn't even a radio, and there wasn't one in the corridor either—a fine state of affairs! At the very least he'd have to see he got *Pravda* every day. Today heavy industry had come up, and yesterday there had been a decree on the increase in output of meat and dairy products. Yes, the economy was advancing by leaps and bounds; and this would mean, of course, major changes in a number of state and economic organizations.

Pavel Nikolayevich had already begun to imagine how the reorganization would be implemented on republic and province level. These reorganizations were always rather exciting; they served as a temporary diversion from everyday work; the officials would be telephoning each other, holding meetings and discussing the possibilities. And whichever direction the reorganizations took—whether this way or that—no one, including Pavel Nikolayevich, ever suffered a drop in rank. There were only promotions.

But affairs of state did not succeed in diverting him or cheering him up either. There was a stabbing pain under his neck—his tumor, deaf and indifferent, had moved in to shut off the whole world. There again: the budget, heavy industry, cattle and dairy farming and reorganization—they were all on the *other* side of the tumor. On *this* side was Pavel Nikolayevich Rusanov. Alone.

A pleasing female voice sounded through the ward. Although nothing could possibly seem pleasant to Pavel Nikolayevich today, this voice was, frankly, delicious.

"Now, let's take your temperature." It was as if she was promising to hand out candy.

Rusanov removed the towel from his face, raised himself slightly and put on his spectacles. Oh, what joy! It wasn't dark, doleful Maria but a trim, firmly built girl, wearing not a folded kerchief but a little cap over her golden hair, like the doctors.

Standing over his bed, she said cheerily to the young man by the window, "Azovkin! Hey, Azovkin!" He lay in an even more awkward position than before—diagonally across the bed, face downward, a pillow under his stomach, resting his chin on the mattress like a dog, and peering through the rails of the bed as if he were in a cage. Shadows of the pain inside him passed across his drawn face. One hand hung down to the floor.

"Now come along, pull yourself together," said the nurse, trying to shame him. "Take the thermometer yourself."

He just managed to raise his hand from the floor—it was like drawing a bucket out of a well—and took the thermometer. He was so exhausted, so taken up with his pain, that it was impossible to believe he was no more than seventeen years old.

"Zoya!" he groaned beseechingly. "Give me a hot-water bottle."

"You're your own worst enemy," she said severely. "We gave you a hot-water bottle but you didn't put it on your injection, you put it on your stomach."

"But it helps me so much," he persisted, in a tone of great suffering.

"It makes your tumor grow, you've been told that already. Hot-water bottles aren't allowed in the oncology department. We had to get one specially for you."

"Well, I won't take my injection, then."

But Zoya was no longer listening. She was tapping her dainty little finger on the rail of Bone-chewer's bed. "Where's Kostoglotov?" she asked.

(Well, well, well! Pavel Nikolayevich had hit the nail on the head! The nickname was perfect!*)

"He's gone for a smoke," Dyomka called over from the door. He was still reading.

"I'll give him 'smoke,'" grumbled Zoya.

Weren't some girls lovely! Pavel Nikolayevich gazed with pleasure at her generous, tightly laced figure and her wide, almost staring eyes. He gazed at her with detached admiration, and felt himself soften. She had held the thermometer out to him with a smile. She was standing right next to the tumor but gave no sign, not even by a raised eyebrow, that she was horrified by the thing or that she had never seen one like it before.

"Hasn't any treatment been prescribed for me?" asked Rusanov.

"Not yet." She smiled apologetically.

"But why not? Where are the doctors?"

"They've finished work for the day."

There was no point in being angry with Zoya, but it must be someone's fault that he was not being treated! He had to do something! Rusanov despised inactivity and ineffectual characters. When Zoya came back to read his temperature he asked her, "Where's your outside telephone? How can I find it?"

After all, he could make up his mind right now and telephone Comrade Ostapenko! The very idea of a telephone brought Pavel Nikolayevich back into his normal world, and restored his courage. He felt like a fighter again.

*Kostoglot in Russian means "bone-swallower."

"Ninety-eight point six." Zoya smiled and made the first mark on the graph of the new temperature chart hanging at the foot of the bed. "There's a telephone in the registrar's office. But you can't go there now, it's the other entrance."

"Forgive me, young lady"—Pavel Nikolayevich raised himself a little and his voice became slightly severe—"but how can the clinic be without a telephone? Suppose something happened now? To me, for instance?"

"We'd run over there and telephone for you." Zoya stood her ground.

"Well, suppose there was a storm, or heavy rain?"

Zoya had already moved on to his neighbor, the old Uzbek, and was filling in his chart.

"In the daytime we go over there straightway, but it's locked now."

All right, she was a sweet girl, but she could also be fresh. She'd refused to hear him out, and even now was moving on to the Kazakh. Raising his voice involuntarily, Pavel Nikolayevich called out after her, "There must be another telephone! It's impossible for there not to be!"

"There is," answered Zoya. She was already squatting by the Kazakh's bed. "But it's in the head doctor's office."

"Well, what's the problem?"

"Dyomka . . . ninety-eight point four. . . . The office is locked. Nizamutdin Bahramovich doesn't like . . ."

And she walked out of the room.

It was logical. Of course, it's not very pleasant to have people going into your office when you're not there. All the same, in a hospital proper arrangements should be made.

For an instant a tiny wire linking him with the outside world had dangled before him—and it had snapped. Once again the tumor under his jaw, the size of a fist, had shut off the entire world.

Pavel Nikolayevich reached out for his little mirror and looked at himself. How the tumor was spreading! Seen through the eyes of a complete stranger it would be frightening enough, but seen through his own . . . ! No, this thing could not be real. No one else around him had anything like it. In all his forty-five years Pavel Nikolayevich had never seen such a deformity . . .

He did not try to work out whether it had grown any more or not.

He just put the mirror away, took some food from his bedside table and started chewing.

The two roughest types, Yefrem and Bone-chewer, were not in the ward. They had gone out. By the window Azovkin had twisted himself into a new position, but he was not groaning. The rest were quiet. He could hear the sound of pages being turned. And some of them had gone off to sleep. All Rusanov, too, had to do was get to sleep, while away the night, think of nothing, and then tomorrow give the doctors a dressing down.

So he took off his pajamas, lay down under the blankets in his underclothes, covered his head with the towel he had brought from home and tried to sleep.

But through the silence there came a particularly audible and irritating sound of somebody whispering somewhere. It seemed to be going straight into Pavel Nikolayevich's ear. He could not bear it, tore the towel away from his face, raised himself slightly, trying to avoid hurting his neck, and discovered it was his neighbor, the Uzbek. He was all shriveled up and thin, an old man, almost brown skinned, with a little black pointed beard, and wearing a shabby skullcap as brown as himself.

He lay on his back with his hands behind his head, staring at the ceiling and whispering—prayers or something, probably, the old fool.

"Hey you! *Aksakal!*"* Rusanov wagged his finger at him. "Stop it. You're disturbing me."

The *aksakal* fell silent. Rusanov lay down again and covered his face with the towel. But still he could not get to sleep. Now he realized that the reason he could not settle down was the penetrating light from the two ceiling lamps. The shades were not made of frosted glass and did not cover the bulbs properly. He could sense the light even through the towel. Pavel Nikolayevich grunted and again raised himself from the pillow with his elbows, carefully, to avoid the stabbing pains from his tumor.

Proshka was standing beside his bed near the light switch and beginning to undress.

"Young man! Turn off the light!" Pavel Nikolayevich commanded.

Aksakal in Uzbek means "village elder," here used mockingly.

"Eh? . . . er . . . Nurse hasn't come with the medicines yet," faltered Proshka, but he reached up one hand toward the switch.

"Turn off the light—what do you mean?" growled Bone-chewer's voice behind Rusanov. "Who d'you think you are, you're not the only person here."

Pavel Nikolayevich sat up straight and put on his spectacles. Carefully nursing his tumor, he turned, making the bedsprings creak, and said, "You might be a bit more *polite.*"

The rude fellow pulled a face and answered in a low voice, "Don't change the subject. You're not my boss."

Pavel Nikolayevich threw him a withering glare, but this had no effect whatever on Bone-chewer.

"OK, but what do you need the light for?" Rusanov went over to peaceful negotiation.

"So I can pick my asshole," said Kostoglotov coarsely.

Pavel Nikolayevich began to have difficulty with his breathing, although by now he was pretty well acclimatized to the air in the ward. The impudent fellow ought to be discharged from hospital at twenty minutes' notice and sent back to work. But at the moment he had no concrete means of action. (He would of course mention him to the hospital administration later on.)

"If you want to read or something, you can go out into the corridor," Pavel Nikolayevich pointed out, trying to be fair. "Why should you take it upon yourself to decide for everyone? There are different sorts of patients here and distinctions have to be made . . ."

"There'll be distinctions." Bone-chewer showed his fangs. "They'll write you an obituary: Party member since the year zero. As for us, they'll just carry us out feet first."

Pavel Nikolayevich had never come across such unrestrained insubordination, such unbridled wilfulness. He could not recall anything like it. He found himself at a loss—how could he counter this sort of thing? He couldn't complain to that girl. The conversation would have to be cut short for the present in the most dignified manner possible. Pavel Nikolayevich took off his spectacles, lay down carefully and covered his head with the towel.

He was exploding with indignation and anguish at the thought of how he had weakly agreed to enter this clinic. But it would not be too late to get a discharge tomorrow.

It was shortly after eight o'clock by his watch. Oh well, for the moment he would put up with it all. Sooner or later they'd quiet down.

But the floor started shaking again as someone paced up and down between the beds. Of course it was Yefrem coming back. The old floorboards vibrated with his footsteps and Rusanov could feel the vibrations through the bedrails and the pillow. However, Pavel Niko-layevich decided not to rebuke him, but to endure it.

There's such bad manners and impudence among our people. We still haven't got rid of it. How can we lead them to a new society carrying this burden?

The evening dragged endlessly. The nurse began her rounds—once, twice, a third and fourth time—a mixture for one, a powder for another, injections for two more. Azovkin uttered a shriek when he was given his injection, and again begged for a hot-water bottle to help the serum disperse more quickly. Yefrem kept tramping up and down, unable to find peace. Ahmadjan and Proshka were talk-ing from their beds. It was as if they were only now coming properly to life, as if they hadn't a care in the world or anything that needed curing. Even Dyomka was not ready to sleep. He came up and sat on Kostoglotov's bed and they began muttering, right by Pavel Niko-layevich's ear.

"I'm going to try to read a bit more," Dyomka was saying, "while there's time. I'd like to go to university."

"That's a good thing. But remember, education doesn't make you smarter."

(What's the point of talking like that? To a child!)

"What do you mean, doesn't make you smarter?"

"It's just one of those things."

"So what does make you smarter?"

"Life, that's what."

Dyomka was silent for a moment, then replied, "I don't agree."

"In our unit there was a commissar, Pashkin. He used to say, 'Education doesn't make you smarter. Nor does rank. They give you another star on your shoulder and you think you're smarter. Well you're not.'"

"So what do you mean, there's no need to study? I don't agree."

"Of course you should study. Study! Only remember, for your own sake, it's not the same as intelligence."

"What is intelligence, then?"

"Intelligence? Trusting your eyes but not your ears. Which subject are you interested in?"

"I haven't decided yet. I am interested in history and literature."

"What about engineering?"

"No . . o."

"Strange. It was like that in our day. But now boys prefer engineering. Don't you?"

"No . . . I think . . . I've a passion for social problems."

Social problems? . . . Oh, Dyomka, you'd better learn to assemble radio sets. Life's more peaceful if you're an engineer."

"What do I care about peace? If I lie here a month or two, I shall have to catch up with the ninth class, for the second half-year."

"What about textbooks?"

"I've got two here. Stereometry's very difficult."

"Stereometry? Bring it here!"

Rusanov heard the lad walk off and get his book.

"Let me see . . . yes . . . yes . . . my old friend, Kiselyov's *Stereometry*. The very same. Straight lines and planes . . . parallel with each other . . . If a straight line is parallel to another straight line in the same plane, then it is parallel to the plane itself . . . Hell, what a book, Dyomka! Wouldn't it be fine if everyone wrote like that? Not fat at all, is it? But what a lot it contains!"

"They teach an eighteen-month course out of this book."

"They taught me too. I used to know it backwards!"

"When?"

"I'll tell you. I was in the ninth class too, the second half-year . . . that would be in '37 and '38. It feels strange to have it in my hands again. Geometry was my favorite subject."

"And then?"

"Then what?"

"After school?"

"After school I read a splendid subject—geophysics."

"Where was that?"

"The same place, Leningrad."

"And what happened?"

"I finished my first year, and then in September '39 there was an order to call up all nineteen-year-olds into the army, and I was hauled in."

"Then what?"

"I was on active service."

"And after that?"

"After that—don't you know what happened? The war."

"You—were you an officer?"

"No, sergeant."

"Why?"

"Because if everyone was made a general there'd be no one to win the war . . . If a plane passes through a straight line parallel to a second plane and intersects that plane, then the line of intersection . . . Listen, Dyomka! You and I will do some stereometry every day. We'll really push ahead! Would you like to?"

"Yes, I would."

(Isn't that the limit? Right under my ear!)

"I'll give you lessons."

"Fine."

"Otherwise you'll really waste time. We'll begin right now. Let's take these three axioms. You see, these axioms are simple in form, but they'll come into every theorem, and you have to spot where. Here's the first one: if two points in a straight line are in a plane, then every point along that line is also in the plane. What's the idea of that? Look, supposing this book is a plane and the pencil a straight line, all right? Now try to arrange them . . ."

They plunged into the subject and droned on about axioms and deductions. But Pavel Nikolayevich resolved to bear it, his back turned on them pointedly. At last they stopped talking and broke up. After his double sleeping draft Azovkin dropped off too and was quiet. Then the *aksakal* started coughing. Pavel Nikolayevich was lying with his face toward him. The light was off by now, but there he was, curse him, coughing away, in such a disgusting manner too, with that whistling noise, on and on, so that it seemed he was going to choke.

Pavel Nikolayevich turned his back on him. He removed the towel from his head, but it still wasn't properly dark; light was coming in from the corridor, and noises, too, people walking about and clanking spittoons and buckets.

He could not get to sleep. His tumor weighed him down. His whole happy life, so well thought out, so harmonious and useful, was now about to crack. He felt very sorry for himself. One little push would be enough to bring tears to his eyes.

It was Yefrem who did not fail to provide the push. Unrestrained even in the dark, he was telling Ahmadjan next to him some idiotic fairy tale:

"Why should man live a hundred years? This is how it happened. Allah gave all the animals fifty years each, and that was enough. But man came last, and Allah had only twenty-five left."

"You mean a twenty-fiver?"* asked Ahmadjan.

"That's right. And man started complaining it wasn't enough. Allah said, 'It's enough!' And man said, 'No, it isn't.' So Allah said, 'All right, go out and ask, maybe someone has some over and will give you some.' Man went off and met a horse. 'Listen,' he said, 'my life's too short. Give me some of yours.' 'All right,' said the horse, 'take twenty-five years.' Man went a bit further and met a dog. 'Listen, dog, let me have some of your life.' 'All right, have twenty-five years.' On he went. He met a monkey, and he got twenty-five years out of him, too. Then he went back to Allah, and Allah said, 'As you wish, it's up to you. The first twenty-five years you will live like a man. The second twenty-five you'll work like a horse. The third you'll yap like a dog. And for the last twenty-five, people will laugh at you like they laugh at a monkey . . .' "

*A twenty-five rouble note. Ahmadjan, an Uzbek, is making a joke to prove how well he speaks Russian.

3. Teddy Bear

Although Zoya was quick and alert, moving very swiftly about the wards from table to beds and back again, she realized she would not be able to deal with all the prescriptions before lights out. So she hurried to finish and put the lights out in the men's ward and the small women's ward. In the large women's ward—it was huge, with more than thirty beds in it—the women never settled down at the proper time anyway, whether the light was turned off or not. Many of them had been there a long time and were thoroughly tired of the hospital. They slept badly, it was stuffy, and there were always arguments about whether the door to the terrace should be kept open or shut. And there were even a few dedicated enthusiasts who talked across the room from one end to the other, discussing everything from prices, goods, furniture, children, men, neighbors, right down to the most shameless subjects imaginable—until midnight or one in the morning.

On top of it all Nellya, the orderly, was washing the floor there that evening. She was a loud-mouthed, round-bottomed girl with thick eyebrows and lips. She had started the job ages ago but would never get through because she butted in on every single conversation. Meanwhile Sibgatov was waiting for his wash. His bed was in the hall next to the entrance to the men's ward. Because of these nightly washes, and also because he felt ashamed of the foul smell from his back, Sibgatov chose to stay out in the hall, even though he had been in the hospital longer than all the other residents. In fact he was less like a patient than a member of the permanent staff.

Dashing around in the women's ward, Zoya gave Nellya a dressing down, and then another, but Nellya just snapped back and carried on slowly: she was no younger than Zoya and thought it beneath her dignity to be under the other girl. Zoya had come to work today in a festive mood, but this defiance on the part of the orderly irritated her. As a rule Zoya felt everyone had a right to his share of freedom and that when one came to work one was under no obligation to work oneself to death. But there was a reasonable limit somewhere, especially when it was sick people you were dealing with.

Finally, when Zoya had taken everything round and was finished and Nellya was through with wiping the floor, they turned off the light in the women's ward and the top light in the hall. It was already after eleven when Nellya had prepared the warm solution on the second floor and brought it from there to Sibgatov in his usual bowl.

"Ooh . . . ah . . . ah . . . ah, I'm dead on my feet." She yawned loudly. "I feel like forty winks. Listen, patient, I know you'll be sitting here a good hour. I'm not waiting for you to finish. What about taking the bowl down and emptying it yourself?"

(The solid old building, with its spacious halls, had no upstairs drain.)

What Sharaf Sibgatov had once been like was impossible to guess; there was nothing to go by. His suffering had been so prolonged that there was practically nothing left of his former self. Yet after three years of continuous, oppressive illness, this young Tartar was the gentlest and most courteous patient in the whole clinic. Often he would smile very weakly, as if to ask pardon for the trouble he had been causing for so long. After the four- and six-month periods he had spent lying there he knew all the doctors, nurses and orderlies as if they were his own family, and they knew him. But Nellya was brand-new. She had only been there a few weeks.

"It will be too heavy for me," Sibgatov objected quietly. "If there was something smaller to put it in I should do it myself, bit by bit."

But Zoya's table was nearby. She heard what was happening and jumped up. "You ought to be ashamed of yourself! He's not allowed to strain his back. And you'd make him carry the bowl, would you?"

She said all this as though she were shouting, but in a half-whisper which only the three of them could hear. But Nellya replied quite calmly, her voice resounding over the whole floor, "Why should I be ashamed? I'm worn out myself."

"You're on duty! You get paid for it!" said Zoya indignantly, even more quietly.

"Huh! Paid! You call that money? I can get more at the textile factory."

"Sh . . . sh! Can't you be quieter?"

"Oooh," Nellya, her mass of hair all over the place, half groaned, half sighed to the whole hall. "My lovely, lovely pillow. I'm so sleepy; I spent last night living it up with the truck drivers. All right, patient, put the bowl under your bed. I'll take it away in the morning."

Without covering her mouth she gave a deep, long-drawn-out yawn. When she had finished she said to Zoya, "I shall be in session in there on the sofa," and without waiting for permission walked off to the corner door which led into a room with upholstered furniture used for doctors' meetings and short daily conferences.

She had left quite a lot of work unfinished; the spittoons had not been cleaned and the landing floor could have done with a wash, but Zoya restrained herself, watching her large back disappear. Zoya had not been working there long, but already she was beginning to understand the annoying principle that the one who doesn't pull her weight is not asked to pull, while the one who does, pulls for two. Elizaveta Anatolyevna would be in in the morning. She'd do the cleaning and washing for Nellya and for herself.

Sibgatov, now alone, uncovered his sacrum and lowered himself uncomfortably onto the bowl on the floor beside his bed. He sat there very quietly. Any careless movement jarred his pelvis. The searing sensation caused by anything touching the injured spot, even the constant contact of his underwear, was agonizing. And of course he tried to avoid lying on his back. Exactly what it was he had on his back he had never actually seen, only groped at occasionally with his fingers. Two years ago he had been brought into the clinic on a stretcher, unable to stand or move his legs. Several doctors had examined him then, but it was always Ludmila Afanasyevna who had treated him. And in four months the pain had gone completely! He could walk and bend freely and had nothing to complain of. When they discharged him Ludmila Afanasyevna had warned him as he kissed her hands, "Be careful, Sharaf! Don't leap about or knock yourself." But he hadn't been able to find the right sort of work and had to become a delivery man again. And as a delivery man could he avoid jumping down from the back of the van on to the ground? Or stand by without helping the loader or driver? Everything had been all right until one day a drum had rolled down off the van and struck Sharaf right on his bad spot. The wound had festered and refused to heal, and from that time on Sibgatov had become chained to the cancer clinic.

It was with a lingering feeling of annoyance that Zoya sat down at her table to check once more that everyone had been given his treatment, and to finish the already blurred lines of her notes with pen strokes that blurred on the poor-quality paper even as she wrote. It would be useless to report her, and against Zoya's nature. She would have to deal with her herself, yet that was just what she could not do with Nellya. There was nothing wrong with having a nap. When she had a good orderly, Zoya would go to sleep for half the night herself. But now she'd have to sit up.

She was sitting looking at her notes when she heard a man come up and stand beside her. She raised her head. It was Kostoglotov, with his gangling frame, his unkempt coal-black hair, and his large hands which hardly fitted into the little side pockets of his hospital jacket.

"You should have been asleep ages ago," Zoya chided him. "What are you doing, walking around?"

"Good morning, Zoyenka," said Kostoglotov as gently as he could, almost singing the words.

"Good night." She gave him a fleeting smile. "It was 'good evening' when I was running after you with the thermometer."

"That was when you were on duty, you mustn't blame me. But now I'm your guest."

"Is that so?" (She didn't consciously flutter her lashes or open her eyes wide. It just happened.) "What gave you the idea I'm receiving guests?"

"Well, every night duty you've always had your nose to the grindstone. But today I can't see any textbooks. Have you passed your last exam?"

"You're observant. Yes, I have."

"What mark did you get? Not that it matters."

"I got four out of five. Why doesn't it matter?"

"I thought you might only have got three and not want to talk about it. So now you're on holiday?"

She winked with light gaiety. And as she winked, it suddenly struck her: what was she worrying about? Two weeks' holiday, what bliss! She didn't have to do anything except go to the clinic! Such a lot of free time! When she was on duty she could read something light, or chat to people.

"So I was right to come and visit you?"

"All right, sit down."

"But, Zoya, as far as I remember in my day the holiday used to start earlier, on January 25."

"In the fall we were picking cotton. We do it every year."*

"How much longer have you got at college?"

"Eighteen months."

"Then where will you be posted to?"

She shrugged her gently rounded shoulders. "Ours is a big country . . ."

Her eyes were enormous even when her face was calm. It was as if there was no room for them under her eyelids, as if they were begging to be let out.

"But they won't leave you here?"

"N-no, of course not."

"How can you leave your family?"

"What family? I've only got a grandmother. I'll take Grandma with me."

"What about your father and mother?"

Zoya sighed. "My mother died."

Kostoglotov looked at her and did not ask about her father. "But you come from round here, don't you?"

"No, from Smolensk."

"Really . . . when did you leave there?"

"During the evacuation . . . when else?"

"You were . . . about nine?"

"Yeah. I was at school for two years there. Then Grandma and I got stuck here."

Zoya reached toward the large orange shopping bag on the floor by the wall, pulled out a mirror, took off her nurse's cap, lightly fluffed up her hair, which was crammed under it, and started to comb out a slightly curling fine golden strand.

A golden reflection from it appeared on Kostoglotov's hard face. He relaxed a little and followed her movements with pleasure.

*In Central Asia there is a shortage of cotton pickers. Every fall students are sent to help, so the school year starts later than in Leningrad, where Kostoglotov had studied, thus making the holidays later too.

"So, where's *your* grandmother?" asked Zoya jokingly, as she finished with the mirror.

"My grandmother"—Kostoglotov was being completely serious—"and my ma" (the word was at odds with his bitter expression) "died in the siege."

"The siege of Leningrad?"

"Uh-huh. And my sister was killed by a shell. She was a nurse just like you, only more of a child."

"Ye-es," sighed Zoya, ignoring the allusion to child, "so many people died in the siege. Damn Hitler!"

Kostoglotov gave a wry grin. "We've had more than enough proof of Hitler being damned. But I wouldn't blame the Leningrad blockade on him alone."

"What do you mean? Why not?"

"Well, listen. Hitler came to annihilate us. Were the besieged supposed to wait for him to open the gate and say: 'Come out one by one, don't crowd together'? He was making war, he was an enemy. But there was someone else responsible for the blockade too."

"Who?" whispered Zoya, quite astounded. She had never heard or imagined anything like it.

Kostoglotov knit his black brows. "Well, let's say those who would have been prepared to fight even if England, France and America had joined Hitler as allies. Those who drew their salaries for decades without seeing how Leningrad was geographically isolated and that this would affect its defense. Those who failed to foresee how heavy the bombardments would be and never thought of stocking up provisions below ground. They strangled my mother too—they and Hitler."

It was all so simple—but somehow terribly new.

Sibgatov was sitting quietly on his bowl in the corner behind them.

"But in that case . . . in that case surely they ought to be put on trial?" ventured Zoya in a whisper.

"I don't know." Kostoglotov grimaced, his lips an even thinner line than before. "I don't know."

Zoya did not put her cap back on. The top button of her uniform was undone and the gold-gray collar of her dress peeped out.

"Zoyenka, I did come to see you partly on business."

"Did you now?" Her eyelashes jerked up. "Well then, it'll have to wait till day duty. Now it's time for sleep. You did say you were just visiting, didn't you?"

"Yes, I . . . I'm visiting too. But before you get spoiled by it all, before you become a fully qualified doctor, just give me a helping hand as a human being."

"Don't the doctors do that?"

"Well, theirs is a different sort of hand and they don't stretch it out. Zoya, all my life I've hated being a guinea pig. They're giving me treatment here, but nobody explains anything. I can't stand it. I saw you with a book the other day—*Pathological Anatomy*. Is that right?"

"Yes."

"And it's about tumors, yes?"

"Yes."

"Do me a favor and bring it to me! I must have a look at it and try to work things out. For myself."

Zoya pursed her lips and shook her head. "It's strictly against the rules for patients to read medical books. Even when we students study a particular disease we always imagine that . . ."

"It may be against the rules for others, but not for me!" Kostoglotov slapped his big paw down on the table. "They've tried to scare me out of my wits so many times, I've stopped being scared. In the regional hospital I was diagnosed by a Korean surgeon. It was New Year's Eve. He didn't want to tell me what was wrong. 'Speak the truth, man!' I said. 'We're not allowed to do that here.' 'Speak!' I said. 'I must put my family affairs in order!' So he blurted out, 'You'll live another three weeks, I won't guarantee you any longer than that!' "

"He didn't have the right to . . ."

"He was a good man. A human being. I shook him by the hand. You see, I had to know! I'd tormented myself for six months before that. The last month I hadn't been able to lie, sit down or stand without it hurting, and I was only sleeping a few minutes a day. So I must have done plenty of thinking. This autumn I learned from experience that a man can cross the threshold of death even when his body is still not dead. Your blood still circulates and your stomach digests, while you yourself have gone through the whole psychological preparation for death—and lived through death itself. Everything around you, you see as if from the grave. And although you've never counted yourself a Christian, indeed the very opposite sometimes, all of a sudden you find you've forgiven all those who trespassed against you and bear no ill-will toward those who persecuted you. You're simply indifferent to everyone and everything. There's nothing you'd put yourself out to change, you regret nothing. I'd even say it was a state of equilibrium, as natural as that of the trees and the stones. Now I have been taken out of it, but I'm not sure whether I should be pleased or not. It means the return of all my passions, the bad as well as the good."

"Ha! What cheek! You've got plenty to be pleased about. When you were admitted here . . . how many days ago was it?"

"Twelve."

"There you were, writhing about on the couch right here in the hall. You were an appalling sight. You had a face like a corpse, wouldn't eat a thing, and a temperature of over a hundred, morning and evening—and now? You go visiting . . . It's a miracle . . . for a man to come to life again like that in twelve days. It hardly ever happens here."

Indeed, his face had been covered in deep, gray creases, as if hacked out with a chisel, evidence of his constant tension. But now there were fewer of them and they had become lighter.

"I was lucky. It turned out I had a high tolerance to X rays."

"Yes, it's very rare. It's a stroke of luck," said Zoya, warmly.

Kostoglotov grinned. "I haven't had all that much luck in my life, so the X-ray business is only fair, isn't it? I've started to dream again—vague, pleasant dreams. I think it's a sign I'm getting better."

"Very possibly."

"Well then, all the more reason why I have to understand and investigate. I want to understand exactly how I'm being treated, what the long-term prospects are, what the complications are. I feel so much better, perhaps the treatment should be stopped altogether. Anyway, I want to understand it. Ludmila Afanasyevna and Van Kornilyevna don't tell me anything, they just give me the treatment as if I were a monkey. Please bring me the book, Zoya, please! I won't give you away. Nobody will see me with it, I promise you."

He was so insistent that he became quite animated.

Zoya hesitated. She took hold of the handle of one of the drawers in her table.

"Is it there?" Kostoglotov guessed at once. "Zoyenka, give it to me."

His hand was outstretched, ready for it. "When are you next on duty?"

"Sunday afternoon."

"I'll give it back to you then, all right? Is it a bargain?"

How pleasant and easygoing she was, with that golden hair and those great wide eyes.

If only he could have seen himself, his hair, matted from lying on the pillow, sticking up in pointed tufts all over his head, one corner of a coarse calico issue shirt showing with hospital informality from under his jacket, which was not buttoned up to the neck.

"Ah yes, yes." He flicked through the book, dipping from time to time into the table of contents. "Yes, good, I can find it all here. Thank you. Otherwise, Christ knows, they might overtreat me. After all, they're only really interested in having something to fill out for their reports. Maybe I'll run away. Even a good doctor shortens your life."

"There, you see." Zoya threw up her hands. "Why did I have to let you see it? Give it back!" And she tugged at the book, first with one hand and then with both. But he hung onto it easily.

"You'll tear it! It's a library copy! Give it back!"

Her firm, round shoulders and small firm, round arms looked as if they had been poured into the close-fitting uniform. Her neck was neither too thin nor too fat, too short nor too long, but just right for her figure.

As they tugged at the book they were drawn together and looked straight into each other's eyes. His uncouth face suddenly blossomed into a smile. The scar on it no longer seemed so terrible; it was paler, like an ancient wound. With his free hand, Kostoglotov softly prized her fingers from the book and spoke to her in a whisper: "Zoyenka. You don't believe in ignorance, you believe in education. How can you stop people becoming wiser? I was joking. I won't run away."

She answered him in an aggressive whisper: "You don't deserve to be allowed to read it. You neglected yourself. Why didn't you come earlier? Why come here when you were practically a corpse?"

"Well," sighed Kostoglotov, this time half aloud. "There wasn't any transport."

"No transport! What sort of a place was it? There are always aeroplanes, aren't there? Why did you have to put it off to the last minute? Why didn't you move earlier to a more civilized place? Wasn't there a doctor or a *feldsher** or something?"

She let go of the book.

"Oh yes, there was a gynecologist. Two, in fact."

"Two gynecologists?" Zoya gasped in amazement. "Are there only women there, then?"

"On the contrary, there aren't enough. There are two gynecologists but no other doctors of any kind. There aren't any laboratories either. It's impossible to get a blood test done. I had a blood count. It turned out to be sixty, and no one knew a thing about it."

"God, what a nightmare! And then you take it upon yourself to decide whether you should be treated or not. If you haven't any pity for yourself at least have some for your family and your children."

"Children?" It was as if Kostoglotov had suddenly come to, as if the whole gay tug-of-war with the book had been a dream and he was now returning to his normal self, with his hard face and his slow way of speaking. "I haven't any children."

"And your wife, isn't she a human being?"

His speech was even slower now.

"No wife either."

"Men always say they've got no wife. Then what about those family affairs that you had to put in order? What was it you told the Korean?"

"I told him a lie."

"How do I know you're not lying to me now?"

"I'm not, I swear it." Kostoglotov's face was growing grave. "It's just that I'm a choosy sort of person."

"I suppose she couldn't stand your personality?" Zoya nodded sympathetically.

Kostoglotov shook his head very slowly. "There never was a wife—ever."

Zoya tried unsuccessfully to work out his age. She moved her lips once, but decided not to put the question. She moved them again, and again did not ask it.

Zoya was sitting with her back to Sibgatov, and Kostoglotov was facing him. He saw him haul himself gingerly out of the little bath, clasp both hands to the small of his back and stand there to dry.

---

*An assistant doctor, not fully qualified, who provides medical treatment in Russian rural areas.

His face was that of a man who had suffered all he could. Acute misery lay behind him now, but there was nothing to lure him on toward happiness.

Kostoglotov breathed in and then out, as if respiration was his whole job in life.

"I'm dying for a smoke! Couldn't I possibly . . ."

"Certainly not. For you smoking means death."

"Not in any circumstances?"

"In no circumstances, especially not in front of me." All the same, she smiled.

"Perhaps I could have just one?"

"The patients are asleep; how can you?"

However, he pulled out a long, empty cigarette holder, hand-made and encrusted with stones, and began to suck it.

"You know what they say: a young man's too young to get married, and an old man's too old." He leaned both elbows on her table and ran his fingers with the cigarette holder through his hair. "I nearly got married after the war, though. I was a student and so was she. I wouldn't have minded getting married, but everything went wrong."

Zoya scrutinized Kostoglotov's face. It didn't look very friendly, but it was strong. Those raw-boned arms and shoulders . . . but that was the disease.

"Didn't it work itself out?"

"She . . . How does one say it? . . . She perished." He closed one eye in a crooked grimace and stared hard with the other. "She perished, although in fact she's still alive. Last year we wrote to each other a couple of times."

He opened his other eye. He saw the cigarette holder between his fingers and put it back into his pocket.

"And, you know, there were some sentences in those letters that set me thinking: was she really as perfect as she seemed to me then? Perhaps she wasn't. What can we possibly understand when we're twenty-five?" His dark-brown eyes looked steadily at Zoya. "You, for instance, what do you understand now about men? Not a damn thing!"

Zoya burst out laughing. "Maybe I understand them very well!"

"That would be quite impossible," Kostoglotov decreed. "What you call understanding isn't understanding at all. You'll get married and you'll make a bi-ig mistake."

"Wet blanket!" Zoya shook her head from side to side. Then she put her hand in the big orange bag and brought out a piece of embroidery, which she unfolded. It was just a small piece, drawn across a frame. A green crane was already stitched in; a fox and tankard were outlined.

Kostoglotov looked at it as if it was something miraculous.

"You do *embroidery*?"

"What's so surprising?"

"I never imagined a modern medical student would do that sort of handwork."

"You've never watched girls doing embroidery?"

"Only when I was a child perhaps, during the twenties. Even then people thought it was bourgeois. You'd have got such a drubbing at the Young Communists' meeting."

"It's very popular these days. Haven't you seen it?"

He shook his head.

"You disapprove?"

"No; why should I? It's nice, gives you a comfortable feeling. I admire it." She stitched away, while he looked on admiringly. She watched her work, he watched her. In the yellow light of the lamp her golden eyelashes glimmered, and the little open corner of her dress shone golden too.

"Teddy bear with the golden hair," he whispered.

"What's that?" Still bent over her work, she raised her eyebrows. He repeated it.

"Oh yes?" Zoya seemed to have expected more of a compliment than that. "If nobody embroiders where you come from, I suppose they have masses of *moulinet* in the stores?"

"What's that?"

"*Moulinet*. These threads here—green, blue, red, yellow. They're very hard to come by here."

"*Moulinet*. I'll remember to ask. If there's any I'll send you some without fail. Or if it turns out we have limited supplies, perhaps it would be simpler for you to move out there?"

"Where's that? Where do you live?"

"I suppose you could say—in the virgin lands."

"So, you're a virgin-lander?"

"I mean, when I went there, nobody thought they were the virgin lands. But now it seems they are and virgin-landers come out to us. When you graduate, why don't you apply to come out? I shouldn't think they'll refuse. They wouldn't refuse anyone who applied to join us."

"Is it that bad?"

"Not at all. Only people have distorted ideas about what's good and what's bad. To live in a five-story cage, with people banging about and walking to and fro above your head and the radio blaring on all sides, is considered good. But to live as a hardworking tiller of the soil in a mud hut on the edge of the steppe—that's considered the height of misfortune."

He wasn't joking at all, his words had the weary conviction of people who have no desire to strengthen their argument even by raising their voice.

"But is it steppe or desert?"

"Steppe. No sand dunes. But there's a bit of grass. *Zhantak* grows there, camel thorn, you know. It's thorn, but in July it produces pinkish flowers and even a very delicate smell. The Kazakhs make a hundred medicines out of it."

"It's in Kazakhstan, then?"

"Uh-huh."

"What's it called?"

"Ush-Terek."

"Is it an *aul*?"*

"Yes, if you like, an *aul*, or a regional administrative center. There's a hospital. Only there aren't enough doctors. Do come."

He narrowed his eyes.

"Doesn't anything else grow there?"

"Oh yes, there's agriculture, but under irrigation. Beets, maize. In the kitchen gardens there's everything you could wish for. Only you have to work hard, with the bucket. In the bazaar the Greeks always have fresh milk, the Kurds have mutton, and the Germans pork.** They're such picturesque bazaars, you should see them! Everyone wears national dress, they come in on camels."

"Are you an agronomist?"

"No. Land surveyor."

"Why do you live there, basically?"

Kostoglotov scratched his nose. "I just adore the climate."

"And there's no transport?"

*A village in the Turkic-speaking part of Russia.
**Greeks, Kurds and Germans were among those deported to the Kazakh steppe during and immediately after the war.

"Of course there is. Motorcars—all you could want."

"But why should *I* go there?"

She looked sideways at him. All the time they had been talking Kostoglotov's face had grown kinder and softer.

"Why should *you*?" He furrowed the skin of his forehead, as though searching for words with which to propose a toast. "Zoyenka, how can you tell which part of the world you'd be happy in, and which you'd be unhappy in? Who can say he knows that about himself?"

4. The Patients' Worries

For the surgical cases, whose tumors were to be arrested by an operation, there was not enough room in the wards on the lower floor. They were put upstairs with the "X-ray" patients, those prescribed radiotherapy or chemical treatment. For this reason there were two different rounds upstairs every morning, one for the radiotherapists, one for the surgeons.

The fourth of February was a Friday, operation day, when the surgeons did not make their rounds. So Vera Kornilyevna Gangart, the radiotherapist on duty, did not start her rounds immediately after the five-minute briefing. She just glanced inside as she passed the door of the men's ward.

Dr. Gangart was shapely and not tall. Her shapeliness was emphasized by her narrow waist, to which all the contours of her body seemed to point. Her hair, gathered in an unfashionable bun on the back of her head, was lighter than black but darker than dark-brown.

Ahmadjan caught sight of her and nodded to her happily. Kostoglotov also had time to raise his head from his large book and bow to her from afar. She smiled to both of them and raised one finger, as if to warn her children to sit quietly while she was away. Then she moved from the doorway and was gone.

Today she was to go round the wards not alone but with Ludmila Afanasyevna Dontsova, who was in charge of the radiotherapy department. But Ludmila Afanasyevna had been called in to see Nizamutdin Bahramovich, the senior doctor, and he was holding her up.

Dontsova would only sacrifice her X-ray diagnostic sessions on the days she did her rounds, once a week. Usually she would spend those two first morning hours, the best of the day, when the eye is at its sharpest and the mind at its clearest, sitting with the intern assigned to her in front of the screen. She saw this as the most complicated part of her work, and after more than twenty years of it, had realized what a high price has to be paid in particular for diagnostic mistakes. In her department there were three doctors, all young women. To ensure that they all became equally experienced and that none of them lagged behind in diagnostic skill, Dontsova changed them round every three months. They worked either in the outpatients' department or in the X-ray diagnosis room or as house physician in the clinic.

Dr. Gangart was at present assigned to the third task. The most important, dangerous and little-researched part of it was to check that the radiation doses were correct. There was no formula for calculating the right intensity of a dose, for knowing how much would be most lethal for an individual tumor yet least harmful to the rest of the body. There was no formula but there was a certain experience, a certain intuition, which could be correlated with the condition of the patient. After all, this was an operation too—but by rays, in the dark and over a period of time. It was impossible to avoid damaging or destroying healthy cells.

As for the rest of her duties, the house physician needed only to be methodical: arrange tests on time, check them and make notes on thirty case histories. No doctor likes filling out forms, but Vera Kornilyevna put up with it because for these three months they became *her* patients, not pale mergings of light and shade on a screen but her own permanent, living charges who trusted her and waited on the encouragement of her voice and the comfort of her glance. And when the time came to give up her stint as house physician, she was always sorry to say goodbye to the ones she had not had the time to cure.

Olympiada Vladislavovna, the nurse on duty, was an elderly, grayish-haired, portly woman who looked more imposing than some of the doctors. She had just gone round the wards telling the radiotherapy patients to stay in their places. But in the large women's ward it was as though the patients had been waiting for exactly this announcement. One after the other, in their identical gray dressing gowns, they filed onto the landing and down the stairs: had the old boy come with the sour cream? Or the old woman with the milk? They would peer from the clinic porch through the theater windows (the lower halves were whitewashed, but through the upper halves they could see the nurses' and surgeons' caps and the bright overhead lamps) or they would wash their clothes in the sink or go and visit someone.

It was the shabby gray dressing gowns of rough cotton, so untidy-looking even when perfectly clean, as well as the fact that they were about to undergo surgery, that set these women apart, deprived them of their womanliness and their feminine charm. The dressing gowns had no cut whatever. They were all enormous, so that any woman, however fat, could easily wrap one around her. The drooping sleeves looked like wide, shapeless smokestacks. The men's pink and white striped jackets were much neater, but the women were never issued dresses, only those dressing gowns without buttons or buttonholes. Some of them shortened the dressing gowns, others lengthened them. They all had the same way of tightening the cotton belt to hide their nightdresses and of holding the flaps across their breasts. No woman suffering from disease and in such a drab dressing gown had a chance of gladdening anyone's eye, and they all knew it.

In the men's ward everyone except Rusanov waited for the rounds quietly and without much movement.

An old Uzbek called Mursalimov, a collective-farm watchman, was lying stretched out on his back on his neatly made bed. As usual, he wore his battered old skullcap. He must have been glad about one thing: his cough was not tearing him to pieces. He had folded his hands across his suffocating chest and was staring at one spot on the ceiling. The dark-bronze skin of his skull-like head was tightly stretched. The small bones of his nose, the jawbone and the sharp chinbone behind his pointed beard were all clearly visible. His ears had thinned and become no more than flat pieces of cartilage. He had only to dry up a bit more and turn a little blacker and he'd be a mummy.

Next to him Egenberdiev, a middle-aged Kazakh shepherd, was not lying but sitting on his bed, legs crossed as though he was sitting on a rug at home. With the palms of his large, powerful hands he held his big, round knees. His taut, tough body was so tightly knit that if he sometimes swayed a little in spite of his immobility, it was like the swaying of a tower or a factory chimney. His back and shoulders stretched the pink and white jacket tight, and the cuffs on his muscular forearms were on the point of tearing. The small ulcer on his lip, the reason for his entering hospital, had been turned by the rays into a large, crimson scab that obstructed his mouth and made it hard for him to eat and drink. But he did not toss about, fidget or shout. He would eat everything on his plate steadily and without fail and then sit like that for hours quite peacefully, gazing into space.

Further down, in the bed by the door, sixteen-year-old Dyomka had his bad leg stretched out. He was continually stroking and lightly massaging the gnawing spot on his shin, his other leg folded up kitten-style, just reading, not noticing a thing. In fact, he read the whole time he was not sleeping or undergoing treatment. In the laboratory where they did all the analyses the senior lab assistant had a cupboard full of books. Dyomka was allowed to go there and change his books for himself without waiting for them to be changed for the whole ward. Now he was reading a thick magazine with a bluish cover,* not a new one but a tattered, faded copy. There were no new ones in the lab. girl's cupboard.

Proshka too had made his bed properly without hollows or wrinkles and was sitting quietly and patiently with his feet on the floor like a man in the best of health. In fact he *was* quite healthy. He had nothing to complain about in the ward. He had no external sign of disease, and there was a healthy tan on his cheeks. A smooth lock of hair lay across his forehead. He was a fit young man, fit enough even to go dancing.

Next to him Ahmadjan had found no one to play with, so he had placed a chessboard diagonally across his blanket and was playing checkers against himself.

Yefrem, his bandage encasing him like a suit of armor, his head immobilized, was no longer stomping along the corridor spreading gloom. Instead, he had propped himself up with two pillows and was completely absorbed in the book which Kostoglotov had forced upon him the day before. He was turning over its pages so slowly one might have thought he was dozing over it.

Azovkin was suffering exactly as he had been the day before. Quite probably he had not slept at all. His things were scattered

---

Novy mir, the famous "liberal" monthly, in which the author's works are normally published. He deliberately does not name it although its identity would be quite clear to any educated Russian.

over the window sill and the bedside table, and his bed was all rumpled. His forehead and temples were covered in perspiration, and his yellow face reflected the pain writhing inside him. Sometimes he stood on the floor, bent double, leaning his elbows against the bed. At other times he would seize his stomach in both hands and fold his whole body around them. For many days he had not even answered the questions people asked him. He said nothing about himself. He used his powers of speech only for begging extra medicine from the nurses and doctors. When people came from home to visit him, he would send them out to buy more of the medicines he had seen in the hospital.

Outside it was a gloomy, still, colorless day. Kostoglotov came back from his morning X ray and without asking Pavel Nikolayevich opened a small window above his head. The air he let in was damp but not cold.

Pavel Nikolayevich was afraid of his tumor catching cold. He wrapped up his neck and sat down by the wall. How dumb they all were, how submissive, wooden almost! Except for Azovkin, nobody really looked as if he was suffering. They were not really worthy of recovery. It must have been Gorky who said the only people worthy of freedom are those prepared to go out and fight for it every day. As for Pavel Nikolayevich, already that morning he had taken certain resolute steps. As soon as the registrar's office was open he had telephoned home and told his wife what he had decided during the night: applications were to made through all possible channels; he must be transferred to Moscow; he would not risk staying and dying in this place. Kapa knew how to get things done, she must already have set to work. Of course, it was sheer weakness—he shouldn't have been afraid of a tumor and stooped to taking a bed in a place like this. Nobody would ever believe it, but it was a fact that since three o'clock yesterday afternoon no one had even come to feel whether the tumor had grown bigger. Nobody had given him any medicine. Assassins in white coats—that was well said.* They'd just hung up a temperature chart for idiots to look at. The orderly hadn't even come in to make his bed. He had had to do it himself! My word, our medical institutions still need a great deal of smartening up!

*This was the standard phrase applied to the accused in the 1953 Doctors' Plot, Stalin's last great purge.

At last the doctors appeared, but they still wouldn't enter the room. They stood over there for quite a while, on the other side of the door, round Sibgatov, who had bared his back and was showing it to them. (Meanwhile Kostoglotov had hidden his book under the mattress.)

Finally, though, they came into the ward: Dr. Dontsova, Dr. Gangart and a portly, gray-haired nurse with a notebook in her hand and a towel over her arm. The entry of several white coats all at once always brings with it a wave of attention, fear and hope; and the strength of these feelings grows with the whiteness of the gowns and caps and the sternness of the faces. The sternest and most solemn of all was that of the nurse Olympiada Vladislavovna. For her the morning rounds were like divine service for a deacon. She was a nurse for whom the doctors were of a higher order than ordinary people. She knew that doctors understood everything, never made mistakes and never gave wrong instructions. She jotted down every instruction in her notebook with a sensation almost of joy— something the young nurses no longer had.

But even after they were in the ward, the doctors made no undue haste toward Rusanov's bed! Ludmila Afanasyevna, a heavy woman with simple, heavy features, her hair already ashen but well trimmed and waved, said a quiet general "Good morning," and then stopped by the first bed, by Dyomka. She peered at him searchingly.

"What are you reading, Dyomka?" (Can't she think of anything more intelligent to say? She's meant to be on duty!)

Dyomka did not name the title. He did what many people do, turned over the magazine with the faded blue cover and showed it to her. Dontsova narrowed her eyes.

"Oh, it's such an old one, it's two years old. Why?"

"There's an interesting article," said Dyomka with a significant air.

"What about?"

"About *sincerity!*" he replied, even more emphatically. "It says literature without sincerity . . ." He was lowering his bad leg onto the floor, but Ludmila Afanasyevna quickly checked him.

"Don't do that. Roll up your pajamas."

He rolled up his trouser leg, and she sat down on the edge of his bed. Carefully, using just two or three fingers, she began to probe gently round the affected part.

Vera Kornilyevna leaned against the foot of the bed behind her, looked over her shoulder and said quietly, "Fifteen sessions, three thousand rads."

"Does it hurt there?"

"Yes, it does."

"And here?"

"It hurts further up, too."

"Well, why didn't you say so? Don't be such a hero! Tell me when it starts to hurt."

She slowly felt around the edges. "Does it hurt without being touched? At night?"

Dyomka's face was smooth. There still was not a single hair on it. But its permanently tense expression made him look much more grown-up than he was.

"It nags me day and night."

Ludmila Afanasyevna and Gangart exchanged glances.

"But have you noticed if it hurts more or less since you've been here?"

"I don't know! Maybe it's a bit better. Maybe I'm just imagining things."

"Blood count?" Ludmila Afanasyevna asked. Gangart handed her the case history. Ludmila Afanasyevna flipped through it, then looked at the boy.

"How's your appetite?"

"I've always liked eating," Dyomka replied grandly.

"He's on a special diet now," broke in Vera Kornilyevna in her lilting voice, kindheartedly, like a nanny. She smiled at Dyomka, and he smiled back.

"Transfusion?" Gangart asked Dontsova the question quickly and quietly. She took back the case history.

"Yes. Well, what do you think, Dyomka?" Ludmila Afanasyevna gave him another searching look. "Shall we go on with the X rays?"

"Of course we go on." The boy's face lit up and he looked at her gratefully.

He thought that the X rays were to be instead of an operation, that that was what Dontsova had meant. (What she had really meant was that before operating on bone sarcoma, its activity has to be suppressed by irradiation to prevent the formation of secondaries.)

Egenberdiev had been getting himself ready for some time. He kept a sharp lookout, and as soon as Ludmila Afanasyevna got up from the next bed he stood bolt upright in the passageway, puffed up his chest and towered soldier-like above her.

Dontsova gave him a smile, leaned toward his lip and inspected the scab. Gangart was quietly reading out figures to her.

"Yes, very good!" she said encouragingly, louder than necessary, as people do when speaking to someone whose native tongue is different from their own. "You're making good progress, Egenberdiev! You'll soon be going home."

Ahmadjan knew what he was supposed to do. He had to translate what she said into Uzbek. (He and Egenberdiev understood one another, although each thought the other was murdering the language.)*

Egenberdiev gazed at Ludmila Afanasyevna. His eyes showed hope and trust, delight even, the delight with which simple souls regard genuinely educated, genuinely useful people. Nevertheless he raised his hand to the scab and said something. "But it's becoming larger? It's grown?" Ahmadjan translated.

"It will all fall off. That's what's meant to happen." Dontsova was articulating the words particularly loudly. "It will all fall away! Three months' rest at home, and then you'll come back to us!"

She went across to the old man Mursalimov, who was already sitting with his feet hanging down. He tried to get up to meet her, but she stopped him and sat down next to him. The emaciated, bronze-skinned old man looked at her with the same faith in her omnipotence. Through Ahmadjan she asked about his cough and told him to lift up his shirt. She felt his chest lightly where it hurt and knocked on it with her fingers over her other hand, meanwhile listening to Vera Kornilyevna telling her about the number of sessions, the blood count and the injections. Then she silently examined the case history herself. Once upon a time every organ had been necessary, everything in its place inside a healthy body. But now it all seemed to be superfluous, knots of muscle and angles of bone protruding from under the skin.

Dontsova prescribed some new injections. Then she asked him to point out among the bottles on his bedside table which pills he was taking. Mursalimov picked up an empty bottle of multi-vitamins.

"When did you buy these?" Dontsova inquired.

---

*Ahmadjan is an Uzbek, Egenberdiev a Kazakh. They speak different Turkic dialects.

Ahmadjan translated: two days ago.

"Well, where are the pills?"

He'd taken them all.

"What do you mean, you've taken them all?" Dontsova was flabbergasted. "All at once?"

"No. Two different times," Ahmadjan relayed to her.

The doctors, the nurses, the Russian patients and Ahmadjan all burst out laughing. Mursalimov bared his teeth—he had not yet understood.

Only Pavel Nikolayevich was filled with indignation at their senseless, untimely, criminal laughter. Well, he'd soon sober them up! He had been debating which pose to use to confront the doctors, and had decided his point could be best made in a semi-reclining position, with his legs drawn up under him.

"It's all right. It doesn't matter!" Dontsova reassured Mursalimov. She prescribed some more vitamin C, wiped her hands on the towel so fervently proffered to her by one of the nurses and turned with a look of concern on her face toward the next bed. Now, as she stood close to the window and facing it, one could see her unhealthy, grayish complexion. There was a very tired, almost sickly, expression on her face.

Sitting up sternly in bed, bald, in his skullcap and glasses, Pavel Nikolayevich looked rather like a schoolteacher, not any old school-teacher but a distinguished one who had brought up hundreds of pupils. He waited until Ludmila Afanasyevna was quite close to his bed, then he adjusted his glasses and declared, "Comrade Dontsova, I shall be forced to inform the Ministry of Health of the way things are conducted at this clinic. And I shall have to telephone Comrade Ostapenko."

She did not tremble or go pale, but perhaps her complexion became a little more pasty. She made a strange movement with her shoulders, a circular movement as though her shoulders were tired and longed to be rid of the harness which held them.

"If you have good contacts in the Ministry of Health," she agreed with him at once, "and if you're in a position to telephone Comrade Ostapenko, I can think of several more things you might add. Shall I tell you what they are?"

"There is nothing that needs to be added. Your display of in-difference is quite enough as it is. I have been in here for *eighteen* hours, and nobody is giving me treatment. And I am a . . ." (There was nothing more he could say to her. Surely she could supply the rest herself!)

Everyone in the room was silent, staring at Rusanov. It was Gangart who was shocked, not Dontsova. Her lips tightened into a thin line. She frowned and knit her brows, as if she had seen something irrevocable take place and been powerless to avert it.

Dontsova, her large frame towering over the seated Rusanov, did not even permit herself a frown. She made another circular movement of her shoulders and said in a quiet, conciliatory tone, "That's why I'm here—to give you treatment."

"No. It's too late now." Pavel Nikolayevich cut her short. "I've seen quite enough of the way things are done here, and I'm leaving. No one shows the slightest interest, nobody bothers to make a diagnosis!" There was an unintended tremble in his voice; he was really offended.

"You've had your diagnosis," Dontsova said slowly, both hands gripping the foot of his bed, "and there's nowhere else for you to go. No other hospital in the republic will take patients with your particular illness."

"But you told me I don't have cancer! . . . What is the diagnosis?"

"Generally speaking, we don't have to tell our patients what's wrong with them, but if it will make you feel any better, very well—it's lymphoma."

"You mean it's not cancer?"

"Of course it's not." Her face and voice bore no trace of the bitterness that naturally comes from a quarrel, for she could see clearly enough the fist-sized tumor under his jaw. Who could she feel bitter against? The tumor? "Nobody forced you to come here. You can discharge yourself whenever you like. But remember . . ." She hesitated. "People don't only die of cancer." It was like a friendly warning.

"What's this? Are you trying to frighten me?" Pavel Nikolayevich exclaimed. "Why are you doing it? That's against the rules of professional etiquette." He was still rattling away as hard as he could, but at the word "die" everything had suddenly frozen inside him. His voice was noticeably softer when he added, "You . . . you mean my condition is all that dangerous?"

"Of course it will be if you keep moving from one hospital to another. Take off your scarf. Stand up, please."

He took off his scarf and stood up on the floor. Gently Dontsova began to feel the tumor and then the healthy side of the neck, comparing the two. She asked him to move his head back as far as it would go. (It wouldn't go very far. The tumor immediately began to pull it back.) Next he had to bend it forward as far as possible, then twist it to the left and the right.

So that was it! His head had apparently already lost practically all its freedom of movement, that amazing effortless freedom which when we possess it goes completely unnoticed.

"Take off your jacket, please."

His green and brown pajama jacket had large buttons and was the right size. No one would have thought it could be difficult to take off. But when he stretched his arms it pulled at his neck, and Pavel Nikolayevich groaned. The situation *was* serious! The impressive, gray-haired nurse helped him untangle himself from the sleeves.

"Do your armpits hurt?" Dontsova asked. "Does anything bother you?"

"Why, might it spread down there as well?" Rusanov's voice had now dropped and was even quieter than Ludmila Afanasyevna's.

"Stretch your arms out sideways." Concentrating and pressing hard, she began to feel his armpits.

"What sort of treatment will it be?" Pavel Nikolayevich asked.

"Injections. I told you."

"Where? Right into the tumor?"

"No. Intravenously."

"How often?"

"Three times a week. You can get dressed now."

"And an operation is . . . impossible?"

(Behind the question lay an overriding fear—of being stretched out on the operating table. Like all patients he preferred any other long-term treatment.)

"An operation would be pointless." She was wiping her hands on the towel the nurse held out to her.

"I'm very glad to hear it," Pavel Nikolayevich thought to himself. Nevertheless he would have to consult Kapa. Using personal influence in a roundabout way was never very easy. In reality, the influence he had was not as much as he might have wished for, or as great as he was now pretending it was. It was not at all an easy thing to telephone Comrade Ostapenko.

"All right, I'll think about it. Then we'll decide tomorrow?"

"No," said Dontsova mercilessly, "you must decide today. We can't give any injections tomorrow, it's Saturday."

More rules! Doesn't she realize rules are made to be broken? "Why on earth can't I have injections on Saturday?"

"Because we have to follow your reactions very carefully, both on the day of the injection and the day after. And we can't do that on a Sunday."

"So you mean . . . it's a serious injection?"

Ludmila Afanasyevna did not answer. She had already moved to Kostoglotov's bed.

"Couldn't we wait till Monday . . . ?"

"Comrade Rusanov! You accused us of waiting eighteen hours before treating you. How can you now suggest waiting seventy-two?" (She had already won the battle. Her steam roller was crushing him; there was nothing he could do.) "Either we take you in for treatment or we don't. If it's yes, you will have your first injection at eleven o'clock this morning. If it's no, then you must sign to the effect that you refuse to accept our treatment and I'll have you discharged today. But we certainly don't have the right to keep you here for three days without doing anything. While I'm finishing my rounds in this room, please think it over and tell me what you've decided."

Rusanov buried his face in his hands.

Gangart, her white coat fitting tightly right up to her neck, walked silently past him. Olympiada Vladislavovna followed like a ship in full sail.

Dontsova, weary of the argument, hoped to be cheered up at the next bed.

"Well, Kostoglotov, what do you have to say?"

Kostoglotov smoothed down a few of his tufts of hair and answered in the loud, confident voice of a healthy man, "I feel fine, Ludmila Afanasyevna. Couldn't be better!"

The doctors exchanged glances. Vera Kornilyevna's lips were smiling faintly, but her eyes—they were fairly laughing with joy.

"Well, all right." Dontsova sat down on his bed. "Describe it in words. How do you feel? What's the difference since you've been here?"

"With pleasure." Kostoglotov was only too willing. "The pain started to go down after the second session. After the fourth it had gone completely. And my temperature went down too. I'm sleeping very well now, ten hours a night, in any position, and it doesn't hurt.

Before, I couldn't find a single comfortable position. I never used to want to look at food, and now I finish everything and ask for second helpings. And it doesn't hurt."

"And it doesn't hurt?" Gangart burst out laughing.

"And they give you the second helpings?" Dontsova was laughing too.

"Sometimes. But what else is there to say? My whole attitude to the world has changed. When I arrived I was a dead man. Now I'm alive."

"No vomiting?"

"No."

Dontsova and Gangart looked at Kostoglotov and beamed, just as a teacher looks at a star pupil and takes more pride in a question excellently answered than in his own knowledge and experience. Teachers become attached to such pupils.

"Can you feel the tumor?"

"It doesn't bother me any more."

"But can you feel it?"

"Well, when I lie down I can feel something heavy, almost as if it's rolling around. But it doesn't bother me," Kostoglotov insisted.

"All right, lie down."

Kostoglotov went through his routine. (During the past month many doctors and medical students had examined his tumor in various hospitals. They used even to call in colleagues from other rooms to feel it. Everyone had been amazed by it.) He lifted his legs onto the bed, drew up his knees, lay on his back without a pillow and uncovered his stomach. He could feel at once how this toad inside him, his companion through life, had dug itself deep in and was pressing against him.

Ludmila Afanasyevna sat next to him. With gentle, circular movements her hand moved closer to the tumor.

"Don't tense up, don't tense up," she kept reminding him. He knew he shouldn't but he still kept tensing himself in instinctive defense, hindering the examination. Finally, having persuaded his belly to relax trustingly, she felt, deep down beside the stomach, the edge of the tumor. Then she went on to feel all round it, gently at first, then more firmly, and then, a third time, more firmly still.

Gangart was looking over her shoulder, and Kostoglotov was looking at Gangart. She was a very likable person. She wanted to be strict, but she couldn't—she got accustomed to her patients so quickly. She tried to be grown-up, but that didn't work either. There was something of the little girl about her.

"I can feel it distinctly, the same as before," Ludmila Afanasyevna announced. "It's a little flatter, there's no doubt about that. It's settled a little further in and released the stomach. That's why it doesn't hurt him. It's softer. But the circumference is almost the same. Will you take a look?"

"No, I don't think so. I do it every day. It's better to take a break from it. Blood count—twenty-five. White cells—five eight hundred. Sedimentation . . . There, you can see for yourself . . ."

Rusanov raised his head from his hands and asked the nurse in a whisper, "The injections? Are they very painful?"

Kostoglotov was also making inquiries. "Ludmila Afanasyevna, how many more sessions will I have?"

"We can't decide that quite yet."

"No, but roughly? When do you think I'll be discharged?"

"*What?*" She raised her head from the case history. "What did you say?"

"When are you going to discharge me?" Kostoglotov repeated just as confidently. He gripped his shins with his hands and assumed an independent air. All trace of admiration for the star pupil had vanished from Dontsova's gaze. He was now just a difficult patient whose face expressed deep-rooted stubbornness.

"I'm just *beginning* to treat you!" she cut him short. "Starting from tomorrow. Up to now we've only been setting our sights."

But Kostoglotov would not give way. "Ludmila Afanasyevna, I'd like to explain something to you. I realize I'm not cured yet, but I'm not aiming at a complete cure."

Well, what a bunch of patients! Each one better than the next! Ludmila Afanasyevna was frowning. This time she was angry. "Whatever are you talking about? Are you in your right mind?"

"Ludmila Afanasyevna." Kostoglotov raised one large hand to wave aside any further accusations. "Discussions about the sanity or insanity of contemporary man will take us far from the point . . . I am really grateful to you for bringing me into this enjoyable state of health. Now I want to make use of it a little and live. But what will happen if I have further treatment . . . I do not know." While he was speaking, Ludmila Afanasyevna's lower lip jutted with impatience and indignation. Gangart's eyebrows had twitched: she was looking from one to the other, eager to intervene and to pacify.

Olympiada Vladislavovna was gazing haughtily down at the rebel. "In fact, I don't want to pay too high a price now for the hope of a life some time in the future. I want to depend on the natural defenses of the organism. . . ."

"You and your natural defenses of the organism came crawling into this clinic on all fours," Dontsova came back with a sharp rebuke. She got up from the bed. "You don't even understand the game you're playing. I won't even talk to you!"

She waved her hand like a man and turned toward Azovkin. Kostoglotov lay there, his knees pulled up under the blanket. He looked implacable, like a black dog.

"Ludmila Afanasyevna, I still want to discuss the matter with you. You may be interested in this as an experiment, in seeing how it will end. But I want to live in peace, if only for a year. That's all."

"Very well." Dontsova threw the words over her shoulder. "You'll be sent for."

She was now looking at Azovkin. She had not yet been able to switch the annoyance from her face or voice.

Azovkin did not get up. He just sat there holding his stomach, merely raising his head to greet the arrival of the doctors. His lips did not form the whole of a mouth: each lip expressed its own separate suffering. In his eyes there was no emotion except entreaty, a plea for help to those who could not hear.

"Well, Kolya, how are things?" Ludmila Afanasyevna encircled his shoulders with her arms.

"Ba-ad," he answered very softly. When he spoke only his mouth moved: he tried not to expel any air from his chest, because the slightest jolt of the lungs was passed on toward the stomach and the tumor.

Six months ago he had been striding along, a spade over his shoulder, at the head of a Young Communists' Sunday working party, singing at the top of his voice. Now he could not raise his voice above a whisper, even when talking about his pain.

"All right, Kolya, let's think about this together." Dontsova was speaking just as softly as he. "Perhaps you're tired of the treatment. Perhaps you're fed up with being in hospital. Is that right?"

"Yes. . . ."

"This is your home town. Perhaps a rest at home would do you good. Would you like that? We can discharge you for a month, or six weeks."

"After that you'd . . . take me in again?"

"Of course we'll take you in. You're one of us now. It'll give you a rest from the injections. Instead you can buy medicine from the chemist and put it under your tongue three times a day."

"Sinestrol?"

"Yes."

Dontsova and Gangart did not realize that for months Azovkin had been frantically begging extra medicine from every duty nurse and night-duty doctor—sleeping pills, painkillers, every sort of extra powder or pill except those prescribed for him orally or by injection. This reserve supply Azovkin crammed into a little cloth bag, which he kept ready to save himself with on the day when the doctors stopped helping him.

"You need a rest, my dear Kolya . . . a rest."

It was very quiet in the ward. Rusanov sighed, and raised his head from his hands. His words rang through the room. "Doctor, I give in. Inject me!"

5. The Doctors' Worries

What name can one give it? Frustration? Depression? When melancholy sets in, a kind of invisible but thick and heavy fog invades the heart, envelops the body, constricting its very core. All we feel is this constriction, this haze around us. We don't even understand at first what it is that grips us.

This was what Vera Kornilyevna felt as she finished her rounds and went down the stairs with Dontsova. She was very upset.

In such circumstances it helps to take stock of oneself and consider what it's all about, to put something up as a protective barrier, too.

But there wasn't time for her to take stock.

This was the position; she was anxious about "Mother." (This was what the three radiotherapy interns called Ludmila Afanasyevna among themselves.) She was like a mother to them partly because of her age—they were all about thirty, while she was nearly fifty—and partly because of the special zeal with which she taught them to work. She herself was keen to the point of being obsessed, and she wanted all her three "daughters" to absorb that same keenness and obsession. She was among the last of the school of doctors with a grasp of X-ray diagnosis as well as X-ray therapy. For some time there had been a general trend toward fragmentation of knowledge, but in spite of this she tried to make her interns keep up with both.

She had no secrets, there was nothing she kept to herself and would not share. And when Gangart occasionally showed herself sharper and quicker than her "mother," Ludmila Afanasyevna was only too pleased. Vera had worked with her for eight years, ever since leaving medical college, and all the power she felt she now possessed—the power to pull back from creeping death those who came and implored her to save them—every atom of it came from her contact with Ludmila Afanasyevna.

This fellow Rusanov might turn out to be a tedious nuisance to Mother. Only a magician can fix a head on a body, but any fool can lop it off.

How she wished there was only one Rusanov. Any patient with bitterness in his heart was capable of behaving like this, and when hounds are in full cry you cannot just call them off at will. These threats left not a footprint on water, but a furrow in the mind. A furrow can always be leveled and filled with sand, but if any drunken huntsman shouts, "Down with doctors," or "Down with engineers," there is always a hunting crop to hand.

The black clouds of suspicion, gathered once over the white coats,* had left shreds behind hovering here and there. Quite recently an M.G.B.** chauffeur had been admitted to the clinic with a stomach tumor. He was a surgical case. Vera Kornilyevna had had nothing to do with him, except that once when she was on night duty, making her evening rounds, he had complained to her of sleeping badly. She had prescribed bromural; however, the sister told her only small doses were available, so she had said, "Give him two powders in one dose." The patient took them from her and Vera Kornilyevna never noticed the peculiar way he looked at her. And no one would have known, if one of the girl laboratory assistants hadn't been living in the same flat as the chauffeur and come to visit him in the ward. She came running to Vera Kornilyevna in great excitement. The chauffeur had not taken the powders. Why were there two together? He'd lain awake all night, and now he was questioning the assistant, "Why is her last name Gangart? Tell me more about her. She tried to poison me. We'd better check up on her."

Vera spent several weeks waiting to be checked up on, several weeks of having to make her diagnoses confidently, impeccably, with inspiration even, of measuring doses accurately, of encouraging her patients with glances and smiles to make up for their finding them-

*A further allusion to the Doctors' Plot.
** The Ministry of State Security, the organization now known as the K.G.B., the Committee for State Security.

selves inside this notorious cancer circle, and all the time expecting one of them to look at her as if to say, "Are you a poisoner?"

Another reason why today's rounds had been particularly difficult was that Kostoglotov, a patient who had made especially good progress and whom Vera Kornilyevna had for some reason treated with particular kindness, had made a point of questioning Mother in that very manner, suspecting that some wicked experiment was being practiced on him.

Ludmila Afanasyevna was also thoroughly depressed as she finished her rounds. She remembered the unpleasant business there had been over Polina Zavodchikova, that prize troublemaker. It wasn't she who had been ill, but her son. She had come into the clinic just to be with him. They operated and removed an internal tumor, and she fell upon the surgeon in the corridor demanding a piece of her son's tumor. If it had not been for Lev Leonidovich, she might well have got it. Her plan was to take the piece to another clinic to have the diagnosis confirmed, and if it hadn't agreed with Dontsova's diagnosis she'd have demanded money or taken them to court.

Every member of the hospital staff could remember some similar incident.

Now that the rounds were over, they were on their way to discuss among themselves what they couldn't talk about in front of the patients, and to take decisions.

Rooms were scarce in the cancer wing, and there was not even a small one to be found for the radiotherapists. There was no accommodation for them either in the gamma-gun unit or in the unit with the long-focus 120,000- and 200,000-volt X-ray installations. There was a room in the X-ray diagnosis unit, but it was always dark in there, so they had to make do with a table in the near-focus X-ray unit. It was here they dealt with their daily problems and wrote out their case histories. As if it wasn't enough to have to spend years working in the nauseating X-ray filled air, with its peculiar smell and heat, they had to do their writing in it too.

They came in and sat down beside each other at the large, rough-surfaced table that had no drawers. Vera Kornilyevna flipped through the inpatients' cards, the women's and the men's, dividing them into cases she would deal with herself and cases they would have to decide about together. Ludmila Afanasyevna looked gloomily down at the table, tapping it with her pencil. Her lower lip stuck out slightly.

Vera Kornilyevna looked at her sympathetically, but could not make up her mind to speak either about Rusanov and Kostoglotov or about the lot of doctors in general, because there was no sense in repeating what they all knew. She would have to be subtle and choose her words carefully, otherwise she might hurt her instead of consoling her.

Ludmila Afanasyevna spoke. "It's infuriating, isn't it, how powerless we are?" (This could be said of many of the patients examined that day.) She started tapping her pencil again. "Of course, there's been no mistake on our side." (This could apply to either Azovkin or Mursalimov.) "We were a bit out in one of our diagnoses, but we gave the right treatment. We couldn't have given a smaller dose. It was that barrel that finished us."

Ah yes, she was thinking about Sibgatov. There are some thankless cases on which you spend three times your usual ingenuity and still can't save the patient. When Sibgatov was first carried in on a stretcher the X rays showed destruction of almost the entire sacrum. The error had been in establishing a bone sarcoma, even though they had consulted a professor. Only later did it gradually emerge that the trouble was caused by a large-celled tumor, which makes fluid appear in the bone and transforms it into a jelly-like tissue. Still, the treatment in both cases was the same.

The sacrum cannot be removed or sawn out. It is the cornerstone of the body. The only thing left was X-ray therapy, which had to be immediate and in large doses. Small ones would not be any good. And Sibgatov got better! The sacrum strengthened. He recovered, but the doses he'd been given were large enough for a horse, and the surrounding tissue became excessively sensitive, developing a tendency to form new malignant tumors. Now his blood and tissue were refusing to respond to radiotherapy, a new tumor was raging and nothing could be done to defeat it. It could only be contained.

For the doctor this meant a sense of helplessness, a feeling that the methods used were not yet effective. And heartfelt pity, simple, ordinary pity. There was Sibgatov, a gentle, well-mannered, mournful Tartar, so ready with his gratitude, and all that could be done for him was to prolong his suffering.

This morning Nizamutdin Bahramovich had summoned Dontsova for a special reason: to increase the turnover of beds. In all doubtful cases, where there was no assurance of improvement, the patient was to be discharged. Dontsova agreed with this. There was a constant line of applicants for admission sitting in the waiting room, sometimes for days on end, and requests were always coming in from provincial cancer clinics asking permission to send patients. She agreed in principle; and there was no one who came so obviously within this category as Sibgatov. But she was incapable of discharging him. The struggle for this single sacrum had been too long and too exhausting. At this point she could not yield to a simple, reasonable suggestion or give up going through the motions, however faint the hope was that death, not the doctor, would be the one to make an error. Sibgatov had even caused a change in Dontsova's scientific interest. She had become absorbed in the pathology of bones for one reason only—to save him. There might well be patients waiting with equally pressing claims, but even so she couldn't let go of Sibgatov. She was ready to use all her cunning with the senior doctor to protect him.

Nizamutdin Bahramovich insisted too on discharging those who were doomed. So far as possible, their deaths should occur outside the clinic. This would increase the turnover of beds, it would also be less depressing for those who remained and it would help the statistics, because the patients discharged would be listed not as "deaths" but as "deteriorations."

Azovkin fell into this category and was to be discharged today. Over the months his case history had become a thick book made of sheets of coarse brown paper all stuck together. In the paper were tiny, whitish flecks of wood that made the pen stick as lines and figures were entered in violet and blue ink. Behind this sheaf of papers both doctors saw a town-raised boy, sweating with pain, sitting doubled up on his bed. However quietly and softly the figures were read out, they were more inexorable than the thunderings of a court-martial, and against them there was no appeal. There were 26,000 rads in him, of which 12,000 were from his last series; he'd had fifty injections of Sinestrol, seven blood transfusions, in spite of which there were still only 3,400 white corpuscles, and as for the red . . . The secondaries were tearing his defenses to pieces like tanks, they were hardening the thoracic wall and appearing in the lungs, inflaming the nodes over the collarbones. The organism was providing no reinforcements, nothing to stop their advance.

The doctors were still flipping through the cards, finishing those they had earlier laid aside. An X-ray laboratory nurse continued treating the outpatients. Just now she had a four-year-old girl in a little blue dress in there with her mother. The girl's face was covered with red vascular swellings; they were still small and nonmalignant, but it was normal to treat these with radiotherapy to stop them degenerating into malignancy. The little girl herself couldn't care less. She had no idea that on her tiny lip she might already be bearing the heavy mask of death. It was not the first time she'd been there, and she'd lost her fear. She chattered like a bird, stretching out her hands to the nickel-plated parts of the apparatus and enjoying the shiny world around her. Her whole session took only three minutes, but she had no desire at all to spend them sitting motionless under the narrow tube precisely pointed at the sore places. She kept extricating herself and turning away. The X-ray technician grew nervous, switched off the current and re-aimed the tube at her again and again. Her mother held out a toy to attract her attention and promised her more presents if she would only sit still.

Then a gloomy old woman came in and spent ages unwinding her scarf and taking off her jacket. She was followed by a woman in-patient wearing a gray dressing gown, with a little spherical pig-mented tumor on the sole of her foot. All that had happened was that a nail in her shoe had pricked her. She was talking merrily away to the nurse, little realizing that this tiny ball no more than a centi-meter wide was the very queen of malignant tumors, a melanoblas-toma. Whether they liked it or not, the doctors had to spend time on these patients as well. They examined them and advised the nurse. And so by now it was long past the time when Vera Kornilyevna was supposed to give Rusanov his embiquine injection. She took out the last card and laid it in front of Ludmila Afanasyevna. It was one she'd been purposely holding back—Kostoglotov's.

"It's an appallingly neglected case," she said, "but our treatment has got off to a brilliant start. Only he's a very obstinate man. I'm afraid he really may refuse to go on with it."

"Just let him try." Ludmila Afanasyevna brought her hand down on the table. "Kostoglotov's disease is the same as Azovkin's. The only difference is that his treatment seems to be working. How dare he refuse it?"

"He won't dare with you," Gangart at once agreed, "but I'm not sure I can outdo him in obstinacy. Can I send him to see you?" She was scratching off some bits of fluff that had stuck to her fingernail.

"Our relations are a bit difficult at the moment . . . I can't seem to manage to speak to him with any authority—I don't know why."

Their relations had been difficult ever since the first time they met.

*   *   *

It was an overcast January day and the rain was pouring down. Gangart had just begun her night as doctor on duty in the clinic. At about nine o'clock the fat, healthy-looking main-floor orderly came to see her with a complaint. "Doctor, one of the patients is making a scene. I can't cope with him on my own. If something isn't done they'll all be round our necks."

Vera Kornilyevna went outside and saw there was a man lying on the floor right by the locked door of the matron's dark little office by the main staircase. He was a lanky fellow dressed in a pair of high boots, a soldier's faded greatcoat and a civilian fur hat with earflaps. It was too small for him, but he'd managed to pull it on. There was a duffel bag under his head, and he was evidently about to go to sleep. Gangart walked right up to him, her well-shaped legs tapering down to a pair of high-heeled shoes (she never dressed carelessly), and looked at him severely, trying to shame him with her stare and make him get up. But although he saw her, he looked back at her quite unconcernedly. He didn't move an inch, in fact it looked as if he'd even closed his eyes.

"Who are you?" she asked him.

"A human being," he answered quietly, unperturbed.

"Do you have an admission card?"

"Yes."

"When did you get it?"

"Today."

The marks on the floor beside him showed that his coat must be wet through. So must his boots and his duffel bag.

"Well, you can't lie here. It's . . . it's not allowed. Besides, it's not seemly . . ."

"It's seemly enough," he answered faintly. "This is my country. Why should I be ashamed?"

Vera Kornilyevna was confused. She felt she couldn't possibly shout at him and order him to get up. And anyway, it wouldn't have any effect.

She cast a look in the direction of the waiting room. During the day it was crowded with visitors and people waiting. There were usually three garden benches for relatives to use as they talked to patients. But at night, when the clinic was locked up, people who had come a long way and had nowhere to go were put up in there. There were only two benches in there at the moment. An old woman was lying on one of them, and a young Uzbek woman in a colorful scarf had laid her child on the other and was sitting beside it.

She could permit him to lie on the waiting-room floor, but it was covered with mud from all the shoes that had trodden on it, and on this side of the glass everything had been sterilized and anyone who came here had to wear hospital dress or white coats.

Once again Vera Kornilyevna glanced at this wild-looking patient. His sharp, emaciated face already registered the indifference of death.

"There's no one in town you can go to?"

"No."

"Have you tried the hotels?"

"Yes, I've tried." He was tired by now of answering her.

"There are five hotels here."

"They wouldn't even listen to me." He closed his eyes, as if to indicate that the audience was over.

If only he'd come earlier, thought Gangart. "Some of our nurses let patients stay the night at their homes. They don't charge much."

He lay there with his eyes closed.

"He says, 'I don't mind if I have to lie here a week,' " the duty orderly went into the attack. "Right in everybody's way! 'Until they give me a bed,' he says! It's disgraceful! Get up, stop playing the fool! This floor's been *sterilized!*" The orderly advanced upon him.

"Why are there only two benches? Wasn't there a third?" said Gangart with surprise in her voice.

"There—they moved the third one over there." The orderly pointed through the glass door.

It was true. One bench had been taken into the corridor leading to the apparatus room. It was now used for the outpatients to sit on when they came for their sessions during the day.

Vera Kornilyevna told the orderly to unlock the door to the corridor. She said to the sick man, "I'll move you somewhere more comfortable. Please get up."

He looked at her, suspiciously at first. Then, tormented and twitching with pain, he started to rise to his feet. It was obvious that every movement, every turn of his body, was an effort. He got up, but left his duffel bag lying on the floor; it would be too painful for him to bend down and pick it up now.

Vera Kornilyevna bent down easily. With her white fingers she picked up the dirty, soaking-wet duffel bag and gave it to him.

"Thank you." He gave her a crooked smile. "Things have come to a pretty pass . . ."

There was a damp, oblong stain on the floor where he had been lying.

"You've been in the rain?" She gazed at him sympathetically. "Take off your coat. It's warm in there in the corridor. You aren't feverish? You don't have a temperature?" His forehead was completely covered by the wretched tight black hat, its fur flaps hanging, so she laid her fingers on his cheek instead.

One touch was enough to tell her that he did have a temperature.

"Are you taking anything?"

The look he gave her was rather different this time. It did not express such utter alienation.

"Analgin."

"Have you any?"

"Um-m."

"Shall I bring you some sleeping pills?"

"If you can."

"Oh yes." She remembered suddenly. "Can I see your admission card?"

Perhaps he smiled, or perhaps his lips moved in obedience to some spasm of pain. "If I don't have the paper, it's back out into the rain, is that it?" He undid the top hooks on his greatcoat and pulled the card from the pocket of the army shirt that showed underneath. It actually had been issued that morning in the outpatients' department. She looked at it: he was one of her patients, a radiotherapy patient. She took the card and went off to get the sleeping pills. "I'll go and get them now. Come and lie down."

"Wait a minute, wait a minute." He suddenly came to life. "Give me back that paper. I know these tricks."

"What are you afraid of?" She turned round, offended. "Don't you trust me?"

He looked at her doubtfully and grunted, "Why should I trust you? You and I haven't drunk from the same bowl of soup. . . ." He went and lay down.

Suddenly she was annoyed. She didn't come back to see him, instead she sent an orderly with the sleeping pills and the admission card. She wrote "urgent" at the top of the card, underlined it and put an exclamation mark.

It was night when next she came past him. He was asleep. The bench was quite good for sleeping on, he couldn't fall off it. The curved back formed a half-trough with the curve of the seat. He had taken off his wet coat, but he'd spread it out on top of him, one side over his legs and the other over his shoulders. The soles of his boots hung over the edge of the bench. There wasn't a single sound inch on them. They were patched all over with bits of black and red leather. There were metal caps on the toes and small horseshoes on the heels.

In the morning Vera Kornilyevna mentioned him to the matron, who then put him on the upper landing.

*   *   *

After that first day Kostoglotov had never been rude to Gangart again. When he spoke to her it was politely and in his normal urbane manner. He was the first to say good morning, and would even greet her with a friendly smile. But she always had the feeling that he might do something a bit strange.

And sure enough, the day before yesterday she'd summoned him for a test to determine his blood group. She prepared an empty syringe to take blood from his vein, and immediately he rolled down his sleeve again and announced firmly, "I'm very sorry, Vera Kornilyevna, but you'll have to get along without the sample."

"For goodness' sake, why?"

"They've drunk enough of my blood already. I don't want to give any more. Someone else can give it, someone who's got plenty of blood."

"You ought to be ashamed of yourself! You're a man, aren't you?" She looked at him with that well-known feminine mockery that men cannot endure. "I'll only take three cubic centimeters."

"Three! Cc.'s? What do you need it for?"

"We'll determine your blood group with a compatibility reaction, and if we have the right kind of blood we'll give you 250 cc.'s."

"Me? Blood transfusion? God forbid! What do I need someone else's blood for? I don't want anyone else's and I'm not giving a drop of my own. Make a note of my blood group. I remember it from the war, when I was at the front."

And nothing she said would change his mind. He refused to give way, finding new and unexpected arguments. He was convinced it was all a waste of time.

At long last she took offense. "You're putting me in a stupid, ludicrous position. For the last time, *please*."

Of course it was a mistake on her part to humiliate herself like that. Why should she do the pleading? But he instantly bared his arm and held it out. "All right, but only for you. You may take three cc.'s."

In fact, she felt ill at ease with him, and one day something funny happened. Kostoglotov said, "You don't look like a German. You must have taken your husband's name?"

"Yes." The word fell involuntarily from her lips.

Why had she said that? Because at that moment it would have hurt to say anything else.

He didn't ask her anything more.

In fact Gangart had been her father's and her grandfather's name. They were Russianized Germans. But what should she have said. "I'm not married . . . I've never been married?"

Out of the question.

6. The Story of an Analysis

First, Ludmila Afanasyevna took Kostoglotov into the treatment room. A female patient had just emerged after her session. The huge 180,000-volt X-ray tube, hanging by wires from the ceiling, had been in operation almost nonstop since 8 A.M. There was no ventilation and the air was full of that sweetish, slightly repellent X-ray warmth.

This warmth (although there was more to it than just warmth) made itself felt in the lungs and became repellent to the patients after half a dozen or so sessions. But Ludmila Afanasyevna had grown used to it and never even noticed whether it was pleasant or not. She had started work there twenty years ago when the machine had no shield of any sort. She had also been caught under a high-tension wire and very nearly killed. Every day she breathed in the air of the X-ray rooms, and she sat in on screening sessions for far longer than was allowed. In spite of all the modern shields and gloves, she had certainly taken in many more rads than even the most acquiescent and seriously ill patients, except that nobody bothered to count the rads or to add them up.

She was in a hurry, not only because she wanted to get out quickly, but also because the X-ray program could not be delayed even for a few minutes. She motioned Kostoglotov to lie on the hard couch under the X-ray tube and to uncover his stomach. Then she went over his skin with some sort of cool, tickly brush. She outlined something and seemed to be painting figures on it.

After this she told the nurse about the "quadrant scheme" and how she was to apply the tube to each quadrant. She then ordered the patient to turn over onto his stomach and she brushed some more lines on his back. "Come and see me after the session," she said.

When she had left the room, the nurse told Kostoglotov to turn over onto his back again and laid sheets around the first quadrant. Then she brought up heavy mats of rubber impregnated with lead, which she used to cover all the surrounding areas which were not for the moment to receive the direct force of the X rays. The pressure of the pliable mats, molded to his body, was pleasantly heavy.

Then the nurse too went out and shut the door. Now she could see him only through a little window in the thick wall. A quiet humming began, the auxiliary lamps lit up, the main tube started to glow.

Through the square of skin that had been left clear on his stomach, through the layers of flesh and organs whose names their owner himself did not know, through the mass of the toadlike tumor, through the stomach and entrails, through the blood that flowed along his arteries and veins, through lymph and cells, through the spine and lesser bones and again through more layers of flesh, vessels and skin on his back, then through the hard wooden board of the couch, through the four-centimeter-thick floorboards, through the props, through the filling beneath the boards, down, down, until they disappeared into the very stone foundations of the building or into the earth, poured the harsh X rays, the trembling vectors of electric and magnetic fields, unimaginable to the human mind, or else the more comprehensible quanta that like shells out of guns pounded and riddled everything in their path.

And this barbarous bombardment of heavy quanta, soundless and unnoticed by the assaulted tissues, had after twelve sessions given Kostoglotov back his desire and taste for life, his appetite, even his good spirits. After the second and third bombardments he was free of the pain that had made his existence intolerable, and eager to understand how these penetrating little shells could bomb a tumor without touching the rest of the body. Kostoglotov could not give himself unreservedly to the treatment until he had grasped for himself the theory behind it and so was able to believe in it.

He had tried to discover the theory of X-ray therapy from Vera Kornilyevna, that sweet woman who had utterly disarmed his prejudice and caution after their first meeting by the stairs when he had been determined that though the fire brigade and the militia might drag him away, he would never leave the place of his own free will. "Don't be afraid, just explain," he used to reassure her. "I'm like an intelligent soldier who has to understand his mission before he'll fight. How is it that X rays can destroy a tumor without touching the other tissues?"

Vera Kornilyevna's feelings always showed first on her lips, not in her eyes. She had such responsive, delicate lips—like little wings. It was on them that her hesitation was now expressed: they fluttered with doubt.

(What could she tell him about the blind artillery which cuts down its own men with the same pleasure as it does the enemy's?)

"Well, I'm not supposed to . . . oh, all right. Of course the X ray smashes everything it meets. Only normal tissues recover quickly, tumor tissues don't."

Maybe what she had said was the truth, maybe it wasn't; anyway Kostoglotov was glad to hear it. "Oh well, in that case I'll join in the game. Thank you. Now I know I'll get better!"

And in fact he was getting better. He lay down eagerly under the X ray and during each session tried to will the tumor cells to believe they were breaking up, that they were *kaput*. At other times he would lie under the tube thinking about whatever entered his head, or he might even doze off.

Just at that moment, his eyes having taken in the mass of hanging pipes and wires, he wanted to know why there were so many of them. And if there was a cooling system there, was it water- or oil-based? But his thoughts did not stay long on this subject; he could not provide himself with any explanation.

As it happened, he began thinking about Vera Gangart. Such a sweet woman would never have been seen in Ush-Terek. And women like that were always married. However, putting the husband as it were in parentheses, he was thinking of her without him. He was thinking how nice it would be to talk to her not just for a moment but for a long, long time, to walk with her in the hospital courtyard, for instance. Sometimes he would shock her by the harshness of his judgments—she looked so funny when she was confused. Every time she smiled her goodness shone like a little sun, even when you met her by chance in the corridor or as she came into the ward. She wasn't professionally kind, she was just naturally kind. Her smile was kind, not so much her smile as the lips themselves. They were vital, separate lips, which seemed about to flutter from her face like a lark into the sky. They were made, as all lips are, for kissing, yet they had other more important work to do: to sing of brightness and beauty.

The tube hummed faintly and musically.

He was thinking about Vera Gangart but he was also thinking about Zoya. The strongest memory he had of last night (it had kept on cropping up all morning) was of her neatly supported breasts which formed, as it were, a little shelf, almost horizontal. While they gossiped yesterday a large, heavy ruler for drawing lines in registers lay on the table beside them. The ruler was made not of plywood but out of a planed block. All evening Kostoglotov had had a temptation —to pick it up and lay it on the shelf of her breasts, to test whether it would slide off or not. He rather thought it wouldn't.

He also remembered, with gratitude, the particularly heavy lead-impregnated mat which they had laid on his body just below his stomach. That mat had pressed against him and reassured him cheerfully, "I'll protect you, don't be afraid!"

But maybe it wouldn't? Maybe it wasn't thick enough? Or perhaps they hadn't positioned it accurately?

During these last twelve days Kostoglotov had returned not simply to life—to food, movement and a cheerful disposition—but also to the loveliest feeling in life which in his agony of the last few months he had completely lost. It proved that the lead mat was holding the defenses!

Nonetheless he had to get out of the clinic while he was still all right.

He didn't even notice that the humming had stopped and the pink wires had begun to grow cold. The nurse came in and began to take off the shields and the sheets. He swung his feet off the couch and then got a good view of the violet squares and figures drawn on his stomach.

"How can I wash with all this?" he asked the nurse.

"Only with the doctors' permission."

"A fine state of affairs. What's the idea? Is it meant to last for a month?"

He went to see Dontsova. She was sitting in the short-focus apparatus room. Through her square glasses, rounded at the four corners, she was examining some large X-ray films against the light. Both machines were switched off, both windows were open and there was no one else in the room.

"Sit down," said Dontsova drily.

He sat down. She went on comparing the X rays.

Although Kostoglotov argued with her, he did it only as a defense against the excesses of medicine, as laid out in a mass of instructions. As for Ludmila Afanasyevna herself, she inspired only confidence, not just by her masculine decisiveness, by the precise orders she gave as she watched the screen in the darkness, by her age and her indisputable dedication to work and work alone, but also, above all, by the confident way in which, right from the very first day, she had felt for the outline of his tumor and traced its circumference so precisely. The tumor itself proclaimed the accuracy of her touch, for it had felt something too. Only a patient can judge whether the doctor understands a tumor correctly with his fingers. Dontsova had felt out his tumor so well that she didn't need an X-ray photograph.

She laid aside the X-ray photographs, took off her glasses and said, "Kostoglotov, there is too big a gap in your case history. We must be absolutely certain of the nature of your primary tumor."

When Dontsova started talking like a doctor, she always spoke much more quickly. In one breath she would leap through long sentences and difficult terms. "What you tell us of your operation the year before last and the position of the present secondaries is in agreement with our diagnosis. However, there are other possibilities which can't be excluded, and this complicates your treatment for us. You'll understand it's impossible now to take a sample of your secondary."

"Thank God! I wouldn't have let you take one."

"I still don't understand why we can't get hold of the slides with the sections of your primary. Are you absolutely sure there was a histological analysis?"

"Yes, I'm sure."

"In that case why were you not told the result?"

She rattled on in the rapid style of a busy person. Some of her words slipped by and had to be guessed at.

Kostoglotov, however, had got out of the habit of hurrying. "The result? There were such stormy goings-on where we were, Ludmila Afanasyevna, such an extraordinary situation that I give you my word of honor. . . . I'd have been ashamed to ask about a little thing like my biopsy. Heads were rolling. And I didn't even understand what a biopsy was for." Kostoglotov liked to use medical terms when he was talking to doctors.

"Of course you didn't understand. But those doctors must have understood. These things can't be played about with."

"Doc-tors?"

He glanced at her, at her gray hair which she did not conceal or dye, and took in the concentrated, businesslike expression of her face with its somewhat prominent cheekbones.

Wasn't that typical of life? Here, sitting in front of him, was his compatriot, his contemporary and well-wisher. They were talking in their own language, common to them both, and still he couldn't explain the simplest thing to her. It seemed one had to start too far back, or else end the explanation too soon.

"Ludmila Afanasyevna, those doctors couldn't do a thing. The first surgeon was a Ukrainian. He decided I was to have an operation and got me ready for it, and then he was taken on a prisoners' transport the night before the operation."

"So?"

"So nothing. They took him away."

"I'm sorry but . . . he must have had warning. He could have. . . ."

Kostoglotov burst out laughing. He thought it very amusing. "Nobody ever warns you about a transport, Ludmila Afanasyevna. That's the whole point. They like to pull you out unexpectedly."

Dontsova's broad forehead creased into a frown. Kostoglotov must be talking nonsense.

"But if he had a patient due for operation . . . ?"

"Huh! Listen to me: they brought in a Lithuanian who'd done an even better job of it than me. He'd swallowed an aluminum spoon, a tablespoon."

"However could he have managed that?"

"He did it on purpose. He wanted to get out of solitary. How was he to know they were taking the surgeon away?"

"So what happened next? Wasn't your tumor growing very fast?"

"That's right, from morning to evening—it was really getting down to it. Then about five days later they brought another surgeon from another compound. He was a German, Karl Fyodorovich. So, he got settled into his new job and after a day or so he operated on me. But words like 'malignant tumor' and 'secondaries'—no one told me anything about them. I'd never even heard of them."

"But he sent away a biopsy?"

"I didn't know then. I didn't know about biopsies or anything. I just lay there after the operation. There were little sacks of sand on top of me. By the end of the week I'd begun learning to move my feet from the bed to the floor, to stand up. Suddenly they went round the camp to collect another transport, about seven hundred men—troublemakers, they said—and Karl Fyodorovich, the gentlest man alive, happened to be in the transport. They took him straight from the hut. They wouldn't even let him do a last round of his patients."

"Absurd!"

"Wait till you hear some real absurdity." Kostoglotov was becoming more than usually animated. "A friend of mine came running in and whispered that I was on the list for the transport too. The woman in charge of the infirmary, Madame Dubinskaya, had given her agreement, knowing I couldn't walk and that they hadn't even taken out my stitches—what a bitch! I'm sorry. . . . Well, I made a firm decision. To travel in a cattle truck with unremoved stitches would mean infection and certain death, so I thought, When they come for me I'll tell them, 'Shoot me here on the bed, I'm not going anywhere.' I'll tell them straight out! But they didn't come for me, and it wasn't because of any kindness on the part of Madame Dubinskaya; she was quite surprised I hadn't been sent. No, they'd checked up in the registration section and found I had less than a year left to serve. But I've got off the point. . . . Anyway I went over to the window and looked out. Behind the hospital woodpile there was a parade ground, twenty meters away, where they were herding everyone with their things ready for the transport. Karl Fyodorovich saw me in the window and shouted, 'Kostoglotov, open the window!' The guards yelled at him, 'Shut up, you bastard.' But he shouted, 'Kostoglotov, remember this, it's very important, I sent the section of your tumor to Omsk for histological analysis, to the department of pathological anatomy, remember!' Well, they herded them away. Those were my doctors, your predecessors. Are they to blame?"

Kostoglotov threw himself back in his chair. He had got himself very worked up, caught up by the atmosphere of that other hospital.

Separating the essential from the superfluous (in patients' stories there is always plenty of the superfluous), Dontsova came back to the point that interested her:

"Well, what was the answer from Omsk? Was there one? Did they tell you anything?"

Kostoglotov shrugged his angular shoulders. "Nobody told me a thing. And I didn't understand why Karl Fyodorovich shouted what he did. But then last autumn, in exile, when the disease had really got hold of me, an old gynecologist fellow, a friend of mine, began to insist that I make inquiries. So I wrote to my camp. No answer. Then I wrote a complaint to the camp administration. About two months later I got an answer: 'After careful investigation of your personal file, there appears to be no possibility of tracing your analysis.' I was already so ill with this tumor that I was ready to abandon the whole correspondence, but since the *komendatura** weren't letting me out for treatment in any case, I thought I'd take a chance and write to Omsk. I wrote to the department of pathological anatomy, and I got an answer in a few days. It was already January, that was before they let me come here."

"Well, come on then! Where is it? Where's the answer?"

"Ludmila Afanasyevna, when I came here I couldn't have cared less about anything. It was a slip of paper without a letterhead, without a stamp, simply a letter from a laboratory worker in the department. She was kind enough to write that on the exact date I mentioned and from the very settlement where I was, a specimen had come in and analysis had been carried out and had confirmed— that's right, the type of tumor you've suspected all along—and that an answer had then been sent to the hospital which had made the inquiry, that is to our camp hospital. What happened next was just typical. I genuinely believe that the answer came, but nobody wanted to know about it, and Madame Dubinskaya. . . ."

No, Dontsova just could not understand this sort of logic! Her arms were crossed and she was impatiently slapping her cupped hands against the upper part of each arm, above the elbow.

"But that answer must have meant you needed X-ray therapy *immediately!*"

"What?" Kostoglotov narrowed his eyes jokingly and looked at her. "X-ray therapy?"

There you are! A quarter of an hour he'd been talking to her, and what had he got across? She still didn't understand a thing.

"Ludmila Afanasyevna," he pleaded with her, "you see, to understand what things are like over there . . . well, very few people have any idea. What X-ray therapy? I was still feeling pain where they had operated, as Ahmadjan is now, for instance. I was already back

*A police office supervising the life of exiles.

on general duties, pouring concrete, and it just didn't occur to me that I have the right to be dissatisfied. Have you any idea how heavy a deep container of liquid concrete is, when two people have to lift it?"

She lowered her head. It was as if it was she who had sent him out to carry concrete. Yes, it might be a bit complicated to clear up the details of this case history.

"All right then. But what about this answer from the department of pathological anatomy? Why did it have no stamp? Why was it a private letter?"

"I was grateful enough to get a private letter." Kostoglotov was still trying to convince her. "That laboratory assistant just happened to be a kind woman. After all, there are more kind women than men, at least that's my impression. . . . Why was it a private letter? Because of our mania for secrecy! She wrote later on, 'The tumor specimen was sent to us anonymously, with no indication of the patient's name. Therefore we cannot give you an official certificate, and we can't let you have slides of the specimen either.'" Kostoglotov was getting annoyed. Annoyance expressed itself in his face more quickly than any other emotion. "What a state secret! Idiots! They're scared that in some department they'll find out that in some camp there's a prisoner languishing called Kostoglotov. The king of France's twin brother! So the anonymous letter will go on lying there, and you'll have to rack your brains about how to treat me. But they've kept their secret!"

Dontsova's look was firm and clear. She stuck to her point.

"I still ought to put the letter in your case history."

"All right, when I go back to my *aul* I'll send it to you."

"No, I need it sooner than that. Can't your gynecologist friend find it and send it?"

"Yes, I suppose he can . . . but I want to know when *I* can go back there." Kostoglotov looked at her somberly.

"You will go home," Dontsova weighed her words one by one with great emphasis, "when I consider it necessary to interrupt your treatment. And then you will only go temporarily."

Kostoglotov had been waiting for this moment in the conversation. He couldn't let it go by without a fight.

"Ludmila Afanasyevna! Can't we get away from this tone of voice? You sound like a grownup talking to a child. Why not talk as an adult to an adult? Seriously, when you were on your rounds this morning I . . ."

"Yes, on my rounds this morning"—Dontsova's big face looked quite threatening—"you made a disgraceful scene. What are you trying to do? Upset the patients? What are you putting into their heads?"

"What was I trying to do?" He spoke without heat but emphatically, as Dontsova had. He sat up, his back firm against the back of the chair. "I simply wanted to remind you of my right to dispose of my own life. A man can dispose of his own life, can't he? You agree I have that right?"

Dontsova looked down at his colorless, winding scar and was silent. Kostoglotov developed his point:

"You see, you start from a completely false position. No sooner does a patient come to you than you begin to do all his thinking for him. After that, the thinking's done by your standing orders, your five-minute conferences, your program, your plan and the honor of your medical department. And one again I become a grain of sand, just as I was in the camp. Once again nothing *depends* on me."

"The clinic obtains written consent from every patient before every operation," Dontsova reminded him.

(Why had she mentioned an operation? He'd never let himself be operated on, not for anything!)

"Thank you! Thank you for that anyway! Even though it's only for its own protection, the clinic at least does that. Unless there's an operation you simply don't ask the patient anything. And you never explain anything! But surely X rays have some effect too?"

"Where did you get all these rumors about X rays?" Dontsova made a guess. "Was it from Rabinovich?"

"I don't know any Rabinovich!" Kostoglotov shook his head firmly. "I'm talking about the principle of the thing."

(It was in fact from Rabinovich that he'd heard these gloomy stories about the aftereffects of X rays, but he'd promised not to give him away. Rabinovich was an outpatient who had already had more than two hundred sessions. He'd made very heavy weather of them and with every dozen he'd felt closer to death than recovery. Where he lived no one understood him, not a soul in his apartment or his building or his block. They were healthy people who ran about from noon till night thinking of successes or failures—things that seemed terribly important to them. Even his own family had got tired of him. It was only here, on the steps of the cancer clinic, that the patients listened to him for hours and sympathized. They understood what it means to a man when a small triangular area grows bone-hard and the irradiation scars lie thick on the skin where the X rays have penetrated.)

Honestly, there he was talking about "the principle of the thing!" Wasn't that just what Dontsova and her assistants needed—to spend days talking to patients about the principles on which they were being treated! Where would they find the time for the treatment then?

Every now and again some stubborn, meticulous lover of knowledge, like this man or Rabinovich, would crop up out of a batch of fifty patients and run her into the ground, prizing explanations out of her about the course of his disease. When this happened, one couldn't avoid the hard task of offering the occasional explanation. And Kostoglotov's case was a special one even from the medical point of view by virtue of the extraordinary negligence with which it had been handled. Up to the time of her arrival on the scene, when he had finally been allowed out to receive treatment, it was as if there had been a malicious conspiracy to drive him to the very borderline of death. His case was a special one too because of the exceptionally rapid revival which had begun under X-ray treatment.

"Kostoglotov! Twelve sessions of X rays have turned you from a corpse into a living human being. How dare you attack your treatment? You complain that they gave you no treatment in the camp or in exile, that they neglected you, and in the same breath you grumble because people *are* treating you and taking trouble over you. Where's the logic in that?"

"Obviously there's no logic." Kostoglotov shook his shaggy black mane. "But maybe there needn't be any, Ludmila Afanasyevna. After all, man is a complicated being, why should he be explainable by logic? Or for that matter by economics? Or physiology? Yes, I did come to you as a corpse, and I begged you to take me in, and I lay on the floor by the staircase. And therefore you make the logical deduction that I came to you to be saved *at any price*! But I don't want to be saved at any price! There isn't anything in the world for which I'd agree to pay *any* price!" He began to speak more quickly. It was something he never liked doing, but Dontsova was making an attempt to interrupt and he still had a great deal more to say on the subject. "I came to you *to relieve my suffering*! I said, 'I'm in terrible pain, help me!' And you did. And now I'm not in pain. Thank you! Thank you! I'm grateful and I'm in your debt. Only now let me go. Just let me crawl away like a dog to my kennel, so I can lick my wounds and rest till I'm better."

"And when the disease catches up with you, you'll come crawling back to us?"

"Perhaps. Perhaps I'll come crawling back to you."

"And we shall have to take you?"

"Yes! And that's where I see your mercy. What are you worried about? Your recovery percentages? Your records? How you'll be able to explain letting me go after fifteen sessions when the Academy of Medical Science recommends not less than sixty?"

Never in her life had she heard such incoherent rubbish. As a matter of fact, from the records' point of view it would be to her advantage to discharge him and make a note of "Marked improvement." This would never apply after fifty sessions.

But he kept hammering away at his point.

"As far as I'm concerned, it's enough that you've driven back the tumor and stopped it. It's on the defensive. I'm on the defensive too. Fine. A soldier has a much better life in defense. And whatever happens you'll never be able to cure me completely. There's no such thing as a complete cure in cancer. All processes of nature are characterized by the law of diminishing returns, they reach a point where big efforts yield small results. In the beginning my tumor was breaking up quickly. Now it'll go slowly. So let me go with what's left of my blood."

"Where did you pick up all this information, I'd like to know?" Dontsova frowned.

"Ever since I was a child I've loved browsing through medical books."

"But what *exactly* are you afraid of in our treatment?"

"Ludmila Afanasyevna, I don't know what to be afraid of. I'm not a doctor. Perhaps you know but don't want to tell me. For example, Vera Kornilyevna wants to put me on a course of glucose injections. . . ."

"Absolutely essential."

"But I don't want it."

"Why on earth not?"

"In the first place, it's unnatural. If I need grape sugar, give it to me through the mouth! Why this twentieth-century gimmick? Why should every medicine be given by injection? You don't see anything similar in nature or among animals, do you? In a hundred years' time they'll laugh at us and call us savages. And then, the way they give injections! One nurse gets it right first time, another punctures your . . . your ulnary flexion to bits. I just don't want it. And now I see you're getting ready to give me blood transfusions. . . ."

"You ought to be delighted! Somebody's willing to give their blood for you. That means health, life!"

"But I don't want it! They gave a Chechen here a transfusion in front of me once. Afterwards he was in convulsions on his bed for three hours. They said, 'Incomplete compatibility'! Then they gave someone else blood and missed the vein. A great lump came up on his arm. Now it's compresses and vapor baths for a whole month. I don't want it."

"But substantial X-ray treatment is impossible without transfusion!"

"Then don't give it! Why do you assume you have the right to decide for someone else? Don't you agree it's a terrifying right, one that rarely leads to good? You should be careful. No one's entitled to it, not even doctors."

"But doctors *are* entitled to that right—doctors above all," exclaimed Dontsova with deep conviction. By now she was really angry. "Without that right there'd be no such thing as medicine!"

"And look what it leads to. You're going to deliver a lecture on radiation sickness soon, aren't you?"

"How do you know that?" Ludmila Afanasyevna was quite astonished.

"Well, it wasn't very difficult. I assumed . . ."

(It was quite simple. He had seen a thick folder of typescript lying on her table. Although the title was upside down, he had managed to read it during the conversation and had understood its meaning.)

". . . Or rather I guessed. There is a new name, radiation sickness, which means there must be lectures about it. But you see, twenty years ago you irradiated some old Kostoglotov in spite of his protests that he was afraid of the treatment, and you reassured him that everything was all right, because you didn't know then that radiation sickness existed. It's the same with me today. I don't know yet what I'm supposed to be afraid of. I just want you to let me go. I want to recover under my own resources. Then maybe I'll just get better. Isn't that right?"

Doctors have one sacred principle: the patient must never be

frightened, he must be encouraged. But with a patient as impor-
tunate as Kostoglotov exactly the reverse tactics were required—
shock.

"Better? No, *you won't get better*! Let me assure you"—her four
fingers slammed the table like a whisk swatting a fly—"that you
won't. You are going—" she paused to measure the blow—"*to die*!"

She looked at him to see him flinch. But he merely fell silent.

"You'll be exactly like Azovkin—and you've seen the condition
he's in. Well, you've got the same disease as him in an almost identical state of neglect. We're saving Ahmadjan because we began
to give him radiotherapy immediately after his operation. But with
you we've lost two years, can you imagine it? There should have
been another operation straight away on the lymph node, next to
the one they operated on, but they let it go, do you see, and the
secondaries just flowed on! Your tumor is one of the most dangerous
kinds of cancer. It is very rapid to develop and acutely malignant,
which means secondaries appear very quickly too. Not long ago
its mortality rate was reckoned at 95 per cent. Does that satisfy you?
Look, I'll show you . . ."

She dragged a folder out of a pile and began to rummage through
it.

Kostoglotov was silent. Then he spoke up, but quietly, without any
of the self-confidence he had shown a few minutes earlier.

"To be frank, I'm not much of a clinger to life. It's not only that
there's none ahead of me, there's none behind me either. If I had a
chance of six months of life, I'd want to live them to the full. But I
can't make plans for ten or twenty years ahead. Extra treatment
means extra torment. There'll be radiation sickness, vomiting . . .
what's the point?"

"Ah yes, I've found it! Here are our statistics." And she turned
toward him a double page taken from an exercise book. Right
across the top of the sheet was written the name of his type of
tumor. Then on the left-hand side was a heading, "Already dead,"
and on the right, "Still alive." There were three columns of names,
written in at different times, some in pencil, some in ink. On the
left there were no corrections, but on the right, crossings out, crossings out, crossings out. . . . "This is what we do. When a patient's
discharged, we write his name in the right-hand list and then transfer
him to the left-hand one. . . . Still, there are some lucky ones who've
stayed in the right-hand one. Do you see?"

She gave him another moment to look at the list and to think about it.

"You *think* you're cured." She returned to the attack with vigor. "You're as ill as you ever were. You're no different than when you were admitted. The only thing that's been made clear is that your tumor *can* be fought, that all is not lost yet. And this is the moment you choose to announce you're leaving! All right, go! Get your discharge today! I'll arrange it for you now. And then I'll put your name down on the list— 'Still alive.' "

He was silent.

"Come on, make up your mind!"

"Ludmila Afanasyevna"—Kostoglotov was ready for a compromise—"Look, if what's needed is a reasonable number of sessions, say, five or ten . . ."

"Not five or ten! Either no sessions at all or else as many as are necessary! That means, from today, two sessions daily instead of one, and all the requisite treatment. And no smoking! And one more essential condition: you must accept your treatment not just with faith but with *joy*! That's the only way you'll ever recover!"

He lowered his head. Part of today's bargaining with the doctors had been in anticipation. He had been dreading that they were going to propose another operation, but they hadn't. X-ray treatment was tolerable, it wasn't too bad.

Kostoglotov had something in reserve—a secret medicine, a mandrake root from Issyk Kul. There was a motive behind his wish to go back to his place in the woodlands—he wanted to treat himself with the root. Because he had the root, he'd really only come to the cancer clinic to see what it was like.

Dr. Dontsova saw she had won the battle and could afford to be magnanimous.

"All right then, I won't give you glucose. You can have another injection instead, an intramuscular one."

Kostoglotov smiled. "I see I'm going to have to give way."

"And please, see if you can hurry up that letter from Omsk."

As he left the room it seemed to him that he was walking between two eternities, on one side a list of the living, with its inevitable crossings out, on the other—*eternal* exile. Eternal as the stars, as the galaxies.

7. The Right to Treat

The strange thing is that if Kostoglotov had persevered with his questions—What sort of injection was it? What was its purpose? Was it really necessary and morally justified?—if he had forced Ludmila Afanasyevna to explain the workings and the possible consequences of the new treatment, then very possibly he would have rebelled once and for all.

But precisely at this point, having exhausted all his brilliant arguments, he had capitulated.

She had been deliberately cunning, she had mentioned the injection as something quite insignificant because she was tired of all this explaining. Also, she knew for sure that this was the moment, after the action of the X rays in their pure state had been tested on the patient, to deal the tumor yet another crucial blow. It was a treatment highly recommended for this particular type of cancer by the most up-to-date authorities. Now that she anticipated the amazing success that attended Kostoglotov's treatment, she could not possibly weaken before his obstinacy or neglect to attack him with all the weapons she believed in. True, there were no slides available with sections of his primary, but all her intuition, her powers of observation and her memory suggested to her that the tumor was the kind she suspected—not a teratoma, not a sarcoma. . . .

It was on this very type of tumor with precisely these secondaries that Dr. Dontsova was writing her doctoral thesis. In fact she was not writing it full-time, she had begun it sometime in the past, dropped it and added a bit more from time to time. Her teacher,

Dr. Oreshchenkov, and her friends tried to convince her it would come out splendidly, but she was always harried and oppressed by circumstances and could no longer foresee a time when she'd be in a position to present it. This wasn't through any lack of experience or material; on the contrary, there was too much of both. Every day they would call her either to the X-ray screen or to the laboratory or to someone's bedside; to combine this with hours of selecting and describing X-ray photographs, with formulations and systematization, let alone with passing the preliminary exams, was beyond human strength.

She could have obtained a six-month sabbatical for research, but there was never a day when her patients were doing quite well enough or when her training sessions with the three young interns could be cut short, so that she could go off for half a year.

Ludmila Afanasyevna believed it was Leo Tolstoy who had said about his brother, he had all the abilities but none of the defects of a real writer. Perhaps she didn't have the defects of a Ph.D. either. She had no particular desire to hear people whisper as she passed, "She's not an ordinary doctor, she's a doctor of philosophy, she's Dontsova," nor to see those tiny, but so weighty, initials added at the head of her articles (more than a dozen of them had already been published, all short but to the point). True, a little extra money never came amiss. But if the thing wasn't going to come off, it just wasn't going to.

When it came to what is called day-to-day scientific work, she had enough to do without the thesis. In their hospital they had conferences on clinical anatomy, analyzing mistaken diagnoses and treatment, and reporting on new methods. Attendance and active participation in these were essential. (Of course the radiotherapists and surgeons in any case consulted daily to sort out mistakes and decide on new methods—but the conferences were a thing apart.) In town too there was a scientific society of X-ray specialists which held lectures and demonstrations. In addition to this, a society of oncologists had recently been started. Dontsova was not only a member but secretary too, and as in all new ventures things were pretty hectic. And then there was the Institute for Advanced Medical Training, and there was correspondence with the *Radiologists' Journal* and the *Oncological Journal* and the Academy of Medical Science and the information center. And so it appeared that although "Big Science" seemed to be confined to Moscow and Leningrad, while out here they simply carried on treating people, nonetheless there was rarely a day devoted just to treatment without bothering about science.

Today had been typical. She had had to call the president of the Radiological Society about her forthcoming lecture. Then she'd had to glance through two short articles in a journal, reply to a letter from Moscow, and to another from a cancer clinic out in the wilds asking for clarification. In a few minutes the senior surgeon, after finishing her day's work in the theater, was due to bring Dontsova one of her gynecological patients for consultation. And then, toward the end of the outpatients' surgery, she had to take one of her interns to see the patient from Tashauz with a suspected tumor of the small intestine. Later on today there was a meeting she had arranged herself with the X-ray laboratory workers to discuss more efficient use of their apparatus: the idea was to process more patients. And Rusanov's embiquine injection had to be kept in mind, too. She'd have to go up and see him. They had only just started treating patients in his condition: up till then they had sent them on to Moscow.

She'd lost a lot of time in that nonsensical wrangle with pigheaded Kostoglotov—an indulgence on her part from a methodical point of view. The technicians in charge of refitting the gamma apparatus had twice peered round the door while they'd been talking. They wanted to show Dontsova that certain work not foreseen in the estimates was now necessary, and to get her to sign a chit for it and to try to square the senior doctor. Now they had finally collared her and were taking her there, but in the corridor on the way a nurse gave her a telegram. It was from Novocherkassk, from Anna Zatsyrko. They hadn't seen each other or written for fifteen years, but she was her dear friend of the old days when they had studied midwifery together in Saratov in 1924, before she went to medical college. Anna's telegram said her eldest son Vadim would be coming to the clinic that day or the next. He had fallen ill on a geological expedition. Would Ludmila Afanasyevna give him friendly attention and write explaining frankly what was wrong with him? Upset by this, she left the technicians and went to ask the matron to reserve Azovkin's bed for Vadim Zatsyrko till the end of the day. Mita, the matron, was as always dashing around the clinic and it wasn't easy to find her. When at last she was found and had promised Vadim a bed, she presented Ludmila Afanasyevna with a new problem: the best nurse in the radiotherapy department, Olympiada Vladislavovna, had been requested for a ten-day seminar of trade union treasurers in town. For those ten days a replacement would have to be found. This was so impossible and impermissible that Mita and Dontsova strode there and then through room after room to the registrar's office to telephone the Party district committee and get it canceled. But the telephone was engaged first at their end, then at the other, and when they got through they were passed on and told to ring the union's area committee, who were absolutely astonished at the doctors' political irresponsibility—did they really suppose trade union finances could be left to run themselves? Clearly neither the Party committee members nor the union committee members, nor their relatives had yet been bitten by a tumor, nor did they expect to be. Ludmila Afanasyevna took the opportunity to ring the Radiological Society, then rushed off to ask the senior doctor to intercede; but he had some outsiders with him and was discussing the most economical way of repairing one wing of the building. So it was all left in the air, and she passed through the X-ray diagnosis department, where she had no work that day, on the way to her own room. The people in the department were taking a break, writing up their results by the light of a red lamp. They reported there and then to Ludmila Afanasyevna that they'd counted the reserves of film and that at the present rate of consumption there was enough for only three more weeks. This meant an emergency, because orders for film were never filled in less than a month. Dontsova realized that either that day or the next she'd have to arrange a meeting between the pharmacist and the senior doctor (not an easy thing to do) and get them to send off an order.

After that the gamma-apparatus technicians barred her way in the corridor, and she signed their chit for them. She felt it was time to look in on the X-ray laboratory assistants, so she sat down and began to make a few calculations. Fundamental technical instructions laid it down that an apparatus should work one hour and then rest thirty minutes, but this rule had long been abandoned and all the apparatuses worked nine hours at a stretch, that is for one and a half X-ray shifts. But even with this overloading, and with the well-trained assistants rushing the patients through under the apparatus, there was still no way of fitting in as many sessions as they wanted. They had to find time for the outpatients once a day and for certain inpatients twice a day (like Kostoglotov from now on), to intensify the attack on their tumors and to speed up the turnover of hospital beds. To do this they had gone on to a twenty-milliamp instead of a ten-milliamp current, concealing the fact from the technical supervisor. This moved things along twice as fast, although the X-ray tubes obviously wore out quicker too. But even so they couldn't fit everyone in. So today Ludmila Afanasyevna had come to mark the lists—for which patients and for how many sessions the millimeter skin-protecting copper filter could be totally dispensed with (which would shorten the sessions by half), and for which a half-millimeter filter could be substituted.

After that she went up to the second floor to see how Rusanov was doing after his injection. Then she went to the short-focus apparatus room where patients were being irradiated again. She was trying to get down to her letters and articles when there was a polite knock on the door and Elizaveta Anatolyevna asked permission to speak to her.

Elizaveta Anatolyevna was just an orderly in the radiotherapy department, but there wasn't a single person there who dared address her familiarly or call her "Liza" or "Aunt Liza," as even young doctors are used to addressing quite elderly orderlies. She was a well-educated woman who spent the hours of her night duty reading French books. For some reason she was working as an orderly in a cancer clinic and did her work very well indeed. It was true the job was paid on a time-and-a-half basis, and for a while the clinic had paid a 50 per cent supplement as radiation danger money. Now the supplement had been reduced to 15 per cent, but Elizaveta Anatolyevna still stuck to the job.

"Ludmila Afanasyevna," she said, slightly bowing her head in apology, as excessively polite people sometimes do, "I'm sorry to trouble you with such a small thing, but it really is enough to drive one to despair. There are no cleaning rags, absolutely none. What am I to clean with?"

So here was something else to worry about! The ministry had the cancer clinic supplied with radium needles, a gamma gun, "Stabili-volt" machines, the newest blood-transfusion equipment and the latest synthetic drugs, but there was no place for ordinary rags and brooms on so elevated a list. Nizamutdin Bahramavich used to say, "If the ministry failed to allow for it, what am I to do? Buy it out of my own pocket?" At one time they used to take worn-out linen and tear it up for dust rags, but the domestic equipment department caught on and forbade it, suspecting that new linen was being plundered. Now they required all worn-out linen to be carried up and delivered to an office where an authorized commission could check it out before tearing it up.

"I have a plan," said Elizaveta Anatolyevna. "Perhaps all of us who work in the radiotherapy department ought to bring one rag each from home. That way we'll solve the problem, won't we?"

"Well, I don't know," sighed Dontsova. "But I suppose there's no other way. All right, I agree. Will you please suggest it to Olympiada Vladislavovna?"

Yes, and what about Olympiada Vladislavovna? How could she get her out of the seminar? It was insane to take their best and most experienced nurse off work for ten days.

She went to telephone about her, and once again she got nowhere. Then she went straight off to have a look at the patient from Tashauz. First of all she sat in the darkness to accustom her eyes. Then she looked at the barium meal in the patient's small intestine— first with him standing, then, lowering the protective screen like a table, she turned him first on one side, then on the other for photographing. Finally she ran her rubber-gloved hands over his stomach, co-ordinating his cries of "It hurts!" with the blurred tones of dim spots and shadows on the film which to her were like a code. Ludmila Afanasyevna bound all this together into a diagnosis.

Somewhere in the midst of all this her lunch break had been forgotten; she never took any notice of it or went out into the garden with a sandwich, even in summer.

At that moment somebody came to call her to a consultation in the dressings room. First of all the senior surgeon briefed her on the case history, then they called in the patient and examined her. Dontsova came to the conclusion there was only one way of saving her—removal of the womb. The patient, who was not more than forty years old, burst into tears. They let her cry for a few minutes. "But this'll be the end for me. . . . My husband is sure to leave me. . . ."

"Well, don't tell your husband what the operation is." Ludmila Afanasyevna drummed it into her. "How will he discover? He'll never know. You can easily hide the whole thing."

She was there to save life, no more and no less. In their clinic it was nearly always life that was at stake, nothing less than that.

Ludmila Afanasyevna was unshakably convinced that any damage to the body was justified if it saved life.

Today, however much she bustled about the clinic, there was something gnawing at her self-confidence, and at her sense of responsibility and authority. Was it the pain she could clearly feel in her stomach? Some days she didn't feel it at all, other days it was weaker, but today it was stronger. If she wasn't an oncologist she'd have dismissed it or else had it investigated without fear. But she knew the road too well to take the first step along it: to tell her relatives, to tell her colleagues. When it came to dealing with herself she kept herself going with typical Russian temporizing: Maybe it'll go away. Maybe it's only my nerves.

But it wasn't just that, it was something else that had been gnawing at her all day, like a splinter in the hand, faintly but persistently. Now that she was back in her own little den, sitting at her own table and reaching out for the file on "Radiation Sickness" which the observant Kostoglotov had noticed, she realized that all day she had been more than upset, really wounded by that argument with him about the right to treat.

She could still hear his words: "Twenty years ago you gave radiation treatment to some old Kostoglotov who begged you not to do it. You didn't know about radiation sickness then!"

And in fact she was due shortly to give a lecture to the society of X-ray specialists on "The Late Aftereffects of Radiotherapy." It was almost exactly what Kostoglotov had reproached her with.

It was only recently, a year or two ago, that she and other X-ray specialists here and in Moscow and in Baku had begun to observe certain cases that could not immediately be understood.

A suspicion arose. Then it became a guess. They began to write letters to each other and to speak about it, not in lectures at this stage but in the intervals between lectures. Then somebody read a paper in an American journal, and somebody else read another. The Americans had something similar brewing. The cases multiplied, more and more patients came in with complaints, until suddenly it was all given a name: "The late aftereffects of radiotherapy." The time had come to speak of them from the rostrum and to reach a decision.

The gist of it was that X-ray cures, which had been safely, successfully, even brilliantly accomplished ten or fifteen years ago through heavy doses of radiation, were now resulting in unexpected damage or mutilation of the irradiated parts.

It was not so bad, or at any rate it was justifiable, in the case of former patients who had been suffering from malignant tumors. Even today there would have been no other solution. They had saved the patient from certain death in the only way possible; they had given large doses because small doses would not help. And if the patient reappeared today with some sort of mutilation, he had to understand that this was the price he must pay for the extra years he had already lived, as well as for the years that still remained ahead of him.

But then, ten, fifteen or eighteen years ago, when the term "radiation sickness" did not exist, X-ray radiation had seemed such a straightforward, reliable and foolproof method, such a magnificent achievement of modern medical technique, that it was considered retrograde, almost a sabotage of public health, to refuse to use it and to look for other, parallel or roundabout methods. They were afraid only of acute, immediate damage to tissue and bone, but even in those days they rapidly learned to avoid that. So—they irradiated! They irradiated with wild enthusiasm! Even benign tumors. Even small children.

And now these children had grown up. Young men and young women, sometimes even married, were coming with irreversible mutilations of those parts of the body which had been so zealously irradiated.

Last autumn a fifteen-year-old boy had come in, to the surgical not the cancer wing, but Ludmila Afanasyevna had heard about the case and had managed to have a look at him. The arm and leg on one side of his body had not kept pace in growth with the other, and the same applied to the bones of his skull, so that from top to bottom he looked bow-shaped, distorted like a caricature.

Ludmila Afanasyevna had checked his case records and identified him as a two-and-a-half-year-old boy who had been brought into the clinic by his mother with multiple lesions of the bones and disturbed metabolism. No one knew the origin of the lesions, but they were certainly not of the tumor type.

The surgeons had sent him to Dontsova on the offchance that X rays might help. Dontsova had taken charge of the case and X rays had indeed helped—so much so that the mother wept with joy and promised she would never forget the woman who had saved him. And now he had come in alone—his mother was no longer alive—and no one had been able to do a thing for him. Nobody could take that early dose of irradiation out of his bones.

Quite recently, no later than the end of January, a young mother had come in complaining that her breast gave no milk. She hadn't come straight to Dontsova but had been sent from one department to another until finally she reached oncology. Dontsova did not remember her, but in the clinic the card index of cases was kept permanently. So someone went to the records annex, rummaged around and found her card, dated 1941. It emerged that she had come in as a child and had lain trustingly under the X-ray tube for treatment of a benign tumor no one would dream of using X rays on today.

All Dontsova could do was make an addition to the old card. She wrote that the soft tissues had become atrophied and that as far as she could see it was a late aftereffect of radiotherapy. Of course no one told the deformed youth or the cheated mother that they had been incorrectly treated as children. Such an explanation would have been useless from the personal point of view, while from the general standpoint it might have done great harm to health propaganda among the population.

But these incidents had greatly shocked Ludmila Afanasyevna. They had left her with a gnawing feeling of deep-rooted and unpardonable guilt. And it was right there that Kostoglotov had struck home today.

She crossed her arms, hugging her shoulders, and walked round the room from door to window and back again, across the free strip of floor between the two apparatuses that were now switched off.

Was it possible? Could the question arise of a doctor's *right* to treat? Once you began to think like that, to doubt every method scientifically accepted today simply because it might be discredited or abandoned in the future, then goodness knows where you'd end up. After all there were cases on record of death from aspirin. A man might take the first aspirin of his life and die of it! By that reasoning it became impossible to treat anyone. By that reasoning all the daily advantages of medicine would have to be sacrificed.

It was a universal law: everyone who *acts* breeds both good and evil. With some it's more good, with others more evil.

Reassure herself as she might—she knew that these accidents,

combined with cases of mistaken diagnosis and of measures taken
too late or erroneously, comprised no more than perhaps 2 per cent
of her activity, while those she had healed, the young and the old,
the men and the women, were now walking through plowed fields,
over the grass, along the asphalt, flying through the air, climbing
telegraph poles, picking cotton, cleaning streets, standing behind
counters, sitting in offices or teahouses, serving in the army and the
navy; there were thousands of them, not all of whom had forgotten
her or would forget her—and yet she knew that she would sooner
forget them all, her best cases, hardest-won victories, but until the
day she died she would always remember the handful of poor devils
who had fallen under the wheels.

It was a peculiarity of her memory.

No, she couldn't do any more preparation today for the lecture.
The day was nearly over anyway. Perhaps she should take the file
home? No, she'd taken it home and brought it back to work hundreds of times, she knew it wouldn't do any good.

This was what she had to find time to do though: she had to
finish *Medical Radiology* and return it to the library, then read a few
short articles, then write and answer that inquiry from the *feldsher*
in Tahta-Kupir.

The light through the gloomy windows was getting bad, so she
lit her table lamp and sat down. One of her internes, who had already
changed out of her white coat, looked in: "Aren't you coming,
Ludmila Afanasyevna?" Then Vera Gangart dropped by: "Aren't
you coming?"

"How's Rusanov?"

"He's asleep. He didn't vomit but he's running a temperature."
Vera Kornilyevna took off her close-buttoned white coat. She was
left in a gray-green taffeta dress, too good for working in.

"Don't you think it's a pity to wear it every day?" Dontsova
nodded at the dress.

"Why should I keep it? . . . What have I got to keep it for?"
Gangart tried to smile but the result was pitiful.

"All right, Verochka, in that case we'll give him a full dose next
time—ten milligrams." Ludmila Afanasyevna pushed the point
home, in her usual quick-fire manner. She felt that words did
nothing but take up time. She continued writing her letter to the
feldsher as she spoke.

"What about Kostoglotov?" Gangart asked quietly. She was already at the door.

"There was a battle, but he was defeated and he surrendered." Ludmila Afanasyevna chuckled, and once again from the sharp intake of breath when she laughed she felt a cutting pain near her stomach. She even felt the urge to complain about it to Vera there and then, making her the first to know. She narrowed her eyes and raised them to Vera's. But then in the twilight depths of the room she saw her in a stylish dress and high heels, as if she were going to the theater.

And she decided—some other time.

Everyone had gone, but she stayed on. It really wasn't good for her to spend even an extra half-hour in these rooms that were daily filled with radiation, but that was the way it always worked out. By the time her annual leave came round her complexion was a pallid gray. Her white corpuscles diminished monotonously throughout the year, going as low as 2,000. It would be criminal to reduce a patient to such a count. Three "stomachs" was the normal daily quota for an X-ray specialist to examine, but she did ten and during the war it had been twenty-five. Before her annual leave she always had to have blood transfusions, and after her leave what had been lost in the past year was never fully restored.

The compelling momentum of her work was very difficult to escape. As each day drew to its end she would note with annoyance that once again she hadn't had time to do everything. In the middle of today's business she had recalled the cruel case of Sibgatov. She had made a note to ask Dr. Oreshchenkov's advice about it when she met him at the society. Just as she had led her interns through their work, so before the war Dr. Oreshchenkov had once led her by the hand, carefully directing her and forming her into a professional all-rounder like himself. "Ludochka," he would warn her, "never overspecialize. Let everyone else specialize to their heart's content, but you stick to what's yours, on the one hand X-ray diagnosis, on the other X-ray therapy. Be that sort of doctor, even if you have to be the last one in the world!" He was still alive, living here in town.

She put out the lamp, but turned back from the door to make a note of some things that needed doing next day. She put on her blue overcoat, no longer new, but on the way out turned aside to call at the senior doctor's office—it was locked.

At last she walked down the steps between the poplars and along the pathways of the Medical Center. Her thoughts, though, remained with her work: she did not even try or want to try to rid herself of them. The weather was nondescript, she didn't notice what it was like. It was just before twilight. On the pathways she passed many people she didn't know, but even here she didn't feel the natural feminine interest in how others were dressed, what they wore on their heads or their feet. She walked on, her brows knit, glancing penetratingly at all these people as if guessing the location of tumors which gave no sign of life today but might appear tomorrow.

So she walked on past the Medical Center's cafeteria, past a little Uzbek boy persistently hawking newspaper cones of almonds, until she reached the main gate.

The unsleeping, bad-tempered, fat old female gatekeeper allowed only the free and healthy through, turning back the patients with loud yells. Once Ludmila Afanasyevna was through the gate, she ought to have made the transition from the working part of her life to the domestic, to her family. But no, her time and energy were not equally divided between work and home. Inside the Medical Center she spent the better and fresher half of her waking hours. Ideas about her work were still circling around her head like bees long after she had left the gates, and in the morning long before she reached them.

She posted the letter to Tahta-Kupir and crossed the road to the streetcar circle. A trolley with the right number swung round with a slight clank. There was a rush through both front and back doors. Ludmila Afanasyevna hurried to grab a seat—and this was the first tiny thought apart from the hospital that began to transform her from an oracle of human destinies into a simple passenger on a trolley jostled like anyone else.

Still, as the trolley clattered down the old, one-way track, or waited long minutes in sidings for another to pass, Ludmila Afanasyevna was looking blankly out of the window, turning over in her mind Mursalimov's pulmonary secondaries or the possible effect of the injections on Rusanov. His offensively didactic manner and the threats he had uttered on her rounds that morning had been overlaid during the day with other impressions. But now, at the end of the day, the oppressive sediment had been uncovered for her to contemplate all evening and all night.

Many of the women in the trolley, like Ludmila Afanasyevna, were carrying not handbags but big bags like small suitcases that could hold a live piglet or four large loaves of bread. At every stop and with every shop that flashed by the window, Ludmila Afanasyevna's thoughts turned more and more to her housework and her home. Home was her responsibility and hers alone, because what can you expect from men? Her husband and son, whenever she went to Moscow for a conference, would leave the dishes unwashed for a whole week. It wasn't that they wanted to keep them for her to do, they just saw no sense in this repetitive, endlessly self-renewing work.

Ludmila Afanasyevna also had a daughter, already married and with a little one on her hands, but now on the point of being unmarried because divorce was in the air. This was the first time today she had remembered her daughter, and the thought did not cheer her.

Today was Friday. On Sunday she absolutely must get through a lot of washing that had piled up. This meant that dinner for the first half of the week had to be got ready and cooked, come what may, on Saturday evening (she prepared it twice a week). As for putting the washing to soak, that had to be done today, whatever time it meant getting to bed. Even though it *was* getting late, now was the only time left to go to the main market. The stalls there were not packed up until later in the evening.

She got out to change trolleys, but, looking through the plate-glass window of a nearby grocery store, decided to go in. The meat department was empty and the assistant had already gone. In the fish department there was nothing worth taking—herring, salt plaice, tinned fish. She walked past the picturesque pyramids of wine bottles and the brown cylindrical rods of cheese that looked just like sausages, on her way to the grocery department. She wanted to get two bottles of sunflower-seed oil (before there had only been cotton-seed oil), and some barley concentrate. From the grocery counter she cut across the quiet shop, paid at the cash desk and went back to collect them.

She was standing in line behind two men when suddenly there was a hubbub in the shop. People were pouring in from the street, forming lines at the delicatessen counter and at the cashier. Ludmila Afanasyevna started, and without waiting to collect her goods in the grocery department hurried across to line up at the delicatessen counter and at the cashier. So far there was nothing to be seen behind the curved glass cover of the counter, but the jostling women were absolutely confident. Minced-ham sausage was going to be sold, one kilo for each buyer.

What a stroke of luck! It was worth going to the back of the line a bit later for a second kilo.

8. What Men Live By

If it hadn't been for the grip of cancer on his throat, Yefrem Podduyev would have been a man in the prime of life. He was on the right side of fifty, firm on his feet, strong shouldered and sound of mind. He was tough, not so much like a carthorse, but more like a two-humped camel; after an eight-hour shift he could put in another just like the first. In his youth on the Kama he used to lug two-hundredweight sacks about, and since then his strength had hardly ebbed. Even now he wouldn't quit when he had to help workmen roll a concrete mixer out on a platform. He had been all over the place and done a mountain of work—pulling down here, digging there, here delivering, and there building. He would think it cheap to take change for ten roubles, he wouldn't reel on a bottle of vodka but wouldn't reach for a third. Yefrem Podduyev knew no end, no bounds, he felt, he would always be the way he was. In spite of his brawn he'd never served at the front; wartime rush construction jobs had kept him back, so he'd never known the taste of wounds and military hospitals. And he'd never had a day's illness in his life—nothing serious, no flu, no epidemic touched him, and he never even had a toothache.

He'd fallen ill for the first time the year before last—and bang! It was this.

Cancer.

"Cancer." Now he could blurt it out just like that; but for years he had been telling himself it was nothing, not worth a damn. While he could bear it, he put off going to the doctor. But once he had

96

gone, they shoved him round from pillar to post until they sent him to the cancer clinic; but the patients there were always told they didn't have cancer, and Yefrem wasn't going to figure out what he had. He couldn't trust the wits he was born with, he believed what he wanted to believe: that he didn't have cancer, that he'd be all right in the end.

It was Yefrem's tongue that had been hit—his quick, ever-ready tongue, which he had never really noticed, but which had been so handy in his life. In fifty years he'd given it a lot of exercise. With it he'd talked his way into pay he'd never earned, sworn blind he'd done things when he hadn't, stood bail for things he didn't believe in, howled at the bosses and yelled insults at the workers. With it he piled filth on everything most dear and holy, reveling in his trills like a nightingale. He told fat-ass stories but never touched politics. He sang Volga songs. He lied to hundreds of women scattered all over the place, that he wasn't married, that he had no children, that he'd be back in a week and they'd start building a house. "God rot your tongue!" one temporary mother-in-law had cursed him, but Yefrem's tongue had never let him down except when he was blind drunk.

And suddenly it had started to bulge. To brush against his teeth. His juicy, soft pharynx had grown too small for it.

But Yefrem shook it off, grinning in front of his pals: "Podduyev? There's nothing can scare him!"

And they would say, "Ah yes, old Podduyev, he's got will power."

But it was not will power, it was sheer blind, cold terror. It was not from will power but from fear that he clung to his job as long as he could, putting off the operation. The whole of his life had prepared Podduyev for living, not for dying. The change was beyond his strength, he did not know how to go about it; he kept pushing it away by staying on his feet, going to work every day as if nothing had happened, and listening to people praising his will power.

He refused an operation, so they started needle treatment: they pushed needles into his tongue as if he were a sinner in Hell, and kept them there for several days. How Yefrem wanted it to stop there, how he hoped! No. His tongue kept swelling. He could no longer muster that famous will power of his; he laid his bull-like head down on the white clinic table, and gave in.

The operation was performed by Lev Leonidovich—and he did

it wonderfully, exactly as he had promised: the tongue was shortened and narrowed, but it was quickly getting used to twisting about again and saying all the things it had before, although perhaps not quite so clearly. They punctured him again with the needles, let him go, recalled him, and Lev Leonidovich said, "Now come back in three months and we'll do one more operation—on your neck. It'll be quite an easy one."

But Yefrem had already seen quite enough "easy" operations on the neck, and he didn't turn up on time. They sent him summonses by post; he ignored them. He was used anyway to not living long in the same place, and could fly off to Kolyma or Khakassia at a day's notice, easy as you like. Neither property, apartment nor family held him anywhere. Two things he liked: a free life and money in his pocket. They were writing from the clinic, "If you don't come yourself the police will fetch you." That's the sort of power the cancer clinic had, even over people who hadn't got any cancer whatever.

He went. Of course, he could still have refused to agree, but Lev Leonidovich felt his neck and gave him a real piece of his mind for putting it off so long. And they cut Yefrem up on the right and on the left of the neck, as hoodlums slash with their knives. He lay there tightly bandaged for a long time, and when they discharged him they were shaking their heads.

He no longer had a taste for the free life: he had gone off work and having a good time, off smoking and drinking. His neck was not softening; it was filling out, and it stung and shot pain right into his head. The disease was creeping up his neck almost to his ears.

Then not much more than a month ago he had returned to the same old gray-brick building, walking up between the poplars to the same porch polished by so many thousands of pairs of feet. The surgeons immediatelly grabbed him like an old friend and put him into the same striped hospital pajamas, in the same ward near the operating theater with windows that gave onto the back fence. And there he waited for a second operation on his poor neck, which would make three in all. Then Yefrem Podduyev could no longer kid himself, and he didn't. He knew he had cancer.

Now, trying to even things up, he began to push it home to all his neighbors in the ward that they had cancer too. That no one would ever escape, that they would all come back in the end. It

was not that he enjoyed crushing people and hearing them crunch—
only why didn't they stop kidding themselves, why didn't they face
the truth?

They did the third operation on him, a deeper and more painful
one, but afterwards, when they were bandaging him up, the doctors
didn't look any more cheerful. They babbled to each other, not in
Russian, either, and bandages got thicker and higher, knitting his
head tightly to his torso. The shooting pains in his head got stronger
and stronger, more and more frequent, almost nonstop.

So why pretend? With cancer he had to take what came after, too.
He'd spent two years turning his back on it, shutting his eyes to
it: it was time for Yefrem to drop dead. When he said it like that,
maliciously, it didn't sound so bad. It wasn't dying, it was dropping
dead.

It was easy enough to say, but his mind and his heart couldn't take
it in. How could it happen to him, to Yefrem? What would happen
and what should be done?

Up to now he had hidden behind work and among other people,
but now it was right there, and he had to face it alone. It was
strangling him with this bandage round his neck.

There was nothing his neighbors could tell him that would help,
in the wards or the corridors, on the lower floor or the upper. It had
all been said many times, and it was all wrong.

Then he started stomping up and down between the door and
the window and back again, five hours a day, sometimes six. He
was running for help.

All Yefrem's life, wherever he'd been (he'd been everywhere
except the big cities, he'd combed all the provinces), he and everyone else had always known what was asked of a man. He had to
have a good trade or a good grip on life. Both would get you money.
When people meet up, "What d'you do?" and "How much d'you
earn?" come straight after "What's your name?" If the earnings
aren't up to scratch—well, he's either a fool or he's unlucky, and
on the whole he's not much of a man.

It was this sort of life, which he understood so well, that Podduyev had seen in Vorkuta, on the Yenisei, in the Far East and in
Central Asia. People earned big money, and then spent it on Satur-
days or else blew the lot on holiday.

This was all right, it suited them fine, until they got cancer or
something fatal like that. But when they did, none of it was worth a

kopeck—their trade, their grip on life, their job, their pay. They all turned out so helpless, wanting to kid themselves to the end that they hadn't got cancer, that they showed up like a lot of poor saps who missed out on life.

But what was it they missed?

When he was young Yefrem had heard, and knew it was right about himself and his friends, that they, the young people, were growing up smarter than the old folk, who never even made it to town, they were scared, while Yefrem rode horses and fired pistols at thirteen, and by the time he was fifty had pawed the whole country about like a woman. But now, as he paced up and down the ward, he remembered how the old folk used to die back home on the Kama —Russians, Tartars, Votyaks or whatever they were. They didn't puff themselves up or fight against it or brag that they weren't going to die—they took death calmly. They didn't stall squaring things away, they prepared themselves quietly and in good time, deciding who should have the mare, who the foal, who the coat and who the boots. And they departed easily, as if they were just moving into a new house. None of them would be scared by cancer. Anyway, none of them got it.

But here in the clinic, sucking an oxygen balloon, eyes hardly able to roll, the tongue keeps on arguing, "I'm not going to die! I haven't got cancer!"

Just like chickens. A knife was ready and waiting for them, but they all carried on cackling and scratching for food. One was taken away to have its head chopped off, but the rest just carried on scratching.

So day after day, Podduyev marched up and down the old floor, rattling the floorboards, without getting it any clearer in his mind how to meet death. He couldn't work it out, and there was no one to tell him. He would never have believed he'd find the answer in a book.

A long time ago he'd done four years in school, and he'd taken a construction course, but he'd never had an urge to read. He didn't read the papers, he listened to the radio, and he couldn't see the use of books in his everyday life. Anyway, in the wild, remote parts of the country where he'd knocked about all his life because they paid a lot, bookworms were thin on the ground. Podduyev read only when he had to—booklets on production experience, descriptions of hoisting mechanisms, operating instructions, administrative orders and the

*Short History** as far as chapter four. He thought spending money on *books* or dragging himself off to a library for them was simply ridiculous. If he was going on a long journey or waiting somewhere and a book came his way, he might read twenty or thirty pages, but he'd always drop it: he never found anything for a man with an intelligent turn of mind.

Here in the hospital there were books on the bedside tables and on the window sills: he never touched them. And he would never have started reading this blue one with the gold signature if Kostoglotov had not palmed it off on him one empty, wretched evening. Yefrem had put two pillows under his back and begun to flip through it. He wouldn't have started reading even then if it had been a novel; but it was a collection of very short stories, you could see what they were getting at in five or six pages, sometimes in just one. Their titles were piled like gravel on the contents page. Yefrem began to read the titles; he had the feeling right away that the book meant business: "Work, Illness and Death," "The Chief Law," "The Source," "Neglect a Fire and It Will Overmaster Thee," "Three Old Men," "Go into the Light While Light There Is."

Yefrem opened it at the shortest one. He read it. He felt like thinking. He thought. He felt like reading the little story again. He did. He felt like thinking again. He thought again.

It was the same with the second story.

Just then they put out the lights. Yefrem shoved the book under his mattress so it wouldn't be pinched and he wouldn't have to go looking for it the next morning. In the darkness he told Ahmadjan the old fable about how Allah had shared out the years of life and how man was given many unnecessary years. (He didn't believe a word of it, of course; he couldn't imagine any years being unnecessary, so long as he was healthy.) Before he went to sleep he thought again about what he had read.

Except that the shooting pains kept going through his head, getting in the way of his thoughts.

Friday morning was dull and, like every other morning in hospital, heavy. Each morning in the ward began with a few of Yefrem's gloomy speeches. If anyone spoke up with a hope or a wish, Yefrem poured cold water on it straightaway and crushed the man. But

---

*Stalin's history of the Soviet Communist Party, which used to be compulsory reading for every Soviet citizen as far as chapter four, the one on Marxist philosophy. Further chapters were for more advanced students.

this morning he wouldn't even open his mouth; instead he settled down to read his calm, quiet book. There wasn't much point in washing, because even his jowls were bandaged. He could eat his breakfast in bed, and there would be no rounds for the surgical patients today. Yefrem slowly turned the rough thickish pages of the book, kept quiet and did his bit of reading and thinking.

The radiotherapy patients' rounds were over. That fellow in the gold-rimmed glasses had barked at the doctor, then got cold feet and had an injection. Kostoglotov pushed for his rights, kept leaving the room and coming back. Azovkin was discharged, said goodbye and left, doubled up and clutching his stomach. Other patients were called—for X rays and blood transfusions. And still Podduyev didn't creep out to stomp up and down the aisle between the beds; he just read to himself and kept silent. The book was talking to him. It was unlike any he had ever read. It really held him.

He had lived his whole life without such a serious book ever coming his way.

Still, it was unlikely he'd ever have started reading if he hadn't been in a hospital bed with this neck shooting pain through his head. These little stories would hardly have got through to a healthy man.

Yefrem had already noticed the title yesterday: *What Men Live By*. The title was so put together that Yefrem felt as though he had made it up himself. Stomping about the hospital floors, thinking his nameless thoughts, he had been thinking that very question during the past few weeks: "What do men live by?"

The story was not very short, but it read easily from the start, speaking softly and simply to the heart:

"A cobbler, with his wife and children, once lodged at a peasant's. He had neither house nor land of his own, and he supported himself and his family by his cobbling. Bread was dear and work was cheap, and what he made by his work went in food. The cobbler and his wife had one fur coat between them, and that was falling into rags."

All this was quite clear, and what followed was clear too: Semyon was gaunt, Mikhailo the apprentice was thin and haggard, but the squire—

"was like a man from another world, with a great red snout, a neck like a bull's, his whole frame was as if of cast iron . . . He could not help getting hard and smooth with the life he led. Even death had no hold upon a clod like that."

Yefrem had seen a lot of people like that. Karashchuk, the boss at the coal complex—he was one, and Antonov was another, and Chechev, and Kukhtikov. And hadn't Yefrem himself started pulling up on them?

Slowly, almost syllable by syllable, Yefrem read the whole story through to the end.

It was then almost time for lunch.

Yefrem just did not feel like walking about or talking. It was as if something had been stuck into him and twisted inside. Where his eyes had once been, there were now no eyes, and where his mouth had been, there was now no mouth.

The hospital had already planed Yefrem down roughly, it was easy to smooth him off now.

Sitting in the same position, supported by pillows, his knees pulled up to his body, the closed book on his knees, he stared at the blank white wall. Outside the day was cheerless.

In the bed opposite that whey-faced holidaymaker was sleeping off his jab. They'd piled blankets on top of him because of his fever.

On the next bed Ahmadjan was playing checkers with Sibgatov. Their languages weren't much alike, and they were talking to each other in Russian. Sibgatov sat carefully so as not to have to bend or twist his bad back. He was still a young man, but his hair was very thin on top.

As for Yefrem, he hadn't lost a single tiny hair. He had a great, wild, fox-colored thatch, so thick you couldn't pull a comb through it. He had almost his full force for women still. Not that that was any good to him now.

No man could tell how many women Yefrem had gone through. In the beginning he had kept a count of them with a separate one for his wives, but later on he hadn't bothered. His first wife was Amina —a white-faced Tartar girl from Yelabuga. She was a very sensitive girl. The skin on her face was so fine you only had to touch it with your knuckles and you'd draw blood. She was unruly too: she left him, taking their little girl. After that Yefrem made up his mind he wasn't going to be disgraced like that again: he always left his women first. His life was footloose and free. He'd take a job in one place, then sign a contract for somewhere else, and if he had to drag a family along too, it would only get in the way. In every new place he found himself a woman to keep house. As for the others he met by the way, willing or unwilling, he didn't even always ask their names, just paid the agreed price. By now faces, habits and the way it happened were all mixed up in his memory, and he could only remember the unusual ones. That was why he remembered Yevdoshka, the engineer's wife, how she had stood under his carriage window on the platform at Alma-Ata One, wiggling her bottom and asking for it. It was during the war and the whole of his gang was going to Ili to open up a new construction site; there was a crowd from work seeing them off. Yevdoshka's husband, a shabby little man, was standing nearby, arguing with somebody over nothing. The engine gave a warning jolt. "Hey, you!" Yefrem shouted, and held out his arms. "If you love me, jump in, let's go!" She grabbed hold of his arms and scrambled through the carriage window in full view of her husband and the whole crowd, and went and lived with him for a couple of weeks. This was what stuck in his memory, how he'd dragged Yevdoshka into the carriage.

One thing about women Yefrem had found out in his life: they cling. It was easy enough to get a woman, but difficult to see the back of her. Nowadays the word "equality" was being bandied about a lot, and Yefrem never said anything against it; still, deep down he never thought of women as fully fledged people—except for his first wife Amina, that is. And he'd been amazed if some other fellow had seriously tried to tell him he treated women badly.

But according to this curious book it turned out that Yefrem was the one to blame for everything.

They put the lights on earlier than usual.

The scrubbed little man with the lump under his jaw woke up, poked his small, bald head out from under the blankets and quickly fitted on the glasses that made him look like a professor. He told everyone the good news right away: the injection had not been too bad, he'd thought it was going to be worse. Then he dived into his bedside table, to get out his bits of chicken.

Milksops like him, Yefrem had noticed, always ask for chicken. Even lamb they call "strong meat."

Yefrem would rather have watched somebody else. To do that he'd have to turn his whole body round, but if he looked straight ahead, all he could see was this shithead wolfing a chicken bone.

Podduyev let out a grunt and gingerly turned himself to the right. "Listen, here's a story," he announced in a loud voice. "It's called 'What Men Live By.'" He grinned. "Who can know a thing like that? What do men live by?"

Sibgatov and Ahmadjan raised their heads from their checkers. Ahmadjan replied confidently and happily, because he was getting better, "Their rations. Uniform and supplies."

Before joining the army he had always lived in the *aul* and spoken only Uzbek. All his Russian words and ideas, his discipline and familiarity with friends, came from his days in the army.

"Anyone else?" Yefrem croaked. The book's riddle had taken him by surprise, and now the rest were finding it difficult too. "Anyone else? What do men live by?"

Old Mursalimov did not understand Russian, otherwise perhaps he'd have given a better answer than any of them. But just then the medical assistant Turgun, who was still a student, came along to give him an injection. "By their pay, that's what," he replied.

The swarthy Proshka, in the corner, stared as if into a shop window. Even his mouth gaped, but he didn't say anything.

"Well? Come on," Yefrem demanded.

Dyomka put down his book and frowned over the question. He had in fact brought Yefrem's book into the ward, but he hadn't managed to read much of it, none of what it said seemed right, it was like talking to a deaf man who gives the wrong answers to your questions. It weakened him and confused everything when what he needed was advice on what to do. And so he hadn't read *What Men Live By* and didn't know the answer that Yefrem was waiting for. He was thinking up his own.

"Well, big boy?" Yefrem prodded him.

"Yes . . . in my opinion," Dyomka announced slowly, as if answering a teacher at the blackboard, trying not to make a mistake, and still thinking it out between the words, ". . . In the first place, air. Then—water. Then—food."

This was the answer Yefrem would have given before, if anyone had asked him. The only thing he might have added was booze. But this was not at all what the book was getting at.

He smacked his lips. "Anyone else?"

Proshka decided to speak. "Professional skill," he said.

Again this was something Yefrem had thought all his life.

Sibgatov sighed and said shyly, "Your homeland."

"What's that?" asked Yefrem in surprise.

"You know, the place you were born in . . . living in the place you were born."

"Ah! Oh no, you don't *have* to have that. I left the Kama when

I was a young man, and now I don't give a damn whether it still exists. One river's the same as another, eh?"

"In the place you were born," Sibgatov insisted quietly, "you don't even get ill. Everything's much easier in the place you were born."

"All right. Anybody else?"

"What, what's this?" asked Rusanov, cheerful again. "What's the problem?"

Yefrem grunted and turned himself round to the left. The beds by the windows were empty, except for Whey-face. He was eating a chicken leg, holding one end of the bone in each hand.

There they sat facing each other, as if the Devil had put them there for his own malicious pleasure. Yefrem screwed up his eyes.

"It's this, Professor. What do people live by?"

Pavel Nikolayevich did not put himself out in the least. He barely looked up from the chicken. "There's no difficulty about that," he said. "Remember: people live by their ideological principles and by the interests of their society." And he bit off the sweetest piece of gristle in the joint. After that all there was left on the bone was the rough skin of the foot and the dangling tendons. These he put on a piece of paper on top of his bedside table.

Yefrem did not answer. He was annoyed that this pipsqueak had managed to wriggle out of it so cleverly. When it came to ideology it was better to keep your trap shut.

He opened the book and stared at it again. He wanted to find the right answer for himself.

"What's the book about? What does it say?" asked Sibgatov, turning from his game of checkers.

"Here, listen . . ." Podduyev read the first few lines: " 'A cobbler, with his wife and children, once lodged at a peasant's. He had neither house nor land of his own . . .' "

But reading aloud was a long and difficult business, so he propped himself up with some pillows and began to tell Sibgatov the story in his own words, trying once again to grasp its meaning.

"Anyway, the shoemaker started hitting the bottle. One night he was going home full of drink when he ran into a guy called Mikhailo who was freezing to death and took him home. His wife scolded him. 'What? Another mouth to feed?' she said. But Mikhailo started working for all he was worth, and learned to sew better than the shoemaker. One winter's day the squire came to see them. He brought a piece of expensive leather and gave them an order—one pair of boots that wouldn't warp or rip. And if the shoemaker spoiled the leather, he'd have to replace it with his own skin. Mikhailo gave a strange smile because he'd seen something over there in the corner behind the squire's back. The squire had just gone out of the door when Mikhailo went and cut the leather and spoiled it. It wasn't big enough now for a pair of welted stretch boots, only for something like a pair of slippers. The shoemaker clapped his hand to his head. 'You've ruined me,' he said, 'you've cut my throat. What have you done?' Mikhailo said, 'A man lays down stores for a year, when he doesn't even know whether he'll be alive that evening.' Sure enough, the squire kicked the bucket on the way home. And the squire's wife sent a boy to the shoemaker to say, 'No need to make the boots. But we want a pair of slippers as quickly as you can. For the corpse.' "

"Good God, what nonsense!" Rusanov spat the words out, with a hiss. "It's time someone changed the record. What a moral! It stinks to high heaven, it's quite alien to us. What does it say there that men live by?"

Yefrem stopped telling the story and moved his swollen eyes across to the bald pate opposite. He was furious that the bald man had almost guessed the answer. It said in the book that people live not by worrying only about their own problems but by love of others. And the pipsqueak had said it was by "the interests of society."

Somehow they both tied up.

"What do they live by?" He could not say it aloud somehow. It seemed almost indecent. "It says here, by love."

"*Love?* . . . No, that's nothing to do with our sort of morality." The gold-rimmed glasses mocked him. "Listen, who wrote all that, anyway?"

"What?" mumbled Podduyev. They were sidetracking him away from the point.

"Who wrote it, who's the author? There, it's up there, look, at the top of the first page."

What's the name got to do with it? What's the name got to do with the point—with their diseases, with their lives or deaths? Yefrem was not used to reading the name at the top of the books he read, and when he did he promptly forgot it. Now he turned to the first page and read aloud, "Tol . . . stoy."

"That's impossible!" Rusanov protested. "Tolstoy? Remember,

Tolstoy* only wrote optimistic and patriotic works, otherwise he wouldn't have been printed: *The Bread, Peter the First*. And, let me tell you, he won the Stalin Prize three times!"

"It's not *that* Tolstoy," retorted Dyomka from the corner. "Our book's by Leo Tolstoy."

"Oh, not tha-a-a-t Tolstoy?" Rusanov drawled, relaxing a little, but curling his lip a little, too. "It's the other one, is it? . . . The mirror of the Russian Revolution? Rice croquettes?** Your namby-pamby Tolstoy, there were plenty of things *he* didn't understand. You *must* resist evil, young man, you *must* fight against it."

"I quite agree," answered Dyomka in a hollow voice.

*Rusanov thinks he means Alexei Nikolayevich Tolstoy (1883-1945).
**Allusions to Lenin's opinion of Tolstoy and to his vegetarianism.

9. *Tumor Cordis*

Yevgenia Ustinovna, senior surgeon, had none of the traits usually ascribed to members of her profession, none of the resolute look, determined lines across the forehead or iron clenching of the jaw, and her appearance as a whole lacked that straightforward wisdom. Although already in her fifties, if she piled her hair on top of her head inside her doctor's cap men who saw her from behind would call out, "Excuse me, Miss, er . . ." She was, as the saying is, a Young Pioneer from behind and an old-age pensioner from in front, with her drooping lower eyelids, puffed-up eyes and perpetually weary-looking face. She tried to make up for this by using lots of bright lipstick, but she had to put it on more than once a day because it always rubbed off on the cigarettes she smoked.

Every moment she was not in the operating theater, the surgical dressing room or the ward, she had a cigarette in her mouth. She would seize every opportunity to dash out and fling herself on a cigarette as though she wanted to eat it. During her rounds she would sometimes raise her first two fingers to her lips. So one might perhaps argue that she smoked even during her rounds.

Apart from the chief surgeon, Lev Leonidovich—a very tall man with long arms—this aged, stringy woman did all the operations in the clinic. She sawed off limbs, put tracheotomy tubes into the wall of the throat, took out stomachs, penetrated to every part of the intestines, plundered the inside of the pelvic girdle. And toward the end of the day's operations it might fall to her lot to remove one or two sets of cancerous lacteal glands—an uncomplicated job that she had mastered like a virtuoso. There was never a Tuesday or a Friday on which Yevgenia Ustinovna did not cut off women's breasts, and she would remark to the orderly who cleaned the theater, a cigarette between her exhausted lips, that if all the breasts she had cut off were collected together and made into a pile, the result would be quite a small mountain.

Yevgenia Ustinovna had been a surgeon all her life: without surgery she would be nothing. Still, she remembered and understood the words of Tolstoy's Cossack, Yeroshka, who said about West European doctors, "All they can do is cut. Well, they're fools. But up in the mountains you get real doctors. They know about the herbs."

And if tomorrow some other kind of therapy were invented—radiation, chemical or herbal, or even something worked by light, color or telepathy—which could save her patients without the knife and would mean that surgery would completely vanish from human practice, Yevgenia Ustinovna would not have defended her craft even for a day, not because of her convictions but simply because she had spent all her life cutting, cutting, all her life had been blood and flesh. It is one of the tiresome but unavoidable facts about humanity that people cannot refresh themselves in the middle of their lives by a sudden, abrupt change of occupation.

They would usually go on their rounds in groups of three or four: Lev Leonidovich, she and the interns. But a few days ago Lev Leonidovich had gone to Moscow for a seminar on thorax operations. For some reason this Saturday she was quite alone when she went into the upper men's ward—without an attendant physician, or even a nurse.

She didn't go right in, she just stood quietly in the doorway, leaning back against the door with a girlish movement. A very young girl can lean against a door and know it looks good, better than standing with a straight back, level shoulders and head erect.

She stood there pensively watching Dyomka playing a game. Dyomka had his bad leg stretched out along the bed and the foot of his good leg laid under it to make a little table. On this he had placed a book, and on the book he was making something out of four long pencils which he held in both hands. He was contemplating this figure and seemed likely to go on doing so for a great while, but just then he heard someone call him. He raised his head and gathered the splayed pencils together.

"What are you building, Dyomka?" Yevgenia Ustinovna asked him sadly.

"A theorem!" he answered cheerfully, louder than necessary.

Those were the words they used, but the looks they gave each other were keen and it was clear that they were really concerned with something quite different.

"Time's slipping away," added Dyomka by way of explanation, but not so cheerfully or loudly.

She nodded. She was silent for a moment, still leaning against the doorway—no, not girlishly but through sheer tiredness.

"Come on, let me have a look at you."

Dyomka was always quite mild, but this time his protest was livelier than usual: "Ludmila Afanasyevna examined me yesterday! She said we'd carry on with the radiation."

Yevgenia Ustinovna nodded. There was a sort of sad elegance about the way she looked.

"Well, that's good, but I'll still take a look at you."

Dyomka frowned. He put away his stereometry, drew himself up in the bed to make room, and bared his bad leg to the knee.

Yevgenia Ustinovna sat down beside him. Without effort she jerked up the sleeves of her coverall and dress almost to the elbow. Her slender, supple hands began to move up and down Dyomka's leg like two live creatures.

"Does it hurt? Does it hurt?" she kept asking.

"Yes . . . Yes, it hurts," he confirmed, frowning more and more.

"Can you feel your leg during the night?"

"Yes . . . but Ludmila Afanasyevna . . ."

Yevgenia Ustinovna again nodded her head understandingly and patted him on the shoulder.

"All right, my friend. Carry on with the radiation."

And once again they looked into each other's eyes.

The ward had fallen quite silent. Every word they spoke could be heard.

Yevgenia Ustinovna got up and turned to the others. Proshka should have been in the bed over there by the stove, but yesterday evening he had moved to the bed by the window (even though there was a superstition against taking the bed of someone who had left the ward to die). In the bed by the stove there was now a short, quiet man with flaxen hair called Friedrich Federau. He was not an entirely new face in the ward since he had already spent three days lying out on the staircase. He stood up, thumbs down the seams of his trousers, and gave Yevgenia Ustinovna a glance of welcome and respect. He was not as tall as she was.

He was in the best of health! He had no pain anywhere! The first operation had completely cured him. He had reported back to the cancer clinic not on account of any complaint but because he was so exact in everything he did. It was written on his certificate: "Checkup on February 1, 1955." And so he had come hundreds of miles, across difficult roads and via awkward connections, first in a sheepskin coat and felt boots in the back of a truck, then from the station to here wearing shoes and a light overcoat, and arrived not on January 31 nor on February 2, but with the exact punctuality with which the moon reports for her scheduled eclipses.

He didn't know why they had put him back in the hospital. He very much hoped they would discharge him today.

Up came Maria, tall and dried up, with dead-looking eyes. She was carrying a towel. Yevgenia Ustinovna wiped her hands and arms, raised them, still bare to the elbows, and in complete silence massaged Federau's neck for a long time with circular movements of her fingers. Then she told him to undo his jacket and continued the movement around the hollows of his collarbones and under his arms. Finally she said, "Very good, Federau. As far as you're concerned, everything's excellent."

His face lit up as though he had been given a reward.

"Everything's fine." She drew the words out with affection and again worked her fingers under his lower jaw. "One more tiny operation, and that'll be it."

"What?" Federau's face fell. "But why, Yevgenia Ustinovna? If everything's fine . . ."

"It'll make you even better." She smiled faintly.

"Here?" He brought his palm down with a cutting movement diagonally across his neck. There was a look of entreaty on his soft face. His eyebrows were fair, almost white.

"Yes, there. But don't worry. Yours isn't one of those neglected cases. We'll get you ready for next Tuesday"—Maria made a note—"and by the end of February you'll be home for good and you'll never have to come back here."

"Will there be another checkup?" Federau tried to smile but did not succeed.

"Well, perhaps a checkup." She smiled apologetically. What else

could she use to reassure him, if not her tired, weary smile? She left
him standing there. Then he sat down and began to think. She moved
on across the room. As she passed Ahmadjan she gave him another
of her slight smiles. She had operated on his groin three weeks ago.
She stopped when she came to Yefrem.

He had already thrown down the blue book he was reading and
was waiting for her. With his broad head, his neck bandaged and
fattened out of all proportion, his wide shoulders, his legs pulled up
and under him, he was sitting up on the bed like some kind of improbable dwarf. He looked at her sullenly, waiting for the blow.

She leaned her elbows against the rail of his bed and held two
fingers to her lips, as though she were smoking.

"Well, what sort of a mood are we in today, Podduyev?"

Hadn't she anything better to do than stand around jabbering
about moods? All she had to do was say her little piece and go. She
just had to do her act.

"I'm fed up with all this cutting," Yefrem blurted out.

She raised her eyebrows, as if surprised that cutting could make
anyone fed up.

She did not say anything.

And he had already said quite enough.

They were both silent, like two lovers after a tiff or before a
breakup.

"The same place again?" It wasn't even a question, it was a statement.

(He wanted to shout, "What did you do before? What were you
thinking about?" He was never very delicate when it came to dealing with bosses. He always jumped down their throats. But he spared
Yevgenia Ustinovna. Let her guess for herself how he felt.)

"Right next door," she made the slight distinction.

(Poor devil, how could she tell him that cancer of the tongue is
not cancer of the lower lip? You take away the nodes under the jaw,
and suddenly it turns out that the deep lymphatic ducts are affected
too. She could never have operated there earlier on.)

Yefrem grunted, like a man pulling a weight too heavy for him.

"I don't need it. I don't need it at all."

She did not try to talk him round.

"I don't want any more cutting. I don't want anything any more."

She looked at him in silence.

"Discharge me!"

She looked into his reddish eyes. They had gone through so much fear that now they were quite fearless. And she too thought, "Why? Why torment him if even the knife can't keep up with his secondaries?"

"We'll unbandage you on Monday, Podduyev. We'll see; all right?"

(He had demanded his discharge, yet he had desperately hoped she'd say, "You're out of your mind, Podduyev. What do you mean, discharge you? We're going to give you treatment. We're going to cure you."

But she had agreed.

Which meant he was a goner.)

He made a movement of his whole body to indicate a nod. He was unable to do it with his head alone.

She went on to Proshka. He got up to meet her and smiled. She did not examine him at all, she just asked him, "Well, how are you feeling?"

"First-class." Proshka's smile broadened. "These tablets have really helped."

He pointed to a bottle of multi-vitamins. If only he knew how to soften her up. If only he could persuade her. She mustn't even think of an operation.

She nodded toward the tablets, then she stretched out a hand toward the left side of his chest.

"Does it hurt here sometimes?"

"Yes, just a bit."

She nodded again. "We're going to discharge you today."

Proshka was overjoyed. His black eyebrows shot up to the ceiling.

"What? You mean, there won't be an operation?"

She shook her head and gave him a faint smile.

They had spent a week feeling him, they had pushed him into the X-ray room four times. They had made him sit down, lie down, stand up. They had taken him to see old men in white coats until he reckoned he must be in a pretty bad way. And now suddenly they were turning him loose without even operating!

"So I'm healthy, am I?"

"Not completely."

"These tablets are good, aren't they?" His black eyes sparkled with understanding and gratitude. He was glad to see how happy she was, too, that his disease had ended so easily.

"You can buy these tablets yourself at the pharmacist's. But I'll prescribe something else for you to take as well. . . ." She turned to the nurse. "Ascorbic acid."

Maria bowed her head severely and noted it down in her book.

"Only you'll have to take care of yourself!" Yevgenia Ustinovna impressed upon him. "You mustn't walk quickly, or lift heavy weights. And when you bend down, be careful about it."

Proshka burst into laughter, happy that there were some things in the world even she didn't understand.

"How can I help lifting things? I'm a tractor driver."

"You won't be able to work for the moment."

"Why? Will I get sick leave?"

"No, we'll give you a certificate to say you're an invalid."

"Invalid?" Proshka's look became almost wild. "Why the hell do I need an invalid's certificate? How can I live on that? I'm still young, I want to work."

He held out his healthy, coarse-fingered hands. They seemed to be begging for work.

But Yevgenia Ustinovna was not convinced.

"Go down to the surgical dressing room in half an hour. They'll have your certificate ready and I'll explain it to you."

She left the room. Maria, lean and unbending, went out after her.

Immediately several of the patients began talking all at once. Proshka asked about his invalid's certificate, what was it for? He had to discuss it with the "boys." But the others were discussing Federau. They were all thunderstruck: here was an unmarked, white, smooth neck, that didn't hurt at all—and an operation!

Podduyev turned over on the bed. He kept his legs pulled up and moved his body with his arms so that he looked like a legless man as he turned. He shouted angrily, his face turning red, "Don't be taken in, Friedrich! Don't be a fool! Once they start cutting, they cut you to death, like they've done to me."

But Ahmadjan had his opinion too. "They have to operate, Federau. They wouldn't say so without a reason."

"Why do they have to operate if it doesn't hurt?" said Dyomka indignantly.

"What's the matter with you, brother?" boomed Kostoglotov. "It's crazy, operating on a healthy neck."

Rusanov screwed up his face as these cries flew round the ward, but he decided not to offer any rebuke. After his injection yesterday he had cheered up considerably because he'd endured it without much difficulty. But all last night and this morning the tumor under his neck had made it just as hard to move his head as before. And today he felt quite miserable since it clearly wasn't going down at all.

True, Dr. Gangart had come to see him. She had questioned him in great detail on every facet of his condition yesterday, during the night, and today. She asked him how weak he felt and explained that the tumor would not necessarily go down after the first injection. Indeed it was quite normal for it not to do so. To some extent she had set his mind at rest. He had taken a good look at Gangart. Her face showed she was no fool (only her last name was open to suspicion). After all, the doctors in this clinic were not the absolute bottom. They must have some experience, you just had to know how to make them do things.

But his mind was not at rest for long. The doctor went away, but the tumor stuck out as before under his jaw, pressing against it. The patients blabbered on. And there was also this talk of operating on a man's neck when it was perfectly healthy. Rusanov's great lump had been so big, yet they weren't operating and didn't mean to. Could it really be as bad as that?

The day before yesterday, when he entered the ward, Pavel Nikolayevich could never have imagined he would so quickly come to feel a sense of unity with all these people. Because it was their *necks* that were at stake. All three of them had their necks at stake.

Friedrich Federau was very upset. He listened to their advice and smiled uneasily. They were all so confident when it came to telling *him* what to do. He was the only one with any doubts about where he stood (just as they had doubts in plenty when it came to their own cases). An operation would be dangerous, but not to operate would be dangerous too. He'd already seen quite a bit and done some investigating last time he was here, when they'd used X-ray treatment on his lower lip, just as they were doing with Egenberdiev now. Since then the scab on his lip had swollen, dried up and fallen off, but he understood why they wanted to operate on his cervical glands: to stop the cancer spreading any further.

But there again, they'd operated twice on Podduyev, and what good had it done? And what if the cancer had no intention of spreading? What if it had gone?

Whatever happened he would have to consult his wife, and especially his daughter Henrietta, who was the most educated and de cisive member of the family. But here he was taking up a bed, and the clinic would not hang around waiting for replies to letters. (From the nearest station to the depths of the steppe where they lived the post was still only delivered twice a week, and then only when the road was good.) To get a discharge and go home for advice would be very difficult, more difficult than either the doctors or the patients who were giving him advice so lightly realized. To do this he'd have to get a final stamp on his travel pass from the town *komendatura* here, the pass he'd gone to such trouble getting hold of, he'd have to get himself taken off the temporary register, and then he could go. First he would have to journey to the little railway station, and he'd have to change there into his fur coat and felt boots that were being kept for him there by some kind strangers he'd met, because the weather there was not like it was here: it was still freezing winds and winter. Then he'd have to bump and jolt along the 150 kilometers of track to his M.T.S.,* perhaps in the back of a truck, not even in the driver's seat. And as soon as he was home he'd have to write to the district *komendatura* and wait two, three, four weeks for permission to leave the area again. When it came he'd have to ask for leave from work, and that would be just when the snow was beginning to thaw. The road would be sodden and the traffic wouldn't be able to get through. Then at the little station where two trains stopped every twenty-four hours for a minute a time he'd have to rush frantically from car attendant to car attendant to try to get onto the train. And when he got back here he'd have to get on the temporary register again at the local *komendatura* and spend several days waiting his turn for a place in the clinic.

Meanwhile they were discussing Proshka. After what had just happened how could anyone believe in superstition? His was the unlucky bed! They congratulated him and advised him to agree to take the invalid's certificate they were offering. "They're giving it, take it! They're giving it, so it must be necessary. They're giving it now, but they'll take it away again later." But Proshka protested that he wanted to work. "All right, you'll have plenty of time to work, you fool. Life is long!"

Proshka went to get his certificates. The ward began to calm down. Yefrem opened his book again, but he was reading the lines without understanding what they meant. He soon realized this.

*A machine and tractor station that provides collective farms with agricultural machinery.

He did not understand what he was reading because he was disturbed and worried by what was happening in the ward and outside in the corridor. In order to understand, he had to remember that he wasn't going to get anywhere any more; that he would never change things or convince anyone of anything, that he had only a few numbered days in which to straighten out his life.

Only then would the book's meaning reveal itself. The lines were printed in the usual small black letters on white paper. But mere literacy was not enough to read them.

Proshka was already coming up the stairs, gleefully clutching his certificates. He met Kostoglotov on the top landing and showed them to him. "Look, great round stamps!" he said.

One certificate was for the railway station, asking them to give such-and-such a person a ticket since he had just undergone an operation. (Unless an operation was mentioned, the patients had to join the general line at the station which meant they could not get away for two or three days.) Another certificate was for the information of the health department in his place of residence. On it was written: *"Tumor cordis, casus inoperabilis."*

"I don't understand." Proshka poked at it with his finger. "What does it say?"

"Just let me think." Kostoglotov screwed up his eyes. "Take it away, I can think better without it."

Proshka took his precious certificates and went to pack his things.

Kostoglotov leaned over the banisters, a lock of hair from his forehead dangling over the stairs.

He had never studied Latin properly, or any other foreign language for that matter, or any subject at all except topography, and then only military topography for sergeants. But although he'd never missed a chance to scoff at education in general, he'd always used his eyes and ears to pick up the smallest thing that might broaden his own. He'd done one year in geophysics in 1938 and one incomplete year in geodesy from 1946 to 1947. Between them there had been the army and the war, circumstances hardly suitable for success in the sciences. But Kostoglotov always remembered his dear grandfather's motto: "A fool loves to teach, but a clever man loves to learn." Even during his years in the army he had always tried to take in useful knowledge and to lend an ear to intelligent conversation, whether it was an officer from another regiment talking or a soldier from his own platoon. True, he lent his ear in such a way that his pride was saved. He would listen as keenly as he could, but pretending all the time there was no real reason for doing so. When he met someone for the first time, he never made an effort to push himself forward or to strike a pose. He first tried to find out who his new friend was, from what background and what part of the world he came, and what sort of a man he was. He would listen and learn a lot like this. But the place where he found he could really get his fill was Butyrka Prison, where the cells were crammed to overflowing after the war. Every evening there were lectures given by professors, doctors of philosophy and people who were experts on some subject, whether it was atomic physics, Western architecture, genetics, poetry or beekeeping. And at all these lectures Kostoglotov was the most eager listener. Under the bunks at Krasnaya Presnya Prison, on the unplaned boards of the prison transport wagons, sitting on his bottom on the ground at the stopping places, or in the marching column in camp—wherever he was he tried to follow his grandfather's motto and acquire what he had never had the chance of learning in academic lecture halls.

In the camp too he cross-questioned the man who kept the records, a shy, aging little man, a penpusher in the hospital department who was sometimes sent to fetch hot water as well. He turned out to be a teacher of classical philology and ancient literature at Leningrad University. Kostoglotov conceived the idea of taking Latin lessons from him. For this they had to go out and walk up and down the camp area in the freezing weather, with no pencil or paper to be had. The recordkeeper would sometimes take off his glove and write something in the snow with his finger. (There was no self-interest in giving these lessons. It was just that for a brief time they made him feel like a human being. Kostoglotov would have had nothing to pay him with anyway. But they both nearly had to pay for it. The chief camp security officer sent for them separately and interrogated them, suspecting they were preparing an escape and drawing a map of the area in the snow. He never believed a word about the Latin. The lessons had to stop.)

Kostoglotov remembered from these lessons that the word "*casus*" meant case* and that "*in-*" was the negative prefix. "*Cor, cordis*" he also knew from the camp, and even if he hadn't, it would not

---

*As it happens, these Latin words are easily understood by an English speaker, but they would not be by a Russian. The Russian words are quite different.

have required great imagination to guess that the word "cardiogram" came from the same root. And the word *"tumor"* he had met on every page of *Pathological Anatomy*, which he had borrowed from Zoya.

So it had not been very difficult to work out Proshka's diagnosis: "Tumor of the heart, case inoperable."

Not only inoperable, but untreatable too, if they were prescribing ascorbic acid.

Kostoglotov, still leaning over the banisters, was not thinking about his translation from Latin, but about his principle, the one he had put forward to Ludmila Afanasyevna the day before—that a patient has the right to know everything.

But this was a principle for people who had seen a bit of the world, like himself.

What about Proshka?

Proshka had hardly anything to carry. He had no property. Sibgatov, Dyomka and Ahmadjan saw him off. They had to go carefully, all three of them. One had to watch out for his back and one for his leg, and the third had a little crutch to help him along. But Proshka walked along cheerfully, his white teeth sparkling.

It was like being back at the camp, on those rare occasions when they saw off a prisoner who had been released.

Was he to tell him he'd be arrested again as soon as he set foot outside the gates?

"What does it say, then?" asked Proshka as he walked past, quite unconcerned.

"G-god knows." Kostoglotov twisted his mouth as he spoke, and his scar twisted with it. "Doctors are so cunning these days, you can't read a word they write."

"Here's to your recovery! All you boys, here's to your recovery! You'll all be going home! Home to your wives!" Proshka shook them all by the hand. Halfway down the stairs he turned round again and gave them a cheerful wave.

He was full of confidence as he went down.

To death.

10. The Children

All she did was run her fingers round Dyomka's tumor and hug his shoulders slightly. Then she moved on. But something fateful happened as she did it: Dyomka felt it. The twigs of his hope were snapped short.

He didn't feel it at once. First there was a lot of talk in the ward and everyone was saying goodbye to Proshka, then he started scheming about how he could move into Proshka's bed by the window, now a lucky one. The light was better there for reading; it was also nearer for talking to Kostoglotov. And then a "new boy" came in.

He was a young man, well tanned, with slightly wavy, tidy, pitch-black hair, probably over twenty years old. He was lugging three books under his left arm, and under his right three more.

"Hello, everyone!" he announced from the doorway. Dyomka took a liking to him, he looked so unassuming and sincere. "Where do I go?" he said, gazing around, for some reason not at the beds but at the walls.

"Will you be reading a lot?" asked Dyomka.

"All the time!"

Dyomka thought for a moment.

"Is it for your work or just reading?"

"For my work."

"Well, take that bed over there by the window, all right? They'll make it up for you in a minute. What are your books about?"

"Geology, pal," answered the newcomer.

121

Dyomka read one of the titles: *Geochemical Exploration of Mineral Deposits*. "Take the bed by the window, then. What's wrong with you?"

"My leg."

"With me it's my leg too."

Yes, the newcomer was moving one leg a bit cautiously. But his figure—it was neat as an ice skater's.

They made up the bed for him, and, as if this was the only reason he had come into hospital, he laid five of his books out on the window sill and stuck his nose into the sixth. He read for an hour or so without asking a question or telling anyone anything. Then he was summoned to see the doctors.

Dyomka too tried to read. First it was stereometry. He tried to build some models out of pencils, but the theorems wouldn't go into his head and the diagrams with their lopped-off straight lines and planes with jagged edges kept on reminding him, hinting at the same thing.

He changed to a book which was a bit easier, *The Water of Life* by someone called Kozhevnikov, which had already picked up a Stalin Prize. It was by A. Kozhevnikov, but there were also an S. Kozhevnikov and a V. Kozhevnikov. Dyomka was rather frightened at the thought of how many writers there were. In the last century there had been about ten, all of them great. In this century there were thousands; you only had to change a letter in one of their names and you had a new writer. There was Safronov and there was Safonov, more than one Safonov, apparently. And was there only one Safronov? No one could have time to read all their books, and when you did read one, it was as if you might just as well not have done. Completely unknown writers floated to the surface, won Stalin prizes, then sank back forever. Nearly every book of any size got a prize the year after it appeared. Forty or fifty prizes popped up every year.

Their titles too kept getting mixed up in Dyomka's head. A lot had been written about two films, *The Big Life* and *The Big Family,* one a very healthy influence, the other a very harmful one, but Dyomka simply couldn't remember which was which, especially as he hadn't seen either. It was the same with ideas; the more he read about them, the more confused they seemed. He had only just grasped that to analyze objectively meant to see things as they are in life. But then he read how Panova, a woman novelist, was being attacked for "treading the marshy ground of objectivism."

Nevertheless he had to cope with it all, understand and remember it.

When Dyomka read *The Water of Life* he couldn't make out whether the book was a drag, or whether it was the mood he was in.

Exhaustion and gloom pressed on him more and more heavily. Did he want someone to talk it over with? Or someone to complain to? Or just someone to have a heart-to-heart talk with, who might perhaps even show him a little pity?

Of course he had read and heard that pity is a humiliating feeling: whether you pity or are pitied.

Even so, he wanted someone to pity him.

Because throughout his life, no one had ever pitied Dyomka.

Here in the ward it was interesting listening and talking to people, but he couldn't talk to them in the way he now wanted. When you're with men you have to behave like a man.

There were women in the clinic, a lot of them, but Dyomka could not make up his mind to cross the threshold of their large, noisy ward. If they had all been healthy women there, it would have been fun to glance in on the way past on the chance of seeing something interesting, but confronted by that great nest of sick women he preferred to turn away from whatever he might see there. Their illness was like a screen of prohibition, much stronger than mere shame. Some of the women he met on the stairs or in the hallways were so depressed, so low-spirited, that they hardly bothered to pull their dressing gowns round them, and he could not avoid seeing their nightdresses round their breasts or below their waists. When this happened, though, he felt no joy, only pain.

This was why he always lowered his eyes when he saw them. It was no easy matter to make friends here.

Aunt Styofa noticed him. She began to ask questions, and they became friendly. She was a mother and a grandmother already, and had, like all grandmothers, wrinkles and an indulgent smile for human weakness. He and Aunt Styofa used to stand about near the top of the stairs and talk for hours. No one had ever listened to Dyomka so attentively and with such sympathy. It was as though she had no one nearer to her than he. And, for him, it was easy to tell her things about himself and even about his mother which he would never have revealed to anyone else.

Dyomka was two years old when his father was killed in the war. Then he had a stepfather, not affectionate but just, and quite possible to live with. His mother became—he had never spoken the word in front of Styofa although he himself had long been certain of it—a whore. His stepfather left her—quite rightly. After that his mother used to bring men to their one room. They always used to drink, and they tried to make Dyomka drink too, but he wouldn't take it. And then the men stayed with her: some till midnight, others till morning. There was no partition in the room, and no darkness because light came in from the street lamps. And it sickened Dyomka so much that the very thought of it, which his friends found so thrilling, seemed to him like so much pigswill.

And so it went on during the fifth and sixth classes. When he reached the seventh class, however, Dyomka went to live with the school watchman, an old man, and the school gave him two meals a day. His mother didn't even try to get him back. She was glad to wash her hands of him.

Dyomka spoke angrily about his mother, he couldn't speak calmly. Aunt Styofa listened to him, shook her head, and said strangely when she'd heard him out: "It takes all sorts to make a world. We're all in the world together!"

Last year Dyomka had moved into a factory housing estate. There was a night school there and they gave him a place in a hostel. He worked as a lathe-operator's apprentice, and later they made him a second-grade operator. He wasn't very good at the job, but as he wanted to be different from his devil-may-care mother, he didn't drink or yell rowdy songs. Instead he studied. He did well in the eighth class and finished the first half of the ninth.

Besides that there was only football. Sometimes he used to run about playing football with the boys. And fate punished him for this, the one little pleasure he enjoyed: in a scramble for the ball someone accidentally hacked him on the shin with his boot. Dyomka didn't even think about it at the time. He limped for a bit and then the pain was gone. But in the autumn his leg started to ache more and more. It was a long time before he went to the doctor with it. They gave him warm compresses for it but it got worse. They sent him along the usual medical obstacle course, first to the provincial center and now here.

"Why is it," Dyomka would ask Aunt Styofa, "that there's such rank injustice in fortune itself? There are people whose lives run smooth as silk from beginning to end, I know there are, while others' are a complete louse-up. And they say a man's life depends on himself. It doesn't depend on him a bit."

"It depends on God," said Aunt Styofa soothingly. "God sees everything. You should submit to him, Dyomusha."

"Well, if it's from God it's even worse. If he can see everything, why does he load it all on one person? I think he ought to try to spread it about a bit. . . ."

But there were no two ways about it—he had to submit. What else was there for him to do?

Aunt Styofa lived locally. Her daughters, sons and daughters-in-law often used to come and visit her and bring her things to eat. She didn't keep them for long. She shared them with her neighbors and the orderlies. She would call Dyomka out of his ward and slip an egg or a pastry into his hand.

Dyomka's appetite was never satisfied. All his life he had never had enough to eat. His constant, anxious thoughts of food had made his hunger seem greater than it really was. Still, he felt embarrassed at taking so much from Aunt Styofa. If he accepted the egg, he would try to refuse the pastry.

"Take it, take it!" she would say, waving it at him. "It's got meat in it. You can eat it now, while it's still Meat Week."

"Why, can't I eat it afterwards?"

" 'Course you can't. Don't you know that?"

"So what comes after Meat Week?"

"Shrovetide, of course."

"That's even better, Aunt Styofa. Shrovetide's even better."

"Better in some ways, worse in others. But no meat!"

"Well, Shrovetide doesn't end then, does it?"

"What do you mean, doesn't end? It's gone in a week."

"So what do we do next?" asked Dyomka cheerfully, as he gobbled up the fragrant homemade meat pie, the like of which had never been baked in *his* home.

"Good heavens, doesn't anybody grow up Christian these days? No one knows anything. After that comes the Great Fast."

"But what's that for—the Great Fast? Why a fast—and why a Great Fast?"

"Because, Dyomusha, if you stuff your belly full it will pull you right down to the ground. You can't go on stuffing like that, you have to have a break sometimes."

"What's a break for?" Dyomka couldn't understand. He'd never known anything else but breaks.

"Breaks are to clear your head. You feel fresher on an empty stomach, haven't you noticed?"

"No, Aunt Styofa, I haven't."

Ever since he had been in the first class, before he could read or write, Dyomka had been taught, knew for certain and fully understood that religion is a drug, a three-time reactionary dogma, of benefit only to swindlers. Because of it the working people in some places had been unable to free themselves from exploitation. But as soon as they got rid of religion, they would take up arms and free themselves. And Aunt Styofa with her funny calendar, with the word "God" always on her lips, with her carefree smile even in that gloomy clinic, and her pastry, was obviously a thoroughly reactionary figure.

Nevertheless on Saturday after lunch, when the doctors had gone and each patient was left alone with his thoughts, when the cloudy day still lent a little touch of light to the wards, while on the landings and in the corridors the lamps were already on, Dyomka would walk about, limping and searching everywhere for none other than the reactionary Aunt Styofa, who could give him no sensible advice except to submit.

He was afraid they'd take it away, amputate it. He'd have to give it up.

To give it up, not to give it up. To give it up, not to give it up. . . .

With the gnawing pain he felt, perhaps to give it up would be easier.

But Aunt Styofa was in none of her usual places. So he went down to the lower corridor, where it broadened out into the little lobby that was regarded as the clinic's "red corner"* (the main-floor duty nurse's table stood there with her medicine cupboard), and then he saw a girl, almost a child, wearing the same kind of faded gray dressing gown. But she was like a film star: yellow hair, the sort you never saw anywhere, with something light and rustling built up from it.

---

*Most Soviet institutions possess a "red corner"—a room with magazines and communist literature.

Dyomka had glimpsed her for the first time the day before and her hair, yellow like a bed of flowers, had made him blink. She seemed so beautiful that he had not dared to let his eyes rest on her. He had turned them away and walked past. Although there was no one closer to him in age in the whole clinic (except for Surhan, the boy whose leg had been amputated), he knew that girls like that were beyond his reach.

This morning he caught sight of her again, from behind. Even in her hospital dressing gown she had a waist like a wasp, you could recognize her at once. And her little sheaf of yellow hair quivered.

Dyomka had certainly not been looking for her. He knew he'd never be able to make up his mind to approach her. He knew that his mouth would stick like paste and he'd bellow something unintelligible and stupid. But he saw her and his heart missed a beat. Trying not to limp, trying to walk as evenly as possible, he made his way to the red corner, where he began to flip through the pile of the local *Pravda,* already thinned out by patients for packing and other uses.

Half the table, which was covered by a red cloth, was taken up by a bronze bust of Stalin with larger-than-lifesize head and shoulders. Opposite, at the corner of the table, stood an orderly, also heavily built and with a large mouth. She seemed to make a pair with Stalin. It was Saturday and she did not expect any rush, so she had spread a newspaper on the table in front of her and poured some sunflower seeds on to it. She was shelling them with relish, spitting out the husks onto the newspaper without any help from her hands. She'd probably only come in for a minute but been unable to tear herself away from the sunflower seeds.

A loudspeaker on the wall was hoarsely blaring dance music. At a small table two patients were sitting playing checkers.

The girl Dyomka was watching out of the corner of his eye was sitting on a chair by the wall, doing nothing, just sitting straight-backed holding together the neck of her dressing gown. They never had any hooks unless the women sewed them on themselves.

She sat there, a delicate yellow-haired angel, untouchable, who looked as though she might melt and vanish. But how good it would be to *talk* to her about something . . . even about his bad leg.

Dyomka was angry with himself. He kept turning the pages of the newspaper. He suddenly realized that when he had had his hair cut he had not asked them to leave the curl on his forehead. Not wanting to waste time, he'd let them clip his head all over with the clippers. Now she must think he looked like an idiot.

Then suddenly the angel spoke. "Why are you so shy? This is the second day you've been around. You haven't come up to me."

Dyomka jumped. He looked round. Well, who else could she be talking to? Yes, she must be, she was talking to *him*! The tuft or plume on her head trembled like the spikes of a flower.

"What's the matter? Are you the scared type? Go on, get a chair, pull it up, let's get to know each other."

"I'm . . . not scared." But something broke in his voice and stopped it ringing out in the normal way.

"Then get a chair. Park it next to me."

Dyomka took the chair. Making an extra effort not to limp, he carried it with one hand and put it next to her by the wall. He gave her his hand.

"Dyomka."

"Asya." She put her soft palm into his and then drew it away.

He sat down, and it struck him as funny: there they were sitting next to each other like bride and groom. He couldn't even see her properly. He got up and moved the chair into an easier position.

"Why do you sit here not doing anything?" Dyomka asked.

"Why should I do anything? Anyway I am doing something."

"What are you doing?"

"I'm listening to music. I'm dancing in the mind. Can't you?"

"In the mind?"

"All right then, on the feet?"

Dyomka sucked his teeth, which meant "no."

"I saw you were rather green. We could have a turn round the floor now." Asya looked around. "Only there's nowhere to do it, and what kind of a dance is this anyway? So I just listen; silence always gets me down."

"Which is a good dance?" Dyomka was enjoying this conversation. "The tango?"

Asya sighed. "The tango! That's what our grandmothers used to dance. The thing today is rock-'n-roll. We don't dance it here yet, but in Moscow they do. Only professionals, of course."

Dyomka did not really take in all she was saying. It was nice just to talk to her and to be allowed to look straight at her. She had strange eyes with a touch of green. But you can't paint eyes, they stay the way they are. Even so they were pretty.

"That really is a dance!" Asya clicked her fingers. "Only I can't give you a demonstration. I've never seen it. How do you spend your time, then? Do you sing songs?"

"No-o, I can't sing."

"Why not? We always sing when silence gets us down. So what *do* you do? Do you play the accordion?"

"No-o," said Dyomka, covered with shame. He wasn't much compared to her, was he? He couldn't just blurt out to her that his passion was for social problems.

Asya was quite at a loss. What a funny type, she thought.

"Are you an athlete, then? I'm not bad at the pentathlon myself, by the way. I can do a hundred and forty centimeters and I can do thirteen point two seconds. . . ."

"No-o, I'm not." Dyomka realized bitterly how worthless he must seem to her. Some people could fix up their lives so easily. Dyomka would never be able to. He played a little football. . . .

And where had it got him?

"You do at least smoke? And drink?" Asya asked, still hoping. "Or is it only beer?"

"Beer . . ." sighed Dyomka. (He had never tasted beer in his life, but he couldn't let himself be completely disgraced.)

"Oh," groaned Asya, as though someone had knocked all the breath out of her. "What a lot of momma's boys you all are! No sporting spirit. The people at school are like you. Last September they moved us to a boys' school,* but the headmaster kept on just a few teachers' pets and bookworms and miserable types. All the best boys he stuck in the girls' school."

She did not mean to humiliate him, in fact she was sorry for him, but all the same he was hurt that she should think him a "miserable type."

"Which class are you in?" he asked.

"The tenth."

"So who lets you wear your hair like that?"

"Who lets us? They fight us! And we fight them!"

It was open-hearted, the way she spoke. But let her tease him, let

*In September 1954 coeducation was reintroduced in Russia.

her even pummel him, the only thing that mattered was that they were talking.

The dance music stopped and the announcer began to speak of the people's struggle against the shameful Paris treaties, which were dangerous for France because they put her at the mercy of Germany, and intolerable for Germany because they put her at the mercy of France.

"So what do you do?" Asya was still trying to find out.

"I'm a turner," Dyomka said casually but with dignity.

Even the turner did not impress Asya. "How much do you earn?"

Dyomka was very proud of his pay, for it was his own and the first he had ever earned. But now he felt he couldn't let on how much.

"Oh, it's nothing. Nothing at all," he forced himself to say.

"It's a complete waste of time," declared Asya quite categorically. "You'd do much better to become a sportsman. You've got what it takes."

"But you have to know how . . ."

"What do you have to know? Anyone can be a sportsman. You've only got to train a lot. And it pays! You travel for nothing. You get thirty roubles a day for food, *and* free hotels, and bonuses thrown in! And think of the places you see!"

"Where have you been?"

"I've been to Leningrad, Voronezh. . . ."

"Did you like Leningrad?"

"You bet! The shops in the Passage and the Gostiny Dvor! They've got separate stores for everything: stores for stockings, stores for handbags. . . ."

Dyomka could not imagine such things and he envied her. Perhaps it was true, perhaps the things this little girl was talking about so freely *were* the good things of life, and everything *he* depended on was musty and provincial.

The orderly was still standing by the table like a statue, spitting out husks without so much as bending her head.

"You're a sportswoman, but you're here?"

He would not have dared ask what part of her body actually hurt. The question might have been embarrassing.

"I'm only here for three days' examination." Asya waved her hand. The collar of her dressing gown kept falling open, and she had to keep holding it together or adjusting it with one hand. "This stupid dressing gown they make you wear here. I'm ashamed to put it on. A week here's enough to make you go crazy. And what have they picked you up for?"

"Me?" Dyomka sucked his teeth. He wanted to tell her about his leg, but he wanted to do it sensibly. Her lightning attack threw him off balance. "It's my leg."

Up to then the words "It's my leg" had been full of deep and bitter meaning for him, but faced with Asya's lightness of heart he was beginning to doubt whether it was really so grave. He spoke of his leg almost as he had of his pay, with embarrassment.

"What do they say about it?"

"Well, they don't really say anything, but they want to . . . to cut it off."

His face darkened as he said these words and he looked at Asya's bright face.

"Nonsense!" Asya slapped him on the back like an old friend. "Cut off your leg? They must be crazy. It's just that they don't want to treat it. Don't let them do it. It's better to die than live without a leg. What sort of life is it for a cripple, do you think? Life is for happiness."

Yes, of course. She was right again. What kind of life was it on crutches? He would be sitting next to her now, but where would he put the crutches? Where would he put the stump? He wouldn't even be able to bring up a chair by himself, she'd have to bring one for him. No, without legs it wouldn't be any sort of a life.

Life was for happiness.

"Have you been here long?"

"How long?" Dyomka thought to himself. "Three weeks."

"How awful!" Asya shook her shoulders. "How boring! No radio, no accordion! And I can imagine the sort of talk there is in the ward!"

Again Dyomka did not want to admit he'd spent whole days reading books and studying. All his values were tottering under the breeze of Asya's words; they seemed exaggerated, cardboard even.

He grinned, although inside he was not grinning at all, and went on, "Well, for instance, we were discussing what men live by."

"What do you mean?"

"Well, why they live, that sort of thing."

"Pah!" Asya had an answer for everything. "We had an essay about that at school: 'What does man live for?' They gave us study material full of cotton growers, milkmaids, Civil War heroes. 'What is your attitude to the brave deed of Pavel Korchagin?' 'What is your attitude to the heroism of Matrosov?' "*

"What *is* your attitude?"

"Well what? Should we do what they did? The teachers said we should. So we all wrote that we would. Why spoil things just before the exams? But Sashka Gromov said, 'Do I have to write all that? Can't I write what I really think?' Our teacher said, 'I'll give you what you really think. You'll get the worst mark you've ever known.' And one girl wrote—you should have been there, 'I don't know yet whether I love my country or not.' Our teacher quacked like a duck: 'What a lousy idea! How dare you *not* love your country?' 'Perhaps I do love it, but I don't know. I must find out for myself.' 'What is there to find out? You ought to drink in love for your country with your mother's milk. Write it all out again by the next lesson.' We call her 'Toad.' She comes to class and never smiles. Everyone knows why. She's an old maid. She hasn't made much of her private life, so she takes it out on us. Most of all she hates the pretty girls."

Asya was throwing the words out casually. She reckoned she knew all right what a pretty face was worth. It was obvious she hadn't been through the disease at all; the pain, the suffering, the loss of appetite and sleep. She hadn't yet lost her freshness or the color in her cheeks. She'd just popped in from one of her gyms or dance floors for a three-day examination.

"But there are *some* good teachers, aren't there?" Dyomka asked, only because he did not want her to fall silent, because he wanted her to keep talking while he sat and looked at her.

"No, not one. They're a lot of puffed-up turkeys. Anyway, school . . . who wants to talk about school?"

Her cheerful healthiness broke over Dyomka. He sat there grateful to her for her chattering, no longer inhibited, relaxed. He did not want to argue with her, he wanted to agree with everything she said in spite of his own beliefs. He'd have felt easier and more at peace with his leg too if it had stopped gnawing at him and reminding him he had done it an injury and that it was about to get its own back on him. Would it be halfway up the shin? Or up to the knee? Or half the thigh? Because of his leg the question, "What do men live by?"

*Korchagin is a character from Nikolai Ostrovski's *How the Steel Was Tempered*. Matrosov was a hero of World War II who threw himself on a German machine gun, covering it with his body.

remained one of the most important things in his life. So he asked her, "No, but seriously, what do you think? What . . . what *do* people live for?"

Oh yes, this little girl understood a thing or two. She turned her greenish eyes toward Dyomka, as if not quite sure whether he was playing a joke on her or being serious.

"What for? What do you mean? For love, of course."

For love! Tolstoy had said "For love" too, but in what sense? And the girl's teacher had made them write "For love" too, but in what sense? After all, Dyomka was used to having things precise in his mind, to working them out for himself.

"But . . ." he began hoarsely. (It was simple enough, perhaps, but rather embarrassing to say.) "After all, love is . . . love isn't the whole of your life. It only happens . . . sometimes. From a certain age, and up to a certain age. . . ."

"What age? From what age?" Asya interrogated him angrily as though he had offended her. "It's best at our age. When else? What is there in life except love?"

Sitting there with her little raised eyebrows, she seemed so certain, it wasn't possible to object. Dyomka didn't object. He just wanted to listen to her, not to argue.

She turned toward him and leaned forward, and, without stretching out either of her arms, it was as if she were stretching them across the ruins of all the walls in the world.

"It is *ours* forever. And it is *today*. Don't listen to them wagging their tongues about whether this'll happen or that'll happen. It's love! That's all!"

She was so frank with him, it was as if they'd spent a hundred evenings talking, talking and talking. And if it hadn't been for the orderly with her sunflower seeds, the nurse, the two checkers players, the patients shuffling along the corridors, she really might have been ready, there and then, in that little corner, at the finest age of their lives, to help him understand what men live by.

His leg had gnawed at him constantly, even in his sleep, even a second ago, but he had forgotten it now, it was as if it didn't exist. He looked at the open collar of Asya's dressing gown and his lips parted a little. What had repelled him so much when his mother did it, now for the first time struck him as innocent before the whole world, unstained, capable of outweighing all the evil on earth.

"What about you?" Asya half-whispered sympathetically, but

ready to burst into laughter. "Haven't you ever . . . ? You silly, haven't you ever . . . ?"

A red-hot wave struck Dyomka, in the ears, the face and the forehead. It was as if he had been caught stealing. In twenty minutes this little girl had knocked him clean off all he had held fast to for years. His throat was dry as he asked her, like a man begging for mercy, "What about you . . . ?"

Just as behind her dressing gown there was nothing but her nightdress, her breasts and her soul, so behind her words there was nothing hidden from him. She saw no reason to hide.

"Oh, me . . . since the ninth . . . There was one in our *eighth class* who got pregnant! And one got caught in an apartment; she was . . . for money, can you imagine? She had her own savings book. How did it come out? She left it in her exercise book and a teacher found it. The earlier you start, the more exciting it is. . . . Why wait? It's the atomic age!"

11. Cancer of the Birch Tree

In spite of everything, Saturday evening came as a sort of invisible relief to everyone in the cancer wing, no one quite knew why. Obviously the patients were not released for the weekend from their illness, let alone from thinking about it; but they *were* freed from talking to the doctors and from most of their treatment, and it was probably this which gladdened some eternally childish part of the human make-up.

After his conversation with Asya, Dyomka managed to climb the stairs, although the nagging pain in his leg was growing stronger, forcing him to tread more carefully. He entered the ward to find it more than usually lively. All those who belonged to the ward were there, Sibgatov too, and there were also some guests from the first floor—new arrivals as well as a few he knew like the old Korean, Ni, who had just been allowed out of the ward. (So long as the radium needles were in his tongue they had kept him under lock and key, like a valuable in a bank vault.) One of the new people was a Russian, quite a presentable man with fair, swept-back hair who had something wrong with his throat. He could only speak in a whisper. As it happened, he was sitting on Dyomka's bed, taking up half of it. Everyone was listening, even Mursalimov and Egenberdiev, who didn't understand Russian.

Kostoglotov was making a speech. He was sitting not on his bed but higher up, on his window sill, emphasizing thereby the importance of the moment. (If any of the strict nurses had been on duty he wouldn't have been allowed to sit there, but Turgin was in charge, a male nurse whom the patients treated as one of themselves. He rightly judged that such behavior would hardly turn medical science upside down.) Resting one stockinged foot on the bed, Kostoglotov put the other leg, bent at the knee, across the knee of the first leg like a guitar. Swaying slightly, he was discoursing loudly and excitedly for the whole ward to hear:

"There was this philosopher Descartes. He said, 'Suspect everything.' "

"But that's nothing to do with our way of life," Rusanov reminded him, raising a finger in admonition.

"No, of course it isn't," said Kostoglotov, utterly amazed by the objection. "All I mean is that we shouldn't behave like rabbits and put our complete trust in doctors. For instance, I'm reading this book." He picked up a large, open book from the window sill. "Abrikosov and Stryukov, *Pathological Anatomy,* medical school textbook. It says here that the link between the development of tumors and the central nervous system has so far been very little studied. And this link is an amazing thing! It's written here in so many words." He found the place. " 'It happens rarely, but there are cases of self-induced healing.' You see how it's worded? Not recovery through treatment, but actual healing. See?"

There was a stir throughout the ward. It was as though "self-induced healing" had fluttered out of the great open book like a rainbow-colored butterfly for everyone to see, and they all held up their foreheads and cheeks for its healing touch as it flew past.

"Self-induced," said Kostoglotov, laying aside his book. He waved his hands, fingers splayed, keeping his leg in the same guitar-like pose. "That means that suddenly for some unexplained reason the tumor starts off in the opposite direction! It gets smaller, resolves and finally disappears! See?"

They were all silent, gaping at the fairy tale. That a tumor, one's own tumor, the destructive tumor which had mangled one's whole life, should suddenly drain away, dry up and die by itself?

They were all silent, still holding their faces up to the butterfly. It was only the gloomy Podduyev who made his bed creak and, with a hopeless and obstinate expression on his face, croaked out, "I suppose for that you need to have . . . a clear conscience."

It was not clear to everyone whether his words were linked to their conversation or were some thought of his own.

But Pavel Nikolayevich, who on this occasion was listening to his neighbor Bone-chewer with attention, even with a measure of sympathy, turned with a nervous jerk to Podduyev and read him a lecture.

"What idealistic nonsense! What's conscience got to do with it? You ought to be ashamed of yourself, Comrade Podduyev!"

But Kostoglotov followed it up straightaway.

"You've hit the nail on the head, Yefrem. Well done! Anything can happen, we don't know a damn thing. For example, after the war I read something very interesting in a magazine, I think it was *Zvezda.** It seems that man has some kind of blood-and-brain barrier at the base of his skull. So long as the substance or microbes that kill a man can't get through that barrier into the brain, he goes on living. So what does that depend on?"

The young geologist had not put down his books since he had come into the ward. He was sitting with one on his bed, by the other window, near Kostoglotov, occasionally raising his head to listen to the argument. He did so now. All the guests from the other wards were listening too, as well as those who belonged there. Near the stove Federau, his neck still unmarked and white but already doomed, lay curled up on his side, listening from his pillow.

". . . Well, it depends, apparently, on the relationship between the potassium and sodium salts in the barrier. If there's a surplus of one of these salts, I don't remember which one, let's say sodium, then nothing harmful can get through the barrier and the man won't die. But if, on the other hand, there's a surplus of potassium salts, then the barrier won't do its work and he dies. What does the proportion of potassium to sodium depend on? That's the most interesting point. Their relationship depends on a man's attitude of mind! Understand? It means that if a man's cheerful, if he is stanch, then there's a surplus of sodium in the barrier and no illness whatever can make him die! But the moment he loses heart, there's too much potassium, and you might as well order the coffin."

The geologist had listened to him with a calm expression, weighing him up. He was like a bright, experienced student who can guess more or less what the teacher is going to write next on the blackboard.

Zvezda (Star) is a well-known literary monthly which attracted official criticism after the war because of its "liberalism."

"The physiology of optimism," he said approvingly. "A good idea. Very good."

Then, as if anxious not to lose time, he dived back into his book.

Pavel Nikolayevich didn't raise any objection now. Bone-chewer was arguing quite scientifically.

"So I wouldn't be surprised," Kostoglotov continued, "if in a hundred years' time they discover that our organism excretes some kind of cesium salt when our conscience is clear, but not when it's burdened, and that it depends on this cesium salt whether the cells grow into a tumor or whether the tumor resolves."

Yefrem sighed hoarsely. "I've mucked so many women about, left them with children hanging round their necks. They cried . . . mine'll never resolve."

"What's that got to do with it?" Pavel Nikolayevich suddenly lost his temper. "The whole idea's sheer religious rubbish! You've read too much slush, Comrade Podduyev, you've disarmed yourself ideologically. You keep harping on about that stupid moral perfection!"

"What's so terrible about moral perfection?" said Kostoglotov aggressively. "Why should moral perfection give you such a pain in the belly? It can't harm anyone—except someone who's a moral monstrosity!"

"You . . . watch what you're saying!"

Pavel Nikolayevich flashed his spectacles with their glinting frames; he held his head straight and rigid, as if the tumor wasn't pushing it under the right of the jaw. "There are questions on which a definite opinion has been established, and they are no longer open to discussion."

"Why can't I discuss them?" Kostoglotov glared at Rusanov with his large dark eyes.

"Come on, that's enough," shouted the other patients, trying to make peace.

"All right, comrade," whispered the man without a voice from Dyomka's bed. "You were telling us about birch fungus . . ."

But neither Rusanov nor Kostoglotov was ready to give way. They knew nothing about one another, but they looked at each other with bitterness.

"If you wish to state your opinion, at least employ a little elementary knowledge." Pavel Nikolayevich pulled his opponent up, articulating each word syllable by syllable. "The moral perfection of Leo Tolstoy and company was described once and for all by Lenin, and by Comrade Stalin, and by Gorky."

"Excuse me," answered Kostoglotov, restraining himself with difficulty. He stretched one arm out toward Rusanov. "No one on this earth ever says anything 'once and for all.' If they did, life would come to a stop and succeeding generations would have nothing to say."

Pavel Nikolayevich was taken aback. The tops of his delicate white ears turned quite red, and round red patches appeared on his cheeks.

(He shouldn't be expostulating, entering into a Saturday afternoon argument with this man. He ought to be *checking up* on who he was, where he came from, where his background was, and whether his blatantly false views weren't a danger in the post he occupied.)

"I am not claiming," Kostoglotov hastened to unburden himself, "that I know a lot about social science. I haven't had much occasion to study it. But with my limited intelligence I understand that Lenin only attacked Leo Tolstoy for seeking moral perfection when it led society away from the struggle with arbitrary rule and from the approaching revolution. Fine! But why try to stop a man's mouth" —he pointed with both his large hands to Podduyev—"just when he has started to think about the meaning of life, when he himself is on the borderline between life and death? Why should it irritate you so much if he helps himself by reading Tolstoy? What harm does it do? Or perhaps you think Tolstoy should have been burned at the stake? Perhaps the Government Synod* didn't finish its work?"

(Kostoglotov, not having studied social science, had mixed up "holy" and "government.")

Both Pavel Nikolayevich's ears had now ripened to a full, rich, juicy red. This was a direct attack on a government institution (true, he had not quite heard *which* institution). The fact that it was made in front of a random audience not hand-picked made the situation more serious still. What he had to do now was stop the argument tactfully and *check up* on Kostoglotov at the first opportunity. So he did not make an issue of it. Instead he said in Podduyev's direction, "Let him read Ostrovsky.** That'll do him more good."

---

*Tolstoy was excommunicated by the Holy Synod, the ruling body of the Russian Orthodox Church under the Tsars.

**Nikolai Ostrovsky, a Soviet writer whose most important character attempted to be of use to the Party even from his deathbed.

But Kostoglotov did not appreciate Pavel Nikolayevich's tact. Without listening or taking in anything the other said, he continued recklessly putting forward his own ideas to an unqualified audience.

"Why stop a man from thinking? After all, what does our philosophy of life boil down to? 'Oh, life is so good! . . . Life, I love you. Life is for happiness!' What profound sentiments. Any animal can say as much without our help, any hen, cat, or dog."

"Please! I beg you!" Pavel Nikolayevich was warning him now, not out of civil duty, not as one of the great actors on the stage of history, but as its meanest extra. "We mustn't talk about death! We mustn't even remind anyone of it!"

"It's no use begging!" Kostoglotov waved him aside with a spade-like hand. "If we can't talk about death *here,* where on earth can we? Oh, I suppose we live forever?"

"So what? What of it?" pleaded Pavel Nikolayevich. "What are you suggesting? You want us to talk and think about death the whole time? So that the potassium salts get the upper hand?"

"Not all the time," Kostoglotov said rather more quietly, seeing he was beginning to contradict himself. "Not all the time, only sometimes. It's useful. Because what do we keep telling a man all his life? 'You're a member of the collective! You're a member of the collective!' That's right. But only while he's alive. When the time comes for him to die, we release him from the collective. He may be a member, but he has to die alone. It's only he who is saddled with the tumor, not the whole collective. Now you, yes, you!"—he poked his finger rudely at Rusanov—"come on, tell us, what are you most afraid of in the world now? Of dying! What are you most afraid of talking about? Of death! And what do we call that? Hypocrisy!"

"Within limits that's true." The nice geologist spoke quietly, but everyone heard him. "We're so afraid of death, we drive away all thought of those who have died. We don't even look after their graves."

"Well, that's right," Rusanov agreed. "Monuments to heroes should be properly maintained, they even say so in the newspapers."

"Not only heroes, everyone," said the geologist gently in a voice which, it seemed, he was incapable of raising. It wasn't only his voice that was thin, he was too. His shoulders gave no hint of physical strength. "Many of our cemeteries are shamefully neglected. I saw some in the Altai Mountains and over toward Novosibirsk. There are no fences, the cattle wander into them, and pigs dig them up. Is that part of our national character? No, we always used to respect graves . . ."

"To revere graves," added Kostoglotov.

Pavel Nikolayevich had stopped listening. He had lost interest in the argument. Forgetting himself, he had made an incautious movement and his tumor had given him such a jab of reverberating pain in the neck and head that he was no longer concerned with enlightening these boobies and exploding their nonsense. After all, it was only by chance he had landed in this clinic. He shouldn't have had to live through such a crucial period of his illness in the company of people like this. But the main, the most terrible thing was that the tumor had not subsided or softened in the least after his injection the day before. The very thought gave him a cold feeling in the belly. It was all very well for Bone-chewer to talk about death. *He* was getting better.

Dyomka's guest, the portly man without a voice, sat there holding his larynx to ease the pain. Several times he tried to intervene with something of his own or to interrupt the unpleasant argument, but nobody could hear his whisper and he was unable to talk any louder. All he could do was lay two fingers on his larynx to lessen the pain and help the sound. Diseases of the tongue and throat, which made it impossible to talk, are somehow particularly oppressive. A man's whole face becomes no more than an imprint of this oppression. Dyomka's guest now tried to stop the argument, making wide sweeps of his arms. Even his tiny voice was now more easily heard. He moved forward along the passageway between the beds.

"Comrades! Comrades!" he wheezed huskily. Even though the pain in his throat was not your own, you could still feel it. "Don't let's be gloomy! We're depressed enough by our illnesses as it is. Now you, comrade"—he walked between the beds and almost beseechingly stretched out one hand as if to a deity (the other was still at his throat) toward the disheveled Kostoglotov sitting on high—"you were telling us such interesting things about birch fungus. Please go on!"

"Come on, Oleg, tell us about the birch fungus. What was it you said?" Sibgatov was asking.

The bronze-skinned Ni could only move his tongue with difficulty because part of it had dropped off during his previous course of treatment and the rest had now swollen, but indistinctly he too was asking Kostoglotov to continue.

The others were asking him to as well.

A disturbing feeling of lightness ran through Kostoglotov's body. For years he had been used to keeping his mouth shut, his head bowed and his hands behind his back in front of men who were *free*. It had become almost a part of his nature, like a stoop you are born with. He hadn't rid himself of it even after a year in exile. Even now it seemed the natural, simple thing to clasp his hands behind his back when he walked along the paths of the hospital grounds. But now these free men, who for so many years had been forbidden to talk to him as an equal, to discuss anything serious with him as one man to another or—even more bitter—to shake hands with him or take a letter from him—these free men were sitting in front of him, suspecting nothing, while he lounged casually on a window sill playing the schoolmaster. They were waiting for *him* to bolster up their hopes. He also realized that he no longer set himself apart from free men, as he used to, but was joining them in the common misfortune.

In particular he had grown out of the habit of speaking to a lot of people, of addressing any kind of conference, session or meeting. And yet here he was, becoming an orator. It all seemed wildly improbable to Kostoglotov, like an amusing dream. He was like a man charging full-tilt across ice, who has to rush forward, come what may. And so carried by the cheerful momentum of his recovery, unexpected but, it seemed, real, he went on and on.

"Friends!" he said, with uncharacteristic volubility. "This is an amazing tale. I heard it from a patient who came in for a checkup while I was still waiting to be admitted. I had nothing to lose, so straightaway I sent off a postcard with this hospital's address on it for the reply. And an answer has come today, already! Only twelve days, and an answer! Dr. Maslennikov even apologizes for the delay because, it seems, he has to answer on an average ten letters a day. And you can't write a reasonable letter in less than half an hour, can you? So he spends five hours a day just writing letters—and he doesn't get a thing for it!"

"No, and what's more, he has to spend four roubles a day on stamps," Dyomka interjected.

"That's right, four roubles a day. Which means a hundred and twenty a month. And he doesn't *have* to do it, it's not his job, he just does it as a good deed. Or how should I put it?" Kostoglotov turned maliciously toward Rusanov. "A *humane* act, is that right?"

But Pavel Nikolayevich was finishing reading a newspaper report of the budget. He pretended not to hear.

"And he has no staff, no assistants or secretaries. He does it all on his own time. And he doesn't get any honor and glory either! You see, when we're ill a doctor is like a ferryman: we need him for an hour and after that we forget he exists. As soon as he cures you, you throw his letters away. At the end of his letter he complains that his patients, especially the ones he's helped, stop writing to him. They don't tell him about the doses they take or the results. And then *he* goes on to ask *me* to write to him regularly—he's the one who asks me, when we should be bowing down before him."

In his heart Kostoglotov was convincing himself that he had been warmly touched by Maslennikov's selfless industry, that he wanted to talk about him and praise him, because it would mean he wasn't entirely spoiled himself. But he was already spoiled to the extent that he would not have been able to put himself out like Maslennikov day after day for other people.

"Tell us everything in the proper order, Oleg!" said Sibgatov, with a faint smile of hope.

How he wanted to be cured! In spite of the numbing, obviously hopeless treatment, month after month and year after year—suddenly and finally to be cured! To have his back healed again, to straighten himself up, walk with a firm tread, be a fine figure of a man! "Hello, Ludmila Afanasyevna! I'm all right now!"

They all longed to find some miracle doctor, or some medicine the doctors here didn't know about. Whether they admitted as much or denied it, they all without exception in the depths of their hearts believed there was a doctor, or a herbalist, or some old witch of a woman somewhere, whom you only had to find and get that medicine from to be saved.

No, it wasn't possible, it just wasn't possible that their lives were already doomed.

However much we laugh at miracles when we are strong, healthy and prosperous, if life becomes so hedged and cramped that only a miracle can save us, then we clutch at this unique, exceptional miracle and believe in it!

And so Kostoglotov identified himself with the eagerness with which his friends were hanging on his lips and began to talk fervently, believing his own words even more than he'd believed the letter when he'd first read it to himself.

"Well, to start from the beginning, Sharaf, here it is. One of our old patients told me about Dr. Maslennikov. He said that he was an old pre-Revolutionary country doctor from the Alexandrov district near Moscow. He'd worked dozens of years in the same hospital, just like they used to do in those days, and he noticed that, although more and more was being written about cancer in medical literature, there was no cancer among the peasants who came to him. Now why was that?"

(Yes, why *was* that? Which of us from childhood has not shuddered at the mysterious? At contact with that impenetrable yet yielding wall behind which there seems to be nothing, yet from time to time we catch a glimpse of something which might be someone's shoulder, or else someone's hip? In our everyday, open, reasonable life, where there is no place for mystery, it suddenly flashes at us, "Don't forget me! I'm here!")

"So he began to investigate, he began to investigate," repeated Kostoglotov. He never repeated anything, but now found pleasure in doing so. "And he discovered a strange thing: that the peasants in his district saved money on their tea, and instead of tea brewed up a thing called *chaga,* or, in other words, birch fungus . . ."

"You mean brown cap?" Podduyev interrupted him. In spite of the despair he'd resigned himself to and shut himself up in for the last few days, the idea of such a simple, easily accessible remedy burst upon him like a ray of light.

The people around him were all southerners, and had never in their lives seen a birch tree, let alone the brown-cap mushroom that grows under it, so they couldn't possibly know what Kostoglotov was talking about.

"No, Yefrem, not a brown cap. Anyway, it's not really a birch fungus, it's a birch cancer. You remember, on old birch trees there are these . . . peculiar growths, like spines, black on top and dark brown inside."

"Tree fungus, then?" Yefrem persisted. "They used to use it for kindling fires."

"Well, perhaps. Anyway, Sergei Nikitich Maslennikov had an idea. Mightn't it be that same *chaga* that had cured the Russian peasants of cancer for centuries without their even knowing it?"

"You mean they used it as a prophylactic?" The young geologist nodded his head. He hadn't been able to read a line all evening, but the conversation had been worth it.

"But it wasn't enough just to make a guess, you see? Everything had to be checked. He had to spend many, many years watching the people who were drinking the homemade tea and the ones who weren't. Then he had to give it to people who developed tumors and take the responsibility for not treating them with other medicines. And he had to guess what temperature the tea ought to be at, and what sort of dose, and whether it should be boiled or not, how many glasses they ought to drink, whether there'd be any harmful after-effects, and which tumors it helped most and which least. And all this took . . ."

"Yes, but what about now? What happens now?" said Sibgatov excitedly.

And Dyomka thought, could it really help his leg? Could it possibly save it?

"What happens now? Well, here's his answer to my letter. He tells me how to treat myself."

"Have you got his address?" asked the voiceless man eagerly, keeping one hand over his wheezing throat. He was already taking a notebook and a fountain pen from his jacket pocket. "Does he say how to take it? Does he say it's any good for throat tumors?"

Pavel Nikolayevich would have liked to maintain his strength of will and punish his neighbor by a show of utter contempt, but he found he couldn't let such a story and such an opportunity slip. He could no longer go on working out the meaning of the figures of the 1955 draft state budget which had been presented to a session of the Supreme Soviet. By now he had frankly lowered his newspaper and was slowly turning his face toward Bone-chewer, making no attempt to conceal his hope that he, a son of the Russian people, might also be cured by this simple Russian folk remedy. He spoke with no trace of hostility—he didn't want to irritate Bone-chewer—yet there was a reminder in his voice. "But is this method officially recognized?" he asked. "Has it been approved by a government department?"

High up on his window sill, Kostoglotov grinned. "I don't know about government departments. This letter"—he waved in the air a small, yellowish piece of paper with green-ink writing on it—"is a business letter: how to make the powder, how to dissolve it. But I suppose if it had been passed by the government, the nurses would already be bringing it to us to drink. There'd be a barrel of the stuff on the landing. And we wouldn't have to write to Alexandrov."

"Alexandrov." The voiceless man had already written it down. "What postal district? What street?" He was quick to catch on.

Ahmadjan was also listening with interest and managing to translate the most important bits quietly to Mursalimov and Egenberdiev. Ahmadjan did not need the birch fungus himself because he was getting better, but there was one thing he didn't understand.

"If the mushroom's that good, why don't the doctors indent for it? Why don't they put it in their standing orders?"

"It's a long business, Ahmadjan. Some people don't believe in it, some don't like learning new things and so are obstructive, some try to stop it to promote their own remedies, but we don't have any choice."

Kostoglotov answered Rusanov and answered Ahmadjan, but he didn't answer the voiceless man or give him the address. So that no one would notice this, he pretended he hadn't quite heard him or didn't have time to answer, but in fact he didn't want to give him the address. He didn't want to because there was something insinuating about the voiceless man's attitude, respectable though he looked. He had the figure and face of a bank manager, or even of the premier of a small South American country. Oleg felt sorry for honest old Maslennikov, who was ready to give up his sleep to write to people he didn't know. The voiceless man would shower him with questions. On the other hand, it was impossible not to feel sorry for this wheezing throat which had lost the ring of a human voice, unvalued when we have it. But there again, Kostoglotov had learned how to be ill, he was a specialist in being ill, he was devoted to his illness. He had already read bits of *Pathological Anatomy* and managed to get explanations out of Gangart and Dontsova, *and* he'd got an answer from Maslennikov. Why should he, the one who for years had been deprived of all rights, be expected to teach these free men how to wriggle out from underneath the boulder that was crushing them? His character had been formed in a place where the law dictated: "Found it? Keep your trap shut. Grabbed it? Keep it under the mattress." If everyone started writing to Maslennikov, Kostoglotov would never get another reply to his own letters.

It was not a deeply thought-out decision. It was all done through a movement of his scarred chin from Rusanov to Ahmadjan, past the man without a voice.

"But does he say how to use it?" asked the geologist. He had pencil and paper in front of him. He always had when he was reading a book.

"How to use it? All right, get your pencils and I'll dictate," said Kostoglotov.

Everyone rushed about asking each other for pencil and paper. Pavel Nikolayevich didn't have anything (he'd left his fountain pen at home, the one with the enclosed nib, the new kind). Dyomka gave him a pencil. Sibgatov, Federau, Yefrem and Ni all wanted to write. When they were ready Kostoglotov began to dictate slowly from the letter, explaining how *chaga* should be dried, but not dried out, how to grate it, what sort of water to boil it in, how to steep it, strain it, and what quantity to drink.

Some of them wrote quickly, some clumsily. They asked him to repeat it, and warmth and friendliness spread through the ward. Sometimes they used to answer each other with such antipathy—but what did they have to quarrel over? They all had the same enemy, death. What can divide human beings on earth once they are all faced with death?

Dyomka finished writing. In his usual rough, slow voice, older than his years, he said, "Yes, but where can we get birch from? There isn't any."

They sighed. All of them, those who had left Central Russia long ago, some even voluntarily, as well as the ones who had never even been there, all now had a vision of that country, unassuming, temperate, unscorched by the sun, seen through a haze of thin sunlit rain, or in the spring floods with the muddy fields and forest roads, a quiet land where the simple forest tree is so useful and necessary to man. The people who live in those parts do not always appreciate their home; they yearn for bright blue seas and banana groves. But no, this is what man really needs: the hideous black growth on the bright birch tree, its sickness, its tumor.

Only Mursalimov and Egenberdiev thought to themselves that here too, in the plains and on the hills, there was bound to be just what they needed; because man is provided with all he needs in every corner of the earth, he only has to know where to look.

"We'll have to ask someone to collect it and send it," the geologist said to Dyomka. He seemed attracted by the idea of the *chaga.*

Kostoglotov himself, the discoverer and expounder of it all, had no one in Russia he could ask to look for the fungus. The people he knew were either already dead or scattered about the country, or he'd have felt awkward about approaching them, others were complete cityites who'd never be able to find the right birch tree, let alone the *chaga* on it. He could not imagine any greater joy than to go away into the woods for months on end, to break off this *chaga,* crumble it, boil it up on a campfire, drink it and get well like an animal. To walk through the forest for months, to know no other care than to get better! Just as a dog goes to search for some mysterious grass that will save him.

But the way to Russia was forbidden to him.

The other people there, to whom it was open, had not learned the wisdom of making sacrifices, the skill of shaking off inessentials. They saw obstacles where there were none. How could they get sick leave or a holiday, to go off on a search? How could they suddenly disrupt their lives and leave their families? Where were they to get the money from? What clothes should they wear for such a journey, and what should they take with them? What station should they get off at, and where should they go then to find out more about it?

Kostoglotov tapped his letter and went on, "He says here there are people who call themselves suppliers, ordinary enterprising people who gather the *chaga,* dry it and send it to you cash on delivery. But they charge a lot, fifteen roubles a kilogram, and you need six kilograms a month."

"What right do they have to do that?" said Pavel Nikolayevich indignantly. His face became sternly authoritative, enough to scare any "supplier" who came before him or even make him mess his pants. "What sort of a conscience do they have, fleecing people for something that nature provides free?"

"Don't shouth!" Yefrem hissed at him. (His way of distorting words was particularly unpleasant. It was impossible to tell whether he did it on purpose or because his tongue could not cope with them.) "D'you think you can just go into the woods and get it? You have to walk about in the forest with a sack and an ax. And in the winter you need skis."

"But not fifteen roubles a kilogram, black marketeers, damn them!" Rusanov simply could not compromise on such a matter. Again the red patches began to appear on his face.

It was wholly a question of principle. Over the years Rusanov had become more and more unshakably convinced that all our mistakes, shortcomings, imperfections and inadequacies were the result of speculation. Scallions, radishes and flowers were sold on the street by dubious types, milk and eggs were sold by peasant women in the market, and yoghurt, woolen socks, even fried fish at the railway stations. There was large-scale speculation too. Trucks were being driven off "on the side" from state warehouses. If these two kinds of speculation could be torn up by the roots, everything in our country could be put right quickly and our successes would be even more striking. There was nothing wrong in a man strengthening his material position with the help of a good salary from the state and a good pension (Pavel Nikolayevich's dream was to be awarded a special, personal pension). Such a man had earned his car, his cottage in the country, and a small house in town to himself. But a car of the same make from the same factory, or a country cottage of the same standard type, acquired a completely different, criminal character if they had been bought through speculation. Pavel Nikolayevich dreamed, literally *dreamed,* of introducing public executions for speculators. Public executions would speedily bring complete health to our society.

"All right, then." Yefrem was angry too. "Stop shouthing and go and organize the supply yourself. A state supply if you like. Or through a coop. If fifteen roubles is too much for you, don't buy it."

Rusanov realized this was his weak spot. He hated speculators, but his tumor would not wait for the new medicine to be approved by the Academy of Medical Science or for the Central Russian cooperatives to organize a constant supply of it.

The voiceless newcomer, who with his notebook looked like a reporter from an influential newspaper, almost climbed onto Kostoglotov's bed. He spoke insistently and hoarsely, "The address of the suppliers? Is the address of the suppliers in the letter?"

Pavel Nikolayevich too got ready to write down the address.

But for some reason Kostoglotov didn't reply. Whether there was an address in the letter or not, he just didn't answer. Instead he got down from the window sill and began to rummage under the bed for his boots. In defiance of all hospital rules he kept them hidden there for taking walks.

Dyomka hid the prescription in his bedside table. Without trying to learn more, he began to lay his leg very carefully on the bed. He didn't and couldn't have that sort of money.

Yes, the birch tree helped, but it didn't help everyone.

Rusanov was really quite embarrassed. He had just had a skirmish with Bone-chewer, not for the first time in the three days, either, and was now patently interested in his story and dependent on him for the address. Thinking he ought to butter Bone-chewer up a bit, he started, unintentionally and involuntarily, as it were, on something that united them, and said with a good deal of sincerity, "Yes, what on earth can one imagine worse than this . . ." (this cancer? He hadn't got cancer!) ". . . than this . . . oncological . . . in fact, cancer?"

But Kostoglotov wasn't in the least touched by this mark of trust coming from someone so much older, senior in rank and more experienced than he was. Wrapping round his leg a rust-colored puttee that he'd just been drying, and pulling on a disgusting, dilapidated rubber-cloth kneeboot with coarse patches on the creases, he barked, "What's worse than cancer? Leprosy."

The loud, heavy, threatening word resounded through the room like a salvo.

Pavel Nikolayevich grimaced, peaceably enough. "Well, it depends. Is it really worse? Leprosy is a much slower process."

Kostoglotov stared with a dark and unfriendly expression into Pavel Nikolayevich's bright glasses and the bright eyes beyond them.

"It's worse because they banish you from the world while you are still alive. They tear you from your family and put you behind barbed wire. You think that's any easier to take than a tumor?"

Pavel Nikolayevich felt quite uneasy: the dark, burning glance of this rough, indecent man was so close to him, and he was quite defenseless.

"Well, what I mean is, all these damn diseases . . ."

Any educated man would have seen at this point that it was time to make a conciliatory gesture, but Bone-chewer couldn't understand this. He couldn't appreciate Pavel Nikolayevich's tact. He rose to his full, lanky height and put on a roomy, dirty gray fustian woman's dressing gown that reached down almost to his boots (it served him as an overcoat when he went for walks). Then he announced in his self-satisfied way, thinking how learned he sounded, "A certain philosopher once said, if a man never became ill he would never get to know his own limitations."

Taking a rolled-up army belt, four fingers wide with a five-pointed star on the buckle, from the pocket of the woman's dressing gown he'd wrapped himself in, he put it round himself, only taking care not to tie it too tight in the place where his tumor was. Chewing a wretched, cheap little cigarette end, the sort that goes out before it's all smoked, he walked to the door.

The interviewer with the wheezing throat retreated before Kostoglotov along the passageway between the beds. Still looking like some sort of banker or minister, he nevertheless kept begging Kostoglotov to answer him, deferring to him as if he were some bright star of oncological science who was about to leave the building forever. "Tell me, roughly, in what percentage of cases does a tumor of the throat turn out to be cancer?"

It is disgraceful to make fun of illness or grief, but even illness and grief must be borne without lapsing into the ridiculous. Kostoglotov looked at the lost, terrified face of the man who had been flitting round the ward so absurdly. He had probably been rather domineering before he got his tumor. Even the understandable habit of holding the throat with the fingers while speaking seemed somehow funny when he did it.

"Thirty-four," said Kostoglotov. He smiled at him and stood aside.

Hadn't he done too much cackling himself today? Hadn't he perhaps said too much, said something he shouldn't have?

But the restless interviewer would not leave him. He hurried down the stairs after him, bending his portly frame forward, still talking and wheezing over Kostoglotov's shoulder: "What do you think, comrade? If any tumor doesn't hurt, is it a good or a bad sign? What does it show?"

Tiresome, defenseless people.

"What do you do?" Kostoglotov stopped and asked him.

"I'm a lecturer." A big-eared man with gray, sleek hair, he looked at Kostoglotov hopefully, as at a doctor.

"Lecturer in what? What subject?"

"Philosophy," replied the bank manager, remembering his former self and regaining some of his bearing. Although he had shown a wry face all day, he had forgiven Kostoglotov his misplaced and clumsy quotations from the philosophers of the past. He wouldn't reproach him, he needed the suppliers' addresses.

"A lecturer, and it's your throat!" Kostoglotov shook his head from side to side. He had no regrets about not giving the suppliers' addresses out loud in the ward. By the standards of the community that for seven years had dragged him along like a slab of metal through a wire-drawing machine, only a stupid sucker would do a thing like that. Everyone would rush off and write to these suppliers, the prices would be inflated, and he wouldn't get his *chaga*. It was his duty, though, to tell a few decent people one by one. He'd already made up his mind to tell the geologist, even though they'd exchanged no more than ten words, because he liked the look of him and the way he'd spoken up in defense of cemeteries. And he'd tell Dyomka, except that Dyomka didn't have any money. (In fact Oleg didn't have any either, there was nothing for him to buy the *chaga* with.) And he would give it to Federau, Ni, Sibgatov, his friends in distress.* They would all have to ask him one by one, though, and anyone who didn't ask would be left out. But this philosophy lecturer struck Oleg as a foolish fellow. What did he churn out in his lectures anyway? Perhaps he was just clouding people's brains? And what was the point of all his philosophy if he was so completely helpless in the face of his illness? . . . But what a coincidence—in the throat, of all places!

"Write down the suppliers' addresses," Kostoglotov commanded. "But it's only for you!" The philosopher, in grateful haste, bent down to write.

After he had dictated it, Oleg managed to tear himself away. He hurried to fit in his walk before they locked the outer door.

There was no one outside on the porch.

Oleg breathed in the cold, damp, still air happily, then, before it had time to cleanse him, he lit up a cigarette. Whatever happened, his happiness could never be complete without a cigarette (though Dontsova was not the only one now to have warned him to stop smoking; Maslennikov too had found room to mention it in his letter).

There was no wind or frost. Reflected in a windowpane he could see a nearby puddle. There was no ice on its black water. It was only the fifth of February and already it was spring. He wasn't used to it. The fog wasn't fog: more a light prickly mist that hung in the air, so light that it did not cloud but merely softened and blurred the distant lights of street lamps and windows.

On Oleg's left, four pyramidal poplars towered high above the roof like four brothers. On the other side a poplar stood on its own,

*They all belonged to deported nationalities and were exiles like Kostoglotov.

but bushy and the same height as the other four. Behind it there was a thick group of trees in a wedge of parkland.

From the unfenced stone porch of Wing 13 a few steps led down to a sloping asphalt pathway lined on both sides by an impenetrable hedge. It was leafless for the moment, but its thickness announced that it was alive.

Oleg had come out for a stroll along the pathways in the park, his leg, with each step and stretch, rejoicing at being able to walk firmly, at being the living leg of a man who had not died. But the view from the porch held him back, and he finished his cigarette there.

There was a soft light from the occasional lamps and windows of the wings opposite. By now there was hardly anyone walking along the paths. And when there was no rumble from the railway close by at the back, you could just hear the faint, even sound of the river, a fast-foaming mountain stream which rushed down behind the nearby wings, under the side of the hill.

Further on, beyond the hill and across the river, there was another park, the municipal one, and perhaps it was from there (except that it was cold) or from the open windows of a club that he could hear dance music being played by a brass band. It was Saturday and there they were dancing. Couples were dancing together . . .

Oleg was excited by all his talking and the way they'd listened to him. He was seized and enveloped by a feeling that life had suddenly returned, the life with which just two weeks ago he had closed all accounts. Though this life promised him nothing that the people of this great town called good and struggled to acquire: neither apartment, property, social success nor money, there were other joys, sufficient in themselves, which he had not forgotten how to value: the right to move about without waiting for an order; the right to be alone; the right to gaze at stars that were not blinded by prison-camp searchlights; the right to put the light out at night and sleep in the dark; the right to put letters in a letterbox; the right to rest on Sunday; the right to bathe in the river. Yes, there were many, many more rights like these.

And among them was the right to talk to women.

His recovery was giving him back all these countless, wonderful rights.

The music from the park just reached him. Oleg heard it—not the actual tune they were playing, but as if it were Tchaikovsky's

Fourth Symphony, its restless strained beginning ringing inside him, one incomparable melody. It was the melody (Oleg interpreted it in his own way, although perhaps it ought to be understood differently) in which the hero is returned to life or perhaps regaining his vision after being blind. He gropes with his fingers, as it were, slides his hand over things or over a face that is dear to him, touching them, still afraid to believe his good fortune: that these things really exist, that his eyes are beginning to see.

12. Passions Return ...

As she dressed hurriedly for work on Sunday morning, Zoya remembered that Kostoglotov had asked her to be sure to wear her gray-and-gold dress next time she was on duty. He'd seen the collar peeping out from underneath her white coat that evening, and he wanted to see it in the daylight. It is always pleasant to fulfill unselfish requests. The dress suited her very well today. It was almost a party dress. In the afternoon she hoped she wouldn't have much to do, and expected Kostoglotov to come and entertain her.

She did a quick change and put on the dress he had asked for. She rubbed it a few times with the palms of her hands to perfume it and combed out her bangs. Time was pressing. She pulled on her overcoat in the doorway, and her grandmother only just had time to slip some lunch into her pocket before she left.

It was a dampish, chilly morning, but not wintry. People would be wearing raincoats on a day like that back in Central Russia, but here in the south people have different ideas of hot and cold. They wear woolen suits in the heat and like to put on their overcoats at the first possible moment and take them off at the last. Those with fur coats spend the winter pining for the few days of frost.

Zoya spotted her trolley as soon as she was out of the gate. She chased it the whole length of the block and was the last to jump in. Flushed and panting, she stood on the rear platform to get some fresh air. The municipal trolleys were all slow and noisy. They screeched hysterically against the rails at every bend. None of them had automatic doors.

The breathlessness, tightness even, that she felt in her chest were pleasant sensations for a young body, because they disappeared almost immediately, thus increasing her feeling of well-being and her holiday mood.

While her medical school was closed for the holidays she found working at the clinic only—three and a half duty sessions a week— very easy, like a rest. Naturally it would have been even easier without the duty sessions, but Zoya had already grown used to the double burden. This was the second year she'd spent working and studying at the same time. Her work in the clinic gave her very little medical experience, but it was the money she was working for, not the experience; her grandmother's pension wasn't enough to buy bread with, her own grant was spent as soon as it came, her father never sent her anything at all, and Zoya never asked him to. She had no wish to be under an obligation to a father like that.

The first two days of the holidays, following her last night duty, Zoya had not spent lolling in bed. She hadn't done that sort of thing since her childhood. First of all she'd sat down to make herself a spring blouse out of some crêpe she had bought in December after she had been paid. (Her grandmother always said to her, "Get the sleigh ready in summer and the cart ready in winter," and the proverb was quite right. The best summer things were only in the shops during winter.) She was making it on her grandmother's old Singer (they'd lugged it with them all the way from Smolensk). It was her grandmother, too, who had first taught her to sew, but her methods were old-fashioned, and Zoya's alert eye was quick to pick things up from neighbors, friends and girls who'd done courses in dressmaking. Zoya had no spare time for them. Two days had not been enough for her to finish the blouse, but she had managed to go round several dry-cleaning shops and had found one that would do her old summer coat. She'd also gone to the market to get potatoes and vegetables, and bargained there like a fishwife, finally bringing back two heavy bags, one in each hand. (Her grandmother could cope with the lines in shops, but she couldn't carry anything heavy.) Then she'd gone to the public bath. In fact there hadn't been a moment to lie down and read a book. Yesterday evening she'd gone with Rita, who was in her year at medical school, to a dance at the House of Culture.

Zoya would have preferred something a bit fresher and more wholesome than these clubs, but there were no houses or parties where you could meet young men, only the clubs. In their year and in their faculty there were plenty of Russian girls, but hardly any boys. This was why she didn't like going to the medical school parties.

The House of Culture, where she and Rita had gone, was spacious, clean and well-heated. It had marble columns, a marble staircase and very tall mirrors with bronze frames. You could see yourself in them from a long way off on the dance floor. There were some very expensive, comfortable armchairs too, only they were kept under covers and you weren't allowed to sit in them. Zoya had not been there since New Year's Eve, when she'd suffered a very humiliating experience. It had been a fancy-dress ball with prizes for the best costumes, and Zoya had made herself a monkey costume with a gorgeous tail. Every detail had been carefully thought out—her hair-do, her light make-up, her color combinations. The result was both attractive and amusing, and the first prize was almost in the bag, even though there was a lot of competition. But just before the prizes were awarded, some toughs cut off her tail with a knife, passed it from hand to hand and hid it. Zoya burst into tears, not because of the boys' stupidity but because everyone round her laughed and said what a clever prank it was. The costume wasn't nearly so effective without the tail. Zoya's face became blotchy with tears, and she didn't win a prize at all.

Yesterday evening she'd gone in there still feeling angry with the club. Her pride had been hurt. But nothing and no one reminded her of the episode of the monkey. There were all kinds of people, students from different colleges and boys from the factories. Zoya and Rita did not have time to dance a single dance together. They were separated from the start, and for three glorious hours they whirled, swung and stamped nonstop to the music of the brass band. Her body reveled in the relaxing twists and turns of the dance, and in the uncensured, public squeezing and cuddling that was its main pleasure. Her partners didn't speak much, and when they did crack jokes Zoya found them a bit silly. Finally Kolya, a technical designer, took her home. On the way they talked about Indian movies and swimming: they'd have thought it ridiculous to talk about anything serious. When they reached the front door of her home, where it was quite dark, they started kissing. It was Zoya's breasts that suffered most. They had never failed to excite young men. And how he mauled them! He tried to find other ways to get at her too. Zoya enjoyed it, but at the same time a detached feeling grew on her that it was a bit of a waste of time. She had to get up early on Sundays too. So she packed him off and scampered up the old stairs.

Most of Zoya's girl friends, especially the medical students, believed that everything possible should be grabbed from life immediately and with both hands. In the face of this prevailing philosophy it was absolutely impossible to survive the first, second and third years as a sort of old maid with an excellent knowledge of theory and nothing more. Zoya had been through it all. Several times with different young men she had passed through the various stages of intimacy, gradually permitting more and more, then capture and finally domination. She had experienced the overwhelming moments, when a bomb might have dropped on the house without making any difference, as well as the calm and sluggish moments when pieces of clothing are picked up from the floor or the chair where they've been thrown—garments which otherwise should never be seen together. Yet they both looked at them, and by now there was nothing at all surprising in it, or in putting hers on in front of him.

Indeed all this was a strong sensation, and by her third year Zoya was well out of the "old maid" category. Still, it was never the real thing. It all lacked that stable, deliberate continuity which gives stability to life, indeed gives life itself.

Zoya was only twenty-three, but she had seen and could remember quite a lot: the long, frenzied evacuation of Smolensk, first in a freight car, then in a barge, then in another freight car. For some reason she remembered particularly the man next to her in the car taking a little piece of string to measure everyone's strip on the plank bed and proving that Zoya's family was taking up two centimeters more than it should. She remembered the hungry, tense life of the war years, when people spoke of nothing but ration cards and prices on the black market, when Uncle Fedya would steal her bread ration from her bedside table. And now there was this malignant suffering from cancer, these lost lives, these wearisome stories from the patients, and their tears.

Compared to all this, the squeezing, hugging and the rest were no more than drops of fresh water in the salt sea of life. But there were never enough to quench the thirst.

Did this mean that marriage was the only alternative, that that was where happiness lay? The young men she met all danced and went for walks with the same aim in mind: to warm themselves up a bit, have their fun and then clear out. They used to say among themselves, "I could get married, but it never takes me more than an evening or two to find a new 'friend,' so why should I bother?"

Indeed, why marry when women were so easy to get? If a great load of tomatoes suddenly arrived in the market, you couldn't just triple the price of yours, they'd rot. How could you be inaccessible when everyone around you was ready to surrender?

A registry office wedding didn't help either. Zoya had learned this from the experience of Maria, a Ukrainian nurse she did alternate shifts with. Maria had relied on the registry office, but a week after the marriage her husband left her, went away and completely disappeared. For seven years she'd brought up her child on her own, and to top it all, she was trapped by her marriage.

When Zoya went to parties and drank wine, and if her unsafe days were coming up, she was as alert as a sapper walking through a minefield.

Zoya had another example, even closer to her than Maria's. She had seen the rotten lives of her own father and mother. She'd watched them quarreling and making up, separating to live in different towns and then coming together again, tormenting each other all their lives. Zoya would sooner have drunk a glass of sulphuric acid than repeat her mother's mistake.

Theirs was yet another example of a registry office marriage turning out worse than useless.

Zoya felt a certain balance and harmony in her body, in the relation of each part of it to the rest, and in her temperament and her outlook on life. Any extension or broadening of her life could only take place within that harmony.

Any man who, in the intervals between sliding his hands over her body, said silly, vulgar things or repeated bits from a film script, as Kolya had done last night, immediately destroyed the harmony, and there was no chance whatever of Zoya really falling for him.

Jolted to and fro by the movement of the trolley, Zoya stood on the rear platform while the conductress railed at a young man who hadn't bought a ticket (he just stood there listening to her, he still wouldn't buy one). She stayed there till the car reached the terminus. Then it began to turn round. On the other side of the turntable a waiting crowd had already gathered. The young man the conductress

had scolded jumped down while the trolley was still moving, followed by a young boy, and Zoya, too, jumped smartly from the
moving car. It made it less far to walk.

It was one minute past eight. Zoya broke into a run along the
winding asphalt path of the medical center. As a nurse she was not
supposed to run, but in a student it was forgivable.

By the time she'd reached the cancer wing, taken off her overcoat, put on her white coverall and run upstairs it was already ten
past eight, and things might have been awkward for her if Olympiada Vladislavovna or Maria had been on duty. Maria would have
scolded her for being ten minutes late as severely as if she'd missed
half the shift. But luckily it was the student Turgun who was on.
Turgun was a Karakalpak,* and always indulgent, especially toward
her. He tried to punish her by smacking her bottom, but she wouldn't
let him, and they both laughed as she pushed him away toward the
staircase.

He was still a student, but because he was a Karakalpak he had
already been appointed senior doctor of a village hospital in that
area. In fact, these were his last few months of irresponsible freedom.

Turgun gave Zoya the treatment book. They also had a special
task assigned to them by Mita, the matron. On Sundays there were
no rounds, treatments were cut short, and there were no post-trans-
fusion patients. Instead there was the added worry of having to see
that relatives did not slip into the wards without the duty doctor's
permission, but in spite of this Mita usually reallocated to whoever
was on day duty on Sunday some of the endless statistical work that
she could not manage to complete herself.

Today the task was to go through a thick stack of patients' cards
from December of the previous year, 1954. Pouting her lips almost
into a whistle, and snapping the corners of the cards, Zoya flicked
through the pile. She was working out how many there were and
whether there'd be any time left over to do a bit of embroidery,
when she sensed a tall shadow beside her. Not in the least surprised,
she turned her head (heads can be turned in all sorts of different
ways) and saw Kostoglotov. Clean-shaven, his hair almost tidy, only
the scar on his chin reminded her as always that he had been a cutthroat.

"Good morning, Zoyenka," he said, the perfect gentleman.

*A Turkic people who live in Central Asia.

"Good morning." She shook her head, as if dissatisfied or doubtful about something, but in fact for no reason at all.

His great dark brown eyes looked at her.

"I can't see, did you do what I asked you?"

"What was that?" Zoya frowned in surprise. (It was an old trick and it always worked.)

"Don't you remember? I made a bet with myself about it."

"You borrowed my *Pathological Anatomy*. I remember that all right."

"Oh yes, I'll give it back to you in a minute. Thank you."

"How did you get on with it?"

"I think I found out what I wanted to know."

"Have I done you any harm?" Zoya asked, quite seriously this time. "I wished afterwards I'd never given it to you."

"No, Zoyenka." He touched her arm lightly to emphasize his point. "On the contrary, the book cheered me up. It was golden good of you to give it to me. But"—he looked at her neck—"could you undo the top button of your coat?"

"Whatever for?" said Zoya in astonishment (that clever trick again). "I'm not hot."

"You are. You've gone quite red."

"So I have." She laughed good-naturedly. In fact she did feel like taking her coat off because she still hadn't got her breath back after running so fast and her tussle with Turgun. So she opened the neck.

The little gold threads shone through the gray.

Kostoglotov widened his eyes, looked at her and said almost in a whisper, "That's fine. Thank you. You'll show me more of it later on, won't you?"

"Depends on what your bet is."

"I'll let you know, but later, all right? We'll have some time together today, won't we?"

Zoya rolled her eyes like a doll. "Only if you come and give me a hand. I look red because I've got so much work today."

"Not me, not if it means sticking needles into living bodies."

"What if it's medical statistics? They won't break your back, will they?"

"I have great respect for statistics, so long as they're not secret."

"Well, come along after breakfast." Zoya threw him a smile. She thought she ought to give him something in advance for his help.

They were already taking breakfast round the wards.

Last Friday morning when the day nurse came on, Zoya had been interested enough in the night's conversation to go along to the admissions register and look up Kostoglotov's record card.

It turned out his name was Oleg Filimonovich (this rather heavy patronymic was a good match for such an unpleasant-sounding last name, although his first name did something to tone the others down). He was born in 1920, and in spite of his thirty-four years was in fact unmarried, which seemed rather improbable. And he *had* lived in a place called Ush-Terek. He had no relatives whatever (in the cancer clinic there was a rule that every patient's close relatives must be listed). He was a topographer by profession but had worked as a land surveyor.

None of this shed any light on the man, it only made things more mysterious.

Then today she'd read in the treatment book that from Friday he was to receive daily intramuscular injections of Sinestrol, two cc.'s. It was the night nurse's job to give it, which meant it wouldn't be hers today. Still, the idea made Zoya twitch her pouting lips like a hedgehog.

After breakfast Kostoglotov arrived with the textbook on pathological anatomy, all ready to help. But just at that moment, Zoya was running in and out of the wards doling out medicines that had to be drunk or swallowed three or four times a day.

At last they sat down at her little table. Zoya produced a large sheet of paper for the rough of the graph. All the information had to be transferred to it by making pen strokes in different columns. She began to explain how it should be done (she'd already forgotten some of it herself) and to draw lines on the paper with a big heavy ruler.

Zoya knew just how useful these "helpers" usually were, these youngsters and unmarried men (married ones, too, sometimes). Their "help" invariably degenerated into giggles, jokes, flirting and mistakes in the register. Zoya was prepared to put up with the mistakes, because even the most unoriginal flirting was infinitely more interesting than the most impressive register. Zoya had no objection to continuing today a game that brightened her duty hours.

Consequently she was quite amazed when Kostoglotov immediately stopped ogling her, dropped his special tone of voice and quickly cottoned on to what was to be done. He even explained some of it back to her. He plunged into the cards, reading out the data on each one while she made pen marks in the columns of the big register.

"Neuroblastoma . . ." he dictated, ". . . hypernephroma . . . sarcoma of the nasal cavity . . . tumor of the spinal medulla . . ." He made a point of asking about everything he did not understand.

They were supposed to count the number of tumors of each type occurring during the time covered by the register, with separate categories for men and women and for each decade of their life, and to list the various types of treatment used and their volume. Then for each category they had to record the five possible results: complete cure, improvement, no change, deterioration or death. Zoya's helper took special note of these five possibilities. He immediately noticed that there were hardly any complete cures; there weren't very many deaths either, though.

"I see they don't allow them to die here. They manage to discharge them in time," said Kostoglotov.

"What else can they do, Oleg? Judge for yourself." (She called him Oleg as a reward for his help. He noticed it and glanced at her.) "If it's obvious a patient is beyond help, and there's nothing left for him but to live out a few last weeks or months, why should he take up a bed? There's a waiting list for beds. People could be cured are being kept waiting. And the irremediable cases . . ."

"The irre- . . . what?"

"The ones we can't cure. The way they look and the way they talk has a very bad effect on those we can cure."

By sitting down at the nurses' table Oleg seemed to have taken a step forward in his social position and his general grasp of things. His other self, the one past help, for whom it hadn't been worth keeping a bed, one of the "irremediables"—Kostoglotov had left it all behind. It was a jump from one status to another, quite undeserved, through some whim of unexpected circumstance. It all reminded him dimly of something else, but it was a line of thought he decided for the moment not to pursue.

"Yes, I suppose it's logical. Well, they've written off Azovkin, and yesterday I was there when they discharged Proshka without a word of explanation, just like that. I even got the feeling I was part of the deception."

As he sat now, the side of his face with the scar was turned away from Zoya, and his face had lost that cruel look.

They worked on amicably and harmoniously, and by lunchtime everything was finished.

But there was another job Mita had left to be done. The laboratory analyses had to be copied on to the patients' temperature charts. This would mean there would be fewer sheets of paper in the case-history books and it would be easier to stick them in. But it was too much if she wanted them done in a single Sunday.

"Thank you," said Zoya, "thank you very much, Oleg Filimonovich."

"Oh no! Please! Call me what you did before. Call me Oleg!"

"Now you must have a rest after lunch . . ."

"I never have rests."

"You *are* ill, you know."

"It's a funny thing, Zoya. As soon as you climb those stairs and come on duty, I'm back in the best of health."

"All right then." Zoya gave in easily (she would rather be with him really). "This time I'll receive you in the drawing room."

She nodded her head toward the doctors' conference room.

After lunch she had to take round the medicines again, and then there were some urgent matters to be seen to in the large women's ward. Zoya was aware of how clean and healthy she was, down to the last pore of skin and the tiniest toenail—in contrast to the decline and disease that surrounded her. She sensed with joy her twin, tightly supported breasts, their weight as she leaned across the patients' beds and their tremor when she walked quickly.

At last the pressure of work eased. Zoya asked an orderly to sit at the table, to admit no visitors to the wards, and to call her if anything happened. She took her embroidery, and Oleg followed her into the doctors' room.

It was a bright corner room with three windows. No one could call the furnishings particularly lavish. The hand of the accountant of the senior doctor could be seen everywhere. There were two upright sofas, not in the collapsible style but strictly in accordance with official taste. They were straight-backed enough to give you a crick in the neck, and the built-in mirrors in the backs were so high that only a giraffe could have seen its face in them. The tables were arranged in the usual depressing institutional way: the huge chairman's writing table, covered with thick plate glass, then, at an angle to it, the long narrow table where people sat during meetings, the two together forming the inevitable letter T. The second table was covered *à la* Samarkand with a cloth of sky-blue plush which brightened the room with a splash of color. There were also some small, comfortable armchairs standing apart from the table in a little random group. These too added a pleasant touch.

There was nothing to remind one that this was a hospital except for a newsletter, *The Oncologist,* pinned to the wall. It was dated November 7.*

Zoya and Oleg sat down in the soft comfortable armchairs in the brightest part of the room. Some flowerpots with agaves in them were standing on pedestals, while beyond the great glass pane of the main window an oak tree spread its branches and strained upward to the next floor.

Oleg did not merely sit. He savored the comfort of the chair with his whole body, its curves fitting his back, his head and neck reclining at ease.

"What luxury!" he said. "I haven't put my weight on anything like this for, oh, fifteen years."

(If he likes the chair so much, why doesn't he go out and buy himself one?)

"Now then, what was your bet?" Zoya asked, with the tilt of the head and expression in the eyes that goes with such questions.

They were now alone in the room, sitting in the chairs with one sole aim in view—to talk together. What turn the conversation took would depend on a word, a tone, a look. Was it going to be just chit-chat, or the kind of conversation that delves right to the heart of things? Zoya was quite prepared for the former, but she had come with the feeling it would be the latter.

Oleg did not let her down. He spoke solemnly, without lifting his head from the back of the chair, directing his voice over her head towards the window.

"I have made a bet about whether or not a certain girl with golden bangs is going to join us in the virgin lands."

Then he looked straight at her—for the first time.

Zoya bore his gaze.

"What will happen to the girl out there?"

Oleg sighed. "I've told you. Nothing particularly cheerful. There's no running water. We heat the iron on charcoal, run the lamps off paraffin. When it's wet, there's nothing but mud. When it's dry

---

*The anniversary of the 1917 Revolution.

there's nothing but dust. There's never any chance to wear nice clothes."

He omitted no unpleasant detail. It was as though he was trying to make it impossible for her to say yes. After all, what sort of life is it if you can never dress decently? But Zoya knew that, however comfortably you can live in a big town, it isn't the town you live with. She would rather understand the man than visualize his village.

"I don't understand what keeps you there."

Oleg laughed. "The Ministry of the Interior, what else?"

He was still lying back enjoying himself, his head resting on the back of the chair. Zoya frowned. "I thought so. But you aren't a Chechen, are you, or a Kalmuck?"

"Oh no, I'm a hundred per cent Russian. Aren't I allowed to have dark hair?" He smoothed it down.

Zoya shrugged her shoulders. "Then why did they send you there?"

Oleg sighed. "Really, modern youth is so uninformed. Where I was brought up we knew nothing about the Penal Code, all those paragraphs, clauses and their extended interpretations. But you, living right in the middle of this district, haven't you even grasped the elementary difference between an exiled settler and an administrative exile?"

"What is the difference?"

"I'm an administrative exile. I wasn't exiled because of my nationality,* I was exiled *personally,* as me, Oleg Filimonovich Kostoglotov. Do you see?" He laughed. "It's like an individual being made an honorary citizen, except that I'm not even allowed to live with honorable citizens."

His dark eyes flashed at her.

But she wasn't frightened. Or, rather, she was a little afraid, but somehow she knew it wouldn't last.

"And . . . how long were you exiled for?" she asked gently.

"In perpetuity." The words seemed to ring out. They tolled like a bell in her ears.

---

*A number of small nationalities—Volga Germans, Chechens, Kalmucks and others—were deported to Central Asia *en masse* during and after the war, suspected of collaborating with the Nazis. These were called "exiled settlers." "Administrative exiles," like Kostoglotov, were usually political prisoners who had served their term in a labor camp but still had to live in a remote region of the country.

"You mean a life sentence?" she asked again, half-whispering.

"No. *In perpetuity,*" Kostoglotov insisted. "Those were the words used on the documents. If it was a life sentence, well, I suppose my coffin could be brought back home to Russia, but since it's perpetual, it means even that won't be allowed back. I won't be allowed back even after the sun goes out. Perpetuity is longer."

Only now did her heart contract. Now she understood, that scar of his, the cruel look he sometimes had. He might be a murderer, some terrifying monster who would strangle her at the slightest provocation.

But Zoya did not turn her chair to make it easier to run away. She just put her embroidery to one side (she hadn't even started on it) and looked boldly at Kostoglotov, who was sitting calm and relaxed in the armchair as comfortably as before. It was she who was excited as she asked him, "Don't tell me if it's difficult to. But if you can, do. Why were you given such a terrible sentence?"

Kostoglotov seemed not a bit shattered by the recollection of his crime. There was even a carefree smile on his face as he answered her. "Zoyenka, there *was* no sentence. I was exiled perpetually 'by order.' "

"By . . . order?"

"Yes, that's what it's called. Something like an invoice. Like when they write a list of goods to be sent from a wholesale to a retail store: so many sacks, so many barrels . . ."

Zoya put her head in her hands. "Wait a minute . . . I understand now. But . . . is it possible? Were you . . . ? Was everyone . . . ?"

"No, one can't say everyone. The people charged under paragraph ten alone weren't exiled; it was only those charged under paragraphs ten and eleven."*

"What's paragraph eleven?"

"Paragraph eleven?" Kostoglotov thought for a moment. "Zoyenka, I seem to be telling you a great deal. You must be careful what you do with this stuff or you might get into trouble yourself. My basic sentence was seven years in the labor camp, according to paragraph ten—and, believe me, anyone who got less than eight years had done nothing: the accusations were based on thin air. But then there was paragraph eleven, which applies to 'group' activity.

*The reference is to Article 58 of the Soviet Penal Code, as it stood until 1959. Paragraph ten dealt with individual "anti-Soviet agitation," paragraph eleven with "group" agitation.

Paragraph eleven by itself doesn't prolong the term in the camp, but because we were a group we were all *exiled perpetually,* scattered in different places, to stop us meeting together again in the old place. Do you understand now?"

No, she still didn't understand a thing.

"So you were a member of what they call"—she tried to find a milder word for it—"a gang?"

Kostoglotov burst into peals of laughter, stopped and just as suddenly frowned.

"It's wonderful, you're just like my interrogator, you can't be content with the word 'group.' He liked to call us a 'gang' too. Yes, we were a gang of students, boys and girls in our first year." He looked at her threateningly. "I know smoking's forbidden here and regarded as a crime, but I am still going to smoke, all right? We used to meet, flirt with the girls, dance, and the boys used to talk about politics. And sometimes we talked about . . . about *him*! Well, you know, there were some things we were dissatisfied with. We weren't, so to speak, ecstatic about everything. Two of us had fought in the war, and afterwards we expected things to be different somehow. In May, before the exams, they pulled the lot of us in, including the girls."

Zoya was panic-stricken. She picked up her embroidery. On the one hand he was saying dangerous things, things it was wrong to repeat or even listen to: her ears ought to be closed to such stuff. On the other hand it was an enormous relief to hear that he'd never lured anyone into dark backstreets and murdered him.

She swallowed. "I don't understand. . . . What was it you actually *did*?"

"What did we do?" He drew on his cigarette and blew out the smoke. What a big man he was, and how tiny the cigarette looked! "I told you, we were students. If our grants allowed it, we drank wine. We went to parties. And you know, they arrested the girls as well. They all got five years." He looked at her intently. "Imagine it happening to you, being taken away just before your second semester's exams and put in a dungeon."

Zoya put down her embroidery.

All the horrors she'd dreaded he was going to divulge had turned out not to be horrors at all. They were almost childish.

"But you boys, why did you have to do it?"

"What do you mean?" Oleg was at a loss.

"Well, why be dissatisfied, why expect anything?"

"Well, really!" Oleg laughed resignedly. "Well, really! I'd never have imagined it possible. Zoyenka, my interrogator said that too. He used exactly those words. Isn't this a lovely little armchair? Sitting up in bed isn't nearly as comfortable as this."

Once more Oleg arranged himself in the chair for maximum comfort. He puffed at his cigarette, gazing through the single glass pane of the great window with narrowed eyes.

Twilight was approaching, but the day, dull as ever, did not get any darker. If anything it was lightening. The layers of cloud in the west, the direction in which the room faced, were parting and thinning.

Now at last Zoya managed to get down to some serious sewing. She took obvious pleasure in the stitching. They sat in silence. Oleg did not praise her for her work as he had the last time.

"What about . . . your girl? Was she one of them?" asked Zoya, without raising her head.

"Y . . . yes," said Oleg. It took some time to complete the word. He seemed to be thinking about something else.

"Where is she now?"

"Now? She's on the Yenisei River."

Zoya glanced at him quickly. "Can't you find some way of joining her?"

"I'm not even trying," he said without interest.

Zoya was watching him as he looked through the window. Why hadn't he married out there, where he lived now?

"Would it really be so difficult? I mean, to join her?" The question had only just occurred to her.

"We were never legally married, so it's practically impossible," he said, "and anyway, there's no point."

"Do you have a photo of her with you?"

"Photo?" he said in surprise. "Prisoners aren't allowed photographs. They get torn up."

"Well, tell me what she looked like."

Oleg smiled and narrowed his eyes a little. "Her hair ran straight down to her shoulders and then—whoops!—it turned up at the end. Your eyes are slightly mocking, but there was a bit of sadness in hers. Can people possibly know their future, do you think?"

"Were you together in the camp?"

"No-o."

"When did you actually leave her?"

"Five minutes before I was arrested. It was in May. We'd been sitting together in the little garden of her house. It was after one o'clock. I said goodnight to her and walked away. They grabbed me at the next block. The car had been waiting there at the corner."

"And her?"

"The next night."

"And you never saw each other again?"

"Just once. The interrogators brought us together for a 'confrontation.' They'd already shaved my head. They hoped we'd give evidence against one another. We didn't."

He was fingering his cigarette butt, not knowing what to do with it.

"Put it over there." She pointed to a shiny, clean ashtray on the table where the chairman sat during meetings.

The light clouds in the west were parting farther and had almost revealed the tender, yellow sun. Its light softened everything, even Oleg's permanently stubborn face.

"But why can't you see her now?" asked Zoya sympathetically.

"Zoya," said Oleg firmly. He paused to think. "Can you imagine what happens to a girl in a labor camp if she's at all pretty? First of all she's probably raped on the way there by some of the criminals, or, if not, they do it as soon as she arrives. Then her first evening some of the camp parasites—those damn work overseers, or else the ones who give out the rations—would have her taken naked to the bathhouse and arrange to have a look at her on the way and decide on the spot who she was to belong to. Before morning they would make her a proposition—you'll live with so-and-so, and you'll get decent work in a place that's clean and warm. Well, if she refuses, they see she gets such a rough time that she'll come crawling back, begging to live with anyone they care to name." He closed his eyes. "She didn't die, she stayed alive, she served out her term all right. I don't blame her for it, I can understand. But . . . that's all there is to it. She understands too."

They were silent for a moment. The sun came out in its full radiance and at once the whole world was cheered and brightened. In the park the trees stood out black and distinct, while in the room the tablecloth burst into blue and Zoya's hair turned to gold.

"One of our girls killed herself. Another's alive. Three of the boys are dead . . . Two others I've no idea what happened to."

He leaned sideways, tipping the chair over, and swung there, reciting:

"The hurricane swept by, few of us survived,
And many failed to answer friendship's roll call . . ."*

He sat there, leaning out of the chair and looking at the floor. His hair stood up on end and stuck out at all angles on his head. Twice a day he had to dampen it and smooth it down, dampen it and smooth it down.

He was silent, but Zoya had heard all she wanted to hear. He'd explained away all the main questions. He was chained to his exile, but not because he was a murderer. He was not married, but not because of his vices. After all these years he could still speak with tenderness of his former fiancée, and clearly he was capable of genuine feeling.

He was silent, and so was she, as she looked from the embroidery to him and back again. There was nothing in the least handsome about him, but she could find nothing ugly about him either.

In the words of her grandmother, "You don't need a handsome one, you need a good one." His stability and strength after all he had endured were what Zoya sensed in him most keenly. His strength had been put to the test. It was something she had never met before in the boys she went with.

She was stitching away when suddenly she became aware that he was scrutinizing her.

She peered at him without raising her head.

He started to speak with great expression, his eyes never leaving her face:

"Whom shall I call on? Who will share with me
The wretched happiness of staying alive?"

"You've already shared it," she whispered, smiling to him with her eyes and mouth.

Her lips were neither pink nor painted. They were somewhere between vermilion and orange, almost like fire, the color of pale flame.

The gentle, yellow, early-evening sun put new life into the un-

*These lines and the ones below are from Sergei Yesenin, perhaps the most popular Russian poet of our century.

healthy tinge of Oleg's thin ill-looking face. In its warm light it seemed he was not going to die, that he would live.

Oleg shook his head, like a guitar player who has finished a sad song and is about to begin a gay one.

"Zoyenka, make it a real holiday for me, will you? I'm fed up with these white coats. I've had enough of nurses, I want you to show me a beautiful city girl. I'll never get the chance to see one in Ush-Terek."

"Where can I find a beautiful girl for you?" said Zoya roguishly.

"Just take off that coat for a minute. And walk around."

He pushed back his chair and showed her where to walk.

"I'm on duty," she objected, "I can't, I'm not allowed to . . ."

Perhaps it was because they'd spent so long talking about gloomy subjects, or perhaps it was the setting sun throwing its cheerful, sparkling rays about the room. Whatever it was, Zoya felt a surging compulsion to do as he asked. She knew it would be all right.

She thrust her embroidery aside, leaped up out of the chair like a little girl, and started to undo her buttons. In her hurry she bent slightly forward, as though she were about to run a race rather than walk through a room.

"Pull!" She flung one of her arms at him, almost as if it were someone else's. He caught hold of it and tugged off one sleeve. "And the other!" Like a dancer she spun around and turned her back on him. He pulled off the other. The white coat fell on to his knees and she . . . walked about the room. She paraded like a model, arching her back and straightening it again just as she should, first swinging her arms as she walked, then raising them slightly.

She took a few steps like this, then turned round and froze, her arms outstretched.

Oleg held Zoya's coat to his chest almost in an embrace, and looked at her with wide-open eyes.

"Bravo!" he boomed. "Magnificent!"

There was something about the glowing blue of the tablecloth, that inexhaustible Uzbek blue exploding in the sunlight, that prolonged in him yesterday's mood of exploration and discovery. All those wayward, tangled and conventional desires were returning to him. After an age of unsettled, shabby, unsheltered existence, the soft furniture and the cozy room were a joy to him. There was joy too in being able to look at Zoya, not simply to admire her from afar. The joy was doubled because his was no indifferent admira-

tion, but one with a claim to her affection. He, who two weeks ago
had been dying!

Zoya moved her flame-colored lips triumphantly, with an expression of sly importance, as if she knew a secret but was not telling.
She walked back across the room toward the window, and again
turned to face him, holding the pose.

He did not get up. He sat there, but his head, with its thick black
mop of hair, strained forward and up to reach her.

There was a certain force about Zoya. There were signs, one
could sense but not name them. It was not the kind of force needed
to push heavy furniture, but one that demands a force in response.
Oleg was happy because he seemed able to meet its challenge and to
measure up to her force.

Now that his body was healing, the passions of life were returning to it. All of them!

"Zo-ya," said Oleg liltingly, "Zo-ya! Do you know what your
name means?"

"Zoya means life," she replied crisply, as though reciting a slogan.
She liked explaining it. She stood there, resting her hands on the
window sill behind her back, leaning a little to one side, her weight
on one leg.

"And what about the 'zo-' in it? Don't you sometimes feel close
to those 'zo-ological' ancestors of ours?"

She laughed in the same mood as he had spoken.

"We're all a little like them. We provide food, feed our young. . . .
Is there anything wrong in that?"

And that is probably where she ought to have ended the conversation. But she was excited by his steady, absorbing admiration.
It was something she'd never encountered among the young men
from the town who cuddled their girls so casually every Saturday
night at the dance. Suddenly she flung out her arms, snapped the
fingers of both hands, her whole body writhing to the urge of the
popular song she began singing from a recent Indian film.

"A-va-rai-ya-a-a! A-va-rai-ya-a-a!"

Oleg's face instantly clouded. "No, don't! Not that song, Zoya,
please!"

In a flash she assumed an air of strict decorum. No one would
have thought that a moment ago she'd been singing and writhing.

"It's from *The Tramp*," she said. "Haven't you seen it?"

"Yes, I have."

"Isn't it a wonderful movie? I saw it twice." (In fact she'd seen it four times, but she didn't quite like to admit it.) "Didn't you like it? After all, the tramp's life was rather like yours."

"It wasn't at all!" Oleg frowned. His radiant expression did not return. The warmth of the yellow sun had left him, and it was obvious what a sick man he was after all.

"I mean, he'd just come out of prison too. And his whole life was ruined."

"That was just a bluff. He was a typical grafter, a hood.*

Zoya stretched out her hand for her white coat.

Oleg got up, smoothed the coat out and helped her into it.

"I can see you don't like people like that." She nodded her thanks and began to do up her buttons.

"I hate them." He looked past her, a cruel expression on his face. His jaw tightened slightly. It was a disagreeable movement. "They're predators, parasites, they live off other people. For the last thirty years we've had it drummed into us that these people are reforming, that they're now almost our social equals, but they work on the same principle as Hitler: 'If *you're* not being'—the next word's an obscenity, it's got punch to it, but it really means—'If *you're* not being beaten, sit quiet and wait your turn.' If your neighbor's being stripped naked and you're not, sit quiet and wait your turn. They're only too happy to kick a man when he's down, and then they have the nerve to wrap themselves up in a cloak of romanticism, while we help them create a legend, and even their songs are sometimes sung on the screen."

"What legends?" Now it was she who was looking up at him, almost as if she felt guilty about something.

"It would take a hundred years to tell you. All right, if you like, I'll tell you one." They were standing at the window now, side by side. Oleg took her by the elbow. It was a dominant gesture, quite unconnected with the words he was uttering. He spoke as one would to a much younger person. "These grafters try to pretend they're noble outlaws. They don't steal from beggars and they never take away a prisoner's 'sacred staff of life,' that is to say, they don't take his basic ration, but they do pinch everything else. Well, in 1947 in

---

*"Grafter" and "hood" are approximate underworld equivalents of the Russian words *blatar* and *urka,* here applied to those prisoners who were professional criminals and formed an underground organization in the labor camps, terrorizing and stealing from the other prisoners.

the Frasnoyarsk transit camp there wasn't a single beaver in our cell, which means there wasn't a soul with anything worth stealing. Half the people in it were these grafters. They got very hungry and started taking all the sugar and bread for themselves. We were an extraordinary collection in our cell: half of them hoods, half of them Japanese, and just two of us Russian politicals, me and a well-known Arctic pilot. There is still an island in the Arctic Ocean named after him, even though he's been in prison. For three days the hoods robbed the Japanese and us mercilessly, they left us with nothing. So the Japs got together and hatched a plot—of course, no one could understand a word they were saying. In the middle of the night they all got up in dead silence, took some of the planks from the beds, yelled '*Banzai!*' and flung themselves on the hoods. They beat them up beautifully, I wish you could have seen it."

"Did they beat you up too?"

"No, why should they? We hadn't been pinching their bread. We were neutral that night, but our sympathies were right behind the 'glorious Japanese army.' In the morning order was restored and we got our full ration of bread and sugar again. But you know what the prison administration did? They took half the Japs out of the cell and reinforced the hoods who'd been beaten up with other hoods who hadn't been. Now that the Japs were completely out-numbered, the hoods threw themselves at them. They'd got knives, they'd got everything, that lot. They were like savages, they fought to kill. The pilot and I couldn't stand it any longer. We joined forces with the Japs."

"Against the Russians?"

Oleg let go of her elbow and drew himself up to his full height. His jaw was working.

"I don't count grafters as Russians."

He raised one hand and ran a finger along his scar, as though he were wiping it clean. It stretched from his chin across the lower part of his cheek and down to his neck.

"That's where they carved me up."

13. . . . and So Do the Specters

Pavel Nikolayevich's tumor still showed no sign of having gone down or softened during Saturday night. He realized this even before he got out of bed. He had been awakened early by the old Uzbek coughing disgustingly into his ear. It started at dawn and went on all through the morning.

Outside the dull, windless day dawned white, like frosted glass, just as it had yesterday and the day before, increasing the melancholy. The Kazakh shepherd had got up early and was sitting cross-legged, aimlessly, on his bed. He looked like a tree stump. The doctors were not expected today, no one was due to be called for an X ray or to have bandages changed, so he could sit there all day if he liked. Yefrem, sinister as ever, was once again immersed in his mournful Tolstoy. Sometimes he would get up and stamp up and down the passageway, making the beds shake, but at least he was no longer picking on Pavel Nikolayevich, or anyone else for that matter.

Bone-chewer had gone. He hadn't been seen in the ward all day. The geologist, that pleasant, well-mannered young man, was reading his geology, not disturbing anyone. The other patients in the ward were behaving quite quietly.

It cheered Pavel Nikolayevich to think that his wife was coming to see him. There was nothing concrete she could do to help him, of course, but it would mean a lot to be able to unburden himself, to tell her how terrible he felt, how the injection hadn't done him any good, and how horrible the people in the ward were. She would

176

sympathize with him, and he would feel better. He might ask her to bring him a book, some cheerful modern book, and his fountain pen, so there'd be no recurrence of that ridiculous situation yesterday when he'd had to borrow the young boy's pencil to write down the prescription. Yes, and most important of all, he could get her to find out about that fungus for him, the birch fungus.

After all, it wasn't the end of the world. If medicines failed, there were other things he could try. The main thing was to feel a Man, with a capital M, to be optimistic.

Gradually Pavel Nikolayevich was becoming acclimatized even here. After breakfast he finished reading the budget report of Minister of Finance Zverev in yesterday's paper. Today's paper had been brought in without any delay. Dyomka had got hold of it first, but Pavel Nikolayevich had requested him to hand it over and derived great pleasure from reading about the fall of Mendès-France's government. (Serves him right for his machinations, and for forcing through the Paris agreements!) He decided he'd keep a long article by Ehrenburg in reserve (he greatly valued Ehrenburg's social significance since the war in spite of some of his deviations which had been put right in good time by the national press); and he buried himself in another article about the fulfillment of the resolutions of the Central Committee's January plenum on sharply increasing the output of meat and dairy products.

Thus Pavel Nikolayevich whiled away the day until the orderly came and told him his wife had arrived. Generally speaking, bed patients' relatives were allowed into the ward, but right now Pavel Nikolayevich could not summon the strength to go and argue that he was a bed patient. Also he knew he would feel freer if he went out into the hall away from these dismal, dispirited people. So he wrapped a little warm scarf around his neck and went downstairs.

It is not every man who, a year before his silver wedding, still loves his wife as dearly as Pavel Nikolayevich did Kapa. Throughout his life there had truly been no one he was closer to, no one with whom he could so frankly rejoice in his successes and mull over his troubles. Kapa was a true friend, an intelligent, energetic woman. "She's got more brains than the whole village council put together," Pavel Nikolayevich used to boast to his friends. He had never felt the need to be unfaithful to her, and she had never been unfaithful to him. It is a fallacy to say that husbands who have progressed up the social ladder always begin to feel ashamed of their youthful past. They had risen far above the level they were at when they married. She'd been a worker in the same macaroni factory where he started work in the dough-kneading shop. But even before their marriage he had risen to membership of the factory trades union committee and was working on safety arrangements. Then through his membership in the Young Communist League he'd been posted to reinforce the Soviet trade organization, and a year later he was made director of the factory's secondary school. During all these years no difference of interests had developed between himself and his wife. Their proletarian sympathies did not change. On festive occasions when they'd had a little to drink, if the people around the table were simple folk, the Rusanovs would recall their days in the factory and break into loud renderings of old workers' songs.

Kapa, with her broad figure, her two silver-fox furs, her large handbag the size of a briefcase and her shopping bag full of provisions, was taking up at least three places on the bench in the warmest corner of the hall. She got up to kiss her husband with her warm, soft lips, and spread the open flap of her fur coat for him to sit on, to make it warmer for him.

"There's a letter here," she said, the corner of her lip twitching. It was a familiar tic and Pavel Nikolayevich immediately concluded the letter was an unpleasant one. Kapa was a cool and reasonable person except for one feminine habit which she could do nothing about: whenever there was news, good or bad, she immediately let the cat out of the bag.

"Well, come on, then," said Pavel Nikolayevich in a hurt voice, "finish me off with it, if it's so important, finish me off."

Now she'd blurted it out, Kapa was free of her burden and could talk like an ordinary human being.

"It's nothing much, nothing at all," she said penitently. "Well, how are you, Pasik? How are you? I know all about the injection. I rang the nurse on Friday and again yesterday morning. If anything had been wrong, I'd have rushed along straightaway. But they told me it went very well, is that right?"

"The injection went very well," Pavel Nikolayevich confirmed, pleased at his own fortitude. "But the conditions here, Kapelka, the conditions!" And at once everything about the place that he found galling and aggravating, starting with Yefrem and Bone-chewer, crowded into his mind. Not knowing which complaint to begin with, he finally said in a tone of agony, "If only there was a separate lavatory I could use! The lavatories here are terrible. There are no cubicles. Everyone can see you!"

(To use a public bath or lavatory inevitably subverts one's authority. In his office Rusanov went to another floor to avoid having to use the general staff lavatory.)

Kapa, realizing how offensive he found it all and that he had to get things off his chest, didn't interrupt but instead steered him on to new complaints, until gradually he'd got them out of his system, right down to the most unanswerable and desperate of them all: "What do they pay these doctors their money for?" She questioned him in detail about how he felt during the injection, and after it, and how his tumor was. She even removed the little scarf, looked at the tumor and gave it as her opinion that it was getting the tiniest bit smaller.

It was not, Pavel Nikolayevich knew this, but even so it was pleasant to hear someone say that it might be.

"Well, at least it's not any bigger, is it?"

"No, of course not, of course not." Kapa was sure it wasn't.

"If only it would stop growing!" said Pavel Nikolayevich, as though begging it to stop. His voice was tearful. "If only it would stop! If it goes on growing like this for another week, goodness only knows. . . ." No, he couldn't say it, he couldn't gaze into the black abyss. How miserable he felt—it was all touch-and-go. "The next injection's tomorrow, then one on Wednesday. But what if it doesn't do any good? What shall I do?"

"Then you'll have to go to Moscow," said Kapa resolutely. "Let's decide that if another two injections don't help, we'll put you on the plane to Moscow. You rang them there on Friday and then changed your mind, but now I've telephoned Shendyapin and been to see Alymov, and Alymov rang Moscow himself. Apparently until recently your illness could only be treated in Moscow, everybody was sent there, but then they started treating it here, you see, to improve the standard of the local specialists. Doctors are a detestable race, anyway. How dare they talk about production achievement when it's living people they're processing? I don't care what you say, I hate doctors."

"Yes, yes," Pavel Nikolayevich agreed bitterly. "Yes, that's just what I told them here."

"I hate teachers too! I'm sick and tired of them because of what's happened to Maika. And what about Lavrik?"

Pavel Nikolayevich wiped his glasses. "I could understand it in my day, when I was a school director. All the trained teachers were hostile to our authority, none of them were on our side. The main problem was to keep them in check. But now we're supposed to be able to count on them and expect things of them."

"All right, now listen! There's nothing particularly complicated about sending you to Moscow, our road isn't completely overgrown with weeds yet, grounds for it can still be found. Alymov got them to agree to make special arrangements. They'll find somewhere good to put you. So what do you think? Shall we wait for the third injection?"

The plans they made were definite, and they raised Pavel Nikolayevich's spirits. Anything so long as he didn't have to sit passively waiting for death in this musty old hole. All their lives the Rusanovs had been people of action and initiative; it was only when they took the initiative that they found inner calm.

There was no reason to hurry today. The longer Pavel Nikolayevich could sit here with his wife without returning to the ward, the happier he would be. He shivered a little as the outside door kept opening and shutting. Kapitolina Matveyevna took off the shawl that was around her shoulders under her coat and wrapped it around him. As it happened, the other people on the bench were clean, cultivated people too. They could sit there for quite a long time.

Moving slowly from subject to subject, they discussed some of the aspects of their life that had been interrupted by Pavel Nikolayevich's illness. The only topic they avoided was the one big possibility hanging over them: that the worst might come to the worst. For this they had no plans, no measures, no guidance ready. They were totally unprepared for such an outcome, and if only for this reason they regarded it as out of the question. (True, now and again it crossed Kapa's mind to wonder what the position of her home and property would be if her husband were to die, but they had both been brought up in such a spirit of optimism that they felt it was better to leave all these problems in a state of confusion than to depress themselves by analyzing the possibilities or by making a morbid last will and testament.)

They talked about the telephone calls she had received, inquiries and good wishes from colleagues on the Board of Industry to which Pavel Nikolayevich had been transferred from the factory's "special department"* the year before last. (He didn't deal in industrial matters himself, of course, he was not such a narrow specialist. Engineers and economists coped with the technical side: his job was to exercise special control over them.) His colleagues all liked him, and it was nice to know how concerned they were.

They also talked about his pension prospects. Somehow or other, in spite of his long, irreproachable service in responsible positions in personnel and special departments, he would probably not achieve his life's dream, the "personal" pension awarded to high officials. He would not even be eligible for the civil servant's lucrative pension, with its high level of payment and favorable starting age, and all because he hadn't made up his mind to put on military uniform in 1939, even though it was offered him. It was a pity, but, considering the unstable situation during the last two years, then again maybe it wasn't. Perhaps it was the price one had to pay for peace.

They also discussed the general desire of the people for a higher standard of living, a trend which had become more marked in recent years, and was now revealing itself in new tastes in clothes, furniture and interior decoration.

At this point Kapitolina Matveyevna mentioned that if her husband's treatment was going to be successful but long-drawn-out (they had been warned it might last six weeks or two months), it might be a good opportunity to have some alterations made in the apartment. One of the pipes in the bathroom ought to have been moved long ago, the kitchen sink would have to be put somewhere else, the wall in the lavatory needed tiling, and the dining room and Pavel Nikolayevich's room absolutely must have a new coat of paint. They would have it a different color (she was already thinking about the exact shade) and it would be overlaid with gilding, which was all the rage now. Pavel Nikolayevich made no objection to this, but immediately a vexing question arose. Although the workers would be assigned by state warrant and paid by the state, they would be bound to extort—not ask for but actually extort—additional payment from the owners. It was not that he begrudged them the money (although it would be a shame to see it go), it was the principle of the thing that was far more important and annoying. Why *should* he pay them? Why was it that all he got was the proper salary for his job, with added bonuses, of course, and that he never

*A euphemism for the K.G.B.

asked for tips or additional payments? And why were these unscrupulous workers, common as they were, such money-grubbers? A concession here would be a breach of principle, an inadmissible concession to the whole petty-bourgeois world and its elements. Pavel Nikolayevich was upset every time the question came up.

"Why is it, Kapa? Don't they care about their honor as workers? When we were working in the macaroni factory, we didn't lay down conditions or try to put the touch on the foreman for money. It would never have entered our heads. Whatever happens, we must not corrupt them. It's nothing less than bribery!"

Kapa agreed with him completely, but at the same time observed that if you didn't pay them and stand them some vodka before they started and halfway through the job, they'd get their own back by doing something badly, and you'd be the one to suffer.

"A retired colonel, I was told, stood his ground and said, 'I'm not paying you an extra kopeck!' The workmen put a dead rat in his bathroom wastepipe. The water couldn't drain away properly and it made a terrible stink."

So they were unable to come to any definite decision about the repairs. Life is complicated, very complicated, whichever side you're on.

They talked about Yuri. He was their eldest son, but he had grown up to be too placid, without the Rusanovs' proper grip on life. They had put him through law school, and they had found him a good job after college, but they had to admit he was not really suited to this type of work. He had no idea of how to consolidate his position or acquire useful contacts. Now he was on a business trip he was probably making mistakes all the time. Pavel Nikolayevich was very worried about it. But Kapitolina Matveyevna was worried about his marriage. His father had made him learn to drive, his father would also see he got a private flat,* but how could they keep an eye on him to prevent him making a mistake in his marriage? He was such a naïve boy, he might be led up the garden path by some ordinary weaver girl from the textile factory. Well, perhaps not a weaver, there'd be nowhere for them to meet, they wouldn't frequent the same kind of places. But what about the danger now, while he was away on his trip? It was such an easy step to take, rashly signing your name in the marriage register, and it

*I.e., not a *communal* flat.

would ruin not only the young man's life, but his family's too, the many years of effort they'd spent on his behalf. Look at Shendyapin's daughter, how she'd very nearly married a student in her year at teachers' training college. He was only a boy from the country, and his mother was an ordinary collective farmer. Just imagine the Shendyapins' flat, their furniture and the influential people they had as guests, and suddenly there's this old woman in a white headscarf sitting at their table, their daughter's mother-in-law, and she didn't even have a passport.* Whatever next? Thank goodness they'd managed to discredit the fiancé politically and save their daughter.

Aviette (Ave or Alla for short) was a different matter. Aviette was the pearl of the Rusanov family. Neither her father nor mother could remember a time when she'd caused them any distress or anxiety, apart from schoolgirl pranks, of course. She was beautiful, intelligent and energetic, with a good understanding of life and how to cope with it. There was no need to check up on her or worry about her. She'd never make a false step in anything, important or unimportant. The only grudge she bore her parents was the first name they had given her. "I don't like verbal trickery," she'd say, "just call me Alla." But on her passport it said quite clearly "Aviette Pavlovna." Such a pretty name! The holidays were nearly over, on Wednesday she'd be flying in from Moscow. She'd be sure to come to the hospital first thing.

Names could be such a bother. Circumstances can change, but names remain forever. Now Lavrik had started resenting his name, too. It was all right for the moment, while he was still at school, nobody picked on him. But later this year he'd be getting his own passport, and what would it say on it? Lavrenti Pavlovich.** At the time his parents had done it on purpose. "Give him the same name as the minister," they'd said, "Stalin's staunch brother-in-arms. Let him be like him in every way." But for over a year now you had to be very careful about saying the words "Lavrenti Pavlovich" aloud. The one thing that would save Lavrik was that he was going to the military academy. His first two names wouldn't be used in the army.

---

*This is the internal identity document without which a Soviet citizen cannot move freely about the country or change his job. City-dwellers possess this passport but collective farmers usually do not, which in practice means they cannot leave their village except for short periods of time.

**These were the first name and patronymic of Beria, Stalin's ruthless security chief, who had recently (July 1953) been branded a "British spy" and liquidated.

One might well ask, in a whisper, "Why was that business handled like that?" This was the way the Shendyapins thought too, although they didn't mention the subject to people they didn't know. All right, let's suppose Beria *was* a double-dealer, a bourgeois nationalist and a seeker after power. Very well, put him on trial and shoot him behind closed doors, but why tell the ordinary people anything about it? Why shake their faith? Why create doubt in their minds? When it was all over, one might perhaps send out a confidential circular down to a certain level to explain the details, but as for the newspapers, wouldn't it be better to say he died of a heart attack and bury him with full honors?

They talked about Maika, their youngest, as well. This year Maika was not getting her usual "five out of five." She was no longer the star pupil, her name had been taken off the roll of honor, and often she wasn't even getting four out of five now. It was all because they'd moved her up to the fifth year. At her elementary school there'd been one teacher looking after her the whole time, who knew her and knew her parents, and Maika had got on superbly. But this year she'd had a dozen different teachers, specialists in various subjects, taking her class for one lesson a week. They didn't know their pupils by sight, all they thought about was the timetable. Did it never occur to them what a shock a change like that could cause a child, or how her character might be damaged? Kapitolina Matveyevna would spare no effort; she would act through the parents' committee and see that things were put right at the school. Though order in the school was being undermined by that new reform as well. Why introduce coeducation, why give up the old system of separate schools for boys and girls—one of the best achievements of mature, Soviet pedagogical science.

And so they talked about this, that and the other for several hours. But there was a listless quality to their gossip. Though neither of them said as much, each realized there was something unpractical about their conversation. Pavel Nikolayevich's spirits had sunk to rock bottom. He could not believe in the reality of the people and events they were discussing. There was nothing he felt like doing. What he wanted most now was to lie down on his bed, rest his tumor against the pillow and cover his head with the blankets.

But Kapitolina Matveyevna was forcing herself to keep up the conversation. This was because the letter was burning a hole in her handbag. She had received it that morning from her brother Minai in K——, the city where the Rusanovs had lived before the war, where they'd spent their youth and married, and where their children had been born. But during the war they'd been evacuated here, and they'd never gone back to K——. They managed to have their flat transferred to Kapa's brother.

She realized that her husband wasn't up to receiving that sort of news at the moment, but at the same time it was the kind of news that she couldn't share with a mere friend. There wasn't a soul in the whole town she could tell this thing to, in its full implications. After all, she had done her best to console her husband, and she was the one who needed support. She could not go home and live on her own, keeping this piece of knowledge all to herself. Of her children, Aviette was the only one she could possibly explain it to. Yuri was out of the question. But before she told Aviette she'd have to ask her husband's advice.

As for him, the longer he sat with her, the wearier he grew, and the more impossible it seemed to discuss the vital subject with him.

It was getting nearer and nearer the time for her to go. She began to take some things out of her shopping bag, to show her husband what she had brought him to eat. The sleeves of her fur coat, with their silver-fox cuffs, were so wide they would hardly go into the open jaws of her bag.

At this point Pavel Nikolayevich saw the provisions, realized he still had plenty left in his bedside table, and suddenly remembered that there was something else far more important than food and drink that he ought to have brought up first of all today: he remembered the *chaga,* the birch fungus. He became animated as he began to tell his wife about this miracle, about the letter and this doctor (although maybe he was a charlatan), and how vital it was to lose no time in thinking of someone to collect this fungus for him back in Central Russia.

"What about back home, around K——? The place is full of birch trees. Minai could arrange it for me. It wouldn't be much trouble. We must write to Minai straightaway. And to other people, too, to some of our old friends. They can join in. Let them all realize the position I'm in."

Well, that made things easier. He'd mentioned Minai and K——, he'd brought the subject up himself! She didn't get out the letter itself, because her brother had written in somewhat gloomy terms. She sat there, clicking open and shut the clasp of her handbag.

"You know, Pasha," she said, "I'm not sure we ought to spread your name about in K——. Minai writes, of course it may not be true, but he says Rodichev has turned up in town. Apparently he's been . . . re-hab-il-it-at-ed. Could he possibly have been?"

While she was enunciating that long, repulsive word "re-hab-il-it-at-ed," staring down at the clasp of her handbag on the point of getting out the letter as well, she missed the moment when Pasha turned whiter than the sheets of his bed.

"What's the matter?" she cried, more alarmed than she had been by the arrival of the letter itself. "What's the matter?"

His body was pressed rigid against the back of the bench. With a feminine gesture he wrapped her shawl more tightly around himself.

"It still may not be true." Her powerful hands were gripping his shoulders. One hand was still holding her handbag, so that it looked as if she were trying to hang it on his shoulder. "It still may not be true. Minai didn't see himself. But people are saying . . ."

Pavel Nikolayevich's pallor gradually subsided, but a weakness had gripped his whole body—his hips, his shoulders; his arms too had grown weak, and the tumor seemed to wrench his head sideways.

"Why did you tell me that?" he moaned in a miserable, feeble voice. "Haven't I had enough misfortune?" And twice his head and chest shuddered with tearless sobs.

"Forgive me, Pashenka! Forgive me, Pasik!" She still held him by the shoulders, shaking her curly copper hair, styled like a lion's mane. "I'm going out of my mind, I really am! Do you think he'll be able to take Minai's room away from him? Goodness knows what all this is going to lead to. You remember we've already heard of two cases like this?"

"What's the room got to do with it? Damn the room! Let him take it!" His voice was a sobbing whisper.

"What do you mean, damn the room? How will Minai like having less space to live in?"

"You'd do better to think about your husband. You'd do better to think of what's going to happen to me. And what about Guzun? Does he mention him in the letter?"

"No, not Guzun . . . But what if they all start coming back? What's going to happen then?"

"How should I know?" answered her husband in a strangled voice. "What *right* have they to let these people out now? Have they no pity? How dare they cause such traumas?"

14. Justice

Rusanov had expected Kapa's visit to cheer him up, but the news she brought sickened him so much that it would really have been better if she hadn't come at all. As he went up the stairs he reeled and clung to the banister, a chill fever sweeping over him with growing power. Kapa was not allowed to go upstairs with him in her coat and outdoor shoes. A lazy orderly was standing there specially to prevent it. So Kapa made her take Pavel Nikolayevich to the ward and carry the bag of provisions. The nurse on duty was lobster-eyed Zoya, who for some reason had caught Rusanov's fancy that first evening. There she was, sitting at her table, fenced off by a pile of registers, flirting with the uncouth Bone-chewer and paying scant attention to the patients. Rusanov asked her for an aspirin, to which she answered glibly that aspirins were given out only in the evening. Still, she took his temperature and brought him some-thing later.

The provisions had been changed in his bedside table but he'd taken no part in it He lay down, as he had longed to do, his tumor against the pillow. It was surprising that the pillows here were soft. He hadn't even had to bring one from home. He pulled the blankets over his head.

The thoughts in his brain were tumbling and jostling, burning him so violently that the rest of his body had lost all sense of feeling. It was as though he were drugged. He could no longer hear the inane conversations going on in the room, and although both he and the floorboards were shuddering from Yefrem's pacing, he was insensible to that as well. He didn't notice that the day had brightened. It was just before sunset and somewhere the sun was creeping through, only not on their side of the building. He didn't notice the hours slipping by either. He kept falling asleep, perhaps because of the medicine he'd just taken, and then waking up again. Once he woke up and the electric light was already on; he went to sleep again. When he woke next it was the middle of the night and the place was dark and silent.

He felt that sleep had vanished forever. Its beneficent veil had slipped away from him. But terror, in full measure, clamped on to the middle of his chest and held it in a vise.

A host of ideas, gradually unraveling themselves, crowded in Rusanov's head, in the room and all around in the spacious darkness.

They weren't ideas at all really, it was just that he was terrified. He was terrified that tomorrow morning Rodichev would suddenly force his way past the nurses, past the orderlies, fling himself into the room and start beating him up. He was not afraid of being brought to justice, or of the judgment of society, or of disgrace, but simply of being beaten up. It had happened only once before in his life, at school, in the sixth class, during his last year. They'd waited for him one evening by the gate, ready to "get" him. None of them had knives, but ever since then he had had a terrible apprehension of cruel, bony fists coming at him from all directions.

When someone dies whom we haven't seen for years, we continue to see him after his death as the young man he was at our last meeting, even though he must in the years between have grown old. Rodichev had been away eighteen years and would probably be an invalid by now, deaf perhaps, or all crippled and bent. But Rusanov still saw him as the sun-tanned healthy he-man he had once been, standing on their joint balcony with his dumbbells and weights that last Sunday before he was arrested. With Kapa's help Rusanov had already written the letter, taken it to the proper authorities and handed it in. Stripped to the waist, Rodichev had called to Rusanov, "Pashka! Come here! Feel my biceps. Don't be shy, press! Now you see what our new-style engineers are made of? We're not a lot of ricket-ridden namby-pambies, like that German Eduard Christoforovich, we're well-co-ordinated men. Look at you, you've become such a weakling you'll wither away behind that leather door of yours. Come down to the factory and I'll get you a job on the shop floor, eh? What about it? Don't you want to? Ha-ha-ha . . ."

He burst out laughing and went off to wash, singing, "Blacksmiths are we, with hearts young and free."

It was this great hunk of man that Rusanov imagined was about to charge into the ward, fists flailing. It was a false picture, but he could not rid himself of it.

He and Rodichev had once been friends. They'd been in the same Young Communist cell and had both been awarded this apartment by the factory. Afterward Rodichev had gone to workers' high school and later to college, while Rusanov had gone into trade-union work and personnel records administration. Then disagreements began, first of all between their wives, then between the men themselves. Rodichev often adopted a very insulting way of talking to Rusanov, generally behaving too independently and setting himself up against public opinion. Living shoulder to shoulder with them became cramped and intolerable. Well, one thing led to another, they had been hasty, of course, and Pavel Nikolayevich wrote the letter. He said they'd had a private conversation in which Rodichev had spoken up in favor of the activities of the recently liquidated Industrial Party and intended to get a group of saboteurs together at the factory.

The one thing Rusanov most particularly requested was that his name should be kept out of the proceedings and that there should be no confrontation. The very idea of such a meeting terrified him. The interrogator had guaranteed that the law would not require Rusanov's name to be mentioned and that a confrontation was not obligatory. It would be sufficient for the accused himself to confess. It would not even be necessary for Rusanov's original letter to be included in the file on the case, so that the accused would not come across his neighbor's name when he signed Article 206.

It would all have gone quite smoothly if it had not been for Guzun, who was secretary of the factory's Party committee. He received a note from the security authorities to the effect that Rodichev was an enemy of the people and must be expelled from the factory Party cell. However, he dug his toes in and started to make a fuss, saying that Rodichev was "our boy" and could he, Guzun, please be given details of the evidence. The fuss he made rebounded on his own head. Two days later he too was arrested during the night. On the third morning both Rodichev and Guzun were duly expelled as members of the same counterrevolutionary underground organization.

What put Rusanov on the spot now was the fact that during the two days when they were trying to talk Guzun round they had been forced to tell him it was Rusanov who had provided the evidence. This meant that if Guzun had met Rodichev *out there* (and since they were involved in the same case it was quite possible they *had* met), he'd have told him everything. This was why Rusanov was now worried about the man's ominous return, about this inconceivable resurrection from the dead.

Possibly, too, Rodichev's wife had guessed the truth. Was she alive, though? Kapa's plan had been to wait till Rodichev was arrested, then have Katka Rodicheva evicted and take over the entire apartment. The whole terrace would then be theirs. (Looking back, it now seemed quite ludicrous that they should have regarded a fourteen-square-meter room in a flat without gas as so important. But they did; the children were growing up.) The operation was all agreed and ready, but when they came to evict Katka she pulled a fast one on them. She claimed she was pregnant. They insisted on a checkup, and she produced a certificate. Perfect! As if she had foreseen it all: it is illegal to evict a pregnant woman. So it was only the following winter that they managed to get her out. And for many long months they had to put up with her, living side by side with her while she carried the child and bore it, and afterwards right to the end of her maternity leave. Of course, Kapa kept her well down in the kitchen and Ava, who was four years old by this time, was very funny the way she teased her and spat in her saucepans.

What about Rusanov's fear? He lay on his back in the darkness of the gently breathing, gently snoring ward. Only a faint gleam from the nurse's table lamp in the lobby penetrated the frosted glass of the door. His mind was clear and sleepless as he wondered why the shades of Rodichev and Guzun had rattled him so much. Would he be frightened if other people came back whose guilt he had also helped to establish? That man Eduard Christoforovich, for instance, whom Rodichev had happened to mention on the terrace. He was an engineer with a bourgeois upbringing who had called Pavel a fool and a rogue in front of the workers (later he confessed that his one dream was the restoration of capitalism). And that stenographer who had been found guilty of distorting the speech of a certain important official, Pavel Nikolayevich's patron, who had in fact used quite different words in his address. And that pigheaded accountant (what's more, it emerged that his father was a priest; it only took them a minute to pin him down after that). Yelchanski and his wife, too . . . and what of the others? . . .

Pavel Nikolayevich was not afraid of any of them. He had helped to establish the guilt of them all, more boldly and openly as time went on. On two occasions he had even gone to the confrontation, raised his voice and denounced them. At that time it was not considered in the least shameful to do such a thing! In that excellent and honorable time, the years 1937 and 1938, the social atmosphere was noticeably cleansed and it became easier to breathe. The liars and slanderers, those who had been too bold in their criticism, the clever-dick intellectuals, all of them disappeared, shut up or lay low, while the men of principle, the loyal and stable men, Rusanov's friends and Rusanov himself, were able to walk with dignity, their heads held high.

Now times had changed, things were bewildering, unhealthy, the finest civic actions of earlier days were now shameful. Would he now have to fear for his own skin?

Fear? What nonsense! Looking back over his whole life, Rusanov could not find a single instance of cowardice to reproach himself with. Indeed, had there ever been anything for him to be afraid of? As a man he was not particularly brave, perhaps, but he could not call to mind an occasion when he had behaved like a coward. There was no ground whatever for suggesting he'd have been afraid if he'd had to fight in the front line. It was simply that he'd been a valuable, experienced official, and so had not been sent to the front. It was impossible to say he'd have lost his head under bombing or in a burning building. He'd left K—— before the bombing started and he'd never been in a fire. Likewise he had never been afraid of justice or the law, because he had never broken the law and justice had always defended and supported him. He had never feared public exposure because the public also had always been on his side. An improper article attacking Rusanov would never have appeared in the local newspaper, because either Kuzma Fotievich or Nil Prokofich would have stopped it, while a national newspaper would never have stooped to Rusanov's level. So he had never been afraid of the press either.

When he traveled by boat across the Black Sea, he was not the least bit afraid of the depths beneath him. Whether or not he was afraid of heights it was impossible to say, because he'd never been such a fathead as to try climbing rocks or mountains, while the nature of his work did not involve bridge building.

The nature of Rusanov's work had been for many years, by now almost twenty, that of personnel records administration. It was a job that went by different names in different institutions, but the substance of it was always the same. Only ignoramuses and uninformed outsiders were unaware what subtle, meticulous work it was, what talent it required. It was a form of poetry not yet mastered by the poets themselves. As every man goes through life he fills in a number of forms for the record, each containing a number of questions. A man's answer to one question on one form becomes a little thread, permanently connecting him to the local center of personnel records administration. There are thus hundreds of little threads radiating from every man, millions of threads in all. If these threads were suddenly to become visible, the whole sky would look like a spider's web, and if they materialized as rubber bands, buses, trams and even people would all lose the ability to move, and the wind would be unable to carry torn-up newspapers or autumn leaves along the streets of the city. They are not visible, they are not material, but every man is constantly aware of their existence. The point is that a so-called completely clean record was almost unattainable, an ideal, like absolute truth. Something negative or suspicious can always be noted down against any man alive. Everyone is guilty of something or has something to conceal. All one has to do is to look hard enough to find out what it is.

Each man, permanently aware of his own invisible threads, naturally develops a respect for the people who manipulate the threads, who manage personnel records administration, that most complicated science, and for these people's authority.

To use yet another analogy, this time a musical one, Rusanov's special position put a set of xylophone keys at his disposal. By choice, desire or necessity he might strike any one of them. Although they were all made of wood, each gave out a different note.

There were keys, that is to say devices, that could be used with gentle precision. For example, if he wished to let a comrade know he was dissatisfied with him, or simply to give him a warning or put him in his place, Rusanov knew well how to say good morning in different tonalities.

When the other man said good morning to him (he had to do it first, of course), Rusanov might reply in a cold, businesslike tone, without a smile. Or he might draw his eyebrows together (he would rehearse this in front of the mirror in his office) and be a little slow about replying, as if he was in doubt as to whether he ought to say good morning to this particular person, whether he was worthy of it. Only then would he say good morning, turning his head toward the man either completely, or only halfway, or even not at all. This small pause, however, always had considerable effect. Every member of the staff who was greeted with this hesitation or coolness would begin to rack his brain for all the sins he might be guilty of. The seed of doubt once sown, the man might well refrain from some false step which he was on the point of taking, but which Pavel Nikolaye-vich would only have learned about later.

There was another stronger method he sometimes used. He would meet a man (or else call him up or have him specially fetched) and say, "Will you please come and see me at ten o'clock tomorrow morning?" "Can't I come now?" the man would always ask, anxious to find out why he was being summoned and to get the interview over. "No, you can't come now," Rusanov would say blandly but severely. He wouldn't say that he had other business or was on his way to a conference; not for anything in the world would he give a simple, straightforward reason that might set the man's mind at rest. This was the whole point of the device. He would pronounce the words, "You can't come now," as though they were fraught with various meanings, not all of them favorable. "What's it about?" the man might ask, either through nerve or sheer lack of experience. "You'll find out tomorrow." The velvet voice of Pavel Nikolayevich would evade the tactless question. But from then until ten o'clock tomorrow was a long time, so many things could happen in between. The man had to finish his day's work, travel home, talk to his family, perhaps go to the movies or to a parents' meeting at his children's school, and finally get to sleep (some did, some didn't), then choke down his breakfast the next morning, while all the time the question was drilling and gnawing at him, "Why does he want to see me?" The long hours would give the man plenty of time for remorse and general misgiving, and he would no doubt vow never again to cross his bosses at meetings. When ten o'clock finally came, it might turn out that nothing more was wanted than to check his date of birth or the number on his diploma.

Like xylophone keys, these devices would mount the wooden scale until they came to the driest and shrillest note of all: "Sergei

Sergeivich" (the director of the whole enterprise, the local boss) "would like you to fill out this form by such-and-such a date." Rusanov would hand the man a form. But this was no ordinary form, it was the most detailed and unpleasant of all the forms and questionnaires kept in Rusanov's cabinet. For example, it was the one that had to be filled out before a man was given access to secret files. There might be no question of the man having access to secrets, and Sergei Sergeivich might not know anything about it all, but who was going to check up when everyone went in mortal fear of Sergei Sergeivich? The man would take the form and try to put on a bold front, but the fact was that if there was anything he had ever concealed from the records center, his insides would be churning. With this questionnaire, it was impossible to conceal anything. It was an excellent questionnaire, the best of the whole lot.

With its help Rusanov had succeeded in making several women divorce their husbands, who were imprisoned under Article 58.* However cleverly the women hid their tracks, sent off their parcels under different names and from different towns, or even sent no parcels at all, the net of questions woven by this form was so fine that further lying became impossible. The only possible way through was for the woman to be finally and legally divorced. There was a specially simplified procedure for such cases: the court did not have to ask the prisoner's agreement to the divorce or inform him that the divorce had been concluded. Rusanov was keenly concerned that such divorces should take place; that the criminals' dirty paws should not drag a woman not yet lost from society's collective path. But the questionnaires were never used and were only shown to Sergei Sergeivich by way of a joke.

The poetic side of his work lay in holding a man in the hollow of your hand without even starting to pile on the pressure.

Rusanov's mysterious, isolated, almost supernatural position in the general production system gave him a satisfyingly deep knowledge of the true processes of life. The life familiar to everybody— work, conferences, factory newssheets, local trade-union announcements pinned up at the checkpoint, applications for various benefits, the cafeteria and the factory club—was not real, it only seemed so to the uninitiated. The actual direction life took was decided without loud publicity, calmly, in quiet offices, by two or three people who

*The main political article of the Penal Code in force at the time.

understood one another, or by dulcet telephone calls. The stream of real life ran on in the secret papers that lay deep in the briefcases of Rusanov and his colleagues. For years this life might follow a man in silence, then suddenly and momentarily it would reveal itself, breathing fire from its jaws as it rose from its underground kingdom, wrenching off a victim's head or belching fire over him, then disappearing, no one know where. Afterward everything remained the same on the surface—club, cafeteria, applications for benefits, newssheets, work—yet as the workers walked past the factory checkpoint one man would be missing—dismissed, removed or eliminated.

Rusanov's office was equipped in a manner suited to the poetic and political nature of the subtle work he performed. It had always been a secluded room. In the early years it had a door upholstered with leather and studded with shiny wallpaper nails, but later on, as society became richer, it was further furnished with a sort of safety device in the doorway, a dark little cubicle like a lobby. This lobby seemed a perfectly simple invention, with nothing particularly cunning about it. It was no more than three feet across, and the caller spent only a second or two in it between closing the first door and opening the second. But to a man facing a critical interview, those few seconds seemed almost like a brief spell in prison. There was no light and no air, and he felt the full weight of his nothingness compared with the importance of the man whose office he was about to enter. If he had any bold or self-assertive ideas he would forget about them right there in the lobby.

Naturally enough, groups were never allowed to burst into Pavel Nikolayevich's office. People were only allowed in one by one after being summoned or given permission to come over the telephone.

This arrangement and admission routine greatly encouraged a properly considered and regulated execution of all duties in Rusanov's department. Without the precautionary lobby, Pavel Nikolayevich would have suffered.

Of course, a dialectic interdependence of all facets of reality*
dictated that Pavel Nikolayevich's behavior at work inevitably had an effect on his way of life in general. Gradually with the years, he and Kapitolina Matveyevna developed an aversion to teeming human beings, to jostling crowds. The Rusanovs found streetcars, buses and

*This is a take-off on pseudo-Marxist Stalinist jargon.

trolley-buses quite disgusting. People were always pushing, especially when they were trying to get aboard. Insults were always flying around. Builders and other workers were always climbing in in dirty overalls, and you could get oil or lime all over your coat. The worst thing was their inveterate habit of clapping you familiarly on the shoulder and asking you to pass a ticket or some change along the car. It meant you were at their beck and call, endlessly passing things on. The distances were too great for going about the town on foot; and anyway it was a bit vulgar, hardly right for a man in his position. Besides, you could always come up against something unexpected among pedestrians. So the Rusanovs gradually changed over to motorcars—first office limousines and taxis, and then their own. They found it quite unbearable, of course, to travel in ordinary railway carriages or even in reserved seats, where people crammed in, wearing sheepskin coats and carrying buckets and sacks. The Rusanovs now traveled only in reserved compartments or "soft class." Naturally, when he stayed in a hotel, he always had a room reserved for him, so there was never any danger of finding himself in a communal room. Naturally too they did not go to just *any* rest home, but only to the places where they knew and respected you, and where it was arranged for the beach and the walks to be fenced off from the general public. And when the doctors told Kapitolina Matveyevna she ought to *walk* more, she positively had nowhere to walk except inside a rest home like this, among her equals.

The Rusanovs loved the People, their great People. They served the People and were ready to give their lives for the People.

But as the years went by they found themselves less and less able to tolerate actual human beings, those obstinate creatures who were always resistant, refusing to do what they were told and, besides, demanding something for themselves.

So they became wary of people who were badly dressed, impudent, or even a bit drunk. You came across people like that in suburban trains, at beer-kiosks, at bus and railway stations. A badly dressed man was always dangerous because it meant he lacked a proper sense of responsibility. He'd also probably be a man with little to lose, otherwise he'd be decently dressed. Of course, the police and the law were there to protect Rusanov against badly dressed men, only this protection would inevitably arrive too late. It would punish the criminal after the event. Up against him on his own, Pavel Nikolayevich was in fact defenseless—neither his position nor his past services could in any way protect him; the lout might insult him for no reason, hurl obscenities at him, bash his face in just for the fun of it, spoil his suit, or even take it away by force.

So although there was nothing in the world Rusanov feared, he did begin to feel a totally normal, justifiable fear of dissolute, half-drunk men, or, to be more precise, of a fist striking him a direct blow in the face.

This was why the news of Rodichev's return had upset him so much at first: Rusanov imagined that the first thing Rodichev would do would be to punch him in the face. He was not afraid of Rodichev or Guzun taking legal action: legally they could probably never get at him; there was nothing they could or should have against him. But what if they were still big, strong, healthy men who might take it into their heads, vulgarly speaking, to poke him in the snout?

As a "new man," intelligent and resolute, Pavel Nikolayevich had to overcome and stifle this fear.

Well, for a start, it might all be pure imagination, and anyway, Rodichev might not even exist any more. God forbid he should ever return. All these stories about people "returning" might be mere inventions. Pavel Nikolayevich was in constant touch with important events, yet so far he had no foreboding that life might assume a new character.

In the second place, even if Rodichev had come back, he wouldn't come here, he'd have gone to K——. Besides, he'd have other things to do than go looking for Rusanov. He'd have to watch his step so as not to be thrown out of K—— yet again. Pavel Nikolayevich's first involuntary fright had been quite unnecessary after all.

And even if he did start looking, it would take him some time to pick up the trail leading here. The train journey took three days, across eight provinces. And even when he arrived, he'd go first to Rusanov's home, rather than the hospital. Pavel Nikolayevich felt he was quite safe so long as he was in hospital.

Safe! That's a joke! A tumor like this, and you call it safe! . . .

Anyway, with a time of such uncertainty ahead, a man might as well die. Better to die than live in fear of every man who returned. What madness it was to let them come back! Why did they do it? They'd grown used to being where they were, they were resigned to it—why let them come back here and upset people's lives?

It looked by now as if Pavel Nikolayevich had at last burned himself out and was ready for sleep. He really ought to try to get some sleep.

But he needed to go down the corridor. This was the most unpleasant procedure in the clinic.

Moving his body very carefully, he turned over. The tumor was squatting on his neck, pressing against him like an iron fist. He clambered out of the bed with its sagging mattress, put on his pajamas, slippers and spectacles and set off, shuffling quietly across the room.

Alert at her table, Maria, severe and swarthy, turned watchfully toward him as he shuffled along.

At the top of the staircase a hefty, long-armed, long-legged Greek, newly arrived, was writhing and groaning in agony on his bed. He couldn't lie down. He was sitting up as if the bed were too small for him. He followed Pavel Nikolayevich with his sleepless, horror-stricken eyes.

On the middle landing a small, yellow-looking man, his hair still neatly brushed, was half sitting in his bed, propped up by two extra pillows and breathing oxygen out of what looked like a waterproof canvas container. On his bedside table he had oranges, cakes, Turkish delight and a bottle of yoghurt; he was quite indifferent to them all—he couldn't get enough clean, ordinary air, which cost absolutely nothing, into his lungs.

In the lower corridor there were more beds with patients in them. Some of them were asleep. An Oriental-looking old woman with a disheveled mane of hair was sprawled across her pillow in agony.

Next, he walked past a small room where all those due for enemas, whoever they might be, were placed on the same short, none-too-clean couch.

Finally, drawing in his breath and doing his best to hold it, Pavel Nikolayevich entered the lavatory. It was a lavatory without cubicles or even proper pedestals, and it made him feel specially vulnerable and humbled in the dust. The orderlies cleaned the place up several times every day, but they never managed to keep pace with it. There were always fresh signs of vomit, blood or other filth. Of course the lavatory was used by savages, unaccustomed to life's comforts, and by patients who were on their last legs. He would have to go to the senior doctor and get permission to use the doctors' lavatory.

But Pavel Nikolayevich's heart was only half in this highly practical plan.

He set off again past the enema room, past the disheveled Kazakh woman and the patients sleeping in the corridor.

Then past the condemned man with the oxygen bag.

On the top landing the Greek wheezed at him in a ghastly whisper, "Hey, brother, listen! Do they cure everyone here? Or do some die?"

Rusanov looked around at him wildly, and the gesture brought him up sharp: he realized that he could no longer turn his head by itself. His whole body, like Yefrem's, had to turn with it. The terrible thing stuck to his neck was pressing up against his chin and down onto his collarbone.

He hurried back to his own bed.

How could he think about anything else? How could he be afraid of anyone else? Who could he rely on? . . .

His fate lay there, between his chin and his collarbone.

There justice was being done.

And in answer to this justice he could summon no influential friend, no past services, no defense.

15. To Each Man His Own

"How old are you?"

"Twenty-six."

"Oh, that's quite old."

"What about you?"

"I'm sixteen. Just think what it's like to lose a leg at sixteen."

"Where do they want to cut it off?"

"At the knee. That's for sure, they never take off any less. I've noticed that. Usually they take off a bit extra. So that's how it is, there'll be a stump hanging down. . . ."

"You can get an artificial leg. What are you going to do with your life?"

"My dream is to get into university."

"What faculty?"

"Either philology or history."

"Will you pass the entrance exam?"

"I think so. I don't get nervous. I'm pretty cool."

"That's good. Having an artificial leg won't be a disadvantage there. You'll be able to work and study—more intensively than the others, in fact. You'll make a better scholar."

"What about life—life in general?"

"You mean, apart from studying? What do you mean, life in general?"

"Well, you know."

"You mean marriage?"

"Well, that too."

"You'll find someone. Every tree can get a bird to perch in it. Anyway, what's the alternative?"

"What d'you mean?"

"It's either your leg or your life, isn't it?"

"Perhaps, yes. But it might get better on its own."

"No, Dyomka, bridges aren't built on perhapses. Perhaps doesn't lead anywhere, only to more perhapses. You can't bank on that sort of luck, it's unreasonable. Have they told you what your tumor's called?"

"It's one of those SA ones."

"That means sarcoma. You'll have to have an operation."

"What? Are you sure?"

"Yes, I am. If they came and told me they wanted to cut off one of my legs, I'd let them do it. Even though the whole point of my life is getting about, on foot and on horseback. Cars are no use where I come from."

"Don't they want to operate on you now?"

"No."

"Does that mean you've missed your chance?"

"How can I put it? I haven't exactly missed my chance . . . or perhaps I have in a way. I was completely wrapped up in my field-work. I should have come in here three months ago, but I didn't want to give it up. All the walking and riding made it worse. It was always being rubbed, it got wet, and then pus started coming out. Once the pus is out you feel better, you want to get back to work again. I thought, I'll wait a bit longer. It's still rubbing so much I feel like cutting off one of my trouser legs or sitting about naked."

"Don't they bandage it?"

"No."

"Can I see it?"

"Take a look."

"O-o-o-gh! What a . . . ! It's all black."

"It's been black ever since I was born. I had a big birthmark here, but you can see it's degenerated."

"What's that there?"

"They're three fistulas that remained after each of the three times it discharged. You see, Dyomka, my tumor's quite different from yours. Mine's a melanoblastoma, a real merciless bastard. As a rule, it's eight months and you've had it."

"How do you know all this?"

"I read a book about it before I came. It was only after I read it that I faced up to what I'd got. But the point is that even if I'd come earlier they still wouldn't have been able to operate. A melanoblastoma is such a swine you only have to touch it with a knife and it produces secondaries. You see, it wants to live too, in its way. Then, because I waited those months, this suddenly appeared in my groin."

"What does Ludmila Afanasyevna say? She saw you on Saturday, didn't she?"

"She says they're going to try to get hold of some colloidal gold. If they do, they may be able to stop it in my groin and then smother the leg with X rays. That way they'll postpone . . ."

"They'll cure you?"

"No, Dyomka, it's far too late to cure me. Nobody's cured of a melanoblastoma. There just aren't any instances of recovery. In my case, cutting off a leg wouldn't be enough, and where could they cut higher up? The question is now, how to postpone it, and how much time do I stand to gain—months or years?"

"That is . . . You mean you're going? . . ."

"Yes, that's what I mean. I've accepted it, Dyomka. But living longer doesn't mean having more life. The real question is, what will I have time to achieve? I must have time to achieve something on this earth. I need three years. If they give me three years, I won't ask more than that. And I don't mean three years lying in the clinic, I mean three years in the field."

Vadim Zatsyrko and Dyomka were talking quite quietly, sitting on Vadim's bed by the window. Only Yefrem, in the next bed, was within earshot, but ever since morning he had been lying there like a block of wood, never taking his eyes off the ceiling. Possibly Rusanov could hear too. Several times he had looked amicably at Zatsyrko.

"What do you think you'll have time to do?" asked Dyomka, frowning.

"Well, try to understand. I'm testing a new, controversial idea. The great scientists in Moscow seem to doubt whether there's anything in it. My theory is that you can discover deposits of polymetallic ore by looking for radioactive water. Radioactive—you know what that means? There are hundreds of different indications, but you can prove or disprove anything you want on paper. However, I feel, that's exactly it, I *feel* I can prove it in practice. It means I have to be out in the field all the time and actually *find* some ore, using this water and nothing else as a guide. Preferably I should do it more than once. But the work! While you're on the job you have to waste your strength on all sorts of trivial things. For example, there's no vacuum pump, only a centrifugal one, and to start it you have to suck out the air. How? By mouth! That means I get mouthfuls of radioactive water. We use it as drinking water, anyway. The Kirghiz workers say, 'Our fathers never drank here, so we won't either.' But we Russians drink it. Why should I be afraid of radioactivity when I've got a melanoblastoma? I'm the obvious one for this work."

"More fool you!" Yefrem's expressionless, rasping voice broke in on their conversation. He didn't even turn his head. Clearly, he'd been listening to every word. "If you're dying, what do you need geology for? It won't do you any good. You'd be better off thinking about what men live by."

Vadim held his leg in one position, but he turned his head freely on its supple neck. His black, vivid eyes flashed and his soft lips trembled slightly before he replied, with no trace of offense, "I know the answer to that already. People live by creative work. It helps a lot. You don't even have to eat or drink!"

He was gently knocking his fluted plastic mechanical pencil between his teeth, watching to see how far they understood him.

"You read this little book here and you'll see, you'll be surprised." Again Podduyev spoke without moving his body or looking at Zatsyrko. He tapped one rough fingernail against the little blue book in his hand.

"I've already gone through it." Vadim's answer came back swiftly. "It doesn't belong to our age. It's too shapeless, not energetic enough. What we say is 'Work harder! And not just for your own profit.' That's all there is to it."

Rusanov started. His spectacles flashed amicably as he asked loudly, "Tell me, young man, are you a Communist?"

In his simple, easy way Vadim turned his eyes toward Rusanov. "Yes," he said gently.

"I was sure you were," declared Rusanov triumphantly, raising one finger. He looked exactly like a teacher.

Vadim clapped Dyomka on the shoulder. "All right, off you go. I've got work to do."

He bent over his *Geochemical Methods*. In it was a piece of paper he was using as a marker, covered with finely written notes and big exclamation and question marks. He began to read, the black, fluted mechanical pencil moving almost imperceptibly between his fingers.

He became absorbed. It was as if he was no longer there. But Pavel Nikolayevich, encouraged by the support Vadim had given him, wanted to bolster himself up before his second injection, and decided to break Yefrem once and for all, to stop him spreading gloom and despondency. He looked at Yefrem straight across the room, from wall to wall, and began to address him:

"It's a good lesson the comrade's just given you, Comrade Podduyev. It's wrong to give in to illness as you've done. And it's wrong to give in to the first priest-ridden booklet that comes your way. It means in effect that you're playing into the hands of . . ." He wanted to say "of the enemy." In ordinary life there was always some enemy to point to, but who could the enemy be here, in a hospital bed? "You should look deep into life, you know, and above all study the nature of achievement. What motivates people to achieve high productivity? What made people fight heroically in the last war against Germany? Or in the Civil War, to take another example? They were hungry, without shoes, clothes or proper arms. . . ."

Podduyev had been strangely immobile all day. He had not got out of bed to stomp up and down the aisle and, what's more, several of his usual movements seemed to have gone. He'd always taken care not to move his neck, and had only turned his body reluctantly, but today he'd moved neither hand nor foot, all he'd done was tap one finger against his book. They had tried to make him take some breakfast, but he said, "It's no good licking the dishes if you haven't eaten enough at the table." Before breakfast and ever since, he had lain there quite motionless. If he hadn't blinked every now and again you might have thought he'd turned to stone.

But his eyes were open.

His eyes were open, and, as it happened, he didn't have to move an inch to see Rusanov. Rusanov with his whey face was the only thing in his line of vision except for the wall and the ceiling.

He heard Rusanov lecturing him. His lips moved and out came that unfriendly voice, but this time the words were more blurred than ever. "What's that? Civil War? You fought in the Civil War, did you?"

Pavel Nikolayevich sighed. "You and I, Comrade Podduyev," he said, "are not of an age to have been able to fight in that particular war."

Yefrem sniffed vigorously. "I don't know why you didn't fight. I did."

Pavel Nikolayevich politely raised his eyebrows behind his glasses. "How can that be possible?"

"Quite simple," said Yefrem slowly, taking a little rest between each phrase. "I picked up a pistol and went and fought. It was quite something. I wasn't the only one."

"And where was it you say that you fought?"

"Near Izhevsk. We were sorting out the Constituent Assembly.* I shot seven Izhevsk chaps with my own hand. I remember it well."

Yes, he really thought he could remember all seven of them, grown men, and exactly where he, a mere boy, had brought each of them down in the streets of a rebel town.

The fellow in the glasses was still lecturing him about something. But today he felt as if his ears were blocked up, and if he surfaced at all it was not for long.

That morning at dawn, when he'd opened his eyes and looked at a patch of bare, white ceiling, for no particular reason a long-forgotten and quite insignificant event had come into his mind with a jolt.

It was a day in November after the war. Snow was falling, turning to slush as soon as it touched the ground, and melting completely on the warmer earth just thrown up from the trench. They were digging for a gas main. The depth had been specified as 1 meter 80 centimeters. Podduyev, walking past, saw it wasn't yet dug to the proper depth. But the foreman came up to him and swore blind that the whole length of the trench had been properly dug. "Very well, do you want us to measure it? It'll be the worse for you!" Podduyev took a measuring stick with a burn mark across it every ten centimeters, every fifth mark longer than the rest, and they went off together to measure, getting continually stuck in the sodden, soggy clay as they went, he in high officers' boots, the foreman in ordinary soldiers' ones. They stopped at one place and measured—1 meter 70. They went on. In the next place three men were digging. One was a tall, thin peasant with a black growth of beard all over his

*The non-Bolshevik majority of the Constituent Assembly, the Russian parliament, organized short-lived resistance to the Bolsheviks during the Civil War.

face. Another was an ex-officer, who still wore his army cap although the little red star had been torn off long ago; it had a patent-leather rim and peak, and the crimson band was caked with lime and clay. The third was a young guy in a cloth cap and a townsman's overcoat (in those days there was a lot of difficulty about providing prison clothes; they weren't issued with regulation ones). What's more, the overcoat must have been made for him when he was a schoolboy because it was short, tight and threadbare. (It seemed to Yefrem now that he was seeing the overcoat clearly for the first time.) The first two were still digging the ground wearily, dragging up the earth with their spades although the sodden clay stuck to the iron. But the third, just a stripling, was leaning his chest against his spade, as though transfixed by it. White with snow, his hands tucked deep into his wretched short sleeves, he was hanging from it like a scarecrow. They'd given the men no gloves. The ex-soldier had a pair of high boots, but the other two had nothing but improvised shoes made out of car tires. "Why are you standing there gaping?" the foreman shouted at the boy. "Do you want to go on punishment rations? OK, that's fine by me!" The young fellow just sighed and sagged. It looked as if the spade handle were going deeper and deeper into his chest. The foreman gave him a clout on the back of the head, and he shook himself, starting to poke about with his spade again.

They began to measure. The earth had been chucked out on both sides of the trench, close beside it. You had to lean right over the ditch to get an accurate view of where the top notch on the measuring stick came. The ex-soldier stood around pretending to help, but in fact he was holding the stick at an angle to gain an extra ten centimeters. Podduyev swore at him obscenely and held the stick up straight himself. The result was quite clear—1 meter 65.

"Citizen commander," the ex-soldier pleaded softly, "please let us off the last few centimeters. We can't manage them. Our bellies are empty, our strength's gone, and the weather—well, look at it."

"And get myself put on a charge just because of you, eh? Think up another one! Those are the specifications. All the sides must be straight, and no dip at the bottom."

As Podduyev straightened up, pulled up the stick and hauled his feet out of the clay, the three turned their faces toward him—the first black-stubbled, the second looking like a winded hound, the third with fluffy down, untouched by a razor. Looking up at him, the three faces no longer seemed alive as the snow fell on them. The young fellow forced his lips open and said, "All right, chief. It'll be your turn to die one day."

Podduyev had not written a report that would have them thrown in the cooler. He merely recorded what they'd earned, so as not to bring their bad luck down on his own head. Looking back, he could think of plenty of people he'd been harder on than them. All that had been ten years ago. Podduyev didn't work in the camps any more, the foreman had been released, that gas main had only been installed temporarily. Probably it wasn't carrying gas any more and the pipes were being used for something else. But what had been said then had stuck in his mind, coming to the surface today. It had been the first sound in his ear that morning: "All right, chief. It'll be your turn to die one day."

There was nothing for Yefrem to set off against this memory and screen him from it. Did he want to go on living? That young fellow had wanted to as well. Did Yefrem have an iron will? Had he learned something new and did he want to live differently? The disease took no notice of any of this. It had its own "specifications."

There was of course the little blue book with the gilt signature, which had already spent four nights under Yefrem's mattress. It was humming to him about the Hindus and their belief that none of us die completely and our souls transmigrate into animals or other people. These "specifications" appealed to Podduyev now: if only he could take something of his own with him, not let the lot go down the drain. If only he could take something of his own through death.

Only to him this "transmigration" of souls was just a lot of hogwash.

Pain was shooting from his neck right into his head, ceaselessly. It had started to throb evenly, in four-beat time, and each beat of the bar was hammering out: "Yefrem—Podduyev—Dead—Stop. Yefrem—Podduyev—Dead—Stop."

There was no end to it. He began to repeat the words to himself, and the more he repeated them, the more remote he felt from the Yefrem Podduyev who was condemned to die. He was getting used to the idea of his own death, as one does to the death of a neighbor. But whatever it was inside him that thought of Yefrem Podduyev's death as of a neighbor's—this, it seemed, ought not to die.

But what about the neighbor? It looked as if he couldn't escape except perhaps by drinking the birch-tree fungus brew. Only it said in the letter you had to drink it regularly for a whole year. For that you'd need two *poods** of dried fungus, four if it was wet. That would mean eight parcels. The fungus should be fresh off the tree, too, it shouldn't have been lying around. So the parcels couldn't be sent all at once, they would have to go one by one, once a month. Who was there who could pack them up and send them off at the right time? Who did he have back there in Russia?

It would have to be someone close to you, a member of your family.

Hundreds of people had passed through Yefrem's life, but no one he'd got close enough to call a member of his family.

That first wife of his, Amina, might be the one to get the stuff together and send it. There was no one on the other side of the Urals he could write to except her. But she'd only write back, "Just drop dead wherever you like, you old wolf." And she'd be right.

She'd be right according to the book of rules. Not according to the little blue book, though. The blue book said Amina ought to pity him, love him even, not as her husband but simply as a man suffering. She ought to send the parcels of fungus.

The book was very right, of course, so long as everyone started living by it at the same time.

Then Yefrem's ears cleared and it got through to him how the geologist was saying he lived for his work, and Yefrem tapped the blue book with his fingernail again.

Once more he sank back into his own thoughts: he didn't hear or see anything and the same shooting pains continued in his head.

All that bothered him now was the shooting pain. If it hadn't been for that it would have been so easy and comforting for him to lie back without moving, without treatment, without eating, talking, hearing, seeing.

Simply to stop existing.

But someone was shaking him by the foot and the elbow. It seemed the girl from the surgical ward had been standing over him for some time, trying to get him to come and have his dressings changed. Now Ahmadjan was helping her.

So for no good reason at all, Yefrem had to get out of bed. He had to pass on the will to stand to all 210 pounds of his body, the will to tense his legs, his arms and his back, to force his flesh-laden bones out of the torpor into which they'd begun to sink, to make

*A *pood* is an old-fashioned Russian measure of weight, equal to 36 lbs.

their joints work and lever their bulk upright, to become a pillar, to robe that pillar in a jacket and shift it along corridors and down a staircase to be uselessly tormented, to have dozens of meters of bandage unwound and replaced . . .

It took so long and was so painful. All around him there was a sort of gray noise. With Yevgenia Ustinovna were two surgeons who never did operations on their own. She was explaining and demonstrating something to them, and talking to Yefrem too. But he did not answer her.

He felt that they had nothing worth talking about. The indifferent gray noise blanketed all their words.

They wound a hoop around his neck, even mightier than the last, and he returned to the ward with it. His head was now smaller than the bandages wrapped around it. Only the top of it stuck out of the hoop. He ran into Kostoglotov, who was on the way out with a tobacco pouch in his hand.

"Well, what have they decided?"

Yefrem thought to himself, "What *have* they decided?" It seemed as if nothing had got through to him, but by now he understood what they had meant and replied as if he'd known all along, "They said, 'Hang yourself where you like, but don't do it in *our* house.' "

Federau gazed in horror at the monstrous neck, which might be his fate too, and asked, "Are they discharging you?"

It was only when he heard the question that Yefrem realized he couldn't do as he wanted and go back to bed. He had to get himself ready for discharge.

After that, although he couldn't even bend down, he had to put on his everyday clothes.

And after that, although it was beyond his strength, he had to trundle his pillar of a body through the streets of the town.

It seemed intolerable to have to bring himself to do all these things, goodness knows who or what for.

Kostoglotov looked at him—not with pity, but with the sympathy one soldier feels for another, as if to say, "That bullet has your name on it, the next may have mine." He knew nothing of Yefrem's past life, he'd not even made friends with him in the ward, but he liked his bluntness and reckoned he was far from the worst man he'd met in his life.

"All right, Yefrem, let's shake on it." He held out his hand.

Yefrem took his hand and grinned. "When you're born, you

wriggle; when you grow up, you run wild; when you die, that's your lot."

Oleg turned to go out for a cigarette, but a lab girl appeared in the doorway. She was taking around newspapers, and since he was the nearest she gave it to him. Kostoglotov took it and opened it, but Rusanov spotted him and loudly, in hurt tones, reprimanded the girl, who had not managed to scuttle away in time. "Listen, there, listen! I told you quite distinctly to give me the paper first."

He sounded really pained, but Kostoglotov had no pity on him. "Why should you have it first?" he barked.

"What do you mean, Why? What do you mean?" Pavel Nikolayevich was suffering aloud, suffering from the indisputable and self-evident nature of his right, which it was impossible, however, to defend in words.

He felt real jealousy if someone else, with unhallowed fingers, opened a fresh newspaper before him. No one here could possibly understand a newspaper as he did. He regarded newspapers as a widely distributed instruction, written in fact in code; nothing in it could be said openly, but a skillful man who knew the ropes could interpret the various small hints, the arrangement of the articles, the things that were played down or omitted, and so get a true picture of the way things were going. This was why Rusanov *had* to read the paper first.

But as none of this could be said aloud, he just complained. "They're going to give me my injection in a minute. I want to see it before I have my injection."

"Injection?" Bone-chewer softened. "All right. . . ."

He cast his eye rapidly over the paper, where reports of the Supreme Soviet session had squeezed the other news into the corners of the page. He was on the point of going for his smoke anyway. The paper rustled as he started folding it to hand it over, when something caught his eye. He dived back into the paper, and almost at once began to utter one long word, repeating it guardedly, as if grating it finely between his tongue and his palate. "In-ter-est-ing . . . In-ter-est-ing . . ."

Beethoven's four muffled chords of fate were thundering above Kostoglotov's head. Nobody heard them in the ward, perhaps they never would. What else could he say out loud?

"What is it? What is it?" Rusanov was getting quite worked up. "Give me the paper immediately!"

Kostoglotov made no attempt to point anything in the paper out to anyone. He didn't answer Rusanov either. He gathered the pages of the newspaper together, folded it in two and then in four, as it had been originally, except that now the six pages were a bit crumpled and the creases didn't fit. He took a step toward Rusanov, as the other took a step to meet him, and handed him the paper. Without leaving the room he took out his silk tobacco pouch. With trembling hands he began to roll a cigarette out of newspaper and crude, home-grown tobacco.

Pavel Nikolayevich's hands were trembling too as he opened the paper. The way Kostoglotov had said "interesting" had struck him like a knife in the ribs. What could it possibly be that Bone-chewer found "interesting"?

Deftly and efficiently he leaped from heading to heading, through the reports of the Supreme Soviet session until suddenly . . .

It was set in quite small type and would have had no significance for the uninitiated, but to him it shrieked from the page. It was an unprecedented, impossible decree! The whole membership of the Supreme Court of the Soviet Union had been changed.

What's this? Matulevich, Ulrich's deputy? Detistov? Pavlenko? And Klopov! Since it had existed Klopov had been a member of the Supreme Court—and now he was dismissed! Who'd look after the state and Party cadre now? A lot of completely new names. All those who'd administered justice for a quarter of a century—gone, at a single stroke.

It couldn't be coincidence.

It was history on the move. . . .

Pavel Nikolayevich broke into a sweat. It was only just before daybreak that morning that he had managed to calm himself down, persuade himself that all his fears were groundless. But now. . . .

"Your injection."

"What?" He jumped like a madman.

Dr. Gangart was standing in front of him with a hypodermic syringe. "Roll up your sleeve, Rusanov. Here's your injection."

16. Absurdities

He was crawling. He was crawling along a concrete tube—no, not a tube, a tunnel, perhaps, with uncovered steel bars jutting out from its sides. Sometimes he'd get caught on them, just at the right of his neck where it hurt. He was crawling on his belly, and what he felt most was the heaviness of his body pressing him against the earth, a heaviness much greater than the weight of his body. He wasn't used to it, it was flattening him. He thought at first it was the concrete crushing him from above, but no, it was his body that was so heavy. As he dragged it along it felt like a sack of scrap metal. He was so heavy he thought he'd never be able to get up on his feet again. Only one thing mattered now, to crawl his way out of this passage for a gulp of air and a look at the light. But the passage was never-ending, never-ending.

Then a voice from somewhere—only it wasn't a voice, but a transmitted thought—ordered him to crawl sideways. "How can I if there's a wall in the way?" he thought. Yet the order was incontestable, and weighed on him as heavily as that other weight flattening his body. With a groan he crawled sideways, and indeed he found he could do it as easily as when he'd been crawling forward. He was just getting used to going to the left when he received an order to crawl to the right. He moaned and got moving. He was weighed down by it all, yet there was still no light, no sign of the tunnel's end. The same distinct voice ordered him to turn right, at the double. He worked his way with his elbows and feet, and in spite of the impenetrable wall on his right, he crawled on and it seemed to work. Then he was called to wheel to the left, again at the double. By now his doubts had gone, he didn't need to think. He worked his way left with his elbows and pushed on. His neck kept getting caught, jarring through his head. He'd never been in such a fix in his life; it would be a pity to die there without reaching the end.

But suddenly his legs lightened, as if they had been inflated with air. They began to rise, although his chest and head were still pressed against the ground. He listened, but no order came. And then he realized that perhaps there *was* a way out: he would let his legs float out of the tube, crawl backwards after them and climb out. Sure enough, he began to move backwards. Pushing himself up with his hands (goodness knows where he found the strength), he began to crawl back after his legs through a hole. It was a narrow hole, but it was made really difficult by the blood flowing down to his head, so that he thought he was going to die right there and that his head would burst. He gave another little push with his hands against the walls and, scratched all over, managed to crawl out.

He found himself sitting on a pipe on a construction site. There was nobody there; the working day was obviously over. The earth was muddy and soggy around him. He had sat down on the pipe for a rest—and saw a girl sitting next to him, in dirty overalls, her head uncovered, her strawlike hair hanging loosely without comb or pin. The girl was not looking at him; she just sat there, but she was expecting him to ask her a question, he knew that. At first he was frightened, but then he realized she was even more afraid of him than he of her. He was not in the mood to talk, but she was so intense, waiting for his question, that he asked her, "Where is your mother, young lady?"

"I don't know," she answered, looking down at her feet and biting her fingernails.

"What do you mean, you don't know?" He began to grow angry. "You must know, and you must tell me truthfully. And write down everything as it is . . . Why don't you say something? For the second time, where is your mother?"

"That's what I'd like to ask you." She looked at him.

She looked at him—and her eyes were all water. It struck right through him and came to him several times, not piecemeal, but all at once: she must be the daughter of Grusha, the press operator who had been run in for gossiping against the Leader of the Peoples, she must have brought him a form that wasn't properly filled out because she'd hidden this fact about her mother. So he'd summoned her and threatened to have her charged with not filling out her form properly. And then she had poisoned herself. She had poisoned herself, but looking at her hair and her eyes now, it struck him that she must have drowned herself. It struck him too that she had guessed who he was. And it also struck him that if she had drowned herself and he was sitting next to her, then he must be dead too. He broke out in a sweat. He wiped the sweat away and said to her, "Whew, it's hot out here. Where can I get a drink of water, do you know?"

"There." The girl nodded.

She pointed to a box or a trough full of stale rainwater mixed with greenish clay. It struck him again that this was the water that she had swallowed, and now she wanted him to choke on it too. If she wanted that, then surely he must still be alive?

"I tell you what." He tried a trick to get rid of her. "Would you run over there and call the foreman? Tell him to bring my boots. How can I walk like this?"

The girl nodded, jumped off the pipe and splashed through the puddles, bareheaded, untidy, in the overalls and high boots girls wear on construction sites.

He was so thirsty he decided to take a drink, even if it was out of the trough. Nothing would happen to him if he drank a little. He climbed down and noticed with amazement that he wasn't slipping on the mud. The soil under his feet was nondescript. Everything around him was nondescript, and in the distance there was nothing to be seen. He could have walked on and on like this, but suddenly he was afraid that he had lost an important document. He went through his pockets, all of them at once, more quickly than his hands could do the job, and he realized—yes, he had lost it.

At once he became frightened, terribly frightened: outsiders must not read documents like that nowadays. He could get into deep trouble. Instantly he realized he'd lost it as he was climbing out of the tube. He walked quickly back, but was unable to find the place; he could not even recognize it, and there was no tube there. Instead there were workers wandering all over the place, and—worst of all —they might find it.

The workers were all young men and he didn't know any of them. One fellow in a welder's canvas jacket with shoulder flaps stopped and looked at him. Why was he staring at him like that? Had he found it?

"Hey, young man, do you have a match?" asked Rusanov.

"But you don't smoke," answered the welder

(They knew everything! How did they know that?)

"I need matches for something else."

"What else?" The welder scrutinized him.

Really, what a stupid answer! A typical saboteur's reply! They might detain him and in the meantime the document would be found. That's what the matches were for, of course: to burn it.

The young man came closer and closer. Rusanov was very frightened. He knew what was going to happen. The young man looked him straight in the eye and said clearly and distinctly, "Since Yelchanskaya has, so to speak, entrusted her daughter to me, I conclude that she regards herself as guilty and that she is awaiting arrest."

Rusanov started to shiver. "How do you know that?"

(It was rather a pointless question because it was clear that the young man had just read his report: his last remark came from it word for word.)

But the welder said nothing and went on his way. Rusanov started rushing about. Obviously his report was lying somewhere nearby. He must find it soon, he must.

Dashing between walls, turning corners, his heart leaped ahead, but his legs couldn't keep up; his legs were moving so slowly. He was desperate, desperate. At last he spotted his paper. He knew at once it must be the right one. He wanted to run and pick it up, but his legs would not carry him. He went down on all fours and, pushing himself mainly with his hands, moved toward the paper. If only no one else grabbed it first! If only no one got there before him and tore it out of his hands! Closer, closer. . . . At last he'd grabbed it! It *was* the paper! But he had no strength left in his fingers, not even to tear it up. He lay face down on the ground, covering it with his body.

Somebody touched him on the shoulder. He resolved not to turn around, not to let the paper escape from under him. But the touch was soft: a woman's hand. It struck Rusanov it must be Yelchanskaya herself.

"My friend," she said softly, bending right down to his ear. "Well, my friend, tell me, where's my daughter? Where did you take her?"

"She is in a good place, Yelena Fedorovna, don't worry," Rusanov replied, without turning his head toward her.

"Where?"

"In a children's home."

"What children's home?" She wasn't interrogating him; her voice was sad.

"I don't know what to tell you, really." He'd have liked to tell her the truth, but he didn't know what it was. He hadn't sent the daughter away himself, and they might easily have transferred her from the original place.

"Is she living under my name?" The questioning voice behind his back was almost tender.

"No," Rusanov told her sympathetically. "They have a rule there: names have to be changed. I can't do anything about it. It's a rule."

Lying there, he remembered how he'd rather liked the Yelchanski couple. He had borne them no ill-will. And if he had had to denounce the old man, it was only because Chukhnenko had asked him to. Yelchanski had been in his way professionally. After the husband was arrested, Rusanov had helped the wife and daughter quite sincerely. And later on, when she was expecting to be arrested herself, she had entrusted her daughter to him. How he had come to denounce the wife as well he couldn't remember.

He turned his head to look at her, but she wasn't there, she wasn't there at all. (How could she be? She was dead.) Something stabbed inside his neck, on the right-hand side. He straightened his head, still lying on the ground. He needed a rest. He was tired, more tired than he'd ever been before. His whole body ached.

He was lying in a mineshaft, in a gallery. His eyes had already got used to the dark, and beside him on the ground, which was littered with small pieces of coal, he noticed a telephone. He was very surprised. How could a telephone have got here? Could it be connected? If so, he could ring and ask someone to bring him a drink. In fact, he'd ask to be taken to hospital.

He lifted the receiver. Instead of a dial tone he heard a vigorous businesslike voice.

"Comrade Rusanov?"

"Yes, yes." Rusanov quickly pulled himself together. (He knew at once that the voice came from above, not below.)

"Please come to the Supreme Court."

"Supreme Court? Yes, of course! Right away! Very good!" He

was about to put down the receiver when he remembered. "Er, excuse me, which Supreme Court? The old or the new?"

"The new one," the voice answered coldly. "Kindly hurry." And the receiver was put down.

He recalled what he knew about the changes in the Supreme Court and he cursed himself for being the first to pick up the receiver. Matulevich was gone . . . Klopov was gone . . . Yes, even Beria was gone. What times these were.

But he had to obey. He was too weak to get up, but now he'd been summoned he knew that he had to. He strained all his limbs, hauled himself up and fell down like a calf that still hasn't learned how to walk. True, they hadn't told him the exact time, but they had said, "Hurry!" At last, supporting himself against a wall, he got to his feet, dragged himself along on weak, unsteady feet, all the time clinging to the wall. He didn't know why, but there was a pain in his neck on the right-hand side.

He walked along wondering, would they really put him on trial? Could they possibly be so cruel as to try him after all these years? What a thing to do, changing the membership of the Court! It wouldn't be a change for the better.

What could he do? With all his respect for the highest court in the land, the only course left to him was to defend himself. He would find the courage to do so.

This is what he would tell them: "I have not been the one to pronounce sentence. Nor have I conducted investigations. I have only signaled my suspicions. If I found a scrap of newspaper in a public lavatory with a torn-up photograph of the Leader, it was my duty to pick it up and signal it. It's the investigator's job to check it out. It may have been a coincidence or it may not. The investigating organs are there to discover the truth. All I did was carry out my simple duty as a citizen."

This is what he would tell them: "All these years it has been vital to make society healthy, morally healthy. This can't be done without purging society, and a purge can't be conducted without men who aren't squeamish about using a dung shovel!"

As these arguments developed in his brain, he got more and more flustered about how he would put them over.

Now he was eager to get there and be summoned to the court as soon as possible; then he would simply shout at them, "I wasn't the only one! Why put *me* on trial? Name one man who didn't do what

I did. How could he hang onto his post if he didn't 'help'? You mention Guzun? He went to prison, didn't he?"

He was as tense as if he was already shouting his speech. But then he noticed that he wasn't really shouting, it was just that his throat was swollen and hurting.

He seemed to be walking along an ordinary corridor now, not a mine gallery. Someone behind him called, "Pashka! What's wrong with you? Are you ill? Why are you dragging yourself along like that?"

He felt more cheerful, and he walked on, it seemed, as if he were quite all right. He turned around to see who it was. It was Zveinek, in a tunic with a shoulder belt.

"Where are you off to, Jan?" asked Pavel, wondering why the other was so young. That is, he was young, of course, but hadn't that been a long time ago?

"Where am I going? Same place as you, of course. To the commission."

"What commission?" Pavel tried to work it out. He knew he'd been summoned somewhere else, but he couldn't quite remember where.

He fell into step with Zveinek and they walked along, cheerfully and briskly, like young men. He felt he was under twenty, not yet married.

Now they were walking through a big office; there sat the intelligentsia behind their desks: old accountants wearing ties and beards that made them look like priests; engineers with little crossed hammers on the lapels of their jackets; elderly, aristocratic-looking ladies; young typists, heavily made up, with skirts above their knees. As soon as he and Zveinek marched in, their four boots thumping in perfect time, all thirty people in the room turned toward them. Some of them stood up, others bowed in their seats. All followed their progress with their eyes, and on every face was a look of terror which Pavel and Jan found flattering.

They entered the next room, greeted the other members of the commission and sat down at a table with a red tablecloth.

"All right, let's get started!" Venka, the president, commanded.

They began. The first to come in was Aunt Grusha, a press operator.

"And what are you doing here, Aunt Grusha?" asked Venka in amazement. "We're purging the administration. How does that concern you? How have you wormed your way into administration?"

Everyone burst out laughing.

"No, nothing like that, you see," Aunt Grusha was not in the least put out, "it's my daughter, she's getting bigger now and I must find a kindergarten for her, you see."

"All right, Aunt Grusha," called Pavel. "Write out your application and we'll arrange things. We'll fix it up for your daughter. Now don't interrupt us any more, we're going to purge the intelligentsia!"

He stretched out a hand to pour himself some water out of a carafe, but the carafe turned out to be empty. He nodded to his neighbor to ask him to pass a carafe from the other end of the table. It was passed to him, but that one was empty too.

He was so thirsty that it felt as if his throat was on fire.

"Give me a drink!" he called out. "I must have a drink!"

"In a moment," said Dr. Gangart. "We'll bring you some water in a moment."

Rusanov opened his eyes. She was sitting beside him on the bed.

"There's some stewed fruit juice in my bedside table," he said weakly. He felt feverish and was aching all over. His head was beating like a drum.

"All right, we'll give you some juice." Gangart's thin lips broke into a smile. She opened the bedside table and took out the bottle and a glass.

To judge from the windows it was a sunny evening.

Out of the corner of his eyes, Pavel Nikolayevich watched Gangart pouring out the juice to make sure she didn't slip anything into it.

The bitter-sweet juice was piercingly delicious. Pavel Nikolayevich lay back on his pillow and emptied the glass Gangart was holding for him.

"I felt awful today," he complained.

"Oh, you came through all right," said Gangart, disagreeing. "It's just that today we increased your dose."

Rusanov was stabbed by another suspicion. "What did you say? You mean you're going to increase it every time?"

"From now on it'll be the same dose as you had today. You'll get used to it. It won't be so bad in future."

"What about the Supreme . . . ?" he began, but cut himself short. He was already confused between delirium and the real world.

17. The Root from Issyk Kul

Vera Kornilyevna was worried about how Rusanov would take the full dose. She visited the ward several times that day and stayed late after work. She wouldn't have had to come so often if Olympiada Vladislavovna had been on duty, as she should have been according to the schedule. But she'd been taken off after all to attend a course for trade-union treasurers. Turgun was on duty instead, and he was a bit too happy-go-lucky.

Rusanov took the injection rather badly, although the effect did not exceed the permissible limits. After it he was given a sleeping draft, so he didn't wake up but kept restlessly tossing and turning, twitching and groaning. Each time Vera Kornilyevna came she stayed, watching over him and taking his pulse. He kept writhing and stretching his legs out.

His face was reddish and damp with sweat. Without his glasses, his head no longer looked like that of an overbearing official, specially lying on the pillow. The few fair hairs that had survived his baldness were slicked down pathetically over the top of his head.

Since she had to come into the ward so often anyway, Vera Kornilyevna took the chance of getting some other things done as well. Podduyev, who had been the ward's "senior patient," was now discharged, and although the duties were practically nonexistent, there was supposed to be one. She walked from Rusanov's bed to the next one along and announced, "Kostoglotov, you are the 'senior patient' as from today."

Kostoglotov was lying fully dressed on top of the blankets reading a newspaper. It was the second time Gangart had come in while he was reading it. She was by now used to his verbal sallies and expected them, so she smiled at him lightly as she spoke, as if to imply that she knew quite well the appointment was meaningless. Kostoglotov raised a cheerful face from the newspaper and, not knowing how best to show his respect for the doctor, drew up his long legs which had been stretched out along the bed. He looked quite friendly as he replied, "Vera Kornilyevna, are you trying to deal me an irreparable moral blow? Administrators always make mistakes. Some of them even succumb to the temptations of power. After years of thought, I've made myself a vow never again to act as an administrator."

"You've been an administrator? An important one?" She was ready to talk and enter into the game.

"My most important position was deputy platoon commander, but I really got further than that. You see, my platoon commander was so stupid and incompetent that they had to send him on a refresher course, after which they'd make him a battery commander, no less, only not in our battalion. The officer they sent instead of him was immediately transferred to the political department as a supernumerary. My battalion commander had no objection to my appointment because I was a good topographer and the boys obeyed me. So I spent two years as acting platoon commander with the rank of senior sergeant, from Yelets to Frankfurt-on-Oder. They were the best years of my life, by the way. I know it sounds funny, but it's true."

He realized it didn't look very polite, sitting there with his legs pulled up, so he transferred them to the floor.

"There, you see." Listening or speaking to him, the friendly smile never left Gangart's face. "Why refuse the job? You might have a few more happy years."

"What wonderful logic! Happy years? What about democracy? You're ignoring the whole principle of democracy. The ward never elected me. The voters don't even know my life history. . . . And you don't know it, either, for that matter."

"Well, tell me then."

As always she spoke softly, and this time he too lowered his voice so that only she could hear. Rusanov was asleep, Zatsyrko was reading, Podduyev's bed was empty now. Their conversation was almost inaudible.

"It'll take a long time. Look, I feel embarrassed to be sitting while you're standing. It's not the proper way to talk to a woman. But it'll look even stupider if I rise to my feet and stand in the passageway like a soldier. Sit down on my bed. Please!"

"I ought to be going really," she said. She sat down on the edge of the bed.

"You see, Vera Kornilyevna, everything that's gone wrong in my life has been because I was too devoted to democracy. I tried to spread democracy in the army, that is, I answered my superiors back. That's why I wasn't sent on an officers' course in 1939, but stayed in the ranks. In 1940 I got as far as the officers' training college, but I was so rude to my superior officers that they threw me out. It was only in 1941 that I somehow managed to complete a course for noncommissioned officers in the Far East. Quite frankly, I regretted it a lot, not being an officer. All my friends were commissioned. When you're young you take things like that to heart. Still, even then I thought justice was more important."

"I had a friend. He was very close to me," said Gangart, looking down at the blanket on the bed. "He went through the same sort of thing. He was an intelligent and educated man, but he was never more than a private." There was a half-pause, a moment of silence that passed between them. She raised her eyes. "But you're just the same now as you were then."

"What do you mean? A private or intelligent?"

"Independent. For instance, look at the way you talk to the doctors, especially me."

She spoke severely, but it was a strange sort of severity, touched with softness, like all her words and movements. It was not a dim, diffused softness, but somehow melodic and based on harmony.

"The way I talk to you? I talk to you with the greatest respect. This is the highest form of conversation I know, but you don't realize that yet. But if you're thinking about that first day, well, you can't imagine what a tight spot I was in then. I was a dying man, and they only just let me leave the district where I'm exiled. I came down here, and instead of winter snow it was pouring with rain. I had to take off my felt boots and carry them under my arm. Where I'd come from the frost was really something. My overcoat got so soaked I could have wrung it out. I checked my boots in the baggage place and took the tram to the old town. I had an address there— one of my soldiers from the front—but it was dark by then and everyone in the trolley kept telling me, 'Don't go, you'll get your throat cut!' After the 1953 amnesty they let all the criminal scum out of prison, and they can't catch them now however much they try. I didn't even know for sure if my soldier friend was there, and no one in the trolley knew where the street was. So I decided to go round the hotels. They had such beautiful lobbies, I felt quite ashamed to walk into them the way my feet were, and one or two of them even had room. But when I showed them an exile's document instead of an ordinary passport, they all said, 'No, we're not allowed to.' Well, what was I to do? I was quite ready to lie down and die, but why die in the open under a fence? I went straight to the police. I said, 'Listen, I'm one of your boys, find me a place to stay for the night.' They hemmed and hawed and finally told me, 'Go to a teahouse and spend the night there. We don't check papers there.' I couldn't find a teahouse, so I went back to the railway station, but they weren't letting anyone sleep there, there was a policeman walking up and down, chasing people away. Then in the morning I came to you, to the outpatients' department. There was a line. They examined me and said I ought to be hospitalized immediately. So I had to go right across the city again, changing street-cars on the way, to get to the *komendatura*. Although working hours are the same everywhere in the Soviet Union, the *komendant* wasn't there. 'Damn the working day,' he'd said. He wouldn't stoop so low as to leave a message for exiles: he might be back in the office or he might not. Then it dawned on me: if I handed in my document I wouldn't be able to get my felt boots back from the station. So I had to take two trolleys again—back to the station. Each trip took an hour and a half."

"I don't remember you having felt boots. Did you?"

"You wouldn't remember, because I sold my boots to a guy at the station. I reckoned I'd be spending the rest of the winter in the clinic and wouldn't live to see the next one. Then I went back to the *komendatura*. I'd already spent ten roubles on trolleys alone. From the carstop I had to wade a whole kilometer more through mud, in such pain I could hardly drag myself along. And everywhere I went I had to lug my duffel bag with me. But, thank God, the *komendant* was back. I deposited the permit from the *komendatura* at my place of exile with him and showed him the admission chit I'd got from your outpatients. He marked up the permission for me to be hospitalized. So I came . . . no, not back here to the clinic, not yet. First I went into town. I'd seen a poster saying *Sleeping Beauty* was on."

"So you decided to go to the ballet? If I'd known that, I'd never have let you in. Definitely not!"

"Vera Kornilyevna, it was like a miracle. I wanted to see a ballet for the last time before I died. Even if I wasn't going to die, I knew I'd never see a ballet in my perpetual exile. But damn it all, they'd changed the program. Instead of *Sleeping Beauty,* they were showing *Agu-Baly.*"*

With a soundless laugh she shook her head. This dying man's venture into the ballet appealed to her, of course. It appealed to her strongly.

"What could I do? There was a graduate giving a piano recital in the *Conservatoire,* but that's a long way from the station, and I knew I'd never be able to get even the corner of a bench at the hospital. And the rain was lashing down, really whipping me. There was only one thing to do—go and give myself up at the clinic. I arrived. 'There's no room,' they said. 'You'll have to wait a few days.' The other patients told me that sometimes people waited as long as a week. But where was there for me to wait? What could I do? Without the tenacity I'd picked up in the camps, I'd have been completely lost. And then you wanted to take my chit away from me, didn't you? . . . How do you expect me to talk to you after all that?"

It all seemed rather amusing in retrospect; they both found it funny.

There'd been no mental effort in telling the story and all the time he'd been thinking about something else: if she'd finished medical school in 1946, she couldn't be less than thirty-one now; she must be roughly the same age as he. Why, then, did she strike him as younger-looking than the twenty-three-year-old Zoya? It wasn't her face, it was her manner—her timidity, her shyness. With a woman like that one always wonders if she has yet. . . . If you look closely you can always spot them from elusive hints in the way they behave. Yet Gangart was married. Why, then . . . ?

She looked at him, wondering why he'd made such an uncouth and unpleasant impression on her at their first meeting. True, he had harsh lines on his face and a dark way of looking at you, but he knew how to look and speak cheerfully and like a friend, as he

*An Italianized Uzbek opera composed during the Stalinist years.

was now for instance. Or rather, he kept both styles of behavior at the ready, using either as the need arose.

"Well, I know all about the felt boots and the ballerinas now." She smiled at him. "But what about your ordinary boots? You realize your boots are an unheard-of breach of the rules?" She narrowed her eyes.

"Rules, more rules." Kostoglotov screwed up his face, and his scar moved with the grimace. "Even in prison a man's allowed exercise, isn't he? I can't go without my walk, I won't get better without it. You wouldn't want to deprive me of fresh air, would you?"

Yes, he liked walking. He spent a lot of time strolling along the lonely remote pathways of the Medical Center; Gangart had noticed. He looked extremely odd on these occasions in the badly made woman's dressing gown which he had begged from the housekeeper (the men weren't issued dressing gowns, there weren't enough). He gathered it in under an army belt with a star buckle, pushing the voluminous folds away from his belly to the sides, but it still flapped open at the hem. He wore army boots but no cap, and his shaggy black head stood out conspicuously as he paced along with great deliberate strides, sometimes slowly, sometimes fast, looking down at the stones at his feet. When he reached the limit he had set for himself, he always turned back. He always kept his hands folded behind his back. And he was always alone, never with anyone else.

"Nizamutdin Bahramovich will be making his rounds in a few days, and you know what'll happen if he sees your boots? I'll get a reprimand."

Once again it was not so much a demand as a request, almost as though she were complaining to him. The tone she used with him wasn't even one of equality but almost of deference. She was surprised herself that it had risen between them. She had never used it with any other patient.

Trying to convince her, Kostoglotov touched her hand with his paw. "Vera Kornilyevna, I give you a one hundred per cent guarantee he'll never find them. He won't even see me wearing them in the hallway."

"What about outside, on the paths?"

"He won't realize I'm from his wing. I've got an idea. Just for fun we'll write an anonymous letter denouncing me for having a pair of boots. Then he'll bring two orderlies in to ransack the place and they won't find a thing."

"That's not a very nice idea, is it—writing anonymous letters?" She narrowed her eyes again.

There was another thing bothering him: why did she use lipstick? It coarsened her, it spoiled her delicacy. He sighed. "People still write them, Vera Kornilyevna. My word, how they write them. And it works! The Romans used to say, 'One witness is no witness,' but in the twentieth century even one witness is superfluous, unnecessary."

She averted her eyes. It was a difficult subject to discuss.

"Where will you hide them?"

"My boots? Oh, I can think of dozens of places. It all depends on the time of day. I might put them in the stove when it's not lit, or I might hang them on a string out of the window. Don't worry about that."

It was impossible not to laugh. He probably *would* manage to pull it off.

"However did you get out of handing them in your first day?"

"Oh, that was easy. I was in that dog kennel where they make us change into pajamas, and I put them behind one of the doors. The orderly collected all the rest of my stuff into a bag with a label and took it away to the central store. I had my bath, came out of the bathroom, wrapped them up in a newspaper and took them along with me."

They went on talking about this, that and the other. It was the middle of the working day. What was she doing sitting there? Rusanov was restlessly asleep, covered in sweat, but at least sleeping and he hadn't vomited. Gangart took his pulse again and was on the point of going when she remembered something and turned back to Kostoglotov. "Oh yes, you're not getting supplementary diet, are you?"

"No, ma'am." Kostoglotov pricked up his ears.

"You will as from tomorrow. Two eggs a day, two glasses of milk and fifty grams of butter."

"What's this? I can't believe my own ears! I've never had food like that in my whole life! I suppose it's only fair, though. You know, I'm not even getting sick benefits while I'm here."

"Why not?"

"Quite simple. It seems I haven't been a member of a trade union for the required six months. Consequently I'm not entitled to anything."

"That's terrible! How did that happen?"

"I'm just not used to life outside any more. When I got to my place of exile I should have known that I ought to join a trade union as soon as possible."

Strange, he was so clever in some things, but so helpless in others. It was Gangart herself who'd insisted on the extra food for him. It hadn't been easy either. . . . But it was time to be off, she couldn't sit chattering all day.

She was almost at the door when he called after her laughingly, "Just a minute. You're not trying to bribe me now that I'm senior patient, are you? You've got me really worried. My first day in the job and I'm corrupted already!"

Gangart left the room.

But after the patients' lunch she had to visit Rusanov again. By that time she'd learned that the senior doctor's rounds would definitely be tomorrow. This meant there was an extra job to be done in the wards: she had to check all the bedside tables, because if there was one thing Nizamutdin Bahramovich kept a zealous eye open for, it was crumbs or illicit food in the bedside tables. Ideally there should be nothing in them except hospital bread and sugar. He would also check on cleanliness, and in that department he was more ingenious than any woman.

Vera Kornilyevna went up to the second floor and, craning her head back, looked alertly around the tops of the walls and the ceiling. In a corner above Sibgatov's bed she thought she spotted a cobweb (there was more light now, the sun had just come out). She called one of the orderlies—it was Elizaveta Anatolyevna; somehow or other she was always around in an emergency—explained to her that everything had to be clean for tomorrow, and pointed at the cobweb.

Elizaveta Anatolyevna took her glasses out of her coat pocket, put them on and said, "Good heavens, you're absolutely right. How disgraceful!" She put away her glasses again and went off to find a brush and a stepladder. She never wore glasses while she was doing her cleaning.

From there Gangart went into the men's ward. Rusanov was in the same position, and running with sweat; however, his pulse had slowed down. Just before she came in Kostoglotov had donned his boots and dressing gown, ready for his walk. Vera Kornilyevna informed the ward of tomorrow's important inspection and asked the patients to take a look inside their bedside tables before she checked them herself.

"We'll begin with our senior patient," she said.

There was no good reason why she should begin with the senior patient, or why she should have gone again to his corner of the room, for that matter.

Vera Kornilyevna's figure resembled two triangles, set apex to apex, the upper one narrow, the lower one broader. Her waist was so narrow that one's hands itched to get one's fingers around it and toss her into the air. But Kostoglotov did no such thing. He obligingly opened the door of his bedside table for her inspection. "Help yourself," he said.

"Now, let's see, let's see." She tried to get to the table and he moved to one side. She sat down on his bed right next to the table and began to look through it.

She was sitting there, he was standing behind her. Now he had a good view of her neck with its tracery of thin, defenseless lines, and her hair, which was fairly dark and tied in a little knot at the back without the slightest attempt at fashion.

Really, he ought to break free of this torment. It was ludicrous that every woman who came along should so utterly cloud his head. She'd just sat with him for a bit, chatted to him and gone away. But in the hours between he couldn't stop thinking about her. While as for her? In the evening she'd be going home to her husband's embraces. . . .

He'd have to break free. But there was only one way to do it— with a woman.

He stood there staring fixedly at the back of her head. The collar of her coat was turned up behind, pouched out like a little hood, over which he could see the little round bone at the top of her spine. He felt like running his fingers around it.

"Of course, your bedside table is one of the most disgraceful in the whole clinic," Gangart was commenting. "Crumbs, bits of greasy paper, shreds of dirty old tobacco, a book and a pair of gloves. Aren't you ashamed of yourself? You must clean it up today, all of it."

He continued to stare at her neck and said nothing.

She pulled out the drawer at the top of the table. In it, among some loose change, was a tightly corked bottle full of brown liquid, about forty milliliters, a small plastic glass, the sort you find in traveling kits, and a medicine dropper.

"What's this? Medicine?"

Kostoglotov whistled under his breath. "Oh, it's nothing," he said.

"What sort of medicine? We didn't issue it, did we?"

"Well, I'm allowed to have my own, aren't I?"

"Of course not, not while you're a patient in our clinic and without our knowledge."

"You see, it's a bit awkward to explain . . . it's for corns."

She started to twist the unlabeled, anonymous bottle in her fingers, to open it and sniff it. At once Kostoglotov intervened. He clamped his two coarse hands onto hers and pushed aside the one attempting to pull out the cork.

(This constant joining of hands which inevitably continues conversations.)

"Careful," he warned her very quietly. "You have to know how to handle that stuff. You mustn't let it get on your fingers, and you mustn't sniff it."

Gently he took the bottle away from her.

Well, really, this is taking a joke a bit too far.

"What is it?" said Gangart, frowning. "Something strong?"

Kostoglotov sat down on the bed next to her. His voice was businesslike but quiet. "Extremely strong," he said. "It's a root from Issyk Kul. You mustn't ever sniff it, either as an infusion or in its dry state. That's why it's so firmly corked. If you got some on your hands, didn't wash it off, forgot about it and licked it later, you might easily die."

Vera Kornilyevna was alarmed. "What do you keep it for?" she demanded.

"That's torn it," Kostoglotov growled. "Now you've found it, I'll be in for trouble, I suppose. I ought to have hidden it . . . I've been taking it for treatment, I still am now and then."

"Purely for treatment?" She questioned him with her eyes, but this time she didn't narrow them, she wore her most professional air.

Yes, she was wearing her most professional air, but her eyes were the same light brown.

"Purely for treatment," he told her honestly.

"Or are you keeping it . . . just in case?" She still didn't entirely believe him.

"Well, all right, if you want to know. On my way here I did have that idea in the back of my mind. I didn't want to suffer unnecessarily. . . . However, the pains went, and I gave up the idea. But I still carried on treating myself with it."

"In secret? When no one was about?"

"What's a man to do if he can't lead his life as he pleases, if he's surrounded by rules and regulations?"

"What sort of doses did you take?"

"It's a graduated system. From one up to ten drops, then from ten down to one, then ten days' interval. It's the interval at the moment. To be honest, I'm not convinced it was the X rays alone that got rid of my pain. It might have been the root as well."

They were both speaking in muffled voices.

"What did you infuse it in?"

"Vodka."

"You did it yourself?"

"That's right."

"What concentration?"

"Concentration. . . . ? Well, he gave me a handful of root and said, 'This'll do for three half-liters of vodka.' So I worked it out from that."

"But how much did it weigh?"

"He didn't weigh it. He measured it by eye."

"By eye? Poison like that and he measured it by eye? It's aconite! Don't you realize that?"

"What was I supposed to realize?" Kostoglotov was beginning to get angry. "You try dying when you're alone in the universe with the *komendatura* not letting you out past the village limits. Would you start thinking, 'Ah yes, aconite; what does it weigh?' Do you know what the weight of that handful of root could have done to me? Twenty years' hard labor! For absence without leave from my place of exile. I went, though. I traveled a hundred and fifty kilometers, into the mountains. There's an old man living there called Krementsov, with a beard like Academician Pavlov's. He's one of the settlers who went there early in the century. He's an honest-to-goodness medicine man who goes out, collects the roots and works out the doses himself. They laugh at him in his own village—no man's a prophet in his own country—but people come to see him from Moscow and Leningrad. Once a *Pravda* correspondent arrived and was convinced, they say. But there are rumors that they've clapped the old man in jail now. Some damn fools made half a liter of it and kept it openly in the kitchen. They had some guests in for the November celebrations,* the vodka ran out, the host and hostess weren't there, so they drank some of the root. Three of them died. In another house some children were poisoned by it too. But why arrest the old man? He warned them . . ."

But by now Kostoglotov had noticed that he was spoiling his own case, so he stopped.

Gangart was upset. "That's the whole point!" she said. "It's strictly forbidden to keep powerful substances like this in a hospital public ward. It's out of the question, absolutely out of the question. There could easily be an accident. Give me the bottle!"

"No," he said firmly.

"Give it to me." She frowned angrily as she reached out toward his tightly clenched fist.

Kostoglotov's strong fingers, which had seen so much work, were closed around the little bottle, completely hiding it.

He smiled. "You won't get it that way."

She relaxed her brows. "Anyway," she said, "I know when you go for your walks. I can take the bottle when you're not here."

"Thank you for warning me. I'll hide it."

"On a string out of the window? What do you expect me to do now, report you?"

"I don't believe you would. You've just told me you don't approve of denouncing people."

"But you don't leave me any alternative."

"Does that mean you have to denounce me? That's not very dignified, is it? Are you afraid Comrade Rusanov here will drink it? I won't let that happen. I'll wrap it in paper and stow it away somewhere. When I leave the clinic I'll want the root extract to treat myself with. I don't suppose you believe it works?"

"No, of course I don't. It's just a lot of dark superstition and playing games with death. I believe in systematic science, practically tested. That's what I was taught and that's the way all oncologists think. Give me the bottle."

Despite what he'd said, she tried to pry off his top finger.

Looking into her angry, light brown eyes, he felt little inclination to dig his toes in and argue. He'd have been only too pleased to

*On November 7, the anniversary of the 1917 Revolution.

give her the bottle and the whole of his bedside table, for that matter, but it went against the grain to betray his principles.

"Oh, I know about your sacred science," he sighed. "If it were all so categorical, it wouldn't be disproved every ten years! What is there for me to believe in? Your injections? And by the way, why have they prescribed these new injections for me? What sort of injections are they?"

"They're absolutely necessary; your life depends on them. We're trying to save your *life*!" She spelled it out with particular insistence, her eyes bright with faith. "And don't imagine that you're cured!"

"Can't you be more precise? What effect will they have?"

"Why should I be more precise? They'll cure you. They'll stop secondaries forming. You wouldn't understand if I explained. . . . Hand over the bottle, and I give you my word of honor I'll return it to you when you leave."

They looked at each other.

He looked really comic, ready for his walk, in his woman's dressing gown and the belt with the star buckle on it.

She was going on and on about it. Damn the bottle. He wouldn't particularly mind handing it over; he still had ten times that amount of aconite stored back at home. No, the trouble really was, here was this lovely woman with the light brown eyes and radiant face, with whom it was wonderful to be talking—and yet he would never be able to kiss her. When he got home to the backwoods he'd hardly believe that he'd been sitting here, right next to such a radiant woman, and that she had wanted to save his life, whatever the cost.

That, however, was just what she couldn't do.

"I'd better think twice before giving it to *you*," he said jokingly. "You'll take it home and someone might drink it."

(Who would? . . . Who would drink it at home? She lived on her own. But it would be clumsy and inept to say so at this moment.)

"All right, let's call it a tie. Let's just pour it away."

He started to laugh. It was a pity he couldn't do more for her than that.

"All right. I'll go outside and pour it away."

(Say what you like, he thought, she's wrong to use lipstick.)

"No, I don't believe you now. I'll have to be there when you do it."

"I've got an idea! Why pour it away? Wouldn't it be better to

give it to some well-deserving fellow you're not going to cure in
any case? It might do him some good."

"Who have you got in mind?"

Kostoglotov nodded toward Vadim Zatsyrko's bed and pitched
his voice even lower. "He's got a melanoblastoma, hasn't he?"

"Now I'm really convinced we've got to pour it away, otherwise
you're bound to poison someone, bound to! How can you have the
heart to suggest giving a bottle of poison to a man who's seriously
ill? What if he poisoned himself? Wouldn't your conscience bother
you?"

She was avoiding calling him anything. Throughout their long
conversation she hadn't once called him anything.

"He won't poison himself. He's a steady sort of guy."

"No! Absolutely no! Come on, we'll go and pour it away."

"Well, I'm in a very good mood today. All right, let's go and
pour it away."

They walked down between the beds and out onto the landing.

"Won't you be cold?"

"No, I've got a cardigan on underneath."

She'd said cardigan underneath! Why had she said it? Now he
wanted to see what sort of cardigan, and what color, but he never
would.

They went out onto the porch. The day had brightened up, it
was almost like spring. No one recently arrived would have believed
it was only the seventh of February. The sun was shining. The high
poplar branches and the low hedge shrubbery were still bare, but
the patches of snow had almost gone, even in the places that didn't
get the sun. Between the trees lay last year's gray-brown beaten-
down grass. The pathways, the paving, the stone and the asphalt
were damp, they hadn't dried off yet. There was the usual lively
traffic of people in the gardens, walking toward each other, crossing
each other's paths or overtaking—doctors, nurses, orderlies, general
staff, outpatients and inpatients' relatives. There were even a couple
of benches occupied. Here and in the other wings a few windows
were open for the first time that year.

They decided not to pour it out right in front of the porch. It
would look odd.

"Come on, we'll go over there." He pointed to a path that ran
between the cancer wing and the ear, nose and throat wing. It was
one of the places where he took his strolls.

They walked side by side along a paved pathway. Gangart's doctor's cap was made like a pilot's. It just came up to Kostoglotov's shoulder.

He watched her out of the corner of his eye. She was walking along with a solemn expression, as if she was engaged in something immensely important. It made him want to laugh.

"Tell me, what did they call you at school?" he asked her suddenly.

She gave him a quick glance. "What's that got to do with it?"

"Nothing, of course. I was just interested."

She took a few more steps in silence, her feet tapping lightly against the paving stones. He had first noticed her slender, gazelle-like legs that day when he had been lying on the floor dying and she had come up to him for the first time.

"Vega," she said.

(Of course, that wasn't really true, or not completely true. She had been called that at school, but only by one man, the educated and intelligent private who never came back from the war. On an impulse, without knowing why, she'd suddenly confided this nickname to someone else.)

They came out of the shadow and onto the walk between the two wings. The sun hit them; a little breeze was blowing there.

"Vega? After the star? But Vega should be dazzlingly white."

They stopped.

"I'm not dazzling or anything." She shook her head. "But I am VE-ra GA-ngart. That's all it is."

For the first time it wasn't she who was embarrassed at something he'd said, but the other way round.

"What I meant was . . ." he began, in an attempt to justify himself.

"I quite understand. Pour it away now," she ordered.

She didn't even permit herself a smile.

Kostoglotov loosened the firmly wedged cork, extracted it with great care, then bent down (he looked absurd with the shirtlike dressing gown over his boots) and pulled up one of the little stones left over from when the path was last paved.

"Watch me! Otherwise you'll say I poured it into my pocket," he said. He was squatting on the ground, close to her legs.

(Those legs, those gazelle-like legs—he'd noticed them that first time.)

He poured someone's murky-brown liquid death—or recovery—into the small damp hole in the dark soil.

"May I put the stone back?" he asked.

She looked down at him and smiled.

There was something boyish in the way he poured the stuff away and put back the stone. It was boyish, but a bit like making a vow, too, or sharing a secret.

"Well, congratulate me," he said, getting up from the ground.

"Congratulations." She smiled, but sadly. "Go for your stroll now."

And she walked off back to the wing.

He stared at her white back: the two triangles, upper and lower.

Any sign of feminine interest stirred him now. He read more than there was into every word, and after every action he waited for the next.

Ve-Ga. Vera Gangart. There was something that didn't quite fit, but for the moment he couldn't work out what. He stared at her back.

"Vega! Ve-ga!" he said half-aloud, trying to suggest it to her from a distance. "Come back, do you hear? Come back! Please turn round!"

But the suggestion failed. She did not turn.

18. At the Grave's Portals*

A bicycle, a wheel, once rolling, retains its balance only so long as it moves. Without movement, it collapses. In the same way the game between woman and man, once begun, can exist so long as it develops. If today didn't continue yesterday's progress, the game would no longer exist.

Oleg could hardly wait for Tuesday evening, when Zoya was due to come on night duty. The gay, multicolored wheel of their game had to roll a little further than it had that first night and on Sunday afternoon. He felt within himself an urge to roll it on and foresaw that same urge in her. Nervously, he waited for her.

At first he went outside, in the hope of meeting her in the garden. He knew the slanting path she always came in by. He smoked two shag cigarettes he'd rolled himself before it occurred to him that he'd look silly in his woman's dressing gown, not at all how he wanted to present himself. It was getting dark, too. He went back into the wing, took off his dressing gown and boots, and stood by the bottom of the stairs in his pajamas, looking no less absurd than he had in the dressing gown. His hair, which usually stuck up on end, was as tamed today as it ever could be.

She came out of the doctors' dressing room, late and in a hurry, but she raised her eyebrows when she saw him, not in surprise but as if noting that things were as they should be, that she'd expected him to be there, that his place was there, at the foot of the stairs.

*The first words of a stanza from one of Alexander Pushkin's poems, which goes on: ". . . unrepining/May young life play, and where I lie may heedless Nature still be shining/With beauty that shall never die."

She did not stop. Not wishing to be left behind, he walked beside her, stretching his long legs up the staircase, two steps at a time. He could move like that without difficulty now.

"Well, what's new?" she asked him as she climbed, as if he were her aide-de-camp.

What was new? The changes in the Supreme Court were new all right. But she would need years of education to understand that, and it wasn't that kind of understanding that Zoya needed at the moment.

"I've found a new name for you. At last I've realized what your name ought to be."

"Really? What?" She continued briskly up the stairs.

"I can't tell you while we're walking. It's too important."

They were at the top now. He lagged back on the last few steps and, looking at her from behind, noted that her legs were a bit thick and heavy, although they seemed to go well with her compact figure. Still, they had a charm of their own, though light and springy legs, like Vega's, put you in a better mood.

He was surprised at himself. He never used to think or look at things that way before; he found it coarse and vulgar. He'd never flitted from woman to woman. His grandfather would have called it "skirt mad." Still, as the saying went, "Eat when you're hungry, love when you're young." Oleg had missed out in his youth, though. Now he was like an autumn plant in haste to extract the last juices from the earth so as not to regret the lost summer. During his short return to life—and his life was already going downhill, yes, downhill—he was impatient to see women and absorb them, in a way which he could never mention to them. He was more sensitive than others to their nature, since for years he hadn't seen one, been near one, or heard a woman's voice: he had forgotten what it sounded like.

Zoya took over the shift and it was as if she'd started whirling like a top. She whirled around her table, around the treatment list and the medicine cabinet, then she'd suddenly spin off sideways toward one of the doors, just like a top.

Oleg watched her and, as soon as he saw she had a moment to herself, was at her side.

"So there's nothing else new in the clinic?" asked Zoya in her delicious voice, meanwhile sterilizing syringes on an electric stove and opening ampoules.

"Oh, there was a great event today at the clinic. Nizamutdin Bahramovich himself made his rounds."

"Did he? That's good. I'm glad I wasn't there . . . So what happened? Did he take away your boots?"

"No, it wasn't the boots. But there *was* a bit of a clash."

"What happened?"

"Oh, it was a grand occasion. Fifteen white coats walked into the ward all at once—heads of departments, registrars, interns, doctors I've never even seen before. The senior doctor pounced on the bedside tables like a tiger. But we'd already had reports from our secret agents. We'd done a little preparation, so there was nothing for him to get his teeth into. He frowned and looked very dissatisfied. At that moment they brought up my case, and Ludmila Afanasyevna made a bit of a gaffe. She was reading out my file. . . ."

"What file?"

"I mean my case history, I always make these mistakes . . . She mentioned my first diagnosis and where it had been made, and it came out I was from Kazakhstan. 'What?' said Nizamutdin. 'He's from another republic? We haven't enough beds; why should we treat foreigners? Discharge him at once!' "

"But half the patients in the ward are 'foreigners.' "

"I know, but he just happened to pick on me. You should have seen Ludmila Afanasyevna. I was amazed: she stuck up for me like a real old mother hen. Her feathers got quite ruffled. 'Scientifically it's an important and complicated case,' she said. 'We need him for fundamental conclusions . . .' It was an idiotic situation for me to be in. A few days ago I argued with her myself, and demanded to be discharged, and she screamed at me, but now she's sticking up for me. All I had to do was say yes to Nizamutdin, and by lunchtime you wouldn't have seen me for dust! I'd never have seen you again either . . ."

"So it was all because of me you didn't say yes?"

"Well, what do you think?" Kostoglotov's voice was muffled. "You hadn't even left me your address. How would I have been able to look for you?"

But she was busy with something, so he couldn't tell how seriously she had taken him.

"I couldn't possibly have let Ludmila Afanasyevna down," he continued, raising his voice again. "I was sitting there like a log saying nothing, while Nizamutdin went on, 'I can go into outpatients' " now and find five men as ill as he is, all of them ours. Discharge him!' And I suppose it was then that I behaved like a fool, missing a wonderful chance of getting away. I was sorry for Ludmila Afanasyevna, she blinked as if she'd been hit and didn't say another word. So I leaned forward with my elbows against my knees, cleared my delicate little throat and asked him quietly, 'How can you think of discharging me? I'm from the virgin lands.' 'Oh, you're a virgin-lander? Really!' said Nizamutdin. He was afraid he'd made a bad political blunder. 'There's nothing our country won't do for the virgin lands.' And they all moved on to the next bed."

"You're a crafty one," said Zoya, shaking her head.

"I never used to be, Zoya. It was the camps, they made me as sharp as an ax. There are plenty of traits in my character that aren't really me, that come from the camps."

"What about your cheerfulness? You didn't acquire that in the camps, did you?"

"Why not? I'm cheerful because I'm used to losing everything. It always strikes me as strange when people here cry during visiting time. What are they crying about? No one's sending them into exile or confiscating their belongings . . ."

"So you'll be staying with us a month or so?"

"God forbid! But I may be here a couple of weeks. It looks as if I've given Ludmila Afanasyevna a blank check. I'll have to put up with anything now . . ."

The hypodermic syringe was now full of warm liquid, and Zoya shot off. She was faced with an awkward problem today and didn't know what to do. She had to give Oleg his new injection, in the usual place, the part of the body that has to put up with every indignity. But the mood that had set in between them made the injection impossible now. It would have wrecked the game. Zoya did not want to spoil the game or the mood, neither did Oleg. The wheel would have to roll some way yet before she was close enough to him to inject him with easy familiarity.

She came back to the table and, while she was preparing one of the new injections for Ahmadjan, asked him, "What about you? Have you come round to the idea of injections? You're not kicking against them any more!"

What a question to ask a patient, especially Kostoglotov! He was just waiting for an opportunity to explain his views.

"You know what I think, Zoyenka. If possible I always prefer to avoid them. Sometimes it works, sometimes it doesn't. With Turgun it's fine. His one ambition is to learn how to play chess. We've made a pact: if I win, no injection; if he wins, injection. The trouble is that when we play I give him odds of a rook. But you can't swing that one with Maria. When she comes up with the syringe her face looks like a block of wood. Sometimes I try to joke with her, but it's always 'Patient Kostoglotov, time for your injection. Turn back your pajamas.' She never says a single kind or unnecessary word."

"She hates you."

"Me?"

"All of you. Men."

"Well, perhaps we deserve it, generally speaking. Now there's a new nurse with whom I can't make any headway either. And when Olympiada comes back it'll be even worse. She doesn't give an inch."

"That's how I'm going to be, too," said Zoya, carefully measuring out two cubic centimeters, but she didn't make it sound very forceful. Off she went to inject Ahmadjan, leaving Oleg alone by the table again.

There was another and more important reason why Zoya did not want Oleg to have injections. Ever since Sunday she had been wondering whether she should tell him what they would do to him.

Supposing something serious suddenly emerged from their banter? It was perfectly possible. What if this time it didn't all end in a depressing search for articles of clothing scattered around a room? What if it developed into something strong and lasting, if Zoya decided to become his Teddy bear and go with him into exile? (And he was right, of course. Who knows in what back-of-beyond happiness may be waiting?) If this happened, the injections prescribed for Oleg would affect not only him, but her too.

And she was against them.

"Well," she said gaily, returning with an empty syringe. "Have you plucked up your courage? Go to the ward. Turn back your pajamas, Patient Kostoglotov. I'll be with you in a minute."

He sat there and gazed at her with eyes that were not the eyes of a patient. He wasn't even thinking about the injection. They had already made a pact.

He looked at her eyes, which bulged slightly, asking to be freed from their sockets.

"Let's go somewhere, Zoya." It was more like a low rumble than speech. The more muffled his voice became, the more hers rang out.

"Where?" Surprised, she laughed. "Into town?"

"The doctors' room."

She absorbed his relentless glance. There was no game in her voice as she said, "I can't, Oleg. I've got too much work."

It was as if he understood her. "Let's go," he repeated.

"Oh yes." She remembered something. "I have to fill an oxygen balloon for . . ." She nodded toward the stairs, she may have mentioned the name of the patient, but he didn't hear. "The trouble is the oxygen cylinder tap's so hard to turn. You can help me. Come on."

She marched down the stairs to the lower landing with him at her heels.

That pitiful, yellow-looking patient with the pinched nose who was being eaten away with cancer of the lungs sat in bed, panting as he breathed through his balloon—you could hear the wheezing in his chest. Had he always been as small as that, or was it the disease that had shriveled him? He was in such a bad way that the doctors on their rounds no longer talked to him or asked him questions. He'd always been in a bad way, but today he was much worse; even an inexperienced eye could see that. He was just finishing one balloon, and another, already empty, was lying beside him.

He was in such a bad way that he didn't even notice people, whether they came up to him or just passed by.

They took the empty balloon from his bedside and went on down the stairs.

"What treatment are you giving him?"

"We're not. He's an inoperable case. And irradiation didn't help."

"Can't you open the thorax?"

"They don't do that here yet, not in this town."

"So he'll die?"

She nodded.

And although the balloon in her hands was needed for the sick man, to prevent him suffocating, they'd already forgotten about him. They were on the verge of something quite out of the ordinary.

The tall oxygen cylinder was standing in a separate corridor which was now locked. It was here, next to the X-ray rooms, that Gangart had once found a soaking-wet and dying Kostoglotov some place to sleep when they first met. ("Once" was only three weeks ago . . .)

As long as the second corridor light was not on (and they'd only switched on the first), the corner where the wall jutted out and the cylinder stood would be in half-darkness.

Zoya was shorter than the cylinder, Oleg taller.

She began to fit the valve of the balloon to the valve of the cylinder. He stood behind her, breathing in the scent of her hair, which was straying from under her cap.

"This is the tap that's stiff," she complained.

He grasped the tap and managed to turn it on at once. The oxygen started to flow. There was a gentle hissing sound.

Then, without any pretext at all, Oleg's hand, the one he'd just used on the tap, grasped Zoya's wrist, the one that wasn't holding the oxygen balloon.

She didn't start. She wasn't surprised. She just watched the balloon inflate.

Gripping her arm, his hand slid upward over the wrist and higher, to the forearm, then beyond the elbow toward the shoulder.

It was an unsubtle reconnaissance, but necessary for them both. It was a test to see whether they had interpreted each other's words rightly.

They had.

He ruffled her hair with two fingers. She did not protest or recoil. She went on watching the balloon.

He grasped her strongly around the shoulders, tilting her whole body toward him, finally reaching her lips, the lips that had smiled at him so often, lips that never stopped chattering.

As they met his, Zoya's lips were not open, soft or slack. They were taut, ready and eager, as he realized in a single flash. A moment before, he hadn't remembered, he'd forgotten that all lips are not the same, that kisses can be different, that one can be worth a hundred others.

It began as a peck, then prolonged itself as they clung to each other, merging. Nothing in the world could end it, and there was no need for it to end. They could have stayed like that forever, their lips crushed together.

But after a time, after two centuries, their lips tore apart and Oleg saw Zoya for the first time and heard her say, "Why do you shut your eyes when you kiss?"

Had he shut his eyes? He had no idea. He hadn't noticed.

"Were you trying to imagine someone else?"

Who else? He couldn't remember anyone . . .

As a diver snatches a quick breath and plunges back to find the pearl lurking on the ocean bed, they kissed again. But this time he noticed that he'd shut his eyes, and he opened them. Close, unbelievably close, he saw two tawny eyes, almost predatory-looking, and each of his eyes looked separately into hers. She was kissing with those confidently taut, experienced lips, never letting them go loose, rocking slightly on her feet and gazing at him steadily as though to judge from his eyes how eternity would sentence him.

Suddenly her eyes swiveled sideways. She tore herself away abruptly from him and shouted, "The tap!"

My God, the tap! His hand shot out to it and hurriedly turned it off.

By a miracle the balloon did not burst.

"You see what happens with kisses!" said Zoya. She had not yet got her breath back; she spoke jerkily. Her hair was disheveled, her cap askew.

Of course she was perfectly right. Nevertheless their mouths joined again; they wanted to drain each other dry.

The corridor had a glass door. Through it someone coming around the corner might easily have seen their raised elbows, hers white, his ruddy. But who cared?

When Oleg had finally got some breath back into his lungs, he scrutinized her, holding her by the nape of her neck, and said, "Goldilocks, that's your real name. Goldilocks."

She repeated the word, shaping her lips to it.

"Goldilocks? Pair of socks? . . ."

(All right, why not?)

"It doesn't worry you that I'm an exile, a criminal?"

"No," she said, shaking her head frivolously.

"Or that I'm old?"

"Old!"

"Or that I'm ill?"

She laid her forehead against his chest and stood quietly.

He pulled her toward him, closer and closer, wondering again whether or not the heavy ruler on her table would slide off those warm curving little shelves or not. "Seriously, you will come to Ush-Terek, won't you? We'll get married. We'll build ourselves a little house."

It looked as if he were going to give her the continuity which she had never had before, and which was part of her Teddy-bear side, the creative stability which sets in after the dazed moment when clothes were scattered around the room. She was pressed close to him, she could feel him with her womb, and was trying to guess, "Will it come from him? Is he really the one?"

She reached up and cradled his neck with her elbow to embrace him again. "Oleg, darling," she said, "you know what these injections are supposed to do?"

"No, what?" he said, rubbing his cheek against hers.

"They . . . how can I explain? . . . Their scientific name is 'hormone therapy'; they're used in reverse; they give women male hormones and men female hormones. They reckon it stops the formation of secondaries. But first of all it suppresses . . . do you understand?"

"What's that? No. Not completely." His voice had changed; it sounded alarmed and jagged. He was holding her by the shoulders differently now, as though trying to shake the truth out of her. "Come on, tell me, tell me!"

"They completely suppress . . . sexual potency. That's the first thing that happens, even before feminization or virulization. With large doses women start to grow beards and men develop breasts."

"Wait a minute! What's all this?" Oleg roared. He was only just beginning to understand. "You mean these injections? The ones they're giving me now? What happens? Do they suppress *everything*?"

"Well, not everything. The libido lasts quite a bit longer."

"How do you mean, the libido?"

She looked him straight in the eyes and ruffled his forelock. "Well, it's what you're feeling for me now: desire."

"So the desire stays, but the ability doesn't? Is that right?" He was completely stunned.

"The ability becomes progressively weaker, and then the desire goes too. Do you understand?" She ran her finger along his scar and stroked his cheek, clean-shaven that morning. "That's why I don't want you to have the injections."

"This is fantastic!" He recovered and drew himself up to his full height. "This is really fantastic! I felt it in my bones. I thought they'd try some dirty trick or other and they have."

He wanted to curse these doctors, swear at them all obscenely for the arbitrary way they disposed of other people's lives, when suddenly he remembered Gangart's radiantly confident face yesterday, when she'd been so warm and friendly to him, when she'd looked at him and said, "They're absolutely necessary. Your life depends on them. We're trying to save your *life*!"

So much for Vega. She wanted to do the best for him, did she? So that was why she was trying to lure him toward this fate?

"That's how you're going to be, isn't it?" He swiveled his eyes toward her.

No, really, why should he blame her? She saw life as he did, she understood that life wasn't worth living without . . . With her avid, flame-colored lips she had just dragged him along the top of the Caucasus. There she stood, there were her lips, and as long as this "libido" flowed in his legs and his loins, he had to kiss her, and the sooner the better.

"Can't you inject me with something that'll have the opposite effect?"

"They'd throw me out if I did . . ."

"But aren't there injections that would do that?"

"Yes, the same sort, hormone injections. But hormones of the same sex."

"Goldilocks, listen, let's go somewhere . . ."

"We've already been somewhere. And we've arrived. And now it's time to go back."

"Let's go to the doctors' room. Come on!'

"No, we can't. There's an orderly there, and people are always coming and going, especially in the evening . . ."

"We can wait till night . . ."

"We mustn't rush things, Oleg. If we do there won't be a . . ."

"What sort of tomorrow can there be if I lose my libido tomorrow? Only that won't happen. Thanks to you, Zoya, I'll keep my libido, won't I? Now come on, think of something, let's go somewhere!"

"Oleg, darling, we must leave something for the future. Don't rush things . . . We have to take the balloon back."

"Yes, that's right, take the balloon back. We'll take it back now . . ."

". . . We'll take it back now . . ."

"Take it back . . . now! . . ."

They walked up the stairs, holding not hands but the balloon, now inflated like a football; through it each jolt was conveyed from him to her. It was as if they were holding hands.

On the landing the yellow, shriveled patient with the weak (it had always been weak) chest was sitting up in his folding bed. Day and night people hurried past him, sick or healthy, busy with their own affairs. Sitting among his pillows, traces of a neat part still left, he had stopped coughing and was beating his forehead against his raised knees as if they were a wall. He was still alive but there were no living men around him.

Today might be the day he was going to die, Oleg's brother and neighbor, abandoned and hungry for sympathy. Perhaps if Oleg sat by his bed and spent the night there, he could provide some solace for his last hours.

All they did was give him the oxygen balloon and walk on. Those last few cubic centimeters of air in the doomed man's balloon had been no more than a pretext for going off into a corner together and getting to know each other's kisses.

Like a chained man, Oleg followed Zoya up the stairs. He wasn't thinking about the doomed man he'd left. He'd been one himself two weeks ago and in six months' time he might be one again. He was thinking about this girl, this woman, this "bit of skirt," and how to persuade her to go off with him again that night.

He had forgotten what it was like, and so it was all the more unexpected to feel that aching sensation again, to feel lips crushed till they were rough and swollen with kisses. It made his whole body young.

19. Approaching the Speed of Light

It is not everyone who calls his mother "Momma," especially in front of strangers. "Boys" over fifteen and under thirty are ashamed of the word. But Vadim, Boris and Yuri Zatsyrko had never been ashamed of their Momma. While their father was alive they had all loved her, and after he was shot they loved her all the more. With only short gaps between their ages, they grew up as three equals, always busy at school and at home, and not given to fooling about in the streets. They never gave their widowed mother cause for concern. Once, when they were little boys, a photograph had been taken of the three of them with their mother, later another one was taken for comparison, then it became a rule that every two years she would take them to be photographed (later they did it with a camera of their own), and picture after picture was stuck into the family album: mother and three sons, mother and three sons. She was fair, but all three of them were dark, probably because of the captive Turk who long ago had married their great-grandmother, a Cossack girl from Zaporozhe. Strangers could not always tell which was which in the photographs. In each successive photograph they had grown noticeably taller and sturdier, overtaking her, while she aged imperceptibly; she held herself erect in front of the camera, proud of this living record of her life. She was a doctor, well known in her town, who had earned widespread gratitude, expressed in the form of pies, pastries and bouquets of flowers. If she had accomplished nothing else, to have reared these three sons would have been sufficient justification for any woman's life. All three of them had been to the same polytechnic. The eldest had studied geology, the middle one electrical engineering; the youngest was just finishing his course in constructional engineering, and his mother was living with him.

That is, she had been until she'd heard about Vadim's illness. Last Thursday she'd been within an ace of rushing away from home to come and see him. On Saturday she'd had a telegram from Dontsova saying he needed colloidal gold, and on Sunday she'd wired back that she was going to Moscow to try to get hold of some. She'd been there since Monday, and she must have spent yesterday and today trying to get interviews with ministers and other important people to whom she could appeal for some gold from the state reserves in the name of her son's fallen father. (When their town was occupied he'd been left behind to pose as an intellectual with a grudge against Soviet power, and the Germans had shot him for being in contact with the partisans and concealing our wounded.)

Soliciting of this kind repelled and offended Vadim, even from a distance. He could not bear string-pulling in any shape or form, whether it was using friends or claiming rewards for services rendered. Even the warning telegram that Momma had sent Dontsova weighed on him. However important his survival might be, he was not prepared to make use of privileges, even when faced with the bogy of death by cancer. But as soon as he saw Dontsova at work, he realized that Ludmila Afanasyevna would have given him the same amount of her time and attention even without his mother's telegram. Except that there would have been no point in sending the telegram about the colloidal gold.

If Momma managed to get the gold, she'd fly here with it, of course. And if she didn't, she'd fly here anyway. He'd written to her from the clinic about the birch fungus, not because he had suddenly come to believe in it but to give her some extra salvation work, to load her with things to do. If she really became desperate, she would even go into the mountains, in spite of her medical knowledge and convictions, to see the medicine man near Lake Issyk Kul and get some of his root. (Oleg Kostoglotov had come over to him yesterday and confessed that to please a woman he'd poured away his root infusion. There hadn't been very much of it anyway, but here was the old man's address. If the old man had already been locked up in jail, he'd give Vadim some out of his own reserve at home.)

Momma's life was a misery while her eldest son was in danger. She was ready to do everything, more than everything, far more than was necessary. She'd even go on a field trip with him, although he already had his girl Galka out there. From snatches of information about his illness, read or overheard, Vadim had come to realize that the flare up of his tumor had actually been caused by Momma's overzealous care and attention. Ever since childhood he'd had this large patch of pigmentation on his leg: as a doctor she should have understood the danger of malignancy setting in. She was always finding reasons to probe the patch, and once she'd insisted on a top surgeon carrying out a preliminary operation. Apparently this was the last thing that ought to have been done.

Although Momma was responsible for the death sentence he was now under, he could not reproach her, either to her face or behind her back. It was wrong to be too pragmatic, to judge people solely by results; it was more humane to judge by intentions. It was unfair to get annoyed at his mother's culpability just because of his unfinished work, his interrupted interests and his unfulfilled opportunities, none of which, let alone the force that drove him to work, would ever have existed if Vadim himself had not been given life—through his mother.

Man has teeth which he gnashes, grits and grinds. But look at plants—they have no teeth, and they grow and die peacefully.

Although Vadim forgave his mother, he could not forgive the circumstances. He was not prepared to concede a single inch of his epithelium. And he could not help grinding his teeth.

This damn illness had cut right across his life, mowing him down at the crucial moment.

True, ever since childhood he had had a sort of foreboding that he would be short of time. It made him nervous when guests or women neighbors came to the house and chattered, taking up Momma's time and his. It exasperated him at school and college when the students were always told to assemble for class, an excursion, a party, or a demonstration, an hour or two earlier than necessary, on the theory that they were bound to be late. Vadim could never stand the half-hour news bulletins on the radio. What was essential or important could easily have been fitted into five minutes, the rest was padding. It made him mad to think that whenever he went to a shop there was a ten-to-one chance of finding it closed for stocktaking, stock renewal or transfer of goods. You could never tell when that was going to happen. Any village council or post office might be closed on a working day, and from twenty-five kilometers away it was impossible to tell when.

Perhaps it was his father who had made him so greedy for time: he hadn't liked inactivity, either. Vadim could remember his father dandling him between his knees and saying, "Vadka, if you don't know how to make use of a minute, you'll fritter away an hour, then a day, and then your whole life."

No, it wasn't only that. From his earliest days this demonic, insatiable hunger for time had been part of his make-up, quite apart from his father's influence. The moment he was bored playing a game with the other boys, he never hung around the gate with them but left at once, paying scant attention to their mockery. If a book struck him as vapid, he would throw it down and go and find something meatier. If the opening scenes of a film were a bit stupid (you can never find out in advance what a film's going to be like, they don't let you know on purpose), disdaining the waste of money, he'd bang his seat behind him and leave, to save time and prevent his mind from being contaminated. He was driven frantic by teachers who spent ten minutes droning at the class and then were unable to cope with the explanations, padding them out or making a complete mess of them, and finally setting the homework after the bell had gone. They just couldn't conceive of one of their pupils planning his break more exactly than they'd planned their lesson.

As a child, without being conscious of it, perhaps he had sensed a vague danger. Totally innocent, from the very beginning he had been under attack from this pigmented patch. As a boy he was always saving time, and he passed on this miserliness to his brothers. He was reading grown-up books before he went to school, and by the sixth grade he'd built himself a chemical laboratory at home. All the time he was running a race against the tumor to come, but racing in the dark, since he couldn't see where the enemy was. But the enemy was all-seeing, and at the best moment of his life it pounced on him with its fangs. It wasn't a disease, it was a snake. Even its name was snakelike—melanoblastoma.

Vadim did not even notice when it began. It was during an expedition to the Altai Mountains. The patch began to harden, then it gave him pain. It burst and seemed to get better, then it started hardening again. It rubbed against his clothes until walking became almost intolerable. But he didn't write to Momma and he didn't give up his work, because he was collecting the first batch of materials which it was essential to take to Moscow.

Their expedition was to investigate radioactive water; their brief did not include work on ore deposits. But Vadim, unusually well read for his age and especially well up in chemistry, a subject not all geologists are versed in, either foresaw or else knew intuitively that a new method of discovering ore deposits was about to be hatched. The expedition leader started to cut up rough over the trend of his work: he had to stick to his brief.

Vadim asked to be sent to Moscow on business, but the leader refused to send him. Then Vadim produced his tumor. He got a sick-leave certificate and turned up at the clinic, where he learned about the diagnosis and was ordered straight to bed. Although they told him his case couldn't wait, he took his hospitalization certificate and at once flew to Moscow, in the hope of seeing Cheregorodtsev at a conference taking place at the time. Vadim had never met Cheregorodtsev, he'd merely read his textbook and other books. People warned him that Cheregorodtsev wouldn't listen to more than one sentence: one sentence was all he needed to decide whether or not to speak to someone. Vadim spent the whole journey to Moscow planning his sentence. He was introduced to Cheregorodtsev on his way into the cafeteria in the interval. He fired off his sentence, and Cheregorodtsev turned back from the cafeteria, took him by the elbow and led him away. Their conversation seemed extremely intense to Vadim. It lasted five minutes and was complicated: he had to rush through his piece without missing a word of the answers, and display his erudition without explaining the idea in detail, since he wanted to keep the main secret to himself. Cheregorodtsev poured out objections, all of them going to show that radioactive water was not a direct indication of ore deposits and that it would be pointless to use it as a basis for search. In spite of what he said, though, he seemed very ready to be persuaded otherwise. He waited a minute for Vadim to persuade him, but when he didn't he let him go. Vadim had the impression that an entire Moscow institute had latched onto the problem while he was pottering about on his own trying to solve it among the pebbles of the Altai Mountains.

He couldn't expect anything better for the time being. He had to get down to the real work now.

He had to get down to the hospital business too, and confide in Momma. He could have gone to Novocherkassk, but he liked it here, and it was closer to his mountains.

Radioactive water and ore deposits weren't the only things he learned about in Moscow. He learned too that people with melano-blastoma died—invariably. They rarely lived as much as a year, usually only eight months.

He became like a moving body approaching the speed of light. His "time" and his "mass" were becoming different from those of other people. His time was increasing in capacity, his mass in pene-tration. His years were being compressed into weeks, his days into minutes. All his life he'd been in a hurry, but now he was really starting to run. Any fool can become a doctor of science if he lives sixty years in peace and quiet. But what can one do in twenty-seven?

Twenty-seven had been Lermontov's* age. Lermontov hadn't wanted to die either. (Vadim knew he looked a bit like Lermontov: they were both short, both had pitch-black hair, a slight, slender build and small hands, but Vadim had no mustache.) Still, Lermon-tov had carved himself a niche in our memory not just for a hundred years, but forever.

Being an intellectual, Vadim had to find a formula for living with the panther of death couched beside him in the same hospital bed, for living next to it like a neighbor. How could he live through the remaining months and make them fruitful if they were only *months*? He had to analyze death as a new and unexpected factor in his life. After the analysis he noticed that he was beginning to get used to the fact, even to absorb it as part of himself.

The falsest line of reasoning would be to treat what he was losing as a premise: how happy he'd have been, how far he'd have got, what he'd have attained if only he'd lived longer. The right view was to accept the statistics which stated that some people are bound to die young. By dying young, a man stays young forever in people's memory. If he burns brightly before he dies, his light shines for all time. In his musings during the past few weeks Vadim had dis-covered an important and at first glance paradoxical point: a man of talent can understand and accept death more easily than a man with none—yet the former has more to lose. A man of no talent

*Mikhail Lermontov (1814–1841), the greatest writer of Russian romanti-cism, who was killed in a duel.

craves long life, yet Epicurus had once observed that a fool, if offered eternity, would not know what to do with it.

Of course it was tempting to imagine that if only he managed to last out three or four years, our age of universal, rapid, scientific discovery was bound to find the remedy even for melanoblastoma. But Vadim had resolved to dismiss all daydreams of recovery or life prolonged. He refused even to waste odd moments of the night on such fruitless speculation. He would clench his teeth, work hard and bequeath the people a new method of discovering ore deposits.

Thus he would atone for his early death, and he hoped to die reconciled.

Throughout his twenty-six years he had found no greater fulfillment, no more satisfying and harmonious feeling than the consciousness of time usefully spent. This, he thought, would be the most sensible way to spend his last months.

Filled with the urge to work, then, Vadim had walked into the ward, clutching his few books under his arm.

The first enemy he was prepared for in the ward was the radio, the loudspeaker. He was ready to fight it by all means, legal or illegal. He planned to begin by trying to convert his neighbors, and go on from there to short-circuiting the wires with a needle or even tearing the socket out of the wall. Compulsory loudspeakers, for some reason generally regarded in our country as a sign of cultural breadth, are on the contrary a sign of cultural backwardness and an encouragement to intellectual laziness. Vadim rarely succeeded in convincing anyone else of this. The permanent mutter—information you hadn't asked for alternating with music you hadn't chosen (and quite unrelated to the mood you happened to be in)—was a theft of time, a diffusion and an entropy of the spirit, convenient and agreeable to the inert but intolerable to those with initiative. Epicurvs's fool with eternity in hand would probably find listening to the radio the only way to bear it.

But as Vadim entered the ward he was happily surprised to discover there was no radio. Indeed, there wasn't one anywhere on this floor. (The reason for this omission was that for years they had been planning to move the clinic into better-equipped quarters, and the new place, of course, was going to be wired for rediffusion points throughout.)

The second enemy Vadim expected was darkness—windows miles away from his bed, lights switched off early and turned on late. But the generous Dyomka had let him have his place by the window, and from the first day Vadim had gone to sleep with the others pretty early, awakened and worked from dawn on, during the best and quietest hours of the day.

The third potential enemy was chattering in the ward. As it turned out, there was a little, but on the whole Vadim liked the setup, especially from the point of view of peace and quiet.

The nicest of them all, in his opinion, was Egenberdiev. He spent most of the time in silence, stretching his fat lips and plump cheeks at one and all in his epic hero's smile.

Mursalimov and Ahmadjan were pleasant, unobtrusive people too. When they spoke Uzbek together it didn't disturb Vadim at all, for they did it quietly and soberly. Mursalimov looked like a real old sage; Vadim had met others like him in the mountains. The two had disagreed only once and then they had argued quite angrily. Vadim had asked them to translate what it was all about. It seemed that Mursalimov didn't like the way people had started messing around with first names, joining several words to make a single name. He declared that there were only forty authentic first names, the ones handed down by the Prophet. All others were incorrect.

Ahmadjan wasn't the sort of fellow to cause trouble. He would always lower his voice if you asked him. Once Vadim told him some stories about the Evenki* which fired his imagination. He spent two days thinking about their inconceivable way of life. Every now and again he would suddenly turn up with a question: "Hey, those Evenki, what sort of uniform do they have?"

Vadim would answer briefly, and Ahmadjan would sink back into thought for several hours. Then he would hobble up again and ask, "What sort of standing orders and timetable do they have, those Evenki?"

And the next morning: "Hey, those Evenki, what set tasks do they have?"

He wouldn't accept the explanation that the Evenki "just live that way."

Sibgatov was also quiet and polite. He often came into the ward to play checkers with Ahmadjan. It was obvious he hadn't had much education, but he seemed to understand that talking loudly was bad manners and unnecessary. Even when he and Ahmadjan argued, he

---

*A small tribe living on the shores of the Arctic Ocean.

always spoke soothingly. "You don't get real grapes here. You don't get real melons."

"Where do you get real ones then?" asked Ahmadjan fiercely.

"In the Crimea, of course, where else? You ought to see them . . ."

Dyomka was a good boy too. Vadim could tell he was no idle chatterbox. Dyomka spent his time thinking and studying; he wanted to understand the world. True, there was no shining talent stamped on his face: he always looked a bit gloomy when an unexpected idea was entering his head. Study and intellectual work would never come easily to him; still, often it was the plodders who turned out to be powerhouses.

Vadim had no objection to Rusanov either. He'd been a good solid worker all his life, although he would never set the world alight. His opinions were basically correct, only he didn't know how to express them flexibly. He stated them as if he'd learned them by heart.

Vadim didn't like Kostoglotov at first. He struck him as coarse and loud-mouthed. But this turned out to be only the surface. He wasn't really arrogant, he could be quite accommodating; it was just that his life had worked out unhappily, which made him irritable. He had rather a difficult temperament, and this, it seemed, was responsible for his failures. His disease was on the mend now, and his life could be too if only he'd concentrate more and make up his mind what he wanted. His prime defect was lack of concentration, and it showed in the way he wasted his time dashing about the place. Sometimes he'd wander aimlessly around the garden smoking cigarettes or he'd pick up a book only to put it down again, and he was too fond of chasing skirts. You didn't have to be particularly observant to notice that something was going on between him and Zoya, and between him and Gangart.

They were both nice enough girls, but Vadim, on the borderline of death, had no desire to chase girls. Galka was with the expedition waiting for him. She dreamed of marrying him, but he no longer had the right to marry. She wouldn't get much of him now.

No one would get any of him now.

That was the price you had to pay. Once a single passion got a grip on you it ousted all others.

The one man in the ward who'd really irritated Vadim was Podduyev. He was a vicious fellow and very strong, and yet he'd cracked and given in to a lot of clerical, Tolstoyan flummery. Vadim couldn't abide mind-sapping fairy tales about humility and loving your neighbor, and your duty to deny yourself and stand around with your mouth open looking for ways to help any Tom, Dick or Harry who came along, any slap-happy Harry or clever-dick Dick or anyone. Such dim, watery little truths contradicted the youthful thrust and fiery impatience in Vadim, his urge to unleash his energies and give of himself. He had sternly set himself not to take but to give, not to fritter himself away, not to falter, but to burn himself out in one great heroic deed for the benefit of the people and all mankind.

He was glad, therefore, when Podduyev was discharged and tow-haired Federau moved from the corner to take his bed. He was a quiet guy, the quietest in the ward. He might not say a word all day, he just lay there watching mournfully, an odd sort of fellow. He made an ideal neighbor. However, the day after tomorrow, Friday, they were due to take him away for his operation.

Yes, they were usually silent, but today they started talking about disease. Federau told him how he'd fallen ill and nearly died of meningeal inflammation. "I see. Did you get a knock?"

"No, I caught a chill. I got very overheated one day and when they took me home from the factory in a car my head was in a draft. I got meningeal inflammation. I couldn't see any more."

He told the story quietly, with a faint smile, without stressing the tragedy and horror of it.

"Why did you get overheated?" Vadim asked, already reading out of the corner of his eye: time was flying. A conversation about disease always finds an audience in a hospital ward. Federau could see Rusanov looking at him from across the room. He looked much milder today, so Federau told his story for him to hear as well.

"There was an accident with the boiler, you see. It was a complicated soldering job. To let out all the steam, cool the boiler and then start it up all over again would have taken a whole day, so the works manager sent a car for me during the night. He said, 'Federau, we don't want all work to come to a stop, do we? Put on your protective suit and get into the steam. OK?' 'All right,' I said. 'If one must, one must!' It was before the war, we were on a tight schedule, it had to be done. So I got into the steam and did it, about an hour and a half's work . . . how could I have refused? I'd always been top of the factory roll of honor."

Rusanov, who had been listening, looked at him approvingly. "An act, I would say, worthy of a Bolshevik," he commented.

"I am a member of the Party." Federau gave him another smile, fainter and even more modest this time.

"You mean you *were,*" Rusanov corrected him. (Give them a pat on the back and they take it seriously.)

"I still am," said Federau very quietly.

Rusanov wasn't in the mood for analyzing other people's lives, arguing with them or putting them in their places, his own had been tragic enough, but when he heard complete and utter nonsense he had to stamp on it. The geologist was lost in his books. Rusanov's voice was weak, low, but perfectly distinct (he knew they'd all be straining their ears and that they'd hear) as he said, "That can't be true. You're a German, aren't you?"

"Yes." Federau nodded. He seemed distressed by the fact.

"Well then?" (I've made it clear enough, but he still won't give in.) "When you were all taken into exile they must have taken away your Party cards."

"No, they didn't." Federau shook his head.

Rusanov screwed up his face. He found it difficult to talk. "Well, they must have made a mistake. They were in a hurry, obviously there was some muddle. You'd better hand it in yourself now."

"No, I won't." Federau was a shy man, but this time he dug his toes in. "I've had my card more than thirteen years, there's no mistake about that. We were brought before the district committee and they explained everything. 'You'll still be members of the Party,' they said, 'but we are making a distinction between you and the masses. A note in the *komendatura* records is one thing, but Party dues are Party dues, they're a different matter altogether. You won't be allowed to hold any important job, but you'll have to set an example as ordinary workers.' That's how it was."

"Well, I don't know," sighed Rusanov. He'd been longing to close his eyelids. Talking was very difficult.

His second injection, the day before yesterday, hadn't done any good. His tumor hadn't gone down or softened, it was still pressing him under the chin like an iron fist. He lay there weakly, anticipating the delirium that would rack him after the third injection. He and Kapa had agreed that after the third injection he should go to Moscow, but he had lost all energy for the struggle. He had only just realized what it meant to be doomed. Three injections or ten, here or in Moscow, what did it matter? If the tumor wasn't going to yield, nothing could be done. Of course, a tumor did not necessarily mean death; it might stay with him, disfiguring him or turning him into an invalid. However, Pavel Nikolayevich had not directly connected the tumor with death until yesterday, when Bone-chewer, who had read all those medical books, had started explaining to someone how a tumor spreads poison throughout the body, and so cannot be allowed to remain.

Pavel Nikolayevich felt a prickling in his eyes. He realized he could not dismiss death entirely. Death was out of the question, of course, but nevertheless it had to be considered.

Yesterday, on the ground floor, with his own eyes he'd seen a postoperative case having a sheet pulled up over his head. He understood now what the orderlies meant when they said among themselves, "This one'll be *under the sheet* pretty soon." So that's what it was. We always think of death as black, but it's only the preliminaries that are black. Death itself is white.

Since men are mortal, Rusanov had always known that one day he too would have to hand over the keys of his office—but "one day," not this very moment. He was not frightened of dying "one day," he was frightened of dying now. What will it be like? What will happen afterward? How will life go on without me?

He felt sorry for himself, as he pictured the purposeful, vigorous life he had been living, a splendid life, one might almost say, knocked flat by this rock of a tumor, this thing so alien in his life which his mind refused to recognize as necessary.

Death, white and indifferent—a sheet, bodiless and void—was walking toward him carefully, noiselessly, on slippered feet. Stealing up on Rusanov, it had caught him unawares. He was not only incapable of fighting it; he could not think, make a decision or speak about it.

Its arrival was illegal, and there was no rule or instruction with which he could defend himself.

He'd grown so weak that he'd lost his civic concern about what went on in the ward. One of the lab. girls had come into the ward today to make up the electoral roll (even here they were getting ready for the elections). She was collecting passports. Everyone handed in a passport or a collective-farm certificate, except for Kostoglotov, who didn't have one. The lab girl was surprised, naturally. She kept asking for his passport, and the insolent fellow started a row. She ought to know the basic political facts—that there are different categories of exiles. Why didn't she ring such-and-such a number to find out? As for him, he *had* the right to vote, that is in principle, but if the worst came to the worst he might not vote at all.

At last it dawned on Pavel Nikolayevich what a den of thieves he'd fallen among in this clinic, and what sort of people he was sharing the ward with. And this scoundrel had the audacity to refuse to have the light off, opened the window whenever he felt like it, passed himself off to the senior doctor as a virgin-lander, and even tried to open the untouched, virgin newspaper before Rusanov. Pavel Nikolayevich's first instinct had been right: that was the sort of man he was.

A fog of indifference enveloped Pavel Nikolayevich. He hadn't enough energy to unmask Bone-chewer. Even the den of thieves somehow no longer repelled him.

The hood of the sheet loomed before him.

From the lobby the rasping voice of Nellya, the orderly, could be heard. There was only one voice like that in the clinic. There she was, asking someone twenty meters away without even having to raise her voice, "Hey, listen, how much are those patent-leather shoes?"

The answer went unheard. Instead Nellya's voice came again. "Hey, if I had a pair of those, I could get all the lover boys I wanted."

The other girl didn't agree, and Nellya half gave in to her. Then she said, "Oh yes, that was the first time I wore nylon stockings. I really fancied them. But Sergei threw a match and burned a hole in them, the bastard."

She came into the ward carrying a broom. "All right, boys," she said. "They told me the place got washed and scrubbed yesterday, so today we'll just give it the once-over, OK?" She remembered something. "Hey, I've got news for you." She pointed to Federau and announced cheerfully, "The one who was over there, he shut up shop, he bought his lunch, he did."

Federau was extremely restrained by nature, but at this he shifted his shoulders, ill at ease.

They didn't understand what Nellya was getting at, so she explained: "You know, that poxy-faced guy, the one with all the bandages. It happened yesterday at the railway station, just by the ticket office. They've just brought him in for a post-mortem."

"Oh God!" Rusanov said pathetically. "How can you be so tact-less, comrade orderly? Why spread such dreadful news around? Can't you find something cheerful to tell us?"

Everyone in the ward became plunged in thought. True, Yefrem had spoken a lot about death, and there had been an air of doom about him. He used to stop there in the aisle and hammer on at them through his teeth. "It's a ter'ble situation we're in," he'd say.

But they had not seen Yefrem's last moment. He had left the clinic and so he remained alive in their memory. They had to picture someone, who the day before yesterday had been treading the floor-boards which they themselves trod, lying in the morgue, slit up the midline like a burst sausage.

"I'll tell you something which will make you laugh if you like. You'll split your sides. Only it's a bit disgusting . . ."

"That's all right, let's have it," begged Ahmadjan. "Let's have it."

"Oh yes." Nellya remembered something else. "You, pretty boy, they want you for X ray. Yes, you!" She pointed at Vadim.

Vadim put his book down on the window sill. Cautiously using his hands to help him, he lowered his bad leg on to the floor, then followed it with the other. Apart from the scarred leg which he nursed carefully, he looked like a ballet dancer as he walked toward the door.

He had heard about Podduyev, but he felt no sympathy for him. Podduyev had not been a valuable member of society. Nor was that sluttish orderly. After all, the value of the human race lay not in its towering quantity, but in its maturing quality.

The lab. girl came in with the newspaper.

Bone-chewer came in behind her. He was always grabbing the newspaper.

"Me! Give it to me!" said Pavel Nikolayevich weakly, stretching out a hand.

He managed to get it.

Even without his glasses he could see that the whole of the front page was covered with large photographs and bold headlines. Slowly he propped himself up, slowly he put on his glasses, and saw, as he'd expected, that the Supreme Soviet session had come to an end. There was a photograph of the presidium and the hall, and the important final resolutions were in large type—so large that there was no need to thumb through the paper looking for the small but significant paragraph.

"What? What?" Pavel Nikolayevich could not contain himself, though there was no one suitable in the ward for him to address and it was bad form to show such amazement at a newspaper item or to query it.

In large print, in the first column, it was announced that chairman of the Council of Ministers, G. M. Malenkov, had expressed a wish to be relieved of his duties, and that the Supreme Soviet had unanimously granted his request.

So this was the end of the session which Rusanov had expected merely to produce a budget!

He felt quite weak. His hands dropped, still holding the paper. He could read no further.

He didn't understand the reason for it. He could no longer follow the instructions now that they were plainly worded. He did realize, though, that things were taking a sharp turn, too sharp a turn.

It was as though somewhere deep in the depths geological strata were beginning to rumble, to shift slightly, shuddering through the town, the hospital and Pavel Nikolayevich's bed.

Oblivious to the quaking of the room and the floor, in through the door, with soft, even tread, walked Dr. Gangart, in a newly pressed white coat, with an encouraging smile on her face and a hypodermic syringe in her hands.

"All right, time for our injection," she invited him coaxingly.

Kostoglotov grabbed the paper from Rusanov's feet. Immediately he spotted the big news and read it.

Then he stood up. He could not remain seated.

He did not understand the full significance of the news either. But if the day before yesterday they had changed the whole Supreme Court, and today had replaced the Premier, it meant that history was on the march.

History was on the march. Was it conceivable that the changes could be for the worse?

The day before yesterday he had held his leaping heart down with his hands, but then he had stopped himself from hoping and believing.

But two days had gone by, and now—as a reminder—the same four Beethoven chords thundered into the sky as though into a microphone.

The patients were lying quietly in their beds. They heard nothing! Vera Gangart was calmly slipping the embiquine into Rusanov's vein.

Oleg darted out of the room. He was running outside.

Into the open!

20. Memories of Beauty

No, he'd forbidden himself faith long ago. He dared not allow himself to take heart.

Only a prisoner in his first years of sentence believes, every time he is summoned from his cell and told to collect his belongings, that he is being called to freedom. To him every whisper of an amnesty sounds like the trumpets of archangels. But they call him out of his cell, read him some loathsome documents and shove him into another cell on the floor below, even darker than the previous one but with the same stale, used-up air. The amnesty is always postponed—from the anniversary of victory to the anniversary of the Revolution, from the anniversary of the Revolution to the Supreme Soviet session. Then it bursts like a bubble, or is applied only to thieves, crooks and deserters instead of those who fought in the war and suffered.

The cells of the heart which nature built for joy die through disuse. That small place in the breast which is faith's cramped quarters remains untenanted for years and decays.

He had had his fill of hoping. He had had his fill of imagining his release and his return home. All he wanted was to go back to his beautiful exile, to his lovely Ush-Terek. Yes, lovely! It was strange, but that was how he saw his remote little place of banishment now, from this hospital in the big city, this world with its complicated rules, to which Oleg felt unable, or perhaps unwilling, to adapt.

"Ush-Terek" means "Three poplars" and is named after three

ancient poplars which are visible for ten kilometers or more across the steppe. The trees stand close together, not straight and slender as most poplars are, but slightly twisted. They must have been about four hundred years old. Once they'd reached their present height they'd stopped trying to grow any higher and branched out sideways, weaving a dense shadow across the main irrigation channel. It was said that there had been more of them in the *aul* once, but that they had been cut down in 1931. Trees like that wouldn't take root these days. No matter how many the Young Pioneers planted. the goats picked them to bits as soon as they sprouted. Only American maple flourished—in the main street in front of the regional Party committee building.

Which place on earth should you love more? The place where you crawled out of the womb, a screaming infant, understanding nothing, not even the evidence of your eyes or ears? Or the place where they first said to you, "All right, you can go without a guard now, you can go *by yourself*"?

On your own two legs. "Take up thy bed and walk!"

Ah, that first night of half-freedom! As the *komendatura* was still keeping an eye on them, they weren't allowed into the village. But they were permitted to sleep on their own in a hay shelter in the yard of the security police building. They shared the shelter with horses who spent the night motionless, quietly munching hay! Impossible to imagine a sweeter sound!

Oleg could not sleep for half the night. The hard ground of the yard lay white in the moonlight. He walked back and forth across the yard like a man possessed. There were no watchtowers, no one to see him stumbling happily over the bumpy ground, head thrown back, and face upturned to the white sky. He walked on and on, not knowing or caring where, as though he were afraid of being late, as though tomorrow he would emerge not into a mean, remote *aul,* but into the wide, triumphant world. The warm, southern early-spring night was far from silent. It was like a huge, rambling railway station where the locomotives call and answer one another all night. From dusk to dawn donkeys and camels brayed and honked in yards and stables throughout the village—solemn, trumpet-like sounds, vibrant with desire, telling of conjugal passion and faith in the continuation of life. And this marital din merged with the roar in Oleg's breast.

Can any place be dearer than one where you spent such a night?

That was the night when he began to hope and believe again, in spite of all his vows to the contrary.

After the camps, the world of exile could not really be called cruel, although here too people fought with buckets to get water during the irrigation season, some of them getting their legs slashed. The world of exile was much more spacious and easier to live in. It had more dimensions. Nevertheless it had its cruel side. It wasn't easy to make a plant take root and to feed it. He had to dodge being sent by the *komendant* a hundred and fifty kilometers or more deeper into the desert. He had to find a straw-and-clay roof to put over his head and pay a landlady, although he had nothing to pay her with. He had to buy his daily bread and whatever he ate in the canteen. He had to find work, but he'd had enough of heaving a pick for the last seven years and didn't feel like taking up a bucket and watering the crops. Although there were women in the village with mud-wall cottages, kitchen gardens and even cows who would have been prepared to take on an unmarried exile, he reckoned it was too early to sell himself as a husband. He didn't feel his life was nearly over; on the contrary, it was only beginning.

Back in the camps the prisoners used to estimate the number of men missing from the outer world. The moment you aren't under guard, they thought, the first woman you set eyes on will be yours. They imagined that all women outside were sobbing their hearts out in solitude and thinking about nothing but men. But in his village there were countless children and the women seemed absorbed in the lives they led. Neither the women who lived alone nor the young girls would go with a man just like that. They wanted to be married honorably first and to build a little house for the village to see. The morals and customs of Ush-Terek went back to the last century.

Although it was a long time now since Oleg had been under guard, he still lived without a woman, just as he had during the years behind barbed wire, even though the village was full of picture-postcard Greek girls with raven hair and hard-working, blond little Germans.

The "invoice" sending him into exile had said in perpetuity, and in his mind Oleg was resigned to the exile being perpetual. He could not imagine it otherwise, yet there was something deep inside him that wouldn't allow him to marry out here. Beria had been overthrown, falling with a tinny clang, like a hollow idol. Everyone had expected sweeping changes, but they had come slowly, and were small. Oleg discovered where his old girlfriend was—in exile in Krasnoyarsk—and they exchanged letters. He also started writing to a girl he'd known in Leningrad. For months he had clung to the hope that she'd come out here. (But who was going to throw up an apartment in Leningrad to come and stay with him in this hole in the ground?) At that point his tumor had appeared, and his life was shattered by continual, overpowering pain. Women ceased to attract him any more than other nice people.

Oleg knew, as everyone had known, if not from experience, from books ever since Ovid, that exile was not simply oppressive (you are neither in the place you love best, nor with the people you most want to see), but he also perceived, as few have, that exile can also bring release—from doubts and responsibilities. The true unfortunates were not the exiles, but the ones who had been given passports with the sordid "Article 39"* conditions. They spent their time blaming themselves for all the false moves they made, constantly on the move looking for somewhere to live, trying to find work and being thrown out of places. This prisoner, on the other hand, entered exile with all his rights intact. As he hadn't picked the place, no one could throw him out. The authorities had planned it all for him; he had no need to worry about whether he was missing a chance of living somewhere else or whether he ought to look for a better setup. He knew he was treading the only road there was, and this gave him a cheerful sort of courage.

Now that he was beginning to recover and was faced once more with the raveled tangle of his life, Oleg enjoyed the knowledge that there was a blessed little place called Ush-Terek, where his thinking was done for him, where everything was clear-cut, where he was regarded almost as a citizen and to which he would soon be going home. For it would be *home*. Threads of kinship were drawing him there, and he wanted to call it "my place."

During the three quarters of a year he'd spent in Ush-Terek, Oleg had been ill. He hadn't observed nature or daily life in much detail, or derived any pleasure from them. To the sick man the steppe seemed too dusty, the sun too hot, the kitchen gardens scorched, the doughy adobe mixture uncomfortably heavy to carry.

But now, as he strolled along the pathways of the Medical Center

*Article 39 restricted work and residence rights of former camp inmates.

with its abundant trees, people, bright colors and stone houses, life was trumpeting inside him, like those donkeys braying in the spring. Deeply stirred, he was reconstructing in imagination every trivial, humble feature of the Ush-Terek world. That humble world was dearer to him for being his own, his own till death, his own *in perpetuity*: the other was temporary, as if rented.

He remembered the *jusan* of the steppe with its bitter smell: it was as if it was an intimate part of him. He remembered the *jantak* with its prickly thorns, and the *jingil,* even pricklier, that ran along the hedges, with violet flowers in May that were as sweet-smelling as the lilac, and the stupefying *jidu* tree, whose scented blossom was as strong and heady as a lavishly perfumed woman.

Wasn't it extraordinary that a Russian, attached with every fiber of his being to the glades and little fields of Russia, to the quiet privacy of the Central Russian countryside, who had been sent away against his will and forever, should have become so fond of that scraggy open plain, always too hot or too windy, where a quiet, overcast day came as a respite and a rainy day was like a holiday? He felt quite resigned to living there until he died. Men like Sarymbetov, Telegenov, Maukeyev and the Skokov brothers had increased his respect for their race, even though he couldn't yet understand their language. Under their veneer of waywardness, in which false and real emotions were mixed, behind their naïve devotion to ancient clans, he saw a fundamentally simple-hearted people who would always answer sincerity with sincerity, good will with good will.

Oleg was thirty-four. Colleges do not accept students over thirty-five. He would never get an education. Well, that was the way it was. Recently he had managed to elevate himself from brickmaker to be land surveyor's assistant. (He'd told Zoya a lie: he wasn't a surveyor, merely an assistant on 350 roubles a month.) His boss, the district surveyor, was only dimly aware of the value of the divisions on a surveyor's pole, and if there had been any work, Oleg could have had all he wanted. In fact he had almost no work at all. The collective farms had deeds assigning them the land they were using "in perpetuity" (there it was again!) and all he had to do was occasionally slice off a plot of land from the farms for the expanding industrial settlements. He could never hope to equal the skill of the *mirab,* the sovereign master of irrigation (his profession was eternal too), who could feel the slightest incline in the soil as he leaned over it with his bucket; oh well, he would probably find himself something better in a few years' time. But why was it that even now he was thinking so warmly of Ush-Terek, longing for the end of his treatment so that he could go back, ready to drag himself back there even if he was only half cured?

Wouldn't it be more natural to become embittered, to hate and curse one's place of exile? No, wrongs that seemed to cry out for the crack of the satirist's whip were for Oleg no more than funny stories, worth a smile. Take, for example, the new headmaster Aben Berdenov who had torn Savrasov's "Rooks" from a classroom wall and tossed it behind a cupboard. (He'd spotted a church in the picture, and thought it was religious propaganda.) Or the local chief health officer, a pert little Russian girl, who used to deliver lectures to the local intelligentsia from a rostrum and then sell *crêpe-de-Chine* of the latest design to the ladies of the village on the quiet at double the retail price, before it appeared in the local shop. And the ambulance that used to bowl along in a cloud of dust, often without any patients inside, requisitioned by the Party secretary for his own use or even for the delivery of noodles and fresh butter around the flats. He remembered the "wholesale" trade run by the small retailer Orembayev. There was never anything to be had in his little general store. It was always piled to the roof with empty boxes of goods already sold, he was continually getting bonuses for overfulfilling his trade plan, and yet he spent the whole time dozing by the door. He was too lazy to use the scales, too lazy to pour out measures, too lazy to wrap anything up. He would supply all the bigwigs first, then make a note of what he thought were the other worthies and put quiet little suggestions to them. "Take a box of macaroni," he would say, "a whole box," or "Take a sack of sugar, a whole sack." The sack or the box would be delivered to the customer's flat straight from the depot, but it would be included in Orembayev's turnover. Finally, there was the third secretary of the district Party committee who, eager to take exams as an extramural student at the high school but ignorant in every branch of mathematics, one night crept up to the teacher's house (he was an exile) and presented him with an Astrakhan pelt as a bribe.

After the wolfish existence of the camps this sort of thing could be taken with a smile. Indeed, what wasn't a joke after the camps? What didn't seem like a rest?

What a joy it was to pull on his white shirt at twilight (it was the only one he had: the collar was frayed, and his trousers and boots were unmentionable) and walk along the village street. The wall under the rush roof of the community center would have a poster announcing a new "Trophy"* film, and the village idiot, Vasya, would be urging all and sundry to come into the cinema. Oleg would try to buy the cheapest ticket in the house—two roubles, right in the front row with all the kids. Once a month he'd have a binge, buy a mug of beer for two and a half roubles and drink it in the teahouse with the Chechen truck drivers.

To Oleg exile was full of laughter and elation, and for that the Kadmins, an old couple he knew, were mainly responsible. The husband, Nikolai Ivanovich, was a gynecologist and his wife was called Elena Alexandrovna. Whatever happened to the exiled Kadmins, they kept saying, "Isn't that fine? Things are so much better than they used to be. How lucky we are to have landed in such a nice part of the world!"

If they managed to get hold of a loaf of white bread—how wonderful! If they found a two-volume edition of Puastovsky in the bookshop—splendid! There was a good movie on at the center that day—marvelous! A dental technician had arrived to provide new dentures—excellent! Another gynecologist had been sent there, a woman, an exile too—very good! Let *her* do the gynecology and the illegal abortions; Nikolai Ivanovich would take care of the general practice. There'd be less money but more peace of mind. And the sunsets over the steppe, orange, pink, flame-red, crimson and purple—superlative! Nikolai Ivanovich, a small, slender man with graying hair, would take his wife by the arm (she was plump and growing heavy, partly through ill-health; he was as quick as she was slow) and they would march off solemnly past the last house of the village to watch the sun go down.

Their life blossomed into steady joy on the day they bought their own tumble-down mud hut with kitchen garden, their last haven, they knew, the roof under which they would live and die. (They decided to die together. When one went, the other would go too: what was there to stay for?) They had no furniture, so they asked Khomratovich, an old man who was also an exile, to fix them an adobe platform in a corner, which became their conjugal bed—beautifully wide and comfortable! Perfect! They stuffed a big, broad

---

*Western films captured by the Red Army in Germany in 1945 and shown throughout Russia for many years after the war.

sack with straw and sewed it up for a mattress. Next, they ordered a table from Khomratovich, a round one into the bargain. Khomratovich was puzzled. Over sixty years he'd lived in this world, and he'd never seen a round table. Why make it round? "Please!" said Nikolai Ivanovich, rubbing his deft, white gynecologist's hands. "It simply *must* be round!" Their next problem was to get hold of a paraffin lamp. They wanted a glass lamp, not a tin one, with a tall stand, the wick had to have ten strands, not seven, and they insisted on spare globes too. Since no such lamp existed in Ush-Terek, it had to be assembled piecemeal, each part brought by kind people from a long way off. Finally, there stood the lamp, with its homemade shade, on the round table. In Ush-Terek in the year 1954, when the hydrogen bomb was already invented and people were chasing after standard lamps in the capitals, this paraffin lamp on the round homemade table transformed the little clay hovel into a luxurious drawing room of two centuries ago. What a triumph! As the three of them sat round it, Elena Alexandrovna would remark with feeling, "You know, Oleg, life is so good. Apart from childhood, these have been the happiest days of my life."

And obviously she was right. It is not our level of prosperity that makes for happiness but the kinship of heart to heart and the way we look at the world. Both attitudes lie within our power, so that a man is happy so long as he chooses to be happy, and no one can stop him.

Before the war they had lived near Moscow with her mother-in-law. She had been so uncompromising and obsessed by detail, and Nikolai Ivanovich had stood in such awe of her, that Elena Alexandrovna had felt crushed. She was already a middle-aged woman with her own life to lead, and this wasn't her first marriage. She called those years her Middle Ages now. It would take some terrible disaster to let a gust of fresh air into that family.

Disaster descended, and it was her mother-in-law who set the wheels turning. During the first year of the war a man with no documents came to their door, asking for shelter. Her mother-in-law considered it her duty to give refuge to the deserter without even consulting the "young couple": she combined sternness toward her family with general Christian principles. The deserter spent two nights in the flat and then left. He was captured somewhere and under interrogation revealed the house which had harbored him. The mother-in-law being nearly eighty, they left her alone, but it was thought convenient to arrest her fifty-year-old son and forty-year-old daughter-in-law. During the investigation they tried to discover whether the deserter was a relative. Had he been, they'd have taken a far more lenient view of the case: a family looking after its own, quite understandable, excusable even. But since he had been a mere passer-by, nothing to them, the Kadmins got ten years apiece, not for harboring a deserter but as enemies of their country who were deliberately undermining the might of the Red Army. The war ended and the deserter was released in Stalin's Great Amnesty of 1945. (Historians will rack their brains, wondering why deserters should have been pardoned before anyone else—and unconditionally.) He'd forgotten in whose house he'd spent two nights on the run, and that he'd dragged others into prison after him. The Kadmins were not affected by the amnesty: they were enemies, not deserters. They'd served their ten years but they were still not allowed to go home: after all, they hadn't acted as individuals, they were a *group*, an *organization*—husband and wife! Therefore they must be exiled in perpetuity. Knowing in advance that this would happen, the Kadmins had made an application to be exiled to the same place. No one seemed to have any particular objection, the request was legitimate enough. All the same, they sent the husband to the south of Kazakhstan and the wife to the Krasnoyarsk region. Did they perhaps want to separate them as members of the same organization? No, it wasn't done out of malice or as a punishment, but simply because there was no one on the staff at the Ministry of the Interior whose job it was to keep husbands and wives together. So they had stayed separated. The wife was nearly fifty, her arms and legs were swelling, yet they sent her out into the *taiga** where the only work was lumberjacking, so familiar from the camps. (Yet she often reminisced about the Yenisei *taiga*—wonderful countryside!) They spent a year bombarding Moscow with complaints until in the end a special guard was sent to bring Elena Alexandrovna out to Ush-Terek.

Of course they enjoyed life now! They loved Ush-Terek and their mud-and-clay hovel! What more could they wish for in the way of worldly goods?

Perpetual exile? Very well. Perpetuity was long enough to make a thorough study of the climate of Ush-Terek. Nikolai Ivanovich hung

*Coniferous forest between the barren Arctic shores and the steppe.

three thermometers outside his house, put out a jar to collect precipitation and consulted Inna Ström, the senior schoolgirl in charge of the state weather station, about the force of the wind. By now Nikolai Ivanovich had a journal full of meticulously kept statistics, whatever happened to the weather station.

His father had been a communications engineer. From him he had imbibed in childhood a passion for constant activity and a love of order and accuracy. Although no one could call Korolenko* a pedant, he had frequently observed (and Nikolai Ivanovich liked to quote his words) that "order in affairs maintains peace of mind." Dr. Kadmin's favorite proverb was "Things know their place." Things know themselves where they belong, and we shouldn't get in their way.

Nikolai Ivanovich's favorite hobby for winter evenings was bookbinding. He liked to take torn, tattered, wilting books and make them blossom anew in fresh covers. Even in Ush-Terek he managed to have a binding press and an extra-sharp guillotine made for him.

As soon as the Kadmins had paid for the mud hut they started economizing, they scraped month after month, wearing out old clothes to save up for a battery radio. First they had to arrange with the Kurd who was the assistant in the cultural-goods store to put some batteries on one side for them. Batteries came separately from the sets, if they came at all. Then they had to overcome the horror that all exiles have of radios. What would the security officer say? Did they want the set for listening in to the BBC? The horror was overcome, the batteries were obtained, the set was switched on—and out came music, sheer heaven to a prisoner's ear, with no disturbances because the battery supplied an even current. Puccini, Sibelius, Bortnyanski were chosen daily from the programs and switched on in the Kadmins' hovel. The radio filled their world and more than filled it: they had no need now to take from the outside world, they could give from their own plenty.

When spring came, there was less time in the evenings to listen to the radio. Instead, they had their little kitchen garden to look after. Nikolai Ivanovich divided up his quarter-acre plot with such energy and ingenuity that old Prince Bolkonski** with his private architect at Bald Hills estates would have had to run to keep up

*A pre-revolutionary Russian writer, popular among members of the intelligentsia eager "to serve the people."
**A character from Tolstoy's *War and Peace*.

with him. At the age of sixty he was still going strong at the hospital, working time-and-a-half and ready to rush out any night to deliver a baby. He never walked in the village, he rushed along with no concern for the dignity of his gray beard, the flaps of the canvas jacket Elena Alexandrovna had made fluttering behind him. When it came to digging, though, he hadn't the strength now. Half an hour in the morning was all he could manage before he was winded. Heart and hands might lag, yet the plan was masterly, barely short of perfection. Boastfully, he would take Oleg around his bare kitchen garden, the boundary carelessly marked by two saplings.

"Oleg," he would say, "I'm going to have an avenue running through it. On the left here there'll be three apricot trees one day. They've already been planted. On the right I'm going to start a vineyard. It'll take root, I'm sure of it. Then at the end of the avenue I'm going to put a summerhouse, a real summerhouse, something Ush-Terek has never seen the like of. I've already laid the foundations, look, over there, that semicircle of adobes"—Khomratovich would have asked, "Why a semicircle?"—"and over here are the hop poles. I'll put tobacco plants next to them, they'll give off a wonderful smell. We'll hide from the heat of the day here, and in the evenings we'll drink tea out of the samovar." (In fact, they hadn't got it yet.) "You'll be welcome whenever you want."

What their garden would grow one day was anybody's guess, but what it *hadn't* got to date—potatoes, cabbages, cucumbers, tomatoes and pumpkins—their neighbors had. "But you can buy all those things," the Kadmins would protest. The Ush-Terek settlers were a businesslike lot; they kept cows, pigs, sheep and hens. The Kadmins were no strangers to livestock breeding either, but they farmed unpractically: they kept dogs and cats and nothing else. They saw it this way—you can get milk and meat in the bazaar, but where can you buy the devotion of a dog? Would lop-eared Beetle, black and brown and big as a bear, or sharp-nosed, pushing little Tobik, white but for two quivering black ears, leap up to greet you for money?

Nowadays we don't think much of a man's love for an animal; we laugh at people who are attached to cats. But if we stop loving animals, aren't we bound to stop loving humans too?

The Kadmins loved their animals not for their fur but for themselves, and the animals absorbed their owners' aura of kindness instantly, without any training. They deeply appreciated the Kadmins' talking to them and could listen to them for hours. They valued their company and took pride in escorting them wherever they went. As soon as Tobik lying in the room (the dogs had the run of the house) saw Elena Alexandrovna putting on her coat and picking up her purse he knew they were going for a walk around the village and, what's more, would jump up, rush off into the garden to fetch Beetle, and be back with him in a trice. He had told Beetle about the walk in dog language, and up would run Beetle, excited and raring to go.

Beetle was an excellent judge of time. After he had escorted the Kadmins to the movies, instead of lying down outside he disappeared, but he was always back before the end of the program. Once there'd been only five reels in the film, and he was late. He was miserable at first, but he jumped for joy after all had been forgiven.

The dogs accompanied Nikolai Ivanovich everywhere except to work, for they realized that wouldn't be very tactful. If they saw the doctor coming out of the gate with his light, youthful step late in the afternoon, they knew unerringly, as if by telepathy, whether he was off to visit a woman in labor, in which case they stayed behind, or going for a swim, in which case they joined him. He used to swim in the Chu River a good five kilometers away. Locals and exiles alike, young or middle-aged, considered it too far to go for a daily trip, but small boys went, so did Dr. Kadmin and his dogs. Actually, this was the one walk that failed to give the dogs complete satisfaction. The track across the steppe was hard and thorny. Beetle's paws got painfully cut, while Tobik, who had once been ducked, was terrified of finding himself in the river again. But their sense of duty was paramount; they followed the doctor all the way. Once within three hundred meters of the river, a safe distance, Tobik would begin to lag behind, to make quite sure that nobody grabbed him. First he would apologize with his ears, then with his tail, and then he sat down. But Beetle went right up to the sloping bank, planted his great body there and like a monument surveyed the people bathing below.

Tobik extended his escort duties to cover Oleg, who was always at the Kadmins. (So much so that the security officer became worried and interrogated them in turn: "Why are you so friendly?", "What do you have in common?", "What do you talk about?") Beetle had a choice in the matter, but Tobik had to escort Oleg, come rain or shine. When it was raining and the streets were muddy and his paws got cold and wet, he hated the idea of going out. He would stretch his forepaws, then his hind paws—but he'd go out all the same. Tobik also acted as postman between Oleg and the Kadmins. If they wanted to let Oleg know that there was an interesting movie on or a good program of music on the radio or something useful for sale in the grocery or the general store, they tied a cloth collar around Tobik with a message inside, pointed in the right direction and announced firmly, "Go to Oleg!" Whatever the weather, off he would trot obediently on his long, stalky legs, and if he didn't find Oleg at home he would wait by the door. It was extraordinary. Nobody had ever taught him, he wasn't trained to do it; but he understood instructions instantaneously, as if by thought waves, and carried them out. (It has to be admitted, though, that on his postal trips Oleg used to strengthen Tobik's ideological loyalty with some material incentive.)

What intrigued Oleg about Tobik were his permanently sad eyes. He never smiled with his teeth, only with his ears.

Beetle was about the size and build of a German shepherd, but he had none of the shepherd's wariness or malice. He overflowed with the goodheartedness of most large, powerful creatures. He had lived a fair number of years and known many owners, but the Kadmins he had chosen himself. Before that he had belonged to Vasadze, a tavernkeeper who had kept him on a chain to guard the crates of empties. Sometimes, for a joke, he unleashed him and set him on the neighbors' dogs. A doughty fighter, Beetle struck terror into the flabby, yellow street dogs, but in fact he was a kindly and peace-loving fellow. On one of the occasions when he was let loose, he attended a dogs' wedding near the Kadmins': the local dogs had all been wooing Dolly, Tobik's mother. Beetle had been rejected because of his ludicrous size and so never became Tobik's stepfather. He sensed sincerity and kindness in the Kadmins' house and garden and began to frequent them, although they never fed him. Then Vasadze left the village and gave Beetle to Emilia, an exile girlfriend of his. Although she gave Beetle plenty to eat, he kept breaking free and going to the Kadmins. Emilia got quite cross with them. She took Beetle back to her house and chained him up again, but he still kept breaking free and running off. Finally she chained him to a car tire. It was then that Beetle saw Elena Alexandrovna walking down the street one day. She deliberately turned her head aside, but he gave a huge jerk, like a drayhorse, and, wheezing as he went, dragged the tire around his neck a hundred meters or so before collapsing. After that Emilia surrendered Beetle. He soon adopted the humane principles of his new owners as a code of behavior. The street dogs no longer went in fear of him, and he began to be friendly toward passers-by, although he was never ingratiating.

But there were people in Ush-Terek, as there are everywhere, who liked to shoot living creatures. Finding no better game, they used to walk the streets drunk, killing dogs. Beetle had been shot twice, and was now afraid of every aperture that was aimed at him, even a camera lens. He would never let himself be photographed.

The Kadmins kept cats too—spoiled, capricious and art-loving cats. But it was Beetle that Oleg would see in his mind's eye as he strolled along the pathways of the Medical Center, Beetle's huge, benevolent head. Not Beetle out in the street but Beetle looming in his window. Suddenly his head would appear, and there he was, standing on his hind legs, peering in just like a human being. Tobik was sure to be jumping up and down beside him, and Nikolai Ivanovich would soon be arriving.

Deeply moved, Oleg knew now that he was completely content with his lot, quite resigned to his exile. Health was all he asked of the heavens. He wasn't asking for any miracle.

He would like to live as the Kadmins lived, happy with what they had. The wise man is content with little.

What is an optimist? The man who says, "It's worse everywhere else. We're better off here than the rest of the world. We've been lucky." He is happy with things as they are and he doesn't torment himself.

What is a pessimist? The man who says, "Things are fine everywhere but here. Everyone else is better off than we are. We're the only ones who've had a bad break." He torments himself continually.

If only Oleg could somehow see the treatment through, escape the clutches of radiotherapy and hormone therapy, and avoid ending up as a cripple. If only he could somehow preserve his libido and all it meant. Without that . . .

Oh, to get back to Ush-Terek, to stop living as a bachelor, to get married! It wasn't likely that Zoya would come out there. Even if she did it wouldn't be for eighteen months. More waiting, more waiting, the whole of his life spent waiting! No, it was impossible.

He could marry Ksana. Her character was firm and her figure rolypoly. Her head was too round, though. But what a wonderful housewife she'd make! Even wiping dishes, with a towel flung over her shoulder, she looked like an empress; you couldn't take your eyes off her. You'd have security with her; you'd have a wonderful home and there'd always be children around.

Or he could marry Inna Ström. She was only eighteen; it was rather a scary thought, but that was precisely the allure. Her smile was pensively abstracted, but with an impudent, provocative quality. That was part of the attraction.

He mustn't trust the tremors, the Beethoven chords. They were nothing but iridescent soap bubbles. He must control his unruly heart and believe nothing, expect nothing from the future, no improvement.

Be happy with what you've got.

In perpetuity? Why not? In perpetuity!

21. The Shadows Go Their Way

Oleg was lucky enough to bump into her right in the doorway of
the clinic. Moving to one side, he held the door open for her. She
was walking so vigorously, her body bent slightly forward, that if he
hadn't moved aside she might well have knocked him down.

He took in the whole picture at a glance: the blue beret on her
dark-brown hair, her head bowed as if she were walking against
the wind, and her coat with its very individual cut. It had a fantastic,
long scarflike collar, buttoned to the throat.

Had he known she was Rusanov's daughter he'd probably have
turned back, but as it was he walked on to take his usual stroll along
the unfrequented paths.

Aviette had no trouble in getting permission to go upstairs to
the ward. Her father was very weak, and in any case Thursday was
visiting day. Taking off her overcoat, she threw over her claret-
colored sweater the white coat they gave her, which was so small
that she would only have been able to get her arms into the sleeves
if she had been a child.

After his third injection the day before, Pavel Nikolayevich had
grown much weaker and no longer felt like taking his legs from
under the blankets unless he had to. He moved about in bed very
little, ate with reluctance, and didn't put on his glasses or butt in
on conversations. The life around him, to which he normally reacted
decisively with approval or censure, had faded. He had become
indifferent to it. His customary strength of will had been shaken and
he had surrendered to his weakness with a kind of pleasure. It was

the wrong kind of pleasure—such as is felt by a man who is freezing to death and powerless to move. The tumor, which had begun by annoying him, then frightening him, had now acquired rights of its own. It was no longer he but the tumor that was in charge.

Knowing that Aviette had flown in from Moscow, Pavel Nikolaye-vich was expecting her. As always he was waiting for her with joy, but this morning the joy was mixed with alarm. It had been decided that Kapa should tell her about Minai's letter and the whole truth about Rodichev and Guzun. There'd been no point in her knowing before, but now her brains and her advice were needed. Aviette was a very clever girl, whose views on things were at least as bright as her parents', usually brighter. Still, it was rather alarming. How would she react? Would she be able to put herself back in time into their position and understand? Mightn't she condemn them thought-lessly, out of hand?

In spite of the heavy bag she was carrying in one hand and the white coat she was holding around her shoulders with the other, Aviette strode energetically into the ward, her head still bent as if against the wind. Her fresh, young face was glowing. It registered none of the pious compassion with which people usually approached the beds of the gravely ill, an expression Pavel Nikolayevich would have been hurt to see on his daughter's face.

"Well, Father, how are things, eh, How are things?" She greeted him brightly, sitting down beside him on the bed. Without forcing herself, she kissed him sincerely, first on one stale, stubbly cheek, then on the other. "Well, how are you this morning? Tell me exactly how you feel. Come on, tell me."

Pavel Nikolayevich's strength seemed to revive at her glowing appearance and her cheerful questioning. He rallied a little.

"Well, how shall I put it?" His voice was weak and measured, as if he were explaining it to himself. "I don't really think it's gone down, no, but I do get the impression I can move my head a little more freely, a little more freely. There's less pressure, if you know what I mean."

Without asking her father's permission, she opened his collar without causing him the least pain and peered at the tumor on his neck as if she were a doctor making a daily inspection.

"There's nothing terrible about that," she declared. "It's a swollen gland, that's all. The way Mother wrote I thought Goodness! You say you can move your head more freely, do you? That means the injections are working, it definitely does. Later on, it'll get smaller. Once it's half the size it is now, it won't bother you so much. You'll be able to leave hospital."

"Yes, you're right." Pavel Nikolayevich sighed. "If it was only half the size, I could live with it, couldn't I?"

"You could be treated at home."

"Do you think I could have the injections at home?"

"I don't see why not. You'll get used to them, you'll get into the way of them, and I'm sure you'll be able to continue them at home. We'll talk about it, we'll work something out."

Pavel Nikolayevich felt more cheerful. Whether or not they let him have his injections at home, his daughter's determination to move into the attack and get what she wanted filled him with pride. Aviette was leaning over him, and even without his glasses he could see her honest, open face, ardent with energy and life, the quivering nostrils and the mobile eyebrows that trembled sensitively at every injustice. Was it Gorky who had said, "If your children are no better than you are, you have fathered them in vain, indeed you have lived in vain"? Pavel Nikolayevich had not lived in vain.

All the same he was worried. Did she know about *it*? What would she say?

In no hurry to bring the conversation around to the subject, she questioned him further about his treatment, asked what the doctors were like, checked his bedside table to see what he'd eaten and replaced the food that had gone bad with fresh supplies.

"I've brought you some tonic wine," she said. "Drink one liqueur glass at a time. And some nice red caviar—you like that, don't you? And some lovely oranges from Moscow."

"That's nice."

Meanwhile she had been looking around the ward and its inmates. The upward jerk of her eyebrows showed how intolerably squalid she found it. Still, he thought, one ought to look at it from the humorous point of view.

Although no one else seemed to be listening, she leaned forward closer to her father, and they began to speak so that only the two of them could hear.

"Yes, I know, Father, it's terrible." Aviette went straight to the point. "It's common knowledge by now, everyone in Moscow's talking about it. It can only be described as a massive review of legal proceedings."

"Massive?"

"Massive is the word for it. It's like an epidemic. The pendulum's swung right the other way. As if the wheel of history can ever be turned back! Who could do it? Who'd dare? All right, granted it was a long time ago they convicted those people, rightly or wrongly, and sent them far away into exile—but why bring them back now? Why transplant them back to their former lives? It's a painful, agonizing process. Above all it's cruel to the exiles themselves. Some of them are dead—why disturb their ghosts? Why raise groundless hopes among their relatives and perhaps a desire for revenge? Again, what does rehabilitated actually mean? It can't mean the man was completely innocent! He must have done *something*, however trivial."

Ah, she was such a clever girl! She had spoken with a passionate assurance that she was right. Although they hadn't yet mentioned his problem, Pavel Nikolayevich could see that his daughter would stand solidly behind him. Alla would never abandon him.

"But do you know of actual cases where people have come back? Even to Moscow?"

"Yes, even to Moscow. That's the point. They're all creeping back there like ants looking for sugar. And there are some terrible, tragic cases! Think of it, there was a man who'd been living in peace and quiet for years and suddenly he was summoned to . . . you know where, to a confrontation! Can you imagine it?"

Pavel Nikolayevich grimaced as if he'd swallowed a lemon. Alla noticed but she couldn't stop herself now; she always carried her train of thought to the finish.

"They told him to repeat what he'd said twenty years ago. Just think! Who could possibly remember? What good would it do anyone? All right, if you've got a sudden urge to rehabilitate them, by all means do so, but don't bring in confrontations! I mean, why shatter people's nerves? The man went home and very nearly hanged himself!"

Pavel Nikolayevich lay there in a hot sweat. That they might confront him face to face with Rodichev or Yelchanski or some other person was one possibility that had never occurred to him.

"Silly fools! Who made them sign those trumped-up confessions about themselves in the first place? They should have refused." Alla's flexible mind sized up the question from every angle. "How *can* they stir up this hell? They should spare a thought for the people who were doing a job of work for society. How are *they* going to come out of all these upheavals?"

"Did Mother tell you . . . about . . . ?"

"Yes, Father, she told me. But there's nothing for you to worry about." Her strong fingers gripped his shoulders. "All right, I'll tell you what I think, if you like. A man who 'sends a signal' is being politically conscious and progressive, he's motivated by the best intentions toward society. The People appreciates this and understands. There are cases where he may make a mistake, but the only people who never make mistakes are the ones who never do anything. Normally a man is guided by his class instinct, and that never lets him down."

"Thank you, Alla, thank you!" Pavel Nikolayevich felt tears welling up inside him, cleansing tears of release. "You've put it well: the People appreciates, the People understands. It's just this stupid habit we've developed of regarding only those at the bottom of society as the People." His sweating hand stroked his daughter's cool one. "It's very important for young people to understand us and not condemn. But tell me, what do you think . . . ? Can they find a clause in the law by which we could be . . . I mean, by which I could be *got* for . . . well, for giving incorrect evidence?"

"Listen," Alla replied animatedly, "I happened to be present at a conversation in Moscow where they were discussing . . . well, just this kind of unpleasant contingency. There was a lawyer present who explained that the law against so-called false evidence used to carry a penalty of only two years, but that since then there have been two amnesties. It's out of the question to get someone on a charge of giving false evidence now. Rodichev won't utter a squeak, you can be sure of that."

Pavel Nikolayevich felt as if even his tumor had eased a little.

"That's my clever little girl!" he said, happily relieved. "You've always got the answer. You're always there at the right moment. You have given me back a lot of my strength."

Taking one of his daughter's hands in both his own, he kissed it reverently. Pavel Nikolayevich was an unselfish man: he always put his children's interests before his own. He knew he had no outstanding qualities except devotion to duty, thoroughness and perseverance, but his daughter was his true achievement, and he basked in her light.

Tired of holding the symbolic white coat which kept slipping off her shoulders, she threw it with a laugh over the foot of the bed across her father's temperature chart. It wasn't the time of day when doctors or nurses came in.

Alla was left in a new claret-colored sweater that he had never seen her in before, a broad white zigzag crossing it gaily from cuff to cuff, up the sleeves and across the breast. The bold zigzag went well with Alla's energetic movements.

Her father had never grumbled if money was spent on dressing Alla well. They got things on the black market, from abroad too, and Alla's clothes were confident and dashing, setting off the sturdy, straightforward attractions that matched her direct, decisive mind.

"Listen," her father said quietly, "do you remember, I asked you to find something out? That strange expression—you come across it sometimes in speeches or articles—'the cult of personality'*—are those words really an allusion to . . . ?"

"I'm afraid they are, Father . . . I'm afraid they are. At the Writers' Congress, for example, the phrase was used several times. And the trouble is, nobody explains what it means, though everyone puts on a face as if they understood."

"But it's pure—blasphemy! How dare they, eh?"

"It's a shame and a disgrace! Somebody whispered it in the wind, and now it's blowing all over the place. But though they talk about 'the cult of personality,' in the same breath they speak of 'the great successor.' So one mustn't go too far in either direction. Generally speaking, you have to be flexible, you have to be responsive to the demand of the times. This may annoy you, Father, but whether we like it or not we have to attune ourselves to each new period as it comes! I saw a lot in Moscow. I spent quite a bit of time in literary circles—do you imagine it's been easy for writers to readjust their attitudes over these last two years? Ve-ry complicated! But what an experienced crowd they are! What tact! You can learn such a lot from them!"

During the quarter of an hour Aviette had been sitting in front of him, routing the grim monsters of the past and opening up vistas of the future with her brisk, precise comments, Pavel Nikolayevich had become visibly healthier. His spirits were now so improved that he no longer had any desire to talk about his tiresome tumor. There

*The Soviet label now given to the negative, criminal aspects of Stalinism. However, Stalin was also called "the great successor" to indicate his positive role as the successor of Lenin.

even seemed no point in making a fuss about his being transferred
to another clinic. All he wanted to do was to listen to his daughter's
cheerful stories, to breathe the current of fresh air she brought with
her.

"Go on, go on," he begged her. "What's happening in Moscow?
What was your journey like?"

"Ah!" Alla shook her head like a horse bothered by a gadfly.
"How can I describe Moscow? Moscow's a place you have to live
in. Moscow's another world. A trip to Moscow is like going fifty
years into the future. In the first place, everyone in Moscow sits
around watching television . . ."

"We'll soon have television too."

"Soon, yes, but it won't be Moscow programs. Ours won't amount
to much. You know, it's like something out of H. G. Wells—everyone sitting watching television. But there's more to it than that.
I've got a general feeling—and I'm very quick at picking up what's
in the air—that there's going to be a complete revolution in our way
of life. I don't mean refrigerators and washing machines—things are
going to change much more drastically than that. For instance, here
and there you see lobbies made out of plate glass. And they're
putting low tables in the hotels, really low, this low, just like the
Americans have. The first time you come across them you don't
know how to cope with them. Then lampshades made out of fabric,
like the ones we have at home—they're something to be ashamed of
now; they're 'vulgar'; they have to be *glass*. And none of the beds
have headboards, headboards are out. It's all wide, low sofas and
couches. They make the room look quite different. Our whole style
of living is changing, you can't imagine what it's like. Mother and
I have talked it over and we've agreed, there's a lot we're going to
have to change. You can't buy things like that out here, of course,
you have to bring them from Moscow. But some of the fashions are
really pernicious and ought to be condemned out of hand—like
that rock-'n'-roll dance, it's absolutely debauched, I can't tell you
what it's like. And those awful, shaggy hair-dos, deliberately in a
mess, as if they'd just got out of bed!"

"That's the West. They want to corrupt us."

"Of course, there's a complete lowering of moral standards, which
is reflected in the arts. Take poetry, for instance. There's this long,
lanky fellow Yevtushenko, a complete unknown, no rhyme or

reason. All he has to do is wave his arms about and yell, and the girls go mad . . ."

Aviette was no longer talking privately. Having switched to a public topic, she had raised her voice without restraint, so that everyone in the ward could hear her. Dyomka, however, was the only one to give up what he was doing to listen intently to her, momentarily distracted from the gnawing pain that was dragging him closer and closer to the operating table. The others either showed no interest or else weren't in the ward. Only Vadim Zatsyrko occasionally lifted his eyes from the book he was reading to gaze at Aviette's back, curved like a great bridge and tightly hugged by her sweater, which was too new to have lost its shape. It was claret-colored all over except for one shoulder which, caught by a sunbeam glancing reflected off an open window, was a rich crimson.

"Tell me some more about yourself."

"Well, Father, I had an excellent trip to Moscow. They've promised they're going to include my collection of poems in their publishing plan! Next year's program, of course, but one can't hope for anything earlier. Sooner than that would be unimaginably quick."

"Alla! Do you really mean it? You mean in a year's time we'll actually have your poems in our hands . . . ?"

"Well, maybe not a year, two perhaps . . ."

His daughter had brought down an avalanche of joy on him today. He knew she'd taken her poems to Moscow, but from those typewritten sheets to a book with ALLA RUSANOVA on the title page had seemed an impassably long distance.

"How did you manage it?"

Alla smiled back firmly at him. She was pleased with herself. "Of course," she said, "I could have just gone into the publishing house and produced my poems, but then I don't suppose anyone would have wasted time talking to me. But Anna Yevgenyevna introduced me to M——, and then to S——. I read them two or three poems, they both liked them, and then, well, they called up somebody and wrote to someone else. It was all quite simple."

"Wonderful!" Pavel Nikolayevich was radiant. He rummaged in his bedside table for his glasses and put them on, as though about to gaze admiringly at the precious book then and there.

For the first time in his life Dyomka had seen a real, live poet. And not just a poet, but a poetess! His jaw dropped.

"I've got such a nice name for a poet too. It's a good, clean, ringing name! I won't use a pseudonym. What's more, I feel I really *look* like a writer."

"Alla, but what if it doesn't work out? You realize, don't you, you'll have to write up every little nobody so that he can be recognized by his friends . . ."

"No, I've got an idea. I'm not going to worry about every individual character, there's no need for that. What I have in mind is something completely new. I'll go straight to the collective, I'll portray whole collectives, with broad strokes. After all, one's whole life is bound up with the collective, not with isolated personalities."

"Yes, that's true enough," Pavel Nikolayevich had to admit. But there was a hazard which his daughter in her enthusiasm might not appreciate. "But have you considered this? The critics may start in on you. You know, in our world criticism is a kind of social reproach, it's dangerous!"

Aviette tossed back her dark-brown locks and, fearless as an Amazon, gazed into the future. "The fact is," she said, "they'll never be able to criticize me *very* seriously because there'll be no ideological mistakes in my work. If they attack me from the artistic point of view—well, heavens alive, who *don't* they attack for that? Take the case of Babayevski. At first everyone loved him, then everyone hated him, they all renounced him, even his most faithful friends. But that's only a temporary phase: they'll change their minds, they'll come back to him. It's just one of those delicate transitions life's so full of. For instance, they used to say, 'There must be no conflict.' But now they talk about 'the false theory of absence of conflict.' If there was a division of opinion, if some people were still talking the old way while others were using the new style, then it would be obvious that there had been a change. But when *everyone* starts talking the new way all at once, you don't notice there's been a transition at all. What I say is, the vital thing is to have tact and be responsive to the times. Then you won't get into trouble with the critics . . . Oh yes, you asked me for some books, Father. I've brought you some. You ought to do some reading now, you don't have time usually.

"I've had a good look at the sort of life writers lead. They have such delightfully simple relationships with each other. They may be Stalin Prize winners, but they're all on first-name terms. They're such unconceited, straightforward people. We imagine a writer

as someone sitting up in the clouds with a pallid brow, unapproach-
able. Not a bit of it! They enjoy the pleasures of life. They tease
each other the whole time, there's plenty of laughter. I should call
their life a merry one. But when the time comes to write a novel,
they lock themselves away in their houses in the country for two
or three months, and there's your novel! Yes, I'm going to put every
ounce of energy into getting into the Writers' Union."

"You mean, you're not going to use your university qualifications
to work professionally?" Pavel Nikolayevich was rather worried.

"Father"—Aviette lowered her voice—"what sort of life does
a journalist have? They give you an assignment—do this, do that—
you've got no *scope*. All you do is go and interview various well-
known personalities. You can't compare that life with the other."

"Bravo!"

"Because it pays."

"Alla, whatever you say, I'm still a bit worried. Suppose it doesn't
work out?"

"How can it fail to work out? You're being naïve! Gorky said,
'Anyone can become a writer.' With hard work anyone can achieve
anything. If the worst comes to the worst, I can become a children's
writer."

"All right, that's fine in principle," said Pavel Nikolayevich
thoughtfully. "In principle that's splendid. Of course, it's perfectly
right for morally healthy people like you to take over literature."

She began to take some books out of her bag. "Here," she said.
"I've brought you *A Baltic Spring* and *Kill Him!*—that one's poetry,
I'm afraid. Will you read it?"

"Kill Him!? All right, leave it."

*"Our Dawn Is Already Here, Light over the Earth, Toilers for
Peace, Mountains in Bloom* . . ."

"Wait a minute, *Mountains in Bloom,* I think I've read that one."

"You read *The Earth in Bloom,* this is *Mountains in Bloom.*
Here's another one, *Youth Is with Us.* That's a must, you'd better
start with it. Even the titles make you feel good. I chose them with
that in mind."

"But didn't you bring anything with a bit of sentiment in it?"

"Sentiment? No, Father. I thought . . . in the sort of mood you
were in . . ."

"I know enough already about books like these." Pavel Nikolayevich waved a couple of fingers at the pile. "But please, can't you find me something that appeals to the heart?"

"All right," said Aviette, pondering. "I'll give Dumas' *La Reine Margot* to Mother to bring when she comes."

"That's just what I need."

She was getting ready to go.

Meanwhile Dyomka had been sitting frowning in his corner, in torment either from the unceasing pain in his leg or else from shyness at the thought of entering into conversation with this dazzling girl who was also a poetess. Finally he plucked up enough courage to ask his question without clearing his throat or coughing in mid-sentence. "Excuse me," he said, "can you tell me, please, what you think about the need for sincerity in literature?"*

"What's that? What did you say?" At once Aviette turned toward him with a regal half-smile, for the hoarseness of Dyomka's voice had told her clearly how shy he was. "That wretched 'sincerity' again! It's wormed its way in here too, has it?"

She looked into Dyomka's face. Obviously the boy was quite uneducated and not very intelligent. She didn't really have the time, but it wouldn't do to leave him under such a bad influence.

"Listen, my boy," she announced in powerful, ringing tones, as though speaking from a platform. "Sincerity can't be the chief criterion for judging a book. If an author expresses incorrect ideas or alien attitudes, the fact that he's sincere about them merely increases the harm the work does. Sincerity becomes *harmful*. Subjective sincerity can militate against a truthful presentation of life. That's a dialectical point. Now, do you understand?"

Dyomka found it hard to absorb ideas. He furrowed his brow. "Not quite," he said.

"All right then, I'll explain." Aviette spread her arms, the white zigzag on her sweater flashing like lightning from arm to arm across her chest. "It's the easiest thing in the world to take some depressing fact and describe it just as it is. What one should do, though, is plow deep to reveal the seedlings which are the plants of the future. Otherwise they can't be seen."

"But seedlings . . ."

*The discussion which follows hinges on Vladimir Pomerantsev's article in the December 1953 edition of *Novy Mir*. Attacked at the time by the Communist Party press, it turned out to be the first indication of the coming "thaw."

"What's that?"

"Seedlings have to sprout by themselves." Dyomka hurried to get his word in. "If you plow seedlings over, they won't grow."

"Yes, I know, but we're not talking about agriculture, my boy, are we? Telling the people the truth doesn't mean telling them the bad things, harping on our shortcomings. On the other hand, one may describe the good things quite fearlessly, so as to make them even better. Where does this false demand for so-called harsh truth come from? Why does truth suddenly have to be harsh? Why can't it be radiant, uplifting, optimistic? Our literature ought to be wholly festive. When you think about it, it's an insult to people to write gloomily about their life. They want life to be decorated and embellished."

"I agree with that, generally speaking," came a pleasant, clear voice from behind her. "True, why spread depression?"

Of course, the last thing Aviette needed was an ally. But she was confident of her luck—if anyone spoke up, it was always on her side. She turned toward the window, and the white zigzag flashed in the sunbeam. A young man of her own age with an expressive face was tapping the end of a black, fluted mechanical pencil against his teeth.

"What exactly is literature for?" He was thinking aloud, perhaps for Dyomka's benefit, or perhaps for Alla's. "Literature is to divert us when we're in a bad mood."

"Literature is the teacher of life," muttered Dyomka, blushing at the awkwardness of his remark.

Vadim tilted his head right back. "Teacher, my foot!" he said. "We manage somehow to sort our lives out all right without it. You're not implying that writers are any cleverer than us practical workers, are you?"

He and Alla exchanged glances: they recognized that they were two of a kind. Although they were the same age and could not help liking each other's looks, each was too firmly set on a definite path to see in a chance exchange of glances the beginning of an adventure.

"The role of literature in life is generally greatly exaggerated," Vadim was arguing. "Books are sometimes praised to the skies when they don't deserve it. Take *Gargantua and Pantagruel*—if you hadn't read it you'd think it was something tremendous. But read it, and it turns out to be nothing but an obscenity and a waste of time."

"Eroticism has its place in literature, even in books by contemporary writers," said Aviette, objecting strongly. "It's not necessarily superfluous. Combined with really progressive ideological thinking, it adds a certain richness of flavor. For example, in . . ."

"It *is* superfluous," Vadim retorted with conviction. "It's not the function of the printed word to tickle the passions. Stimulants can be bought at the pharmacist's."

Without giving the Amazon in the claret-colored sweater another glance or waiting for her to convince him to the contrary, he lowered his eyes to his book.

It always upset Aviette when people's ideas failed to fall into one of two clear-cut categories: the soundly argued and the unsoundly argued. She hated it when they ranged vaguely through all the shades of the spectrum. It only led to ideological confusion. Right now she couldn't make out whether this young man was for her or against her. Ought she to argue with him or let it go at that?

She let it go. "Now, my boy," she said, turning back to Dyomka to finish with him. "You must understand this. Describing something that exists is much easier than describing something that doesn't exist, even though you know it's going to exist. What we see today with the unaided human eye is not necessarily the truth. The truth is what we *must* be, what is going to happen tomorrow. Our wonderful tomorrow is what writers ought to be describing today."

"But what will they describe tomorrow, then?" The slow-witted Dyomka frowned.

"Tomorrow? . . . Well, tomorrow they'll describe the day after tomorrow."

The young man must be a bit weak in the head. It wasn't worth wasting her arguments on him. However, Aviette wound up:

"That article was extremely harmful. It groundlessly and insultingly accused writers of insincerity. Only a philistine could treat writers with such disrespect. What matters is that writers should be appreciated for what they are—honest toilers. It's only Western writers who can be accused of insincerity, because they are mercenary. If they weren't, nobody would buy their books. Everything depends on money over there."

She had got up and was standing in the aisle now—the strong, sturdy, good-looking daughter of Rusanov. Pavel Nikolayevich had been listening with pleasure throughout the lecture she'd just given Dyomka.

She had kissed her father and now she raised her hand, fingers spread, to give him a cheerful wave. "Fight for your health, Daddy," she said. "Fight hard, go on with the treatment, get rid of your tumor, and don't worry about *anything*." She emphasized the word. "Everything's going to be all right, *everything*."

PART TWO

PART TWO

22. The River that Flows into the Sands

March 3, 1956.
Dear Elena Alexandrovna and Nikolai Ivanovich,

Here's a puzzle picture for you: what is it and where am I? Bars on the windows (only on the first floor, it is true, to keep the burglars out, and they are in a geometric pattern like rays of light coming out of one corner, and there are no shields to bar the view either). The rooms are full of bunks, complete with bedding, and on each bunk lies a little man terrified out of his wits.

In the morning you get a bread roll, sugar and tea (this is a breach of regulations because they give you breakfast later on). All through the morning people are gloomy and silent, no one talks to anyone else, but in the evenings there is a constant hum and lively discussion: about opening and closing windows, about who can hope for the best and who can expect the worst, and about how many bricks there are in the mosque at Samarkand.

During the day they pull you in, one by one, for talks with officials, "processing," and for visits from relatives. We play chess and read books. Parcels are allowed and those who get them nurse them carefully. Some people even get extra food, and not only the "squealers" (I can tell you that for sure because I've had some myself).

Sometimes they come in and search the place. They take away personal belongings, so we have to hide them and fight for our right to go out and exercise. Bath time is a major event, but also an ordeal. Will it be warm? Is there enough water? What sort of underclothes will you get? The funniest thing is when they bring in someone "new" and he starts asking the most absurd questions, having no idea what he is in for . . .

Well, have you guessed? Of course you'll say I must be lying: if it's a transit prison, why the bedclothes? And if it's a prison, why are there no night-time interrogations?

I am assuming this letter will be checked by our "protectors" in the Post Office, so I shall not embark on any other analogies.

So this is the life I've lived for five weeks in the cancer ward. There are moments when it seems I am back again in my former life. And there is no end to it. The most depressing thing is that I have no fixed term, I am in "at the pleasure of the state." (And the *komen-datura,** you remember, gave me permission for only three weeks, so strictly speaking I am already overdue and they could put me on trial for trying to escape.)

They don't say a thing about when they are going to discharge me, they make no promises. Of course their medical instructions make them squeeze the patient of everything that can be squeezed, and they will not let him go till his blood can't take any more.

So here are the results: that wonderful improved state, "euphoric" you called it in your last letter, which I was in after two weeks of treatment when I was so simply and joyfully returning to life, has all disappeared, there's not a trace of it left. It's a great pity I didn't insist on being discharged then. The useful part of my treatment has come to an end, now the harmful part's beginning.

They're battering me with X-ray treatments, two sessions a day, twenty minutes each session at 300 rads, and although the pain I had when I left Ush-Terek is long forgotten, I have now come to know what nausea is. My friends, X-ray nausea (or maybe it comes from the injections, everything here gets mixed), you have no idea how loathsome it is. It gets you right in the chest and it goes on for hours. Of course I gave up smoking, that happened by itself. It's such a disgusting state to be in, I can't go for walks, I can't sit down, there's only one comfortable position I can find (I am in it now as I write to you, which is why it is with a pencil and not very even): no pillow, flat on my back, legs slightly raised and head hanging a bit over the end of the bed. When they call you for your next session and you go into the apparatus room with that thick X-ray

*The office which supervises the lives of exiles.

smell, you're afraid you're going to spew your guts out. The only things that help the nausea are pickled cucumbers and pickled cabbage, but of course they're unobtainable either in the hospital or in the Medical Center and patients aren't allowed out of the gates. "Your relatives can bring you some," they say. Relatives! Our relatives are all running about the Krasnoyarsk *taiga* on all fours, as is well known.*

What can a poor prisoner do? I put on my boots, fasten my woman's dressing gown round me with an army belt, and creep to the place where the Medical Center wall is half destroyed. I get through the wall, cross the road, and in five minutes I'm in the bazaar. My appearance causes no surprise or laughter either in the alleyways near the bazaar or in the bazaar itself. I see this as a sign of the spiritual health of our nation, which has become accustomed to everything. I walk round the bazaar grimly bargaining, as only old prisoners know how. (They look at some fat, yellow-white hen and say, "All right, Granny, how much do you want for that tubercular chicken?") But how many roubles have *I* got? And how do I get them? My grandfather used to say, "A kopeck will save a rouble, and a rouble will save you worry." He was clever, my grandfather.

Cucumbers are the one thing that gives a kind of respite. At the start of the treatment my appetite suddenly came back to me. But now it's gone again. I was even putting on weight under the X rays, but now I am losing it. My head feels heavy and once I had a real dizzy spell. Still, it is true that half my tumor has gone, the edges have softened so I can hardly feel it myself. But meanwhile my blood is being destroyed. They're giving me special medicines that are supposed to increase the white corpuscles (and presumably destroy something else at the same time) and they want to give me milk injections "to provoke white-corpuscle augmentation" (that's what they call it in their jargon). Sheer barbarity, isn't it? Why not just give me a jug of fresh milk straight from the cow in the usual way? I won't let myself be injected, come what may.

On top of that, they're threatening to give me blood transfusions. I am fighting that one too. What's saving me is the fact that my blood is Group A, which they rarely bring here.

---

*An allusion to the mocking retort—well known in Russia—security police officers make to prisoners who try to call them comrade: "The wolf in the *taiga* is your comrade."

Generally speaking, my relations with the doctor in charge of the radiation department are rather strained. Whenever I see her, we have an argument. She is a very strict woman. Last time she started probing my chest and declaring there was "no reaction to the Sinestrol," implying that I was avoiding the injections and deceiving her. Naturally I was indignant. (In fact, of course, I *am* deceiving her.)

I find it much harder to be firm with the doctor in charge of treatment. You know why? Because she is so soft and gentle. (You once started to explain to me, Nikolai Ivanovich, the origin of the expression "Soft words will break your bones." Try and remind me of it, please.) Not only does she never raise her voice, she can't even get her eyebrows to frown properly. When she prescribes something I don't want, she lowers her eyes and for some reason I give in to her. There are details, too, we find it difficult to discuss together. She's still a young woman, younger than I am, and there are some things she tries not to call by their proper names and somehow I feel too embarrassed to press her for an answer.

By the way, she's a good-looking, attractive woman. She introduced herself to me as married, I remember quite well, and then it suddenly transpired she had no husband at all. It seems she regards her unmarried state as a humiliation, and this is why she lied.

She seems to have a schoolgirlish belief in book learning left in her. Like the rest of them she believes unquestioningly in their established methods and treatments and I can't implant the tiniest doubt in her mind. Generally speaking, no one will condescend to discuss such methods with me. There's no one willing to take me on as a reasonable ally. I have to listen in on the doctors' conversations, make guesses, fill in the guessed parts, get hold of medical books— this is how I try to establish the situation.

Still, it is hard for me to make up my mind. What should I do? What is the best way of behaving? For instance, they often probe under my collarbones, but how true is it what they say, that this is where secondaries are to be found? Why is it they bombard me with these thousands and thousands of X-ray units? Is it really to stop the tumor growing again? Or is it just to make sure, to build a fivefold or tenfold reserve of strength like they do when they build bridges? Or is it just carrying out senseless, pointless instructions which they can't ignore on pain of losing their jobs? But I could ignore them! I am the one who could smash this vicious circle if only they would tell me the truth—but they don't.

After all, I am not asking for a long life. Why should I want to peer deep into the future? First I lived under guard, then I lived in pain, and now I want to live just a little while without guards and without pain, simultaneously without one or the other. This is the limit of my ambition.

I am not asking for Leningrad or for Rio de Janeiro, all I want is our little place out in the wilds, humble Ush-Terek. Soon it will be summer, and this summer I want to sleep on a folding bed under the stars, to wake up at night and know by the positions of Cygnus and Pegasus what time it is, to live just this one summer and see the stars without their being blotted out by camp searchlights—then afterward I would be quite content never to wake again.

Yes, and one other thing, Nikolai Ivanovich, I want to walk with you (and with Beetle and Tobik, of course) after the heat has abated, along the steppe track to the Chu River. Then where the water's deepest, where it comes above your knees, I shall sit on the sandy bottom, legs floating in the current, sit hour after hour, as still as the heron on the opposite bank.

Our Chu reaches no sea, no lake, no expanse of water at all. It is a river that ends life in the sands, a river flowing nowhere, shedding the best of its water and strength haphazardly along its path.

My friends, isn't this a fine picture of our lives as prisoners? We are given nothing to accomplish, doomed to be stifled in ignominy, while the best left to us is a single reach of water which has not yet dried up, and the only memory of us will be the two little handfuls of water we hold out to each other, as we held out human contact, conversation and help.

A river flowing into the sands! But the doctors even want to deprive me of this last stretch of water. By some right (it never enters their heads to question this right) they have decided, without my consent and on my behalf, on a most terrible form of treatment —hormone therapy. It is a piece of red-hot iron with which they brand you just once and make you a cripple for the rest of your life. But what an everyday event that is in the routine of the clinic.

Even before this I thought a lot about the supreme price of life, and lately I have been thinking about it even more. How much can one pay for life, and how much is too much? It's like what they teach you in schools these days, "A man's most precious possession is his life. It is only given to him once." This means we should cling to life at any cost. But the camps have helped many of us to establish that the betrayal or destruction of good and helpless people is too high a price, that our lives aren't worth it. As for bootlicking and flattery, the voters in the camp were divided. Some said it was a price one could pay, and maybe it is. But what about this price? To preserve his life, should a man pay everything that gives it color, scent and excitement? Can one accept a life of digestion, respiration, muscular and brain activity—and nothing more? Become a walking blueprint? Is not this an exorbitant price? Is it not mockery? Should one pay? Seven years in the army and seven years in the camp, twice seven years, twice that mythical or biblical term, and then to be deprived of the ability to tell what is a man and what is a woman—is not such a price extortionate?

I wouldn't have hesitated for a minute, I'd have quarreled with them and left long ago, but then I'd lose their certificate, the great Goddess Certificate! The *komendant* or security chief may want to send me another three hundred kilometers into the desert tomorrow. I can stop that happening as long as I have my certificate. Please, sir, I'm in need of constant observation and medical treatment, sir! Thank you, sir! Get an old prisoner to give up his medical certificate? It's unthinkable!

So once more I have to be cunning, pretend, deceive, drag things out—and one gets so sick of it after a lifetime! (Incidentally, too much cunning makes one tired and prone to error. I brought everything down on my own head with that letter from the Omsk lab. assistant I asked you to send me. I handed it in. They seized it, wove it into my case history, and when it was too late I realized how the senior doctor had deceived me about it. Now she can be confident about giving me hormone treatment, whereas otherwise she would probably have had doubts.)

When I get back to Ush-Terek I'll give my tumor another pummeling with that mandrake root from Issyk Kul, just to make sure it doesn't start throwing secondaries about. There's something noble about treating oneself with a strong poison. Poison doesn't pretend to be a harmless medicine, it tells you straight out, "I'm poison! Watch out! Or else!" So we know what we're in for.

I was quite excited by your last letter (it got here pretty quickly —five days; all the ones before have taken eight). Is it true? A geodetic expedition in our area? What a joy that would be, getting behind a theodolite, working like a human being for a year or so, even if no more. But will they take me on? It would be bound to go beyond the limits of my place of exile, wouldn't it? And anyway, these things are top secret, without exception, and I'm a man with a record.

I'll never see *Waterloo Bridge* or *Open City* now, those movies you thought were so good. They won't come back to Ush-Terek a second time, and to go to the cinema here I'd have to find somewhere to stay the night after being discharged from hospital. Where could I stay? Anyway, I probably won't be discharged till I'm crawling on all fours.

You offer to send me a little money. Thank you very much. First of all, I wanted to refuse; all my life I have tried to avoid being in debt, and I have succeeded. But then I remembered that I shan't die with nothing to bequeath. There is an Ush-Terek sheepskin jacket—that's something, after all! And what about a two-meter length of black cloth I use as a blanket? And a feather pillow, a gift from Melchuk? And three packing cases nailed together to make a bed? And two saucepans? My camp bowl? And my spoon? Not to mention my bucket! There's still some *saksaul** for the stove! An ax! And lastly a paraffin lamp! It was just an oversight that I forgot to make a will.

And so I would be most grateful if you could send me 150 roubles (no more than that). I will undertake your commission to try to find some manganate, soda, and cinnamon. Write to me if you think of anything else. Perhaps you would like a portable iron after all? I'll get it home, don't be afraid to ask.

I see from your weather report, Nikolai Ivanovich, that it's still quite cold at home, the snow hasn't gone yet. It's such a wonderful spring here, it's almost indecent and incomprehensible.

By the way, about the weather report. If you see Inna Ström please give her my best wishes. Tell her I often think about her and . . .

Or maybe you'd better not . . .

There are such vague feelings singing inside me, I don't know what I want myself. Or what I have the right to want.

---

*A desert tree that provides excellent fuel.

But when I remember our consolation, that great saying "Things have been worse," I always cheer up straightaway. We aren't ones to hang our heads! We'll muddle along somehow!

Elena Alexandrovna says she has written ten letters in two evenings. It made me think what a wonderful thing it is—this sympathetic, steadfast consideration for people you have. Who nowadays remembers distant friends and gives up evening after evening for them? This is why it's so pleasant writing you long letters, because I know you will be reading them aloud, and then reading them again, and then going over them sentence by sentence and answering each point.

So may you continue to flourish, my friends, and may your light shine.

Your
OLEG.

23. Why Not Live Well?

March 5 was a murky sort of day outside, with a fine cold drizzle, but in the ward it was a day of surprises and events. The evening before Dyomka had signed his agreement to the operation, so he was moving down to the surgical ward. That day they also moved in two new patients.

The first took Dyomka's bed, the one in the corner by the door. He was a tall man, but he had a terrible stoop, a crooked spine and a worn face like a very old man's. His eyes were so swollen, his lower eyelids so pulled down that instead of the horizontal oval everyone has in their eyes he had something more like a circle, and in each circle the white had an unhealthy reddish tinge. They were bright, brownish iridescent rings larger looking than usual because of the distended lower eyelids. With these great round eyes the old man seemed to be examining everyone with an unpleasant, attentive gaze.

During the past week Dyomka had not been himself; he had had unceasing aches and shooting pains in his leg so that he could no longer sleep or take part in anything. It was a real effort holding himself together so as not to cry out and disturb his neighbors. All this had worn him out to the point where he no longer thought of his leg as precious, but as a cursed burden he ought to get rid of as quickly and easily as possible. A month ago the operation had seemed like the end of life, but now it seemed like salvation. Thus do our standards change.

Dyomka had taken the advice of every single man in the ward

before signing his agreement. Still, even today, as he was tying up his bundle of belongings and saying his goodbyes, he was trying to turn the conversation, to make people calm him down and reassure him. So Vadim had to repeat what he had already said, that Dyomka was lucky to get off so easily, that he, Vadim, would have taken his place with pleasure.

Dyomka still managed to find objections. "But the bone—they saw it through with a saw. They just saw it through like a log. They say you can feel it under any anesthetic."

But Vadim was unable to console anyone for long, nor did he wish to. "Come on now," he said, "you're not the first one it's happened to. Others have to put up with it, you'll put up with it too."

In this case, as in every other, he was being just and impartial. He had asked for no consolation himself, and if offered it, he would not have accepted it. There was something spineless, religious even, about every attempt to console.

Vadim was just as proud, collected and courteous as he had been during his first days in the hospital. The only difference was that his swarthy mountaineer's skin had started to turn yellow. Occasionally, too, his lips would tremble with pain, his forehead twitch with impatience and bewilderment. So long as he had just been *saying* he was doomed to die in eight months, but had still gone riding, and flying to Moscow and meeting Cheregorodtsev, he had been convinced at the bottom of his heart that he would escape the trap. But now here he was, he had been here a month—one month out of the eight he had left, and maybe not the first, but the third or the fourth out of the eight. And every day walking became more painful. Already he found it difficult even to imagine mounting a horse and riding out into the field. Already the pain had spread to his groin. He had by now read three of the books he had brought with him, but he was losing his conviction that the discovery of ores by radioactive water was the only essential thing in his life. Therefore he was reading less intently than before, making fewer question and exclamation marks.

Vadim had always reckoned life was at its best when he was so busy that there were not enough hours in the day. But now, somehow, he found the days quite long enough, too long even, only there was not enough life. His tightly strung capacity for work had begun to sag. Seldom now did he wake early and read his books in the quiet of the morning. Sometimes he would just lie there, the blankets pulled up over his head, and the idea would seep into his mind that perhaps to give in and end it all would be easier than to struggle. He began to feel the terrifying absurdity of these paltry surroundings and idiotic conversations, and the urge to rip apart his polished self-control and howl as a wild animal howls at its snare, "All right, stop playing the fool, let go of my leg!"

Vadim's mother had been to see four highly placed officials but had still not managed to get any colloidal gold. She had brought some *chaga** from Russia and arranged for the nurse to bring him jugs of infusion every other day. Then she went back to Moscow for more interviews to try to get some gold. She could not come to terms with the possibility that radioactive gold might exist somewhere and yet her son's secondaries were still penetrating his groin.

Dyomka went up to Kostoglotov to say or to hear some word of farewell. Kostoglotov was lying diagonally across his bed, his feet up on the rail and his head hanging over the mattress into the aisle. They saw each other upside down. Oleg held out his hand and said quietly in parting (he now found it hard to speak loudly, he could feel something reverberating under his lungs): "Don't lose your nerve, Dyomka. Lev Leonidovich is here. I saw him. He'll have it chopped off in no time."

"Is he?" Dyomka's face lit up. "Did you see him yourself?"

"That's right."

"Well, that's something! What a good thing I held out!" Indeed, it was enough for this lanky surgeon with his over-long drooping arms to appear in the clinic corridors and immediately the patients began to take heart, as though realizing that this long-legged fellow was just the man they had been missing all month. If they had paraded all the surgeons in front of the patients and let the patients take their pick, there is little doubt that each one would have signed on for Lev Leonidovich. He always looked so bored the way he walked about the clinic, but this expression they interpreted as a sign that it was not the day for operations.

Although Yevgenia Ustinovna was quite good enough for Dyomka, although little, fragile Yevgenia Ustinovna was a splendid surgeon, still it was an entirely different feeling lying underneath the hairy, apelike hands of Lev Leonidovich; because however it turned out, whether he saved you or not, it wouldn't be because

*A birch-tree fungus, believed by many to be a cure for cancer.

he'd made a mistake. Of this Dyomka was somehow quite convinced.

The intimacy between patient and surgeon is short-lived, but closer than between a son and his own father.

"He's a good surgeon, is he?" came a muffled question from the "new boy" with the swollen eyes in the bed that had once been Dyomka's. He looked absentminded, and as if someone had taken him by surprise. He was shivering. Even inside the ward he wore a fustian dressing gown over his pajamas, unfastened and unbelted. The old man stared about him as if, alone in a house, he had been awakened by a knock on the door in the middle of the night, had got out of bed and couldn't make out what was threatening him.

"Uh-huh!" Dyomka grunted. His face was brightening all the time. He looked as if his operation was already half over. "He's a champ, that boy! Are you for an operation too? What have you got?"

"Yes, I'm for one too," was all the "new boy" replied. It was as if he had not heard the whole of Dyomka's question. His face in no way mirrored Dyomka's relief, there was no change in his great, round, fixed eyes. Either they gazed much too intently or else they were completely unseeing.

Dyomka went away. They made up the bed for the "new boy," who sat down on it and leaned against the wall. Once more his enlarged eyes gazed in silence. He did not move them about, but would focus them on some man in the ward and gaze at him for ages. Then he would turn his head and gaze at someone else, or else perhaps look straight past him. He did not move or react to the sounds and stir in the ward. He did not speak, did not ask or answer questions. An hour went by and all they could get out of him was that he came from Fergana. Then one of the nurses called him, revealing that his name was Shulubin.

He was an eagle owl, that's what he was. Rusanov at once recognized those fixed, round, completely immobile eyes. The ward was not a particularly merry place as it was, so the last thing they needed was this eagle owl. Gloomily Shulubin fixed his gaze on Rusanov and stared at him for so long that it became quite unpleasant. He gazed at everyone like this, as though each man in the ward had done him a bad turn. Life in the ward could no longer continue in its normal unconstrained way.

The day before, Pavel Nikolayevich had had his twelfth injection. He was now used to these injections and could take them without going into delirium, but he kept getting headaches and felt generally weaker. The main thing that had emerged was that there was no danger of his dying. Of course, the whole thing had been no more than a family panic. Half his tumor had already disappeared, while the part that remained straddling his neck had softened so that, although it still got in his way, it was not as bad as before. His head had recovered its freedom of movement. The only thing left was the weakness, and one can put up with weakness, there's even something agreeable about it—just lying there and reading, reading *Ogonyok* and *Krokodil*,* taking tonics and choosing some tasty thing he felt like eating. If only he could talk to some agreeable people and listen to the radio—but he'd have that when he went home. The weakness would have been the only thing if it hadn't been for Dontsova's painful probing into his armpits, the hard pressure of her fingers poking as though with a stick. She was looking for something, and having been there a month he could guess what it was—another tumor. She would also call him down to her surgery, lay him out on the couch and probe his groin, again pressing him painfully and sharply.

"Might it really start up somewhere else?" Pavel Nikolayevich would ask her in alarm, his joy over the collapse of his tumor quite dimmed.

"That's why we're treating you, to stop that happening," Dontsova would shake her head. "But we'll have to give you a lot more injections."

"How many?" Rusanov would ask in terror.

"We'll see."

(Doctors never tell you anything straight out.)

He was so weak from the twelve he had had—already they were shaking their heads over his blood count—might he really have to endure the same number again? By hook or by crook the disease was overpowering him. The tumor had abated, but this was no real cause for joy. Pavel Nikolayevich passed his days listlessly, mostly lying down. Incidentally, even Bone-chewer had become quite tame. He had stopped roaring and snarling and it was obvious now he wasn't pretending; the disease had laid him low too. More and more often he would let his head hang dangling over the end of the bed and lie there like that for hours, screwing up his eyes. Pavel

Ogonyok is a Soviet illustrated weekly magazine; *Krokodil* is the leading Soviet satirical and cartoon journal.

Nikolayevich would be taking powders for his headaches, slapping a wet rag over his forehead and covering up his eyes against the light. And so they would lie side by side for hours on end, quite peaceably, without joining battle.

They had hung a banner across the wide staircase landing. (The little fellow who had spent his time sucking oxygen balloons had been taken away from there to the morgue.) The message was written in the usual way in white letters on a long piece of red calico: "Patients, do not discuss each other's illnesses!"

Of course with such a grand piece of calico hanging in such a prominent spot, some slogan to celebrate the October Revolution or First of May anniversaries would have been more suitable. But this was an important appeal for the people who lived here. Pavel Nikolayevich had mentioned the matter several times, to stop patients upsetting himself and each other.

(Generally speaking, it would have been more statesmanlike, more correct, not to keep the tumor patients all in one place, but to spread them out among ordinary hospitals. They wouldn't frighten one another then and one would be able to hide the truth from them, which would be much more humane.)

The people in the ward came and went, but no one ever seemed to be happy. They were always so dejected and withered. Only Ahmadjan, who had already abandoned his crutch and was soon to be discharged, showed his white teeth in a grin. But this did not cheer anyone else except himself. Probably the only effect it had was to make people jealous.

Then suddenly, a couple of hours after the gloomy "new boy's" arrival, on this gray, depressing day when everyone was lying on their beds, when the windowpanes washed by the rain let in so little light that one felt like turning on the electric lights even before the midday meal and longed for the evening to come more quickly— suddenly a shortish, energetic-looking man walked briskly and healthily into the ward, straight past the nurse who was showing him in. He didn't really enter the ward, he burst into it as hurriedly as if there was a guard of honor drawn up in ranks to greet him, men who had been waiting for him and getting tired. When he saw how listlessly everyone was lying on their beds, he stopped dead. He even whistled. Then, in a voice of energetic reproach, he announced proudly, "Hey, boys, you're a lot of dopes, aren't you? Have your feet shriveled up or something?"

Even though the men were not exactly a welcoming guard of

honor, he greeted them with a semi-military gesture, like a salute. "Chaly, Maxim Petrovich! It's a pleasure! Stand at ease!"

There was nothing of the exhaustion of cancer on his face. His smile twinkled with confidence and *joie de vivre,* and some of the men smiled back at him. Pavel Nikolayevich was one of these. A month with all these nincompoops, and now it looks as if we have got a man at last.

"Well then . . ." He did not ask anyone, but his quick eyes spotted his bed and he strode boldly across to it. It was the bed next to Pavel Nikolayevich, the one that had been Mursalimov's. The new man went in on the side he shared with Pavel Nikolayevich. He sat down on the bed, bounced it up and down, and it creaked.

"Sixty per cent worn out," he quipped. "The senior doctor's no rat catcher, you can see that."

He started to unload his belongings, but it turned out there was nothing to unload. He carried nothing in his hands. He had a razor in one pocket and a pack in another pocket, not a cigarette pack but a pack of playing cards, almost new ones. He took out the pack, flipped through it with his fingers and turned his clever-looking eyes toward Pavel Nikolayevich. "Do you indulge?" he asked him.

"Yes, sometimes," Pavel Nikolayevich admitted amiably.

"Do you play Preference*?"

"Not really. I like Casino best."

"That's not a game," said Chaly sternly. "What about whist? Or twenty-one? Or poker?"

"Well, not really." Rusanov waved one arm in embarrassment. "There was no place to learn."

"We'll teach you here, where else?" Chaly said enthusiastically. "It's like they say: If you can't we'll teach you, if you won't we'll make you!"

He was laughing. His nose was too big for his face. It was a great, soft, reddened nose. But it was this that gave his face its simple-hearted, attractive and open quality.

"Poker's the best game in the world!" he declared authoritatively. "You bet blind in poker."

He had already counted Pavel Nikolayevich in and was looking around for more players. But there was no one nearby to inspire him with hope.

"Me! I'll learn!" Ahmadjan shouted from behind him.

*A form of contract bridge.

"Fine," said Chaly encouragingly. "Try and find something we can put between the beds for a table."

He looked around the ward once more, saw the frozen gaze of Shulubin, then spotted a Uzbek in a pink turban with a drooping mustache as fine as though made of silver thread. It was then that Nellya came in with a bucket and cloth. She had been told to give the floors an extra wash.

"Aha!" said Chaly appreciatively straightaway. "What a girl we've run across here! Hey, where were you before? We'd have had a ride on the swings together, wouldn't we?"

Nellya stuck out her thick lips, which was her way of smiling. "Well, it's not too late, is it?" she said. "Only you're sick, aren't you? What use are you to a girl?"

"A woman a day keeps the doctor away," Chaly retorted. "Why, are you afraid of me?"

"Why should I be afraid of you? You're not much of a man!" said Nellya, getting him in her sights.

"I'm man enough to get through you, don't you worry!" Chaly exclaimed. "Come on, hurry up then, get down and wash the floor, we want to inspect the façade!"

"Look as much as you like, we don't charge for that," said Nellya. She was enjoying herself. She slapped the wet cloth under the first bed, bent down and started washing.

Maybe the man wasn't ill at all. There were no visible sores on him, and judging by his face there was no internal pain either. Or was he controlling himself with a great effort of will, showing an example unprecedented in the ward, but one which a Soviet man really ought to set? Pavel Nikolayevich looked at Chaly enviously.

"But . . . what's wrong with you?" he asked Chaly quietly, so that only he could hear.

"Me?" Chaly shook himself. "I've got polyps!"

None of the patients knew exactly what polyps were, even though they came across them quite often in one another.

"Does it hurt?"

"Well, as soon as it started to hurt I came along here. You want to cut it out? All right, go ahead. Why stall?"

"Where is it, then?" Rusanov asked him with increasing respect.

"In my stomach, I think," Chaly remarked casually. He even smiled. "I reckon they'll cut out my beautiful old stomach. They'll hack away three quarters of it."

With the edge of his hand he sawed away at his stomach and squinted.

"What will you do then?" asked Rusanov in amazement.

"Not a thing. I'll just have to get used to it. As long as it still soaks up the vodka!"

"But you have such wonderful self-control."

"Listen to me, neighbor." Chaly nodded his head up and down. His face with its big reddish nose was kindness itself. Simplicity shone in his eyes. "If you don't want to croak, you shouldn't get yourself upset. Less talk, less pain. That's my advice to you!"

At that moment Ahmadjan appeared with a board made of plywood. They set it up between Rusanov and Chaly's beds. It was quite firm.

"That's more civilized," said Ahmadjan happily.

"Turn on the light," Chaly ordered.

They turned on a light. The room brightened up.

"Well, what about a fourth?"

But there was no fourth to be found.

"Never mind, explain it to us," said Rusanov. He was becoming quite cheerful. There he sat, legs on the floor, just like a healthy man. When he turned his head the pain in his neck was much less than before. Maybe it was only a piece of board, but he imagined himself sitting at a nice little card table with a cheerful, bright lamp shining from the ceiling. The signs of the gaily inscribed red and black suits stood out sharp and precise on the polished white surfaces of the cards. Maybe Chaly was right, maybe if you tackled your illness the way he did it would slip away of its own accord. Why mope? Why go around with gloomy thoughts all the time?

"We wait longer, yes?" Ahmadjan was as eager as the rest now.

"Look at this!" Chaly let the whole pack slip through his sure fingers with the speed of a filmstrip. The unnecessary ones he discarded to one side, the others he stacked in front of him.

"The cards we use are from the ace down to the nine. Here's the order of suits: clubs, then diamonds, then hearts, then spades." He pointed the suits out to Ahmadjan. "Do you understand?"

"Yes, sir. I understand!" Ahmadjan answered with great satisfaction.

Maxim Petrovich bent the chosen part of the pack between his fingers, flipped through it, shuffled it lightly and went on explaining.

"Each man gets five cards, the rest are for drawing. Now you must learn the order of the hands. These are the combinations: one pair . . ." he showed them, ". . . two pairs. A straight—that's five cards in a sequence. Like this or like that. Then threes. Full house . . ."

"Which one's Chaly?" someone asked, appearing in the doorway. "Get on parade, your wife's here!"

"Did she bring a bag by any chance? . . . All right, boys, take a break." He walked boldly and nonchalantly toward the door.

It became quite quiet in the ward. The lights were burning as though it was evening. Ahmadjan went off to his own bunk. Nellya carried on slopping water quickly across the floor, so everyone had to pull their feet up onto their beds.

Pavel Nikolayevich lay down. He could physically feel that eagle owl staring at him from the corner, like a stubborn, reproachful pressure on the side of his head. To relieve the pressure he asked him, "What's the matter with you then, comrade?"

But the gloomy old man would not make even the merest polite gesture in answer to the question. It was as if it had never been asked. His huge round eyes, red and tobacco-brownish, seemed to stare straight past Pavel Nikolayevich's head. After waiting for an answer but not getting one, Pavel Nikolayevich had started flipping the glossy cards through his hands when he heard the man's hollow voice. "The usual!" he said.

What was "the usual"? Boorish fellow! This time Pavel Nikolayevich did not even look at him. He lay down on his back and just stayed like that, lying there and thinking.

The arrival of Chaly and the cards had distracted him, but of course the newspapers were what he was really waiting for. Today was a memorable day,* a very significant day for the future, and there was a lot he ought to be working out and deducing from the newspapers. Because your country's future is, after all, your own future as well. Would the whole paper carry a black mourning edge? Or just the first page? Would there be a full-page portrait or only a quarter-page one? And what would be the wording of the headlines of the leading article? After the February dismissals this was particularly important. If he'd been at work Pavel Nikolayevich could have gathered the news from someone, but here all he had was the newspaper.

*March 5, 1955, was the second anniversary of Stalin's death.

Nellya was fussing and pushing between the beds. None of the spaces between them was wide enough for her, but she did the washing quite quickly. In no time she was finished and rolling out the strip of carpet.

Then in walked Vadim along the strip on his way back from the X-ray room. He was carefully nursing his bad leg, his lips twitching with the pain.

He had the newspaper.

Pavel Nikolayevich beckoned him over. "Vadim," he said, "come over here. Sit down."

Vadim hesitated, thought for a minute, turned and walked into Rusanov's bed-space. He sat down, holding his trouser leg to stop it chafing.

It was obvious that Vadim had already opened the paper, because it wasn't folded as a fresh paper would be. Even while he was taking hold of the paper, Pavel Nikolayevich could see at once that there were no borders around the edges and no portrait in the first column. He looked more closely, rustling hurriedly through the pages, on and on, but however far he looked he could not find a portrait, a black border or a big headline anywhere. In fact, it looked as though there wasn't even an article!

"There's nothing in it, is there?" he asked Vadim. He was frightened and neglected to say exactly what there was nothing of.

He scarcely knew Vadim. Although the man was a Party member he was still too young, not a leading official but a narrow specialist, and what might be tucked away inside his head it was impossible to guess. But on one occasion he had given Pavel Nikolayevich excellent grounds for hope. The men in the ward were talking about the exiled nationalities. Vadim had raised his head from his geology, looked at Rusanov, shrugged his shoulders and said so quietly that only Rusanov could hear, "There must have been something in it. They wouldn't exile people for nothing in our country."

By making such a correct observation Vadim had shown himself a thoroughly intelligent man of unshakeable principles.

It seemed that Pavel Nikolayevich had not been mistaken. He did not have to explain what he was talking about. Vadim had already looked for it himself. He indicated the special feature which Pavel Nikolayevich, overcome by emotion, had not spotted.

It was an ordinary feature, quite undistinguished from the others. No picture, just an article by a member of the Academy of Sciences.

And the article itself was not about the second anniversary or about the whole nation's grief. Nor did it say he was "alive and will live forever!" It merely said, "Stalin and Some Problems of Communist Construction."*

Was that all? Just "Some Problems"? Just those few problems? Problems of Construction? Why Construction? They might as well be writing about protective forest belts.** What about the military victories? What about the philosophical genius? What about the giant of the sciences? What about the entire people's love for him?

Knitting his brow, Pavel Nikolayevich gazed sufferingly through his spectacles at the swarthy face of Vadim.

"How could it happen? Eh? . . ." He peered cautiously over his shoulder at Kostoglotov, who seemed to be asleep. His eyes were shut and his head was hanging down from the bed as usual.

"Two months ago, just two months, isn't that right? You remember, his seventy-fifth birthday! Everything the way it's always been. A huge picture and a huge headline, 'The Great Successor.' Isn't that right? Isn't that right?"

It wasn't the danger, no, it wasn't the danger that now threatened those who were left after his death—it was the ingratitude. It was this ingratitude that wounded Rusanov most of all, as though his own great services, his own irreproachable record were what they were spitting on and trampling underfoot. If the Glory that resounds in Eternity could be muffled and cut short after only two years, if the Most Beloved, the Most Wise, the One whom all your superiors and superiors' superiors obeyed, could be overturned and hushed up within twenty-four months—then what remained? What could one rely on? How could a man recover his health in such circumstances?

"You see," Vadim said very softly, "officially there was an order issued recently to commemorate only the anniversaries of births, not those of deaths. But of course, to judge from the article . . ."

He shook his head sadly from side to side.

He too felt somehow insulted, most of all because of his late father. He remembered how his father loved Stalin. He'd loved him much more than he'd loved himself (his father never tried to get anything for himself), more even than he loved Lenin, and probably

---

*The word "Construction" is here used in the communist sense of "constructing a new society."

**A feature of Stalin's "Plan for the Transformation of Nature," the last of his grandiose schemes. It has now been abandoned.

more than he'd loved his wife and his sons. He could speak calmly or jokingly about his family, but about Stalin—never! His voice would shake at the mention of him. He had one portrait of Stalin hanging in his study, one in the dining room and yet another in the nursery. As the boys grew up they always saw hanging over them those thick eyebrows, that thick mustache, that firm, steadfast face seemingly incapable either of fear or of frivolous joy, all emotions seeming concentrated in those glittering velvety-black eyes.

Every time Stalin made a speech his father would first read it right through, then read pieces aloud to the boys, explaining how profound their thought was, how subtly it was expressed and how fine the Russian was. Only later, when his father was no longer alive and Vadim was grown up, did he begin to find the language of the speeches a trifle insipid. He began to feel the thought was not concentrated at all, that it could have been set out much more concisely and that judging by the volume of words there should have been more of it. Despite his discovery, he would never have spoken of it aloud, he still felt himself a more complete person when professing the admiration instilled in him as a child.

It was still quite fresh in his memory—the day of Stalin's death. They had wept—old people, young people and children. Girls burst into sobs and young men were wiping their eyes. To judge from the widespread tears, you would think that a crack had appeared in the universe rather than that one man had died. He felt that if humanity was able to survive this day, it would for centuries be carved in man's memory as the blackest day of the year.

And now, on its second anniversary, they wouldn't even spend a drop of printer's ink on giving him a black border. They couldn't find the simple words of warmth: "Two years ago there passed away . . ." the man whose name was the last earthly word uttered by countless soldiers as they stumbled and fell in the Great War.

But it was not merely a question of Vadim's upbringing—he might have outgrown that. No, the fact was that all reasonable considerations demanded that one honor the great man who had passed away. He had been clarity itself, radiating confidence in the fact that tomorrow would not depart from the path of the preceding day. He had exalted science, exalted scientists and freed them from petty thoughts of salary or accommodations. Science itself required his stability and his permanence to prevent any catastrophe happening that might distract scientists or take them away from their work, which was of supreme interest and use—for settling squabbles about the structure of society, for educating the underdeveloped or for convincing the stupid.

Vadim walked miserably back to his bed, nursing his bad leg.

Then Chaly reappeared, very pleased with himself, carrying a bag full of provisions. He put them into his bedside table, on the side away from Rusanov's bed-space, and smiled at him sheepishly. "The last time I'll have something to eat with! Goodness knows what it will be like when I've nothing left but guts!"

Rusanov couldn't have admired Chaly more. What an optimist he was! What an excellent fellow!

"Pickled tomatoes . . ." Chaly carried on unpacking. He pulled one straight out of the jar with his fingers, swallowed it and screwed up his eyes. "Ah, they're delicious!" he said. "And a piece of veal, all juicy and fried, not dried up." He felt it and licked his fingers. "The golden hands of a woman!"

Silently he slid a half-liter bottle of spirit into his bedside table. Rusanov saw him, although Chaly's body screened what he was doing from the rest of the room. He winked at Rusanov.

"So, you're a local boy, are you?" said Pavel Nikolayevich.

"No-o. I'm not local. I just pass through here sometimes, on business."

"But your wife lives here, does she?"

But Chaly was already out of earshot, taking away the empty bag.

He came back, opened the bedside table, screwed up his eyes, had a look, swallowed one more tomato and closed the door. He shook his head from side to side with pleasure.

"Well, what did we stop for? Let's get on with it."

By this time Ahmadjan had found a fourth, a young Kazakh from out on the staircase. He had spent the time sitting on his bed heatedly gesticulating and telling the Kazakh in Russian the story of how "our Russian boys" beat the Turks. (He had gone to another wing the previous evening and seen a movie there called *The Capture of Plevna.**)

Both men now came over and set the board up again between the beds. Chaly, even merrier than before, dealt out some cards with his quick, clever hands to show his friends some examples.

---

*Plevna was captured by the Russians in the Russo-Turkish War of 1877–78. The irony is that both Ahmadjan and his partner belong to Turkic nationalities, and can understand one another's dialect.

"Now, that's a full house, do you see? That's when you get three of one kind and two of another. Do you see, *chechmek*?"*

"I'm no *chechmek*," said Ahmadjan, shaking his head but not taking offense. "I was a *chechmek* before I joined the army."

"All right, fine. Now, the next one's a flush. That's when all five are the same suit. Then we have fours: four of the same kind, with an odd one out as fifth. Then straight flush. That's a straight of the same suit from nine to the king. Here, look, like this . . . or like this . . . Then higher still is the royal straight flush . . ."

Of course it wasn't all clear at once, but Maxim Petrovich promised them it would be when they actually started. The main thing was that he talked so amiably, in such a straightforward, sincere tone of voice that it made Pavel Nikolayevich's heart warm to hear him. He had never counted on meeting such a pleasant, obliging fellow in a public hospital. Here they were sitting together, a nice, friendly little "cell," and so it would go on hour after hour, perhaps every day. Why bother about illness? Why think about unpleasant facts? Maxim Petrovich was right.

Rusanov was just about to stipulate that they wouldn't play for money until they had properly mastered the game when suddenly someone appeared in the doorway. "Which of you is Chaly?" he asked.

"I'm Chaly."

"Get on parade, your wife's here!"

"Ah, silly bitch!" Maxim Petrovich spat without malice. "I told her, don't come on Saturday, come on Sunday. She nearly bumped into the other one, didn't she? Oh well, friends, you'll have to excuse me."

So the game was disrupted again. Maxim Petrovich went off and Ahmadjan and the Kazakh took the cards across to their corner to go through them and practice.

And once more Pavel Nikolayevich thought about his tumor and about March the fifth. Again he could feel the eagle owl staring at him disapprovingly from the corner. He turned round and was hit by the open eyes of Bone-chewer. Bone-chewer had not been asleep at all.

Kostoglotov had been awake all the time. Rusanov and Vadim had been rustling through the paper and whispering to each other, and

---

*A racially insulting word for Uzbeks, used by Russians.

he had heard every word. He had deliberately not opened his eyes. He wanted to hear what they would say about it, what Vadim would say about it. He didn't need to fight for the paper, open it and read it, because everything was already explained.

More knocking. His heart was knocking. His heart was banging against an iron door which ought never to open, but which was now for some reason emitting faint creaks. It was beginning to shake slightly, and rust was beginning to flake off the hinges.

Kostoglotov found it impossible to comprehend what he had heard from men in the outside world: that on this day two years ago old men had shed tears, young girls had wept, and the whole world had seemed orphaned. He found this preposterous to imagine because he remembered what the day had been like for them. Suddenly they were not taken out to their daily work. Barracks blocks were not unlocked and the prisoners were kept shut up. The loudspeaker just outside the camp grounds, which they could always hear, had been turned off. Altogether it showed that the bosses had lost their heads, that they had some great trouble on their hands. And the bosses' troubles meant the prisoners' delight! No need to go to work, just lie on your bunk, all rations delivered to the door! First they had a good sleep, then they wondered what was happening, then played their guitars and bandores for a bit, then went from bunk to bunk trying to guess what had happened. You can dump prisoners in any out-of-the-way place you like, but somehow the truth will get through to them every time—via the bread-cutting room or the water-boiling room or the kitchen. So the news spread and spread. Not very decisively at first. People were moving along the bunks, sitting down on them and saying, "Hey, kids, it looks like the old cannibal has kicked the bucket . . ."—"What did you say?"—"I'll never believe it!"—"About time!" and a chorus of laughter. Bring out your guitars, strum your balalaikas! They didn't open the barracks blocks for twenty-four hours, but the next morning (it was still frosty in Siberia) the whole camp was formed up in ranks on parade. The major, both captains and the lieutenants—everyone was there. The major, somber with grief, began to announce, "It is with deep sorrow . . . that I must tell you . . . that yesterday in Moscow . . ."

And they all started to grin, they were all but openly crowing in triumph, those coarse, sharp-boned, swarthy prisoners' mugs. The major saw them as they started to smile. Beside himself, he ordered, "Caps off!"

Hundreds of men hesitated on the verge of obeying. To refuse to take them off was still out of the question, but to take them off was too painfully ignominious. One man showed them the way—the camp joker, the popular humorist. He tore off his cap—it was a *Stalinka* made of artificial fur—and hurled it up into the air. He had carried out the order!

Hundreds of prisoners saw him. They too threw their caps in the air!

The major choked.

And now after all this Kostoglotov was finding out that old men had shed tears, young girls had wept, and the whole world had seemed orphaned . . .

Chaly came back looking even merrier than before, once again with a bag full of provisions, but a different one this time. Someone grinned, but Chaly himself was the first one to laugh openly. "Well?" he said. "What can you do with these women? Why not, if it gives them pleasure? Why not comfort them? What harm does it do?

> "Kitchen maid or Lady Muck,
> They're all the same, they like a fuck."

He burst into loud laughter, in which his listeners joined. With a gesture, Chaly waved away the surfeit of laughter. Rusanov too joined in the good, honest laughter. It sounded so clever the way Maxim Petrovich had said it.

"So your wife . . . ? Which one's she?" asked Ahmadjan, choking with mirth.

"Don't ask me that, brother," sighed Maxim Petrovich. He was transferring the food into the bedside table. "We need a reform in the law. The Moslem arrangement's much more humane. And as from last August they're allowing abortions again—that'll make life much more simple! Why should a woman live on her own? Someone ought to visit her, even if it is only once or twice a year. It's useful for people traveling on business, too. It's nice to have a room in every town, where you can get chicken and noodles."

Once again a dark bottle of something flashed into the closet of provisions. Chaly closed the door and took away the empty bag. Obviously he wasn't going to pamper this one with his attention. He came straight back. He stopped in the aisle where Yefrem had once stood, looked at Rusanov and scratched the curls at the back of his neck. (His hair grew quite wild, its color a cross between flax and straw.) "How about a bite to eat, neighbor?"

Pavel Nikolayevich smiled sympathetically. The ordinary lunch was a bit late, and he didn't really want to eat it after seeing Maxim Petrovich laughingly handling each piece of food he'd been brought. There was something agreeable, something of the flesheater about Maxim Petrovich and the way his fat lips smiled. It made one feel drawn toward sitting down with him at a dinner table.

"All right." Rusanov invited him to come to his table. "I've got a few things in here too . . ."

"What about glasses?" Chaly leaned across and his agile hands carried the jugs and parcels across to Rusanov's table.

"But we're not allowed to . . ." said Pavel Nikolayevich, shaking his head. "With our disease it's strictly forbidden to . . ."

During the past month no one in the ward had even dared to think of doing this but with Chaly it seemed natural and unavoidable.

"What's your name?" He was already across in Rusanov's bed-space, sitting opposite him, knee to knee.

"Pavel Nikolayevich."

"Pasha." Chaly laid a friendly hand on Rusanov's shoulder. "You mustn't listen to the doctors. They'll cure you, but they'll lead you to the grave. What we want is to live, and to keep our tails up!"

Chaly's artless face, with its big, ruddy nose and fat, juicy lips, shone with friendliness and firm conviction.

It was Saturday in the clinic and all treatments were held over until Monday. Outside the graying windows the rain poured down, cutting Rusanov off from friends and family. The newspaper had no mourning portrait, and a murky resentment congealed in his soul. The bright lamps were shining, switched on well before the start of the long, long evening. He could now sit with this agreeable man, have a drink, have a bite to eat, and then play some poker. (Poker! What a piece of gossip for Pavel Nikolayevich's friends!)

Chaly, the artful dodger, already had his bottle under the pillow. With one finger he knocked off the stopper and poured out half a glass each, holding the bottle down by their knees. They held the glasses down there and clinked them together.

Like a true Russian, Pavel Nikolayevich now scorned his former fears, reservations and vows. All he wanted was to swill the despair out of his soul and to feel a little warmth.

"We'll have a good time! We'll have a good time, Pasha!" Chaly impressed it on him. His funny old face became filled with sternness, ferocity even. "Let the others croak if they want to. You and I'll have a good time!"

They drank to that.

Rusanov had grown much weaker over the past month, he had drunk nothing but weak red wine, so now he was on fire at once. As each minute passed the heat dissolved and floated through his body, convincing him that it was no use hanging your head, that people managed to live even in the cancer ward, and then leave it behind them.

"Do they hurt a lot then, these . . . polyps?" he asked.

"Yes, a bit. But I don't give in! Pasha, vodka can't make it any worse, you've got to realize that. Vodka's a cure for all illnesses. I'll drink some pure spirit before the operation, what do you think? Here, I've got it in a little bottle. Why spirit? Because it gets absorbed right away, it doesn't leave any surplus water. When the surgeon turns out my stomach, there'll be nothing there. Clean as a whistle! And I'll be drunk! You fought at the front yourself, didn't you? You know how it is: before an attack they give you vodka. Were you wounded?"

"No."

"Bad luck. I was, twice. Look, here and here . . ." Another hundred grams of liquid had appeared in each glass.

"We shouldn't have any more," said Pavel Nikolayevich, resisting mildly. "It's dangerous."

'What's so dangerous? What's put the idea into your head that it's dangerous? Have some tomatoes. Ah, tomatoes!"

And indeed what difference was there—a hundred or two hundred grams—once you'd gone over the edge anyway? Two hundred or two hundred and fifty grams, what did it matter if the Great Man had died and they were now going to ignore him? Pavel Nikolayevich downed another glass in memory of the Leader. He drank as though drinking at a wake, and his lips twisted sadly. Then he stuffed little tomatoes between them. The two men leaned forward, foreheads almost touching, and he listened to Maxim Petrovich sympathetically.

"Yes, lovely and red!" Maxim declared. "Here they're a rouble a kilo, but take them up to Karaganda and you can get thirty. They tear them out of your hands! You aren't allowed to take them, though. The baggage car won't accept them. Why won't they, eh? You tell me, why won't they?"

Maxim Petrovich grew quite excited. His eyes widened. Where's the sense of it? they seemed to imply. The sense of existence.

"A little man in an old jacket comes into the stationmaster's office. 'You want to live, do you, chief?' The stationmaster grabs the telephone, he thinks they've come to kill him. But the man slaps three hundred-rouble notes down on the table. 'Why won't you let me do it?' he asks. 'Why all this "not allowed"? You want to live . . . I want to live too. Tell them to take my basket into the baggage car.' Life will conquer, you see, Pasha. Off goes the train, they call it a 'passenger' train, and it's full of tomatoes, baskets of them, on the racks and under the racks too. The guard gets his cut, the ticket collector gets his cut. When we cross the railway boundaries they put on new ticket collectors, and they get their cut too."

Rusanov's head was beginning to spin. He was glowing with warmth and felt he was stronger than his illness now. Maxim seemed to be saying something that didn't tie up with . . . that didn't tie up with . . . that went right against . . .

"That's against the rules!" objected Pavel Nikolayevich. "What do you do it for? It's not right . . ."

"Not right?" Chaly was quite amazed. "Try the dill pickle, then. And some caviar . . . In Karaganda there's an inscription, stone inlaid on stone: 'Coal is bread.' Bread for industry, that is. But when it comes to tomatoes for the people, they're just aren't any, and there won't be any unless businessmen bring them. People snap them up at twenty-five a kilo, *and* give you a thank you into the bargain. At least they get a few tomatoes that way. Otherwise they would get nothing. They're real morons out there in Karaganda, you can't imagine! They get squads of guards and musclemen together and instead of sending them out to get apples and bring them in by the wagonload they post them on every road in the steppe to catch the men who are trying to bring apples to Karaganda, to stop them getting through. And they just stand there and guard, stupid fools!"

"And . . . you do that . . . you do it, do you?" Pavel Nikolayevich was distressed.

"Why me? I don't carry baskets around, Pasha. I've got my brief-case. And my suitcase. Train tickets are always sold out, always! I don't knock on the glass window, I can always get on the train. I know who to go to at every station, how to find where the right tea-brewer or baggage man is. Life will always conquer, Pasha, remember that."

"But what do you do exactly? What's your job?"

"Me? I'm a technician, Pasha, even though I didn't finish technical school. I do a bit of middleman work on the side. I do it so I can always have a bit left in my pocket. And when they stop paying the right money I leave and go somewhere else. See?"

Pavel Nikolayevich was beginning to realize that things weren't turning out quite as they ought to be. It wasn't proper, in fact it was wrong. But Maxim was such a pleasant, merry fellow you felt at home with him. The first one he'd met in a whole month. He didn't have the heart to hurt him.

"But is it right, what you're doing?" Pavel Nikolayevich pressed him.

"It's all right, it's fine!" said Maxim reassuringly. "Now have a bit of this delicious veal. We'll guzzle some of your compote in a minute. You see, Pasha, we only live once, so why not live well? What we want to do is live well!"

Pavel Nikolayevich could not help agreeing with this. Maxim was quite right. We only live once, so why not live well? It was just that . . .

"You see, Maxim, people don't approve of . . ." he reminded him gently.

"Well, Pasha," he answered as amiably as ever, gripping him by the shoulder, "that depends on how you look at it. It's one thing here, another thing somewhere else.

"A mote in the eye
Makes everyone cry,
But no woman's hurt
By a yard up her skirt."

Chaly was roaring with laughter and slapping Rusanov on the knee. Rusanov could not contain himself. He shook with laughter too. "Hey, you know a few funny lines, don't you? You know what you are, Maxim, you're a poet!"

"What are you, then? What's your job?" asked his new friend inquisitively.

They were almost embracing each other by now, but at this point Pavel Nikolayevich unwittingly became rather dignified. His position imposed certain obligations.

"Well, I'm in personnel." He was being modest. Of course he was higher up than that really.

"Where's that?"

Pavel Nikolayevich told him.

"Listen," said Maxim delightedly. "I know a good man we ought to try and arrange something for! As for the entrance fee, that will come through as usual, don't you worry about that."

"What do you mean? How can you think that?" Pavel Nikolayevich took offense.

"What is there to think?" said Chaly in surprise. And again that search for the meaning of life could be seen trembling in his eyes, only this time slightly blurred with drink. "If the personnel boys didn't take entrance fees, what do you think they would live on? What would they bring their children up on? How many children have you got?"

"Have you finished with the paper?" came a hollow, unpleasant voice from above their heads.

Eagle Owl had dragged himself out of his corner, his eyes harsh and swollen and his dressing gown wide open.

It turned out that Pavel Nikolayevich was sitting on the paper. It was all crumpled.

"Certainly, by all means," said Chaly at once, pulling the paper out from under Rusanov. "Move over there, Pasha. Here you are, Dad. I don't know about anything else, but we won't begrudge you this, will we, Pasha?"

Gloomily Shulubin took the paper and made as if to go, but Kostoglotov restrained him. He began to stare at Shulubin in just the same way as Shulubin had been staring at them all, silently and persistently. He examined him and now saw him particularly clearly and closely.

Who could this man be? And with such an extraordinary face? He looked like an exhausted actor who had just taken off his make-up. Kostoglotov had picked up a trick of familiarity in the transit prisons, where the first minute you met a man you could ask him anything you liked. Lying there in his half-upside-down position, he asked Shulubin, "Hey, Dad, what was your job, eh?"

It wasn't only Shulubin's eyes but his whole head that turned to look at Kostoglotov. For some moments he looked at him unblinkingly, meanwhile twisting his neck in a strange circular movement, as though his collar were too tight. But his collar couldn't have been getting in his way: his nightshirt was quite roomy. This time he didn't ignore the question. "A librarian," he answered abruptly.

"Where?" Kostoglotov grabbed the chance to slip in another question.

"In an agricultural technical college."

For some unknown reason, the heaviness of his gaze or his owl-like silence as he sat in his corner, Rusanov felt the urge to humiliate him, to put him in his place. Or perhaps it was the vodka speaking inside him. His voice was louder and more frivolous than it need have been as he said, "You're not a Party member, are you?"

Eagle Owl turned his tobacco-brownish eyes on Rusanov. He blinked, as though he couldn't believe the question, and blinked again. Suddenly he opened his beak: "On the contrary."

And he strode off across the room.

His walk was oddly unnatural. Something must have been pricking or chafing him somewhere. He hobbled away, the flaps of his dressing gown wide apart, bent forward clumsily, reminding one of a large bird whose wings have been unevenly clipped to prevent it from taking off into the air.

24. Transfusion of Blood

Kostoglotov was sitting in a sunny spot on a stone below a garden bench. He was wearing his boots, and his legs were curled uncomfortably underneath him, knees just off the ground. His arms were dangling lifelessly down to the ground. His uncovered head was hanging forward. He was sitting there warming himself, his gray dressing gown open, as unmoving and angular as the gray stone. His head with its cap of black hair was baking hot. The sun was scorching his back as he sat there motionless, soaking in the March warmth, doing nothing and thinking nothing. He could sit blankly like that for a long time, gleaning from the sun's warmth what had not been provided for him earlier in the bread and soup.

From a distance one could not even see his shoulders rising and falling as he breathed, but he had not toppled to one side; somehow he held himself up.

A fat orderly from the main floor came along the path. She was a large woman who had once tried to chase him out of the corridor for contaminating it. She was addicted to sunflower seeds. Now that she was out in the garden she was making the most of her chance to crack a few seeds. She came up to him and called out in her good-natured fishwife's voice, "Hey, Uncle! Can you hear me, Uncle?"

Kostoglotov raised his head and screwed up his face against the sun. Her figure looked distorted through his half-closed eyes.

"Go to the dressings room. Doctor wants you."

He had sat there so long he was like just another warm stone. The last thing he wanted was to move or get up. He felt like a man who had to go to some job he hated. "What doctor?" he growled.

"The one who wants you, the one who says you're to go!" The orderly raised her voice. "It's not my job to come out and round you all up in the garden. Get inside."

"But I haven't anything that needs dressing. It can't be me they want," said Kostoglotov, refusing to go in.

"It's you all right!" The orderly was stuffing sunflower seeds into her mouth in between sentences. "I wouldn't mix you up with anyone, you long-nosed stork. There's no one else like you round here, darling."

Kostoglotov sighed, straightened his legs and began to get up, groaning and supporting himself with his hands.

The orderly looked at him disapprovingly. "Walk, walk, walk—you should've saved your strength. You should have been lying down."

"Oh," sighed Kostoglotov. "We don't know everything before it happens, do we?" And he dragged himself along the garden path. He wasn't wearing his belt now. There was nothing left of his military bearing. His back was all bent.

He walked toward the dressings room, expecting to encounter some new unpleasantness and ready to fight it off, though he didn't know what it might be.

Waiting for him in the dressings room was not Ellya Rafailovna, who had taken Vera Kornilyevna's place for the past ten days, but a plump young woman. She was more than apple-cheeked, her cheeks were positively crimson with health. It was the first time he had seen her.

"What's your name?" she asked right away while he was still in the doorway.

The sun was no longer in Kostoglotov's eyes, but he was still screwing them up and looking as displeased as ever. He was eager to figure out what was going on, to get an idea of the situation, but he was in no hurry to answer questions. Sometimes a man has to hide his name or to lie about it. He didn't yet know what was the right thing to do.

"Well? What's your name?" the plump-armed doctor asked again.

"Kostoglotov," he confessed reluctantly.

"Where have you been? Get your clothes off quickly. Come here and lie down on the table."

It was only now that Kostoglotov remembered, saw and understood—all at once. It was a blood transfusion! He had forgotten they did it in the dressings room. First of all he wanted to stick to his former principles: he didn't want anyone else's blood, and he wouldn't give his own. In the second place this pert little woman, who looked as if she had drunk her fill of donors' blood herself, inspired no confidence in him. Vera had gone away. Once more there was a new doctor with different habits and fresh mistakes. What the hell was the use of this merry-go-round? Why wasn't anything permanent?

Sullenly he took off his dressing gown. He didn't know where to hang it—the nurse showed him where—and all the time he was trying to think up a pretext for not giving in. He hung up his dressing gown. He took off his jacket and hung that up. He pushed his boots into the corner. He walked barefoot across the clean linoleum floor and lay down on the high padded table. He still couldn't think of any reason to refuse, but he knew he'd be able to think something up presently.

The transfusion apparatus, rubber tubes and glass pipes with water in one of them, towered above the table on a shining steel support. On the same stand there were several rings for different-sized bottles: half-liter, quarter-liter and one-eighth-liter. The last ring was full. The brownish-colored blood was partly covered by a label to mark the blood group, the donor's name and the date on which it had been taken.

Kostoglotov was used to looking at things he wasn't supposed to look at, so while he was climbing onto the table he read what was written on the label. Instead of laying his head back against the headrest, he announced, "Ah-hah! February 28! Old blood. You can't use that."

"Who are you to say that?" said the doctor indignantly. "Old blood, new blood, what do you understand about preservation? Blood can be kept over a month."

Her anger stood out a bright raspberry color against her pink face. Her arms, bare to the elbow, were plump and rosy, but the skin was covered in goose pimples. It was not because of the cold; they were permanent.

For some reason it was these goose pimples that finally convinced Kostoglotov not to give in.

"Roll up your sleeve," the doctor ordered. "Lower your arm and let it relax."

This was the second year she had been working on blood transfusions and she could not remember a single patient who had not been suspicious. They all behaved as though theirs was the purest aristocratic blood and they were afraid of it being tainted. Invariably they looked sideways at the blood and claimed the color wasn't right, or the group wasn't right, or that it was too hot or too cold, or that it was congealed. Or else they would ask straight out, "Why are you giving me bad blood?" "Why should it be bad?" "Because it's written on it—'Do not touch.'" "Yes, that's because it was earmarked for someone else, but he doesn't need it any more." Even after the patient had let her put the needle in, he would go on muttering to himself, "That means it's not proper quality." Firmness was the only way of breaking down these stupid suspicions. Furthermore, she was always in a hurry because she had a blood transfusion quota to get through every day in various different places.

Kostoglotov had already seen people with bloody swellings in the clinic—hematomas, they were called—because a vein had been double-punctured or the end of the needle misdirected. He had seen people trembling and feverish after transfusions because the blood had been introduced too hastily. And he had no inclination whatever to entrust himself to those impatient, pink, puffy, goose-pimply arms. His own sluggish, diseased blood, ruined by the X rays, was still more precious to him than any fresh addition. His own blood would sooner or later recover. And if his bad blood made them stop the treatment, so much the better.

"No," he said grimly, refusing to roll up his sleeve or to let his arm relax. "Your blood's old blood. Anyway, I don't feel well today."

Of course he knew he shouldn't give two excuses at the same time, only one. But the two came out together.

"We'll check the pressure right away," said the doctor, quite unabashed. The nurse was already handing her the instrument.

The doctor was a complete newcomer, but the nurse belonged to the clinic. She worked in the dressings room, Oleg had never had dealings with her before. She was no more than a girl, but quite tall, with a dark complexion and a Japanese slant to her eyes. Her hair was piled on top of her head in such a complicated way that no cap or scarf would ever have been able to cover it. Every lock and turret of her tower of hair had been patiently bound with innumerable bandages. She must have come on duty fifteen minutes early to get the bandaging done.

None of this was much use to Oleg, but still he studied her white tiara with interest, trying to imagine what her hair looked like under the bandages. The one in charge here was the doctor, and instead of delaying he ought to be defending himself against her, making objections and trying to talk his way out. Yet here he was losing the rhythm of his arguments by watching the girl with the Japanese slant to her eyes. Like every young girl she embodied some sort of an enigma simply because she was young. She carried it with every step she took and was conscious of it at every turn of her head.

Meanwhile they had wrapped a great black snake round Kostoglotov's arm to squeeze it and to check that he had the right pressure . . .

He opened his mouth to raise another objection, but just then someone in the doorway called the doctor to go to the telephone. She gave a start and walked off. The nurse began to put the black tubes back into their case. Oleg stayed lying on his back.

"Where does that doctor come from, eh?" he asked.

Every tone in the girl's voice was part of the enigma that surrounded her. She knew this, and when she spoke she seemed to be listening to her own voice with great attention. "From the blood transfusion station," she said.

"Why did she bring that old stuff, then?" asked Oleg. She was only a girl, but he wanted to test his guest.

"It's not old." The girl turned her head smoothly and carried the white tiara across the room.

The little girl was quite convinced she knew everything she needed to know.

And maybe she did.

The sun had come round to the side of the building where the dressings room was. It didn't come straight in through the windows, but two of the panes were shining brightly and part of the ceiling was covered by a large patch of light reflected off something shiny. It was very bright and clean, and quiet too.

It was nice being in the room.

A door opened outside Oleg's field of vision. Someone came in, another woman.

She walked in. Her shoes made hardly any noise. Her little heels didn't tap out her identity.

And Oleg guessed.

No one else walked like that. It was she he was missing in the room, she and no one else.

Vega!

Yes, it was she. She walked into his field of vision, walked into it so simply, as though it was hardly any time at all since she'd stepped out of it.

"Where have you been, Vera Kornilyevna?" Oleg was smiling.

He didn't exclaim, he asked the question quietly and happily. And he didn't sit up, even though they hadn't tied him down to the table.

The room became quiet, bright and comfortable—just perfect!

Vega too had her own question to ask him. "Are you rebelling?" She too was smiling.

But his plan to resist had already weakened. He was enjoying himself, lying there on the table; he wouldn't be got off it as easily as that. He answered her, "Me? No, I'm through with rebellions . . . Where have you been? It's been more than a week."

She spoke distinctly, as though dictating unusual or new words to someone particularly slow-witted. She stood over him and said, "I've been traveling round setting up oncological stations. Health propaganda, trying to fight cancer."

"Somewhere out in the wilds?"

"Yes."

"And now you've finished traveling?"

"For the time being. But what about you? You aren't feeling well?"

What was it in those eyes? Unhurried attentiveness. The first unverified note of alarm. The eyes of a doctor.

But apart from that they were light-brown eyes, like a glass of coffee with two fingers of milk in it. But of course it was years since Oleg had last drunk coffee. Friendly—that's what they were! The eyes of a very old friend.

"Oh no, it's nothing. I've probably got a touch of the sun. I sat there for ages, I almost fell asleep."

"How *could* you sit in the sun! Haven't you learned during all the time you've been here that it's forbidden, exposing tumors to heat?"

"I thought it was only hot-water bottles."

"Sun's even more strictly forbidden."

"You mean I'm not allowed to go to the Black Sea beaches?"

She nodded.

"What a life! I'd better have my exile transferred to Norilsk . . ."*
She lifted her shoulders, then dropped them. It was something
beyond her power, even beyond her comprehension. "So why have
you been unfaithful?"

"What's that?"

"To our agreement. You promised you'd give me blood transfusions yourself, not hand me over to some student."

"She's not a student; to the contrary, she's a specialist. We have
no right to do transfusions when she's here. But she's gone away
now."

"What do you mean—gone?"

"She was sent for."

What a merry-go-round! A merry-go-round that didn't even
protect him from other merry-go-rounds.

"So you'll do it?"

"Yes, I will. But what's all this about old blood?"

He nodded his head toward it.

"It's not old. But it's not for you either. We'll give you two
hundred and fifty grams. Here!" Vera Kornilyevna brought it
over from the other table and showed it to him. "Read this, check
the label for yourself."

"You know, Vera Kornilyevna, it's a miserable, cursed life I
lead: never believe anything, check everything. Don't you think
I'm happier when I *don't* have to check?"

He said this in a weary voice, like a dying man. But his alert
eyes couldn't restrain themselves from making sure. They took in
the words "GROUP A. YAROSLAVTSEVA, IRENA L. MARCH 5."

"Aha, March 5! That'll be just right!" Oleg cheered up. "That's
bound to do us good."

"So, you *do* realize what good it does you. At last! And you made
such a fuss before." She didn't understand what he meant. Oh well,
never mind.

He rolled his shirt sleeve up over his elbow and let his arm fall
relaxed alongside his body.

It was true. For a man like Oleg who had to be permanently
suspicious and watchful it was the greatest pleasure in the world
to be able to trust, to give himself to trust. And he trusted this
woman, this gentle ethereal creature. He knew she'd move softly,

*The most northerly large city in the Soviet Union.

thinking out her every action, and that she wouldn't make the slightest mistake.

And so he lay there and felt as though he was having a rest.

The large patch of sunlight on the ceiling, weak as though filtered through lace, formed an uneven circle. This patch, reflected off he didn't know what, was contributing to his happiness and beautifying the clean, quiet room.

Vera Kornilyevna had perfidiously drawn some blood out of his vein with a needle. She was turning the centrifuge and breaking up the blood into four sectors.

"Why four?" He only asked because all his life, everywhere he went, he had been in the habit of asking questions. In fact at the moment he felt he couldn't even be bothered to know.

"One for compatibility, and three to check the distribution center for group accuracy. Just in case."

"But if the group's the right one, why check the compatibility?"

"In case the patient's serum congeals after contact with the donor's blood. It's rare, but it does happen."

"I see. But why do you turn it?"

"To push back the red corpuscles. You have to know everything, don't you?"

Of course he didn't really have to know everything. Oleg looked at the patch hovering on the ceiling. You can't know everything in the world. Whatever happens you'll die a fool.

The nurse with the white tiara inserted the upturned March 5 bottle into the clamps on the stand. Then she put a little pillow under his elbow. She pulled tight the red rubber sling over his arm above the elbow and began to twist it. Her Japanese eyes gauged how far she could go.

It was strange that he had seen some sort of an enigma in this girl. There just wasn't one. She was a girl like any other.

Up walked Vera Gangart with the syringe. It was an ordinary one full of a colorless liquid, but the needle was unusual, a tube rather than a needle, a tube with a triangular end. There was nothing wrong with a tube in itself, just so long as no one was going to drive it into you.

"Your vein stands out well," Vera Kornilyevna began to say. One of her eyebrows twitched as she looked for it. Then, with concentration, puncturing the skin so that he could scarcely feel it, she introduced the monstrous needle. And that was all.

There was still a lot he didn't understand. Why did they twist the sling above his elbow? What was that water-like liquid in the syringe for? He could ask, of course, but he could also try to work it out for himself. It was probably to stop air rushing into the vein and blood rushing into the syringe.

Meanwhile the needle remained in his vein. The pressure of the sling was released and it was taken off. The syringe was skillfully removed and the nurse shook the tip of the instrument over a little bowl to get rid of the first drops of blood. Now Gangart was fixing this tip to the needle instead of the syringe. She held it in place, at the same time slightly opening the screw on the top.

Inside the widening glass pipe of the instrument a number of transparent bubbles began to rise slowly, one by one, through the transparent liquid.

Questions kept occurring to him, floating up like the bubbles, one after the other. Why such a wide needle? Why did they shake off the blood? What did those bubbles mean? One fool can ask enough questions to keep a hundred wise men too busy to answer them all.

If he was going to ask questions, he wanted to ask them about something else.

There was a festive air about everything in the room, especially that sun-bleached patch on the ceiling.

The needle had to stay in a long time. The level of the blood in the bottle had hardly dropped, indeed it hadn't dropped at all.

"Do you need me, Vera Kornilyevna?" asked the nurse, the Japanese girl. She spoke with deference, still listening to her own voice.

"No, I don't need you," Gangart answered quietly.

"I'll go out for a bit . . . Can I take half an hour?"

"Yes, as far as I'm concerned. *I* don't need you."

The nurse with the white tiara almost ran out. They were left, just the two of them.

Slowly the bubbles rose. Then Vera Kornilyevna touched the screw and they stopped rising. Not one single bubble remained.

"You've turned it off?"

"Yes."

"But why?"

"You always have to know, don't you?" She smiled at him, this time encouragingly.

It was very quiet in the dressings room. They were old walls and the doors were sturdy. One could speak in a voice slightly over a whisper, just breathe effortlessly out and talk while doing it. That was the way he wanted to speak.

"Yes, I know I'm difficult to deal with. I always want to know more than I'm allowed to know."

"It's good you still want to . . ." she observed. Her lips were never uninvolved in the words they were pronouncing. Tiny movements of her mouth, quirks in the right-hand or left-hand corner, a slight pout or a slight twitch, emphasized each thought and illuminated it.

"After the first twenty-five cubic centimeters we're supposed to pause for a time and see how the patient is feeling." One hand still held the tip against the needle, just one hand. She shifted her smile slightly, welcomingly and inquiringly, and looked into Oleg's eyes as she leaned over him. "How do you feel?"

"At this precise moment—excellent."

"Isn't that putting it rather strongly?"

"No, I really feel excellent. Much better than 'well.' "

"No shivering, no unpleasant taste in the mouth, nothing of that?"

"No."

The bottle, the needle and the transfusion formed a task that united them in a common concern for someone quite apart from themselves, someone whom they were trying to treat together and cure.

"And apart from this precise moment?"

"Apart from this precise moment?" It was wonderful just being there, looking minute after minute into each other's eyes at a time when they had a perfect right to do so, when there was no need to look away. "Well, generally I feel awful."

"Awful? Why?"

She asked it sympathetically and anxiously, like a friend. But . . . she had deserved the blow. And Oleg felt that now was the time to deliver it. However soft her bright, light-brown eyes were, she wouldn't escape.

"It's my morale that's awful. Awful because I know that I'm paying too high a price for my life, and that even you—yes, you— are involved in the process and are deceiving me."

"Me!"

When eyes gaze endlessly into each other, they acquire an entirely new quality. You see things never revealed in passing glances. The eyes seem to lose their protective-colored retina. The whole truth comes splashing out wordlessly, it cannot be contained.

"How *could* you have assured me so fervently that the injections were necessary, and that I wouldn't understand the point of them? What is there to understand? It's hormone therapy. What is there to understand about that?"

Of course it wasn't fair, it wasn't fair to take those defenseless brown eyes so unawares, but it was the only way of really asking the question. Something in her eyes jumped; she was quite staggered.

And Dr. Gangart (no, it wasn't Dr. Gangart, it was Vega) turned away her eyes.

So they withdraw a company from the field of battle before its final rout.

She looked at the bottle, but what was there to look at when the blood flow had stopped? She looked at the bubbles, but the bubbles weren't rising either.

Then she turned on the screw. The bubbles started. It was time it was done anyway.

Her fingers stroked the rubber tube that hung down from the instrument to the needle. It was as if they were helping to remove all obstructions in the tube. She put some more absorbent cotton under the tip to make sure the tube wouldn't bend. He saw she had some adhesive tape. She took a strip of it and stuck the tip to his arm. Then she threaded the rubber tube through his fingers, the fingers of the same hand. They were stuck up in the air like hooks. Thereafter, the tube held itself in position.

There was now no need for Vega to hold it, or to stand by his side, or to gaze into his eyes.

Her face was stern and clouded as she adjusted the flow of bubbles to make it more frequent. "That's the way," she said, "just lie still." And she left.

She didn't go completely offstage, she only left that part of it in his field of vision. He had to lie quite still. It meant that the only things in sight were the instrument stand, the bottle of brown blood, the shiny bubbles, the tops of the sunlit windows, the reflections of the windows with their six panes in the frosted glass of the lamp globe, and the whole expanse of ceiling with its shimmering patch of faint sunlight.

Vega was no longer there.

The question seemed to have fallen flat, like an object passed carelessly, clumsily, from hand to hand.

And she hadn't picked it up.

It was up to Oleg to go on working on it.

Looking up at the ceiling, he began slowly thinking aloud: "If my life is totally lost, if I can feel in my bones the memory that I'm a prisoner in perpetuity, a perpetual 'con,' if Fate holds out no better prospect, if the only expectation I have is being consciously and artificially killed—then why bother to save such a life?"

Vega heard everything, but she was offstage. Perhaps it was better this way, it was easier to speak.

"First my own life was taken from me, and now I am being deprived even of the right . . . to perpetuate myself. I'll be the worst sort of cripple! What use will I be to anyone? An object of men's pity—or charity? . . ."

Vega said nothing.

That patch on the ceiling—from time to time it seemed to quiver, to contract at the edges. It was as if a frown was passing over it, as if it too was thinking but couldn't understand. Then it would become motionless once more.

The gay transparent bubbles kept gurgling. The level of blood in the bottle was falling. A quarter of it was already transfused. It was woman's blood. The blood of "Yaroslavtseva, Irena L." Was she a girl? An old woman? A student? Or a market woman?

"Yes, charity . . ."

Keeping out of sight, Vega didn't start arguing with him. Instead she suddenly launched out from where she was standing: "No, it's not true! You don't really believe that, do you? I know you don't! Examine yourself—those aren't *your* ideas, you've borrowed them from somewhere else, haven't you?"

She spoke with more force than he had heard in her voice before. It was full of wounded feeling, more than he would ever have expected.

Suddenly she cut herself short and fell silent.

"What do you expect me to believe, then?" Oleg tried cautiously to draw her out.

Goodness, what a silence! You could even here the little light bubbles in the glass balloon. They made a faint ringing noise.

It was hard for her to speak. Her voice was shattered. She was trying to pull herself up out of the ditch, but it was beyond her strength.

"There must be some people who think differently! Maybe a few, maybe only a handful, but differently all the same! If everyone thought your way, who could we live with? What would we live for? Would we be able to live at all?"

She had pulled herself up and over the edge. The last words came crying from her with a new sort of despair. It was as if her protest had jolted him, as if she had jolted him with all the petty strength she possessed, moving his heavy reddened body to reach the only place of salvation possible.

Like a stone thrown boldly from a boy's sling made out of a sunflower stem that lengthens his arm, or like a shell fired out of one of those long-barreled guns in the last year of the war, a whooshing, whistling shell shuddering noisily through the air—Oleg shot up and flew in a crazy parabola, breaking loose from everything he had memorized and sweeping away everything he'd borrowed from other people, high over the wastelands of his life, one wasteland after the other, until he came to some land of long ago.

It was the country of his childhood. He didn't recognize it at once, but the moment his blinking, still-clouded eyes did recognize it he was ashamed. He remembered how he used to believe the same when he was a boy, and he was ashamed she had had to rediscover it for him instead of him telling her.

There was something else coming back to him too, out of his memory. It was perfect for the occasion. He simply had to get it into his mind. Then he remembered!

He remembered it in a flash, but when he began to speak it was slowly and reasoningly, taking one thing at a time: "In the 1920's there were some books by a certain venereologist, Dr. Friedland. They were immensely successful. In those days people thought it a good thing to open people's eyes, the eyes of the youth and the whole nation. It was medical information about the most unmentionable of subjects. And very likely it was necessary, better than hypocritical silence. There was a book called *Behind the Closed Door,* and another one called *The Sufferings of Love.* You didn't read them, by any chance, did you? Being a doctor, I thought perhaps you . . ."

The odd bubble was still gurgling. Offstage perhaps it was her breathing one could hear.

"I must admit," he said. "I read them at a very early age. I was probably about twelve. Of course I didn't let the grownups see me. Reading them made a shattering impression on me, but it was somehow emptying as well. I had the feeling I didn't really want to live any more . . ."

Suddenly she answered his question. "I . . . read them too," she said expressionlessly.

"You did, did you? You too?" said Oleg delightedly. He said the words "You too?" as though he still felt he was the first to make that particular point. "Such consistent, logical, irrefutable materialism and the result was . . . the point of living? Everything totted up in exact percentages, how many women experience nothing at all, how many women experience ecstasy? Those stories about how women . . . move from category to category in search of their own identity . . ." As he remembered more and more he drew in his breath as though he had been hit or had hurt himself. ". . . Such heartless certainty that psychology is of secondary importance in marriage. The writer makes the point that physiology is the sole cause of incompatibility. But, of course, you remember, don't you? When did you read them?"

She didn't answer.

He shouldn't have interrogated her like that. He'd probably put it much too crudely and bluntly. He had absolutely no experience of talking to women.

The strange patch of pale sunlight on the ceiling suddenly began to ripple. A flashing cluster of silver spots appeared from somewhere. They began to move about. Oleg watched the fast-moving ripples and wavelets. He had finally realized that the mysterious flash high up on the ceiling was no more than a reflection of a puddle, a patch of ground outside the window by the fence that hadn't dried up yet. The image of an ordinary puddle. But now a little breeze had begun to blow.

Vega was silent.

"Please forgive me," Oleg begged. He found it agreeable, almost a delight, to plead with her. "Somehow I don't think I put it right . . ." He tried to twist his head toward her but still he couldn't see her. "You see, that sort of attitude destroys everything human on earth. If you give in to it, if you accept it and everything it entails . . ." He was now surrendering joyfully to his former faith. He was trying to persuade *her!*

Vega came back. She returned on stage, her face showing none of the despair or harshness he had thought he detected in her voice. There was the usual friendly smile. "I don't want you to accept it either," she said. "I was sure you didn't accept it."

She shone. She actually shone.

Yes, she was that little girl from his childhood, his school friend. Why hadn't he recognized her before?

He felt like saying something quite simple and friendly to her, something like "Let's shake hands on it." Then he would take her hand and—"My God, it's wonderful just talking to you!"

His right arm was under the needle, though.

If only he could call her Vega. Or Vera.

But it wasn't possible.

The blood in the bottle had already dropped by more than half. It had once flowed in someone else's body, a body with its own personality, its own ideas, and now it was pouring into him, a reddish-brown stream of health. Surely it must be bringing some of its own characteristics?

Oleg watched Vega bustling about. She straightened the little pillow under his elbow and the absorbent cotton under the tip. She stroked the rubber tube with her fingers and began to raise the upper part of the stand which held the bottle.

He wanted to do more than shake that hand, he wanted to kiss it, even though it would have been a contradiction of everything he had said.

25. Vega

She was in a festive mood as she left the clinic, humming quietly to herself, her mouth closed so that only she could hear. She was wearing a light-gray spring coat, but no rubbers because the streets were quite dry. She felt light and springy. Everything was light, especially her legs. Walking was so easy, a girl could cross the whole town when she felt like this.

The evening was just as sunny as the day had been. One could feel it was spring even though it was getting cooler. It would be silly to climb onto a crowded bus. She felt much more like walking. So she walked.

There was no time more beautiful than when the apricot trees were in bloom in town. All of a sudden she felt she had to see one, now, before spring came, just one apricot tree in bloom, for luck, even if from a distance, or perhaps sheltered behind a fence or a clay wall. You could always tell them by their airy pinkness.

But it was too early. The trees were only just beginning to change from gray to green. The moment had come when the trees already had some green on them, but gray still predominated. Behind the clay walls, the few patches of garden that had managed to assert their rights against the stones of the city showed their dried, reddish earth, but nothing more.

It *was* early.

Vera always seemed to be in a hurry, but when she got into a bus she would sit herself down as comfortably as possible on the broken springs of the seat, or else reach out for a strap, hang onto it and think to herself, "I don't want to do *anything*."

In spite of common sense she knew that she merely had to kill the hours of the evening, then hurry back to work the next morning in an identical bus.

But today she walked unhurriedly, and she wanted to do everything, everything there was to do. A lot of things had suddenly appeared that needed doing: at home, in the shops or the library, or perhaps sewing or some other pleasant task. There was nothing forbidden or banned about them, they were just things she had for some reason avoided doing. She felt like doing them all now, immediately. On the other hand, she didn't feel like rushing to get home, or doing any single one of them straightaway. Instead she walked slowly along, delighting in every step her little shoes took along the dry pavement. She walked past shops that were not yet locked up, but she didn't go into any of them to buy the food or the things she needed. She walked past some theater placards but didn't read a single one, even though in her present mood she wanted to read them.

And so she just walked, walked on and on. This was her delight. It was all there was to her pleasure.

And occasionally she smiled.

She'd have liked to have seen an apricot tree in bloom, but there wasn't one; it was too early.

Yesterday had been a holiday, but she had felt downtrodden and despised. Today was an ordinary working weekday, and she was in such a carefree, happy mood.

She had this holiday feeling because she felt she was in the right. Suddenly your powerful arguments, unspoken because everywhere ridiculed and rejected, which are the little thread by which you hang all alone over a terrible chasm, turn out to be a rope of steel wire. And its reliability is recognized by a worldly-wise, suspicious, hardheaded man who is ready to hang by it himself in complete confidence.

They were gliding, as in a cable car, over an unimaginable abyss of human incomprehension, and they had trust in each other.

This absolutely entranced her!

She knew now she was normal and not insane, but knowing this is not enough. She needed to hear she was normal and not insane, which she had now heard—and what a man to hear it from! All she really wanted to do was to say "thank you" to him for saying it, for thinking it and for having remained himself through all the setbacks in his life.

He deserved to be thanked, but in the meantime it was her duty to make excuses to him. She had to make excuses for the hormone therapy. He rejected Friedland, but he rejected hormone therapy as well. There was a logical contradiction here. Still, one expects logic from a doctor, not from a patient.

Whether or not there was a contradiction here, she had to persuade him to submit to this treatment. She couldn't give him up, surrender him to the tumor. She was becoming more and more passionately concerned. This was a patient she had to outdo in persuasiveness and stubbornness, until she finally cured him. But to spend hours trying to convince such an unruly, pigheaded man she would have to have great faith.

When he attacked her about the hormone therapy she had suddenly remembered that it had been introduced into their clinic to conform with a general nationwide instruction, which applied to a broad range of tumors. She couldn't for the moment remember the actual scientific paper that described how hormone therapy should be used to combat seminoma. There might be more than one such paper, foreign ones too. To persuade him she had to read them all. Normally she didn't have time to read very many.

But now she'd have time for everything! She'd certainly read them now!

Kostoglotov had once thrown out the argument that he didn't see why his medicine man with the roots was any less of a doctor than she was. He told her that he hadn't noticed anything very mathematical about medicine. Vera had taken slight offense at the time, but later it occurred to her he was partly right. When they used X rays to destroy cells did they know, approximately even, what percentage of healthy cells as compared to diseased ones would be destroyed? Was this method any more certain than the medicine man's way of scooping up his dried root by the handful, without using scales? Or to take another example—everyone was furiously prescribing penicillin treatment because penicillin produced results. But who in the medical world had actually succeeded in explaining why penicillin acted as it did? These were dark waters, weren't they? One had to keep following the medical journals, reading them and pondering them.

But she'd have time for all that now.

And now—it was amazing, she just hadn't noticed how quickly she'd walked—here she was home in the courtyard outside her apartment block. She walked up the few steps to a spacious communal veranda with railings thickly hung with rugs and doormats. She walked across the dented cement floor and, not in the least depressed, unlocked the outside door to her communal apartment. The floor-covering was torn in places. Then she walked down a corridor. It was rather dark; she couldn't turn on all the lights because they were on different meters.

She used another key to open the door to her room. It didn't depress her in the least, this convent cell. It had bars in the window to protect it from thieves, like all ground-floor windows in town. The room was by now almost in twilight. It never had any bright sunlight except briefly in the morning. Vera stopped in the doorway, and without taking off her coat looked round the room in amazement, as if it was all new to her. In a room like this, life could be fine and enjoyable! All there was to do was to change the tablecloth straightaway, flick a dustcloth around, and perhaps rehang the pictures on the wall—one of Petropavlovsk Fortress during a white night, and one of some black Crimean cypresses.

But first she took off her coat, put on an apron and went into the kitchen. She vaguely remembered she had to begin by doing something in the kitchen. Oh yes, she had to light the oil stove and cook herself something.

But her neighbor's son, a big strong lad who had dropped out of school, had installed his motorcycle in the kitchen like a kind of barrier. He was in there taking it to bits, whistling as he laid the parts all over the floor and oiled them. The room had the benefit of the setting sun and was still quite light. There was space to squeeze through and get to her table, but Vera suddenly felt she didn't want to bother about things in the kitchen: she just wanted to be alone in her room.

She wasn't hungry either, not hungry at all. So she went back to her room and snapped the lock shut with satisfaction. There was no reason for her to leave it again today. There were some chocolates in one of the tins, she could nibble at them.

She squatted down in front of the chest, the one she'd got from her mother, and pulled out the heavy drawer that contained her other tablecloth.

But no, first of all the dusting had to be done.

And before that she ought to change into something simpler.

Vera took delight in every new movement. It was like changing step during a dance. Each new movement delighted her, because that was what the dance was about.

Or perhaps she ought to rehang the fortress and the cypresses? No, that would mean getting a hammer and some nails, and there was nothing more unpleasant than a man's work. Let them hang the way they were for a while.

So she shook the dustcloth and went around the room with it, humming softly to herself.

Almost at once she came upon a colored postcard she had received the day before, propped up against a pot-bellied bottle of scent. It had red roses, green ribbons and a blue figure 8 on the front of it, while on the back there was a typewritten message of greeting. Her trade-union committee were sending her their best wishes on the occasion of International Women's Day.*

National holidays are hard for a lonely person to live through, but a women's holiday, for lonely women whose years are slipping away, is quite unbearable. Widowed or unmarried, they get together to drink a lot of wine, sing songs and pretend how merry they are. Last night there had been a crowd of them celebrating uproariously out in the yard. There was one husband among them, and when they got drunk they all lined up to kiss him.

Her trade-union committee, without in the least trying to be amusing, were wishing her success in her work and happiness in her private life.

What private life?

She tore the postcard into four pieces and threw it into the waste-basket.

She went on dusting, first some bottles of scent, then the little glass cabinet with views of the Crimea in it, then the box of records by the radio, then the electric phonograph in its angular plastic case.

Now she could listen to any of the records she possessed, and they no longer hurt. She could put on that intolerable tune, "So now I'm alone, alone as before . . ." But she was looking for another

---

*March 8 is celebrated in the Soviet Union as International Women's Day. Originally the date was to mark the solidarity of the world's female proletariat, but now it has become simply an occasion for flower-giving and greetings from men to women.

one. She put it on, turned the knob for the phonograph part, withdrew herself into her mother's deep armchair and curled her stockinged legs up underneath her. Her hand was still idly clutching one corner of the dustcloth. It hung down from her hand to the floor.

The light in the room was already gray. The radio's green-lit dial stood out clearly.

It was a suite from *The Sleeping Beauty*. First the Adagio, then "The Entry of the Fairies."

Vera listened to it, but not for herself. She was trying to imagine how that Adagio would have struck the doomed man who had never known what human happiness was, as he listened from the operahouse balcony, soaked with rain and isolated by the pain of his disease.

She put it on again.

And yet again.

She began *talking,* only not aloud. She was talking to him in her imagination, as though he was sitting right there, across the round table from her in the room's greenish light. She was saying all that she should have said, and she was listening to him. She had an unerring ear for what he might have replied. He was a difficult one to foresee, the way he twisted and turned, but she felt she was getting used to him.

She was finishing the conversation they had had today, telling him what couldn't have been said, their relationship being what it was. But it could be said now. She was developing her theory about men and women. Hemingway's supermen were creatures who had not yet raised themselves to human level. Hemingway was a shallow swimmer. (Oleg would be bound to bark back at her that he'd never read any Hemingway. He would even make it into a boast: none of that stuff in the army, none of that in the camp.) This wasn't at all what a woman needed from a man. She needed attention and tenderness and a sense of security when he was with her, a feeling that he was her shield and her shelter. (And it was Oleg, a man without rights who had been deprived of all significance as a citizen, who for some reason made Vera feel protected.)

Ideas on what women should be like were even more confused. The most feminine of them all, people thought, was Carmen. They reckoned the most feminine was the one most aggressive in her search for pleasure. But this type is a pseudo-woman, a man in woman's clothes.

On this point there was a lot more that needed explaining. It seemed he'd been taken by surprise, he hadn't been ready for the idea, but he was thinking about it now.

While she put on the same record yet again.

It was quite dark by now and she had forgotten about her dusting. The green light of the dial was deepening, casting its glow further and further over the whole room.

She had no desire to turn the light on, not for anything in the world, but she simply had to have a look.

In semi-darkness her hand reached out confidently for the little framed photograph on the wall. She lifted it up with affection and brought it close to the dial. Even without its green starry light, even if it went out now, Vera could still have made out every detail: the neat face of a young boy: those unclouded, vulnerable, inexperienced eyes; the tie hanging down over the neat white shirt, the first tie he'd ever worn. It was his first suit too. Yet he still hadn't minded spoiling the lapel, for there was a severe-looking little badge screwed into it, a small white circle enclosing the black profile of a man. The photo was six by ten centimeters, so the badge was tiny, but in the daytime one could distinctly see (her memory was so clear that she could see it even now) that the profile was Lenin's.

The boy was smiling. "This is the only medal I need," he seemed to be saying.

It was this boy who had thought up the name "Vega" for her.

The agave blooms once in its lifetime. Soon afterward it dies.

This was the way Vera Gangart had fallen in love. She had been quite young, just a schoolgirl.

But he had been killed in the war.

After that, whatever aspect—just, heroic, patriotic or holy—the war took on, for Vera Gangert it was the last war ever, the war in which she, as well as the man she loved, had been killed.

When it happened, how she had longed to be killed as well! She left medical college immediately. She would have liked to go to the front, but they wouldn't take her because she was a German.

They had still been together during the first two or three months of the war's first summer. It was obvious that he would go into the army quite soon. Now, a generation later, it would be impossible to explain how it was that they hadn't got married. How could they have wasted those months, even if they weren't married, the last and only months they were to have? Surely there should have been no barrier at such a time, when everything was cracking and falling apart?

But there was.

It was something she couldn't now justify to anyone, not even to herself.

"Vega! My Vega!" he had cried to her from the front line. "I can't die and leave you not my own. If only I could tear myself away for three days' leave, or three days in hospital, we could get married. Couldn't we? Couldn't we?"

"Don't let such thoughts break your heart. I shall never belong to anyone else. I am yours."

This was how she wrote to him, confidently. But he was still alive then.

He wasn't wounded. He didn't go into hospital or on leave. He was simply killed.

He was dead but his star burned, it kept burning . . .

But its light was wasted.

It wasn't the sort of star that still gives light after being extinguished. It was the sort of star that shines, still shines with all its light, yet no one sees the light or needs it.

They wouldn't take her, they wouldn't let her be killed too. The only thing left was for her to live, to go back to medical college. She even became group monitor there.* She was always first to volunteer for harvesting, for cleaning up or for Sunday work. What else was there to do?

She graduated with a first-class degree. Dr. Oreshchenkov, whose practice she had worked in, was very satisfied with her. (It was he who had given her a recommendation to Dontsova.) There was now only one thing that mattered—her patients and their treatment. Here was her salvation.

Of course, if one thought on the Friedland level the whole thing was nonsense, madness, a complete anomaly. Fancy remembering a dead man instead of looking for someone who was alive!

*Students in Soviet colleges are divided into groups, each of which has its monitor. Part of the monitor's duty is to organize participation in "volunteer tasks," such as helping the collective farmers with the harvest or construction workers with their extra work on Sundays.

It just wasn't possible. After all, the laws of tissues, the laws of hormones and the laws of growing old were indisputable.

Were they? But Vega knew that none of these laws applied to her. They were abolished as far as she was concerned.

It was not that she felt eternally bound by her promise, "I shall always be yours." It was more that someone you have once been very close to never entirely dies. He is still present, seeing a little, hearing a little; in fact he exists. Helpless and wordless, he will see you betray him.

So what was the significance of the laws of cell growth, reaction or secretion? What relevance did they have if there was no other man like him? And there wasn't. So what did cells have to do with it? Or cell reactions?

It was simply that we grow dull with the passing years. We grow tired. We lose all true talent for grief or for faithfulness. We surrender to time. Yet every day we swallow food and lick our fingers—in this respect we are unyielding. If we're not fed for two days we go out of our minds, we start climbing up the wall.

Fine progress we've made, we human beings.

Vega had not changed, but she was crushed. Her mother had died too; she used to live with her mother, just the two of them. Her mother died because she too was crushed. Her son, Vera's elder brother, had been an engineer. In 1940, he'd been arrested. For a few years he still wrote. For a few years they sent him parcels somewhere out in Buryat-Mongolia. Then one day they received a strange notification from the Post Office, and they gave Mother her parcel back. It was ink-stamped all over and the writing was crossed out. She carried the parcel home like a coffin. When he was born he would just have fitted that little box.

It crushed Vera's mother. Then to cap it all, shortly afterwards her daughter-in-law remarried. Mother could not understand at all. She understood Vera.

So Vera stayed on all alone.

Not exactly alone, of course, she wasn't the only one. She was alone among millions. There were so many lonely women in the country, it made one want to count up those who knew—who were there more of, those on their own or those who were married? These lonely women were all about her age, all born in the same decade, the same age as the men who were killed in the war.

The war was merciful to the men, it took them away. The women it left to suffer to the end of their days.

The bachelors who managed to drag themselves back from the ruins of war did not choose wives of their own age, but younger girls. As for those who were a few years younger still, they were a whole generation younger, like children. War hadn't crawled over them like a tank.

So there they were, those millions of women. No one ever formed them into an army. They had come into the world to accomplish nothing. They were a fallow patch left behind by history.

Those among them who could take life as it came were not the doomed ones.

Long years of ordinary peaceful life went by. Vera lived and went about like someone in a permanent gas mask. It was as if her head was enclosed by a skin of tight, hostile rubber. The gas mask drove her mad, it made her weak. So she tore it off.

It looked then as though her life had become more human. She allowed herself to be agreeable. She dressed carefully and did not avoid meeting people.

There is great satisfaction in remaining faithful; perhaps it is the greatest satisfaction of all. Even if no one knows about your faithfulness, even if no one values it.

If only it made some impression!

But what if it made no impression, if no one needed it?

However large the round goggles of a gas mask are, you see very little through them and what you see you see badly. Now without the goggles in front of her eyes, she might be able to see more clearly.

But she didn't. She was inexperienced and she hurt herself badly. She was incautious and made false steps. Short, unworthy intimacy brought no light or relief into her life. It soiled and humiliated her, it smashed her wholeness and destroyed her harmony.

To forget was by now impossible. To obliterate was out of the question.

No, taking life as it comes was not her forte. The more fragile a person was, the more dozens and hundreds of coincidences were needed to bring him closer to another. Each new coincidence can only fractionally increase this closeness, whereas a single discrepancy can destroy everything in a flash. With her this discrepancy always managed to appear early and to stand out clearly. There was no one at all to advise her what to do or how to live.

Each man has his own path in life.

She was strongly urged to adopt a child. She talked about this at length and in detail with a number of women. They persuaded her. She warmed to the idea and was already going round visiting children's homes.

But in the end she gave it up. She couldn't start loving a child just like that, out of despair or because she had decided to. There was a great danger—she might stop loving it later. And a greater danger still—it might grow up a stranger to her.

If only she had a daughter, a real daughter of her own. (A daughter, because then she could bring her up in her own image: she wouldn't be able to do that with a little boy.)

She couldn't bring herself to walk along that long, miry road again and with a complete stranger.

She sat in the armchair until midnight. She hadn't done any of the things crying to be done since early evening. She didn't even turn on the light. She had enough light from the dial on the radio. Her thoughts flowed freely as she watched the green of its light and the black markings of the dial.

She listened to a great many records and was not upset even by the most melancholy. She listened to marches too. Marches were like a triumph unfolding before her in the dark, while she sat like a victor in her old armchair with its high thronelike back, her delicate legs curled underneath her.

She had crossed fourteen deserts, but now she had come home. She had crossed fourteen years of insanity, and she had been right all along!

It was on this day that her years of faithfulness had acquired a new, final meaning.

Near-faithfulness. One could regard it as faithfulness—faithfulness in what counted.

Today, too, she became aware that the one who had died was a boy, that he wasn't her age now, not a man. He hadn't had that unwieldy heaviness men have, which is a woman's only refuge. He hadn't seen either the war as a whole or its end, or the many difficult years that followed. He had remained a young boy with unclouded, vulnerable eyes.

She went to bed, but although she didn't fall asleep straightaway she wasn't worried that she wouldn't get enough sleep that night. After she fell asleep, however, she woke up several times and had a great many dreams, too many perhaps for a single night. Some of them were merely disturbing, but others she tried to keep in her mind for the next morning.

She woke up in the morning and she smiled.

She was squeezed, jostled and pushed all over the bus. People stepped on her feet, but she put up with it all without taking offense.

She put on her white coat. On her way to the daily five-minute conference, she was pleased to see a powerful, amiable, awkward, gorilla-like figure in the distance coming toward her along the lower corridor. It was Lev Leonidovich; she hadn't seen him since his return from Moscow. His large arms seemed too heavy for him, they hung down, almost dragging his shoulders down with them. It looked as if there was something wrong with them, but in fact they were the most handsome thing about him. His head was modeled with bold strokes on many different levels, its crown set well back and topped by a funny white cap like the ones pilots wear. As always it had been slapped on carelessly: it looked rather useless with its two pig ears sticking up at the back and its hollow, crumpled top. His chest under the tight white coat with no opening at the front was like the front of a tank camouflaged for snow conditions. His eyes were narrowed as usual and he walked along looking stern and threatening, but Vera knew he only had to shift his features slightly and they would turn into a grin.

This is exactly what he did when he and Vera emerged simultaneously from the corridor in different directions and met at the foot of the staircase. "I'm so glad you're back," she said, "we really missed you."

His smile widened. His dangling hand caught her by the elbow and turned her toward the staircase. "Why are you so happy?" he asked her. "Make me happy too."

"Oh no, it's nothing really. Well, how was your trip?"

Lev Leonidovich sighed. "It was all right, but a bit upsetting. Moscow's a disturbing place."

"You can tell me more about it later."

"I brought you some records. Three."

"Did you? Which ones?"

"Well, you know, I'm never too sure about Saint-Saëns and those people . . . they've got a new LP record department in GUM* now.

*The biggest department store in Moscow.

I gave them your list and they wrapped three of them up for me. I'll bring them in tomorrow. Verusya, let's go to the trial today."

"What trial?"

"Didn't you know about it? They're putting one of the surgeons on trial. He's from Number 3 Hospital."

"A real court?"

"No, it's a comradely court* so far. But the investigation took eight months."

"What's he charged with?"

Nurse Zoya was coming down the stairs, having just finished her night duty. She said good morning to them both, her golden eyelashes flashing in the light.

"A child died after an operation . . . I'd better go while I've got a bit of Moscow energy in me. I want to make a hell of a fuss. A week in this place and you're back with your tail between your legs. Shall we go?"

But Vera didn't have time to reply or to make up her mind.

It was time to go into the conference room. There was the same bright blue cloth on the table and round it some little armchairs covered with sheets.

Vera put a high value on her good relationship with Lev. He and Ludmila Afanasyevna were closer to her than anyone else in the clinic. The most precious thing about their relationship was that it was one that hardly ever existed between an unmarried man and woman. Lev never gave her that special look men give, he never dropped any hints, never overstepped the mark, never staked out any claims—and of course neither did she. They had a harmless, tension-free friendship. There was one subject they always avoided, never mentioned and never discussed: love, marriage and the rest. It was as if these things did not exist.

Lev Leonidovich presumably guessed this was the type of relationship Vera needed as well. He had married once, stopped being married, then had a "friendship" with someone else. The female part of the clinic (which meant the whole place) loved talking about him. At the moment they suspected he was having an affair with one of the operating-theater nurses. One of the young surgeons, Angelica, emphatically declared that this was the case, but some people suspected she was after Lev herself.

---

*A group of colleagues who try a man for social misdemeanors. Its decision has no legal power but it can refer a case to a regular court.

Ludmila Afanasyevna spent the five-minute conference drawing angular figures on a piece of paper which she managed to tear with her pen. On the other hand, Vera sat more quietly than ever before. She felt an unfamiliar steadiness in herself.

The conference ended and Vera began her round in the big women's ward. She had a lot of patients there and always took her time. She would sit down on each bed, examine the patient and talk softly to her. She did not insist on complete silence in the ward during her rounds because it was impossible to stop the women from talking for so long. One had to be even more tactful and circumspect in the women's wards than in the men's. Her status and distinction as a doctor were not accepted so unconditionally here. She only had to turn up in a slightly better mood than usual or be a bit too cheerful about promising them that everything was going to be all right—trying to apply the principles of psychotherapy—and she could feel the women staring at her blatantly or enviously looking sideways at her. "What do you care?" the glances seemed to say. "You aren't ill. How can you understand?" The same principles that made her advise these diseased women, frightened out of their wits, not to let their appearance go to pot. She made them do their hair and put on make-up. But if she spent too much time on her own make-up, the women would not have given her a particularly warm welcome.

Today was the same as ever. She moved from bed to bed, looking as modest and collected as she could, ignoring the general noise in the ward and attending to the patient she was examining. Suddenly a particularly coarse and unrestrained voice reached her ears from over by the opposite wall: "Don't talk to me about patients! Some of the patients here are on the job morning, noon and night! You take that scruffy one, the one with the belt round his middle— every night duty he gives that nurse Zoya a bit of a cuddle!"

"What's that? What did you say?" Gangart asked the woman she was examining. "Will you say that again, please?"

The patient started to repeat it.

(Zoya had been on duty *last night!* So last night, while the green dial was burning . . .)

"Excuse me, would you mind repeating that, please? Right from the beginning and in detail!"

26. *Superb Initiative*

When is a surgeon (not a new one, but an experienced one) nervous? Not during operations. During an operation he works honestly and openly. He knows what he is doing, his task is merely to remove what has to be removed as cleanly as possible, so that later on there are no regrets about an unfinished job. True, there are sometimes unexpected complications. There may be a rush of blood and he may remember how Rutherford died while having a hernia repaired. But basically a surgeon's nervousness begins *after* the operation, when for some reason the patient's temperature refuses to drop or a stomach remains bloated and one has to open it not with a knife, but in one's mind, to see what has happened, to understand and put it right. When time is slipping away, you have to grab it by the tail.

This was why Lev Leonidovich was in the habit of dropping in on his postoperative cases before the five-minute conference, just to have a look. As usual before an operation day the ordinary rounds would last a long time, and he could not go another hour and a half without knowing what had happened to his stomach case and how Dyomka was. He called on the stomach case, who wasn't doing too badly. He told the nurse what drink to give him and how much. Then he looked into the next room, a tiny one for only two people, to see Dyomka.

The other patient in the room was already on the mend and due for discharge, but Dyomka was lying there on his back with the blanket pulled up to his chest, looking very gray. He was staring at the ceiling, only it wasn't a calm, relaxed stare. He was straining all the muscles round his eyes as though there was a minute object up there which he wanted to see but couldn't. He looked alarmed.

Lev Leonidovich stood in silence, legs slightly apart and arms dangling, just to one side of Dyomka. He looked sullen. He even appeared to pull his right arm back slightly, as if measuring what would happen if he gave Dyomka a right-handed hook to the jaw.

Dyomka turned his head, saw him, and burst out laughing.

The surgeon's stern, threatening expression soon turned to laughter as well. Lev Leonidovich winked at Dyomka, an understanding, man-to-man sort of wink. "All right, then?" he asked him. "Everything under control?"

"Under control?" There was plenty Dyomka had to complain about, but when it came to a man-to-man exchange there were no complaints at all.

"Does it hurt?"

"Yeah."

"In the same place?"

"Yeah."

"And so it will for a long time yet, Dyomka. You'll still be clutching at it next year, even though there's nothing there. But when it hurts you, try to remember: *It's not there!* It'll make you feel better. The most important thing is you're going to live now, see? As for your leg—to hell with it!"

Lev Leonidovich made it sound so easy. He was right, to hell with the nagging painful thing! He felt better without it.

"Well, we'll call and see you later on."

Leonidovich rushed off to the five-minute conference, clearing the air like a shell. (He was late, the last one to arrive, and Nizamutdin Bahramovich didn't like latecomers.) His white coat hugged him tightly. It had no opening in front, while at the back its two edges were pulled tight across his jacket but still wouldn't meet. When he walked through the clinic on his own, he always went fast and took the stairs two at a time, moving his legs and arms boldly. It was these positive, rapid movements that made the patients realize he didn't hang about the place killing time.

The five-minute conference began and lasted half an hour. Nizamutdin liked to conduct the proceedings with dignity and without undue haste (or so he thought). Obviously he loved listening to the sound of his own voice. Every time he made a gesture or turned toward someone, it was plain he was regarding himself. He thought he looked like a man of authority, reputation, education and intellect. Legends would be springing up about him back in the *aul* where he was born. He was well known throughout the town too, and even occasionally got a mention in the newspaper.

Lev Leonidovich was sitting on a chair he had moved slightly back from the table. He crossed one long leg over the other and stuffed his splayed paws under the white tabs tied tightly round his belly. He wore a crooked frown under his pilot's cap, but since he almost always frowned in his boss's presence, the senior doctor didn't guess the frown was meant for him.

The senior doctor viewed his position not as an unremitting, exhausting job, but as a constant opportunity to parade himself, to gain rewards and a whole range of special privileges. "Senior doctor" was his title, and he believed that the name really made him the most important doctor, that he knew more than the rest of the doctors (well, not perhaps down to the last detail), that he was fully aware of every treatment his subordinates were administering and that only his guidance and corrections prevented them from making mistakes. This was why he had to spend so long presiding over his five-minute conferences, although of course everyone else seemed to enjoy them well enough. The privileges of the senior doctor were fortunately much greater than his duties, which meant he need not be over-particular about choosing administrative personnel, doctors or nurses to come and work in his clinic. He could hire people recommended by telephone calls from the regional health services or the city Party committee or the medical college where he hoped soon to be submitting his thesis, or people he'd promised to take in some moment of dinnertime bonhomie, or members of the same branch of his own ancient clan. Then when the heads of departments came and complained about some new man who knew nothing and was thoroughly incapable, Nizamutdin Bahramovich would be even more surprised than they were. "Well, teach them, comrades," he'd say. "What do you think you're here for?"

He had a head of white hair, the sort of hair that gives a man of a certain age, whether genius or fool, saint or rascal, man-of-action or idler, an aura of calm nobility. He had the impressive, soothing appearance which is nature's reward to those who have not suffered the pangs of thought, and the even, dark complexion that goes particularly well with gray hair. Nizamutdin Bahramovich was telling his medical staff what was wrong with their work and how they should intensify their struggle for precious human lives. Thus he was wont to hold the attention of the men and women who sat behind the peacock-blue tablecloth in their straight-backed official sofas, armchairs and hard-backed chairs, the staff he had already managed to appoint, as well as those he had not yet managed to get rid of.

Lev Leonidovich could see curly-haired Halmuhamedov particularly well from where he sat. He looked like an illustration from the travels of Captain Cook, a savage straight out of the jungle. His hair was a dense mat, his bronzed face was spotted with jet-carbon blackheads, his ferociously gleeful smile revealed a set of large white teeth—there was only one thing missing: a ring through his nose. Of course it was not his appearance that mattered, or the neatly inscribed certificate he had received from medical college, it was that he could not carry out a single operation without bungling it. Lev Leonidovich had let him operate a couple of times, but now swore he would never let him do it again. To fire him, however, was equally out of the question. That would be called undermining the policy of training native personnel. So the man had now spent more than three years writing case histories, only the simple ones of course. He went on doctors' rounds and looked important, visited the dressings room and did night duty (during which he slept). Lately he'd even started drawing his salary on a time-and-a-half basis, even though he left the hospital at the end of the ordinary working day.

There were also two ladies in the room with surgeons' certificates. One was Pantyokhina, an extremely plump lady of about forty. She was always in a state of anxiety. Her worry was that she had six growing children by two different husbands, and there was never enough money for them or time to look after them. These cares never left her face, even during so-called working hours, which meant the hours she had to spend inside the clinic to get her pay. The other one was Angelica, a young woman qualified for only two years. She was small, reddish-haired and rather pretty, and she hated Lev Leonidovich for not paying her enough attention. She was the one mainly responsible for the intrigues against him in the surgical ward. These two women could do no more than receive outpatients and they could never be trusted with a scalpel, yet there were weighty reasons why the senior doctor would never fire either of them.

On paper the department had five surgeons, and the number of operations was calculated on the basis of five.

Yet only two were actually capable of operating.

There were some nurses in the room too, some of them no better than these doctors. Again, it was Nizamutdin Bahramovich who had taken them on and protected them.

There were times when the pressure of it all got Lev Leonidovich down and he felt he couldn't carry on another day. All he wanted was to break with the clinic and go somewhere else. But where could he go? Any new place would have its own senior doctor who might be even worse than the one here, its own puffed-up fools and its own drones filling the place of workers. It would be different if he could take over the clinic on his own, and, just for a change, organize things on an efficient basis. He would make everyone who had the capacity do a proper job of work and employ only as many as were needed. But Lev Leonidovich wasn't in a position to be entrusted with a senior doctorship, unless it was in some place miles from anywhere. Out here was close enough to Moscow for someone to be sent.

Anyway, he didn't really want to be in charge. He knew that administrators were seldom efficient in their actual profession. At one period in his life he had seen some great men who were down and out, and he had recognized what a futile thing power is. He had seen former divisional commanders whose dream it was to get work as kitchen orderlies. His first practical teacher had been the surgeon Koryakov, whom he had once literally had to pull out of a rubbish heap.

At other times things calmed down, smoothed themselves out, and Lev Leonidovich reckoned he could put up with it all and wouldn't have to leave. His fears would then go to the opposite extreme. He was frightened lest they might get rid of Dontsova, Gangart, and himself. This was the way things seemed to be going; every year the situation became not simpler but more complicated. It was no longer easy for him to tolerate abrupt breaks in his life. He was nearly forty and his body now craved a degree of comfort and security.

His own life was a source of great puzzlement to him. He didn't know whether to make a heroic charge forward or to swim quietly with the current. It wasn't here that his serious work had begun. In the beginning, his career had been full of scope. One year he'd fallen only a few yards short of a Stalin Prize. Then suddenly their whole establishment had burst like a bubble. Certain areas of research had been stretched too far, there had been too much haste. After the collapse, he never actually submitted his thesis. It was partly Koryakov who had put him into this frame of mind. "You just keep working," he had said to him. "There'll always be time to write it down." But when would there be time?

And what was the use of writing it all down?

Lev Leonidovich's face showed no disapproval of the senior doctor. He screwed up his eyes, pretending to listen, particularly as they were suggesting that he carry out the first-ever operation on the thorax next month.

Everything comes to an end, and so did the five-minute conference. The surgeons filed slowly out of the room and gathered on the upper landing. His paws still tucked into the narrow belt round his belly, Lev Leonidovich set off like a grim, absentminded colonel, leading his team on the main rounds: Yevgenia Ustinovna, gray-haired and simple-looking, Halmuhamedov with his luxuriant curls, fat Pantyokhina, red-haired Angelica, and two nurses.

Some rounds were like flying visits, everyone in a hurry to get the job done. They should have hurried today as well, only the time-table decreed that there should be a slow, general round, taking in every single surgical case. They walked into the wards one after the other, all seven of them, diving into an atmosphere stale from the stifling medical smells, the reluctant use of ventilation and the patients' bodies. They squeezed in, making way for each other in the narrow passage between the beds and looking over each other's shoulders. Gathered in a little circle round each bed, they were supposed to spend either one, three or five minutes penetrating each patient, just as they had already penetrated the heavy air of the ward. They had to penetrate his pains, his emotions, his anamnesis, his case history, the progress of his treatment, his present condition —in fact, everything theoretically and practically possible for them to do.

If there had been fewer of them, if each had been the best specialist available and not merely a man who drew a doctor's salary, if there hadn't been thirty patients to every staff member, if they hadn't had to bother about the most tactful thing to put in a case history (a document which might one day find itself on the desk of a state prosecutor), if they hadn't been human beings, that is to say firmly attached to their skin and bones, their memories and intentions, and if they hadn't derived a vast relief from the knowledge that they weren't the ones in pain—then very probably such a system of doctors' rounds would have been the best conceivable solution.

But as Lev Leonidovich very well knew, things were as they were. Still, the rounds could neither be cancelled nor replaced. He therefore led his team round the wards, as he always did, narrowing his eyes (one eye more than the other) and tamely listening as his staff recited (not speaking off the cuff but reading out of files) the facts about each patient: where he was from, when admitted (he already knew this about the senior patients), reason for admittance, type of treatment being administered and in what intensity, blood count, whether he was already down for an operation or wasn't to be operated on, and if so why, or whether the question hadn't yet been decided. He heard some of the patients out and sat down on their beds. Some of them he asked to show him the diseased place. He examined it, felt it, and covered the patient up himself with a blanket or else invited the other doctors to feel it.

The really difficult cases couldn't be resolved on rounds like these, you had to call the patient in and examine him on his own. You couldn't be too outspoken during rounds either, you couldn't call a spade a spade and come to an agreement with each other. You couldn't even say that a patient's condition had worsened, all you could say was "The process seems somewhat more acute." Everything was discussed in euphemisms and half-allusions (sometimes even in substitutes for substitutes), or else in a way that was in direct antithesis to the truth. No one ever said "cancer" or "sarcoma," nor could they use terms that patients half understood, like "carcinoma," "CR" or "SR." Instead they had to use harmless words like "ulcer," "gastritis," "inflammation," or "polyps." What these terms actually meant could be explained in full only after the rounds. Sometimes, for the sake of better understanding, they were allowed to use expressions like "The shadow in the mediastinum has widened," or "The case is not respectable," "We cannot exclude a lethal outcome" (which meant the man might die on the operating table). When in spite of everything he ran out of expressions, Lev Leonidovich used to say, "Put that case history to one side," and then they would move on.

During the rounds they would reach very little understanding of the disease or of each other, but the less agreement reached, the more important Lev Leonidovich attached to improving the patient's morale. He began to see the improvement of morale as the main aim of the rounds.

"*Status idem*," someone might say to him. ("No change.")

"Is that so?" he would reply happily. At once he would check the remark with the patient herself. "You feel a bit better, do you?"

"Yes, perhaps," the patient would agree, slightly surprised. She hadn't noticed it herself, but if the doctors had noticed it, it must be true.

"There, you see! Little by little, you'll soon get better."

But another patient sounded the alarm.

"Tell me," she said "why do I have these pains in the spine? Perhaps I've got a tumor there as well?"

"O-oh, no-o." Lev Leonidovich smiled as he drawled out the words. "That's a subsidiary development." (He was telling the truth: a secondary tumor *was* a subsidiary development.)

He stood over an old man with a terrible, sharpened face and the gray complexion of a corpse, who could hardly move his lips. "Patient is receiving general tonics and sedatives," they told him.

It meant the end. It was too late to treat him. There was nothing to treat him with; the only aim was to reduce his suffering.

Then Lev Leonidovich would knit his heavy eyebrows, as if making up his mind to lift the curtain and explain what had to be explained: "All right, Grandpa, let's be quite frank and open about this. What you're feeling now is a reaction to your earlier treatment. Don't push us too hard, just lie there quietly and we'll see you get better. Just lie there. You may think we're not doing very much, but we're helping your organism to defend itself."

The doomed man would nod his head. The doctor's frankness had turned out to be less lethal than expected. It kindled his hope.

"You can observe a tumorous formation of such-and-such a type in the iliac region," someone might report, showing Lev Leonidovich an X ray.

He would hold the murky, black transparent X-ray film up to the light and nod encouragingly. "That's a very good photo! Very good!"

And so the patient would be encouraged. As far as she was concerned, it wasn't merely good, it was very good. The photograph *was* very good, but only because there was now no need to take another. It clearly showed the size and boundaries of the tumor.

Throughout the ninety-minute general round, the senior surgeon would make a point of never saying what he really thought. He took care to prevent his tone expressing his feelings. At the same time, the staff doctors had to make accurate notes for the case histories, those files of reference cards, filled out in longhand with pen and ink, which might later provide the basis for one of them being put on trial. Never once did Leonidovich turn his head abruptly, never once did he look alarmed, his benevolent, bored expression indicating to patients how simple their diseases were. They were all well-known disorders, and not a single one was serious.

An hour and a half of acting combined with scientific analysis was enough to exhaust Lev Leonidovich. He frowned, straining the skin on his forehead.

Then an old woman complained she hadn't had her chest tapped for some time, so he tapped it.

An old man announced, "Look, there's something I want to tell you."

He started a confused story about his interpretation of the origin and development of his pains. Lev Leonidovich listened patiently, even nodding occasionally.

"There was something you were going to say, wasn't there?" said the old man, allowing him to speak.

The surgeon smiled. "What is there for me to say? Our interests are exactly the same. You want to be cured, we want you to be cured too. Let's carry on in agreement."

He knew a few words of Uzbek, enough to say simple things to them. There was one very sophisticated-looking lady who wore glasses. Even seeing her on a hospital bed in a dressing gown was somehow embarrassing, so he decided not to examine her in front of the others. He gravely offered his hand to a little boy who had his mother with him. Then he gave a seven-year-old a flick on the tummy, and they both had a laugh together.

There was only one patient he treated with a certain lack of politeness, a schoolmistress who demanded the right to consult a neurologist.

By now he was in the last ward. He came out as exhausted as if he'd done a full operation. "Smoke break, five minutes," he said.

He and Yevgenia Ustinovna puffed out two big clouds of smoke after throwing themselves on the cigarettes as if they were the climax of the round. (Yet they told the patients that tobacco was carcinogenic and strictly contraindicated!)

Then they all went into a small room and sat down round a table. The names mentioned during the rounds now came up for discussion once again, but the general impression of improvement and recovery that an outside listener might have gathered during the rounds was now completely exploded and disintegrated. The man with *status idem* was an inoperable case being given symptomatic X-ray treatment to suppress the immediate pain, but without any hope of a cure. The little boy Lev Leonidovich had offered his hand to was incurable too, suffering from a widely dispersed tumor, and it was only because his parents insisted on it that he had to stay in hospital a while longer. As for the old woman who'd demanded to have her chest tapped, Lev Leonidovich said, "She's sixty-eight. If we give her X-ray treatment, we may put it off till she's seventy. If we operate, she won't live a year. What do you think, Yevgenia Ustinovna?"

If even such a staunch supporter of the knife as Lev Leonidovich was giving the case up, Yevgenia Ustinovna would certainly be in agreement.

In fact he wasn't a supporter of the knife, but he was a skeptic. He knew that there was no instrument as good as the naked eye for letting you see a clear picture, and that nothing could remove what had to go more radically than the knife.

There was one patient who, not wanting to decide on an operation himself, asked if he could consult with his family. Lev Leonidovich said, "His family live in the depths of the wilds. In the time it takes to get in touch and for them to come here and give their opinion, the man will die. We must persuade him and get him on the operating table, not tomorrow but the next time round. Of course it is a risk. We'll give him a lookover, then maybe we'll just sew him up without doing anything."

"What if he dies on the table?" asked Halmuhamedov with an air of importance, as though he were the one taking the risk.

Lev Leonidovich moved his long, intricately shaped eyebrows, which had grown together in the middle. "An if is an if, but if we do nothing he'll die for sure." He paused to think. "We've got a good death rate so far, we can take the risk."

After every discussion he would ask, "Does anyone disagree?"

However, the only opinion that interested him was Yevgenia Ustinovna's. Their experience, age and approach were quite different, but their views almost always coincided, which showed it was easy enough for sensible people to understand one another.

"What about that girl with the straw-colored hair?" asked Lev Leonidovich. "Isn't there some other way we can help her, Yevgenia Ustinovna? Must we amputate?"

"It's unavoidable," said Yevgenia Ustinovna, drawing in her curved, heavily made-up lips. "And we'll have to give her a dose of X ray afterwards."

"It makes you feel wretched," Lev Leonidovich suddenly sighed. His odd-shaped head was crowned with the funny little cap. He bowed his head and seemed to be examining his fingernails, drawing his thumb, which was enormous, across the forefingers. "The hand literally rebels against doing an amputation on someone so young," he mumbled. "You have a feeling you're going against nature."

He drew his index finger round his thumbnail. Whatever he did, nothing would help. He raised his head. "Well, comrades," he said, "do you understand Shulubin's case now?"

"*CR recti*?" said Pantyokhina.

"Yes, *CR recti*. But you know how they found out about it? It shows how much all our cancer propaganda and oncological stations are worth. Oreshchenkov was right when he once said at a conference, 'A doctor who's squeamish about putting his finger in a patient's anus isn't a doctor at all.' The number of things our people neglect! Shulubin dragged himself from one outpatient's clinic to another complaining about frequent calls of nature, rectal blood and then pains. They did every imaginable test on him except the simplest one of all, feeling with the finger. They treated him for dysentery and piles, but it didn't help. Then he read a cancer poster hanging on the wall in one of the outpatients' clinics. He's an educated man, he read it and he guessed. So with his own finger he felt his own tumor. Now why couldn't the doctors have done it six months earlier?"

"Is it deep?"

"About seven centimeters, just behind the sphincter. If we'd caught it earlier we could have kept the rectal muscle controlled and he'd have remained a normal human being. But now the sphincter's affected we'll have to remove the rectum. It means he'll lose control of his stool, and it means we'll have to take the colon out to one side. What sort of a life is that? And he's a good fellow . . ."

They began to prepare the list of tomorrow's operations. On it they marked which of the operations required pre-operative treatment, what with, who should be bathed, who prepared and in what way.

"Chaly hardly needs pre-operative treatment!" said Lev Leonidovich. "It's cancer of the stomach. But he's such a cheerful character, it's almost unheard of."

(If he only knew it, Chaly was planning to treat himself the next morning with a bottle of alcohol!)

They worked out who was going to assist whom, and who would take care of the blood count. Inevitably it worked out that Lev Leonidovich would be assisted by Angelica. This meant that once again she would be standing there across the table, with the theater nurse moving back and forth on one side, and instead of devoting herself to the job would spend the whole time watching out of the corner of one eye to see what he was up to with the theater nurse.

She was a bit of a psycho as well, you only had to cross her to see that. So there was no way of being certain whether her silk thread was properly sterilized or not. And this was what the whole operation depended on . . . Damn these women! They didn't know the simple masculine rule: working and sex don't mix.

The girl's parents had made a mistake in calling her Angelica when she was born. Of course they could hardly have foreseen what a demon she would grow up to be. Lev Leonidovich took a sideways peek at her pretty, though foxy, little face and felt like saying to her peaceably, "Listen, Angelica—or Angela, or whatever name you want us to call you—you're not entirely without qualifications and ability, you know. If you applied yourself to surgery instead of scheming to get yourself married, you might be doing a decent job of work by now. Listen, there's no point in our having a quarrel. After all, we stand side by side at the operating table . . ."

But she'd have interpreted this to mean that he was exhausted by the campaign and was surrendering.

He also felt like giving a detailed account of yesterday's trial. He had begun telling Yevgenia Ustinovna the story briefly while they were smoking. But he didn't feel much like telling these particular colleagues about it.

The moment the conference was over, Lev Leonidovich stood

up, lit a cigarette and strode down the corridor toward the radio-therapy department. He swung his excessively long arms boldly as he walked, cleaving the air with his glazed white-coated chest. Vera Gangart was the one he felt like talking to. He found her in the near-focus X-ray unit. She was sitting at a table with Dontsova, doing some paperwork.

"It's time for your lunch break," he declared. "Give me a chair."

He threw the chair under him and sat down. He was in the mood for a gay, friendly chat, but then he noticed something. "You're not very pleased to see me, are you?" he said.

Dontsova smiled lightly, twisting her hornrimmed spectacles round her fingers. "On the contrary, I'm doing my best to get on good terms with you. Will you operate on me?"

"Operate on you? Not for anything in the world!"

"Why not?"

"Because if I hack you to death they'll say I did it out of jealousy, because your department's more successful than mine."

"No jokes, Lev Leonidovich. I'm being serious."

It was true, one could hardly imagine Ludmila Afanasyevna making jokes. Vera was sitting there looking very sad. She had shrunk into herself, her shoulders hunched as if she was cold.

"Ludmila Afanasyevna will have to be examined during the next few days, Lev. It seems she's had pains in her stomach for some time, but she didn't tell anyone. Fine oncologist she is!"

"And of course you've already collected your evidence and you can prove it's cancer, is that right?" Lev Leonidovich curved those extraordinary eyebrows stretching from temple to temple. He always wore a mocking expression, even during the most ordinary conversation when there was nothing to laugh at. But you could never tell whom he was mocking.

"Not all of it, not yet," Dontsova admitted.

"Well, what evidence is there? For example?"

She told him.

"That's not enough!" was Lev Leonidovich's verdict. "Let Verochka here sign the diagnosis, then we'll talk. They're giving me my own clinic soon, so I'll take Verochka away from you to be my diagnostician. Will you give her up?"

"I won't give Vera up for anything. Get yourself someone else."

"I won't take anyone else, I only want Verochka. Why should I operate on you, if you won't give her up?"

He was finishing the last few puffs of his cigarette, looking about him and chatting jokingly, but in his thoughts he was completely serious. As his old teacher Koryakov used to say, "When you're young you haven't the experience, when you're old you haven't the strength." But just at the moment Gangart was like himself, at the peak age when the ear of experience had already ripened and yet the stem of energy is still strong. Before his eyes she had developed from a girlish intern into a diagnostician so acute that he believed in her no less than he believed in Dontsova herself. With a diagnostician like her a surgeon, however skeptical, knew no cares. The trouble was that for a woman this peak time of life was even shorter than it was for a man.

"Have you got your lunch with you?" he asked Vera. "You won't be eating it anyway, you'll be taking it back home, won't you? Let me eat it."

Amid much joking and laughing some cheese sandwiches appeared. He began eating them and offering them round. "You have one! . . . Oh yes, I went to the trial yesterday. You should have come, too, you'd have learned something. It was in a school building. About four hundred people were there, they knew it was going to be interesting. I'll tell you what happened. A child suffering from volvulus and twisted bowels was operated on. He lived several days after it was done. He even started going out and playing games— this is established. Then his bowels got partially twisted again and he died. The wretched surgeon had to put up with eight months of investigation—goodness knows how he went on operating all that time. Present at the trial were a representative of the city health service, the city's chief surgeon, and a public prosecutor* from the medical college. Can you imagine? He went on and on about the surgeon's criminally negligent attitude. The parents were brought forward as witnesses—fine witnesses they made! They said something about a blanket not being straight, it was all nonsense. As for the public, the doctor's fellow citizens, they just sat there staring, saying to themselves, 'What bastards these doctors are!' Yet some of the public are doctors. We know how stupid it all is, we can see the whirlpool that's going to draw us in; it's bound to get us in the end, you today, me tomorrow. But still we say nothing. If I hadn't just come from Moscow I'd probably have said nothing either, but

---

*In a "comradely court" this would not be an official public prosecutor but someone put forward by "medical public opinion" for the purpose.

after two refreshing months there values seem to change, both the Moscow values and the local ones here. Cast-iron barriers turn out to be made of rotten wood. So I stuck my neck out. I got up and made a speech."

"Are you allowed to make speeches?"

"Well, yes, it's a sort of debate. I told them, 'You ought to be ashamed of yourselves, organizing this circus'—I really gave it to them! They tried to stop me, they threatened to cut me short. 'How do you know a judicial error's any easier to make than a medical error?' I said. 'This whole case should be under *scientific* investigation, not judicial at all. You should've got a group of doctors together, doctors and no one else, and had them do a qualified scientific analysis. Every Tuesday and every Friday we surgeons take enormous risks, we walk into a minefield. Our work is entirely based on trust. A mother ought to entrust her child to us, not stand up as a witness against us in a courtroom.' "

Lev Leonidovich was getting excited all over again, he could feel something trembling in his throat. He had forgotten the unfinished sandwich. He tore his half-empty pack as he took out a cigarette and lit it.

"And this surgeon was Russian! If he'd been a German, or, let's say, a Y-yid"—his lips protruded as he drew out the soft "y" and at length—"they'd all be crying 'Hang him! Why wait?' They clapped after I'd finished, but how could I have kept silent? If they're putting a noose round your neck, you have to tear it off, there's no point in waiting."

Vera had been shaking her head from side to side all the time he was recounting his story. She was shocked. Her eyes expressed understanding, intelligence and strained dismay—which was why Lev Leonidovich liked telling her such things. Ludmila Afanasyevna had looked puzzled as she listened. Now she shook her large head with its ashen, short-cropped hair.

"I don't agree with you," she said. "What other way is there of dealing with us doctors? I remember once a surgeon sewed up a swab into a patient's stomach—they just forgot about it! Somewhere else they injected a physiological saline solution instead of Novocain. There was another case where they let a leg go dead inside a cast. Somebody else made a mistake about dosage, gave ten times the right amount. We do sometimes transfuse blood of the wrong group. We do inflict burns. What other way can they deal with us? They should pull us up by the hair, like children!"

"Ludmila Afanasyevna, you're killing me!" said Lev Leonidovich, raising one large hand to his head as if to protect it. "How can you talk like this, you of all people? This is a problem that goes beyond medicine. It's a struggle that concerns the nature of our whole society."

"Here's the answer, here's the answer!" said Gangart, trying to make peace. She seized their arms to stop them waving them at each other. "Of course doctors must carry greater responsibility, but at the same time their patient quota ought to be lowered by two or three times. Look at outpatients: nine an hour! Isn't it appalling! Give us a chance to talk to each patient in peace and quiet, and to think in peace and quiet as well. When it comes to operations, a surgeon should do one a day—not three!"

But Ludmila Afanasyevna and Lev Leonidovich carried on shouting at each other. They couldn't agree. Finally Vera managed to calm them down. "What was the result, then?" she asked.

Lev Leonidovich unscrewed his eyes and smiled. "We saved him!" he said. "The whole trial fizzled out. The only thing the court recognized was incorrect entries in the case history. But wait! That wasn't the end of it. After the verdict was pronounced the city health service director made a speech, you know, about how we aren't educating our doctors properly, or our patients, and how we don't hold enough trade-union meetings. Then finally we had a speech from the chief city surgeon. What was his conclusion after all this? What was his message? 'Comrades,' he said, 'putting doctors on trial shows superb initiative, truly superb!' "

27. Each Has His Own Interests

It was an ordinary weekday and ordinary rounds were in progress. Vera Kornilyevna was going to see her radiotherapy cases. She was by herself, but on the upper landing she was joined by one of the nurses.

The nurse was Zoya.

They stood for a while beside Sibgatov, but they didn't stay with him long because every new step in his case was decided by Ludmila Afanasyevna herself. They went into the ward.

As it happened, they were both exactly the same height. Their lips, eyes, and caps were on the same level. But since Zoya was the more thickset she seemed the larger as well. One could foresee that in two years' time when she became a doctor she'd look more imposing than Vera Kornilyevna.

They walked down the row opposite Oleg's. He could see only their backs, the dark-brown knot of hair sticking out from under Vera Kornilyevna's cap and the golden ringlets under Zoya's.

Today the row consisted entirely of radiotherapy cases. Progress was slow. Vera Kornilyevna was sitting down beside every patient, examining him and talking to him.

Vera Kornilyevna looked at Ahmadjan's skin, checked on his case history and his latest blood test, then said, "All right, we'll soon be finishing the X-ray treatment. You'll be going home."

Ahmadjan flashed his teeth.

"Where do you live?"

"Karabaïr."

"Well, that's where you'll be going."

"Have I recovered?" Ahmadjan was literally shining.

"Yes, you've recovered."

"Completely?"

"So far, yes, completely."

"You mean I won't be coming back here any more?"

"You'll be coming back in six months' time."

"Why? If I'm cured, why?"

"We'll want to see you again."

And so she covered the whole row without turning toward Oleg once, keeping her back to him all the time. Zoya threw just one brief glance into his corner.

Vera Kornilyevna stayed some time with Vadim. She looked at his leg and felt his groin on one side and the other. Then she felt his belly and diaphragm, inquiring all the time how it felt. She also asked a question that was new to him: what sensations did he have after eating various types of food?

Vadim was concentrating. She talked to him quietly and he answered quietly. He hadn't expected her to feel in the right-hand side of his diaphragm or to ask him about eating. "Are you examining my liver?" he asked.

He remembered how, as if by chance, his mother had felt him there before she left the hospital.

"He has to know everything, doesn't he?" said Vera Kornilyevna, shaking her head from side to side. "These days our patients are so educated, we'll be handing them over our white coats soon."

Vadim was watching the doctor with a stern, prophetic air, like a young boy on an icon. His head, with its pitch-black hair and yellowish, swarthy features, lay straight across the white pillow.

"I do understand," he said quietly. "I've read about it, I know what it's like." He said it without pressing her in any way, without insisting that she agree and explain everything straightaway. But his attitude made her feel awkward. Unable to think of anything to say, she just sat there on the bed as if she was guilty of doing him some injury. He was handsome, young and probably very talented. He reminded her of a young man in a family they knew well who had spent a long time dying, completely conscious the whole time, while no doctor was able to do a thing to help him. Vera had only been in her eighth year at school at the time; it was this young man who had made her change her mind and decide to become a doctor instead of an engineer.

She was a doctor now, but there was still nothing she could do to help.

On Vadim's window sill stood a jug containing a dark-brown infusion of *chaga*. The other patients used to come up and look at it enviously.

"Are you drinking it?"

"Yes, I am."

Gangart herself didn't believe in *chaga*. She had simply never heard of it, never been told about it before. In any case it was harmless, not like the mandrake root from Issyk Kul. And if a patient believed in it, it had its uses.

"How are things with the radioactive gold?" she asked.

"They're making promises still. Perhaps they'll give it to us in the next few days." He was speaking in his usual intense, somber manner. "But it seems they don't give it to you directly, they have to send it through official channels. Listen . . ." he gazed demandingly into Gangart's eyes, "if they bring it in two weeks' time, there'll be secondaries in my liver by then, won't there?"

"Good heavens no, why should there? Of course not!" Gangart lied very persuasively and animatedly. She seemed to have convinced him. "Secondaries take months to form, if you must know."

(Why was she feeling his diaphragm, then? Why did she ask him how he responded to food?)

Vadim was inclined to believe her.

It made it easier if he did . . .

While Gangart was sitting on Vadim's bed Zoya, having nothing to do, turned her head toward Oleg since he was so near, glanced sideways at his book lying on the window sill, then at Oleg himself. She was asking him something with her eyes, but it was impossible to tell what. Her inquiring eyes with their little raised brows looked very pretty indeed, but Oleg looked back without expression or reply. She always found a moment during rounds when he was the only one who could see her eyes, and then they would send him short, cheerful flashes like Morse signals, flashes of welcome. But just lately the dot flashes had become much fewer, while the dash flashes had ceased altogether.

Oleg was angry with Zoya because of those few days when he had reached out for her and begged her to yield, but she hadn't.

The next nights when she was on duty he had gone through the same motions as before with his lips and hands, but without feeling the same emotion. It had become forced. After that, whenever she was on duty he hadn't even gone to see her, he'd gone to sleep instead. Now it was all in the past he couldn't see the point of all these eye games. His calm gaze was meant to show her that he didn't understand. He considered himself a bit too old for that sort of game.

He had prepared himself for the thorough examination usual on such days. He had taken off his pajama jacket and was ready to pull off his undershirt as well.

Vera Kornilyevna had finished with Zatsyrko. Wiping her hands, she turned her face toward Kostoglotov, but she didn't smile at him, nor did she invite him to tell her the details, nor did she sit down on his bed. She merely glanced at him briefly, just enough to let him know he was next on the list. But in the moment it took her to shift her gaze, Kostoglotov saw how alienated it had become. The special brightness and joy her eyes had radiated on the day he'd had his blood transfusion, their affectionate friendliness before that day, the attentive sympathy they had shown earlier still—all had disappeared at once. The eyes had become empty.

"Kostoglotov," Gangart noted, looking not so much at him as at Rusanov. "Same treatment. But here's an odd thing . . ." She turned and looked at Zoya. "Reaction to hormone therapy's a bit weak."

Zoya shrugged her shoulders. "Perhaps it's a peculiarity of his organism," she said.

Zoya, who was only a year away from being qualified, probably thought Dr. Gangart was asking her advice as a colleague. But Gangart ignored her suggestion. "How regularly does he receive the injections?" she asked, in a tone that showed this was clearly no consultation.

Zoya was quick to grasp what was in the air. She threw back her head slightly and looked straight at the doctor, widening her eyes a little. They were yellow-hazel and bulging. They showed honest surprise.

"What possible doubt can there be?" she asked. "All the required treatments are invariably . . ." One more step and she would consider herself literally insulted. "At least when I'm on duty."

Obviously they couldn't ask her about when others were on duty. She pronounced the words "at least" in one whistling breath, and the blurred, hasty sound somehow convinced Gangart that Zoya was lying. If the injections weren't having their full effect, someone must be failing to give them. It couldn't possibly be Maria. It couldn't possibly be Olympiada Vladislavovna. And she knew that during night duty Zoya . . .

Zoya's stare, ready to rebuff her, was so bold that Vera Kornilyevna realized that it would be impossible for her to prove anything and Zoya had already decided as much. Zoya's rebuff and her determination were so strong that Vera Kornilyevna couldn't understand them. She lowered her eyes.

She always lowered her eyes when she was thinking unpleasant thoughts about someone.

She lowered her eyes guiltily while Zoya, having won the battle, continued to test her with her straightforward gaze.

Zoya had won the battle, but she realized at once she shouldn't have taken a risk like that. Dontsova might begin her own inquiries and if one of the patients, Rusanov, for example, confirmed that she wasn't giving Kostoglotov any injections she could easily lose her job in the clinic and have a bad report sent to her college.

It was a risk, but what had been the point of it? It was a game which had in fact exhausted itself; no new moves could be played, there was no more room for the wheel to roll. It would be quite ridiculous to go outside the limits of the game, take a job in that stupid Ush-Terek and tie her life to a man who . . . No, it was out of the question, it didn't even exist in her mind as a possibility. Zoya looked Oleg up and down, and by this look she cancelled their agreement not to give him the injections.

Oleg saw clearly that Vera didn't even want to look at him, but he was quite unable to understand why, or how it could happen so suddenly. As far as he knew, nothing had taken place which could explain the change. It was true she'd turned away from him in the lobby yesterday, but he'd thought that was accidental.

These women's tempers, he'd forgotten what they were like! They were all the same: one whiff and off they flew. Only with men could a man have long-standing, even normal relationships.

Now Zoya too was getting at him, fluttering her eyelids in reproach. She had taken fright. If they began the injections what would be left between them, what secret would they have?

What did Gangart want, then? Did she want him to have every single injection without fail? Why were they so important to her?

Her sympathy was all very well, but wasn't this too high a price to pay for it? To hell with her!

But meanwhile Vera Kornilyevna was talking to Rusanov. Her tone was warm and solicitous, in sharp contrast to the abrupt way she had spoken to Oleg. "We've got you used to the injections now," she was saying. "You take them so well you probably won't want to stop them," she said jokingly.

(All right, lick the bastard's boots, see if I care!)

While waiting for the doctor to reach him, Rusanov had seen and heard the clash between Gangart and Zoya. Being Oleg's neighbor, he knew perfectly well that the young lady was lying for the sake of her lover-boy. He knew she had a pact with Bone-chewer. If it had concerned Bone-chewer and no one else, Pavel Nikolayevich would probably have whispered a few words to the doctors— well, perhaps not during the rounds in front of everyone, the doctors' room would be a better place. But he simply didn't dare do the dirty on Zoya. It was strange, but during the past month he had come to realize that even the most insignificant nurse could get her revenge by causing him a great deal of inconvenience. Here in hospital they had their own system of command, and while he was inside he oughtn't to start trouble even with a nurse over some trifle that didn't concern him.

If Bone-chewer was fool enough to refuse injections, well, let him get worse. Let him drop dead, it was all right by him.

As for himself, Rusanov now knew for certain he wasn't going to die. His tumor was rapidly going down, and every day he looked forward to the rounds, when he could hear the doctors confirming it. Today Vera Kornilyevna had confirmed that the tumor was going well, and as for the headaches and the general weakness, he would get over them in time. She would give him another blood transfusion too.

Pavel Nikolayevich now set a high value on the testimony of those patients who had known his tumor from the start. Ahmadjan had been the only one of these left, if you didn't count Bone-chewer, but then a few days ago Federau had returned from the surgical ward. His neck, unlike Podduyev's a few weeks ago, was making good progress, and they were reducing the bandages round it layer by layer. Federau had taken Chaly's bed, which made Pavel Niko-layevich's other neighbor.

Of course, for Rusanov to have to lie between two exiles was in itself a humiliation and a mockery on the part of fate. If things had been as they were before he entered hospital, he'd have gone straight to the authorities and taken it up as a matter of principle— should leading officials be thrown together with dubious, socially harmful elements? But for five weeks the tumor had dragged him along like a fish on a hook, and he had become kinder, or perhaps simpler. He could always turn his back on Bone-chewer, especially since he didn't make much noise now, just lay there hardly moving. As for Federau, looking at it from the charitable point of view one could say he was a tolerable neighbor. First and foremost, he was delighted at the way Pavel Nikolayevich's tumor had gone down, right down to one third of its former size. At Pavel Nikolayevich's request he would inspect it again and again, appraise and reappraise it. He was patient, never insolent and always ready to listen to what Pavel Nikolayevich told him. He never contradicted. For obvious reasons, Pavel Nikolayevich couldn't talk in detail about his work in a place like this, but was there any reason why he shouldn't intimately describe his apartment, which he loved so earnestly and to which he was about to return? There was no secret about it, and of course Federau found it agreeable listening to disquisitions on the fine way people could live (one day everyone would be able to live like that). After the age of forty, a man's apartment gives a good indication of what he is and what he has deserved. So Pavel Nikolayevich had told him, in various stages, how the first room had been arranged and furnished, then the second, and then the third, what sort of terrace it had and how the terrace was fitted out.

Pavel Nikolayevich, who had a good memory, clearly recollected every sofa and cupboard—where and when he'd bought it, how much he'd paid for it and what its particular advantages were. As for his bathroom, he described it in even greater detail. He told Federau what sort of tiles he had put on the floor and on the walls, he described the ceramic baseboard, the little shelf in the bathtub for the soap, the rounded headrest, the hot-water tap, the shower control and the towel rail. These weren't mere trifles, they were part of one's daily life and being, and "Being determines consciousness."* A man's life had to be good and pleasant to give him the right kind of consciousness. To quote the words of Gorky, "A healthy mind in a healthy body."

*This saying of Karl Marx has become a proverb in communist countries.

Colorless, tow-haired Federau listened to Rusanov's stories, his mouth open in admiration, never contradicting him. Sometimes he even nodded his head, as far as his bandaged neck would allow.

Though a German and an exile, he was a quiet chap, one might say quite a decent fellow. There was no harm in being in the next bed to him, one could get along with him. He was even a Communist, technically speaking. Pavel Nikolayevich explained it all in his usual blunt way. "Federau," he said, "you realize it was necessary for the state to send you into exile? You understand that?"

"I understand, I understand," said Federau, bowing his inflexible neck.

"There was no other way of dealing with the situation."

"Of course, of course."

"One must have a clear idea of the reasons behind all official measures, including exile. One thing you should appreciate: you were allowed, one might say, to remain inside the Party."

"Certainly! Of course I . . ."

"And as for your Party appointments, you never held any before you were exiled, did you?"

"No, I didn't."

"You were an ordinary worker the whole time, weren't you?"

"I was a maintenance mechanic. The whole time."

"I was an ordinary worker myself once. Look at the way I got on."

They talked in detail about their children, too. It turned out that Federau's daughter Henrietta was in her second year at regional teachers' college.

"Just think of it!" Pavel Nikolayevich exclaimed. He was really quite touched. "You must appreciate that. Here you are, an exile, and your daughter is about to graduate from college! Who could've dreamed of such a thing in Russia under the Tsars? You have no restrictions at all."

At this point Friedrich Jakobovich contradicted him for the first time. "The restrictions were only lifted this year," he said. "Before that we had to get permits from the *komendatura*. And the colleges kept returning her application forms, saying she hadn't passed the entrance exam. How could we check whether it was true?"

"But you said your daughter's in her second year?"

"Ah well, you see, she's good at basketball. That's why they took her."

"Whatever they took her for, one must be fair in one's judgment, Federau. As from this year there are absolutely no restrictions."

After all, Federau had been an agricultural worker and it seemed natural for Rusanov, a worker in industry, to take him under his protection.

"Things will be much better for you now after the January Plenum decisions," Pavel Nikolayevich explained benevolently.

"Oh yes, of course."

"The main link is the establishment of groups of instructors in each tractor station zone.* Everything depends on that."

"Yes, yes."

But saying "Yes, yes" wasn't enough, he had to understand as well. So Pavel Nikolayevich explained to his tractable neighbor in greater detail how it was that tractor stations, after the groups of instructors had been set up, would become veritable fortresses. He also discussed the appeal issued by the Central Committee of the Young Communist League about the cultivation of maize, how this year the young people were expected to come to grips with the problem of maize and how this would completely change the agricultural picture.** They had also read in yesterday's paper about changes in the basic practice of agricultural planning. They could look forward to many conversations on the subject.

In general, Federau turned out to be a positive sort of neighbor. Sometimes Pavel Nikolayevich would simply read aloud to him newspaper items he would never have got through himself but for the leisure of being in hospital. There was a statement about why an Austrian peace treaty couldn't be concluded without a German peace treaty, Rakosi's speech in Budapest, a fresh stage in the struggle against the infamous Paris Agreements, and an article about the inadequacy and lenience of the West German trials of those who had helped to run concentration camps. Sometimes he would offer Federau some of his private food, when there was too much for him, or give him part of his hospital meal.

---

*At that time tractor stations had the function of lending agricultural machinery to collective farms. Their management had a decisive say in the management of agriculture. The allusion is to one of countless reorganizations in the management of these stations.

**Khrushchev had just become Party Leader. He believed that wide cultivation of maize in the north of Russia would solve grain and fodder problems, and called upon Young Communists to fight those who didn't believe maize could be grown there. His scheme, however, was defeated by the climate.

But however quietly they talked, there was still a certain atmosphere of strain because Shulubin was obviously listening in to their conversation all the time. There he sat, that eagle owl, silent and motionless on the bed next to Federau's. Ever since the man had appeared in the ward, his presence had been impossible to forget—the way he looked at you with his great, drooping eyes, clearly hearing every word. And when he blinked it seemed like a mark of disapproval. Pavel Nikolayevich found his presence a constant pressure. He tried to draw him out and discover what was in his mind or at least what was wrong with him physically, but Shulubin would utter no more than a few gloomy words. He saw no reason to discuss even his tumor.

And when he sat he didn't relax like everyone else, he adopted a strained, wound-up pose, as though sitting was hard labor. He seemed constantly on the alert, and his tense way of sitting was his means of showing this. Sometimes he would grow tired of sitting and rise to his feet, but he found walking painful. He would hobble about for a while and then stand erect, motionless, for half an hour or so at a time. Rusanov found this equally strange and depressing. Furthermore, Shulubin couldn't stand beside his own bed because he would have blocked the doorway, nor could he stand in the aisle because he would have blocked that too, so he chose the space between Kostoglotov's and Zatsyrko's windows. This became his favorite place. He would tower there like an enemy sentry watching everything Pavel Nikolayevich ate, did, or said, standing there for ages, his back barely touching the wall.

He had taken up his position today after the rounds and stayed there in the crossfire of Oleg and Vadim's glances, sticking out from the wall like an *alto-rilievo*.

Oleg and Vadim's beds were so placed that their glances often met, even though they didn't talk to each other much. In the first place they were both in low spirits and they had little energy left for idle chat. In the second place, some weeks ago Vadim had cut everyone short by declaring, "Comrades, to warm one single glass of water requires the energy of two thousand years of quiet talking or seventy-five years of loud shouting, and then only if heat is retained in the glass. So you see, gossiping is not particularly useful, is it?"

Moreover, each man had made a remark that had annoyed the other, though possibly unintentionally. Vadim had said to Oleg,

"You should've *fought*! I can't understand why people like you didn't fight." (He was right, but Oleg didn't yet dare open his mouth and come out with the story of how they had fought.) Oleg had said to Vadim, "Who are they saving the gold for, anyway? Your father gave his life for his country. Why won't they give it to you?"

And he was right, too. The thought had occurred to Vadim himself, and he was beginning to ask himself the same question. But it was annoying to have it asked by a complete stranger. Only a month ago he'd felt that his mother had been wrong to try to pull strings like that, he'd felt awkward about her making use of his father's memory. But now that the trap had snapped round his leg he was beginning to cast about wildly while he waited for his mother's good-news telegram. "If only Mama can get it," he thought to himself. It was true it didn't seem fair for him to be saved merely because of what his father had achieved, but it would be more than fair if he were to be saved because of his own talent—unfortunately, however, the men who distributed the gold knew nothing of this. It was a torment and a responsibility to carry within himself a talent which filled him to the brim but which could not yet be poured out into the world. For him to die before his talent had burst forth and found expression would be a much greater tragedy than an ordinary man's death, in fact more tragic than the death of any other man in the ward.

Vadim felt a throbbing, fluttering sense of loneliness. It wasn't because no one visited him or because he didn't have his mother or Galka with him, it was because neither the patients, nor those who were treating him, nor the officials who held his salvation in their hands, had any idea how much more important it was for him to survive than for the others.

These hopes and despairs beat so insistently in his head that he found he was no longer fully grasping what he read. He would read a whole page and then realize he hadn't understood it. He'd grown heavy, he could no longer scale other people's thoughts as a goat scales a mountain. He was sitting stock-still over a book. From the outside it might look as though he were reading, but in fact he wasn't.

His leg was in a trap, and with it his whole life.

So he sat there, while over him, in his space between the windows, stood Shulubin absorbed in his own pain and his own silence. Kostoglotov was lying on his bed, also in silence, his head dangling over one side.

Like the three storks in the fairy tale, they could maintain their silence forever.

Shulubin was usually the most persistently silent of the three, yet strangely enough it was he who suddenly asked Vadim, "Are you sure you're not kidding yourself? Do you really need all that stuff? Why that? Why not something else?"

Vadim raised his head. His dark, almost black eyes stared at the old man as if unable to believe he could have uttered such a long question. Or perhaps they were surprised at the question itself.

There was nothing to indicate that the preposterous question hadn't been asked, or that the old man was not the one who'd asked it. The old man's baggy, reddened eyes were squinting at Vadim in curiosity.

He had to answer him. He knew how to answer, of course, but for some reason he didn't feel the usual spring-coiled impulse to make the required reply. He answered quietly, in the same meaningful tone the old man had used, "It's . . . it's interesting. It's the most interesting thing I know in the world."

Despite the pain inside him, however agonizingly his leg throbbed, however fast those eight fatal months seemed to be melting away, Vadim still took pleasure in the way he kept himself under control, behaving as though there were not the least danger in the air, as though it was a rest home that they were all in, not a cancer hospital.

Shulubin stood there gazing dismally at the floor. His body still motionless, he made an odd circular movement of the head and a spiral movement of the neck as though he wanted to make someone let go of his head, but couldn't. " 'Interesting'—that's no argument," said Shulubin. "Business is interesting too: making money, counting it, acquiring property, building things and surrounding yourself with comforts. It's all very interesting. If that's your explanation science becomes no different from the ordinary run of selfish, thoroughly unethical occupations."

It was a strange point of view. Vadim shrugged his shoulders. "But what if it really *is* interesting?" he asked. "What if it's the most interesting thing there is?"

"Here in hospital? Or in general?"

"In general."

Shulubin straightened the fingers of one hand. They made a

cracking noise. "If that is the premise you start from," he said, "you'll never create anything that's ethically good."

This was a really cranky argument. "It's not the duty of science to create ethical values," explained Vadim. "Science creates material values, that's how it earns its keep. Anyway, what values do you call ethical?"

Shulubin closed his eyes for a space, opened them, and closed them once again. Then he spoke, quite slowly. "Values directed toward the mutual illumination of human souls," he said.

"Well, science illuminates, doesn't it?" Vadim smiled.

"Not souls!" said Shulubin, wagging his finger. "Now you used the word 'interesting.' Have you ever spent five minutes inside a collective farm chickenhouse?"

"No."

"Well, just imagine—a long, low barn, dark because the windows are only slits, and covered with netting to stop the hens flying out. There are two thousand five hundred hens per poultry maid. The floor's made of earth, the hens scratch it all the time, and the air's so full of dust you need a gas mask. And all the time the girl's steaming stale sprats in an open vat—you can imagine the stink. She works without a break. In summer her working day lasts from three in the morning till twilight. When she's thirty she looks like fifty. What do you think? Do you think this girl finds her work *interesting*?"

Vadim was taken aback. He moved his eyebrows. "Why should I ask myself the question?" he said.

Shulubin pointed his finger at Vadim. "That's a businessman's answer," he said.

"What she suffers from is an underdevelopment of science," said Vadim. He had found himself a strong argument. "When science advances, all chickenhouses will be clean and decent."

"But until science advances you'll go on cracking three eggs into your frying pan every morning, will you?" said Shulubin. He closed one eye, making the other one's stare even more baleful. "Wouldn't you like to work in a chickenhouse for a bit, while science advances?"

"He's not *interested* in that!" came the gruff voice of Kostoglotov, his head still hanging down over the side of the bed.

Rusanov had already noticed Shulubin's arrogant opinion on matters of agriculture. He had been explaining something about cereals when Shulubin had interrupted the conversation and corrected him. He now saw his chance to needle Shulubin. "Did you graduate from Timiryazev Academy,* by any chance?"

Shulubin started. He turned his head toward Rusanov. "That's right, Timiryazev," he confirmed in a surprised voice.

Suddenly he stopped, puffed himself up and looked all sulky. Like a bird with clipped wings trying to take off, he hobbled, hobbled his way back to his bed. His movements were as awkward as ever.

"Then why do you work as a librarian?" Rusanov called after him triumphantly.

But once Shulubin stopped talking, he stopped talking. He was silent as a tree stump.

Pavel Nikolayevich had no respect for such men who had come down in the world instead of going up.

*The best-known agricultural college in the Soviet Union.

28. Bad Luck All Round

The first time Kostoglotov saw Lev Leonidovich in the clinic, he recognized him as a man who meant business. Having nothing better to do during rounds, Oleg spent the time sizing him up. There was much that disposed him in his favor. That cap he always wore on top of his head had obviously not been put on in front of a mirror. His arms were too long, and sometimes he shoved his fists into the front pockets of his blind-fronted white coat. His lips were pinched at the corners, which made him look as if he was about to whistle. And in spite of his obvious strength and ferocity he had a joking, facetious way of talking to the patients. It all made Kostoglotov think he would like to have a heart-to-heart talk with him and ask him a few of the questions that the women doctors would be neither able nor willing to answer.

But there was no time to ask them. During rounds Lev Leonidovich noticed no one except his surgical cases. The radiotherapy patients' beds he passed by as though they were empty. When people said "Good morning" to him in the corridors or on the stairs his answer would be light enough, but his face was never free of care and he was always in a hurry.

One day Lev Leonidovich had been talking about a patient who had confessed to some offense after first denying everything. Lev Leonidovich had laughed and said, "Ah! So he 'sang' in the end, did he?" This really staggered Oleg; it wasn't every man who knew this sense of the word and was capable of using it.

Kostoglotov had spent less time lately wandering round the

clinic, so his and the senior doctor's paths had crossed even less than before. One day, though, he saw Lev Leonidovich unlock the door of the little room next to the operating theater and go in. This meant there couldn't be anyone else in the room. Oleg knocked on the white-painted glass door and opened it.

Lev Leonidovich had sat down on the stool. He was sitting sideways, as people do when they're only going to sit for a few minutes, but already he was writing something.

"Yes?" He raised his head, but didn't look particularly surprised. Evidently he was still busily thinking what to write next.

Everybody always in a hurry! Whole lives to be decided in a single minute!

"Excuse me, Lev Leonidovich." Kostoglotov was trying to be as polite as he could contrive. "I know you're in a hurry, only there's nobody except you . . . Can you give me two minutes?"

The surgeon nodded. But he was still thinking about his own problems, that was obvious.

"They're giving me a course of hormone therapy by reason of. . . . Intramuscular Sinestrol injections, in doses of . . ." (Kostoglotov took pride in his ability to talk to doctors in their language, with full precision. It was the basis of his claim that they should talk to him with complete frankness.) "What interests me is this: is the effect of hormone therapy cumulative or not?"

Of the one hundred and twenty seconds he obtained he had spent less than twenty on this introductory speech. From now on the number of seconds no longer depended on him. He stood there in silence, hands behind his back, looking down at the sitting man. It made Oleg look humpbacked in spite of his lankiness.

Lev Leonidovich furrowed his forehead, screwing up his whole face.

"No, I don't think so. It shouldn't be," he replied. But it didn't sound very decisive.

"Somehow I feel it may be cumulative," said Kostoglotov, continuing to press his point home. It sounded as though he wanted the effect to be cumulative, or else as though by now he didn't really believe Lev Leonidovich.

"No, not really, it oughtn't to be," the surgeon replied, sounding as uncategorical as before. Either it wasn't his particular field or else he hadn't yet been able to switch his mind over to the subject.

"It's very important for me to understand," said Kostoglotov. He looked and talked as if he was threatening the other. "After this treatment will I lose the ability to . . . well, I mean, as far as women are concerned? Or will it be just for a limited period? Will the injected hormones leave my body or will they stay forever? Or perhaps the therapy can be reversed after a while by cross injections?"

"No, I wouldn't advise that. That's not possible," said Lev Leonidovich. He was observing this patient with the shaggy black hair. The main thing he noticed was his scar. It was an interesting scar; he could imagine it freshly cut, like a case recently brought to him in the surgical ward. He wondered what would have had to be done. "But why would you need cross injections?" he said. "I don't understand."

"What do you mean, you don't understand?" Kostoglotov couldn't make this out. Was it simply that, being businesslike and loyal to medical etiquette, Lev Leonidovich wanted to persuade the patient to accept his lot? "You really don't understand?" Oleg asked again.

They'd already gone far beyond the two minutes, as well as beyond the doctor-patient relationship. Then suddenly Lev Leonidovich spoke to Oleg with that lack of arrogance he had already noticed and appreciated. He addressed him like an old friend, in a lowered, unofficial voice. "Listen to me," he said, "do you really think women are the flower of life? You know, you can get fed up with them after a while . . . All they do is stop you achieving anything serious."

He spoke with great sincerity. His voice sounded almost weary. He was remembering the most important moment of his life, when he had not had the strength to make one final effort, perhaps because it had been diverted in precisely this way. But Kostoglotov couldn't understand him at all. He couldn't imagine ever having more than enough. His head swung vacantly from left to right, his eyes stared vacantly too. "There's nothing more 'serious' in my life," he said.

But this conversation was no part of an oncological clinic's schedule. Consultative deliberations on the meaning of life, especially with a doctor from another department, were not in the timetable. That little fragile woman surgeon put her head round the door and walked straight in without asking permission. She was wearing high heels and her whole body swayed slightly as she walked. She didn't stop but crossed the room, stood close to Lev Leonidovich, put a laboratory test form in front of him and leaned over it (from where

Oleg was she seemed actually to touch Lev Leonidovich). She didn't call him by his name. "Listen to this," she said, "Ovdienko has a white-corpuscle count of ten thousand."

The loose strands of her hair drifted in front of Lev Leonidovich's face like thin reddish smoke.

"What of it?" said Lev Leonidovich, shrugging his shoulders. "It doesn't point to a good leucocytosis. It simply means there's a process of inflammation which will have to be suppressed by X-ray therapy."

She went on talking and talking (and it was true, her right shoulder *was* pressing against Lev Leonidovich's arm!). The paper Lev Leonidovich had begun to write on was lying there. His pen was hanging idle, upside down between his fingers.

Obviously it was time for Oleg to leave. The long and secretly planned conversation had been interrupted at the most interesting point.

Angelica turned round, surprised to see Kostoglotov still there. Lev Leonidovich glanced at him too, peering over her head, a rather humorous expression on his face. There was something indefinable in his face that made Kostoglotov decide to go on. "I'd also like to ask you, Lev Leonidovich," he said, "whether you've heard about this birch-tree fungus, this *chaga*?"

"Yes, I have," he confirmed quite willingly.

"What's your attitude to it?"

"It's hard to say. I accept that some particular kinds of tumor react to it, stomach tumors for example. In Moscow they're going crazy about it. They say the forests have been stripped of it for two hundred kilometers round the city."

Angelica leaned back from the table, picked up her form and walked out of the room. She looked contemptuous and as independent as ever, and she walked with a swaying motion that was extremely attractive.

She left the room but, alas, the conversation they had begun was in ruins. To a certain extent his question had been answered, but to return to a discussion of woman's contribution to life would have been out of place.

But the light, momentary, humorous glance Lev Leonidovich had given him and the unstrained manner in which he'd been treated had paved the way for Oleg to ask a third prepared question, again one of some importance. "Lev Leonidovich," he began, shaking his head from side to side, "forgive my lack of discretion, if I'm wrong forget what I've said. Have you ever . . ." he lowered his voice as Lev Leonidovich had before, and screwed up one of his eyes. "Have you ever been where there's 'nonstop singing and dancing'?"

Lev Leonidovich came alive. "Yes, I have," he said.

"Is that so?" said Kostoglotov, pleasantly surprised. They were now equals! "What did they get you for?"

"They didn't get me for anything. I was a free man. I just worked there."

"Oh, a free man!" Kostoglotov sounded disappointed. It seemed they weren't equals after all.

"How did you guess?" the surgeon asked curiously.

"It was a word you used. You said someone 'sang,' meaning he confessed. You also described someone else as a 'fence.' "

Lev Leonidovich laughed. "I'll never get out of the habit," he said.

Equal or not, they already had much more in common than a moment ago.

"Were you there long?" asked Kostoglotov unceremoniously. He even managed to straighten up; he didn't look so sickly now.

"About three years. They sent me after I was demobilized—I couldn't get out of it."

He needn't have added the last remark, but he had. It was a job like any other, an honorable and respectable one. Why did decent people think they had to make excuses for it? Men still have an indicator somewhere inside them; even if it is short-circuited, it works in spite of everything.

"What did you do exactly?"

"I was in charge of the sick bay."

Aha! The same job as Madame Dubinskaya's—lord over life and death. Only she'd never have felt she had to make excuses, whereas this man had given up the job.

"So you managed to finish medical school before the war?" Kostoglotov stuck to him like a burr. He didn't really need the information, it was just a habit he'd picked up in prison, reviewing the life of any stranger he happened to meet between one rattle of the cell-door feeding hatch and the next. "How old are you, then?"

"No, I didn't qualify. After my fourth year I volunteered to go to the front as an ordinary doctor." Lev Leonidovich stood up, leaving his writing unfinished, walked up to Oleg and began to feel his scar with interest, kneading it between his fingers. "Did you get this 'out there'?"

"That's right."

"They did a good job on it, a very good job. Was the doctor a prisoner?"

"That's right."

"You don't remember his name? It wasn't Koryakov?"

"I don't know, we were in transit. This Koryakov, what was he in for?" Oleg was getting onto Koryakov now, eager to try to sort out his life story as well.

"They locked him up because his father was a colonel in the Tsarist army."

But just then the nurse with the Japanese eyes and the white crown came in to call Lev Leonidovich to the dressings room.

Kostoglotov resumed his stoop and wandered down the corridor.

Here was another life story, drawn in outline, two life stories, in fact. The missing parts he could imagine for himself. There were so many different ways of being sent 'out there' . . . No, it wasn't *that* he was thinking about, it was something else. Here you are, he thought, in your bed in the ward, you walk down the corridor or stroll in the garden and next to you, or coming toward you, there's a man, just a man, and it never occurs to either of you to say, "Hey, you, turn back the lapel of your jacket!" That's where it would be, the badge of their secret society. And he was one of them, he belonged, he was part of it and knew about it! How many of them were there? It was no good asking, they were all struck dumb. You couldn't guess anything from the outside. How well it was all concealed!

What an absurd idea, to live to see the day when women seem superfluous! Surely a man could never get his fill of women? It was impossible to imagine.

But basically there was nothing to be overjoyed about. Lev Leonidovich's denial had not been insistent enough to make one believe him.

So he must presume that he had lost everything.

Everything . . .

Kostoglotov felt as if his death sentence had been commuted to life imprisonment.

He would live, only God knows for what purpose.

He had forgotten where he was going. He hesitated in the lower corridor, then stood there idly.

A little white coat appeared out of one of the doors, three doors away from him. It was very narrow at the waist, it was immediately familiar.

Vera!

She was coming his way! It wasn't far in a straight line, but she had to walk round two beds by the wall. Oleg, however, hadn't moved toward her; he had to think—one second, two seconds and a third.

For three days since her last rounds her manner with him had been dry and official. Not one single friendly glance.

At first he thought: To hell with her! He'd give as good as he got. He had no desire to bow and scrape, to look for explanations.

It was a pity, though. It seemed a pity to hurt her. He was sorry for his own sake too. Were they supposed to walk past one another like strangers?

Was it his fault? It was her fault: she had deceived him about the injections, she had wished him ill. He was the one who might be unable to forgive.

Unseeing, without looking at him, she came alongside, and in spite of his resolutions Oleg found himself speaking to her, quietly, as though asking a favor. "Vera Kornilyevna . . ."

(It was a ludicrous tone to adopt, but he enjoyed using it.)

She raised her cold eyes, and she saw him.

(No, really, why was he forgiving her?)

"Vera Kornilyevna . . . wouldn't you like to . . . to give me another blood transfusion . . . ?"

(It sounded as if he was groveling. Still, he was enjoying it.)

"I thought you were refusing to take them," she said, looking at him with the same unforgiving sternness. But a kind of uncertainty trembled in her eyes, in those dear, dark-brown eyes.

(All right, according to her own lights she wasn't to blame. And they couldn't go on living in the same clinic together like complete strangers.)

"But I liked it *then*. I want more."

He smiled. Whenever he smiled, his scar shortened and the line of it went all wavy.

(He'd forgive her now. They'd straighten it out sometime later.)

Still, something was stirring in her eyes—a sort of repentance.

"Maybe they'll bring more blood tomorrow."

She was still resting her hand against an invisible pillar, yet it seemed to be melting or bending under the pressure.

"Only it has to be you," he said, "it must be you." His demand sounded heartfelt. "Otherwise I won't let them do it."

She shook her head, trying not to look at him, to evade the whole issue. "It depends how it works out," she said.

She walked on.

She was wonderful, in spite of everything she was wonderful.

Only what was he hoping for with her? A doomed man with a life sentence, what was he trying to achieve?

Oleg stood there in the corridor like a fool, trying to remember where he was going.

Oh yes, he was on his way to visit Dyomka.

Dyomka was lying in a tiny double room. His neighbor had been discharged and he was expecting a new one to arrive the next day from the operating theater. Meanwhile he was alone.

A week had passed, and with it had gone the first agony of his amputated leg. The operation was receding into the past, but his leg stayed with him torturing him as if it hadn't been removed. He could feel each toe separately.

Dyomka was delighted to see Oleg and greeted him like an elder brother. Of course they were like relatives, those friends of his from his former ward. Some of the women patients had sent him food too; there it was on his bedside table under a napkin. None of the new arrivals could come and visit him or bring him anything.

Dyomka was lying on his back nursing his leg (or rather what remained of a leg, less than a thigh), still with his huge turban-shaped bandage. But his head and arms were free.

"Well, hello, Oleg, how are you?" he said, taking Oleg's hand in his. "Sit down, tell me how things are in the ward."

The upstairs ward he'd recently left was the world he was used to. Here, downstairs, the nurses and the orderlies were different and so was the routine. There was constant bickering about who had to do what.

"Well, what can you expect in the ward . . . ?" Oleg was looking at Dyomka's yellowed face. It seemed whittled, as if grooves had been planed in his cheeks. His eyebrows, nose and chin had been planed down and sharpened. "It's still the same."

"Is 'Personnel' still there?"

"Oh yes, 'Personnel's' there."

"What about Vadim?"

"Vadim's not too good. They didn't get the gold. And they're frightened of secondaries."

Dyomka frowned his concern in a way that made Vadim his junior. "Poor fellow," he said.

"So, Dyomka, you ought to thank God they amputated yours in time."

"I could still get secondaries."

"Oh, I don't think so."

But who could tell? Even doctors, how could they detect whether the solitary, destructive cells had or hadn't stolen through the darkness like landing craft, and where they had berthed?

"Are they giving you X rays?"

"They roll me in on a small cart."

"You've got a clear road ahead now, my friend. You must get better and get used to using a crutch."

"No, it'll have to be two. Two crutches."

Poor boy, he'd already thought of everything. Even in the old days he'd frowned like a grown man. Now he seemed to have grown even older.

"Where are they going to make them for you? Right here?"

"Yes, in the orthopedic wing."

"They'll be free of charge, at least?"

"Well, I've made an application. What have I got to pay with?"

They sighed. The sighs came easily from them, two men who year in, year out had had very little to cheer them.

"How are you going to finish school next year, then?"

"I'll finish or bust."

"What'll you live on? You can't work in a factory now."

"They've promised me a disability rating. I don't know if it'll be Group 2 or Group 3."

"Which one is Group 3, then?" asked Kostoglotov. He didn't understand these disability groups, or any other civil regulations for that matter.

"It's one of these groups—enough to buy you bread, but not enough for sugar."

He was a real man, Dyomka, he'd thought of everything.

The tumor was trying hard to sink him, but he was still steering his course.

"Will you go to the university?"

"I'll do my best."

"You'll study literature?"

"That's it."

"Listen to me, Dyomka, I'm talking seriously, you'll just ruin yourself. Why don't you work on radio sets? It's a quiet life, and you can always earn something on the side."

"Oh, to hell with radio sets!" Dyomka blinked. "Truth is what I love."

"Well, you can repair radio sets and tell the truth at the same time, you old fool!"

They couldn't agree. They argued it this way and that. They talked about Oleg's problems as well. That was another grown-up thing about Dyomka, he was interested in others. Normally, youth is only concerned with itself. Oleg spoke to him about his own situation as he might to an adult.

"Oh, that's awful . . ." Dyomka mumbled.

"I don't reckon you'd change places with me, would you?"

"G-g-god knows."

The upshot of it all was that, what with the X rays and the crutches, Dyomka would have to spend another six weeks lounging about the hospital. He would get his discharge in May.

"Where will you go first?"

"I'll go straight to the zoo," said Dyomka, cheering up. He'd already spoken to Oleg several times about this zoo. They would stand together on the clinic porch and Dyomka would describe exactly where the zoo was, how it was lurking over there, across the river, behind those thick trees. He had spent years reading about animals and listening to stories about them on the radio, but he had never actually seen a fox or a bear, let alone a tiger or an elephant. He had always lived in places where there was no menagerie, circus or forest. His cherished dream was to go out and meet the animals, and it was a dream that did not fade as he grew older. He expected something extraordinary from this encounter. On the very day he'd come to hospital with his aching leg, the first thing he'd done was visit the zoo, only it happened to be the one day of the week it was closed. "Listen, Oleg," he said, "you will be discharged soon, won't you?"

Oleg sat there, hunching his back. "Yes, I expect so. My blood won't take any more. The nausea's wearing me out."

"But you will go to the zoo, won't you?" Dyomka couldn't let the matter go. He would have thought the worse of Oleg otherwise.

"Yes, I may."

"No, you must. I'm telling you, you must go! And you know what? Send me a postcard afterwards, will you? It'll be easy enough for you, and it'll give me such pleasure. Write and tell me what animals they have now and which is the most interesting, all right? Then I'll know a month before they let me out. You will go, won't you? And write to me? They say they have crocodiles and lions and . . ."

Oleg promised.

He left the room to go and lie down himself, leaving Dyomka alone in the small room with the door closed. For a long time Dyomka didn't pick up his book, he just looked at the ceiling and through the window, and thought. He couldn't see anything through the window. Its bars converged into one corner and it looked out on a nondescript corner of the yard bounded by the wall of the Medical Center. There was not even a strip of direct sunlight on the wall now. But it wasn't an overcast day either. The sun was slightly veiled, not completely covered by clouds, and gave out a sort of diffused, angular light. It must have been one of those dullish days, not too hot and not too bright, when Spring was doing her work without undue fuss or noise.

Dyomka lay motionless, thinking pleasant thoughts: how he'd learn to walk on crutches, briskly and smartly; how one really summery day shortly before May Day he'd go out and explore the zoo from morning until the evening train; how he'd have plenty of time now to get quickly through his subjects at school and do well and read all the essential books he'd hitherto missed. There would be no more wasted evenings with the other boys, going off to a dance hall after tormenting himself about whether to go or not, even though he couldn't dance anyway. No more of that. He would just turn on his light and work at his books.

There was a knock at the door.

"Come in," said Dyomka.

(Saying "Come in" gave him a feeling of satisfaction. He had never known a situation where people had to knock at his door before entering.)

The door was flung open, letting in Asya.

Asya came in, or rather burst in. She rushed into the room as though someone was chasing her, pushed the door shut behind her and stood there by the door, one hand on the knob, the other holding the front of her dressing gown together.

She was no longer the Asya who had dropped in for a "three-day checkup," who was expected back in a few days' time by her track friends at the winter stadium. She had sagged and faded. Even her yellow hair, which couldn't change as quickly as the rest of her, hung down pitifully now.

She was wearing the same dressing gown, an unpleasant one without buttons that had covered many shoulders and been boiled in goodness knows what boilers. It looked more becoming on her now than before.

Asya looked at Dyomka and her eyelashes trembled a little. Had she come to the right place? Would she have to rush on somewhere else?

She was utterly crushed now. No longer Dyomka's senior by a full year in school, she had lost her advantage of extra experience, her knowledge of life and the three long journeys she had made. She seemed to Dyomka almost like part of him. He was very pleased to see her. "Aysa, sit down! What's the matter?" he said.

They had had many talks together in hospital. They had discussed his leg (Asya had come out firmly against giving it up). After the operation she had come to see him twice, brought him apples and cookies. Natural though their friendship had been that first evening, it had since then become even more so. And she'd told him, although not all at once, exactly what was wrong with her. She had had a pain in her right breast, they had found some sort of hard lumps in it, they were giving her X-ray treatment for it and making her put pills under her tongue.

"Sit down, Asya. Sit down."

She let go of the dooknob and walked the few steps to the stool at the head of Dyomka's bed, dragging her hand behind her along the door, along the wall. It was as though she had to hold onto them and grope her way.

She sat down.

She sat down, and she didn't look Dyomka in the eye. She looked past him at the blanket. She wouldn't turn to face him, and he couldn't twist his body round to see her directly either.

"Come on now, what's the matter?" He had to play the "older man" again, that was his role. He threw his head back, craning his neck over the pile of pillows so that he could see her, still lying on his back.

Her lip trembled. Her eyelashes fluttered.

"As-asyenka!" Dyomka just had time to say the word. He was overcome with pity for her, he wouldn't have dared call her "Asyenka" otherwise. Suddenly she threw herself onto his pillow, her head against his, her little sheaf of hair tickling his ear.

"Please, Asyenka!" he begged her, fumbling over the blanket for her hand. But he couldn't see her hands and so he didn't find it.

She sobbed into the pillow.

"What is it? Come on, tell me, what is it?"

But he'd almost guessed what it was.

"They're going to c-c-cut it off . . . !"

She cried and she cried. And then she started to groan, "O-o-oh!"

Dyomka couldn't remember ever hearing such a long-drawn-out moan of grief, such an extraordinary sound, as this "O-o-oh."

"Maybe they won't do it after all," he said, trying to soothe her. "Maybe they won't have to." But he knew somehow that his words wouldn't be enough to comfort her sorrow.

She cried and cried into his pillow. He could feel the place beside him; it was already quite wet.

Dyomka found her hand and began to stroke it. "Asyenka," he said, "maybe they won't have to."

"They will, they will! They're going to do it on Friday . . ."

And she let out such a groan that it transfixed Dyomka's soul.

He couldn't see her tear-stained face. A few locks of hair found their way through to his eyes. It was soft hair, soft and ticklish.

Dyomka searched for words, but they wouldn't come. All he could do was clasp her hand tighter and tighter to try to stop her. He had more pity for her than he had ever had for himself.

"What have I got to live for?" she sobbed.

Dyomka's experiences, vague as they were, provided him with an answer to this question, but he couldn't express it. Even if he could have done, Asya's groan was enough to tell him that neither he, nor anyone, nor anything at all would be able to convince her. Her own experience led to only one conclusion: there was nothing to live for now.

"Who in the world will w-w-want me n-n-now?" She stumbled the words out inconsolably. "Who in the world . . . ?"

She buried her face in his pillow once again. Dyomka's cheek was by now quite wet.

"Well, you know." He was still trying to soothe her, still clasping her hand. "You know how people get married . . . They have the same sort of opinions . . . the same sort of characters . . ."

"What sort of fool loves a girl for her character?" She started up angrily, like a horse rearing. She pulled her hand away, and Dyomka saw her face for the first time—wet, flushed, blotched, miserable and angry. "Who wants a girl with one breast? Who wants a girl like that? When she's seventeen!" She shouted the words at him. It was all his fault.

He didn't know how to console her.

"How will I be able to go to the beach?" she shrieked, as a new thought pierced her. "The beach! How can I go swimming?" Her body corkscrewed, then crumpled. Her head clutched between her hands, she slumped down from Dyomka toward the floor.

Unbearably, she began to imagine bathing suits in different styles —with or without shoulder straps, one-piece or two-piece, every contemporary and future fashion, bathing suits in orange and blue, crimson and the hue of the sea, in one color or striped with scalloped edges, bathing suits she hadn't yet tried on but had examined in front of a mirror—all the ones she would never buy and never wear.

She could never show herself on the beach again. It had suddenly struck her as the most excruciating, the most mortifying fact of her existence. Living had lost all meaning, and this was the reason why.

Dyomka mumbled something clumsy and inept from his pile of pillows. "Of course, you know, if no one will have you . . . Well, of course, I realize what sort of a man I am now . . . But I'll always be happy to marry you, you know that . . ."

"Listen to me, Dyomka!" A new thought had stung Asya. She stood up, faced him and looked straight at him. Her eyes were wide open and tearless. "Listen to me, you'll be the last one! You're the last one who can see it and kiss it. No one but you will ever kiss it! Dyomka, *you* at least must kiss it, if nobody else!"

She pulled her dressing gown apart (it wasn't holding together anyway). It seemed to him that she was weeping and groaning again as she pulled down the loose collar of her nightdress to reveal her doomed right breast.

It shone as though the sun had stepped straight into the room. The whole ward seemed on fire. The nipple glowed. It was larger than he had ever imagined. It stood before him. His eyes could not resist its sunny rosiness.

Asya brought it close to his face and held it for him.

"Kiss it! Kiss it!" she demanded. She stood there, waiting.

And breathing in the warmth her body was offering him, he nuzzled it with his lips like a suckling pig, gratefully, admiringly. Nothing more beautiful than this gentle curve could ever be painted or sculptured. Its beauty flooded him. Hurriedly his lips took in its even, shapely contour.

"You'll remember? . . . You'll remember, won't you? You'll remember it was there, and what it was like?" Asya's tears kept dropping onto his close-cropped head.

When she did not take it away, he returned to its rosy glow again and again, softly kissing the breast. He did what her future child would never be able to do. No one came in, and so he kissed and kissed the marvel hanging over him.

Today it was a marvel. Tomorrow it would be in the trash bin.

29. Hard Words, Soft Words

The first thing Yuri did after returning from his official trip was to visit his father and spend two hours with him. Before Yuri set off, Pavel Nikolayevich telephoned him and asked him to bring his warm shoes, overcoat and hat. He was sick and tired of this vile ward, the blockheads that inhabited its beds and their idiotic conversations. The hospital lobby he found no less repulsive. Although he was very weak he had a longing to go out into the fresh air.

So this is what they did. They wrapped a scarf lightly round his tumor, which he could still feel when he moved his head, but much less than before. He was unlikely to run into anyone he knew in the paths of the Medical Center grounds. Even if he did, they would never recognize him in these motley clothes. So Pavel Nikolayevich felt no embarrassment or uneasiness as he strolled along. Yuri took his arm and Pavel Nikolayevich leaned on him heavily. He enjoyed taking step after step across the clean, dry asphalt, particularly as it presaged a speedy return first to his beautiful apartment where he would rest, and later to the work and activity he enjoyed so keenly. It was not only the treatment that had worn Pavel Nikolayevich down, but the dull inactivity. He was no longer a vital cog in a large, important mechanism. In fact, he felt he had lost all power and significance. He wanted to get back as soon as possible to the place where he was loved and where people couldn't do without him.

During the week there had been some cold and rainy spells, but today the warm weather had begun to reassert itself. It was still cool in the shade of the buildings, and the earth there was damp.

But it was so warm in the sun that Pavel Nikolayevich could scarcely bear even the weight of the autumn coat he was wearing. He began to undo it button by button.

It was a specially good opportunity for him to have a sober, serious talk with his son. Today, Saturday, was considered the last day of Yuri's official trip. Yuri was in no hurry to get to work, which was all the more reason for Pavel Nikolayevich to take his time too. His son's affairs had taken a turn which might become dangerous. His paternal heart realized this; he acknowledged that he had neglected them. Clearly, his son had not returned from his assignment with a clear conscience. He kept averting his gaze instead of looking his father in the eye. As a child, Yuri had been quite different, a straightforward boy; he had only developed this shy, evasive manner toward his father during his years as a student. It irritated Pavel Nikolayevich tremendously, and sometimes he would shout at him, "Hey, you, hold your head up straight!"

But today he decided he would refrain from such sharpness. He would speak to him tactfully. He asked Yuri to describe in detail how he had acquitted and distinguished himself as a representative of the republic's legal inspection team in the remote towns it had been his duty to visit.

Yuri began to tell him, but without much enthusiasm. He related one case, then another, but he kept turning his eyes aside.

"Come on, tell me more, tell me more!"

They sat down in the sun for a while on a bench which had dried off. Yuri was wearing a leather jacket and a warm woolen cap. He looked serious and manly enough, but there was that streak of weakness inside him which was ruining him.

"Yes, well, there was a case involving a truck-driver . . ." he said, staring at the ground.

"What about the truck-driver?"

"It was winter and he was driving a truckload of cooperative foodstuffs. He was supposed to drive seventy kilometers but he was stopped halfway by a snowstorm. Everything was covered in snow, the wheels wouldn't grip, it was freezing cold and not a soul in sight. The snowstorm whirled round him for more than twenty-four hours. He couldn't stand it any longer in the cab, so he abandoned the truck as it was, with a full load, and went to find somewhere to spend the night. The next morning the storm had died down and he came back with a tractor to pull the truck out. But there was one case of macaroni missing."

"What about the delivery man?"

"As it happened, he was doubling up for him. He was on his own."

"Disgraceful negligence!"

"Yes, of course."

"So he grabbed his chance and made a quick profit."

"Father, it was too high a price to pay for a case of macaroni," said Yuri, and he raised his eyes at last. A stubborn, unpleasant expression had appeared on his face. "It got him five years, that case of macaroni. There were cases of vodka in the truck too, and they weren't touched."

"You shouldn't be so gullible, Yuri, so naïve. Who else could've taken it during a snowstorm?"

"Someone might have come along on a horse, who knows? There'd be no tracks left by the morning."

"Well, even supposing he didn't take it himself, he did leave his post, didn't he? What sort of behavior is that, abandoning state property and just walking away?"

Guilt was beyond doubt, the sentence was transparently correct, perhaps even a little on the lenient side. But what infuriated Pavel Nikolayevich was that his son didn't see it that way. He had to ram the point down his throat. Yuri was weak and flabby in most things, but when it came to arguing some stupid point he was as stubborn as a mule.

"Try to imagine, Father: a snowstorm, ten degrees below—how could he spend the night in the cab? He'd have died, wouldn't he?"

"What do you mean, 'died'? What about sentries in the army?"

"Sentries are relieved every two hours."

"Well, what if a sentry isn't relieved? What about at the front? It doesn't matter about the weather, sentries just have to stand there, die if necessary, but abandon their post, never!" Pavel Nikolayevich even pointed a finger to show where they stood and died rather than desert. "Think what you're saying. If this one gets off, all the truck-drivers will start leaving their posts, they'll pinch things till there's nothing left of the state. Don't you understand?"

No, Yuri didn't understand. It was apparent from his duncelike silence that he didn't understand.

"All right, I know you have these childish opinions, it's because you're young. You may even have mentioned them to someone else, but I hope at least you had the sense not to put your views down in the official report?"

Yuri's chapped lips moved, then moved again. "I . . . I made out an official objection. I suspended execution of the sentence."

"You suspended it! And now they're going to review it? Oh no! No!" Pavel Nikolayevich covered his face, half hiding it with his hands. It was just what he'd dreaded. Yuri was making a mess of his job, ruining himself and casting a shadow over his father's reputation. Pavel Nikolayevich felt positively sick with fury, the helpless fury of a father who knows he can never pass his own intelligence or efficiency on to a lout of a son.

He got up and Yuri rose as well. They started walking and once again Yuri tried to support his father by the elbow. Pavel Nikolayevich knew that even if he used both hands he would never be able to beat into his son's head any understanding of the blunder he had committed.

He began by explaining to him about the law, about legal observance, about the unshakeable foundation on which it was based, a foundation not lightly to be questioned, especially if one was considering working as a legal inspector in a state prosecutor's office. All truth was specific; the law is the law, but one should also take into account the specific moment and the specific situation—the course of action required at any given time. He particularly tried to make Yuri understand the organic interrelationship of all levels and all branches of the state's machinery. Consequently, it would be wrong for him to assume an attitude of arrogance even when arriving in an out-of-the-way corner of the world with the mandate from the republic's authorities. On the contrary, he should be sensitive to the local context and try not to cross the paths of local officials who knew the situation and its requirements better than he did. If they gave the truck-driver five years, it meant that this must be the sentence deemed necessary in this particular area.

And so they walked into the shadow of the buildings and out of it, along pathways straight and crooked, then beside the river. Yuri listened, but all he said was, "Aren't you getting tired, Father? Perhaps we should sit down again."

He was a pigheaded boy and no mistake! The whole business had not taught him a thing. All he had retained were those ten degrees of frost in the driver's cab!

Pavel Nikolayevich was naturally getting tired and it was dread-
fully hot in his overcoat. They sat down again on a bench among
some thick bushes. They weren't in leaf yet, just twigs; you could
see right through them, but the first tiny ear-shaped leaves were
beginning to twist themselves out of their buds. The sun was very
warm.

Pavel Nikolayevich was not wearing his spectacles on the walk.
His face was relaxing and his eyes were resting. He screwed up his
eyes as he sat there silently in the sunlight.

Not far away, below the steep bank, the river was roaring along
like a mountain stream. Pavel Nikolayevich listened to it, warmed
himself and thought how pleasant it was to be getting back to life,
to know for sure he'd still be alive while all this was turning green,
and next spring as well.

But he had to complete the picture of Yuri's situation. He had to
pull himself together and restrain his anger, otherwise he would
frighten him off. He sighed, then asked his son to carry on and tell
him about a few more cases.

However slow he was on the uptake, Yuri knew perfectly well
what would provoke his father's praise or abuse. The next case he
described, Pavel Nikolayevich could not but approve. All the same,
Yuri kept averting his eyes. He hadn't learned to lie, and his father
sensed there was yet another bad case in store for him. "Tell me
everything," he said. "I want to know everything. You know, all I
want to do is give you sensible, reasonable advice. I'm only doing
it for your own good, you know. I don't like to see you make mistakes."

Yuri sighed and told his story. In the course of his inspection he
had to go through a good many old court records and documents,
some of them as much as five years old. He had begun to notice that
some of the one-rouble or three-rouble duty stamps were missing
from the documents, or, to be more exact, traces of them remained
but the stamps themselves were gone. Where had they got to? Yuri
thought it over and began to dig around. He discovered that some
of the stamps stuck on recent documents looked defective and
slightly torn in places. He then guessed that one of the girls who
had access to the court archives, Katya or Nina, must be pasting on
old stamps instead of new stamps, and pocketing the clients' money.

"Think of that!" said Pavel Nikolayevich. He grunted and threw
up his hands. "Just think of all the loopholes there are for stealing

from the state. You wouldn't think of that one straight off, would you?"

Yuri had conducted his investigation quietly, without breathing a word to anyone. He had made up his mind to get to the bottom of it, to find out which of the two girls was the embezzler. He formed a plan. He made dates with them both, first Katya, then Nina. He would take each girl to the cinema and then to her home. The one who had expensive furniture and carpets would be the thief.

"Well done!" said Pavel Nikolayevich, clapping his hands and smiling. "Very clever! Combining business with pleasure, you might say. Good boy!"

But Yuri had discovered that neither girl seemed to have much to spare. One lived with her parents, the other with her younger sister. They didn't even have many of the things Yuri regarded as necessities, let alone carpets. It made him wonder how they lived at all. He thought it over, then went and told the story to the judge they worked for. He asked the judge not to bring the matter to a court of law, simply to reprimand the girls and have done with it. The judge was very grateful to Yuri for preferring the matter to be handled privately. The publicity would have harmed him too. They called both girls in, separately, and scolded them angrily for several hours. First one confessed, then the other. Both had been making a hundred roubles a month out of the business.

"Oh dear, it should have been done officially, it really should," said Pavel Nikolayevich. He was as distressed as though he had missed the chance himself. But then, on the other hand, it was right not to have embarrassed the judge; Yuri had been very tactful in that respect. "At least they should have been made to pay back what they took," he said.

Yuri could hardly bring himself to mention how the story ended. He simply couldn't grasp the meaning of what had happened. When he had gone to the judge and suggested dealing with the matter privately, he had been conscious of acting with great magnanimity. He was proud of his decision. He imagined the joy every girl would feel after the horror of being made to confess. They would be expecting punishment, then suddenly they would be offered forgiveness. He would vie with the judge in telling them how shamefully they had behaved. He would cite examples, from his own twenty-three years of experience, of honest men who had every opportunity to steal but who didn't. Yuri lashed the girls with hard words, knowing the effect would be softened by forgiveness afterwards. The girls were forgiven and they left, but in the days that followed they did not beam with delight every time they met Yuri. Not only did they not come up to thank him for his noble act, they even did their best to ignore him. He was astounded, he simply couldn't understand it. Perhaps they didn't realize what they had been spared—but no, working in a lawyer's office they must have known perfectly well. Unable to restrain himself, he went up to Nina and asked her point-blank whether she was happy about the way things had gone. "Why should I be happy?" Nina replied. "I'll have to change my job now. I'll never live on my wages alone." Then he asked Katya, who was the prettier of the two, to come to the cinema with him again. Katya replied, "No, I like to be honest when I go out with men. I can't do it the way you do."

So this was the puzzle he had brought back from his assignment, and it still exercised his mind. He had been deeply hurt by the girls' ingratitude. He knew life was more complicated than it seemed to his father, who was straightforward and had a one-track mind, but apparently life was even more complicated still. What should Yuri have done? Refused to spare them? Or said nothing and over-looked the fact that the stamps were being reused? But in that case was there any point in his work at all?

His father asked no more questions, and Yuri was only too pleased to hold his tongue.

In Pavel Nikolayevich's eyes it was just another disaster brought about by his son's clumsy touch. He was finally convinced that if one doesn't develop a backbone as a child, one never will. It was hard being angry with one's own son, but he was very annoyed and very upset for him.

They had probably stayed too long outside. Pavel Nikolayevich's feet began to feel cold and he had a terrible urge to lie down. He let Yuri kiss him, then sent him on his way and went back to the ward.

A lively discussion was going on there in which everyone had joined, except that the main speaker had no voice. It was the imposing-looking philosopher, that assistant professor who used to visit them in the ward. He had since undergone an operation on his larynx. A few days before, he'd been transferred from the surgi-cal to the X-ray ward on the second floor. A metal gadget like a toggle from a Young Pioneer's scarf had been inserted conspicuously into the front of his throat. The professor was an educated, likable man and Pavel Nikolayevich made every effort not to hurt his feelings, not to wince visibly at the clasp in his larynx. Every time he spoke, the philosopher placed one finger on it. It made his voice at least semi-audible. He was fond of speaking, indeed accustomed to it, and now, after the operation, was delighted to make use of the ability which had been restored to him.

He was standing in the middle of the ward telling a story. His voice was hollow but louder than a whisper. "The amount of stuff he's got piled up!" he was saying. "You can't imagine! In one room there's a suite of furniture made of pale-gilded wood with backs, seats, and arms upholstered in lilac velvet plush. He thinks he's a serious collector! He's got four armchairs like that, and a small sofa. Where did he pinch them from, I'd like to know? From the Louvre, I suppose!" The philosopher laughed. He was greatly amused. "In the same room he's got another set with hard seats and high black backs. The piano he brought from Vienna. He has a table inlaid with ivory—it's like something out of Goethe's Weimar —and yet he covers it with a blue and gold tablecloth that hangs down to the floor. On another table he's got a bronze statue, a curvaceous, naked girl with a ring of torches in her hand, but the lamps don't work. The statue's too large for the room, it almost reaches the ceiling. It was probably meant for a park. Then he's got clocks—wall clocks, watches, grandfathers, some coffee-table size, some as high as the ceiling. Most of them don't go. There's a huge bowl that came from a museum, with one single orange in it. I only went into two rooms, but I counted five mirrors, some in carved oak frames, some with marble stands. Then there were pictures—seascapes, views of mountains, views of Italian streets . . ." The philosopher was laughing.

"Where does he get it all from?" wondered Sibgatov, both hands as usual propping the small of his back.

"Some of it's war booty, some of it he bought in second-hand shops. He met a girl who worked in one of them; originally he came in to ask her to value some of his furniture, but he ended up marrying her. After that they joined forces, and everything valuable that came along they reserved for themselves."

"But where does he work himself?" Ahmadjan insisted.

"Nowhere. He got his pension when he was forty-two, but he's still a great ox of a man, he'd be a good fellow for cutting down trees. He has his stepdaughter and granddaughter living with him, and you should see the way he talks to them. 'I order you!' he says. 'I'm in charge here! This is my house, I built it!' He sticks his hands under the lapels of his overcoat and walks about the house like a field marshal. His name's Yemelyan according to his passport, but for some reason he makes everyone at home call him Sashik. But can one say he's happy with his lot? No, he's not. What gets him on the raw is that the general commanding the army he was in has a house in Kislovodsk,* with ten rooms, two cars and his own man to stoke the boiler. Sashik hasn't got as far as that!"

They laughed.

Pavel Nikolayevich found the story out of place and thoroughly unamusing.

Shulubin didn't laugh either. He looked at the others as if he wished they'd let him get some sleep.

"All right, maybe it's funny," said Kostoglotov from his prostrate position. "But how is it that . . . ?"

"There was a feature in the local paper. When was it? A few days ago," someone in the ward remembered. "It was about a man who built himself a villa with government funds. Then it all came out. And you know what happened? He confessed he'd made a 'mistake,' handed the place over to a children's home, and all he got was an official reprimand. He wasn't even expelled from the Party."

"Yes, that's right!" Sibgatov remembered the case as well. "Why only a reprimand? Why wasn't he put on trial?"

The philosopher hadn't read the article and was not ready to undertake to explain why the man hadn't been tried. It was left to Rusanov. "Comrades," he said, "if he repented, realized his error and turned the place over to be a children's home, why take extreme measures? We must be humane, it's a fundamental feature of our . . ."

"All right, maybe it's funny," Kostoglotov continued in his drawl, "but how do you explain it all from the philosophical point of view— I mean Sashik and the villa?"

The professor made a spreading gesture with one hand, the other he held to his larynx. "Unfortunately," he said, "these are survivals of bourgeois mentality."

"Why bourgeois?" grumbled Kostoglotov.

*A fashionable resort in the Northern Caucasus.

"Why, what else do you think it is?" said Vadim, switching on his attention. He was in the mood for reading, but now obviously the whole ward was about to be embroiled in a brawl.

Kostoglotov raised himself from his prone position, hauling himself up to his pillow to get a better view of Vadim and the others.

"What else? Why, it's human greed, that's what it is, not bourgeois mentality. There were greedy people *before* the bourgeoisie and there'll be greedy people *after* the bourgeoisie."

Rusanov was not yet lying down. He surveyed Kostoglotov across his bed and declared didactically, "If you dig deep into such cases you'll always find a bourgeois social origin."

Kostoglotov jerked his head as if he was spitting. "That's a lot of nonsense, all that about social origin."

"What do you mean, 'nonsense'?" There was a stabbing pain in Rusanov's side, and he clutched it. He had never expected a brazen assault like this, even from Bone-chewer.

"Yes, what *do* you mean, 'nonsense'?" asked Vadim, lifting his dark eyebrows in puzzlement.

"I mean what I say," growled Kostoglotov. He hauled himself up a bit further so that he was now sitting upright. "It's a lot of nonsense that's been stuffed into your head."

"What do you mean, 'stuffed'? Are you responsible for what you're saying?" Rusanov brought the words out shrilly, his strength unexpectedly returning.

"Whose heads have been stuffed?" asked Vadim, straightening his back but keeping his book balanced on one leg.

"Yours."

"We aren't robots," said Vadim, shaking his head. "We don't take anything on trust."

"Who do you mean by 'we'?" Kostoglotov scowled. His forelock was hanging over his face.

"I mean us, our generation."

"Well, why do you swallow all this talk about social origin then? That's not Marxism. It's racism."

"What did you say?" shouted Rusanov, almost roaring with pain.

"Exactly what you heard." Kostoglotov threw the reply back at him.

"Listen to this! Listen to this!" shouted Rusanov, staggering and waving his arms as if calling everyone in the ward to gather round him. "I call you as witnesses, I call you as witnesses! This is ideological sabotage!"

Quickly Kostoglotov lowered his legs off the bed. Swinging both elbows, he made a highly indecent gesture at Rusanov, at the same time exploding with one of the filthiest words written up on walls: "Go and——— yourself, you and your ideological sabotage! A fine habit you've developed, you mother- . . . . Every time someone disagrees with you, you call it ideological sabotage!"

Hurt and insulted by this impudent hoodlum with his obscene gesture and foul language, Rusanov choked, making an attempt to straighten his slipping spectacles. Now Kostoglotov was yelling so loudly his words could be heard by the whole ward, even in the corridor (Zoya looked in round the door): "Why do you keep cackling on about social origins like a witch doctor? You know what they used to say in the twenties? 'Show us your calluses! Why are your hands so white and puffy?' Now that *was* Marxism!"

"I've been a worker, I've worked!" cried Rusanov, but he could hardly see his assailant since he couldn't get his spectacles on right.

"I believe you!" Kostoglotov bellowed unpleasantly. "I believe you! You even started to lift a log during Saturday Work,* only you stopped halfway. All right, maybe I *am* the son of a merchant, third class, but I've sweated blood all my life. Here, look at the calluses on my hands! So what am I? Am I bourgeois? Did my father give me a different sort of red or white corpuscles in my blood? That's why I tell you yours isn't a class attitude but a racial attitude. You're a racist!"

"What! What am I?"

"You're a racist!" Kostoglotov spelled the word out for him, leaping to his feet and drawing himself up to his full height.

The thin voice of the unjustly insulted Rusanov had reached a shriek. Vadim was also speaking, rapidly and indignantly, but he didn't get up from his bed and no one caught what he was saying. The philosopher was reproachfully shaking his big, well-shaped head with its cap of well-groomed hair, but who could hear his diseased voice?

The philosopher now came up close to Kostoglotov, waited for him to draw breath, and just had time to whisper to him, "Have you heard of the expression, 'a hereditary proletarian'?"

---

*Voluntary, unpaid manual labor was a feature of communist education and applied to everyone, including some white-collar officials.

"It makes no difference if you had ten proletarian grandfathers, if you're not a worker yourself you're no proletarian," boomed Kostoglotov. "He's not a proletarian, he's a son of a bitch. The only thing he's after is a special pension, I heard him say so himself." He saw Rusanov opening his mouth, so he decided to give it to him straight in the guts. "You don't love your country, you love your pension, and the earlier you get it the better. Why not when you're forty-five? And here am I, wounded at Voronezh, and all I've got is a pair of patched boots and a hole in a doughnut. But I love my country! I'm not getting a kopeck in sick benefits for these two months, but I still love my country!"

He waved his long arms until they nearly reached Rusanov. Suddenly furious, he threw himself raging into debate just as he'd done dozens of times in prison. His mind overflowed with phrases and arguments he'd heard from other men who were probably no longer alive.

In the heat of the fray the scene seemed to shift in his mind. The crowded, enclosed room, crammed with beds and people, became a prison cell, which made it easier for him to use obscene language. And if it came to a fight, he was ready for that too.

Kostoglotov was now in such a state that he might easily have punched Rusanov in the face. Rusanov, sensing this, cringed away and fell silent under the fury of the assault, but his eyes burned with rage.

"I don't need any pension," shouted Kostoglotov, finishing what he had to say. "I haven't got a bean, and I'm proud of it. I'm not trying to get anything, I don't want a huge salary, I *despise* such things."

"Sh-sh," hissed the philosopher, trying to stop him. "Socialism provides for differentiation in the wage structure."

"To hell with your differentiation!" Kostoglotov raged, as pig-headed as ever. "You think that while we're working toward communism the privileges some have over others ought to be increased, do you? You mean that to become equal we must first become unequal, is that right? You call that dialectics, do you?" He was shouting, but his shouts echoed painfully above his stomach. His voice was shaken with pain.

Several times Vadim tried to intervene, but Kostoglotov managed to draw on a hidden reserve. He threw more and more arguments into the field, like balls in a bowling game, and Vadim had no time to dodge them all.

"Oleg!" Vadim cried, trying to stop him. "Oleg! It's the easiest thing in the world to criticize a society which is still establishing itself, but you must remember it's only forty years old, it's not yet forty."

"I'm no older than that," Kostoglotov retorted insistently. "I'll always be younger than this society. What do you expect me to do, keep silent all my life?"

Again the philosopher tried to check him with a gesture of his hand. Beseeching him to have mercy on his stricken larynx, he whispered a few reasonable sentences about people making different contributions to the national product and the need to distinguish between those who washed hospital floors and the men in charge of the health service.

Kostoglotov was about to roar something incoherent in reply when suddenly Shulubin, whom everyone had forgotten, began to move in on them from his far corner by the door. He hobbled toward them awkwardly, looking as slovenly and disheveled as ever, his dressing gown in such disorder that he looked like a man roused from sleep in the middle of the night. They all saw him and looked at him in surprise. He stood in front of the philosopher, raised a finger and waited till the room was silent. "Are you familiar with the April Theses?"* he asked.

"Why, aren't we all?" The philosopher smiled.

"Can you list them point by point?" continued Shulubin, interrogating him in his guttural voice.

"My dear sir, there's no need to go through them one by one. The April Theses discussed the methods of transition from the bourgeois-democratic revolution to the socialist revolution. In this sense . . ."

"There's one point I remember," said Shulubin, moving the bushy brows above his unhealthy, tired, tobacco-colored, bloodshot eyes. "It runs, 'No official should receive a salary higher than the average pay of a good worker.' That's what they began the Revolution with."

"Is that so?" said the professor in surprise. "I don't remember that."

*The revolutionary program expounded by Lenin in April, 1917, after his return to Russia from Switzerland.

"Go home and check it. The regional health service director shouldn't get any more than Nellya here."

He wagged his finger reprovingly in front of the philosopher's face, then limped back to his corner.

"Aha, you see!" said Kostoglotov. He'd enjoyed this unexpected support. It was just the sort of argument he'd been in need of, and the old man had rescued him. "Put that in your pipe and smoke it!"

The philosopher straightened the toggle on his larynx. He couldn't think of anything to say. "You don't think Nellya's a good worker, do you?" he brought out finally.

"All right then, what about that orderly who wears glasses? They all get the same pay."

Rusanov was just sitting there. He had turned his back on the whole thing. He couldn't bear the sight of Kostoglotov any more. He was shaking with disgust, but Kostoglotov's long arms and fists meant he could not take administrative action. As for that repulsive owl from the corner, he'd been right to take an immediate dislike to him. Imagine paying the health service director and the floor-scrubber the same rate! Couldn't he think of anything cleverer than that? There was absolutely nothing to be said.

Suddenly the whole debate fell apart and Kostoglotov found no one to go on arguing with. Anyway, he'd already shouted all he wanted to say. Besides, shouting had made him feel sore inside. It was now painful for him to speak.

At that point Vadim, who hadn't got up from his bed throughout the debate, beckoned Kostoglotov over to him. He asked him to sit down and began to explain quietly, "You use the wrong scale of values, Oleg. Your mistake is comparing the present day with the ideal of the future; you should rather compare it with the festering sores that plagued Russia's history before 1917."

"I wasn't alive then, I don't know." Kostoglotov yawned.

"You don't have to have lived then, you can find out easily enough. Read Saltykov-Shchedrin,* he's the only textbook you need. Or compare us with these showcase Western democracies where a man can never get his rights or justice or even lead a normal, human life."

Kostoglotov yawned once more, wearily. The anger that had flared and thrown him into argument had subsided. The exercise of

*The best-known Russian satirist of the nineteenth century (1826–1889).

his lungs made his stomach or his tumor very sore. He mustn't talk so loudly.

"Were you in the army, Vadim?"

"No, I wasn't. Why?"

"Why weren't you?"

"We were doing an officers' training course at university."

"Oh, I see . . . I was in for seven years, as a sergeant. It was called the Workers' and Peasants' Army then. The section commander made twenty roubles a month, but the platoon commander made six hundred. And at the front they gave the officers special rations: cookies and butter and tinned food. They hid somewhere where we other ranks couldn't see them, and ate the stuff there. Do you see? They did it because they were ashamed. And we had to build the officers' shelters before we built our own. I was a sergeant, I told you that, didn't I?"

Vadim frowned. He didn't know about all this, but of course there must be some reasonable explanation for it.

"Why are you telling me this?"

"Because I want to know where the bourgeois mentality comes in. Who's got the bourgeois mentality?"

Oleg had already said more than enough today, even without this remark. He felt a bitter relief that there was now very little for him to lose.

He yawned loudly again and walked back to his bed. He gave another yawn, and another.

Was it weariness or illness that gave him this urge to yawn? Or was it because these arguments, counterarguments, technical terms, bitter, angry glances suddenly seemed so much squelching in a swamp? None of this was to be compared with the disease that afflicted them or with death, which loomed before them.

He yearned for the touch of something different, something pure and unshakeable.

But where he would find that, Oleg had no idea.

This morning he'd received a letter from the Kadmins. Among other things Nikolai Ivanovich had answered his question about the origin of the expression "Soft words will break your bones." It came from a collection of didactic fifteenth-century Russian chronicles, a sort of manuscript book. In it there was a story about Kitovras. (Nikolai Ivanovich always knew about things that were old.) Kitovras lived in a remote desert. He could only walk in a straight line. King Solomon summoned him and by a trick contrived to bind him with a chain. Then they took him away to break stones. But since Kitovras could only walk in a straight line, when they led him through Jerusalem they had to tear down the houses which happened to be in his way. One of them belonged to a widow. The widow began to weep and implore Kitovras not to break down her poor, pitiful dwelling. Her tears moved him and he gave in. Kitovras began to twist and turn to left and right until—he broke a rib.

The house remained intact, but Kitovras said, "Soft words will break your bones, hard words will rouse your anger."

Oleg thought it over. We must be raging wolves compared to Kitovras and those fifteenth-century scribes. Who today would let himself break a rib for the sake of a few soft words?

The Kadmins' letter hadn't begun with this story, though. Oleg groped for it on his bedside table and found it. They had written:

Dear Oleg,
 We are in great distress.
 Beetle has been killed.
 The village council hired two hunters to roam the streets and shoot dogs. They were walking down the streets, shooting. We hid Tobik, but Beetle broke loose, went out and barked at them. He'd always been frightened even when you pointed a camera lens at him, he had a premonition. They shot him in the eye. He fell down beside an irrigation ditch, his head dangling over the edge. When we came up to him he was still twitching—such a big body, and it was twitching. It was terrifying to watch.
 You know, the house seems empty now. We feel guilty about Beetle, for not keeping him in, for not hiding him.
 We buried him in the corner near the summerhouse.

Oleg lay there imagining Beetle. But he didn't picture him shot to death with one bleeding eye, his head dangling into the irrigation ditch. He saw two paws and a great kind, affectionate head with bearlike ears hanging like the drapes over the tiny window of Oleg's hut, just as he was when he came to see him and wanted him to open the door.

So now they had killed the dog as well.

Why?

30. The Old Doctor

In his seventy-five years of life and half century of treating disease Dr. Oreshchenkov had raised himself no stone mansion, but he had bought himself, back in the twenties, a one-story wooden house with a small garden. He had lived in it ever since. The little house stood in one of the quiet streets, a wide boulevard with a spacious sidewalk which put a good fifteen meters between the street and the houses. Back in the last century, trees with thick trunks had taken root in the pavement. In the summertime their tops met to make a continuous green roof. The base of each tree was dug round, cleared and protected by a neat cast-iron grill.

However scorching the sun, the people walking along the sidewalk felt none of its severity. Cool irrigation water ran along in a tiled ditch. This arch-shaped street ran round the most solid, attractive part of town, and was itself one of the town's finest adornments. (However, the town council grumbled that these one-story houses weren't close enough together, and this made the public utility models too expensive. It was time to pull them down and build five-story apartment blocks.)

The bus did not stop near Oreshchenkov's house, so Ludmila Afanasyevna went there on foot. It was a very warm evening, dry and not yet twilight, and she could see the trees preparing themselves for the night. The first tender fuzz of leaves had appeared on their branches, denser on some, thinner on others, while there was as yet no green at all in the candle-shaped poplars. But Dontsova was looking not upward but down at her feet. This year spring brought

416

her no joy. Joy had been suspended as far as she was concerned, and no one knew what was going to happen to Ludmila Afanasyevna while all these trees were breaking into leaf, and while the leaves turned yellow and were finally shed. Even before her illness she'd been so busy the whole time that she'd never had a chance to stop, throw back her head, crinkle her eyes and look upward.

Dr. Oreshchenkov's house was guarded by a wooden-slatted door, alongside which stood an old-fashioned front door with a brass handle and heavy pyramid-shaped panels. In houses like these the old doors were usually nailed up and one entered by the new door. But here the two stone steps that led up to the old door were not overgrown with grass and moss. There was a copper plate with sloping calligraphic writing on it. "Dr. D. T. Oreshchenkov" it read, and it was polished as brightly as it had been in the old days. The electric bell was set in a little cup. It did not look unused.

Ludmila Afanasyevna pressed the button. She heard a few steps and the door was opened by Oreshchenkov himself. He had on a well-worn brown suit (it had once been a good one) and an open-necked shirt.

"Aha, Ludochka!" he said, raising the corners of his lips slightly. But with him this was the broadest of smiles. "Come in, I've been waiting, I'm very glad to see you. I'm glad, but I'm also not glad. You wouldn't come visiting an old man if it was something good."

She had telephoned him and asked permission to call. She could have told him what it was about on the telephone, but that wouldn't have been very polite. She was now guiltily trying to convince him that she would have called anyway, even if she hadn't been in trouble, while he was refusing to let her take off her coat by herself. "Please, allow me," he said. "I'm not an old ruin yet."

He hung her coat on one of the pegs of a long, dark, polished coat rack ready to receive any number of guests or visitors, and led her across the smoothly painted wooden floor. The corridor took them past the best and brightest room in the house. In it was a grand piano with a raised music stand, the pages of the score open and gay-looking. It was here that Oreshchenkov's eldest granddaughter lived. They walked across into the dining room. It had windows draped with dry grapevines and giving out onto the yard. In the room was a large and expensive radio-phonograph. After this they came to the consulting room, which had walls lined with bookshelves, a heavy old-fashioned writing desk, an old sofa and some comfortable armchairs.

"Well, Dormidont Tikhonovich," said Dontsova, gazing round the walls and narrowing her eyes. "It looks as though you've got even more books than before."

"Oh no, not really," Oreschenkov replied, shaking his head fractionally. His head seemed to have been cast out of metal. He shook it very slightly; all his gestures were slight. "Oh, it's true, I did buy a couple of dozen lately, and you know who from?" He looked at her merrily, just a shade merrily; you had to know him to notice all these nuances. "I got them from Kaznacheyev. He's retired, he's just turned sixty, you know. And on the actual day of his retirement it turned out he wasn't a radiologist at heart at all, he didn't want to spend another day of his life on medicine. He'd always wanted to be a beekeeper, and now bees are the only thing he'll take an interest in. How do these things happen, do you think? If you're really a beekeeper, how is it that you waste the best years of your life doing something else? Well now, where would you like to sit, Ludochka?" She was a grandmother with graying hair, but he spoke to her as he would to a little girl. He made up her mind for her. "Take this armchair, you'll be comfortable here."

"I won't stay long, Dormidont Tikhonovich, I only dropped in for a minute," said Dontsova, still protesting, but by now she had sunk deep into a soft armchair. Immediately she felt calm. She felt almost confident that in this room only the best possible decisions could be taken. The burden of permanent responsibility, the burden of administration, the burden of choosing what she ought to do with her life, had been lifted from her shoulders at the coat rack in the corridor. Now she was deep in the armchair her problems had finally collapsed. Calm and relaxed, she let her eyes travel slowly round the room which, of course, she know of old. It touched her to see the old marble washstand basin in the corner, not a modern washbasin but one with a bucket underneath it. It was all covered, though, and very clean.

She looked straight at Oreshchenkov, glad that he was alive, that he was there and would take all her anxiety upon himself. He was still on his feet. He stood upright without the faintest stoop, shoulders and head set as firmly as ever. He always had this look of confidence. It was as though, while he treated other people, he was absolutely sure he could never fall ill himself. A small, neatly cut silvery beard streamed from the middle of his chin. His head was not yet bald, not even completely gray, and the smooth part of his hair seemed to have changed hardly at all over the years. He had the kind of face whose features are not moved by emotion. Every line remained smooth, calm and in place, except for his habit of raising his eyebrows almost imperceptibly into archlike angles. Only his eyebrows expressed the full range of his emotions.

"If you'll forgive me, Ludochka," he said, "I'll sit at the desk. It's not that I want it to look like a formal interview, it's just that I'm used to sitting there."

It would be a miracle if he hadn't been. It was to this room that his patients had always come, frequently at first, almost every day, then more rarely. But they still came, even now. Sometimes they would sit through long, painful conversations on which their whole future depended. As the conversation twisted and turned, the green baize of the table, outlined by the margins of dark-brown oak, might engrave itself on their memories for the rest of their lives. So might the old wooden paperknife, the nickel-plated spatula which helped him see down throats, the flipover calendar, the inkpot under its copper lid, or the very strong tea he drank—the color of deep claret —which grew cold in the glass. The doctor would sit at his desk, occasionally getting up and walking toward the washstand or the bookshelves to give the patient a chance to relax from his gaze and to think things over. Dr. Oreshchenkov would never look to one side without good reason. His eyes reflected the constant attention he gave both patient and visitor; they never missed a moment for observation, never wandered toward the window or stared down at the desk or the papers on it. His eyes were the chief instrument he used to study his patients and students, to convey his decisions or wishes.

Dormidont Tikhonovich had suffered from persecution several times during his life: for revolutionary activities in 1902 when he and some other students spent a week or so in jail; again, because his late father had been a priest; then for having been a brigade medical officer in the Tsarist army during the First Imperialist War.* (It was not just because he'd been a medical officer; according to the testimony of witnesses, he had mounted a horse while his regiment was in panic retreat, rallied the regiment and dragged it back to take

---

*The term used in the Soviet Union to describe World War I.

part in the imperialist slaughter of German workers.) The most persistent and oppressive persecution had been due to his stubborn insistence on his right to maintain a private medical practice in the face of stricter and stricter prohibitions. What he did was forbidden as a source of private enterprise and enrichment, as an activity, divorced from honest labor, that served as a daily breeding ground for the bourgeoisie. There were years when he had had to take down his copper plate and turn away every patient, no matter how much they implored him or how ill they were. This was because the neighborhood was full of spies from the tax office, paid or voluntary, and because the patients themselves could never refrain from talking. As a result, the doctor was threatened with the loss of all work, even with the loss of his house.

But it was precisely this right to run a private practice that he valued most in his profession. Without the engraved plate on the door he lived as if illegally or under an assumed name. He refused to submit either his Master's or Doctor's thesis as a matter of principle, on the ground that a thesis was no indication whatever of the success of day-to-day treatment, that it made a patient uneasy having a doctor who was a professor, and that the time spent on the thesis could be much more usefully spent picking up an extra branch of medicine. During Oreshchenkov's thirty years at the local medical college, quite apart from his other jobs, he had helped provide general treatment and also worked in the pediatric, surgical, epidemic, urological and even ophthalmological clinics. It was only after all this that he became a radiologist and oncologist. He would employ a one-millimeter compression of the lips to express his opinion about "Honored Scientists." He claimed that if a man was called a "Scientist" during his lifetime, and an "Honored" one at that, it was the end of him as a doctor. The honor and glory of it all would get in the way of his treatment of his patients just as elaborate clothing hinders a man's movements. These "Honored Scientists" went about with a suite of followers, like some new Christ with his Apostles. They completely lost the right to make mistakes or not to know something, they lost the right to be allowed to think things over. The man might be self-satisfied, half-witted, behind the times, and trying to conceal the fact, and yet everyone would expect miracles from him.

Oreshchenkov wanted none of this sort of thing for himself. All he needed was a brass plate on his door and a bell which any passer-by could ring.

Luckily for him, Oreshchenkov had once happened to save a local VIP's son who was at death's door. On a different occasion he had saved another big shot, not the same one but a very important person nevertheless. There were several members of other important families as well who owed their lives to him. It had all taken place here in the one town, since he had never gone away. As a result, Dr. Oreshchenkov's reputation became established in influential circles and a certain aura of protection was built up around him. In a purely Russian city this might well not have helped, but the East was more easygoing and they were willing to overlook the fact that he had hung up his plate and was accepting patients again. After the war he no longer held a regular permanent appointment, but served as consultant in several clinics and attended meetings of scientific societies. So it was that after the age of sixty-five he began to lead the sort of unhindered life he regarded as right for a doctor.

"So, Dormidont Tikhonovich, I came to ask you to come down and give me a gastrointestinal examination. Any day that suits you, we'll arrange it."

She looked gray and her voice faltered. Oreshchenkov watched her steadily, his glance never wavering and his angular eyebrows expressing not one millimeter of surprise.

"Of course, Ludmila Afanasyevna. We shall arrange the day. However, I should like you to explain what your symptoms are, and what you think about them yourself."

"I'll tell you my symptoms right away, but as for what I think about them—well, you know, I try *not* to think about them. That is to say, I think about them all too much, and now I've begun not sleeping at nights. The best thing would be if I knew nothing! I'm serious. You decide whether I'm to go into hospital or not and I'll go, but I don't want to know the details. If I'm to have an operation I would rather not know the diagnosis, otherwise I'll be thinking the whole time during the operation, 'What on earth are they doing to me now? What are they taking out now?' Do you understand?"

Whether it was the size of the armchair or the way her shoulders sagged, somehow she no longer looked a big, strong woman. She had shrunk.

"Understand? Well, perhaps I do understand, Ludochka, but I

don't share your opinion. Anyway, why is an operation your first thought?"

"Well, we have to be ready for . . ."

"Why didn't you come here earlier, then? You of all people?"

"Well, you see, Dormidont Tikhonovich . . ." Dontsova sighed. "That's the way life is, one whirl after another. Of course I should've come earlier . . . But you mustn't think I've let it go too far." She was protesting vigorously more to herself than to anyone else. She had regained her brisk, businesslike way of talking. "Why does it have to be so unjust? Why should I, an oncologist, be struck down by an oncological disease, when I know every single one of them, when I can imagine all the attendant effects, consequences and complications?"

"There's no injustice there," he replied. His bass voice was measured and very persuasive. "On the contrary, it is justice in the highest degree. It's the truest of all tests for a doctor to suffer from the disease he specializes in."

(What's just about it? Why is it such a true test? He only talks like this because he's not ill himself.)

"Do you remember that nurse Panya Fyodorova?" he continued. "She used to say, 'Oh dear, why am I being so rude to the patients? It's time I went in as a patient again . . .'"

"I never thought I'd take it so hard," said Dontsova, cracking her interlocked fingers.

Yet in these few minutes she had felt much less anguish than during recent weeks.

"So what have you observed in the way of symptoms?"

She began to tell him in general outline, but he wanted to know the precise details.

"Dormidont Tikhonovich, the last thing I want to do is to take up the whole of your Saturday evening. If you're coming to give me an X-ray examination anyway . . ."

"Well, you know what a heretic I am, don't you? You know I worked for twenty years before X rays were invented. And, my dear, you should have seen the diagnoses I made! It's like when you have an exposure meter or a watch, you completely lose the knack of estimating exposure by eye or judging time by instinct. When you don't have them, you soon acquire the trick."

Dontsova began to explain, grouping and differentiating the symptoms and forcing herself not to omit any details which might point toward a crushing diagnosis. (But in spite of herself she was tempted to omit some of them, just to hear him say, "It's nothing serious, Ludochka, it's nothing at all.") She told him her blood composition, which wasn't at all good, and her blood count, which was too high. At first he listened to her without interrupting, then he asked her some questions. Sometimes he nodded his head to indicate that something was readily understandable and frequently encountered, but he never said "It's nothing." The thought flashed through Dontsova's mind that he must have made his diagnosis already, that she might as well ask him straight out without waiting for the X ray. But it was terrifying, the idea of asking him here and now and getting an answer, whether correct or incorrect or even tentative. She had to put it off, she had to soften the blow by a few days of waiting.

They talked as friends talk when they meet at a scientific conference. Yet having confessed to being ill was like having confessed to a crime: immediately they had lost the key to the equality they had once possessed. No, perhaps not equality; there had never been equality between her and her teacher. It was more drastic than that. By her confession she had excluded herself from the noble estate of medical men and transferred herself to the taxpaying, dependent estate of patients.

It was true that Oreshchenkov did not at once ask if he could feel where it hurt her. He continued to talk to her as to a guest. He seemed to be inviting her to join both estates at once. But she had been crushed, she had lost her former bearing.

"Quite frankly, Verochka Gangart is such a good diagnostician now that I'd normally have had complete confidence in her," said Dontsova, firing out sentences in the rapid manner her crowded working day forced her to adopt. "But it's you, Dormidont Tikhonovich, I thought I'd . . ."

"I'd be a fine one if I turned down my own students," Oreshchenkov replied, looking at her steadily. Dontsova couldn't see him very well at the moment, but for the last two years she'd noticed a certain gleam of detachment in his unswerving gaze. It had appeared after the death of his wife. "But if you have to . . . take sick leave for a bit, will Verochka take your place?"

(Take sick leave! He had chosen the mildest term of all! Did it mean, did it mean there was nothing wrong with her?)

"Yes, she will. She's a mature specialist now, she's quite capable of running the department."

Oreshchenkov nodded. He gripped his narrow beard. "Yes," he said, "she may be a mature specialist, but what about her getting married?"

Dontsova shook her head.

"My granddaughter's like that too," Oreshchenkov went on, his voice dropping to a whisper, quite unnecessarily. "She can't find anyone right for her. It's a difficult business."

The angles of his eyebrows shifted slightly to register his concern.

He made a point of insisting there should be no delay. He would examine Dontsova on Monday.

(Why was he in such a hurry? . . .)

Then came the pause when, presumably, it was time for her to say "Thank you" and take her leave. She stood up, but Oreshchenkov insisted she take a glass of tea with him.

"Really, I don't want any tea," Ludmila Afanasyevna told him.

"Well, I do. It's just time for my tea." He was making a determined effort to pull her out of the category of the criminally ill into the category of the hopelessly healthy.

"Are your young people at home?" she asked him.

The young people were the same age as Ludmila Afanasyevna.

"No, they're not. My granddaughter isn't here either. I'm on my own."

(Still, it was in his consulting room that he had received her as a doctor. It was only here that he could impress her with the true significance of what he said.)

"Are you going to play the hostess for me, then?" she said. "Because I won't let you."

"No, there's no need for that. I've got a full thermos. There are some cakes and plates for them in the cupboard; you can get them if you like."

They moved into the dining room and sat down to drink their tea at one corner of a square oak table, big enough for an elephant to dance on and much too big to be got through any of the doors. The wall clock, not in its first youth, showed that it was still quite early.

Dormidont Tikhonovich began to talk about his granddaughter, who was his favorite. She had recently finished a course at the Conservatoire. She played charmingly and she was both intelligent (a rarity among musicians) and attractive. He showed Ludmila Afanasyevna a new photo of her, but he didn't talk about her excessively, he didn't insist on Ludmila Afanasyevna giving his granddaughter her undivided attention—not that she could have given her undivided attention to anything; it had been smashed to pieces now and would never be put together again. How odd it was to be sitting here, carefree, drinking tea with someone who already knew the extent of the danger and could probably foresee how the illness would develop. Yet there he sat, and not one word would he utter. All he did was to pass the cookies.

She had someone to talk about too, not her divorced daughter—that was much too painful a subject—but her son. Having finished his eighth year in school, he had announced that he had come to the conclusion that he saw no point in further study. Neither his father nor his mother could find a single argument to sway him; arguments just bounced off his head. "You have to have an education!"—"Why should I?"—"Education and culture are the most important things in life."—"The most important thing in life is to have a good time."—"But you'll never get a decent job without education."—"I don't need one."—"You mean you're happy to be an ordinary laborer?"—"No, you won't catch me working like a donkey."—"Well, what will you live on, then?"—"I'll always find something. You only have to know what's what." He had fallen in with some very suspicious characters and Ludmila Afansyevna was worried.

The expression on Oreshchenkov's face indicated that he heard stories like this before. He said, "You know, one of the problems is that our young people have lost one of their most important preceptors—the family doctor! Girls of fourteen and boys of sixteen need to have a doctor to talk to—not in a classroom forty at a time (though they don't even have that these days), and not in the school surgery either, with people coming in at three-minute intervals. It had to be the same 'uncle' who examined their throats when they were little children and came to tea at their house. Now what if this kind, stern, impartial 'uncle' of a doctor, who never gives in to your temper or wheedlings as parents do, were suddenly to take the youngster into his surgery, lock the door and gently start an obscure sort of conversation, both embarrassing and interesting, and then, without any prompting, were to guess all his or her most important and difficult questions and answer them himself? And what if he invited them back for another talk? Surely this would not only guard them against making mistakes, against giving in to bad urges, against harming their bodies? Mightn't it also cleanse and correct their whole view of the world? Once their chief anxieties and desires are understood, they will no longer imagine they're so hopelessly incomprehensible in other respects. From that moment on, they will find the arguments their parents produce much more impressive too."

Ludmila Afanasyevna had herself prompted him to this discourse by telling the story of her son. Since her son's problems were still unsolved, she ought now to be listening to what Oreshchenkov said and thinking how best to apply it to the case. When he spoke it was in a full, pleasant voice which had not yet cracked with age. His eyes were bright and lively with meaning which added conviction to his words. But Dontsova noticed that as the minutes went by she was losing the blissful calm that had refreshed her in his consulting room armchair; there was an unpleasant dreary feeling rising in her chest, a sensation of something lost, of something being lost even as she listened to his well-thought-out speech, an urge to get up and run away, although she had no idea where to, why, or for what purpose.

"You're right," she agreed. "We *have* neglected sex education."

"We seem to think children ought to pick it all up for themselves like animals. And that's exactly how they do—like animals. We seem to think it's unnecessary to warn children against perversion, because we work from the assumption that in a healthy society they should all be normal. So they have to learn from one another, and what they learn is vague and distorted. In all other fields we regard it as essential that our children be guided. It's only in this field that guidance is considered 'shameful.' That is why you sometimes meet grown women who have never experienced the full range of emotion, for the simple reason that the man didn't know how to treat her on their first night."

"Hmm, yes," said Dontsova.

"Yes indeed!" said Oreshchenkov firmly. He had noticed the momentary troubled, confused, impatient expression on Dontsova's face. But since she wasn't eager to know the nature of her disease, why keep going over the symptoms on Saturday night when she would only have to step behind an X-ray machine on Monday? It was his job to distract her by conversation, and what better topic could there be for doctors to talk about? "Generally speaking," he remarked, "the family doctor is the most comforting figure in our lives, and now he's being pulled up by the roots. The family doctor is a figure without whom the family cannot exist in a developed society. He knows the needs of each member of the family, just as the mother knows their tastes. There's no shame in taking to him some trivial complaint you'd never take to the outpatients' clinic, which entails getting an appointment card and waiting your turn, and where there's a quota of nine patients an hour. And yet all neglected illnesses arise out of these trifling complaints. How many adult human beings are there, now, at this minute, rushing about in mute panic wishing they could find a doctor, the kind of person to whom they can pour out the fears they have deeply concealed or even found shameful? Looking for the right doctor is the sort of thing you can't always ask your friends for advice about. You can't advertise for one in a newspaper either. In fact, it's a matter as essentially intimate as a search for a husband or a wife. But nowadays it's easier to find a good wife than a doctor ready to look after you personally for as long as you want, and who understands you fully and truly."

Ludmila Afanasyevna frowned. These were abstract ideas. Meanwhile her head was whirling with more and more symptoms arranging themselves in the worst possible pattern.

"That's all very well, but how many family doctors would you need? It simply doesn't fit into the system of a free universal national health service."

"It'll fit into a universal national health service, but it won't fit into a free health service," said Oreshchenkov, rumbling on and clinging confidently to his point.

"But it's our greatest achievement, the fact that it's a free service."

"Is this in fact such a great achievement? What does 'free' mean? The doctors don't work for nothing, you know. It only means that they're paid out of the national budget and the budget is supported by patients. It isn't free treatment, it's depersonalized treatment. If a patient kept the money that pays for his treatments, he would have turned the ten roubles he has to spend at the doctor's over and over in his hands. He could go to the doctor five times over if he really needed to."

"But he wouldn't be able to afford it?"

"He would say, 'To hell with the new drapes and spare pair of shoes. What's the use of them if I'm not healthy?' Is it any better as things are now? You would be ready to pay goodness knows how much for a decent reception at the doctor's, but there's no one to go to get it. They all have their schedules and their quotas, and so it's 'Next patient, please.' As for the clinics that do charge fees, the turnover's even faster than in the others. Why do people go there? Because they want a chit or certificate or sick leave or an invalid's pension card. The doctor's job there is to catch the malingerers; patients and doctors are like enemies. Do you call that medicine? Or take actual drugs and medicine, for instance. In the twenties all medicines were free. Do you remember?"

"Is that right? Yes, I think they were. One forgets."

"You'd really forgotten, have you? They were all free of charge, but we had to give it up. Do you know why?"

"I suppose it must have been too expensive for the government," said Dontsova with an effort, closing her eyes for a short while.

"It wasn't only that, it was also that it was extremely wasteful. The patient was bound to grab all the drugs he could since they cost him nothing and the result was he threw half of them away. Of course I'm not saying all treatments should be paid for by the patient. It's the primary treatment that ought to be. After a patient has been directed to enter hospital or undergo treatment that involves complicated apparatus, then it's only fair it should be free. But even so, take any clinic: why do two surgeons do the operations while the other three just gape at them? Because they get their salaries come what may, so why worry? If they got their money from the patients, nobody would ever consult them. Then your Halmuhamedov and your Pantyokhina would be running round in circles, wouldn't they? One way or the other, Ludochka, the doctor should *depend* on the impression he makes on his patients, he should be dependent on his popularity. Nowadays he isn't."

"God help us if we had to depend on every single patient, that scandalmonger Polina Zavodchikova, for instance . . ."

"No, we should depend on her as well."

"That's sheer humiliation!"

"Is it any worse than depending on the senior doctor? Is it any less honest than drawing a government salary like some bureaucratic civil servant?"

"But some of these patients dig down into every detail—Rabinovich and Kostoglotov, for example. They wear you out asking theoretical questions. Are we supposed to answer every single one?"

Not a crease furrowed Oreshchenkov's high forehead. He had always known Ludmila Dontsova's limitations: they were not narrow, either. She was quite capable of considering and treating the trickiest cases, all on her own as well. The two hundred or so unassuming little items she had published in medical journals were examples of the most difficult type of diagnosis, which was the most difficult aspect of medicine. Why should he expect any more of her?

"That's right," he said, "you must answer every single one."

"Well, where do we find the time?" objected Dontsova indignantly, warming up to the argument. It was all very well for him, walking up and down the room in his slippers. "Have you any idea what the pace of work is like at medical institutions nowadays? It was different in your day. Just think how many patients there are for every doctor."

"With the right kind of primary system," Oreshchenkov countered, "there'd be fewer cases altogether, and no neglected ones. The primary doctor should have no more patients than his memory and personal knowledge can cover. Then he could treat each patient as a subject on his own. Treating diseases separately is work on the *feldsher** level."

"Oh dear!" sighed Dontsova wearily. As if there was any chance of their private conversation changing or reforming anything of consequence! "It's a frightening thought, treating each patient as a subject on his own."

Oreshchenkov too sensed that it was time he stopped. Verbosity was a vice he had developed in his old age.

"But the patient's organism isn't aware that our knowledge is divided into separate branches. You see, the organism isn't divided. As Voltaire said, 'Doctors prescribe medicines about which they know little for an organism about which they know less.' How can we understand the patient as a single subject? After all, the anatomist who draws the charts operates on corpses; the living aren't his province, are they? A radiologist makes a name for himself on bone fractures; the gastrointestinal tract is outside his field, isn't it? The patient gets tossed from 'specialist' to 'specialist' like a basketball.

---

*An assistant doctor, not fully qualified, who provides medical treatment in rural areas of the Soviet Union.

That's why a doctor can remain a passionate beekeeper, all through his career. If you wanted to understand the patient as a single subject, there'd be no room left in you for any other passion. That's the way it is. The doctor should be a single subject as well. The doctor ought to be an all-rounder."

"The doctor as well?" It was almost a plaintive groan. If she'd been able to keep her spirits up and a clear head no doubt she would have found this exhaustive discussion interesting. But as things were they merely broke her morale even further. She found it so hard to concentrate.

"Yes, Ludochko, and you're just such a doctor. You shouldn't undersell yourself. There's nothing new about this, you know. Before the Revolution we municipal doctors all had to do it. We were clinical specialists, not administrators. Nowadays the senior doctor of a district hospital insists on having ten specialists on his staff, otherwise he won't work."

He could see it was time to finish. Ludmila Afanasyevna's exhausted face and blinking eyes showed that the conversation designed to distract her had done her no good at all. Just then the door from the veranda opened and in came . . . it looked like a dog but it was such a big, warm, unbelievable creature that it resembled even more a man who had for some reason gone down on all fours. Ludmila Afanasyevna's first impulse was to be afraid he might bite her, but one could no more be afraid of him than of an intelligent, sad-eyed human being.

He moved across the room softly, almost as though he were deep in thought, without the faintest inkling that anyone in the house might be surprised at his entrance. He raised his luxuriant white brush of a tail, waved it once to say hello and lowered it. Apart from two black drooping ears he was ginger-white, two colors alternating in his fur in a complicated pattern. On his back he was wearing what looked like a white horse blanket, but his sides were bright ginger and his rear almost orange. True, he did come up to Ludmila Afanasyevna and sniff her knees, but he did it quite unobtrusively. He did not sit down on his orange hindquarters next to the table as one would expect a dog to do. He expressed no interest in the food on the table just above the top of his head. All he did was stand there on all fours, his great liquid-brown eyes peering up over the edge of the table in transcendental detachment.

"Good heavens, what breed's that?" Ludmila Afanasyevna was

so amazed that for the first time that evening she had completely forgotten herself and her pain.

"He's a Saint Bernard," replied Oreshchenkov, looking at the dog encouragingly "He'd be all right except that his ears are too long. Manya gets furious when she feeds him. 'Shall I tie them up with string for you?' she says. 'They keep slopping into the dish!' "

Ludmila Afanasyevna inspected the dog and was struck with admiration. There was no place for such a dog in the bustle of the streets. They'd never allow a dog like that onto public transport. If the Himalayas were the only place left where an abominable snowman could live, the only place for this dog was the garden of a one-story house.

Oreshchenkov cut a slice of cake and offered it to the dog. But he didn't throw it to him as one throws things for fun or out of pity to other sorts of dogs, to see them stand on their hind legs or jump up, teeth chattering. If this one stood on his hind legs it would not be to beg, but to put his paws on human shoulders as a sign of friendship. Oreshchenkov offered him the cake as an equal, and he took it as an equal, his teeth calmly and unhurriedly removing it from the doctor's palm as though from a plate. He might not even have been hungry; he might have taken it out of politeness.

The arrival of this tranquil, thoughtful dog somehow refreshed Ludmila Afanasyevna and cheered her up. She rose from the table thinking that maybe she wasn't in such a bad state after all, even if she did have to undergo an operation. She hadn't been paying Dormidont Tikhonovich enough attention, though.

"I've become absolutely unscrupulous," she said. "I've come here bringing you all my aches and pains and I haven't even asked how *you* are. How are you?"

He stood facing her, straightbacked, on the portly side; his eyes had not yet begun to water; his ears could hear every sound. It was impossible to believe he was twenty-five years older than she was.

"All right so far," he said, smiling. It was an amiable smile but not a very warm one. "I've decided I'm never going to be ill before I die. I'll just give up the ghost, as they say."

He saw her out, came back into the dining room and sank into a rocking chair of black bentwood and yellow wickerwork, its back worn by the years he had spent in it. He gave it a pushoff as he sat and let the movement die down. He did not rock it any more. He was sitting in the odd position peculiar to rocking chairs. It was almost off balance but free. He froze like that for a long time, completely motionless.

He had to take frequent rests nowadays. His body demanded this chance to recoup its strength and with the same urgency his inner self demanded silent contemplation free of external sounds, conversations, thoughts of work, free of everything that made him a doctor. Particularly after the death of his wife, his inner consciousness had seemed to crave a pure transparency. It was just this sort of silent immobility, without planned or even floating thoughts, which gave him a sense of purity and fulfillment.

At such moments an image of the whole meaning of existence—his own during the long past and the short future ahead, that of his late wife, of his young granddaughter and of everyone in the world —came to his mind. The image he saw did not seem to be embodied in the work or activity which occupied them, which they believed was central to their lives, and by which they were known to others. The meaning of existence was to preserve unspoiled, undisturbed and undistorted the image of eternity with which each person is born.

Like a silver moon in a calm, still pond.

31. Idols of the Market Place

An inner tension had built up inside him—not an exhausting tension but a joyful one. He could even feel the exact place where it was: in the front of his chest, under the bones. The tension was pressing lightly on him like warm air in a balloon, producing a sort of pleasant ache. It was somehow even audible too, except that its sound was not of this earth, not the sort of sound that is heard by ears.

It was a different feeling from the one which had sent him chasing after Zoya during those evenings of recent weeks. That feeling had not been in his chest; it was in a different part of his body altogether.

He carried this tension inside him, nursed it and listened to it constantly. He now remembered he'd known it as a young man as well, but then completely forgotten it. What sort of feeling was it? How lasting? Might it not be deceptive? Did it depend entirely on the women who had aroused it, or did it depend also on the mystery inherent in not yet being accustomed to the woman or intimate with her? Mightn't it completely disappear lately?

But the expression "To become intimate with" had no meaning for him now.

Or did it? This feeling in his chest was the only hope he had left, which was why he preserved it so carefully. It had become the chief fulfillment, the chief adornment of his life. He was amazed at what had happened—Vega's presence endowed the whole cancer wing with interest and color; the only thing that stopped the cancer wing withering on the stem was the fact that they were . . . friends. Still,

Oleg saw her quite seldom, and then only for a short while. A few days ago she'd given him another blood transfusion. They'd had another good talk, although not as free as the last one because this time there was a nurse present.

He had done everything he could to get out of this place, but now the moment of discharge was approaching he felt sad about leaving. In Ush-Terek he would no longer see Vega. What would happen then?

Today was Sunday, the one day on which he had no hope of seeing her. It was warm and sunny, the air was still, ready to be warmed up and overheated. Oleg went out for a walk in the hospital grounds. He breathed in the thickening warmth which seemed to knead his body. He tried to imagine how *she* would be spending this Sunday. What would she be doing?

His movements were sluggish nowadays, not as they once were. He no longer strode firmly along a straight line that he had marked out for himself, turning sharply whenever it came to an end. His steps were weak and cautious. Every now and then he stopped and sat down on a bench, and if no one else was there he stretched himself out along it.

This was how it was today. He dragged himself along, his dressing gown unbuttoned and hanging open, his back sagging. Often he would stop, throw back his head and look up at the trees. Some of them were already half in leaf, others a quarter of the way out, while the oak trees hadn't broken into foliage at all. It was all so . . . good!

Unheard and unnoticed, a mass of bright green grass had pushed its way up. In places it was so tall that it might have been taken for last year's if only it hadn't been so green.

On one of the pathways open to the sun's glare Oleg spotted Shulubin. He was sitting on a wretched-looking, backless narrow-plank bench. Perched on his thighs, he was so twisted that he seemed to be bent backward and forward at the same time, his arms stretched out and his interlocked fingers clasped between his knees. Sitting there, head bowed, on the lonely bench in the sharp lights and shadows, he looked like a monument to uncertainty.

Oleg wouldn't have minded joining Shulubin on the bench. He hadn't yet managed to have a proper talk with him, but he wanted to because the camps had taught him that people who say nothing carry something within themselves. Besides, Oleg's sympathy and interest were aroused by the way Shulubin had supported him in the argument.

However, he decided to walk past him. The camps had also taught him that each man had a sacred right to be left on his own. He recognized this right and would not violate it.

He was walking past, but slowly, raking his boots through the gravel. Stopping him would be no problem. Shulubin saw the boots and his eyes followed them up to see whose they were. He gave Oleg a look of indifference, implying no more than the recognition "We're from the same ward, aren't we?" Oleg had taken two more measured steps before Shulubin suggested to him in a half-question, "Will you sit down?"

Shulubin was wearing a pair of high-sided house shoes, not the ordinary hospital slippers that just hung on your toes. It meant he could go outside for walks and sit outside. His head was uncovered; on it a few tufts of gray hair were sticking up.

Oleg turned toward the bench and sat down, giving the impression that it was all the same to him whether he sat or walked on, but, come to think of it, sitting down would be better.

However their conversation began he knew he could ask Shulubin one crucial question, and the answer would provide the key to the whole man. But instead he simply asked, "So, it's the day after to-morrow, is it, Aleksei Filippovich?"

He didn't need an answer to know that it was the day after to-morrow. The whole ward knew that Shulubin's operation was sched-uled for then. The important thing, though, was that he had called him "Aleksei Filippovich." No one in the ward had yet addressed the silent Shulubin in this way. It was spoken as though by one old soldier to another.

Shulubin nodded. "It's my last chance to get a bit of sunshine."

"Oh no, not the last," boomed Kostoglotov.

But looking at Shulubin out of the corner of his eyes he thought it might well be the last. Shulubin ate very little, less than his appe-tite demanded. He was preserving himself so as to diminish the pain he would feel after eating. But this undermined his strength. Kosto-glotov already knew what Shulubin's disease was. "So it's decided, is it? They're diverting the excreta through one side?" he asked him.

Shulubin compressed his lips as though about to smack them, then nodded again. They were silent for a while.

"Whatever you say there's cancer and cancer," Shulubin declared, looking straight ahead of him instead of at Oleg. "There's one kind of cancer beats all the others. However miserable one is, there's always someone worse off. Mine's the sort of case you can't even discuss with other people, you can't ask their advice about it."

"Mine's the same, I think."

"No, mine's worse, whichever way you look at it. My disease is something specially humiliating, specially offensive. The consequences are terrible. If I live—and it's a very big if—simply standing or sitting near me, like you are now, for instance, will be unpleasant. Everyone will do their best to keep two steps away. Even if anyone comes closer I'll still be thinking to myself, 'You see, he can hardly stand it, he's cursing me.' It means I'll lose the company of human beings."

Kostoglotov thought about it for a while, whistling slightly, not with his lips but through his clenched teeth, absentmindedly letting air out through them. "Well, it's hard to work out which of us is worse off," he said; "it's even harder than competing over achievement or success. One's own troubles are always the worst. For instance, I might conclude that I've led an extraordinarily unlucky life, but how do I know? Maybe yours has been even harder. How can I judge from the outside?"

"Don't judge, you're sure to be wrong," Shulubin answered. At last he turned his head and peered at Oleg with his disturbingly expressive round bloodshot eyes. "The people who drown at sea or dig the soil or search for water in the desert don't have the hardest lives. The man with the hardest life is the man who walks out of his house every day and bangs his head against the top of the door because it's too low . . . As far as I can gather, you fought in the war and then you were in the labor camps, is that right?"

"Yes, and a few more things: no higher education, no officer's commission, exile in perpetuity"—Oleg listed the points thoughtfully and uncomplainingly—"Oh yes, and one more thing: cancer."

"Well, let's call it quits about the cancer. As regards the other things, young man . . ."

"Who the hell's the young man! I suppose you think I'm young just because I've got my original head on my shoulders or because I haven't had to get a new skin?"

"As regards the other things, I'll tell you something. You haven't had to do much lying, do you understand? At least you haven't had to stoop so low—you should appreciate that! You people were arrested, but we were herded into meetings to 'expose' you. They executed people like you, but they made us stand up and applaud the verdicts as they were announced. And not just applaud, they made us demand the firing squad, *demand* it! Do you remember what they used to write in the papers? 'As one man the whole Soviet nation arose in indignation on hearings of the unprecedented, heinous crimes of . . .' Do you know what 'as one man' meant for us? We were individual human beings, and then suddenly we were 'as one man'! When we applauded we had to hold our big strong hands high in the air so that those around us and those on the platform would notice. Because who doesn't want to live? Who ever came out in your defense? Who ever objected? Where are they now? I knew one—Dima Olitsky—he abstained. He wasn't opposed, good heavens no! He *abstained* on the vote to shoot the Industrial Party members.* 'Explain!' they shouted. 'Explain!' He stood up, his throat was dry as a bone. 'I believe,' he said, 'that in the twelfth year of the Revolution we should be able to find alternative methods of repression . . .' Aaah, the scoundrel! Accomplice! Enemy agent! The next morning he got a summons to the G.P.U.,** and there he stayed for the rest of his life."

Shulubin twisted his neck and turned his head from side to side in that strange motion of his. Bent both forward and backward, he sat on the bench like a large bird on a perch it wasn't accustomed to.

Kostoglotov tried not to feel flattered by what Shulubin had said. "Aleksei Filippovich," he said, "it all depends on the number you happen to draw. If the position had been reversed it would have been just the opposite: you'd have been the martyrs, we'd have been the time-servers. But there's another point: people like you who understood what was happening, who understood early enough, suffered searing agonies. But those who believed were all right. Their hands were bloodstained, but then again they weren't bloodstained because they didn't understand the situation."

The old man flashed him a sidelong scorching glance. "Who are these people, the ones who believed?" he asked.

---

*In November, 1930, several leading Soviet scientists and economists were sentenced to death as "wreckers" for working for a counterrevolutionary Industrial Party. The party was, in fact, nonexistent. Their trial was one of the signs of the coming Great Purge.

**The "Chief Political Administration," one of the many names held by the Soviet security police during its history.

"Well, I did. Right up to the war against Finland."*

"But how many are they, these people who believed, the ones who didn't understand? I know you can't expect much from a young boy, but I just cannot accept that our whole people suddenly became weak in the head. I can't believe it, I won't! In the old days the lord of the manor stood on the porch of his mansion and talked a lot of nonsense, but the peasants only smirked quietly into their beards. The lord of the manor saw them, so did the bailiffs standing at his side. And when the time came to bow down, true, they all bowed 'as one man.' But does that mean the peasants believed the lord of the manor? What sort of person do you have to be to believe?" Shulubin began to grow more and more angry. He had the kind of face which is violently changed and distorted by strong emotion, not one feature remaining calm. "What sort of man are we talking about?" he continued. "Suddenly all the professors and all the engineers turn out to be wreckers, and he believes it! The best Civil-War divisional commanders turn out to be German and Japanese spies, and he believes it! The whole of Lenin's old guard are shown up as vile renegades, and he believes it! His own friends and acquaintances are unmasked as enemies of the people, and he believes it! Millions of Russian soldiers turn out to have betrayed their country, and he believes it all! Whole nations, old men and babies, are mown down, and he believes it! Then what sort of man is he, may I ask? He's a fool. But can there really be a whole nation of fools? No, you'll have to forgive me. The people are intelligent enough, it's simply that they wanted to live. There's a law big nations have—to endure and so to survive. When each of us dies and History stands over his grave and asks 'What was he?' there'll only be one possible answer, Pushkin's:

"In our vile times
. . . Man was, whatever his element,
Either tyrant or traitor or prisoner!"

Oleg started. He didn't know the lines, but there was a penetrating accuracy about them. Poet and truth became almost physically tangible.

Shulubin wagged his great finger at him. "The poet had no room

*This war, fought during the winter of 1939–40, revealed a terrible unpreparedness within the Red Army. The result was a certain disillusionment with Stalin's rule.

in his line for 'fool,' even though he knew that there are fools in this world. No, the fact is there are only three possibilities, and since I can remember that I've never been in prison, and since I know for sure that I've never been a tyrant, then it must mean . . ." Shulubin smiled, then started to cough. "It must mean . . ."

As he coughed he rocked back and forth on his thighs.

"Do you think that sort of life was any easier than yours? My whole life I've lived in fear, but now I'd change places with you."

Like Shulubin, Kostoglotov was rocking forward and backward, slumped on the narrow bench like a crested bird on a perch.

Their slanting black shadows, legs tucked underneath them, lay starkly on the ground in front of the two men.

"No, Aleksei Filippovich, you're wrong, it's too sweeping a condemnation, it's too harsh. In my view, the traitors were those who wrote denunciations or stood up as witnesses. There are millions of them too. One can reckon on one informer for every, let's say, two or three prisoners, right? That means there *are* millions. But to write every single one off as a traitor is much too rash. Pushkin was too rash as well. A storm breaks trees, it only bends grass. Does this mean that the grass has betrayed the trees? Everyone has his own life. As you said yourself, the law of a nation is to survive."

Shulubin wrinkled up his face, so much so that his eyes disappeared and there was only a trace of his mouth left. One moment his great, round eyes were there, the next they had gone, leaving only puckered, blind skin.

He let his face relax. In his eyes were the same tobacco-brown irises, the same reddened whites, but there was now a blurred look about them as well. He said, "All right, then, let's call it a more refined form of the herd instinct, the fear of remaining alone, *outside the community*. There's nothing new about it. Francis Bacon set out his doctrine of idols back in the sixteenth century. He said people are not inclined to live by pure experience, that it's easier for them to pollute experience with prejudices. These prejudices are the idols. 'The idols of the tribe,' Bacon called them, 'the idols of the cave' . . ."

When he said "idols of the cave," the image of a real cave entered Oleg's mind, smoke-filled, with a fire in the middle, the savages roasting meat, while in the depths of the cave there stood, almost indiscernible, a bluish idol.

". . . 'The idols of the theater' . . ." Where was this particular idol to be found? In the lobby? On the curtains? No, a more appropriate place would probably be the square in front of the theater, in the center of the garden there.

"What are the idols of the theater?"

"The idols of the theater are the authoritative opinions of others which a man likes to accept as a guide when interpreting something he hasn't experienced himself."

"Oh, but this happens very often."

"But sometimes he actually has experienced it, only it's more convenient not to believe what he's seen."

"I've seen cases like that as well . . ."

"Another idol of the theater is our overwillingness to agree with the arguments of science. One can sum this up as the voluntary acceptance of other people's errors."

"That's good," said Oleg. He liked the idea very much. "Voluntary acceptance of other people's errors! That's it!"

"Finally, there are the idols of the market place."

This was the easiest of all to imagine: an alabaster idol towering over the swarming crowd in a market place.

"The idols of the market place are the errors which result from the communication and association of men with each other. They are the errors a man commits because it has become customary to use certain phrases and formulas which do violence to reason. For example, 'Enemy of the people!' 'Not one of us!' 'Traitor!' Call a man one of these and everyone will renounce him."

Shulubin emphasized each of these exclamations by throwing up first one hand, then the other. Again he looked like a bird with clipped wings making crooked, awkward attempts to fly.

The sun was hotter than it should be in springtime, and it was burning their backs. The branches of the trees had not yet become interwoven, each still standing out separately in its pristine greenery, and they gave no shade. The sky had not yet been scorched pale by the southern sun; between the white flakes of the small, passing clouds of day it kept its blueness. But Shulubin didn't see it or else he didn't believe what he saw. He raised one finger above his head and shook it as he said, "And over all idols there is the sky of fear, the sky of fear overhung with gray clouds. You know how sometimes in the evenings thick low clouds gather, black and gray clouds, even though no storm is approaching? Darkness and gloom descend before their proper time. The whole world makes you feel ill at ease, and all you want to do is to go and hide under the roof in a house made of bricks, skulk close to the fire with your family. I lived twenty-five years under a sky like that. I saved myself only because I bowed low and kept silent. I kept silent for twenty-five years—or maybe it was twenty-eight, count them up yourself. First I kept silent for my wife's sake, then for my children's sake, then for the sake of my own sinful body. But my wife died. And my body is a bag full of manure—they're going to drill a hole for it on one side. And my children have grown up so callous it's beyond comprehension. And when my daughter suddenly started writing to me—in the past two years she's sent three letters up to now, I don't mean here, I mean to my home—it turned out it was because her Party organization demanded that she *normalize* her relationship with her father, do you understand? But they made no such request of my son . . ."

Shulubin turned toward Oleg and twitched his bushy eyebrows. His whole figure was disheveled. Oleg suddenly knew who he was— he was the Mad Miller from *The Mermaid:* "Me, a miller? I'm no miller, I'm a raven!"*

"I don't remember any more, maybe I dreamed those children up, maybe they never existed . . . Listen to me, do you think a man can become like a log of wood? A log of wood doesn't mind whether it lies by itself or among other logs. The way I live, if I lose consciousness, fall down on the floor and die, no one will find me for days, not even my neighbors. But listen! Listen!" He grabbed Oleg hard by the shoulder, as if he was frightened Oleg wouldn't hear him. "I'm still on my guard, just as I was before, I keep looking behind me. I know I spoke out in the ward, but I'd never dare say anything like that in Kokand, or where I work. As for what I'm telling you now, I'm only doing it because they're wheeling in a little table to take me to my operation. Even now I'd never say it if there was a third person present. No, never! That's the way it is. This is the wall they've pushed me up against . . . I graduated from agricultural academy, then did advanced courses in historical and dialectical materialism. I was a university lecturer in several subjects, and in Moscow at that. But then the oak trees began to topple. There was the fall of Muratov at the agricultural academy. Professors were being arrested by the dozen. We were supposed to confess our 'mistakes'? I confessed them! We were supposed to renounce them? I renounced them! A certain percentage managed to

---

*A line from the classical Russian opera by Dargomyzhski.

survive, didn't they? Well, I was part of that percentage. I withdrew into the study of pure biology, I found myself a quiet haven. But then the purge started there as well, and what a purge! The professorial chairs in the biological department got a thorough sweeping with the broom. We were supposed to give up lecturing? Very well, I gave up lecturing. I withdrew even further, became an assistant. I agreed to become a little man!"

He was always so silent in the ward, and yet now he was speaking with extraordinary ease. Words poured out of him as though public speaking were his daily occupation.

"They were destroying textbooks written by great scientists, they were changing the curricula. Very well, I agreed to that too; we would use the new books for teaching! They suggested we reshape anatomy, microbiology and neuropathology to fit in with the doctrines of an ignorant agronomist and an expert in horticulture.* Bravo! I agreed! I voted in favor! 'No, that's not enough. Will you please give up your assistantship as well?' 'All right, I'm not arguing. I'll work on methods of biology teaching in schools.' But no, the sacrifice wasn't accepted, I was sacked from that job as well. 'Very well, I agree, I'll be a librarian, a librarian in remote Kokand.' I retreated a long, long way! Still, I was alive, and my children were university graduates. But then librarians receive secret instructions from the authorities: for the destruction of books by this or that author. Well, this was nothing new for us. Had I not declared a quarter of a century earlier from my chair of dialectical materialism that the relativity theory was counterrevolutionary obscurantism? So I draw up a document, my Party secretary and special-branch representative signs it, and we stuff the books into the stove. Into the stove with all your genetics, leftist aesthetics, ethics, cybernetics, arithmetic . . ."

He could still laugh, that mad raven!

". . . Why set up bonfires in the streets? Superfluous histrionics! Let's do it in some quiet corner, let's shove the books into the stove, the stove will keep us warm! The stove's what I've been pushed up against—I've been pushed back against a stove . . . And yet I man-

---

*By "ignorant agronomist" he means Trofim Lysenko, the scientist who dominated Soviet biology until the fall of Khrushchev in 1964 and destroyed many of his opponents by denouncing them to the security police. The "horti-culturist" is Ivan Michurin, a specialist in growing new varieties of fruit trees whose name was misused by Lysenko.

aged to raise a family and my daughter edits a provincial newspaper. She wrote a little lyrical poem:

"No, I don't wish to retreat!
To ask pardon I'm unable.
If we must fight, then we fight!
As for my father—under the table!"

His dressing gown hung on him like a pair of helpless wings.

"Ye-e-e-s, I agree," was all Kostoglotov could say. "Your life hasn't been any easier than mine."

"That's right," said Shulubin, catching his breath. He relaxed his posture and began to speak more calmly. "I wonder, what is the riddle of these changing periods of history? In no more than ten years a whole people loses its social drive and courageous impulse. Or rather, the impulse changes the sign from plus to minus, from bravery to cowardice. You know, I have been a Bolshevik since 1917. I remember how we charged in and dispersed the local council of Social Revolutionaries and Mensheviks in Tambov, even though all the weapons we had were a couple of fingers to put in our mouths and whistle with. I fought in the Civil War. You know, we did nothing to protect our lives, we were happy to give them for world revolution. What happened to us? How could we have given in? What was the chief thing that got us down? Fear? The idols of the market place? The idols of the theater? All right, I'm a 'little man,' but what about Nadyezhda Konstantinovna Krupskaya?* Didn't she understand, didn't she realize what was happening? Why didn't she raise her voice? How much a single statement from her would have meant to us all, even if it did cost her her life! Who knows, we might have changed, might have dug our heels in and stopped it from going any farther. Then what about Ordzhonikidze?** He was a real eagle of a man, wasn't he? They couldn't break him by locking him up in the Shlisselburg fortress or by sending him to hard labor in Siberia. What kept him from speaking up once, just once, against Stalin? But no, they preferred to die in mysterious circumstances or to commit suicide. Is that courage? Will you tell me, please?"

"How can I be the one to tell you, Aleksei Filippovich? How can I? You explain it to me."

*Lenin's widow.
**An old Bolshevik, in charge of industrialization in the Soviet Union during the thirties, who committed suicide in 1937.

Shulubin sighed and tried to change his position on the bench, but it hurt no matter how he sat.

"There's something else that interests me. Here you are, you were born after the Revolution, but they put you in prison. Well, have you lost your faith in socialism, or haven't you?"

Kostoglotov smiled vaguely.

"I don't know. Things got so tough out there, you sometimes went further than you wanted to, out of sheer fury."

Shulubin freed the hand he had been using to prop himself up with on the bench. With this hand, now enfeebled by disease, he clung to Oleg's shoulder. "Young man," he said, "don't ever make this mistake. Don't ever blame socialism for the sufferings and the cruel years you've lived through. However you think about it, history has rejected capitalism once and for all!"

"Well, out there, out there in the camps, we used to argue that there was a lot of good in private enterprise. It makes life easier, you see. You can always get everything. You know where to find things."

"You know, that's a philistine's way of reasoning. It's true that private enterprise is extremely flexible, but it's good only within very narrow limits. If private enterprise isn't held in an iron grip it gives birth to people who are no better than beasts, those stock-exchange people with greedy appetites completely beyond restraint. Capitalism was doomed ethically before it was doomed economically, a long time ago."

"Well, to be quite honest," replied Oleg, twitching his forehead, "I've found people whose greedy appetites are beyond restraint in our society as well. And I don't mean state-licensed craftsmen or repairmen. Take Yemelyan-Sashik, for example . . ."

"That's true!" said Shulubin, his hand weighing more and more heavily on Oleg's shoulder. "But is socialism to blame? We made a very quick turnaround, we thought it was enough to change the mode of production and people would immediately change with it. But did they? The hell they did! They didn't change a bit. Man is a biological type. It takes thousands of years to change him."

"Can there be socialism, then?"

"Can there indeed? It's an enigma, isn't it? They talk about 'democratic' socialism, but that's just superficial, it doesn't get to the essence of socialism. It only refers to the form in which socialism is introduced, the structure of the state that applies it. It's merely a declaration that heads will not roll, but it doesn't say a word about what this socialism will be built on. You can't build socialism on an abundance of material goods, because people sometimes behave like buffaloes, they stampede and trample the goods into the ground. Nor can you have a socialism that's always drumming on about hatred, because social life cannot be built on hatred. After a man has burned with hatred year in, year out, he can't simply announce one fine day, 'That's enough! As from today I'm finished with hatred, from now on I'm only going to love!' No, if he's used to hating he'll go on hating. He'll find someone closer to him whom he can hate. Do you know the poem by Herwegh?*

> *"Bis unsre Hand in Asche stiebt,*
> *Soll sie vom Schwert nicht lassen?"*

Oleg took up the lines:

> *"Wir haben lang genug geliebt*
> *Und wollen endlich hassen!*

"Of course I know it, we learned it at school."

"That's right, you learned it at school, that's what's so terrifying. They taught you that poem at school when they should've taught you the opposite: *To hell with your hatred; now, finally, we wish to love!* That's what socialism ought to be like."

"You mean Christian socialism, is that right?" asked Oleg, try-ing to guess.

"It's going too far to call it 'Christian.' There are political parties that called themselves Christian Socialists in societies that emerged from under Hitler and Mussolini, but I can't imagine with what kind of people they undertook to build this kind of socialism. At the end of the last century Tolstoy decided to spread practical Christianity through society, but his ideals turned out to be impossible for his contemporaries to live with, his preaching had no link with reality. I should say that for Russia in particular, with our repentances, confessions and revolts, our Dostoyevski, Tolstoy and Kropotkin, there's only one true socialism, and that's ethical socialism. That is something completely realistic."

---

* Georg Herwegh (1817–1875), a German revolutionary poet, at one time a friend of Karl Marx. The lines quoted mean: "Until our hand turns to ashes,/ Shall it let drop the sword?/We have loved long enough;/Now, finally, we wish to hate."

Kostoglotov screwed up his eyes. "But this 'ethical socialism,' how should we envisage it? What would it be like?"

"It's not very difficult to imagine," said Shulubin. His voice had become lively again and he had lost his startled expression of the "miller-raven." It was a cheerful liveliness; clearly he was eager to persuade Kostoglotov. He spoke very distinctly, like a master giving a lesson. "We have to show the world a society in which all relationships, fundamental principles and laws flow directly from ethics, and from them *alone*. Ethical demands must determine all considerations: how to bring up children, what to train them for, to what end the work of grownups should be directed, and how their leisure should be occupied. As for scientific research, it should only be conducted where it doesn't damage morality, in the first instance where it doesn't damage the researchers themselves. The same should apply to foreign policy. Whenever the question of frontiers arises, we should think not of how much richer or stronger this or that course of action will make us, or of how it will raise our prestige. We should consider one criterion only: how far is it ethical?"

"Yes, but that's hardly possible, is it—not for another two hundred years?" Kostoglotov frowned. "But wait a moment. I'm not with you on one point. Where is the material basis for your scheme? There has to be an economy, after all, doesn't there? That comes before everything else."

"Does it? That depends. For example, Vladimir Soloviëv* argues rather convincingly that an economy could and should be built on an ethical basis."

"What's that? Ethics first and economics afterwards?" Kostoglotov looked bewildered.

"Exactly! Listen, you're a Russian, but I bet you haven't read a single line of Vladimir Soloviëv, have you?"

Kostoglotov twisted his lips to indicate "No."

"Well, you've at least heard of his name?"

"Yes, when I was inside."

"But at least you've read a page or two of Kropotkin, haven't you? His *Mutual Aid Among Men*?"

Kostoglotov made the same movement with his lips.

"Yes, of course, his views are incorrect, so why read him? What

---

*A Russian religious thinker (1853–1900) whose ideas are an important influence on modern Russian non-Marxist thought.

about Mikhaylovski?* No, of course you haven't. He was refuted, wasn't he, banned and withdrawn from the libraries?"

"When could I have read them? What books could I have read?" asked Kostoglotov indignantly. "All my life I've sweated blood and still people keep asking me, 'Have you read this? Have you read that?' When I was in the army the shovel was never out of my hand. It was the same in the camps. And now I'm an exile it's exactly the same, only now it's a hoe. When have I had time to read?"

But Shulubin's face, with its round eyes and furry eyebrows, shone with the excitement of an animal about to overtake its quarry. "So you see," he said, "that's what ethical socialism is. One should never direct people toward happiness, because happiness too is an idol of the market place. One should direct them toward mutual affection. A beast gnawing at its prey can be happy too, but only human beings can feel affection for each other, and this is the highest achievement they can aspire to."

"Oh no, I want happiness, you'd better leave me with happiness," Oleg insisted vigorously. "Just give me happiness for the few months I have before I die. Otherwise to hell with the whole . . ."

". . . Happiness is a mirage." Shulubin was emphatic, straining his strength to the utmost. He had turned quite pale. "I was happy bringing up my children, but they spat on my soul. To preserve this happiness I took books which were full of truth and burned them in the stove. As for the so-called 'happiness of future generations,' it's even more of a mirage. Who knows anything about it? Who has spoken with these future generations? Who knows what idols they will worship? Ideas of what happiness is have changed too much through the ages. No one should have the effrontery to try to plan it in advance. When we have enough loaves of white bread to crush them under our heels, when we have enough milk to choke us, we still won't be in the least happy. But if we share things we don't have enough of, we can be happy today! If we care only about 'happiness' and about reproducing our species, we shall merely crowd the earth senselessly and create a terrifying society . . . You know, I don't feel very well . . . I'd better go and lie down . . ."

All this time Shulubin's face had looked exhausted. Oleg hadn't noticed how pale, how deathly it had become.

"Come on then, Aleksei Filippovich, come on, I'll take your arm."

*A leading ideologist of populist socialism (1840–1904).

It wasn't easy for Shulubin to get up from the position he was in. They dragged themselves along very slowly. All around them was the lightness of spring, but gravity weighed heavily on both men. Their bones, the flesh that remained to them, their clothes, their shoes, even the stream of sunlight pressed upon them heavily and burdened them.

They walked in silence. They were tired of talking.

Only when they had reached the porch steps and were standing in the shadow of the cancer wing did Shulubin speak again. Still leaning on Oleg, he lifted his head to look up at the poplar trees and the patch of merry sky. He said, "The only thing is, I don't want to die under the knife. I'm frightened . . . No matter how long you live or what a dog's life it's been, you still want to live . . ."

They walked into the lobby. It was hot and stuffy. Very slowly, one step after the other, they began to climb the long staircase.

Then Oleg asked him, "Tell me, did you think of this during those twenty-five years, while you were bowing low and renouncing your beliefs?"

Shulubin replied, his voice empty and flat, growing weaker and weaker, "Yes, I did. I renounced everything, and I went on thinking. I stuffed the old books into the stove and I turned things over in my mind. Why not? Haven't I earned the right to a few thoughts through my suffering, through my betrayal?"

32. The Other Side of the Coin

Dontsova had never imagined that something she knew inside and out and so thoroughly could change to the point where it became entirely new and unfamiliar. For thirty years she had been dealing with other people's illnesses, and for a good twenty she had sat in front of the X-ray screen. She had read the screen, read the film, read the distorted, imploring eyes of her patients. She had compared what she saw with books and analyses, written articles and argued with colleagues and patients. During this time what she had worked out empirically for herself had become more and more indisputable, while in her mind medical theory grew increasingly coherent. Etiology, pathogenesis, symptoms, diagnosis, the course of the disease, treatment, prevention, prognosis—all these were real enough. The doctor might have sympathy with the patient's resistance, doubts and fears; these were understandable human weaknesses, but they didn't count for anything when it came to deciding which method should be used. There was no place left for such feelings in the squares of logic.

Until now all human bodies had been built identically, as described in the standard anatomy text. The physiology of the vital processes and the physiology of sensations were uniform as well. Everything that was normal or deviated from the norm was explained in logical terms by authoritative manuals.

Then suddenly, within a few days, her own body had fallen out of this great, orderly system. It had struck the hard earth and was now like a helpless sack crammed with organs—organs which might at any moment be seized with pain and cry out.

Within a few days everything had been turned inside out. Her body was, as before, composed of parts she knew well, but the whole was unknown and frightening.

When her son had been small they used to look at pictures together. Ordinary household objects—a tea kettle, a spoon or a chair—were unrecognizable to him if drawn from an unusual angle. The course of her disease and her new place in the system of treatment had now become equally unrecognizable to her. As from today she ceased to be a rational guiding force in the treatment, she had become an unreasoning, resistant lump of matter. The moment she admitted the disease existed, she was crushed by it like a frog underfoot. Adjusting to the disease was at first unbearable. Her world had capsized, the entire arrangement of her existence was disrupted. She was not yet dead, and yet she had had to give up her husband, her son, her daughter, her grandson, and her medical work as well, even though it was her own work, medicine, that would now be rolling over her and through her like a noisy train. In a single day she had to give up everything and suffer, a pale-green shadow, not knowing for a long time whether she was to die irrevocably or return to life.

It had once occurred to her that there was a lack of color, joy, festivity in her life—it was all work and worry, work and worry. But how wonderful the old life seemed now! Parting with it was so unthinkable it made her scream.

Already the whole of this Sunday had been unlike any other Sunday: it had consisted of a preparation of her intestines for the next day's X ray.

On Monday at a quarter past nine, as agreed, Dormidont Tikhonovich, Vera Gangart and another intern turned off the lights in the X-ray room and began to adapt themselves to the dark. Ludmila Afanasyevna undressed and went behind the screen. An orderly handed her the first glass of barium meal. As she took it she spilled some. The hand that held the glass was quite used to pressing and kneading patients' stomachs, in this very room, clad in a rubber glove, but today it was shaking.

They went through the familiar routine: feeling her, pressing her, turning her round, making her raise her arms and breathe in. Then they lowered the camera, placed her on the table and photographed her from various angles. They had to allow time for the contrast mass to spread into the digestive tract. Of course the X-ray apparatus wasn't allowed to stand idle meanwhile; the intern was letting her regular patients through. Ludmila Afanasyevna even sat down and tried to help a few times, but her mind wouldn't concentrate and she wasn't much use. Again the time came for her to go behind the screen, to drink the barium, lie down and be photographed.

It was an examination like any other, only it didn't take place in the usual businesslike silence, interrupted by brief commands from the doctors. Oreshchenkov kept up a humorous banter with his young assistants, making jokes at their expense, at Ludmila Afanasyevna's and at his own. He told them how as a student he had been ejected for bad behavior from the Moscow Arts Theatre, just after it came into existence. It was a première of *The Power of Darkness.** Akim was blowing his nose and undoing his puttees so realistically that Dormidont and the friend he was with began to hiss. After that occasion, he said, every time he went to the Moscow Arts Theatre he was afraid he might be recognized and thrown out again. They were all trying to talk as much as possible to relieve the painful pauses between the moments of silent examination. Dontsova could tell, though, that Gangart's throat was dry and that it was an effort for her to speak. She knew her well enough to be sure about that.

But of course this was the way Ludmila Afanasyevna wanted it. She drank the barium meal, wiped her mouth and reaffirmed, "No, the patient shouldn't know everything. I always thought so and I still do. When the time comes for discussion, I shall leave the room."

They accepted this arrangement. Each time the doctors wanted to talk, Ludmila Afanasyevna went out and tried to find herself some work with the X-ray lab. assistants or with the case histories. There was plenty to be done, but today she found she could not complete anything. Every time they called her in she went with pounding heart, hoping that they would greet her with good news, that Verochka Gangart would throw her arms around her with relief and congratulate her. But it didn't happen; there were only more instructions, more twists and turns under the camera, more examinations.

As Ludmila Afanasyevna obeyed each new order she couldn't help pondering and trying to explain it. "I can see what you're looking for, I can tell from your methods." She let the words slip out.

As she saw it, they suspected a tumor not of the stomach or of the duodenum but of the oesophagus. This was the most difficult

---

*Tolstoy's drama about peasant life.

type of all because the operation required partial opening of the chest cavity.

"Come on, Ludochka," Oreshchenkov boomed through the darkness. "First you want an early diagnosis and now you say you don't like our methods! Would you rather wait three months or more? Then we'll tell you the result outright."

"No, thank you, I can do without a three-months' wait!"

She refused, too, to look at the large, most important X ray, which they had received from the laboratory by the end of the day. She had dropped her decisive, masculine gestures and was sitting there limply on a chair under the bright overhead lamp, waiting for Oreshchenkov's concluding words—for his words and his decision, not for his diagnosis.

"Well then, my respected colleague," Oreshchenkov drawled the words out benevolently, "the celebrities are divided in their opinion."

As he said this his eyes kept watch from under his angular eyebrows. They saw how confused she was. One might have expected the resolute, unyielding Dontsova to show more strength in such a trial. Her sudden collapse confirmed Oreshchenkov's opinion that modern man is helpless when confronted with death, that he has no weapon to meet it with.

"Which one of you is it who thinks the worst?" asked Dontsova, making an effort to smile.

(I hope it's not him!)

Oreshchenkov spread the fingers of one hand to show his doubt. "Your 'daughters' are the ones who believe the worst," he said; "see how you've brought them up? I take a more cheerful view."

The corner of his lips curved slightly—a sign of good humor and benevolence. Gangart sat there, pale as a ghost, as though *her* fate was being decided.

"I see. Thank you." Dontsova felt a little better. "So now what?"

How many times had patients sat there waiting for her to announce her decision after a similar moment of respite? Invariably the decision was based on science and statistics, a conclusion crosschecked and attained by logic. What a cask of horrors, she now thought, lies concealed in this moment of respite!

"Well, Ludochka," Oreshchenkov rumbled on soothingly, "it's an unjust world, you know. If you weren't one of us we'd be turning you straight over to the surgeons with an alternative diagnosis. They would hack away at you a bit and slice something out in the process.

You know what miserable creatures they are, they can't open up an abdomen without taking out a souvenir. They'd cut you open and then it would transpire which of us was right. But you *are* one of us after all, and we have our friends Lenochka and Seryozha in the Radiology Institute in Moscow. So what we've decided is this: we want you to go there. All right? They'll read what we write about you and give you a lookover. We'll have more opinions to go by. Also if there has to be an operation they'll do it better there. In fact, everything can be done better there, isn't that so?"

(He had said, "If there has to be an operation." Was he trying to say it mightn't be necessary? Or perhaps he meant that . . . No, it must be worse than that . . .)

"You mean," Dontsova hazarded, "that the operation's so complicated you daren't do it here?"

"Oh no, of course not," replied Oreshchenkov, frowning and raising his voice a little. "You mustn't look for a hidden meaning behind what I said. It's just that we're arranging a little . . . what's the word? . . . a little extra 'pull' for you. If you don't believe us"—he nodded toward the table—"take the film and look for yourself."

It was simple, wasn't it? All she had to do was reach out for it and make her own analysis.

"No, no," said Dontsova, drawing an imaginary line between herself and the X-ray plate. "I don't want to."

And so the decision was taken. They talked to the senior doctor, then Dontsova went to the Republic's Ministry of Health. Strangely enough, there was no delay there, they gave her a leave pass and an admission chit to the Moscow clinic. It was suddenly apparent that there was no reason whatever to keep her in the town where she had worked these past twenty years.

Dontsova had known what she was doing when she had concealed her pain from everyone. You only had to tell one person and irresistibly the avalanche was set in motion, nothing depended on you any more.

Her ties in life, which had seemed so strong and permanent, were loosening and breaking, all in a space of hours rather than days.

In the clinic and at home she was unique and irreplaceable. Now she was being replaced.

We are so attached to the earth, and yet we are incapable of holding onto it.

There was no point in further delay. On Wednesday that same

week she went on her last rounds of the wards with Gangart. She was transferring the administration of the radiology department to her.

The rounds began in the morning and continued almost until lunchtime. Dontsova relied on Verochka Gangart, who was familiar with the cases of all her inpatients. Yet as she began to walk past their beds, knowing it would be at least a month before she returned to them, if she ever did, for the first time for days she felt lucid and a little stronger. She regained her interest in work and her ability to reason. In the morning she had intended to go through her affairs and sign the last necessary papers as quickly as possible, then go home and prepare for the journey, but the plan had gone by the board. She was so used to taking personal charge of everything that even today she couldn't leave a single patient without making at least a month's mental forecast. She had to foresee the course of the disease, and what treatment and emergency measures might become necessary. She walked through the wards almost exactly as usual. It gave her the first hours of relief she had had in the whirl of the last few days.

She was getting acclimatized to her misfortune.

Yet as she passed through the wards, she felt as if she had been deprived of her rights as a doctor, as if she had been disqualified because of some unforgivable act, fortunately not yet announced to the patients. She examined, prescribed and issued instructions, gazing at each patient like a false prophet, while all the time there was a chill running down her spine. She no longer had the authority to pass verdicts of life and death upon others. In a few days' time she would be lying in a hospital bed, as helpless and as dumb as they were, neglecting her appearance, awaiting the pronouncements of her more experienced seniors, afraid of the pain, perhaps regretting that she had entered that particular clinic at all. She might even come to doubt whether they were giving her the right treatment and long to get rid of her hospital pajamas and go home in the evening, as most people do, as though this were the greatest happiness in the world.

These were the thoughts that plagued her and weakened her normal resolute cast of mind.

Meanwhile Vera Kornilyevna was taking on a joyless burden she did not want at this price. In fact she didn't want it at all.

They called her "Mother," and for Vera this was no empty word.

She had produced the worst diagnosis of the three doctors. She expected Ludmila Afanasyevna to have to undergo an exhausting operation which she might not survive, undermined as she was by chronic radiation sickness. As she walked through the wards beside her it occurred to her that this might well be the last time, that she might spend many more years walking daily between these beds recalling with a pang of sorrow the woman who had made a doctor of her.

Unobtrusively she lifted a finger and brushed aside a tear.

But today of all days Vera's prognoses had to be accurate as never before. She couldn't miss asking a single important question, because henceforward for the first time these fifty or so lives would be her responsibility entirely. There would be no one to turn to or ask advice from.

And so, upset and worried, the doctors carried on their rounds for half the day. First they went through the women's wards, then they visited the patients whose beds were out on the landing or in the corridor. Naturally enough, they lingered beside Sibgatov.

They had given so much of themselves to try to save this quiet Tartar, yet all they had won was a few months' delay. And what miserable months—a pitiful existence in an unlit, unventilated corner of the landing! His sacrum could no longer support him, he could only hold himself upright by pressing against his back with his two strong arms. His only exercise was a walk into the next-door ward where he would sit and listen to the conversation. His only air was what reached him from a distant window. His only sky was the ceiling.

But even this miserable life, consisting of nothing but medical treatments, orderlies' quarrels, hospital food and games of dominoes, even life with that gaping wound in his back was good enough for his pain-racked eyes to light up with gratitude every time the doctors came on their rounds.

It made Dontsova realize that if she rejected her own yardstick and adopted Sibgatov's, she could still count herself lucky.

Somehow Sibgatov had already heard that it was Ludmila Afanasyevna's last day.

They peered at each other in silence, defeated but staunch allies, knowing that the conqueror's lash was soon to drive them to different corners of the earth.

"You see, Sharaf," Dontsova's eyes were saying, "I did everything I could. But now I'm wounded, I'll soon be falling too."

"I know that, Mother," the Tartar's eyes answered. "The man who gave me life did no more for me than you did. But now here I am, I can do nothing to save you."

In the case of Ahmadjan they had had a brilliant success. There had been no neglect there; they had acted exactly according to theory and everything had come out precisely as it should. They totted up how much radiation he had had and Ludmila Afanasyevna announced, "We're discharging you."

They should have told him in the morning so that he could have let the nurse know and allow time for his uniform to be brought from the clothes store. Nevertheless, disdaining the use of his crutches, he dashed down the stairs to see Mita. The idea of spending one night longer than necessary here was intolerable. His friends were waiting for him that same evening in the Old Town.

Vadim also knew that Dontsova was handing over her department and going to Moscow. This was how it had happened. The previous evening a telegram had arrived from his mother, addressed to Ludmila Afanasyevna and himself, announcing that the colloidal gold was being dispatched to the clinic. Immediately, Vadim hobbled downstairs. Dontsova was at the Ministry of Health, but Vera Kornilyevna had already seen the telegram. She congratulated him and introduced him there and then to Ella Rafailovna, their radiologist, whose job it would be to start his treatment as soon as the gold reached the radiological room. At that moment Dontsova appeared and read the telegram. She looked crushed and defeated, yet she did her best to give Vadim an encouraging nod.

The previous night Vadim had been so overwhelmed with joy he'd been unable to sleep. But toward morning he began to have second thoughts. When would the gold arrive? If they had actually handed it over to Mama, it would have come that morning. Would it take three days? Or a week? This was the question Vadim asked as soon as the doctors approached him. "It'll take a few days, just a few days," Ludmila Afanasyevna told him. (But she knew what these "days" were like. She recalled a case where a Moscow institute had asked for a medical preparation to be sent to a clinic in Ryazan, but in the covering letter the girl in the office had written "Kazakh" and sent the parcel to Alma-Ata.*

*The capital of Kazakhstan, one of the republics of the Soviet Union.

Good news can do a lot for a human being. Vadim's dark eyes, so gloomy of late, now shone with hope. Those pouting lips with the indelible furrow had became smooth and young again. Vadim was clean-shaven, neat, collected and polite. He glowed as if it were his birthday and he had awakened to find all his presents around him.

How could he have become so depressed? How could he have let his will power slide so far during the last two weeks? After all, his will was his salvation, his will was everything! And now, the race was on! Only one thing mattered: the gold had to fly its three thousand kilometers faster than the secondaries could crawl their thirty centimeters. Then the gold would clear his groin and protect the rest of his body. As for the leg, well, the leg would have to be sacrificed. Or perhaps the radioactive gold might move down (since in the final resort science can never destroy faith entirely) and cure his leg as well?

After all, it was only rational and fair that he should be the one to survive! To accept death, to let the black panther tear him to pieces, was stupid, weak, unworthy. Because of his brilliant talent, he believed more and more that he would survive, that he would survive come what may. Half the night he could not sleep for the joyous excitement welling up inside him. He was picturing the lead container bringing the gold. Was it in the baggage car? Was it on its way to the airport? Or was it already in the airplane? His eyes moved up toward those three thousand kilometers of dark, nocturnal space, and with all his will he hastened the gold on its way. He would have summoned angels to his aid, if angels had existed.

But during the rounds he watched the doctors suspiciously to see what they would do. They said nothing bad, in fact they were doing their best to keep any expression out of their faces, but—they kept prodding him. True, it wasn't only his liver; they prodded him in several places, exchanging casual remarks. Vadim tried to calculate whether they were prodding his liver more than they prodded the other places.

(They had spotted how tense and attentive the patient was and so, quite unnecessarily, they ran their fingers over his spleen. But the real aim of their skillful probing was to test whether there had been any change in his liver.)

There was no chance of their slipping past Rusanov. He expected his special "officer's ration" of attention. He had lately begun to develop a liking for these doctors. It was true they weren't Honored Scientists or professors, but the fact was they had cured him. The tumor on his neck hung loosely, unswollen, small now. Even at the beginning, the danger had probably not been as great as they had made out.

"You know something, comrades," he announced to the doctors. "I'm tired of these injections. I've had more than twenty of them, isn't that enough, eh? Maybe I could finish off the treatment at home?"

In fact his blood was in a bad way, even though they had given him four transfusions. He looked sallow, exhausted and shriveled. Even the skullcap seemed too large for his head.

"I mean to say, doctor, I know I ought to thank you. It's true, I was wrong in the beginning," Rusanov announced candidly to Dontsova. He enjoyed admitting his errors. "You've cured me, and I thank you."

Dontsova nodded vaguely, not out of modesty or embarrassment, but because she didn't understand what he was talking about. They still expected an outbreak of tumors in many of his glands, and it depended on the speed of the process whether or not he would live out the year.

In fact, he and she were in the same position.

She and Gangart prodded him hard in the armpits and round the collarbones. They pressed so hard they made him twitch.

"Honestly, there's nothing there!" he assured them. It was quite clear now that they had merely been trying to frighten him with the disease. But he had kept his nerve and had come through easily. He was particularly proud of his new-found strength of character.

"So much the better, but you must be very careful and look after yourself, Comrade Rusanov," Dontsova warned him. "We'll give you another injection or two and then we'll probably discharge you. But you'll have to come every month for a checkup. And if you notice anything yourself, come along immediately."

But the delighted Rusanov knew from his own experience that these compulsory checkups were only for the record. They were merely to enable the people in charge to put a mark in the appropriate column. Off he went to telephone the good news to his family.

It was Kostoglotov's turn. He was awaiting the doctors with mixed feelings. In one sense they saved him, in another sense they had destroyed him. Oil and water was what they offered, in equal proportions, and the resulting mixture was no good either for drinking or for oiling the wheels.

When Vera Kornilyevna came to his bedside on her own she was Vega. Whatever she said to him in the course of her duties, whatever she prescribed for him, he would look at her and the sight would gladden him. Since last week, he had managed to forgive her for the part she had played in damaging his body. He had begun to take it for granted that she had some sort of right over his body, and this gave him an obscure satisfaction. Whenever she came to see him on her rounds he felt a desire to stroke her little hands or rub his muzzle against them like a dog.

But now here they were, two of them, a team of doctors bound by their own regulations, and Oleg could not rid himself of his sense of bewilderment and injury.

"How are you?" Dontsova asked, sitting down on his bed.

Vega stood behind her. She gave him the slightest of smiles. By inclination, or perhaps necessity, she had resumed her habit of smiling at him, if only very faintly, whenever she met him. But this morning her smile seemed shrouded.

"Not so good," Kostoglotov replied wearily, lifting his dangling head and letting it rest on the pillow. "I've started feeling a sort of pressure, here in my diaphragm, whenever I move clumsily. All in all, I feel I've been doctored to death. I want you to let me go."

He did not press the demand with his old fire and fury. He spoke with indifference, as though the problem were really not his and the solution too obvious to need restating.

Indeed Dontsova did not even bother to restate the case herself. Besides, she was tired. "It's your decision," she said; "you do what you want. But the treatment's not yet finished."

She started examining the irradiated part of his skin. The skin virtually screamed that it was time to stop the treatment. The surface reaction could increase even after the end of the radiation sessions.

"We aren't giving him two a day any more, are we?" Dontsova asked.

"No, it's one now," answered Gangart.

(She pronounced those simple words "It's one now" pushing her thin neck forward. She sounded as though she was making some tender declaration to touch the heart!)

Strange living threads, like a woman's long hair, linked her to this patient and entangled her with him. She was the one who felt pain when the threads were tugged and broken. He felt no pain. No one near them could see what was happening. The day Vera heard about his nighttime sessions with Zoya she had felt as though a tuft of hair had been torn out of her head. Perhaps it would have been better to end it then and there. This tearing of the threads reminded her of the law that men have no need for women of their own age, they need women who are younger. She shouldn't forget that her time was past, past.

But then he had started blatantly bumping into her in the corridors, hanging on her every word, talking to her and looking at her so wonderfully that those hairs, those threads, began to separate one by one and get entangled all over again.

What were these threads? They were inexplicable and inconvenient. He would have to leave now and go somewhere else, and there'd be a strong attraction to keep him there. He'd return only if he became very ill, when death bent him to the ground. The healthier he was, the less often he would come. Perhaps he never would.

"How much Sinestrol have we given him?" Ludmila Afanasyevna inquired.

"More than enough," answered Kostoglotov aggressively before Vera Kornilyevna could speak. He stared at them dully. "Enough for a lifetime."

At any other time Ludmila Afanasyevna wouldn't have let him get away with such a rude reply, she would have given him a good dressing down. But right now her will had sagged, she was scarcely able to complete her rounds. Outside her line of duty, to which she was now bidding farewell, she couldn't really object even to Kostoglotov. It was true, it was a barbarous treatment.

"I'll give you some advice," she said, trying to appease him, speaking softly so that the other patients could not hear. "You shouldn't hope to achieve the happiness of a family. It'll be many more years before you can have a normal family life . . ." here Vera Kornilyevna lowered her eyes, ". . . because remember, your case was terribly neglected. You came to us very late."

Kostoglotov knew things were bad, but hearing this straight out from Dontsova made him gape in amazement. "Er, yes," he mumbled. Then he found a thought to console himself with. "Well, I daresay the authorities would've taken care of that anyway."

"Carry on giving him Tezan and Pentaxil, please, Vera Kornilyevna. But you'll have to give him some time off for a rest. I'll tell you what we'll do, Kostoglotov, we'll prescribe you a three-months' supply of Sinestrol; it's in the pharmacists' now, you can buy it. Be sure and see you take it at home. If there's no one there to give you the injections, take it in tablet form."

Kostoglotov began moving his lips to remind her that in the first place he had no "home," in the second place he had no money, and in the third place he was not such a fool as to commit slow suicide.

But there was a gray-green look about her, she was exhausted. He thought better of it and said nothing.

And that was the end of the rounds.

Ahmadjan came running in. Everything was arranged, they had even gone to get his uniform. That same evening he'd be out drinking with his friends! Tomorrow he'd come back to get those papers of his. He was wildly excited, speaking more rapidly and loudly than anyone had heard him before. His movements were so strong and decisive that he might almost never have been ill, never spent those two months with them in the ward. He had thick black crew-cut hair and two coal-black eyebrows, under which his eyes burned like a drunkard's, and his back quivered as he scented the new life that lay just across the hospital threshold. He dashed off to get his things, decided not to, then ran off (he had to get special permission) to eat his lunch with the second-floor patients.

Kostoglotov was called out for an X-ray session. He waited his turn and then lay down under the apparatus, after which he went out to the porch to see why the weather was so gloomy.

The whole sky was boiling with fast-moving gray clouds. Behind them crawled a cloud deep violet in color, promising heavy rain. But it was very warm. It would only be a spring shower.

This was no time to go out for a walk, so he went back upstairs to the ward.

Walking down the corridor, he could hear the excited Ahmadjan telling a story in a loud voice. "Damn it," he was saying, "they feed them better than they feed soldiers. At least, not worse. Rations— twelve hundred grams a day. They should give them shit to eat! Work? They no work! We take them out to zone, they run off, hide and sleep whole day!"

Quietly Kostoglotov stepped into the doorway. Ahmadjan was standing with his bundle of belongings by the bed stripped of sheets and pillowcases, his white teeth shining, waving one arm, confidently treating the ward to the last story.

The ward had completely changed. Federau was gone, so was the philosopher, so was Shulubin. Strangely enough, Oleg had never heard Ahmadjan tell this particular story to the old ward's inhabitants.

"So they don't build anything?" asked Kostoglotov quietly. "So nothing gets built in the zone, is that right?"

"Yes, they build," Ahmadjan said, a bit taken aback. "But they build bad."

"Then you could have . . . helped them . . ." Kostoglotov said even more quietly, as if his strength was ebbing.

"My job—rifle; their job—shovel!" replied Ahmadjan cheerfully.

Oleg looked at his fellow patient's face. He seemed to be seeing him for the first time, and yet he had seen him for years, framed by the collar of a sheepskin coat, carrying an automatic rifle. Ahmadjan was uneducated above the checker-playing level, but he was sincere and straightforward.

If decade after decade no one can tell the true story, each person's mind goes its own separate way. One's fellow countrymen become harder to understand than Martians.

Kostoglotov didn't give up. "How do you view it?" he said. "Feeding human beings on shit? You were joking, weren't you?"

"I no joke! They no human beings! They no human beings!" Ahmadjan insisted heatedly.

He hoped to convince Kostoglotov, to make him believe like the others in the ward. He knew Oleg was an exile, but he did not know he had been in the camps.

Kostoglotov glanced out of the corner of his eye at Rusanov's bed. He couldn't understand why Rusanov wasn't speaking up for Ahmadjan. But Rusanov wasn't in the ward.

"And to think I took you for a soldier!" Kostoglotov drawled. "Whose army were you in, I'd like to know? You were in Beria's Army,* isn't that so?"

"I don't know no Beria!" said Ahmadjan. He became angry and red in the face. "Those up top—not my business. I swear oath—I serve. They force you—you serve . . ."

*Lavrenti Beria was responsible for sentencing millions of men to forced labor.

33. Happy Ending ...

That day it started to pour with rain. It poured all night as well. It was windy too, and the wind grew colder and colder. By Thursday morning it was a mixture of snow and rain, and those in the clinic who had predicted spring and unsealed the windows, Kostoglotov among them, felt as if slapped with a wet rag. On Thursday afternoon the snow ceased, the rain stopped abruptly and the wind fell. The weather became still, cold and gloomy.

But at sunset the western edge of the sky brightened, turning into a thin strip of gold.

On Friday morning Rusanov was due to be discharged. On that day the sky opened out and was cloudless. The early sun began to dry the big puddles on the asphalt and on the earthen paths which cut across the lawns.

Everyone felt that here was the true, irreversible beginning of spring. They cut through the paper pasted over the cracks, knocked off the bolts, opened the inner portion of the storm windows. Bits of dry putty fell onto the floor for the orderlies to sweep up.

Pavel Nikolayevich had never handed his things into store. He had taken no issue clothing and so was free to discharge himself any time during the day. Immediately after breakfast his family came to fetch him with the car.

And what a surprise! It was Lavrik driving the car, he'd got his driving license the day before!

School holidays had started the day before too. There were parties for Lavrik and long walks for Maika—his younger children were in a state of great excitement. Kapitolina Matveyevna arrived with just the two of them, leaving the older ones behind. Lavrik had persuaded his mother to let him take his friends for a drive afterwards. He had to show he could drive perfectly well, even without Yuri.

Like a film played backward, the whole process was being repeated in reverse, only this time it was all so cheerful! Pavel Nikolayevich walked into the nurse's little room under the stairs in his pajamas and emerged in his gray suit. Lavrik was in an excellent mood. A handsome and sporty young man in a new blue suit, he would have looked quite grown up if he hadn't started fooling around with Maika in the lobby. He kept proudly swinging the car key on a little strap round his finger.

"Have you locked all the doors?" Maika kept asking him.

"Yes, all of them."

"And you closed all the windows?"

"Go and look for yourself."

Maika ran off, tossing her dark curls, and returned right away. "Yes, it's all right," she said. Then immediately she pretended alarm again. "But did you lock the trunk?"

"Go and look for yourself."

Off she ran again.

There were still men carrying jars of yellow liquid through the lobby toward the laboratory. There were other people, faceless and exhausted, sitting there waiting for a bed to become free. One of them was lying stretched out on a bench. Pavel Nikolayevich watched it all with a certain benevolent condescension. He proved himself a man of courage, stronger than circumstances.

Lavrik carried his father's suitcase. With her beige spring coat and mane of copper-colored hair, Kapa seemed to have grown younger with happiness. She dismissed the nurse with a nod, took her husband's arm and walked along beside him. Maika hung onto her father's other arm.

"Have you seen her new hood? Just look at it, brand-new! It has stripes!"

"Pasha. Pasha!" someone called from behind. They turned round.

Chaly was emerging from the surgical corridor. He looked in good spirits and well, not in the least sallow. The only sign that he was a patient was his hospital pajamas and slippers.

Pavel Nikolayevich shook his hand cheerfully. "Look, Kapa,"

he said, "this is our hero from the hospital front line, I want to introduce you. They scooped out his stomach and all he does is smile!"

When he was introduced to Kapitolina Matveyevna, Chaly gracefully clicked his heels and inclined his head to one side, half in play and partly as a mark of respect. "Pasha, your telephone number! Give me your telephone number!" Chaly accosted him.

Pavel Nikolayevich pretended he'd got stuck in the doorway and hadn't heard the question. Chaly was a good fellow, but they moved in different circles, had different ideas, and it might not be quite respectable to get involved with him. He tried to think up a way of refusing politely.

They came out onto the porch and at once Chaly caught sight of the Moskvich.* Lavrik had turned it round ready to move off. Chaly cast his eye over it. He did not ask, "Is it yours?" All he said was, "How many on the clock?"

"Just under fifteen thousand."

"Why are the tires so worn, then?"

"Oh, you know, we just happened to get a bad set . . . It's the way these workers make them . . ."

"Shall I get you some?"

"Can you? Maxim, that's wonderful!"

"You bet your life I can! No trouble at all! Write down your phone number, go on!"—he poked a finger at Rusanov's chest. "As soon as I'm discharged I guarantee you'll have them in a week."

There was no need to think up an excuse now! Pavel Nikolayevich tore a page out of his notebook and wrote down his office and home telephone numbers.

"Good, that's settled then, I'll give you a call," said Maxim in farewell.

Maika leaped into the front seat, the parents got into the back.

"We'll be friends!" Maxim gave them this parting encouragement. The doors slammed shut.

"We'll have a good time!" shouted Maxim, holding up his fist in a Red Front salute.

"Well, what do I do now?" said Lavrik to Maika. He was giving her a test. "Turn on the ignition?"

"No, first you check that it's in neutral!" Maika's answer came out pat.

*A small, popular make of Russian automobile.

They drove off, splashing through the occasional puddle, and turned the corner of the orthopedic wing. There, in a gray dressing gown and boots, a long, lanky patient was walking down the middle of the asphalt road, enjoying an unhurried stroll.

"Blow your horn at him! Give him a good toot!" said Pavel Nikolayevich as soon as he noticed him.

Lavrik gave a short, loud burst. The lanky fellow moved briskly to one side and looked round. Lavrik stepped on the gas and drove past, missing him by about ten centimeters.

"I call him Bone-chewer. A really unpleasant, envious type, if only you knew him! You saw him, Kapa, didn't you?"

"Why does it surprise you, Pasik?" Kapa sighed. "You'll find envy wherever there's good fortune. There are always people who will envy you if you're happy."

"He's a class enemy," Rusanov grumbled. "If circumstances were different . . ."

"I ought to have run over him, then. Why did you tell me to blow the horn?" Lavrik laughed, turning round for a moment.

"Don't you dare turn round when you're driving!" cried Kapitolina Matveyevna in terror.

And it was true, the car had swerved.

"Don't you dare turn round!" repeated Maika with a ringing laugh. "But I can, can't I, Mama?"

She turned her head back to look at them, first to the left, then to the right.

"I'll stop him taking his girls for a drive, that'll teach him!" said Kapitolina Matveyevna.

As they drove out of the Medical Center, Kapa wound down the window and threw a piece of trash out on the road. "Damn the place, I hope we never come back!" she said. "Don't anyone turn round!"

Kostoglotov flung a long stream of obscenities at them as they drove away, carrying on to his heart's content.

The conclusion he had come to was that they were right, he must get himself discharged in the morning. It would be inconvenient to leave in the middle of the day when everyone was discharged. It would be impossible to get anything done outside.

They had promised him his discharge tomorrow.

It was an agreeable, sunny day and growing hotter. Everything was drying up quickly, absorbing the heat. In Ush-Terek too they were doubtless digging their gardens and cleaning the irrigation ditches.

He strolled along, letting his thoughts wander.

How lucky he was! Last winter during fierce frost he had left Ush-Terek to go away and die. Now he'd be back there at the height of spring, he'd be able to plant his little garden. It was wonderful sticking something in the ground and watching it come up.

Except that the gardens were worked in couples, and he was on his own.

He strolled on a bit further and then had an idea: he'd go and see Mita. Some time had passed since the day she had stopped him and kept telling him there were "no vacancies" in the clinic. They had known each other well for some time now.

Mita was sitting in her windowless den under the stairs. The only light came from the electric bulb. His lungs and eyes found it intolerable after walking in the grounds. Mita was stacking and restacking some record cards.

Kostoglotov stooped to squeeze through the low door. "Mita," he said, "I have a favor to ask. Something important."

Mita lifted her long, sharply chiseled face. She had always had an ill-proportioned face, ever since she was born. For forty years no man had been attracted enough to kiss it or stroke it with his hand. The tenderness which might have enlivened it had never had a chance to express itself. Mita had become a packhorse.

"What is it?" she asked him.

"They're discharging me tomorrow."

"I'm very glad for you!" Mita was a kind woman. It was only at first glance she seemed grumpy.

"But it's not about that. There are things I must do in town tomorrow, before I leave in the evening. But they always bring our clothes so late in the day from the store. Couldn't we do it this way, Mitochka—get my things out today, hide them away somewhere, and I'll come down at crack of dawn, change into them and leave?"

"Oh no, that's impossible, really," said Mita. "If Nizamutdin finds out . . ."

"He won't find out! I know it's against the rules, but you know, Mitochka, you're only alive when you're breaking rules!"

"But what if they decide not to discharge you tomorrow?"

"It's definite. Vera Kornilyevna said so."

"But I must have it from her."

"All right, I'll go and see her about it now."

"Have you heard the news?"

"No, what news?"

"They say we're all going to be released by the end of the year! They're positive!"

Her unattractive face became prettier as she talked of the rumor she had heard.

"What do you mean, 'we.'* You mean 'you'?"

"No, it'll mean us *and* you! Don't you believe it?" She waited apprehensively to hear his opinion.

Oleg scratched his head and made a face. He closed one eye completely. "It's possible," he said. "I mean, it isn't out of the question. Only I've lived through so many of these false alarms, my ears can't take any more."

"But this time it's definite. They say it's absolutely definite!" She wanted so much to believe it, it was impossible to say no to her.

Oleg put his top lip over his lower and thought for a moment. Of course there was something in the wind. The Supreme Court had been sacked. But it was all happening too slowly, nothing more had happened for a month. He had become skeptical again. History moves too slowly for our lives or our hearts.

"Well, God willing," he said, mostly for her benefit. "What will you do, then? Will you leave here?"

"I don't know," Mita declared faintly, almost voicelessly, her big fingernails spread over the well-thumbed cards. She had had enough of them.

"You're from around Salsk, aren't you?"

"Yes."

"Well, do you think things are any better there?"

"It means *freedom*," she whispered.

Or, more likely, she still counted on finding a husband in her own part of the world.

Oleg set off to find Vera Kornilyevna. At first he did not succeed. They told him she was in the X-ray room, then that she was with the surgeons. In the end he spotted her walking down the corridor with Lev Leonidovich. He hurried to catch them up.

*Mita is also an exile, because she is of German origin, though in a different category from Kostoglotov, exiled for a personal reason.

"Vera Kornilyevna, have you a spare moment?"

It was nice being able to address her, and her alone. He noticed that the voice he used for her wasn't the voice he used for others.

She turned round. One could tell what a busy day it had been from the posture of her hands, the preoccupied look on her face and the droop of her body.

But she was always attentive toward everyone. She stopped. "Yes?"

She didn't add "Kostoglotov." She only called him this when speaking in the third person, to the doctors or the nurses, never when addressing him directly.

"Vera Kornilyevna, I've something very important to ask you. Can you tell Mita I'm definitely being discharged tomorrow?"

"Why?"

"It's essential. You see, I have to leave town tomorrow evening and that means . . ."

"All right. Lev, you go on ahead. I'll be with you in a minute."

Lev Leonidovich went on, his body stooping and rocking from side to side, his hands jammed into the front pockets of his white coat, his back straining at the tapes. "Come into my office," Vera Kornilyevna said to Oleg.

She went ahead of him. She was light, light in her joints.

She led him into the X-ray room, the one where he had had that long argument with Dontsova. She sat down at the same badly planed table and mentioned him to sit too. But he remained standing.

There was no one else in the room. The sunlight flowed in, a slanting golden column of dancing specks, reflecting off the nickel-plated parts of the apparatus. It was so cheerful and bright you felt like shutting your eyes.

"But what if I don't have time to discharge you tomorrow? The epicrisis has to be written, you know."

He couldn't tell whether she was being official or just teasing him. "Epi-what, did you say?"

"The epicrisis—that's a resumé of the whole treatment. You can't be discharged until the epicrisis is ready."

What a mass of work there was piled on those frail shoulders! Everywhere there were people calling her and waiting for her. Once again he had disturbed her; she still had the epicrisis to write.

But there she sat, literally glowing. It wasn't just her, it wasn't just the kind, tender look she gave him, there was a sort of bright reflected light surrounding her and radiating from her figure. "What about you? Do you want to leave immediately then?"

"It's not what I want to do that counts, I'd be happy to stay on. But there's nowhere for me to spend the night. I don't want to spend another at the railway station."

"Yes, of course, they won't let you into the hotel," she said, nodding her head. She frowned. "What a nuisance, that old orderly who puts patients up at her apartment is absent from work at the moment on sick leave. What can we do about it?" She drew the words out, running her upper lip along her lower teeth and doodling what looked like two overlapping little rings on the paper in front of her. "You know . . . there's no reason at all why you shouldn't stay . . . at my place."

What was that? Had she really said that? He couldn't have heard properly. Should he ask her to repeat it?

Her cheeks were noticeably blushing, and she was avoiding his eyes just as she had before. She had said it quite simply, as though it were an everyday occurrence for a patient to spend the night at his doctor's apartment. "Tomorrow's rather an unusual day for me," she went on. "I'll only be two hours in the clinic, during the morning, and the rest of the day I'll be at home. Then after four o'clock I'm going out again . . . I can quite easily spend the night with friends . . ."

Then she did look at him. Her cheeks were aglow, but her eyes were bright and innocent. Had he understood her properly? Was he worthy of what was being offered?

Oleg simply couldn't understand. How could one possibly understand a woman when she said something like that? . . . It might be earth-shaking or it might be much less than that. But he didn't think, there was no time for thinking.

There was an aura of nobility about her as she waited.

"Thank you very much," he blurted out. "Of course . . . that's wonderful." He had completely forgotten what he'd been told a hundred years ago as a child about how to behave properly and answer politely. "That's splendid. But I don't want to deprive you of your . . . I wouldn't want to do that."

"Don't let that worry you," said Vega with a reassuring smile. "And if you have to stay two or three days, we'll think of some way of arranging it. Are you sorry to be leaving town?"

"Yes, of course I'm sorry . . . But there's one other thing. If I stay, you'll have to date my discharge certificate the day after tomorrow, not tomorrow, otherwise the *komendatura* will want to know why I didn't leave. They might put me back in prison."

"That's all right, we'll do shady things all round. So I'm to tell Mita today to discharge you tomorrow and to write the day after tomorrow on your certificate? What a complicated man you are!"

But her eyes weren't in the least troubled by the complications, they were laughing.

"It's not me that's complicated, Vera Kornilyevna, it's the system! *And* I have to have two certificates, not one like everyone else."

"Why?"

"The *komendatura* will take one to justify my travel authorization. I'll keep the other one." (He'd do his best not to give the *komendatura* their copy. He'd shout and swear it was the only one he had. A spare copy would do him no harm. After all, he had suffered from so long at the hospital for the sake of the certificate, hadn't he?)

"Then you'll need a third copy for the railway station," she said. She jotted a few words down on a slip of paper. "This is my address. Shall I tell you how to get there?"

"I'll find it, Vera Kornilyevna." (Was she being serious? Was she truly inviting him?)

"And . . ." —she took a few rectangular slips of paper and attached them to the one with her address—" . . . here are the prescriptions Ludmila Afanasyevna mentioned. There are three copies, so you can draw the supply little by little."

The prescriptions. *Those* prescriptions!

She mentioned them as if they were some small insignificant supplement to her address. In two months of treatment she had contrived not to mention the subject once.

That's what we call tact.

She stood up, she was on her way to the door.

She had to get to work, Lyova was waiting for her . . .

And suddenly in the scattered fan of light which filled the whole room he saw her as if for the first time. She was radiant and slender at the waist. She was so understanding, she was a friend, he needed her so badly. It was as if he had never seen her before.

It made him feel cheerful. He wanted to be frank. He asked, "Vera Kornilyevna, why were you angry with me for such a long time?"

She looked at him from the light that surrounded her. She smiled, somehow a wise sort of smile. "You mean you can't think of anything you've done wrong?"

"No."

"Nothing at all?"

"Not a thing."

"Try to remember."

"I can't think of anything. At least give me a hint."

"I have to go . . ."

She had the key in her hand. She'd have to lock the door and leave. It had been so wonderful being with her! If only it could have gone on all day.

She looked very small as she walked down the corridor. He stood there and watched her go.

Immediately he went out for another stroll. Spring had broken through and he couldn't get enough fresh air. He walked about aimlessly for two hours, breathing his fill of air and warmth. Already he felt sorry at the thought of leaving this garden where he'd been a prisoner. It was sad he wouldn't be here when the Japanese acacias bloomed and the first, late leaves of the oak unfolded.

For some reason he felt no nausea today, no weakness either. He would have liked to do some digging in his garden. There was something he wanted, something, but he couldn't think what. He noticed his thumb moving of its own accord toward his index finger, craving for a cigarette. But no, however often he dreamed of smoking, he had given it up and that was that.

He'd had enough of walking, so he went to see Mita. Mita was a splendid woman. His knapsack had already been removed from the store and hidden in the bathroom. The key to the bathroom would be held by the old orderly who came on duty in the evening. Before the working day ended, he would have to go to the outpatients' clinic to get all his certificates.

His discharge from hospital seemed to be gradually becoming irreversible.

He climbed the staircase. It wasn't the last time, but nearly the last time he would do so.

At the top of the stairs he met Zoya.

"Well, how are things, Oleg?" Zoya asked unaffectedly.

Her manner was amazingly unforced, quite natural in fact. It was as though nothing had ever happened between them—no tender nicknames, no dance from *The Tramp,* no oxygen balloon.

And she could be right. Why should they keep coming back to it the whole time? Why remember? Why sulk?

One night when she'd been on duty he'd gone to sleep instead of going out and hanging around her. Another evening she'd come up to his bed with the syringe, as if it was the most normal thing in the world. He'd turned round and let her inject him. Everything that had grown up between them, taut and strained like the oxygen balloon they had once carried together, had suddenly subsided little by little, until there was nothing. All that remained was her friendly greeting, "Well, how are things, Oleg?"

He leaned forward over a chair, bracing himself with his long arms. His black forelock hung down. "White corpuscle count—two thousand eight hundred," he said, "no X rays since yesterday. Tomorrow I'm being discharged."

"Tomorrow?" she said, fluttering her golden eyelashes. "Well, good luck! Congratulations!"

"What is there for you to congratulate me on?"

"You ungrateful thing!" said Zoya, shaking her head. "Try and remember your first day here, out on the landing. You didn't think you were going to last more than a week, did you?"

That was also true.

No, really, she was a fine girl, Zoya—cheerful, hardworking, sincere. She said what she thought. Once they had got rid of the awkwardness between them, this feeling that they had deceived each other, and begun again with a clean slate, was there any reason why they shouldn't be friends?

"There, you see." He smiled.

"There, you see." She smiled.

She didn't remind him about the *moulinet.*

So there it was. Four times a week she would come to the clinic on duty. She would stick her nose in her textbooks, occasionally she'd do embroidery. Back in town, she'd go to dances, and afterwards stand in the shadows with some man . . .

One couldn't be angry with her for being twenty-two years old and healthy, healthy to the last cell, to the last drop of blood.

"Good luck!" he said, without resentment.

He'd already moved on when suddenly in her old simple and easy manner she called after him, "Hey, Oleg!"

He turned round.

"Do you have anywhere to spend the night? Write down my address." (What? Her too?)

Oleg looked at her in bafflement. It was beyond his powers of comprehension.

"It's very convenient, just by the trolley-car stop. It's just the two of us, Grandma and me, but we have two rooms."

"Thank you very much," he said in confusion, taking the little piece of paper. "But I hardly think . . . Well, we'll see how things go . . ."

"Who knows?" She smiled.

It's easier to find your way in the *taiga* forest than to know where you are with women. He went on a couple of steps and saw Sibgatov lying miserably on his back on the hard plank bed in his musty corner of the landing. Even today's raging sun only reached him as a feeble reflection of a reflection. He was gazing upward, up at the ceiling. He'd grown thin these last two months.

Kostoglotov sat down beside him on the edge of the plank bed.

"Sharaf, there are rumors going about that all exiles are to be released. Both groups—'specials' and 'administratives.' "

Sharaf didn't turn his head toward Oleg, only his eyes. It was as if he had taken in nothing except the sound of Oleg's voice.

"Did you hear? It means both you and me. They're absolutely definite."

Sibgatov didn't seem to understand.

"Don't you believe it? Will you be going home?"

Sibgatov turned his eyes back to the ceiling. His lips parted indifferently. "It's not much good to me; it ought to have happened earlier."

Oleg placed a hand on one of his. The hand he took was laid across Sibgatov's chest as though he were a corpse.

Nellya rushed briskly past them into the ward. "Any dishes left in here?" she shouted. Then she turned round to him. "Hey, you, hairy-top, why aren't you eating your lunch? Hurry up, I have to collect the dishes. Why should I wait for you?"

Incredible! Kostoglotov had missed his lunch and hadn't even noticed. His head must be in a whirl. There was only one thing he didn't understand. "Why, what have the dishes got to do with you?" he asked Nellya.

"What do you mean? I'm food orderly now, I hand round the

meals!" Nellya announced proudly. "Look at my coat, isn't it clean?"

Oleg got up and went off to eat his last hospital lunch. Insidiously, invisibly, soundlessly, the X ray had burned out his appetite. But the prisoner's code made it impossible for him to leave anything on the plate.

"Come on, come on, hurry up!" Nellya commanded.

It wasn't just her new coat, she had her hair curled differently as well.

"Well, look at you now!" said Kostoglotov in amazement.

"Well, I mean to say, what a fool I was crawling round the floor for three-fifty a month. What a job! No free grub either . . . !"

34. . . . and One a Bit Less Happy

It is time, it is time for me too to depart. Like an old man who has outlived his contemporaries and feels a sad inner emptiness, Kostoglotov felt that evening that the ward was no longer his home, even though the beds were all occupied and there were the same old patients asking the same old questions again and again as though they had never been asked before: Is it or isn't it cancer? Will they cure me or won't they? What other remedies are there that might help?

Vadim was the last to leave, toward the end of the day. The gold had arrived and he was being transferred to the radiological ward.

Oleg was left on his own to survey the beds, to remember who had originally occupied them and how many of those had died. It turned out that not very many had.

It was so stuffy in the ward and warm outside that Kostoglotov went to bed leaving the window half-open. The spring air flowed across the window sill and over him. The fresh, lively sounds of spring could be heard from the little courtyards of the tiny old houses, huddled right up against the wall on the other side of the Medical Center. He couldn't see what was happening in these little courtyards beyond the brick wall, but the sounds were now clearly audible—doors slamming, children yelling, drunks roaring, records screeching, and then, after lights out, the deep, powerful voice of a woman singing the lines of a song, in anguish or in pleasure, one couldn't tell which:

> So this yo-u-ung and handsome mi-i-ner
> She esco-o-orted to her ho-o-ome . . .

476

All the songs were about the same thing. So were the thoughts everyone was thinking. But Oleg needed to divert his mind.

On this night of all nights, when he had to get up early and save his energy, Oleg couldn't get to sleep. A succession of thoughts, idle as well as important, kept running through his head: the unresolved argument with Rusanov; the things Shulubin hadn't got round to saying to him; the points he should have made during his talks with Vadim; the head of murdered Beetle; the faces of the Kadmins, animated in the yellow light of the paraffin lamp, as he described to them his million impressions of the town and they told him the news of the *aul* and what concerts they had heard on the radio while he'd been away. The three of them would feel as if that little low hut contained the whole universe. He lay there imagining the supercilious, absentminded look on the face of eighteen-year-old Inna Ström, whom Oleg would not now dare to approach, and those two invitations to spend the night from two different women. It was something new for him to rack his brains about—how was he supposed to interpret them?

The icy world which had shaped Oleg's soul had no room for "unpremeditated kindness." He had simply forgotten that such a thing existed. Simple kindness seemed the most unlikely explanation of their having invited him.

What did they have in mind? And what was he expected to do? He had no idea.

He turned from side to side, then back again, while his fingers kept rolling an invisible cigarette.

Oleg got up and dragged himself out for a walk.

The landing was in half-darkness. Just by the door Sibgatov was sitting, as usual, in the tub, struggling to save his sacrum. He was patient and hopeful no longer. Hopelessness had cast its spell over him.

Sitting at the duty nurse's table with her back to Sibgatov was a short, narrow-shouldered woman in a white coat bending under the lamp. She wasn't one of the nurses, though. Tonight was Turgun's night for duty and presumably he was already asleep in the conference room. It was the remarkably well-mannered orderly who wore glasses, Elizaveta Anatolyevna. She had managed to complete all her jobs for the evening and was sitting there, reading.

During the two months Oleg had spent in hospital, this painstaking orderly with the quick, intelligent expression had often crawled under their beds to wash the floor while they lay above her. She would always move Kostoglotov's boots, which he kept secretly in the dark depths under his bed, carefully to one side, and never cursed him for it. She wiped the wall panels, cleaned the spittoons and polished them until they shone. She distributed jars with labels to the patients. Anything heavy, inconvenient or dirty that the nurses were not supposed to touch she had to carry to and fro.

The more uncomplainingly she worked, the less notice they took of her in the wing. As the two-thousand-year-old saying goes, you can have eyes and still not see.

But a hard life improves the vision. There were some in the wing who immediately recognized each other for what they were. Although in no way distinguished by uniform, shoulder insignia or armband, they could still recognize each other easily. It was as if they bore some luminous sign on their foreheads, or stigmata on their feet and palms. (In fact there were plenty of clues: a word dropped here and there; the way it was spoken; a tightening of the lips between words; a smile while others were serious or while others laughed.) The Uzbeks and the Kara-Kalpaks had no difficulty in recognizing their own people in the clinic, nor did those who had once lived in the shadow of barbed wire.

Kostoglotov and Elizaveta Anatolyevna had long ago recognized each other, and since then they had always greeted one another understandingly. There had never been a chance for them to have a talk, though.

Oleg walked up to her table, slapping with his slippers so as not to alarm her. "Good evening, Elizaveta Anatolyevna."

She was reading without glasses. She turned her head in some indefinably different way from usual, ready to answer the call of duty.

"Good evening." She smiled with all the dignity of a lady of a certain age receiving a welcome guest under her own roof.

Agreeably and without hurry they regarded one another. The look meant that they were always ready to give one another help.

But there was no help either of them could give.

Oleg inclined his shaggy head to get a better view of the book. "Another French one, is it?" he asked. "What is it?"

"Claude Farrère," replied the strange orderly, pronouncing the "l" softly.

"Where do you get all these French books?"

"There's a foreign-language library in town. And there's an old woman I borrow them from too."

Kostoglotov peered sideways at the book as a dog might examine a stuffed bird. "Why always French?" he asked.

The crow's-feet round her eyes and lips revealed her age, her intelligence, and the extent of her suffering.

"They don't hurt you so much," she answered. Her voice was never loud; she enunciated each word softly.

"Why fear pain?" Oleg objected. It was hard for him to stand for any length of time. She noticed this and pulled up a chair.

"How many years is it? For the last two hundred years, I suppose, we Russians have been oohing and ahing, 'Paris! Paris!' It's enough to burst your eardrums," Kostoglotov growled. "We're supposed to know every street, every little café by heart. Just to be spiteful, I don't want to go to Paris at all!"

"Not at all?" She laughed, and he laughed with her. "You'd rather be an exile?"

They laughed identically: a laugh which began but then seemed to trail off.

"It's true, though," grumbled Kostoglotov. "They're always twittering, blowing themselves up into rages and going in for trivial repartee. It makes you want to take them down a peg or two and ask them, 'Hey, friends, how would you make out at hard labor? How would you do on black bread without hot food, eh?' "

"That's not fair. I mean, they managed to avoid black bread, and deservedly so."

"Well, maybe. Maybe I'm just jealous. But I still want to put them down."

Kostoglotov was shifting from side to side as he sat there. It was as though his body was too tall and a burden to him. Making no attempt to bridge the gap, he suddenly asked her easily and directly, "Was it . . . because of your husband, or you yourself?"

She answered at once and as straightforwardly as if he was asking her about tonight's duty, "It was the whole family. As for who was punished because of whom—I haven't any idea."

"Are you all together now?"

"No, my daughter died in exile. After the war we moved here and they arrested my husband for the second time. They took him to the camps."

"And now you're alone?"

"I have a little boy. He's eight."

Oleg looked at her face. It hadn't trembled with pity.

Why should it? It was a purely businesslike conversation. "The second time was in '49, was it?" he asked her.

"Yes."

"As one would expect. Which camp?"

"Taishet station."

Again Oleg nodded. "I know," he said, "that'll be Camp Lake. He might be right up by the Lena River, but the postal address is Taishet."

"You've been there, have you?" she asked, unable to restrain her hope.

"No, I've only heard about it. Everyone bumps into everyone else."

"His name's Duzarsky. You didn't meet him? You never met him anywhere?"

She was still hoping. He must have met him somewhere . . . he'd tell her about him . . . Duzarsky . . . Oleg smacked his lips. No, he hadn't met him. You can't meet everyone.

"He's allowed two letters a year!" she complained.

Oleg nodded. It was the old story.

"Last year there was only one, in May. I've had nothing since then . . ."

Look, she was hanging on a single thread, a single thread of hope. She was only a woman, after all.

"It doesn't mean anything," Kostoglotov explained confidently. "Everyone's allowed two letters a year, and you know how many thousands that makes? The censors are lazy. At Spassk camp when a prisoner was checking the stoves during the summer he found a couple of hundred unposted letters in the censors' office stove. They'd forgotten to burn them."

He'd done his best to explain it gently. It had been going on for so long she ought to be accustomed to it by now. But she was still looking at him in that wild, terrified way.

Surely people should eventually cease to be surprised at anything? And yet they continue to be.

"You mean your son was born in exile?"

She nodded.

"And now you have to bring him up on your own salary? And no one will give you a skilled job? They hold your record against you everywhere? You live in some hovel?"

They were framed as questions, but there was no element of curiosity in his questions. It was all so clear, clear enough to make you sick. Elizaveta Anatolyevna's small hands, worn out from the everlasting washing, the floorcloths and the boiling water, and covered in bruises and cuts, were now resting on the little book, soft-covered and printed in small, graceful format on foreign paper, the edges a bit ragged from being cut many years ago.

"If only living in a hovel was my only problem!" she said. "The trouble is, my boy's growing up, he's clever and he asks about everything. How ought I to bring him up? Should I burden him with the whole truth? The truth's enough to sink a grown man, isn't it? It's enough to break your ribs. Or should I hide the truth and bring him to terms with life? Is that the right way? What would his father say? And would I succeed? After all, the boy's got eyes of his own, he can see."

"Burden him with the truth!" declared Oleg confidently, pressing his palm down on the glass tabletop. He spoke as though he had brought children up himself, as though he had never made a single slip.

She propped up her head, cupping her temples in her hands, which were tucked under her headscarf. She looked at Oleg in alarm. He had touched a nerve.

"It's so difficult, bringing up a son without his father," she said. "A boy constantly needs something to lean on, an indication where to go, doesn't he? And where is he to get that from? I'm always doing the wrong thing, doing this or doing that when I shouldn't . . ."

Oleg was silent. It wasn't the first time he had heard this point of view, but he couldn't understand it.

"That's why I read old French novels, but only during night duty, by the way. I have no idea whether these Frenchmen were keeping silent about more important things, or whether the same kind of cruel life as ours was going on outside the world of their books. I have no knowledge of the world and so I read in peace."

"Like a drug?"

"A blessing," she said, turning her head. It was like a nun's in that white headscarf. "I know of no books closer to our life that wouldn't irritate me. Some of them take the readers for fools. Others tell no lies; our writers take great pride in that achievement. They conduct deep research into what country lane a great poet traveled along in the year 1800 and something, or what lady he was referring to on page so-and-so. It may not have been an easy task working all that out, but it was safe, oh yes, it was safe. They chose the easy path! But they ignored those who are alive and suffering today."

In her youth she might have been called "Lily." There could have been no hint then of the spectacle marks on the bridge of her nose. As a girl she had made eyes, laughed and giggled. There had been lilac and lace in her life, and the poetry of the Symbolists. And no Gypsy had ever foretold that she would end her life as a cleaning woman somewhere out in Asia.

"These literary tragedies are just laughable compared with the ones we live through," Elizaveta Anatolyevna insisted. "Aïda was allowed to join her loved one in the tomb and to die with him. But we aren't even allowed to know what's happening to them. Even if I went to Camp Lake . . ."

"Don't go. It won't do any good."

"Children write essays in school about the unhappy, tragic, doomed, and I-don't-know-what-else life of Anna Karenina. But was Anna really unhappy? She chose passion and she paid for her passion—that's happiness! She was a free, proud human being. But what if during peacetime a lot of greatcoats and peaked caps burst into the house where you were born and live, and order the whole family to leave house and town in twenty-four hours, with only what your feeble hands can carry?"

Her eyes had shed all the tears that could be shed. No drop would ever flow from them now. Yet perhaps they could still flare up with a tense, dry flame—her last curse upon the world.

"You open your doors, call in the passers-by from the streets and ask them to buy things from you, or, rather, to throw you a few pennies to buy bread with. Then those sharp black marketeers arrive who knew everything except that the thunder and lightning are going to strike them down too one day. A ribbon in her hair, your daughter sits down at the piano for the last time to play Mozart. But she bursts into tears and runs away. So why should I read *Anna Karenina* again? Maybe it's enough—what I've experienced. Where can people read about us? *Us*? Only in a hundred years' time?"

She was almost shouting now, but her years of training by fear didn't desert her. It wasn't a real shout, she didn't cry out. The only one who had heard her was Kostoglotov.

And perhaps Sibgatov in his tub.

There weren't many points of reference in her story, but there were enough. "Leningrad?" Oleg asked her. "Nineteen thirty-five?"

"You recognize it?"

"What street did you live in?"

"Furshtadskaya," Elizaveta Anatolyevna replied, lingering plaintively but with a hint of pleasure over the word. "What about you?"

"Zakharyevskaya. Just next door!"

"Just next door . . . How old were you then?"

"Fourteen."

"Do you remember anything about it?"

"Very little."

"You don't remember? It was like an earthquake. Apartment doors were flung wide open, people went in and took things and left. No one asked any questions. They deported a quarter of the city. Don't you remember?"

"Yes, I do. But the shameful thing is, at the time it didn't seem the most important thing in the world. They explained it to us at school—why it was necessary, why it was expedient."

Like a tightly reined mare, the aging orderly shook her head up and down. "Everyone talks about the Siege," she said. "They write poems about it. That's allowed. But they behave as if nothing ever happened before the Siege."

Yes, he remembered. Sibgatov had been there as usual in his tub, Zoya was sitting there in that chair and Oleg in this one. It had been at this table, by the light of this lamp, that they had talked about the Siege. What else were they supposed to talk about? The time before the Siege?

Kostoglotov sat there, propping his head sideways on one elbow and looking despondently at Elizaveta Anatolyevna. "It's shameful," he said quietly. "Why are we so calm? Why did we just wait quietly until it struck down our friends, our relatives and ourselves? Why is human nature like that?"

He suddenly felt ashamed of having exaggerated his own misery and blown it up out of all proportion. What does a woman need of a man? What is her minimum need? He had behaved as though this problem was all that life hinged on, as though apart from this his country had endured no torment, enjoyed no happiness. He was ashamed, but at the same time more at peace. Another person's misery had rolled over him and washed his own away.

"A few years before that," Elizaveta Anatolyevna recalled, "they deported all members of the nobility from Leningrad. There were a hundred thousand of them, I suppose. But did we pay much attention? What kind of wretched little ex-nobles were they, the ones who remained? Old people and children, the helpless ones. We knew this, we looked on and did nothing. You see, we weren't the victims."

"You bought their pianos?"

"We may even have bought their pianos. Yes, of course we bought them."

Oleg could now see that this woman was not yet even fifty. Yet anyone walking past her would have said she was an old woman. A lock of smooth old-woman's hair, quite uncurlable, hung down from under her white headscarf.

"But when you were deported, what was it for? What was the charge?"

"Why bother to think up a charge? 'Socially harmful' or 'Socially dangerous element'—'S.D.E.' they called it. Special decrees, just marked by letters of the alphabet. So it was quite easy, no trial necessary."

"And what about your husband? Who was he?"

"Nobody. He played the flute in the Philharmonic. He liked to talk when he'd had a few drinks."

Oleg remembered his late mother, just as prematurely aged, just as meticulous and ladylike, just as helpless without her husband.

If they'd lived in the same town he might have been able to help this woman to put her son on the right track.

But they were like insects pinned inside separate compartments, each in its own set place.

"One family we knew . . ." she went on. Poor soul, she had been silenced for so long and now it had broken through, she was ready to talk and talk. ". . . We knew one family with grown-up children, a son and a daughter, both keen Komsomol members. Suddenly the whole family was put down for deportation. The children rushed to the Komsomol district office. 'Protect us!' they said. 'Certainly we'll protect you,' they were told. 'Just write on this piece of paper: *As from today's date I ask not to be considered the son, or the daughter, of such-and-such parents. I renounce them as socially harmful elements and I promise in future to have nothing whatever to do with them and to maintain no communication with them.'* "

Oleg slumped forward. His bony shoulders stuck out and he hung his head. "Many people signed letters like that . . ." he said.

"Yes, but this brother and sister said, 'We'll think about it.' They went home, threw their Komsomol cards into the stove and started to pack their things for exile."

Sibgatov stirred. He grasped the bed and began to raise himself out of his tub. The orderly hurried over to take the tub and carry it out.

Oleg got up too. Before going back to bed he walked down the inevitable staircase.

In the lower corridor he passed the door of the room where Dyomka was lying. The second occupant had been a postoperative case who had died on Monday. They had moved him out and put Shulubin in after his operation.

The door was usually shut tight, but at the moment it was slightly ajar. It was dark inside. In the darkness he could hear a heavy gasping noise. There was no nurse in sight. Either they were with other patients or they were asleep.

Oleg opened the door a bit more and edged his way in.

Dyomka was asleep. Shulubin was the one gasping and groaning.

Oleg went right into the room. Now the door was open there was a little light coming in from the corridor. "Aleksei Filippovich . . ." he said.

The gasping stopped.

"Aleksei Filippovich . . . Do you feel bad?"

"What?" The word came out in another gasp.

"Do you feel bad? Do you want your medicine? Shall I turn the light on?"

"Who is it?" Terrified, the man breathed out and coughed. Then the groaning began again because coughing was too painful.

"It's Kostoglotov. Oleg." He was now right by the bed, bending over it. He was beginning to distinguish Shulubin's great head lying on the pillow. "What can I get you? Shall I call a nurse?"

"No-thing." Shulubin breathed the word out.

He didn't cough or groan again. Oleg could distinguish more and more detail. He could even make out the little curls of hair on the pillow.

"Not all of me shall die,"* Shulubin whispered. "Not all of me shall die."

*A quotation from a Pushkin poem.

He must be delirious.

Kostoglotov groped for the man's hot hand lying on the blanket. He pressed it lightly. "Aleksei Filippovich," he said, "you're going to live! Hang on, Aleksei Filippovich!"

"There's a fragment, isn't there? . . . Just a tiny fragment," he kept whispering.

It was then it struck Oleg that Shulubin was not delirious, that he'd recognized him and was reminding him of their last conversation before the operation. He had said, "Sometimes I feel quite distinctly that what is inside me is not all of me. There's something else, sublime, quite indestructible, some tiny fragment of the universal spirit. Don't you feel that?"

35. The First Day of Creation...

Early in the morning while everyone was still asleep Oleg got up quietly, made his bed, folding the four corners of the blanket cover into the middle, as regulations required, and walked on tiptoe in his heavy boots out of the ward.

Turgun was asleep at the duty nurse's table, his head of thick black hair resting on folded arms over an open textbook.

The old orderly on the lower floor opened the bathroom for Oleg. The clothes he changed into there were his own, but they felt strange after two months in store, his old trousers, his army riding breeches, his cotton-and-wool blouse and his greatcoat. They had also been kept in store for him in the camps, so there was something left of them, they weren't completely worn. His winter hat was a civilian one he'd bought in Ush-Terek; it was too small for him and squeezed his head. The day promised to be a warm one, so Oleg decided not to put his hat on at all, it made him look too like a scarecrow. His belt he tied not round his greatcoat but round the blouse he wore under his greatcoat. To the ordinary passer-by he must have looked like a demobilized soldier, or one who had escaped from the guardroom. He tucked his hat into his old duffel bag, which was covered with grease stains and had a sewn-up shrapnel hole and a burn hole as well. He had had it in the front line and had asked his aunt to bring it to the prison in a parcel. He didn't want to take anything good with him to the camp.

After what he'd worn in hospital even clothes like these gave him a cheerful bearing. They made him feel healthy.

Kostoglotov was in a hurry to leave, afraid something might crop up to detain him. The old orderly removed the bar from across the handle of the outer door, and let him out.

He walked onto the porch and stood still. He breathed in. It was young air, still and undisturbed. He looked out at the world—it was new and turning green. He raised his head. The sky unfolded, pink from the sun rising somewhere unseen. He raised his head higher. Spindle-shaped, porous clouds, centuries of laborious workmanship, stretched across the whole sky, but only for a few moments before dispersing, seen only by the few who happened to throw back their heads that minute, perhaps by Oleg Kostoglotov alone among the town's inhabitants.

Through the lace, the cutout pattern, the froth and plumes of these clouds sailed the shining, intricate vessel of the old moon, still well visible.

It was the morning of creation. The world had been created anew for one reason only, to be given back to Oleg. "Go out and live!" it seemed to say.

But the pure, mirror-bright moon was not young. It was not the moon that shines on those in love.

His face radiated happiness. He smiled at no man, only at the sky and the trees, but it was with that early-morning springtime joy that touches even the old and the sick. He walked down the well-known pathways, meeting no one but an old street sweeper.

He turned round and looked at the cancer ward. Half hidden by the long brooms of the pyramidal poplars, the building was a towering mass of bright gray brick, brick upon brick and none the worse for seventy years of age.

Oleg walked on, bidding farewell as he went to the trees in the Medical Center. Already tassels hung in bunches from the maple trees, already the first flowers had appeared on the wild plum trees— white blossoms but given a greenish tinge by the leaves.

But there wasn't a single apricot tree, although he'd heard that they would be in flower by now. He might see one in the Old Town.

The first morning of creation—who can act rationally on such a day? Oleg discarded all his plans. Instead, he conceived the mad scheme of going to the Old Town immediately, while it was still early morning, to look at a flowering apricot tree.

He walked through the forbidden gates and came to the half-empty square where the trolley cars turned round, the same gates he had once entered as a hopeless, despondent man, soaked by the January rain, expecting only to die.

He walked out through the hospital gates thinking to himself, It's just like leaving prison.

Last January, when he had been struggling to make his way to the hospital, the screeching, jolting, overcrowded trolley cars had shaken him almost to death, but sitting there now with a window to himself he even began to enjoy the rattle of the machine. Going by trolley was a sort of life, a sort of freedom.

The trolley car dragged its way along a bridge across the river. Down below, weak-legged willow trees were bending over, their branches hanging into the tawny swift-moving water, already green, trusting in nature.

The trees along the sidewalk had also turned green, but not enough to hide the houses—one-story houses of solid stone, built unhurriedly by men who were in no hurry. Oleg looked at them enviously—lucky people who had actually lived in them! It was an amazing part of town flashing past the window now; very wide sidewalks and spacious boulevards. But what town does not look wonderful in the rosy early morning?

Gradually the style changed. The boulevards ended, the two sides of the street began to converge and hastily constructed buildings to flash by. They made no pretense to beauty or strength. Probably they had been built before the war. Oleg read the name of the street; it seemed familiar.

Then he knew why he recognized it—it was the street where Zoya lived!

He took out his rough-paper notebook and found the number. He looked out through the window again, and as the trolley car slowed down he spotted the house itself—two-story, with irregular-shaped windows and gates either permanently open or broken. There were a few outbuildings in the yard.

He could get out here, somewhere here.

He was by no means homeless in this town. He had an invitation, an invitation from a girl.

He didn't move from his seat. He sat there, almost enjoying the jolts and rumblings of the trolley car. It was not yet full. Opposite Oleg sat an old Uzbek in glasses—no ordinary Uzbek but a man with an air of ancient learning about him.

The lady conductor gave the man a ticket, which he rolled into a tube and stuck in his ear, and on they went, the twist of pink paper jutting out of his ear. It was an elementary touch that made Oleg feel gayer and more at ease as they entered the Old Town.

The streets grew even narrower. The tiny houses were crowded together, pushed shoulder to shoulder. Later on, even the windows disappeared. High clay walls rose blindly from the street. Some houses were built up higher than these walls; their backs were smooth, windowless and smeared all over with clay. There were a few gates or little tunnels in the walls, so low that you'd have to stoop to enter. It was only a jump from the runningboard of the trolley car to the pavement, and only another step across the pavement before it ended. The whole street seemed to be falling under the trolley car.

So this must be the Old Town, where Oleg wanted to be. But there were no trees growing in the naked streets, let alone a flowering apricot.

Oleg couldn't let the streets go by any more. He got off.

What he saw now was the same scene as before, except that he was moving at walking pace. Without the rattle of the trolley car he could hear, he was sure he could hear, a sort of iron knocking noise. A moment later he spotted a Uzbek in a black and white skullcap and a long black quilted coat with a pink waist sash. He was squatting in the middle of the street hammering a hoe into a circle against one of the rails of the single trolley track.

Oleg stood there. He was touched—atomic age indeed! Even now in places like this, and in Ush-Terek, metal was such a rarity that there was nothing better than a trolley rail to use as an anvil. Oleg watched to see if the Uzbek would finish before the next trolley came. But he was in no hurry whatever. He hammered on carefully. When the oncoming trolley car sounded its horn he moved half a step to one side, waited for it to pass and then squatted down again.

Oleg watched the Uzbek's patient back and the pink sash (which had drained the blue sky of its previous pinkness). He couldn't exchange two words with this Uzbek, but he still felt for him as a brother worker.

Hammering out a hoe on a spring morning—a real restoration of life that would be, wouldn't it?

Very good!

He walked slowly on, wondering where all the windows were. He wanted to peep behind the walls and look inside, but the doors, or rather the gates, were shut and it would be awkward just to walk in.

Suddenly Oleg saw light emerging from a small passageway in the wall. He bent down and walked along a dampish tunnel into a court-yard.

The courtyard hadn't yet woken up, but one could see that people lived here. Under a tree stood a bench dug into the ground and a table. Some toys were scattered about, quite modern ones, there was a water pump to provide the moisture of life, and a washtub too. There were many windows all around, all looking out in this direc-tion, onto the courtyard. There wasn't one that faced the street.

He walked a bit further down the street and went into another courtyard through a similar sort of tunnel. Everything was the same, but there was also a young Uzbek woman looking after her little children. She wore a lilac shawl and her hair hung down to her waist in long, thin black braids. She saw Oleg and ignored him. He left.

It was completely un-Russian. In Russian villages and towns all the living-room windows looked straight onto the street, so that the housewives could peer through the curtains and the windowbox flowers, like soldiers waiting in a forest ambush, to see the stranger walking down the street, and who was visiting who and why. Yet Oleg immediately understood and accepted the Oriental way: I don't want to know how you live, and don't you peep in on me!

What better way of life could an ex-prisoner choose for himself after years in the camps, constantly exposed, searched and examined, under perpetual observation?

He was getting to like the Old Town more and more.

Earlier on he'd noticed an empty teahouse in a space between two houses and the man who ran it just beginning to wake up. He now came across another one on a balcony above street level. He walked up into it. There were several men inside wearing skullcaps—purple or blue and some made of rug cloth—and an old man in a white turban with colored embroidery. There wasn't a single woman there. Oleg remembered he'd never seen a woman in a teahouse. There was no sign up to say woman were forbidden, it just that they weren't invited.

Oleg thought it all over. It was the first day of his new life. Every-thing was new and had to be understood afresh. Did these men, by gathering together apart from women, mean to demonstrate that the most important part of life does not concern women?

He sat down by the balcony rail. It was a good point from which to observe the street. It was coming to life now, but no one seemed to be in the hurry habitual in towns. The passers-by moved along sedately, the men in the teahouse sat in endless calm.

One might imagine that Sergeant Kostoglotov, or Prisoner Kostoglotov, had served his time, had paid his debts to society, had sweated out the torment of his illness and had died in January, and that some new Kostoglotov, tottering on two uncertain legs, had emerged from the clinic "so lovely and clean you can see through him," as they said in the camps, to live not an entire life but an extra portion, like the piece of bread they used to pin onto the main ration with a pine twig to make up the weight; it was part of the ration, but a separate bit.

As he embarked on this little additional piece of life, Oleg longed for it to be different from the main part he had lived through. He wished he could stop making mistakes now.

However, he'd already made one mistake, in choosing his tea. Instead of trying to be clever he should have chosen the ordinary black tea he knew well, but in his pursuit of the exotic he'd chosen *kok*—green tea. It turned out to have no strength, it didn't pep him up, it didn't really taste like tea at all, and when he poured some into the bowl it was full of tea leaves. He didn't want to swallow them, he'd rather pour it away.

Meanwhile the day was warming up and the sun was rising. Oleg wouldn't have minded a bite to eat, but this teahouse served nothing but two sorts of hot tea. They didn't even have sugar.

But he decided to adopt the changeless, unhurried manner of those about him. He didn't get up or set off in search of something to eat, but stayed sitting, adjusting his chair into a new position.

And then from the teahouse balcony he saw above the walled courtyard next door something pink and transparent. It looked like a puff dandelion, only it was six meters in diameter, a rosy, weightless balloon. He'd never seen anything so pink and so huge.

Could it be the apricot tree?

Oleg had learned a lesson. This was his reward for not hurrying. The lesson was—never rush on without looking around first.

He walked up to the railings and from on high gazed and gazed through this pink miracle.

It was his present to himself—his creation-day present.

It was like a fire tree decorated with candles in a room of a northern home. The flowering apricot was the only tree in this courtyard enclosed by clay walls and open only to the sky. People lived in the yard, it was like a room. There were children crawling under the tree, and a woman in a black headscarf with a green-flowered pattern was hoeing the earth at its base.

Oleg examined it—pinkness, that was the general impression. The tree had buds like candles. When on the point of opening, the petals were pink in color, but once open they were pure white, like apple or cherry blossoms. The result was an incredible, tender pink. Oleg was trying to absorb it all into his eyes. He wanted to remember it for a long time and to tell the Kadmins about it.

He'd planned on finding a miracle, and he'd found one.

There were many other joys in store for him today in this newly born world . . .

The vessel of the moon had now disappeared.

Oleg walked down the steps into the street. His uncovered head was beginning to feel the sun. He ought to go and buy four hundred grams or so of black bread, stuff himself with it without any water and then go downtown. Maybe it was his civilian clothes that put him in such good spirits. He felt no nausea and sauntered along quite easily.

Then he saw a stall set into a recess in the wall so that it didn't break the line of the street. It had an awning raised as a sun shield and propped up by two diagonal struts. Gray-blue smoke was blowing out from under the shield. Oleg had to bend low to get under. He stood stooping beneath, unable to straighten up.

A long iron grill ran across the whole length of the counter. In one place there was a fire of red-hot coals, the rest was full of white ashes. Across the grill and above the fire lay fifteen or so long, pointed aluminum skewers strung with pieces of meat.

Oleg guessed—it must be *shashlik!* Here was another discovery in his newly created world—the dish he'd heard so much about during those gastronomical discussions in prison. But in all his thirty-four years he had never had the chance to see it with his own eyes. He'd never been to the Caucasus or eaten in restaurants. In the pre-war canteens they had served nothing but stuffed cabbage and pearl-barley porridge.

Shashlik!

It was an enticing smell, the mixed odor of smoke and meat. The meat on the skewers wasn't charred, it wasn't even dark brown, it was the tender pinky-gray of meat nearly just right. The stallkeeper, round and fat of face, was unhurriedly turning the sticks round or moving them away from the fire and over the ashes.

"How much?" asked Kostoglotov.

"Three," the stallkeeper answered dreamily.

Oleg couldn't understand—three what? Three kopecks was too little, three roubles seemed too much. Perhaps he meant three sticks for a rouble? It was a difficulty he was always coming across since his release from the camp: he couldn't get the proper scale of prices into his head.

"How many for three roubles?" Oleg guessed, trying to find a way out.

The stallkeeper was too lazy to speak. He lifted one skewer up by the end, waved it at Oleg as one would to a child, and put it back on the fire.

One skewer, three roubles? Oleg shook his head. It was a scale beyond his experience. He only had five roubles a day to live on. But how he longed to try it! His eyes examined every piece of meat, selecting one for himself. Each skewer had its own special attraction.

There were three truck drivers waiting nearby, their trucks parked in the street. A woman came up to the stall, but the stallkeeper said something to her in Uzbek and she went away looking annoyed. Suddenly the stallkeeper began laying all the skewers out on a single plate. He sprinkled some chopped scallions on them with his fingers and splashed something out of a bottle. Oleg realized that the truck drivers were taking the whole stock of *shashlik,* five skewers each.

It was another example of the inexplicable, two-tiered price and wage structure that prevailed everywhere. Oleg couldn't even conceive of this second tier, let alone imagine himself climbing up to it. These truck drivers were just having a snack, fifteen roubles apiece, and very likely this wasn't their main breakfast either. No wage was enough to support such a life. Wage earners didn't buy *shashlik.*

"All gone," said the stallkeeper to Oleg.

"Gone? All gone?" asked Oleg miserably. Why on earth had he hesitated? It might be the first and last chance of a lifetime!

"They didn't bring any in today," said the stallkeeper, cleaning up his things. It looked as if he was getting ready to lower the awning.

"Hey, boys, give me one skewer!" Oleg begged the truck drivers. "One skewer, boys!"

One of them, a heavily tanned but flaxen-haired young man, nodded to him. "All right, take one," he said.

They hadn't paid yet. Oleg took a green note from his pocket, the flap of which was fastened with a safety pin. The stallkeeper didn't even pick it up. He just swept it off the counter into his drawer, as one sweeps crumbs or scraps off a table.

But the skewer was Oleg's! Abandoning his duffel bag on the dusty ground, he took the aluminum rod in both hands. He counted the pieces of meat—there were five of them, the sixth was a half—and his teeth began to gnaw them off the skewer, not whole chunks at a time but morsel by morsel. He ate thoughtfully as a dog eats after taking his food into a safe corner, and he thought how easy it was to whet human desires and how difficult it was to satisfy them once aroused. For years he had regarded a hunk of black bread as one of the most precious gifts on earth. A moment ago he had been ready to go and buy some for his breakfast, but then he had smelled the gray-blue smoke and the roast meat, the men had given him a skewer to gnaw and already he was beginning to feel contempt for bread.

The drivers finished their five skewers each, started up their engines and drove off, leaving Oleg still licking the last of his skewer. He was savoring each morsel with his lips and tongue—the way the tender meat ran with juice, the way it smelled, how perfectly it was cooked, not at all overdone. It was amazing the primeval pleasure, quite undulled, he derived from every mouthful. And the deeper he dug into his *shashlik* and the greater his enjoyment, the more he was struck by the cold fact that he wasn't going to see Zoya. The trolley car had been about to take him past her house, but he wouldn't get off. It was while lingering over the skewer of *shashlik* that he finally realized this.

The trolley car dragged him back along the same route into the town center, only this time it was jammed with passengers. Oleg recognized Zoya's stop and let two more go by. He didn't know which stop was best for him. Suddenly a woman appeared selling newspapers through the trolley-car window. Oleg decided to have a good look and see what was happening; he hadn't seen people selling newspapers in the street since he was a child. (The last time was when Mayakovsky* shot himself and little boys ran about selling a

*Vladimir Mayakovsky, the great Futurist poet and supporter of the Russian Revolution, who shot himself in 1930.

late-extra edition.) But on this occasion it was an aging Russian woman selling them, not at all briskly, taking her time over finding the right change. Still, her enterprise stood her in good stead and as each new trolley came along she managed to get rid of a few copies. Oleg stood there just to see how she was doing.

"Don't the police chase you away?" he asked her.

"They haven't got round to it yet," the newspaper woman replied.

He hadn't been able to get a look at himself for a long time and he'd forgotten what he looked like. Any policeman who looked closely at them both would have demanded his documents before bothering about the woman's.

The electric clock in the street showed only nine, but the day was already so hot that Oleg began to unbutton the top loops of his greatcoat. Unhurriedly, letting himself be overtaken and pushed, he walked along the sunny side of the street near the square, screwing up his eyes and smiling into the sun.

There were many more joys in store for him today!

It was the sun of a spring he had not reckoned on living to see. And although there was no one around to rejoice after his return to life—in fact, no one knew about it—still, somehow the sun knew, and Oleg smiled at him. Even if there were never another spring, even if this were the last, nevertheless it was like a surprise gift, and he was grateful.

None of the passers-by was particularly pleased to see Oleg, but he was happy to see them all. He was delighted to have come back to them, to everything there was in the streets. He could find nothing in this newly made world of his that was uninteresting, unpleasant, or ugly. Whole months, years of life could not compare with today, this one supreme day.

They were selling ice cream in paper cups. Oleg could not remember the last time he'd seen those little cups. Goodbye to another one and a half roubles, off you go! His duffel bag, scorched and bullet-riddled, hung from his back leaving both hands free to skim the freezing layers off the top with the little wooden spoon.

Walking even more slowly, he came across a photographer's shop-window in the shade. He leaned against the iron railings and stood there for a time stock still, gazing at the purified life and the ideal-ized faces arranged in the window, especially the girls of course—they were in a majority. Originally, each girl had been dressed in her best clothes, then the photographer had twisted her head and adjusted the light ten times, then taken several shots and chosen the best one and retouched it, and then selected one shot each of ten such girls. That was how the window had been composed, and Oleg knew it, but still he found it pleasant to look in and believe that life actually was composed of girls like these. To make up for all the years he had lost, for all the years he would not live to see, and for all he was now deprived of, he gazed and gazed quite shamelessly.

The ice cream was finished and it was time to throw away the little cup. But it was so neat and clean and smooth that it occurred to Oleg it might be useful for drinking out of on the way. So he put it in his duffel bag. He put the little spoon in, too. That might come in handy as well.

Further on, he came across a pharmacist's. A pharmacist's is also a very interesting institution. Kostoglotov went inside immediately.

The counters were very clean—one right angle after another. He could have spent all day examining them. The goods on display looked bizarre to his camp-trained eye. He had never come across such things during the decades he had spent in the other world, while the objects he had seen as a free man he now found difficult to name. He could hardly remember what they were in. Overawed like a savage, he gazed at the nickel-plated glass and plastic shapes. There were herbs, too, in little packets with explanations of their properties. Oleg was a great believer in herbs—but where was the herb he wanted?

Next, there was a long display of pills. There were so many new names on them, names he had never heard before. All in all, the pharmacist's shop was opening up a complete new universe of observation and reflection. But all he did was walk from counter to counter, then ask for a thermometer, some soda, and some manganate, as the Kadmins had asked him to. There was no thermometer and no soda, but they sent him to the cashier, to pay three kopecks for the manganate. Afterward, Kostoglotov joined the line at the dispensary and stood there about twenty minutes. He had taken his bag off his back; he was still oppressed by a feeling of stuffiness. He was undecided—should he take the medicine? He pushed one of the three identical prescriptions Vega had given him the previous day through the little window. He hoped they would not have the medicine, in which case there would be no problem, but they did. They counted up on the other side of the window and wrote him out a bill for fifty-eight roubles and a few kopecks.

Oleg was so relieved he actually laughed as he left the window. The fact that at every stage in his life he was pursued by the figure 58 did not surprise him one jot.* But the idea of paying a hundred and seventy-five roubles for three prescriptions—that really was too much! He could feed himself for a month on money like that. He felt like tearing up the prescriptions and throwing them into the spittoon there and then, but it occurred to him that Vega might ask him about them, so he put them away.

He was sorry to leave the pharmacist's shop with its mirrored surfaces, but the day was already far advanced and calling him. It was his day of joy.

There were even more joys in store for him today!

He trudged on unhurriedly, moving from one shopwindow to the next, clinging like a burr to everything he saw. He knew he would meet something unexpected at every step.

Sure enough, there was a post office, and in the window an advertisement: "Use our photo-telegraph!" Fantastic! It was something people had written about ten years ago in science-fiction stories, and here it was being offered to passers-by in the street. Oleg went in. There was a list hanging up of about thirty towns where photo-telegrams could be sent. Oleg started to work out where he could send one to and to whom, but among all those big towns scattered over one sixth of the world's land surface he could not think of a single person who would be glad to see his handwriting.

He wanted to find out more, so he walked up to the window and asked them to show him a form and tell him what length the letters had to be.

"It's broken," the woman answered; "it doesn't work."

Aha, it doesn't work! Well, to hell with them! That's more like what we're used to. That's reassuring somehow.

He walked on a bit further and read some billboard posters. There was a circus advertised and a few cinemas. There were matinees in all of them, but he couldn't waste the day he had been given to observe the universe on something like that. Of course, if he had plenty of time to spend in town, then it would do him no harm to go to the circus. After all, he was like a child, he had only just been born.

*Oleg had originally been sentenced under Article 58 of the Soviet Penal Code.

It was getting near the time when it would be all right to go and see Vega.

If he was going at all . . .

Well, why on earth shouldn't he go? She was his friend. Her invitation had been sincere. She'd even felt embarrassed about giving it. She was the only soul close to him in the town, so why shouldn't he go?

To go and see her was, secretly, the one thing in the world he most wanted to do. He wanted to go to her before he went on to inspect the universe of the town. But something held him back and kept producing counterarguments: Wasn't it a bit early? She might not be back yet, or she might not have had time to tidy the place up.

All right, a bit later . . .

At every street corner he stopped and pondered. How could he avoid taking the wrong turning? Which was the best way to go? He did not ask anyone, but chose his streets by whim.

And so he ran across a wineshop, not a modern store with bottles but an old-fashioned vintner's with barrels. It was half dark, half damp, with a peculiar sourish atmosphere. They were pouring the wine out of the barrels straight into glasses. And a glass of the cheap stuff cost two roubles. After the *shashlik* this was cheap indeed! Kostoglotov pulled one more ten-rouble note out of the depths of his pocket and handed it over to be changed.

The taste turned out to be nothing special, but his head was so weak the wine made it turn even as he was finishing the glass. He left the shop and walked on. Life seemed even better, even though it had been good to him ever since morning. It was so easy and pleasant that he felt nothing could possibly upset him. For he had already experienced and left behind all the bad things of life, as many as there are, and he was left with the better part.

There were still more joys in store for him today.

For instance, he might run across another wineshop and be able to drink another glass.

But he did not see one.

Instead, there was a dense crowd occupying the whole sidewalk, making passers-by step into the road to go round. Oleg decided it must be a street incident. But no, they were all standing facing a broad flight of steps and some big doors, just waiting. Kostoglotov craned his neck and read: "Central Department Store."

He understood now. They must be giving out something important. But what exactly was it? He asked one man, then a woman, then another woman, but they were all very vague. No one would give him a straight answer. The only thing Oleg found out was that it was due to open very soon. Oh well, if that's the way it is . . . Oleg pushed his way into the crowd.

A few minutes later two men opened the wide doors. With timid gestures they tried to restrain the first row of people, but then leaped aside as though avoiding a cavalry charge. The front rows of waiting men and women were all young; they galloped in through the doors and up the straight staircase to the second floor at the same speed as they would have left the building if it had been on fire. The rest of the crowd pushed their way in too, each running up the steps as fast as his age or strength allowed. One tributary flowed off across the ground floor, but the main stream was up on the second. As part of this attacking surge it was impossible to walk up the stairs quietly. Dark and ragged-looking, Oleg ran up with them, his duffel bag hanging from his back.

"Damn soldier!" the crowd kept swearing at him.

At the top of the stairs the flood separated at once. People were running in three different directions, but turning carefully on the slippery parquet floor. Oleg had a moment to choose in, but how could he decide? He ran blindly on, following the most confident of the racing streams.

He found himself in a growing line near the knitwear department. The assistants, however, in their light-blue uniforms were yawning and talking calmly, apparently quite unaware of the crush. To them it was just another boring, empty day.

As he regained his breath, Oleg discovered they were lining up for women's cardigans or sweaters. He whispered an obscenity and walked away.

Where the other two streams had run off to he could not discover. There was movement on all sides and people crowding at every counter. In one place the crowd was thicker and he decided it must be here. They were waiting for cheap blue soup plates. There they were unpacking boxes of them. Now that was something! There were no soup plates in Ush-Terek. The Kadmins ate off chipped ones. It would be quite something to bring a dozen plates like that to Ush-Terek. But he'd never manage to get them there, they'd all get broken on the way.

Oleg began to walk at random across the two floors of the department store. He looked at the photography department. Cameras, quite unobtainable before the war, were piled all over the shelves, together with all their accessories, teasing him and demanding money. It was another unfulfilled childhood dream of his, to take up photography.

He liked the men's raincoats very much. After the war he had dreamed about buying a civilian raincoat; he reckoned that was what a man looked his best in. But now he would have to lay out three hundred and fifty roubles, a month's wages. He walked on.

He did not buy anything anywhere, but in this mood he felt he had a wallet full of money and no needs. The wine inside him was evaporating, making him merry.

They were selling staple-fiber shirts. Oleg knew the words "staple-fiber." All the housewives in Ush-Terek would run off to the district store whenever they heard them. Oleg looked at the shirts, felt them and fancied them. Mentally he decided to buy one of them, a green one with a white stripe. But it cost sixty roubles; he couldn't afford it.

While he was thinking about the shirts a man in a fine overcoat came up to the counter. He was not after these shirts, but the silk ones. He politely asked the assistant, "Excuse me, do you have size 40, collar size 16?"

Oleg winced. It was as if he were being scraped with iron files on both sides of his body. He started and turned round to look at this cleanshaven man, skin completely unscarred, wearing a fine felt hat with a tie hanging down his white shirt front. He looked at him as if the other had hit him across the ear, and one of them would soon be sent flying down the stairs.

What was this? There were men rotting in trenches, men being thrown into mass graves, into shallow pits in the perma frost, men being taken into the camps for the first, second and third times, men being jolted from station to station in prison trucks, wearing themselves out with picks, slaving away to be able to buy a patched-up quilt jacket—and here was this neat little man who could remember the size not only of his shirt but of his collar too!

It was the collar size that really stunned Oleg. He could not imagine a collar possibly having its own special number. Stifling a wounded groan, he walked right away from the shirts. Collar size too—really! What good was this refined sort of life? Why go back to it? If you remember your collar size, doesn't it mean you're bound to forget something else, something more important?

That collar size had made him feel quite weak . . .

In the household goods department Oleg remembered how Elena Alexandrovna had dreamed of owning a lightweight steam iron, even though she had not actually asked him to bring her one. He hoped there would not be one, just as none of the other household necessities were available. Then both his conscience and his shoulders would be free of a great burden. But the assistant showed him just such an iron there on the counter.

"This iron, is it really a lightweight one, miss?" Kostoglotov was weighing it doubtfully in his hand.

"Why should I tell you a lie?" said the assistant, curling her lips. There was something metaphysical about her gaze. She was plunged deep in faraway thought, as if the customers hanging around the counter were not real people but shadows detached from this world.

"I don't mean you'd lie to me, but you might be making a mistake," suggested Oleg.

The assistant returned unwillingly to this mortal life. Undertaking the intolerable effort of shifting a material object, she put another iron down in front of him. After that she had no strength left to explain anything in words. Once again she floated off into the realm of the metaphysical.

Well, comparison reveals the truth. The lightweight one was in fact a full kilo lighter. Duty demanded that he buy it. She was quite exhausted after carrying the iron, yet her weary fingers still had to write him out a bill, her weakening lips to pronounce the word "Control." (What control was this? Who were they going to check? Oleg had completely forgotten. Goodness, it was difficult getting back into this world!)

But wasn't it she who was supposed to carry this lightweight iron all the way to the control point, her feet barely touching the floor? Oleg felt quite guilty at having distracted the assistant from her drowsy meditations.

He tucked the iron away in his duffel bag and immediately his shoulders felt the weight. Already he was beginning to feel hot and stuffy in his thick overcoat. He must get out of the store as soon as possible.

But then he saw himself in a huge mirror reaching from floor to ceiling. He knew it wasn't right for a man to stand gazing at himself, but the fact was there wasn't a mirror like that in the whole of Ush-Terek, he hadn't seen himself in a mirror that large for ten years. So, not caring what people thought, he just stood gazing at himself, first from a distance, then a little closer, then closer still.

There was no trace of the military man he considered himself to be. His greatcoat and boots only vaguely resembled a greatcoat and boots. His shoulders had drooped long ago and his body was incapable of holding itself straight. Without a hat and without a belt, he looked less like a soldier than a convict on the run or a young lad from the country in town for the day to do a bit of buying and selling. But for that you needed a bit of bravado, and Kostoglotov looked exhausted, devastated, fearfully neglected.

It was a pity he had caught sight of himself. Until then he had been able to imagine himself a bold, soldierly figure who could look condescendingly down on the passers-by and ogle a woman as an equal. This terrible duffel bag on his back had stopped looking soldierly long ago, it now looked like a beggar's bundle. In fact, he could have sat there in the street and held out his hand and people would have thrown kopecks to him.

But he had to be going . . .

Only how could he go to her looking like this?

He walked on a bit further and found himself in the haberdashery or gifts department. They were selling women's costume jewelry.

The women were twittering, trying things on, going through things and rejecting them, when this half-soldier, half-beggar, with the scar low down on his cheek stopped among them and stood dully on the spot, gazing around.

The assistant smiled. What did this chap want to buy for his country sweetheart? She kept an eye on him, too, in case he pinched anything.

But he did not ask to be shown anything or pick anything up. He just stood there looking dully round.

The whole department was glittering with glass. Precious stones, metals and plastic. He stood before it, his head lowered like an ox before a road barrier smeared with phosphorus. Kostoglotov's head could not break through this barrier.

Then he understood. He understood how wonderful it is to buy something pretty for a woman, to pin it on her breast or hang it round her neck. So long as he had not known or remembered, he had been innocent. But he was conscious now, very acutely, that from this moment on he could not go to Vega without taking her a present.

He couldn't give her anything, he just didn't dare. He couldn't give her anything at all. There was no point in even looking at the expensive gifts. And as for the cheap stuff, what did he know about it? Those brooches, for instance—no, not brooches, those decorated pendants with pins, especially that hexagonal one with the sparkling glass crystals—wasn't that a good one?

But perhaps it was trashy and vulgar? . . . Perhaps a woman of taste would be ashamed even to take such a thing in her hand? . . . Perhaps they had given up wearing that type of thing long ago, it might be out of fashion? . . . How was he to know what they were not wearing?

How could he possibly manage it—arrive to spend the night and then offer her a brooch, tongue-tied and blushing?

Waves of confusion were battering him like a succession of balls in a bowling-alley.

The dense complexity of this world was too much for him, a world where one had to know women's fashions, be able to choose woman's jewelry, look respectable in front of a mirror and remember one's collar size . . .

Yet Vega actually lived in this world, she knew everything about it and felt at home in it.

He felt embarrassed and depressed. If he was going to see her the time to go was now, now!

But . . . he couldn't.

He . . . he had lost the impulse. He . . . he was afraid.

They were separated by this department store . . .

And so Oleg staggered out of the cursed temple into which, obedient to the idols of the market place, he had run so recently and with such coarse greed. He was weighed down by depression, as exhausted as if he had spent thousands of roubles, as if he had tried something on in every single department, had it all wrapped up for him and was now carrying on his bent back a mountain of boxes and parcels.

But he only had the iron.

He was so tired, it was as if he had spent hours buying one vain object after another. And what had become of the pure, rosy morning promising him a completely new, beautiful life? Those feathery clouds which took centuries to design? And the diving vessel of the moon?

Where was it he had traded in his untouched soul of this morning? In the department store . . . No, earlier on, he had drunk it away with that wine. Or even earlier, he had eaten it away with the *shashlik*.

What he should have done was to take one look at the flowering apricot and rush straight off to see Vega . . .

Oleg began to feel nauseous, not only from gaping at the shop-windows and signs, but also from jostling his way along the streets among that ever-thickening swarm of worried or cheerful people. He wanted to lie down somewhere in the shade by a stream, just lie there and purify himself. The only place in town he could go to was the zoo, the place Dyomka had asked him to visit.

Oleg felt that the animal world was more understandable anyway, more on his own level.

He was feeling weighed down too because he was appallingly hot in the heavy greatcoat. He didn't feel much like dragging it along with him separately, though. He started to ask people the way to the zoo, and was led there by a succession of well-laid-out streets, broad and quiet, with some paving slabs and spreading trees. No stores, no photographs, no theaters, no wineshops—nothing like that here. Even the trolley cars were rumbling somewhere far away. Here it was a nice, peaceful, sunny day, warming him through even under the trees. Little girls were jumping about playing hopscotch on the sidewalks. Householders were planting their front gardens or putting in sticks for climbing plants.

Near the zoo gates it was a veritable children's kingdom. It was a school holiday, and what a day!

The first thing Oleg saw as he walked into the zoo was the spiral-horned goat. There was a towering rock in its enclosure with a sharp slope and then a precipice. Right there, its front legs on the edge of the precipice, the proud goat stood motionless on its strong, slender legs, with its fantastic horns—long and curved, as though wound spiral after spiral out of a ribbon of bone. It wasn't a beard it had, but a luxuriant mane hanging low on each side to its knees, like a mermaid's hair. Yet the goat had such dignity that the hair did not make it look either effeminate or comic.

Anyone who waited by the spiral-horn goat's cage in the hope of seeing its self-assured little hoofs change position on the smooth rock would have despaired. It had stood there a long time just like a statue, like a continuation of the rock itself. And when there was no breeze to make its straggly hair flutter it was impossible to prove it was alive, that it wasn't just a trick.

Oleg stood there for five minutes and departed in admiration. The goat had not even stirred. That was the sort of character a man needed to get through life.

Walking across to the beginning of another path, Oleg saw a lively crowd, children mostly, gathered round one of the cages. There was something charging frantically about inside, rushing around, but always on the same spot. It turned out to be a squirrel in a wheel—exactly like the one in the proverb. But the proverb was by now a bit stale—and one had never really been able to picture it. Why a squirrel? And why in a wheel? But here was the squirrel, acting it out. It had a tree trunk inside its cage too and dry branches spreading out at the top. But someone had perfidiously hung a wheel next to the tree, a drum with one side open to the viewer. Along the inside rim were fixed cross pieces so that the whole rim was in fact a continuous, endless staircase. And there, quite oblivious of its tree and the slender branches up above, stood the squirrel in its wheel—even though no one had forced it there or enticed it with food—attracted only by the illusion of sham activity and movement. It had probably begun by running lightly up the steps out of curiosity, not knowing then what a cruel, obsessional thing it was. (It hadn't known the first time, but now at the thousandth time it knew well enough, yet it made no difference.)

The wheel was revolving at a furious pace. The squirrel's russet, spindly body and smoky-red tail unfurled in an arc of mad galloping. The cross pieces of the wheeled staircase rippled until they melted together with speed. Every ounce of the animal's strength was being used. Its heart was nearly bursting, but still it couldn't raise its front paws higher than the first step.

The people who had been standing there before Oleg saw it running just as Oleg did during those few minutes. Nothing ever changed. There was no external force in the cage to stop the wheel or rescue the squirrel. There was no power of reason to make it understand. "Stop! It's all in vain!" No, there was clearly only one inevitable way out, the squirrel's death. Oleg didn't want to see that, so he walked on. Here were two meaningful examples, on the right and left of the entrance, two equally possible modes of existence with which the zoo greeted young and old alike.

Oleg walked past the silver pheasant, the golden pheasant, and the pheasant with red and blue feathers. He admired the indescribably turquoise neck of the peacock, the meter-wide spread of its tail and its pink and gold fringe. After his monochrome exile and life in hospital, his eye feasted on the colors.

It wasn't particularly hot here. The zoo was spaciously laid out and the trees were beginning to give shade. Oleg felt more and more rested as he walked past a whole poultry farm—Andalusian hens, Toulouse and Kholmogory geese—and climbed up the hill where they kept the cranes, hawks and vultures. Finally, on a rock covered by a tentlike cage towering high over the whole zoo, he came to where the white-headed vultures lived. If it hadn't been for the sign, they might have been taken for eagles. They had been housed as high up as possible, but the roof of the cage was quite low over the rock, and these great, gloomy birds were in torment, spreading their wings and beating them although there was nowhere to fly.

When Oleg saw the tormented vultures he moved his shoulder-blades as if about to spread his wings. (Or was it just the iron beginning to press into his back?)

Everything round him he explained in his own way. One of the cages had a notice on it: "White owls do not thrive in captivity." So they know that! And they still lock them up! What sort of degenerate owls, he wondered, did thrive in captivity?

Another notice read: "The porcupine leads a nocturnal life." We know what that means: they summon it at half-past nine in the evening and let it go at four in the morning.

Again: "The badger lives in deep, complicated burrows." Aha— just like us! Good for you, badger; how else can one live? He's got a snout of striped ticking, like an old bum's clothes.

Oleg had such a perverse view of everything that it was probably a bad idea for him to have come, just as he shouldn't have gone into the department store.

Much of the day had already gone by, but the promised joys had still not appeared.

Oleg emerged at the bears' den. A black one with a white "tie" was standing poking its nose into the wiring between the bars. Suddenly it jumped up and hung by its forepaws from the grill. It wasn't so much a white tie as a kind of priest's chain with a cross over the chest. It jumped up and hung there. What other way did it have of showing its despair?

In the next-door cell its mate was sitting with her cubs.

In the one after that a grizzly lived in misery. It kept stamping the ground restlessly, longing to walk up and down its cell, but there was only room for it to turn round and round, because the length from wall to wall was no more than three times its own.

So, according to a bear's measuring scale, it was a punishment cell.

The children were amused by the spectacle, saying to each other. "Hey, let's throw him some stones, he'll think they're candies."

Oleg did not notice the children looking at him. For them he was an animal too, an extra one free of charge. He couldn't see himself.

The path led down to the river where they kept the polar bear. At least they kept a couple there together. Several irrigation ditches flowed into their pit to form an icy basin into which they jumped every few minutes to refresh themselves, then climbed out again onto the cement terrace, squeezed the water out of their muzzles with their paws, and paced to and fro along the edge of the terrace above the water.

What must the summer down here be like for polar bears? It's forty degrees Centigrade. Oh well, the same as it was for us in the Arctic Circle.

The most confusing thing about the imprisoned animals was that even supposing Oleg took their side and had the power, he would still not want to break into the cages and liberate them. This was because, deprived of their home surroundings, they had lost the idea of rational freedom. It would only make things harder for them, suddenly to set them free.

This was the odd way Kostoglotov reasoned. His brain was so twisted that he could no longer see things simply and dispassionately. Whatever he experienced from now on, there would always be this shadow, this gray specter, this subterranean rumbling from the past.

Past the miserable elephant, the animal most deprived of space, past the sacred Indian zebu and the golden aguti hare, Oleg walked on up the hill, this time toward the monkeys.

Children and grownups were amusing themselves round the cages, feeding the monkeys. Kostoglotov walked past them without smiling. Quite hairless, as if clipped bare, sitting sadly on their plank beds, wrapped in their primitive sorrows and delights, they reminded him of many of his former acquaintances. In fact, he could even recognize individuals who must still be in prison somewhere.

One lonely, thoughtful chimpanzee with swollen eyes, hands dangling between his knees, reminded Oleg of Shulubin. It was exactly how he often used to sit.

On this bright, hot day Shulubin would be writhing in his bed between life and death.

Kostoglotov didn't think he would find anything interesting in the monkeyhouse. He moved quickly on and had begun to pass it when he noticed an announcement fixed to one of the further cages, and several people reading it.

He went there. The cage was empty but it had the usual notice reading "Macaque Rhesus." It had been hurriedly scrawled and nailed to the plywood. It said: "The little monkey that used to live here was blinded because of the senseless cruelty of one of the visitors. An evil man threw tobacco into the Macaque Rhesus's eyes."

Oleg was struck dumb. Up to then he had been strolling along, smiling with knowing condescension, but now he felt like yelling and roaring across the whole zoo, as though the tobacco had been thrown into his own eyes, "Why?" Thrown just like that! "Why? It's senseless! Why?"

What went straight to his heart was the childish simplicity with which it was written. This unknown man, who had already made a safe getaway, was not described as "anti-humanist," or "an agent of American imperialism"; all it said was that he was evil. This was what was so striking: how could this man be simply "evil"? Children, do not grow up to be evil! Children, do not destroy defenseless creatures!

The notice had been read and read again, but still the grownups and little children stood looking into the empty cage.

Oleg moved on, drawing his greasy, scorched, shrapnel-riddled duffel bag with the iron inside into the kingdom of reptiles, vipers and beasts of prey.

Lizards were lying in the sand like scaly pebbles, leaning against each other. What had they lost in the way of freedom of movement?

A huge Chinese alligator with a flat snout, black as cast iron, was lying there. Its paws seemed twisted in the wrong direction. A notice announced that during hot weather it did not eat meat every day. It probably quite liked the well-organized zoo world with its ever-ready food.

There was a powerful python attached to a tree, like a thick dead branch. It was completely motionless except for its little sharp, flickering tongue. A poisonous ethis was coiled under a bell glass. There were ordinary vipers too, several of them.

But he had no wish to inspect all these. He was obsessed with picturing the face of that blinded macaque monkey.

He was already in the alley where they kept the beasts of prey. They were magnificent, vying with each other for the richest pelt: a lynx, a snow leopard, an ash-brown puma and a tawny jaguar with black spots. They were prisoners, of course, they were suffering from lack of freedom, but Oleg felt toward them as he had toward the camp gangsters. After all, one can work out who are the guilty ones of this world. A notice said that the jaguar ate one hundred and forty kilograms of meat every twenty-four hours. Really, it was past all imagining! Their camp did not get as much meat in a week, and the jaguar had it every twenty-four hours. Oleg remembered the "trusties" in the camp who worked in the stables. They robbed their horses, ate their oats and so survived.

A little further on he spotted "Mr. Tiger." His whiskers—yes, it was the whiskers that were most expressive of his rapacious nature. But his eyes were yellow . . . Strange thoughts came to Oleg's mind. He stood there looking at the tiger with hatred.

In the camps, Oleg had met an old political prisoner who had once been in exile in Turukhansk.* He had told Oleg about those eyes—they were not velvet black, they were yellow.

Welded to the ground with hatred, Oleg stood in front of the tiger's cage.

Just like that, just like that . . . but why?

He felt sick. He didn't want to stay in the zoo any longer. He wanted to run away from it. He didn't go to see the lions. He began to look for the exit—where was it?

A zebra raced past. Oleg glanced at it and walked on.

Then suddenly . . . he stopped dead in front of a miracle.

After all that carnivorous coarseness it was a miracle of spirituality: the Nilgai antelope, light brown, on fine, light legs, her head keen and alert but not in the least afraid. It stood close to the wire

*The place of Stalin's exile before the Revolution.

netting and looked at Oleg with its big, trustful and . . . gentle, yes, gentle eyes.

The likeness was so true it was unbearable. She kept her gentle, reproachful eyes fixed on him. She was asking him, "Why aren't you coming to see me? Half the day's gone. Why aren't you coming?"

It was witchcraft, it was a transmigration of souls, she was so obviously waiting for Oleg standing there. Scarcely had he walked up to her than she began asking him with those reproachful but forgiving eyes, "Aren't you coming? Aren't you coming? I've been waiting . . ."

Yes, why wasn't he coming? Why wasn't he coming?

Oleg shook himself and made for the exit.

He might still find her at home.

36. ... and the Last Day

He could not think of her either with greed or with the fury of passion. His one joy would be to go and lie at her feet like a dog, like a miserable beaten cur, to lie on the floor and breathe on her feet like a cur. That would be a happiness greater than anything he could imagine.

But such kind animal simplicity—arriving and prostrating himself at her feet—was of course something he could not allow himself. He would have to utter polite, apologetic words, then she'd have to do the same, and she would, because this was the complicated way things had been arranged for many thousands of years.

Even now he could see her as she was yesterday, with that glow, that flush on her cheeks as she said, "You know, you could quite easily come and stay with me—quite easily!" That blush would have to be redeemed. He couldn't let it touch her cheeks again, he would have to get round it with laughter. He couldn't let her make herself embarrassed again, and that was why he had to think up a few first sentences, sufficiently polite and humorous to soften the strangeness of the situation: his calling to see his doctor, a young woman living on her own, with the intention of staying the night—goodness knows why. But he'd rather not think up sentences, he'd rather open the door, stand there and look at her, and call her Vega from the start, that was essential—"Vega! I've come!"

But whatever happened it would be an uncontainable joy being with her, not in the ward or the doctor's consulting room but in an ordinary room, talking about something or other, he didn't know

512

what. He would probably blunder, say the wrong things. After all he was no longer used to living among the human race. But his eyes would let him express what he wanted to say: "Have pity on me! Please, have pity on me, I am so unhappy without you!"

How could he have wasted so much time? Why ever hadn't he gone to Vega? He should have gone long ago. He was walking along briskly now, unhesitatingly, afraid only that he might miss her. After strolling round the town for half the day, he had grasped the layout of the streets and knew the way.

If they got on well together, if it was pleasant being with each other and talking, if there was a chance that at some point he might even take her by the hands, put his arms round her shoulders and look closely, tenderly into her eyes—wouldn't that be enough? And if there was to be even more, much more than that—wouldn't that be enough?

Of course with Zoya it wouldn't have been enough. But with Vega? The Nilgai antelope?

The very thought of taking her hands in his gave him a tense feeling inside his chest. He began to be quite excited about how it was going to happen.

Surely this would be enough?

He grew more and more excited the closer he came to her house. It was really fear, but a happy fear, a fainting delight. This fear was in itself enough to make him happy.

He kept walking, noticing only the street names, ignoring the shops, shopwindows, trolley cars, people, when suddenly he came to a street corner. There was an old woman standing there; he couldn't get past her at first because of the crush. He saw she was selling bunches of little blue flowers.

In no remote corner of his drained, plowed-over, adjusted memory was there a shadow of a notion that when calling on a woman one should bring her flowers. He had forgotten the convention as profoundly and finally as though it had never existed. He had been walking calmly along with his threadbare, patched, heavy duffel bag, not one doubt causing his step to hesitate, and now he had seen some flowers. For some reason these flowers were being sold to people. He frowned, and a vague recollection began to swim up in his mind like a drowned corpse out of a pool of murky water. That's right, that's right! In the long-past, almost nonexistent world of his youth, it had been the custom to give women flowers!

"These . . . What are they?" he asked the flowerseller shyly.

"They're violets, that's what," she said in an insulted tone. "One rouble a bunch."

Violets? Could they be those same violets, the ones in the poem? For some reason he remembered them differently. Their stems should be more graceful, taller, and the blooms more bell-shaped. But perhaps his memory was at fault. Or maybe it was some local variety. In any case there were no others to choose. Now he'd remembered, he realized it would be impossible to go without flowers, shameful too.

How could he possibly have walked along so calmly without flowers?

But how many should he buy? One? One didn't seem enough.

Two? Even two would be on the mean side. Three? Four? Appallingly expensive. A flash of labor camp cunning darted through his mind, like an adding machine ticking over. He could probably knock her down to one and a half roubles for two bunches or four for five bunches. But this sharp streak was apparently not the true Oleg. He held out two roubles and handed them over quietly.

He took the two bunches. They had a scent, but there again it wasn't the way the violets of his youth should have smelled, the violets of the poets. He could carry them along sniffing them like this, but it would look odd if he just carried them in his hands: a sick, demobilized, bareheaded soldier, carrying a duffel bag and some violets! There was no proper way of arranging them, so the best thing was to pull his hand up his sleeve and carry them inside, out of sight.

Vega's house—yes, this was the one!

Straight into the courtyard, she had said. He went into the courtyard, then turned left.

(Something in his chest seemed to be lurching from side to side.)

There was a long concrete veranda used by the whole house, open, but with an awning of slanting, interlaced ironwork under the railings. Things were thrown over the railings to air: blankets, mattresses, pillows, and some linen hanging on lines strung from pillar to pillar.

All in all, it was a very unsuitable place for Vega. The approaches were cluttered and untidy. Anyway, that wasn't her responsibility. A little further on, behind all that washing hanging out to dry, would be the door to her apartment, and behind that door the private world of Vega.

He ducked under some sheets and looked for the door. It was a door like any other, painted bright brown and peeling in places. It had a green box for mail.

Oleg produced the violets from the sleeve of his overcoat. He tried to tidy his hair. He was anxious and excited, and very glad to be so. He tried to imagine her without her doctor's white coat and in her home surroundings.

It wasn't just those few blocks from the zoo that his heavy boots had tramped. He had walked the far-flung roads of his country for twice seven years. And now here he was, demobilized at last, at the very door where for those past fourteen years a woman had been silently waiting for him.

He touched the door with the knuckle of his middle finger.

But he didn't have time to knock properly. The door was already beginning to open. (Could *she* have noticed him already through the window?) It opened and out came a great loutish, snout-faced young man with a flat, bashed-in nose, pushing a bright red motorcycle straight at Oleg. It looked enormous in that narrow doorway. He did not even ask what Oleg was doing or whom he had come to see. He wheeled it straight on as if Oleg wasn't there (he wasn't the sort to give way) and Oleg stepped to one side.

Oleg tried to figure it out but couldn't: what was the young man doing here if Vega lived on her own? Why should he be coming out of her apartment? Surely he couldn't have forgotten, even though it was years ago, that people didn't usually live by themselves, they lived in communal apartments? He couldn't have forgotten, and yet there was no reason why he should have remembered. In the labor camp barracks room one forms a picture of the outside world that is the barracks room's complete opposite, certainly not a communal apartment. Even in Ush-Terek people lived on their own, they didn't have communals there.

"Er, excuse me . . ." he said, addressing the young man. But he had pushed his motorcycle under the hanging sheet and was already taking it down the steps, the wheels bumping hollowly.

He had left the door open, though. Down the unlit depths of the corridor Kostoglotov could now see a door, and another, and a third. Which one? Then he made out a woman in the half-darkness. She didn't turn on the light.

"Who do you want?" she asked him aggressively.

"Vera Kornilyevna." Oleg spoke shyly, in a voice quite unlike his own.

"She's not here," the woman snapped back at him with sharp, confident hostility, without bothering to look or to try the door. She walked straight at Kostoglotov, forcing him to squeeze backward.

"Will you knock, please?" Kostoglotov recovered his old self. The expectation of seeing Vega had softened him, but he could still yap back at yapping neighbors. "She's not at work today," he said.

"I know. She's not here. She was, but she's gone out." The woman looked him over. She had a low forehead and slanting cheekbones.

She had already seen the violets, it was too late to hide them.

If it weren't for the violets in his hand he'd be able to stand up for himself. He'd be able to knock by himself, assert his independence, insist on asking how long she had gone out for, whether she would be back soon, and leave a message for her. Perhaps she had already left one for him?

But the violets had turned him into a suppliant, a bearer of gifts, a lovesick fool . . .

The assault of the woman with the slanting cheekbones was so intense that he retreated onto the veranda.

She drove him from his bridgehead, pressing hard at his heels and observing him. There seemed to be a bulge in the old bum's bag. He might pinch something. (In here too!)

Out in the yard the motorcycle gave a number of impudent, explosive bursts. It had no silencer. The motor died, roared out and died again.

Oleg hesitated.

The woman was looking at him with irritation.

How could Vega not be there? She had promised. But what if she had waited earlier on and then gone out somewhere? What a disaster! It wasn't a mere misfortune or a disappointment, it was a disaster.

Oleg drew his hand with the violets back into his overcoat sleeve, so that it looked as if his hand had been cut off.

"Excuse me, will she come back or has she gone to work?"

"She's gone," the woman cut him short.

It was no sort of an answer.

It would be equally absurd just to stand there opposite her, waiting.

The motorcycle twitched, spat, barked and then died away.

Lying on the railings were heavy pillows, mattresses, and blankets inside envelope-shaped covers, out to dry in the sun.

"What are you waiting for then, citizen?" Those enormous bastions of bedding had made Oleg's mind go blank.

The woman with the slanting cheekbones was staring at him. He couldn't think.

And that damn motorcycle was tearing him to shreds. It wouldn't start.

Oleg edged away from the bastions of pillows and retreated down the steps to where he'd come from. He was repulsed.

If it hadn't been for that pillow—one corner of it all crumpled, two corners hanging down like cows' udders and the fourth sticking up like an obelisk—if it hadn't been for that pillow he could have collected himself and decided something. He couldn't leave suddenly like this. Vega might be coming back soon. And she'd be sorry he'd left. She'd be sorry.

But those pillows, mattresses, blankets, envelope-shaped blanket covers and banner-like sheets implied such stable, tested experience that he hadn't the strength to reject it. He had no right.

Especially now. Especially him.

A man alone can sleep on planks or boards so long as his heart has faith or ambition. A prisoner sleeps on naked planks since he has no choice, and the woman prisoner, too, separated from him by force. But when a man and a woman have arranged to be together, the pillows' soft faces wait confidently for what is their due. They know they will not miss what is theirs.

So Oleg walked away from this unassailable fortress he could not enter, the lump of iron still weighing his shoulders down. He walked, one hand amputated, trudging toward the gate. The pillow bastions riddled him joyfully in the back with machine guns.

It wouldn't start, damn it.

Outside the gate the bursts sounded muffled. Oleg stopped to wait a little longer.

He still hadn't given up the idea of waiting for Vega. If she came back, she couldn't avoid passing this point. They'd smile and be so glad to see each other: "Hello . . ." "Do you know that . . . ?" "Such a funny thing happened . . ."

Was he to produce from his sleeve those crumpled, faded violets?

He could wait for her and then they'd go back into the courtyard, but they wouldn't be able to avoid those swollen, self-confident bastions again.

They would have to pass them whatever happened.

Someday, if not today, Vega, lightfooted and ethereal with those bright dark-brown eyes, her whole being a contrast to the dust of this earth, would carry her own airy, tender, delightful little bed out onto the same veranda. Yes, Vega too.

No bird lives without its nest, no woman lives without her bed.

However immortal, however rarefied she may be, she cannot avoid those eight inevitable hours of the night, going to sleep and waking up again.

It rolled out! The crimson motorcycle drove out through the gate, giving Kostoglotov the *coup de grâce*.

The lad with the bashed-in nose looked like a conqueror in the street.

Kostoglotov walked on his way, defeated.

He took the violets out of his sleeve. They were at their last gasp. In a few minutes they'd be unpresentable.

Two Uzbek schoolgirls with identical braids of black hair plaited tighter than electric wire were walking toward him. With both hands Oleg held out the two bunches.

"Here, girls, take these."

They were amazed. They looked from one to the other. They looked at him. They spoke to each other in Uzbek. They realized he wasn't drunk and wasn't trying to molest them. They may even have realized that some misfortune had made the old soldier give them flowers.

One of the girls took her bunch and nodded.

The second girl took hers and nodded.

Then they walked quickly, rubbing shoulders and chattering excitedly.

He was left with nothing but the dirty, sweat-soaked duffel bag on his shoulder.

Where could he spend the night? He'd have to think of something all over again.

He couldn't stay in a hotel.

He couldn't go to Zoya's.

He couldn't go to Vega's.

Or rather, he could, he could. And she'd be pleased. She'd never show how disappointed she'd been.

But it was a question of "mustn't" rather than "couldn't."

Without Vega the whole of this beautiful town with its wealth and its millions of inhabitants felt like a heavy bag on his back. Strange to think that this morning he had liked the place so much he'd wanted to stay longer.

And even stranger still, what had he been so happy about this morning? His cure no longer seemed like some special gift.

Oleg had walked less than a block when he felt how hungry he was, how sore his feet were, how utterly physically exhausted he was, and that still unbeaten tumor rolling around inside him. All he wanted was to get away as quickly as possible.

But even returning to Ush-Terek, to which the road was now open, no longer attracted him. Oleg realized he would sink even deeper into the gloom until he drowned.

At the moment he couldn't imagine any place or thing that could cheer him up.

Except—going back to Vega.

He would have to fall at her feet: "Don't turn me out, don't turn me out! It's not my fault!"

But it was a question of "mustn't" rather than "couldn't."

He asked a passer-by the time. After two o'clock. He ought to come to some decision.

He caught sight of a trolley car, the number that went toward the *komendatura*. He started to look around for a nearby stop.

With an iron screech, especially on the bends, as though gravely ill itself, the trolley car dragged him along the narrow stone streets. Oleg held onto the leather strap and bent his head to try and see something out of the window, but they were going through a part of town that had no greenery, no boulevards, only sidewalks and shabby houses. They flashed past a billboard poster advertising matinee shows at an outdoor moviehouse. It would have been interesting to see how it worked, but something had snuffed out his interest in the world's novelties.

She was proud to have withstood fourteen years of loneliness. But she didn't know what six months of the other thing could do to them: together, yet not together.

He recognized his stop and got off. He would now have to walk one and a half kilometers along a wide, depressing street in a factory neighborhood. A constant stream of trucks and tractors rumbled along both sides of the roadway. The footpath was lined by a long stone wall, then cut across a factory railway track and a coal-slack embankment, ran past a wasteland pitted with hollows, then across some more rails, then along another wall, and finally past some wooden, one-story barracks blocks—the sort described in official files as "temporary civilian accommodation" but which had remained standing for ten, twenty or even thirty years. At least there was none of the mud there had been in January during the rain, when Kostoglotov was looking for the *komendatura* for the first time. All the same, it was a depressing, long walk. One could hardly believe this street was in the same town as those ring boulevards, huge-girthed oak trees, buoyant poplars and wondrous pink apricots.

However hard she tried to convince herself she ought to do it, that it was the right thing to do, it would merely mean that when it did break through the surface it would be all the more heart-rending.

Whose idea could it have been to place the *komendatura,* the office that decided the fate of all the city's exiles, in such a tucked-away corner of town? But here it was, among the barracks blocks and the muddy pathways, the windows broken and boarded up with plywood, among the endless lines of washing. Here it was.

Oleg remembered the repulsive expression on the face of the *komendant,* who hadn't even been at work on a weekday, and how he had been received the last time. As he walked along the corridor of the *komendant's* barracks block, he slowed down and composed his features into a close, independent look. Kostoglotov would never permit himself to smile at his jailers even if they smiled at him. He considered it his duty to remind them that he remembered everything.

He knocked and went in. The first room was bare and empty: only two long, wobbly, backless benches and, behind a board partition, a desk where presumably twice every month they performed the sacred rite of registering the local exiles.

There was no one there now, but further on was a door wide open with a notice on it: *Komendant.*

Oleg walked across so he could see through the door. "Can I come in?" he asked anxiously.

"Certainly, certainly!" A pleasant, welcoming voice invited him in.

Unbelievable! Oleg had never heard an N.K.V.D. man use such a tone. He went in. There was no one in the room but the *komendant,* sitting at his desk. But it wasn't the same one, not that enigmatic idiot with the wise-looking expression; it was an Armenian with the soft face of a well-educated man, not at all arrogant, wearing no uniform but a good suit that looked out of place in the barracks surroundings. The Armenian gave him a merry look, as if his job was selling theater tickets and he was glad to see that Oleg had come with a big order.

After his years in the camps Oleg couldn't be very well disposed toward Armenians. Few in number, they had looked after one another jealously and always taken the best jobs—in the storeroom or the bread room, or even where they could get at the butter. But to be fair, Oleg couldn't object to them because of that. It wasn't they who had invented the camps, they hadn't invented Siberia either. After all, what high ideal forbade them to help and save one another? Why should they give up commerce and peck away at the earth with pickaxes?

Seeing this merry-looking, friendly Armenian sitting behind his official desk, Oleg thought warmly that informality and enterprise must be the Armenians' special qualities.

Oleg gave him his name and that he was here on a temporary registration. The *komandant* got up eagerly and with ease, although he was a heavily built man, and began flipping through the cards in one of the files. At the same time, as though trying to provide Oleg with some diversion, he kept up a constant chatter: sometimes meaningless interjections, but occasionally naming people, which the most stringent instructions prohibited him from doing.

"Ye-es, now, let's have a look . . . Kalifotides . . . Konstantinides . . . Yes, do please sit down . . . Kulayev . . . Karamuriev. Oh dear, I've torn off the corner . . . Kazmagomayev . . . Kostoglotov!"

And again in blatant disregard of N.K.V.D. rules, he did not ask Oleg his first name and patronymic, but gave them himself. "Oleg Filimonovich?"

"Yes."

"I see. You've been under treatment in the cancer clinic since January 23. . . ." And he lifted his keen, kindly eyes from the paper. "Well, how did it go? Are you better?"

Oleg was genuinely moved; there was even a tightness in his throat. How little was needed. But a few humane men behind these vile desks and life became completely different. He no longer felt constrained. He answered simply, "Well, how shall I put it . . . in one way better, in another way worse . . ." (Worse? What an ungrateful creature man is! How could he be worse off than he had been lying on the clinic floor, longing to die?) "I mean, better on the whole."

"Well, that's good," said the *komendant* happily. "Why don't you sit down?"

Even filling out theater ticket orders takes a bit of time. You have to stamp them and write in the date in ink, then copy it into a thick book, and of course cross it out of another. All this the Armenian did happily and without fuss. He took Oleg's certificate with the travel permit from the file and held it out to him. His glance was expressive, his voice unofficial and a little quieter as he said, "Please . . . don't let it depress you. It'll all be over soon."

"What will?" asked Oleg in surprise.

"What do you mean? These registrations, of course. Your exile. *Komendant's* too!" he said with a carefree smile.

Obviously he had some more congenial job up his sleeve.

"What? Is there already . . . an instruction?" Oleg hastened to extract the information.

"Not an instruction." The *komendant* sighed. "But there are certain signs. I'll tell you straight out, it's going to happen. Get better, and you will soon be going up in the world."

Oleg gave him a crooked smile. "I'm almost out of this world," he said.

"What's your profession?"

"I haven't one."

"Are you married?"

"No."

"That's good," said the *komendant* with conviction. "Those who marry in exile almost always get divorced afterwards and it's a terrible business. But you can get released, go back to where you came from and get married."

"Well, in that case, thank you very much." Oleg got up to go.

The *komendant* nodded amiably but still didn't offer Oleg his hand.

As he walked out through the two rooms, Oleg wondered about

the *komendant*. Had he always been like that or was it the changing times? Was he a permanent or a temporary? Or had they started specially appointing ones like him? It was very important to find out, but he couldn't go back now.

Back past the barracks again, past the railway lines, past the coal, Oleg set off along the long streetful of factories at a brisk pace, his step quicker and more even. He soon had to take off his overcoat because of the heat, and slowly the bucket of joy which the *komendant* had poured into him began to flood his whole being. Only gradually did he realize the full meaning of it all.

Only gradually because Oleg had lost the habit of believing the men who sat behind those desks. How could he forget the lies deliberately spread by officials, captains and majors in the years after the war, about how a sweeping amnesty for political prisoners was in preparation? Prisoners had believed them implicitly: "The captain told me so himself!" But the officials had simply been ordered to raise the prisoners' morale, to get them to carry on as before and fulfill their norms, to give them something to aim at and live for.

But as for this Armenian, if there was anything to suspect it was that he knew too much, more than his post warranted. Still, hadn't Oleg himself expected something of the sort from the scraps of information he had read in the newspapers?

For heaven's sake, it was about time! It was long overdue. How could it be otherwise? A man dies from a tumor, so how can a country survive with growths like labor camps and exiles?

Oleg felt happy again. After all, he hadn't died. And here he was, soon he'd be able to buy himself a ticket to Leningrad. Leningrad! Would be really be able to go up and touch one of the columns of St. Isaac's? His heart would burst!

But what did St. Isaac's matter? Everything was changing now between him and Vega. It was enough to make his head spin. If he could really . . . if he could seriously . . . No, it wasn't mere fantasy any longer. He'd be able to live here, with her.

To live with Vega! Together! Just imagining it was enough to burst his ribcase.

How glad she'd be if he went to her now and told her this. Why shouldn't he tell her? Why shouldn't he go? Who in the world was he to tell if not her? Who else was there interested in his freedom?

He had already reached the trolley-car stop. He'd have to choose which trolley to take—the one to the station, or the one to Vega's?

And he'd have to hurry because she'd be going out. The sun was already quite low in the sky.

Again he began to feel agitated, and again he felt drawn toward Vega. Nothing remained of the convincing arguments he had amassed on his way to the *komendant's*.

He was not guilty, he was not covered in dirt, why should *he* avoid *her*? She'd known what she was doing, hadn't she, when she'd given him that treatment? Hadn't she become all silent, hadn't she left the stage when he was arguing with her and begging her to stop the treatment?

Why shouldn't he go? Why shouldn't they try to rise above the common level? Why shouldn't they aim higher? Weren't they human beings after all? At least, Vega was.

He was already pushing through the crowd to get to the trolley. There were a lot of people waiting at the stop, all surging forward to get to the one he wanted, all traveling his way. Oleg had his overcoat in one hand and his duffel bag in the other, so he couldn't grab hold of the handrail. He was squashed, spun round and finally shoved onto the platform and into the car.

People were leaning on him savagely from all sides. He found himself behind two girls who looked like students. One fair, the other darkish, they were so close to him they must be able to feel him breathing. His arms were pulled apart and separately pinioned so that he could not pay the irate lady conductor, in fact he could not even move. His left arm, the one with the coat in it, seemed to be embracing the dark girl, while his whole body was pressed against the blonde. He could feel her all over, from knee to chin, and she couldn't possibly avoid feeling him in the same way. The greatest passion in the world could not have joined them as intimately as that crowd. Her neck, her ears and her little curls were thrust closer to him than he would ever have thought possible. Through her worn old clothes he was absorbing her warmth, her softness and her youth. The dark girl was still chatting to her friend about something going on at college. The blond girl had stopped answering her.

In Ush-Terek they had no trolley cars. Only in the shell holes had he ever been as close to people as this. But there hadn't always been women there. This sensation—he hadn't felt it, he hadn't had it confirmed for decades. It was all the more primeval for that, all the stronger.

It was a happiness, and it was a sorrow. There was in the sensation a threshold he could not cross whatever his powers of self-suggestion.

They had warned him, hadn't they? The libido remains, the libido but nothing else . . .

They went past a couple of stops. After that it was still a crush, but there were not so many people pressing from behind. Oleg could have moved away from them a bit, but he didn't. He had no will left to put an end to this blissful torture. At this moment he wanted no more than to stay as he was for just a little longer, even if the trolley took him right back to the Old Town, even if it went out of its mind and took him clattering and circling nonstop until nightfall. Even if it ventured on a voyage round the world, Oleg had no will left to be the first to break away. As he prolonged this happiness, the greatest joy to which he could now aspire, he remembered gratefully the little curls of hair on the back of the blond girl's neck. Her face he hadn't even glimpsed.

She broke away from him and began to move forward.

And as he straightened his bent, weakened knees Oleg realized his journey to see Vega would end as a torture and a deceit.

It would mean his demanding more from her than he could ask from himself.

They had come to a high-minded agreement that spiritual communion was more valuable than anything else; yet, having built this tall bridge by hand together, he saw now that his own hands were weakening. He was on his way to her to persuade her boldly of one thing while thinking agonizingly of something else. And when she went away and he was left in her room alone, there he'd be, whimpering over her clothes, over every little thing of hers, over her perfumed handkerchief.

No, he should be more sensible than some teen-age girl. He should go to the railway station.

He fought his way through to the rear platform—not forward, not past the student girls—and jumped off. Someone swore at him.

Not far from the trolley stop someone else was selling violets . . .

The sun was already going down. Oleg put on his overcoat and took another trolley to the station. This time it wasn't so crowded.

He pushed his way all over the station, asking questions and getting the wrong answers. Finally he reached a sort of pavilion like a covered market, where they were selling tickets for the long-distance trains.

There were four booking-office windows, at each a line of a hundred and fifty to two hundred people. And there must be others in the line who were away for the moment.

The picture of railway station lines going on for days was one Oleg recognized at once, as though he'd always been familiar with it. Much had changed in the world: fashions, street lamps, the habits of young people, but this had remained constant for as long as he could remember. It had been like this in 1946, it had been the same in 1939, and in 1934 and in 1930. Shopwindows bursting with food he could even remember from the N.E.P.* period, but he couldn't imagine station booking offices that were easy to get to. The difficulties of travel were unknown only to those who had special cards or official vouchers.

As it happened, he had a voucher—not a very impressive one perhaps, but it would suit the occasion.

It was stuffy and he was sweating, but he pulled from his duffel bag a tight fur hat and squeezed it over his head as a hatmaker would over a stretching block. He slung his bag over one shoulder and assumed the expression of a man who less than two weeks earlier had lain on the operating table under Lev Leonidovich's knife. In this assumed condition of exhaustion, a dull stare in his eyes, he dragged himself between the lines right up to the booking-office window. There were no fights going on solely because a policeman was standing nearby.

In full view of everyone, Oleg made a feeble gesture to pull the voucher out of the slanting pocket under his greatcoat. Trustfully he handed it over to the "comrade militiaman."

The policeman was a fine upstanding Uzbek with a mustache, who looked like a young general. He ceremoniously read it through and announced to the people at the head of the line, "Let this man through. He's had an operation."

He made a sign to Oleg to take third place in the line.

Oleg glanced exhaustedly at his new neighbors in the line. He didn't even try to squeeze in, he just stood on one side, head bowed. A fat, elderly Uzbek, his face bronzed in the shadow of a brown velvet hat with a saucer-like brim, took him and pushed him into line.

He felt cheerful standing there near the window. He could see the

*The New Economic Policy of limited private enterprise, begun by Lenin in 1921.

girl's fingers as she pushed out the tickets. Clutched in the passengers' hands, he could see the sweat-drenched money, as much as was needed or more, that had been extracted from their sewn-up pockets or belts. He could hear the passengers making timid requests, all of which the girl refused mercilessly. It was clear that things were moving, and quickly.

Now it was Oleg's turn to bend down to the window.

"Please may I have one ordinary ticket to Khan-Tau," he said.

"Where?" the girl asked.

"Khan-Tau."

"Never heard of it." She shrugged her shoulders and started looking through a huge directory.

"Why do you want an ordinary ticket, dear?" a woman behind him asked sympathetically. "An ordinary ticket after you've had an operation? You'll split your stitches climbing up to your bunk. You should have got a reservation."

"I haven't any money," Oleg sighed.

It was the truth.

"There's no such station!" shouted the girl behind the window, slamming the directory shut. "Take a ticket to some other station."

"There must be." Oleg smiled weakly. "It's been working a whole year. I came from there myself. If I'd known, I'd have kept my ticket to show you."

"I don't know anything about that. If it's not in the directory it means there's no such station."

"The trains stop there. They do!" Oleg was beginning to argue more heatedly than someone who had just had an operation ought to. "It's even got a booking office."

"Move on, then, if you don't want a ticket, citizen. Next!"

"That's right, why should he hold us up?" came a disapproving murmur from behind. "Take a ticket to the station they give you ... He's just had an operation, all right, but why should he be so choosy?"

My God, Oleg could've given them an argument! How he longed to go the whole hog, demand to see the passenger-service director and the stationmaster. How he would have loved to get through to these thick skulls and see his bit of justice, a tiny, miserable bit but nevertheless justice. So long as he was fighting for it, he would feel like a human being.

But the law of supply and demand was an iron one, and so was the law of transport planning. The kind woman behind him, who had tried to persuade him to take a reservation, was already pushing her money over his shoulder. That policeman who had only just sent him to the front of the line was already lifting a hand to take him to one side.

"The one I want is thirty kilometers from where I live, the other's seventy." Oleg went on complaining into the window, but his words had become, in camp language, mere belly-aching. He was now eager to agree. "All right, give me one to Chu Station."

The girl recognized the station straightaway and knew what the price was. And there was a ticket left. All Oleg had to do was bless his good luck. He moved a little away from the window, checked the punchholes on the ticket against the light, checked the car number, checked the price, checked his change and walked slowly away.

The further he got from the people who knew him as a post-operation case, the straighter he stood up. He took off his wretched little hat and put it back into his duffel bag. There were two hours before the train left and it was wonderful to be able to spend them with a ticket in his pocket. Now he could really celebrate: eat an ice cream (there was no ice cream in Ush-Terek), drink a glass of *kvas** (there was no *kvas* either), and buy some black bread for the journey. Sugar too, he mustn't forget that. He'd also have to line up patiently and pour some boiled water into a bottle (it was a great thing, having your own water!). As for salt herrings, he knew he mustn't take any. How much more free and easy it was than traveling in those prison transports, in converted freight cars. They wouldn't search him before he got on, they wouldn't take him to the station in a paddy wagon, they wouldn't sit him on the ground surrounded by guards and make him spend forty-eight hours tormented by thirst. And if he managed to grab the luggage rack above the two bunks, he'd be able to stretch his whole length along it. This time there wouldn't be two or three people in the rack, there'd be just one! He'd lie down and feel no more pain from his tumor. This was happiness! He was a happy man. What was there to complain about?

That *komendant* had blabbed out something about an amnesty . . . It was here, his long-awaited happiness, it was here! But for some reason Oleg hadn't recognized it.

---

*A Russian national drink, a fermentation usually of bread.

After all, he'd heard Vega calling the surgeon "Lyova," speaking quite familiarly to him. And if not him, there might be someone else. There were so many opportunities. It's like an explosion when a man enters another person's life.

When he'd seen the moon this morning, he'd had faith! But that moon had been on the wane . . .

He ought to go out onto the platform now, a good long time before they started letting passengers onto the train. When the train came in empty he'd have to watch out for his car, run to it and get to the head of the line.

Oleg went to look at the timetable. There was a train going in the opposite direction, Number 75. The passengers must already be getting in. Pretending to gasp for breath, he pushed his way quickly toward the door, asking everyone he met, including the ticket collector, half-hiding the ticket with his fingers, "Seventy-five, is this it? Is this it?"

He was terrified of being late for Number 75. The ticket collector didn't bother to check his ticket, he just pushed him on, slapping the heavy, bulging bag on his back.

Oleg began to walk quietly up and down the platform. Then he stopped and threw his duffel bag down on a stone ledge. He remembered another equally funny occasion in Stalingrad in 1939 during his last days of freedom. It was after the treaty with Ribbentrop had been signed, but before Molotov's speech and before the order to mobilize nineteen-year-olds.

He and a friend had spent the summer going down the Volga in a boat. In Stalingrad they sold the boat and had to get back by train to where they studied. But they had quite a lot of stuff left over from the boat trip, so much that they could hardly carry it in their four hands. And on top of that, Oleg's friend had bought a loudspeaker in some out-of-the-way village store. You couldn't buy them in Leningrad at that time.

The loudspeaker was a large, cone-shaped funnel without a case, and his friend was frightened it would get crushed as they got on the train. They went into the station at Stalingrad and immediately found themselves at the end of a long, bulky line that took up the whole station hall, cluttering it with wooden trunks, bags and boxes. It was quite impossible to get through to the platform before their train came in, and it looked as if they would have to spend two nights without anywhere to lie down. Also a close watch was being kept to see they didn't get through onto the platform.

Suddenly Oleg had an idea: "Make an effort and get these things to the car door, even if you're the last man through." He took the loudspeaker and walked up to the staff door, which was locked. He waved the loudspeaker importantly through the glass at the girl on duty. She opened it. "Just this one to fix and I'm through," Oleg said. The woman nodded understandingly as if he'd spent the whole day carrying loudspeakers to and fro. The train pulled in and he got on first before all the others and grabbed two luggage racks.

That was sixteen years ago and nothing had changed.

Oleg wandered along the platform and saw there were others just as cunning as himself. They had also got through for a train that wasn't theirs and were waiting with their luggage. There were quite a few of them, but still there was much less of a crush on the platform than in the station and in the gardens in front of it. There were also some people from train Number 75 walking around carefree on the platform. These well-dressed types had no worries. They had numbered places which no one could grab from them. There were women with bunches of flowers they had been given, men with bottles of beer and someone taking a photograph. It was a life quite inaccessible to Oleg. He could hardly understand it. The warm spring evening and the long platform under the awning reminded him of some place in the South he had known as a child, perhaps Mineralniye Vody.*

Then Oleg noticed a post office with an entrance onto the platform. There was even a little four-sided sloping desk on the platform for people to write letters at.

It suddenly dawned on him. He had to. And he'd better do it now before the day's impressions got blurred and faded.

He pushed his way in with his bag and bought an envelope—no, two envelopes and two sheets of paper—yes, and a postcard as well. Then he pushed his way back onto the platform, put his bag with the iron and the black bread between his feet, leaned against the sloping table and began with the easiest task, the postcard:

Hello there, Dyomka! Well, I went to the zoo. It was quite something, I can tell you. I've never seen anything like it. You must go. There are

*A spa in the Northern Caucasus.

white bears, can you imagine? Crocodiles, tigers, lions. Allow a whole
day and go right round. They even sell pies in the place. Don't miss the
spiral-horned goat. Don't be in a hurry, just stand and look at it—and
think. And if you see the Nilgai antelope, do the same. There are lots
of monkeys—they'll make you laugh. But there's one missing. An evil
man threw tobacco into the Macaque Rhesus's eyes. Just like that, for
no reason. And it went blind.

The train's coming, I must dash.

Get better and live up to your ideals. I'm relying on you.

Give Aleksei Filippovich all the best from me. I hope he's getting
better.

Best wishes,
OLEG.

He was writing quite easily, except that it was a very smudgy pen.
The nibs were all crossed or broken, they tore the paper and dug
into it like a spade, and the inkwell was a storehouse of scraps of
paper. However hard he tried, the letter ended up looking terrible:

Zoyenka, my little Teddy bear, I'm so grateful for you for allowing
my lips to get a taste of genuine life. Without those few evenings I
should have felt absolutely, yes absolutely, robbed.

You were more sensible than I was, and I can go away now without
any feelings of remorse. You asked me to come and see you but I
didn't.

Thank you for that. You see, I thought—we'll stick with what we've
had. We won't ruin it. I'll always remember everything about you with
gratitude.

Honestly and sincerely I wish you the happiest of marriages!

OLEG.

It had been the same in the N.K.V.D. remand prison. On official
complaint days they provided the same vile rubbishy inkwell, the
same sort of pen and a piece of paper smaller than a postcard. The
ink swam all over the place and went through the paper. Given that,
you could write to anyone you liked about anything you liked.

Oleg read through the letter, folded it and put it in the envelope.
He wanted to seal the envelope—he remembered as a child reading
a detective story where everything started with a mixup in some
envelopes—but that wasn't so easy. There was only a dark line
along the edges of the flap to mark the place where, according to

State All-Union Regulations, there should have been glue—but of course there wasn't.

Oleg worked out which of the three pens had the best nib, wiped it clean and thought about what he was going to write in his last letter. Until then he had been standing there firmly enough, even smiling, but everything became unsteady now. He was sure he was going to write "Vera Kornilyevna" but instead he wrote:

Darling Vega (all the time I was dying to call you that, so I will now, just this once), I want to write to you frankly, more frankly than we've ever spoken to each other. But we have thought it, haven't we? After all, it's no ordinary patient, is it, to whom a doctor offers her room and her bed?

Several times today I set out to walk to your place. Once I actually got there. I walked along as excited as a sixteen-year-old—an indecency for a man with a life like mine behind him. I was excited, embarrassed, happy and terrified. It takes many years of tramping to realize the meaning of the words "God sent you to me."

You see, Vega, if I'd found you in, something false and forced might have started between us. I went for a walk afterwards and realized it was a good thing I hadn't found you in. Everything that you or I tormented ourselves with at least has a name and can be put into words. But what was about to begin between us was something we could never have confessed to anyone. You and I, and between us *this thing*: this sort of gray, decrepit yet ever-growing snake.

I am older than you, I don't mean in years so much as in life. So believe me, you are right, right in everything, right in your past and in your present. Your future is the only thing you do not have the power to guess. You may disagree, but I have a prediction to make: even before you drift into the indifference of old age you will come to bless this day, the day you did not commit yourself to share my life. (I'm not just talking about my exile. There are even rumors it's going to come to an end.) You slaughtered the first half of your life like a lamb. Please spare the second half!

Now that I'm going away anyway (if they end my exile I won't come back to you for checkups or treatment, which means we must say goodbye), I can tell you quite frankly: even when we were having the most intellectual conversations and I honestly thought and believed everything I said, I still wanted all the time, *all the time,* to pick you up and kiss you on the lips.

So try to work that out.

And now, without your permission, I kiss them.

It was the same thing with the second envelope: a dark strip but no glue. Oleg had always suspected that for some reason this was done on purpose.

Meanwhile, behind his back—that was the result of all his scheming and cunning—the train had pulled into the platform and the passengers were running toward it.

He grabbed his bag, seized the envelopes, and squeezed his way into the post office. "Where's the glue? Have you got any glue, miss? Glue!"

"People are always taking it away," the girl shouted in explanation. She looked at him, then hesitatingly offered him the glue pot. "Here you are, glue it down now while I'm watching. Don't go away."

In the thick black glue there were dried-up lumps like those a schoolchild would make. It was almost impossible to use and he had to employ the whole body of the brush to spread the glue— moving it across the envelope flap like a saw—wipe off the extra glue with his fingers, then stick it down, then use his fingers again to remove the extra glue pressed out by the flap.

All this time the people were running.

Now—glue back to the girl, pick up the duffel bag (he'd kept it between his legs to stop it being snatched), letters into the mailbox, and run!

He might be a prisoner on his last legs, completely worn out, but, goodness, how he ran!

He cut through some people who had dashed from the main exit gates and were dragging heavy luggage from the platform down onto the tracks and then up again onto the second platform. He reached his car and joined the line. He was about twentieth in the line, but then the ones in front were joined by friends and relations and he ended up about thirtieth. He'd never get a top bunk now, but his legs were so long he didn't really want one. He should be able to get hold of a luggage rack, though. They'd all have baskets thrown up on them—all right, he'd shove them out of the way.

They all carried the same sort of baskets, buckets as well. Maybe they were all full of spring vegetables? Were they on their way to Karaganda, as Chaly had described, to make up for mistakes in the supply system?

The old gray-haired car attendant was shouting at them to stand in line along the car and not climb in because there'd be room for everyone. But the last remark did not sound too confident—the line behind Oleg was still growing. Then Oleg noticed the beginning of what he'd been afraid of, a movement to jump the line. The first one to make a move was some wild, raving creature. The ignorant eye might have taken him for a psychopath and let him go to the front of the line, but Oleg at once recognized him as a self-styled camp hoodlum. He was trying to frighten people, as his sort always does. The loudmouth was backed up by a number of ordinary quiet people: if he's allowed through, why aren't we? Of course it was a ruse Oleg could have tried, and he'd have had a proper bunk to himself. But the past years had made him tired of such tricks. He wanted things done honestly and in the proper way, just as the old car attendant did.

The attendant was still not letting through the maniac, who was pushing him in the chest and using foul language, quite naturally, as though they were the most ordinary words in the world. The people in the line were murmuring sympathetically, "Let him through! He's a sick man!"

Oleg lurched forward. In a few enormous strides he was beside the maniac. Then he yelled right in his ear, without sparing his eardrums, "Hey! You! I'm from 'out there' too!"

The maniac jumped back, rubbing his ear. "Where's that?" he said.

Oleg knew he was too weak to fight, he was at his last gasp. But at least he had both hands free; the maniac had a basket in one. Towering over the maniac, he measured out his words quite softly: "The place where ninety-nine weep but one laughs."

The people in the line could not understand how the maniac was so suddenly cured. They saw him cool down, wink, and say to the tall chap in the overcoat, "I'm not saying anything. I don't mind. All right, get in first if you like."

But Oleg stayed there beside the maniac and the car attendant. If the worst came to the worst he could get on from here, but the ones who had been pushing were beginning to go back to their places in the line.

"That's all right by me," the maniac said with reproachful sarcasm. "I don't mind waiting."

On they came, carrying their baskets and their buckets. Under a sacking cover one caught the occasional glimpse of a long lilac-pink radish. Two out of three presented tickets to Karaganda. So these were the people Oleg had arranged the line for! The ordinary passengers were getting in too, including a respectable-looking woman in a blue jacket. Oleg got in and the maniac climbed confidently in behind him.

Oleg walked quickly along the car. He spotted a luggage rack—not one of the uncomfortable ones along the windows—which was still almost empty.

"Right," he announced. "We'll have to shift that basket."

"Where to? What's going on?" a man asked in alarm. He was lame but a sturdy fellow.

"Here's what's going on," Oleg replied. He was already up in the rack. "There's nowhere for people to lie down."

At once he made himself at home on the rack. He put his duffel bag under his head as a pillow, but only after removing the iron. He took off his overcoat and spread it out. He threw off his army jacket too. A man could do what he liked up here. Then he lay down to cool off. His feet and large-sized boots hung down over the corridor. They jutted out almost to calf length, but they were high enough not to get in anyone's way.

People were sorting themselves out down below as well, cooling off and getting to know each other.

The lame man seemed a sociable type. He told them he'd once been a vet's assistant. "Why did you give it up?" they asked him in surprise.

"What do you mean? Why should I get run in for every little sheep that dies? I'm better off on an invalid's pension carrying vegetables," he explained in a loud voice.

"Yes, what's wrong with that?" said the woman in the blue jacket.

"It was in Beria's day they rounded people up for fruit and vegetables. They only do it for household goods now."

The sun's last rays would be shining on them if they hadn't been hidden by the station.

It was still quite light down below, but up where Oleg was it was twilight. The "soft"- and "hard"-class sleeper passengers were strolling along the platform, but in here they were sitting wherever they had managed to grab seats, arranging their things. Oleg stretched out full length. That was good! It was terrible traveling forty-eight hours with your legs tucked under you in those converted freight cars. Nineteen men in a car like this would be terrible. Twenty-three would be even worse.

The others hadn't survived. But he had. He hadn't even died of cancer. And now his exile was cracking ilke an eggshell.

He remembered the *komendant* advising him to get married. They'd all be giving him advice like that soon.

It was good to lie down. Good.

The train shuddered and moved forward. It was only then that in his heart, or his soul, somewhere in his chest, in the deepest seat of his emotion, he was seized with anguish. He twisted his body and lay face down on his greatcoat, shut his eyes and thrust his face into the duffel bag, spiky with leaves.

The train went on and Kostoglotov's boots dangled toes down over the corridor like a dead man's.

An evil man threw tobacco in the Macaque Rhesus's eyes.

Just like that . . .

Appendix

Afterword

BY VLADIMIR PETROV

The story of the publication of *Cancer Ward* in the West—and of its non-publication in the Soviet Union—is closely interwoven with political developments in that country and with the fate of the author, Alexander Solzhenitsyn. Solzhenitsyn's fame came to him late in the period of the Thaw, following the death of Stalin, which probably reached its zenith in 1956–1957. The publication of the sensational *One Day in the Life of Ivan Denisovich* in the liberal monthly *Novy mir* in November 1962 was sponsored by Nikita Khrushchev himself and approved by the party's Politburo. The novel, which appeared shortly thereafter in book form, attracted immediate attention both in Russia and abroad by its highly realistic portrayal of the subhuman conditions in concentration camps of the late Stalin era. At the same time it came under a barrage of criticism from the unreconstructed Stalinists still controlling most of the Soviet press. Although Solzhenitsyn and his book were received enthusiastically in leftist circles in Europe as a manifestation of a decisive break by the Soviet leadership with the inglorious deeds of Stalin, the principal charge leveled against Solzhenitsyn was that he supplied grist to the anti-Soviet propaganda mill, a charge similar to that made in 1958 against Boris Pasternak for *Doctor Zhivago.*

For a while it seemed that Solzhenitsyn would weather the storm. Although during the spring of 1963 it became evident that the Communist Party leadership had decided to put an end to further liberalization of Soviet literature, some critics rallied to Solzhenitsyn's side. *Novy mir* published several of his short stories, and in December

1963 there began a lively public debate: should he be awarded the cherished Lenin Prize in literature? The debate ended in April 1964 when a *Pravda* editorial revealed that the Party leaders has decided against honoring the acknowledged leader of liberal Soviet writers in this manner.

No further works by Solzhenitsyn have been published in the Soviet Union. Yet under the uncertain conditions of the mid-sixties he continued to write, and his two novels, *Cancer Ward* and *The First Circle,* although finally rejected by the Soviet publishers, circulated widely among Russian intellectuals in manuscript form—as did many other literary works that failed to pass the official censorship. Inevitably, copies of Solzhenitsyn's manuscripts found their way out of the Soviet Union.

Like many of his literary colleagues, Solzhenitsyn continued to struggle against overwhelming odds, protesting the tightening of censorship and elimination of the liberties the Party had granted at its 20th Congress in 1956. He wrote "open letters," which also circulated by the hundreds in Moscow and elsewhere, and held his own in personal confrontations with the managers of Soviet literary affairs—the bureaucrats of the Union of Soviet Writers.

It should be stressed that in his struggle Solzhenitsyn remained a loyal and patriotic Soviet citizen, notwithstanding the attacks on him by Party hacks. His protests were directed against the bureaucracy's excesses and abuses, not against Soviet authority and the communist society. His aim was to improve and perfect the Soviet system, not to destroy it. We may suspect that he considered the utilization of world public opinion as a legitimate means of putting pressure on Soviet authorities, hoping that this pressure would help the more moderate elements in the Party hierarchy. He insisted that *Cancer Ward* be published in the Soviet Union, arguing that this, more than anything else, would take the wind out of the sails of anti-Soviet propaganda.

In some of his "open letters," Solzhenitsyn expressed disapproval of the publication of his books abroad. We can only speculate whether he protested in order to free himself of the blame of aiding and abetting the "imperialists." He was probably aware that his admirers abroad—the liberal intellectuals of the West—were the same people who had for years hoped for the liberalization of the Soviet state and worked hard for the reduction of East–West tensions. And he probably was not immune to the natural desire of an author to see his works in print.

Some Western intellectuals have expressed concern that foreign publication of Solzhenitsyn's novels in the face of the author's protests puts him in direct and immediate danger of police persecution, ignoring the fact that the author had already cast the die by writing the books. The publishers, much as they were aware of the dilemma, had to answer a broader question, namely whether they should in effect collaborate with the Soviet authorities and acquiesce in the repression of literature in Russia, or follow their own code and publish Solzhenitsyn's works because they merited publication. If it were a question of waiting until these works first appear in the Soviet Union, there would perhaps be a valid argument in favor of such delay. But it can be taken for granted that the chances for the publication of Solzhenitsyn's books in his own country are zero.

The author's two letters at the beginning of the book, and the documents reproduced below, all of which are my translations, reflect the struggle of Alexander Solzhenitsyn for his rights as an author and a citizen of the Soviet Union, and his concern about the future of Soviet literature. They also tell the story, in Solzhenitsyn's own words, of how *Cancer Ward,* Part One of which was initially accepted for publication, failed to appear in print in his country. All the documents belong to the period 1967–1968, and their authenticity is beyond doubt. They shed light on the general atmosphere in Soviet literature today and on the pathetic plight of one of the most talented and forceful writers of our time. Whatever Solzhenitsyn himself might feel, whatever punishment the increasingly brutal Soviet bureaucrats, fearful for their power, might inflict on him, the story of his struggle belongs on public record. It is another notable page in the long history of the battle of Russian writers for the cause of literature.

Letter of Pavel Antokolsky

To Comrade P. N. Demichev, Secretary of the Central Committee of the Communist Party of the Soviet Union.

Dear Piotr Nilych!

Like other delegates to our congress, I too have received the famous letter written by Alexander Isaevich Solzhenitsyn, and it has perturbed me, as it has several other comrades.

As an old writer and a Communist, I feel obliged to share my feelings with you.

I consider Alexander Solzhenitsyn a writer endowed with rare talent, a rising hope of our realistic literature, an heir to the great and humanistic traditions of Gogol, Lev Tolstoy, and Alexey Maximovich Gorky. We ought to cherish such contributors to our culture. Criticism of those works of Solzhenitsyn which have been published has shocked me because it is biased, unjust, and unconvincing.

The ban on Solzhenitsyn's manuscripts, described in detail in his letter, strikes one as an incredible occurrence unworthy of our socialist society and our Soviet state. It is all the more dreadful in view of the fact that the same thing happened several years ago to the manuscript of the second part of the novel by the late Vassily Grossman.

Is it possible that such reprisals against the manuscripts of our writers are threatening to become a custom sanctioned by law in our country?

This cannot and must not happen!

Such savagery toward works of art is incompatible with our fundamental laws and unthinkable in any normal human community.

If Solzhenitsyn's works contain controversial and unclear elements, if political mistakes have been discovered in them, they should be submitted to the public for open discussion. Writers have many opportunities to do this.

I have worked in the field of literature for fifty years. I have written many books and lived out my life, a life full of vicissitudes. I have experienced periods of burning anxiety for the fate of our entire literature, and sometimes for various comrades: Bulgakov, Pasternak, Titsian Tabidze—I recall the names of those who were close to me.

Having lived out my life, I would never have thought that such anxiety would recur in the evening of my life, and on the eve of the great and glorious anniversary!*

If a Soviet writer is compelled to turn to his fellow writers with a letter like Solzhenitsyn's, this means that we are all morally responsible to him and to our own readers. If he cannot tell his readers the truth, then I too, old writer that I am, have no right to look my readers in the eye.

PAVEL ANTOKOLSKY

Session of Soviet Writers' Secretariat

This is a transcript of the proceedings of a session of the secretariat of the Board of the Union of Soviet Writers, held on September 22, 1967, at which Solzhenitsyn himself was present. The session was attended by approximately thirty secretaries of the Union of Writers, and by Comrade Melentiev of the Cultural Department of the Central Committee. K. A. Fedin was chairman. The session, which discussed the two letters of Solzhenitsyn, lasted four hours.

FEDIN: I was shaken by Solzhenitsyn's second letter. His allegation that things have come to a standstill seems to me to be without foundation. I feel that this was an insult to our collective. Three and a half months are by no means a long time to spend examining his manuscript. I sensed something in the nature of a threat in his letter. This strikes me as offensive! Solzhenitsyn's second letter seems to urge us to take up his manuscripts in all haste and to publish them immediately. The second letter continues the line of the first, but the first letter spoke more concretely and with more fervor about the fate of the writer, while the second, I feel, was offensive. Where do we stand with regard to the complex question of publishing Solzhenitsyn's works? None of us denies that he is talented. Yet the tenor of the letter veers in an impermissible direction. His letter is like a slap in the face to us, as if we were dullards and not representatives of the creative intelligentsia. In the final analysis, he himself is slowing down the examination of the question of his demands. I did not find the idea of literary comradeship in his letters. Whether we want to or not, today we must get into a discussion of Solzhenitsyn's works, but it seems to me that we should start by discussing the letters.

Solzhenitsyn requests permission to say a few words about the subject under discussion. He reads the following written statement.

SOLZHENITSYN: It has become known to me that, in preparation for the discussion of *Cancer Ward*, the secretaries of the Board were instructed to read

*The fiftieth anniversary of the October Revolution.

the play, *Feast of the Conquerors,* which I myself have long since renounced; I have not even read it for ten years. I destroyed all copies of it except the one that was confiscated and that has now been reproduced. More than once I have explained that this play was written not by Solzhenitsyn, member of the Union of Writers, but by a nameless prisoner, Sh-232, in those distant years when there was no return to freedom for political prisoners, and at a time when no one in the community, including the writers' community, either in word or deed spoke out against repression, even when such repression was directed against entire peoples. I now bear just as little responsibility for this play as many other authors bear for speeches and books they wrote in 1949 but would not write again today. This play bears the stamp of the desperation of the concentration camp in those years when a man's whole conscious being was determined by his social being, and at a time when the conscious being was by no means uplifted by prayers for those who were being persecuted. This play bears no relationship whatsoever to my present work, and the critique of it is a deliberate departure from a businesslike discussion of the novel, *Cancer Ward.*

Moreover, it is beneath a writer's ethics to discuss a work that was seized in such a way from a private apartment. The critique of my novel, *The First Circle,* is again a separate matter and should not be substituted for a critique of the novel, *Cancer Ward.*

KORNEICHUK: I have a question to put to Solzhenitsyn. How does he regard the licentious bourgeois propaganda that his first letter evoked? Why doesn't he dissociate himself from the propaganda? Why does he put up with it in silence? How is it that his letter was broadcast over the radio in the West even before the congress of Soviet writers started?

Fedin calls upon Solzhenitsyn to reply. Solzhenitsyn replies that he is not a schoolboy who must jump up to answer every question, and that he will deliver a statement like the others. Fedin says that Solzhenitsyn can wait until there are several questions and then answer them all at the same time.

BARUZDIN: Even though Solzhenitsyn protests against the discussion of *Feast of the Conquerors,* we shall have to discuss this play whether he wants to or not.

SALYNSKY: I would like Solzhenitsyn to tell us by whom, when, and under what circumstances these materials were removed. Has the author asked for their return? To whom did he address his request?

Fedin asks Solzhenitsyn to answer these questions. Solzhenitsyn repeats that he will answer them when making his statement.

FEDIN: But the Secretariat cannot begin the discussion until it has the answers to these questions.

VOICE: If Solzhenitsyn wants to refuse to talk at all to the Secretariat, let him say so.

SOLZHENITSYN: Very well, I shall answer these questions. It is not true that the letter was broadcast over the radio in the West before the congress: it was broadcast *after* the congress closed, and then not right away. Very significant and expressive use is made here of the word "abroad," as if it referred to some higher authority whose opinion was very much cherished. Perhaps this is understandable to those who spend much creative time traveling abroad, to those who flood our literature with sketches about life abroad. But all this is alien to me. I have never been abroad, but I do know that I don't have time enough left in my life to learn about life there. I do not understand how one can be so sensitive to opinion abroad and not to one's own country, to pulsing public opinion here. During my entire life I have had the soil of my homeland under my feet; only *its* pain do I hear, only about *it* do I write.

Why was the play, *Feast of the Conquerors,* mentioned in the letter to the congress? This can be seen from the letter itself: in order to protest against the illegal "publication" and dissemination of this play against the will of the author and without his consent.

Now, concerning the confiscation of my novel and papers. Yes, I did write several times beginning in 1965 to protest this matter to the Central Committee of the Communist Party. But in recent days a whole new version of the confiscation of my archives has been invented. The story is that Teush, the person who was keeping my manuscripts, had some tie with another person who is not named, that the latter was arrested while going through customs (where is not mentioned), and that something or other was found in his possession (they do not say what); it was not something of mine, but they decided to protect me against such an acquaintanceship. All this is a lie. Teush's friend was investigated two years ago, but no such accusation was made against him. The items I had in safekeeping were discovered as a consequence of police surveillance, wire-tapping, and eavesdropping. And here is the remarkable thing: barely does the new version of the confiscation appear than it crops up in various parts of the country. Lecturer Potemkin has just aired it to a large assemblage in Riga; and one of the secretaries of the Union of Writers has passed it on to writers in Moscow, adding his own invention, namely, that I supposedly acknowledged all these things at the last meeting of the Secretariat. Yet not a single one of these things was discussed. I have no doubt that I will soon start getting letters from all parts of the country about this spreading version.

VOICE: Has the editorial board of *Novy mir* rejected or accepted the novel, *Cancer Ward?*

ABDUMOMUNOV: What kind of authorization does *Novy mir* require to print a story, and from whom does it come?

TVARDOVSKY: Generally, the decision to print or not to print a particular thing is a matter for the editorial board to decide. But in the situation that has developed around this author's name, the Secretariat of the Union must decide.

VORONKOV: Not once has Solzhenitsyn appealed directly to the Secretariat of the Union of Writers. After Solzhenitsyn's letter to the congress, some of the comrades in the Secretariat expressed the desire to meet with him, to answer questions, to talk with him and help. But after the letter appeared in the dirty bourgeois press and Solzhenitsyn did not react in any way . . .

TVARDOVSKY (*interrupting*): Nor did the Union of Writers!

VORONKOV: . . . this desire died. And now the second letter has come. It is written in the form of an ultimatum; it is offensive and a disrespect to our writers' community. Just now Solzhenitsyn referred to "one of the secretaries" who addressed a party meeting of Moscow writers. I was that secretary. (*To Solzhenitsyn*) People hastened to inform you but they did a bad job of it. As to the confiscation of your things, the only thing I mentioned was that you had admitted at the last meeting that the confiscated items were yours and there had been no search made of your house. Naturally, after your letter to the congress, we ourselves wanted to read all your works. But you should not be so rude to your brothers in labor and writing! And you, Alexander Trifonovich (Tvardovsky), if you consider it necessary to print *Cancer Ward*, and if the author accepts your corrections, then go ahead and print it yourself; why should the Secretariat be involved?

TVARDOVSKY: And what happened in the case of Bek?* The Secretariat was also involved then and made its recommendations, but all the same nothing was published.

VORONKOV: What interests me most of all now is the civic image of Citizen Solzhenitsyn: Why doesn't he give answer to the malicious bourgeois propaganda? And why does he treat us as he does?

MUSREPOV: I have a question, too. How can he possibly write in his letter: "Prominent persons persistently express regret that I did not die in the camp." What right does he have to write such a thing?

SHARIPOV: And by what channels could the letter have reached the West?

Fedin asks Solzhenitsyn to answer these questions.

SOLZHENITSYN: Lots of things have been said about me. A person who right now occupies a very high position publicly declared that he is sorry he was not one of the "troika" that sentenced me in 1945, that he would have sentenced me to be shot then and there! Here at the Secretariat my second letter is interpreted as an ultimatum: either print the story, or it will be printed in the West. But it isn't I who presents this ultimatum to the Secretariat; life presents this ultimatum to you and me both. I write that I am disturbed by the distribution of the story in hundreds—in hundreds of typewritten copies.

*The writer Alexander Bek became prominent during the war. His novel, referred to here, was first approved for publication in *Novy mir,* and then rejected.

VOICE: How did this come about?

SOLZHENITSYN: My works are disseminated in one way only: people persistently ask to read them, and having received them to read, they either use their spare time or their own funds to copy them and then give them to others to read. As long as a year ago the entire Moscow section of the Writers' Union read the first part of *Cancer Ward,* and I am surprised that Comrade Voronkov said here that they didn't know where to get it and that they asked the KGB. About three years ago my *Prose Poems* were disseminated just as rapidly: barely had I given the manuscript to people to read when it quickly reached various cities in the Union. And then the editors of *Novy mir* received a letter from the West from which we learned that these writings had already been published there.* It was in order that such a fate might not befall *Cancer Ward* that I wrote my insistent letter to the Secretariat. I am no less astonished that the Secretariat could fail to react in some way to my letter to the congress before the West did. And how could it fail to respond to all the slander that surrounds me? Comrade Voronkov has used the remarkable expression, "brothers in writing and labor." Well, the fact of the matter is that these brothers in writing and labor have for two and a half years calmly watched me being hounded, persecuted, and slandered.

TVARDOVSKY: Not everyone has been indifferent.

SOLZHENITSYN: And newspaper editors, also like brothers, contribute to the web of falsehood that is woven around me by not publishing my denials. I'm not speaking about the fact that people in the concentration camps are not allowed to read my book, *One Day in the Life of Ivan Denisovich.* It was banned in the camps; searches were made and people were put in solitary confinement for reading it, even during those months when all the newspapers were loudly acclaiming it and promising that "this kind of thing will not happen again." But in recent times the book has secretly been withdrawn from libraries outside the camps as well. I have received letters from various places telling me of the prohibition against circulating the book: the order is to tell readers that the book is in the bindery, or that it is out, or that there is no access to the shelves where the book is kept, and to refuse to circulate it. Here is a letter recently received from Krasnogvardeiskii Region in the Crimea:

> In the regional library, I was confidentially told (I am an activist in this library) of an order that your books be removed from circulation. One of the women workers in the library wanted to present me with *One Day* in a newspaper edition as a souvenir, since the library no longer needs it, but another woman immediately stopped her rash friend: "What are you doing, you mustn't! Once the book has been assigned to the Special Section, it is dangerous to make a present of it."

*In *The New Leader,* January 18, 1965.

I am not saying that the book has been removed from *all* libraries; here and there it can still be found. But people coming to visit me in Riazan were unable to get my book in the Riazan Oblast Reading Room! They were given various excuses but they did not get the book . . .

The circle of lies becomes ever wider, having no limits; they are even charging me with having been taken prisoner during the war and having collaborated with the Germans. But that's not the end of it! This summer, in the political education schools, e.g., in Bolshevo, the party propagandists were told that I had fled to the United Arab Republic and that I had changed my citizenship. Naturally, all this was written down in the propagandists' notebooks and is disseminated one hundred times over. And this took place no more than a few miles from the capital! Here is another version. In Solikamsk, a Major Shestakov declared that I had fled to England, having taken advantage of a tourist visa. This man is the deputy for political affairs in his army unit—who'd dare to disbelieve him? Another time, the same man stated: "Solzhenitsyn has officially been *forbidden* to write." Well, at least here he is closer to the truth.

The following is being said about me from the rostrums: "He was set free prematurely, for no reason." Whether there was any reason can be seen in the court decision of the Military Collegium of the Supreme Court, Rehabilitation Section. This document has been presented to the Secretariat . . .

TVARDOVSKY: It also contains the combat record of Officer Solzhenitsyn.

SOLZHENITSYN: And the expression "prematurely," isn't it really something? After having served the eight-year sentence, I was kept an additional month in prison, but of course it is considered shameful even to mention such a petty detail. I spent three years in exile with that eternal feeling of doom. It was only thanks to the 20th Party Congress that I was set free—and this is called "prematurely"! The expression is so reminiscent of the conditions which prevailed in the 1949–53 period: if a man did not die beside a camp rubbish heap, if he was able even to crawl out of the camp, this meant he had been set free "prematurely"—after all, the sentence was for eternity and anything earlier was "premature."

Former Minister Semichastny, who was fond of speaking on literary issues, also singled me out for attention more than once. One of his astonishing, even comical, accusations was the following: Solzhenitsyn is materially supporting the capitalist world; else why doesn't he collect his royalties from the publishers of his well-known book? Obviously, the reference was to *Ivan Denisovich,* since no other book of mine had been published at that time. Now if you knew, if you had read somewhere that Comrade Semichastny felt that it was absolutely necessary for me to wrest the money from the capitalists, then why didn't you inform me about it? This is a farce; whoever collects royalties from the West has sold out to the capitalists; whoever does not take the money is materially supporting them. And the third alternative? To go to heaven. While Semichastny is no longer a minister, his idea has not died: the All-Union Society for the Dissemination of Scientific Information has carried it further. To illustrate, the idea was repeated on July 16 of this year by Lecturer A. A. Freifeld at the Sverdlovsk Circus. Two thousand persons sat there and marveled: "What a crafty bird, that Solzhenitsyn! Without leaving the Soviet Union, without a single kopeck in his pocket, he contrived to support world capitalism materially." This is indeed a story to be told at a circus.

We had a talk on June 12, right here, at the Secretariat. It was quiet and peaceful. We seemed to make some progress. A short time passed, and suddenly rumors were rampant all over Moscow. Everything that actually took place was distorted, beginning with the fabrication that Tvardovsky had been shouting and waving his fist at me. But everyone who was there knows that nothing like that took place. Why these lies, then? And right now we are all hearing what is said here, but where is the guarantee that after today's meeting of the Secretariat everything will not be distorted again? If you really are "brothers in labor and writing," then my first request is that when you talk about today's session, don't fabricate and distort things.

I am one person; my slanderers number in the hundreds. Naturally I am never able to defend myself, and I never know against whom I should defend myself. I wouldn't be surprised if I were declared to be an adherent of the geocentric cosmic system and to have been the first to light the pyre of Giordano Bruno.

SALYNSKY: I shall speak of *Cancer Ward*. I believe that it should be printed —it is a vivid and powerful work. To be sure, it contains descriptions of diseases in pathological terms, and the reader involuntarily develops a phobia about cancer—a phobia which is already widespread in our century. Somehow this aspect of the book should be eliminated. The caustic, topical-satirical style should also be eliminated. Another negative feature is that the destinies of almost all the characters are connected with the concentration camp or with camp life in one form or another. This may be all right in the case of Kostoglotov or Rusanov, but why does it have to be applied to Vadim, to Shulubin, and even to the soldier? At the very end we learn that he is no ordinary soldier from the army, that he is a camp guard. Still, the basic orientation of the novel is to discuss the end of the difficult era of our past. And now a few words about moral socialism, a concept expounded in the novel. In my opinion, there is nothing bad about this. It would be bad if Solzhenitsyn were preaching *amoral* socialism. If he were preaching national socialism or the Chinese version of national socialism—it would have been bad. Each person is free to form his own ideas on socialism and its development. I personally believe that socialism is determined by economic laws. But of course there is room for argument. Why not print the story then? (*He subsequently calls upon the Secretariat to issue a statement resolutely refuting the slanders against Solzhenitsyn.*)

SIMONOV: I do not accept the novel, *The First Circle,* and oppose its publication. As for *Cancer Ward,* I am in favor of publishing it. Not everything in the story is to my liking, but it does not have to please everyone. Perhaps the author should take into account some of the comments that have been made, but naturally he cannot adopt all of the suggestions. It is also our duty to refute the slander about him. Furthermore, his book of stories should be published. The foreword to the latter would be a good place in which to publish his biography, and in this way the slander would die by itself. Both we and he himself can and must put an end to false accusations. I have not read *Feast of the Conquerors,* nor do I desire to do so, since the author doesn't wish it.

TVARDOVSKY: Solzhenitsyn's position is such that he cannot issue a statement. It is we ourselves, the Union, who must make a statement refuting the slander. At the same time, we must sternly warn Solzhenitsyn against the inadmissible, unpleasant way in which he addressed the congress. The editorial board of *Novy mir* sees no reason why *Cancer Ward* should not be printed, naturally with certain revisions. We only wish to receive the Secretariat's approval or at least word that the Secretariat does not object.

He asks Voronkov to produce the Secretariat's draft communiqué which was prepared back in June. Voronkov indicates that he is in no hurry to produce the communiqué. During this time exchanges are heard: "They still haven't decided. There are those who are opposed!"

FEDIN: No, that isn't so. It isn't the Secretariat that has to print or reject anything. Are we really guilty of anything? Is it possible, Alexander Trifonovich, that you feel guilty?

TVARDOVSKY (*quickly, expressively*): I? No.

FEDIN: We shouldn't search for some trumped-up excuse to make a statement. Mere existence of the rumors does not provide sufficient grounds for doing so. It would be another matter if Solzhenitsyn himself were to find a way to resolve the situation. What is needed is a public statement by Solzhenitsyn himself. (*To Solzhenitsyn*) But think it over, Alexander Isaevich— whose interest will be served by our publishing your protests? You must protest above all against the dirty use of your name by our enemies in the West. Naturally, in the process you will also have the opportunity to vent some of the complaints you've uttered here today. If this proves to be a fortunate and tactful document, we will print it and help you. It is precisely from this point that your justification must proceed, and not from your works, or from this bartering as to how many months we are entitled to examine your manuscript. Three months, four months, is that really so important? It is far more frightening that your works are used there, in the West, for the basest of purposes.

(*Approval expressed among members of the Secretariat.*)

KORNEICHUK: We didn't invite you here to throw stones at you. We summoned you in order to help you out of this trying and ambiguous situation. You were asked questions but you declined to answer. By our writings we are protecting the interests of our government, our party, our people. Here you have sarcastically referred to trips abroad as if they were pleasant strolls. We travel abroad to wage the struggle. We return home from abroad, worn out and exhausted, but with the feeling of having done our duty. Don't think that I was offended by the comment concerning travel sketches. I don't write them. I travel on the business of the World Peace Council. We know that you suffered a great deal, but you are not the only one. There were many other comrades in the camps besides you. Some were old Communists. From the camps they went to the front. Our past consists not of acts of injustice alone; there were also acts of heroism—but you didn't notice them. Your works consist only of accusations. *Feast of the Conquerors* is malicious, vile, offensive! And this foul play is disseminated, and the people read it! When were you imprisoned? Not in 1937. In 1937 *we* went through a great deal, but nothing stopped us! Konstantin Alexandrovich Fedin was right in saying that you must speak out publicly and strike out against Western propaganda. Do battle against the foes of our nation! Do you realize that thermonuclear weapons exist in the world and that despite all our peaceful efforts the United States may employ them? How then can we, Soviet writers, not be soldiers?

SOLZHENITSYN: I have repeatedly declared that it is dishonest to discuss *Feast of the Conquerors,* and I demand that this argument be excluded from our discussion.

SURKOV: You can't stop everyone from talking.

KOZHEVNIKOV: The long time lapse between the receipt of Solzhenitsyn's letter and today's discussion is in fact an expression of the *seriousness* with which the Secretariat approaches the letter. If we had discussed it at the time, while the impact was still hot, we would have treated it more severely and less thoughtfully. We ourselves decided to find out just what kind of anti-Soviet manuscripts these were, and we spent a good deal of time reading them. The military service of Solzhenitsyn has been confirmed by relevant documents; yet we are not now discussing the officer but rather the writer. Today, for the first time, I have heard Solzhenitsyn renounce the libelous depiction of Soviet reality in *Feast of the Conquerors,* but I still cannot get over my first impression of this play. For me, this moment of Solzhenitsyn's renunciation of *Feast of the Conquerors* still does not jibe with my perception of the play. Perhaps this is because in both *The First Circle* and *Cancer Ward* there is a feeling of the same vengeance for past suffering. And if it is a question of the fate of these works, the author should remember that he is indebted to the Party organ that discovered him. Some time ago, I was the first to express apprehension concerning "Matriona's House." We spent time reading your gray manuscript, which you did not even venture to give to any editorial board. *Cancer Ward* evokes revulsion from the abundance of naturalism, from the surfeit of all manner of horrors. All the same, its basic orientation is not medical, but rather social . . . And it is apparently from this that the title of the work is derived. In your second letter, you demand the publication of your story, which still requires further work. Is such a demand worthy of a writer? All of our writers willingly listen to the opinions of the editors and do not hurry them.

SOLZHENITSYN: Despite my explanations and objections, despite the utter senselessness of discussing a work written twenty years ago, in another era, in an incomparably different situation, by a different person—a work, moreover, which has never been published or read by anyone, and which was stolen from a drawer—some of the speakers have concentrated their attention on this very work. This is even more senseless than the action of the First Congress of Writers when it rebuked Maxim Gorky for *Untimely Thoughts* or Sergeyev-Tsensky for the *osvagovskie* correspondence,* which had been published a good fifteen years earlier. Korneichuk has stated here that "such a thing has never happened and will not happen in the history of Russian literature." Precisely!

OZEROV: The letter to the congress proved to be a politically irresponsible act. First of all, the letter reached our enemies. It contained things that were incorrect. Zamyatin was put in the same heap together with unjustly repressed writers. As regards the publication of *Cancer Ward*, we can make an agreement with *Novy mir* that the thing be printed only if the manuscript is corrected and the corrections are discussed. There remains some other very important work to be done. The story is uneven in quality. There are good and bad points in it. Most objectionable is the penchant for sloganeering and caricatures. I would ask that quite a number of things be deleted, things which we simply do not have time to discuss now. The philosophy of moral socialism does not belong merely to the hero. One senses that it is being defended by the author. This cannot be permitted.

SURKOV: I, too, have read *Feast of Conquerors*. The mood of it is, "Be damned, the whole lot of you!" The same mood pervades *Cancer Ward* as well. Having suffered so much, you had a right to be angry as a human being, Alexander Isaevich, but after all you are also a writer! I have known Communists who were sent to camps, but this in no measure affected their world-view. No, your story does not approach fundamental problems in philosophical terms, but in political terms. And then there is the reference to that idol in the theater square, even though the monument to Marx had not yet been erected at that time.

If *Cancer Ward* were to be published, it would be used against us, and it would be more dangerous than Svetlana's memoirs. Yes, of course it would be good to forestall its publication in the West, but that is difficult. For example, in recent times I have been close to Anna Andreyevna Akhmatova. I know that she gave her poem "Requiem" to several people to read. It was passed around for several weeks, and then suddenly it was printed in the West. Of course, our reader is now so developed and so sophisticated that no measly little book is going to alienate him from Communism. All the same, the works of Solzhenitsyn are more dangerous to us than those of Pasternak: Pasternak was a man divorced from life, while Solzhenitsyn, with his animated, militant, ideological temperament, is a man of principle. We represent the first revolution in the history of mankind that has changed

*Both Gorky and Sergeyev-Tsensky had initially expressed misgivings about the October Revolution.

neither its slogans nor its banners. "Moral socialism" is a philistine socialism. It is old and primitive, and (*turning to Solzhenitsyn*) I don't understand how anyone could fail to understand this, how anyone could find anything in it.

SALYNSKY: I do not defend it in the least.

RIURIKOV: Solzhenitsyn has suffered from those who have slandered him, but those who have heaped excessive praise on him and have ascribed to him qualities that he does not possess have also done him harm. If Solzhenitsyn is renouncing anything, then he should renounce the title of "standard-bearer of Russian realism." The conduct of Marshal Rokossovsky and General Gorbatov is more honest than that of his heroes.* The source of this writer's energy lies in bitterness and wrath. As a human being, one can understand this. (*To Solzhenitsyn*) You write that your things are prohibited, but not a single one of your novels has been censored. I marvel that Tvardovsky asks permission from us. I, for example, have never asked the Union of Writers for permission to print or not to print. (*He asks Solzhenitsyn to heed the recommendations of* Novy mir *and promises page-by-page comments on* Cancer Ward *from "anyone present."*)

BARUZDIN: I happen to be one of those who from the start has not been captivated by the works of Solzhenitsyn. "Matriona's House" was already much weaker than his first work, *One Day in the Life of Ivan Denisovich.* And *The First Circle* is much weaker, so pitifully naïve and primitive are the depictions of Stalin, Abakumov, and Poskrebyshev. But *Cancer Ward* is an anti-humanitarian work. The end of the story leads to the conclusion that "a different road should have been taken." Did Solzhenitsyn really believe that his letter "in place of a speech" would be read from the rostrum of the congress? How many letters did the congress receive?

VORONKOV: About five hundred.

BARUZDIN: Well! And would it really have been possible to get through them in a hurry? I do not agree with Riurikov: it is proper that the question of permission be placed before the Secretariat. Our Secretariat should more frequently play a creative role and should willingly advise editors.

ABDUMOMUNOV: It is a very good thing that Solzhenitsyn has found the courage to repudiate *Feast of the Conquerors.* He will also find the courage to think of ways of carrying out the proposal of Konstantin Alexandrovich Fedin. If we publish *Cancer Ward,* there will be more commotion and harm than there was from his first letter to the congress. Incidentally, what's the meaning of the expression "threw tobacco into the eyes of the Rhesus monkey—just like that"? Why the "just like that"? This is against our entire style of narration. In the story there are the Rusanovs and the great martyrs from the camp—but is that all? And where is Soviet society? One shouldn't lay it

*Gorbatov's memoirs, *Years of My Life,* have been published in English.

on so thick and make the story so gloomy. There are many tedious passages, twists and turns, and naturalistic scenes—all these should be eliminated.

ABASHIDZE: I was able to read only 150 pages of *Cancer Ward* and therefore can make no thoroughgoing assessment of it. Yet I didn't get the impression that the novel should not be published. But I repeat, I can't make a thorough assessment. Perhaps the most important things are further on in the book. All of us, being honest and talented writers, have fought against embellishers even when we were forbidden to do so. But Solzhenitsyn tends to go to the other extreme: parts of his work are of a purely essayist, exposé nature. The artist is like a child, he takes a machine apart to see what is inside. But genuine art begins with putting things together. I have noticed him asking the person sitting next to him the name of each speaker. Why doesn't he know any of us? Because we have never invited him. The proposal of Konstantin Alexandrovich was correct: let Solzhenitsyn himself answer, perhaps first of all for his own sake.

BROVKA: In Belorussia there are also many people who were imprisoned. For example, Sergei Grakhovsky was in prison for twenty years. Yet he realized that it was not the people, not the Party, and not the Soviet authorities that were responsible for illegal acts. The people have already seen through Svetlana's notes—that fishwife twaddle—and are laughing at them. But before us stands a generally acknowledged talent, and therein lies the danger of publication. Yes, you feel the pain of your land, even to an extraordinary degree. But you don't feel its joys. *Cancer Ward* is too gloomy and should not be printed.

(*Like all preceding and subsequent speakers, he supports Fedin's proposal that Solzhenitsyn himself speak out against the Western slander concerning his letter.*)

YASHEN: The author is not tortured by injustice; he is rather poisoned by hatred. People are outraged that there is such a writer in the ranks of the Union of Writers. I would like to propose his expulsion from the Union. He is not the only one who suffered, but the others understand the tragedy of the time better. The hand of a master is discernible in *Cancer Ward*. The author knows the subject better than any physician or professor. As for the siege of Leningrad, he now blames "still others" besides Hitler. Whom? We don't know. Is it Beria? Or today's outstanding leaders? He should speak out plainly.

(*All the same, the speaker supports Tvardovsky's courageous decision to work on the story with the author, remarking that it can then be shown to a limited number of people.*)

KERBABAEV: I read *Cancer Ward* with a feeling of great dissatisfaction. Everyone is a former prisoner, everything is gloomy, there is not a single word of warmth. It is downright nauseating to read. Vera offers the hero her home and her embraces, but he renounces life. And then there is the remark, "twenty-nine weep and one laughs"—how are we to understand this? Does this refer to the Soviet Union? I agree with what my friend Korneichuk said. Why does the author see only the black? Why don't I write about the black? I always strive to write only about joyful things. It is not enough that he has repudiated *Feast of the Conquerors.* I would consider it courageous if he would renounce *Cancer Ward.* Then I would embrace him like a brother.

SHARIPOV: I wouldn't make any allowances in his case—I'd expel him from the Union. In his play, not only everything Soviet but even Suvorov* is presented negatively. I completely agree: let him repudiate *Cancer Ward.*

NOVICHENKO: The letter with its inadmissible appeal was sent to the congress over the head of the formal addressee. I approve Tvardovsky's stern words that we should resolutely condemn this kind of conduct. I disagree with the principal demands of the letter: it is impossible to let everything be printed. Wouldn't that also mean the publication of *Feast of the Conquerors?* Concerning *Cancer Ward,* I have mixed feelings. I am no child, my time will come to die, perhaps in an agony like that of Solzhenitsyn's heroes. But then the crucial issue will be: how is your conscience? What are your moral reserves? If the novel had been confined to these things, I would have considered it necessary to publish it. But there was the base interference in our literary life—the caricatured scene with Rusanov's daughter, which is not congruent with our literary traditions. In the ideological and political sense, moral socialism is the negation of Marxism-Leninism. All these things are completely unacceptable to us, to our society and to our people. Even if this novel were put into some kind of shape, it would not be a novel of socialist realism, but only an ordinarily competent work.

MARKOV: This has been a valuable discussion. (*The speaker notes that he has just returned from Siberia, where he spoke before a mass audience five times.*) I must say that nowhere did Solzhenitsyn's name create any particular stir. In one place only was a note submitted to me. I ask your forgiveness, but this is exactly the way it was written: "Just when is this man Solzhenitsyn going to stop reviling Soviet literature?" We await a completely clear answer from Solzhenitsyn to the bourgeois slander; we await his statement in the press. He must defend his honor as a Soviet writer. As for his dedication with regard to *Feast of the Conquerors,* he took a load off my mind. I view *Cancer Ward* in the same light as Surkov does. After all, the thing does have some practical worth. But the social and political settings in it are utterly unacceptable to me. Its culprits remain nameless. What with the excellent collaboration that has been established between *Novy mir* and Alexander Isaevich, this story can be finished, even though it requires very serious work. But of course it would be impossible to put it into print today. So what next? Let me suggest some constructive advice: Alexander Isaevich must prepare the kind of statement for the press that we talked about. This would be very good, on the very eve of the fiftieth anniversary of the Great October Revolution. Then it would be possible to issue some kind of com-

---

*Russia's military hero, Suvorov waged successful campaigns against the Turks and the French late in the eighteenth century.

muniqué from the Secretariat. All the same, I still consider him our comrade. But, Alexander Isaevich, it's your fault and no one else's that we find ourselves in this complicated situation. As to the suggestions concerning expulsion from the Union—given the conditions of comradeship that are supposed to prevail, we should not be unduly hasty.

SOLZHENITSYN: I have already spoken out against the discussion of *Feast of the Conquerors* several times today, but I shall have to do so again. In the final analysis, I can rebuke all of you for not being adherents of the theory of development if you seriously believe that in the span of twenty years and in the face of a complete change in all our circumstances, a man does not change. But I have heard an even more serious thing here: Korneichuk, Baruzdin, and someone else mentioned that the people are reading *Feast of the Conquerors*, as if this play was being disseminated. I shall now speak very slowly; let my every word be taken down accurately. If *Feast of the Conquerors* is being widely circulated or printed, I solemnly declare that the full responsibility lies with the organization which had the only remaining copy—one not read by anyone—and used it for "publication" of the play during my lifetime and against my will; it is this organization that is disseminating the play! For a year and a half I have repeatedly warned that this is very dangerous. I imagine that there is no reading room there, that one is handed the play and takes it home. But at home there are sons and daughters, and desk drawers are not always locked. I had already issued a warning before, and I am issuing it again today!

Now, as to *Cancer Ward*, I am being criticized for the very title of the story, which is said to deal not with a medical case but with some kind of symbol. I reply that this symbol is indeed harmful, if it can be perceived only by a person who had himself experienced cancer and all the stages of dying. The fact is that the subject is specifically and literally cancer, a subject avoided in literature, but nevertheless a reality as its victims know only too well from daily experience. These may include your relatives—or soon perhaps someone among those present will be confined to a ward for cancer patients, and then he will understand what kind of a "symbol" it is.

I absolutely do not understand why *Cancer Ward* is accused of being antihumanitarian. Quite the reverse is true: life conquers death, the past is conquered by the future. Were this not the case, I would not by my very nature have undertaken to write it. But I do not believe that it is the task of literature to conceal the truth, or to tone it down, with respect either to society or the individual. Rather, I believe that it is the task of literature to tell people the real truth as they expect it. Moreover, it is not the task of the writer to defend or criticize one or another mode of distributing the social product, or to defend or criticize one or another form of government organization. The task of the writer is to select more universal and eternal questions, the secrets of the human heart and conscience, the confrontation of life with death, the triumph over spiritual sorrow, the laws of the history of mankind that were born in the depths of time immemorial and that will cease to exist only when the sun ceases to shine.

I am disturbed by the fact that some comrades simply did not read certain passages of the story attentively, and hence formed the wrong impressions. For example, "twenty-nine weep and one laughs" was a popular concentration-camp saying addressed to the type of person who would try to go to the head of the queue in a mess-hall. Kostoglotov comes out with this saying only so that he may be recognized, that's all. And from this people draw the conclusion that the phrase is supposed to apply to the entire Soviet Union. Or the case of "the Rhesus monkey." She appears twice in the story, and from the comparison it becomes clear that this evil person who throws tobacco in the animal's eyes is meant to represent Stalin specifically. And why the protest over my "just like that"? If "just like that" does not apply, does that mean that this was normal or necessary?

Surkov surprised me. At first I couldn't even understand why he was talking about Marx. Where does Marx come into my story? Alexei Alexandrovich, you are a poet, a man with sensitive taste, yet in this case your imagination played a trick on you. You didn't grasp the meaning of this scene. Shulubin cites Bacon's ideas and employs his terminology. He says "idols of the market," and Kostoglotov tries to imagine a marketplace and in the center a gray idol; Shulubin says "idols of the theater," and Kostoglotov pictures an idol inside a theater—but that doesn't work, and so it must be an idol in a theater square. How could you imagine that this referred to Moscow and to the monument to Marx that had not yet even been built?

Comrade Surkov said that only a few weeks after Akhmatova's "Requiem" had been passed from hand to hand, it was published abroad. Well, *Cancer Ward* has been in circulation for more than a year. And this is what concerns me, and this is why I am hurrying the Secretariat.

One more piece of advice was given to me by Comrade Riurikov: to repudiate Russian realism. Placing my hand on my heart, I swear that I shall never do it.

RIURIKOV: I did not say that you should repudiate Russian realism, but rather that you should repudiate your role as it is interpreted in the West.

SOLZHENITSYN: Now concerning the suggestion of Konstantin Alexandrovich. Well, of course I do not welcome it. Publicity is precisely what I am relentlessly trying to attain. We have concealed things long enough—we have had enough of hiding our speeches and our manuscripts under seven locks. Now, we had a previous discussion of *Cancer Ward*.* The Prose Section decided to send a transcript of the discussion to interested editorial boards. Some likelihood of that! They have hidden it; they barely agreed to give me, the author, a copy. As for today's transcript, Konstantin Alexandrovich, may I hope to receive a copy?

Konstantin Alexandrovich Fedin has asked: "What interest would be served should your protests be printed?" In my estimation, the answer is

---

*This discussion took place early in 1967.

clear: the interest of Soviet literature. Yet it's strange that Konstantin Alexandrovich says that I should resolve the situation. I am bound hand and foot and my mouth is closed—how am I to resolve the situation? It seems to me that this would be an easier matter for the mighty Union of Writers. My every line is suppressed, while the entire press is in the hands of the Union. Still, I don't understand and don't see why my letter was not read at the congress. Konstantin Alexandrovich proposes that the fight be waged not against the causes but rather against the effects and against the furor of the West surrounding my letter. You wish me to print a refutation—of what, precisely? I can make no statement whatsoever concerning an un-printed letter. And, most important, my letter contains a general part and a personal part. Should I renounce the general part? Well, the fact is that I am still of the same mind as I was then, and I am not renouncing a single word. After all, what is the letter about?

VOICE: Censorship!

SOLZHENITSYN: You haven't understood anything if you think it is about censorship. This letter is about the destiny of our great literature, which once conquered and captivated the world but which has now lost its stand-ing. In the West they say the Russian novel is dead, and we gesticulate and deliver speeches saying that it is not dead. But rather than make speeches we should publish novels—truly good novels. Thus, I have no intention of repudiating the general part of my letter. Should I then declare that the eight points in the personal part of my letter are unjust and false? But they are all just. Should I say that some of the wrongs I protested against have already been eliminated or corrected? But not one of them has been elimi-nated or corrected. What, then, can I declare? No, it is you who must clear at least a little path for such a statement: first, publish my letter, then issue the Union's communiqué concerning the letter, and then indicate what is being corrected. Then I will be able to make my statement, and will do so gladly. If you wish, you can also publish my statement of today concerning *Feast of Conquerors,* though neither the discussion of a stolen play nor the refutation of unprinted letters makes any sense to me. On June 12, here at the Secretariat, I was assured that the communiqué would be printed un-conditionally, and yet today conditions are posed. What has changed?

My book *Ivan Denisovich* is banned. New slanders continue to be directed at me. You can refute them, but I cannot. The only comfort I have is that I will never get a heart attack from this slander because I've been hardened in Stalinist camps.

FEDIN: No, this is not the proper sequence. You must make the first public statement. Since you have received so many approving comments on your talent and style, you will find the proper form, you can do it. Your idea of our acting first has no sound basis.

TVARDOVSKY: And will the letter itself be published in this process?

FEDIN: No, the letter should have been published right away. Now that foreign countries have beat us to it, why should we publish it?

SOLZHENITSYN: Better late than never. So nothing will change regarding my eight points?

FEDIN: We'll see about that later.

SOLZHENITSYN: Well, I have already replied and I hope that everything has been accurately transcribed.

SURKOV: You should state whether you renounce your role of leader of the political opposition in our country—the role they ascribe to you in the West.

SOLZHENITSYN: Alexei Alexandrovich, it really makes me sick to hear such a thing—and from you, of all persons: an artist with words and a leader of the political opposition? How does that jibe?

Several brief statements follow, demanding that Solzhenitsyn accept what was said by Fedin. A voice from the hall: "Well, what do you say?"

SOLZHENITSYN: I repeat once again that I am unable to provide such a statement, since the Soviet reader would have no idea what it is all about.

Letter to Newspapers and Writers

April 18, 1968

To: The Secretariat of the Union of Writers of
     the USSR
    The journal *Novy mir*
    Literaturnaya gazeta
    Members of the Union of Writers

At the editorial offices of *Novy mir* I was shown the following telegram:

IM0177. Frankfurt-am-Main. Ch 2 9 16.20. Tvardovsky. *Novy mir.* This is to inform you that the Committee of State Security, acting through Victor Louis, has sent one more copy of *Cancer Ward* to the West, in order thus to block its publication in *Novy mir.* Accordingly we have decided to publish this work immediately. The editors of the journal *Grani.**

I should like to protest both against the publication of my work in *Grani* and against the actions of V. Louis, but the turbid and provocative nature of the telegram requires, first of all, the clarification of the following:

---

*A literary journal published in West Germany by an organization of Russian emigrés known as NTS.

1) Whether the telegram was actually sent by the editors of the journal *Grani* or whether it was sent by a fictitious person (this can be established through the international telegraph system; the Moscow telegraph office can wire Frankfurt-am-Main).

2) Who is Victor Louis, what kind of person is he, of what country is he a citizen? Did he really take a copy of *Cancer Ward* out of the Soviet Union, to whom did he give it, and where else are they threatening to publish it? Furthermore, what does the Committee of State Security (KGB) have to do with this?

If the Secretariat of the Writers' Union is interested in establishing the truth and in stopping the threatened publication of *Cancer Ward* in Russian abroad, I believe that it will help to get prompt answers to these questions.

This episode compels us to reflect on the terrible and dark avenues by which the manuscripts of Soviet writers can reach the West. It constitutes an extreme reminder to us that literature must not be brought to such a state that literary works become a profitable commodity for any scoundrel who happens to have a travel visa. The works of our authors must be printed in their own country and must not become the plunder of foreign publishing houses.

A. SOLZHENITSYN

Letter to the Literaturnaya Gazeta

April 21, 1968

I have learned from a news story published in *Le Monde* on April 13 that extracts and parts of my novel, *Cancer Ward,* are being printed in various Western countries, and that the publishers—Mondadori (Italy) and The Bodley Head (England)—are already fighting over the copyright to this novel—since the U.S.S.R. does not participate in the Universal Copyright Convention—despite the fact that the author is still living!

I would like to state that no foreign publisher has received from me either the manuscript of this novel or permission to publish it. Thus I do not recognize as legal any publication of this novel without my authorization, in the present or the future, and I do not grant the copyright to anyone. I will prosecute any distortion of the text (which is inevitable in view of the uncontrolled duplication and circulation of the manuscript) as well as any unauthorized adaptation of the work for the cinema or theater.

I already know from my own experience that all the translations of *One Day in the Life of Ivan Denisovich* suffered because of the haste with which they were made. Evidently the same fate awaits *Cancer Ward* as well. Besides the question of money, literature itself is involved here.

A. SOLZHENITSYN

K7